KINGDOM
COME

KINGDOM COME

ROB MURPHY

authorHOUSE®

AuthorHouse™ UK Ltd.
1663 Liberty Drive
Bloomington, IN 47403 USA
www.authorhouse.co.uk
Phone: 0800.197.4150

Kingdom Come is a work of fiction and the creation of the author's imagination. Any organisation which exists is referred to in a fictional context and the book is in no way a reflection on the views of the organisations or their staff. All characters in the book are fictional and any resemblance or similarity of same to people currently alive is coincidental and not intentional.

Published by AuthorHouse   08/06/2013

ISBN: 978-1-4567-8211-5 (sc)
ISBN: 978-1-4567-8212-2 (e)

PROLOGUE

The mood at the meeting of the National Defence Council was grim. The President of Iran, Mohammed Khoramzadeh, had a face like thunder. The following day, he was due to attend a meeting of the Supreme Council and would have to explain to the Ayatollahs how the Iranian Defence Forces, supposedly the most formidable in the Middle East and the claimed vanguard for Islam had been comprehensively routed in battle by the combined forces of the USA, Great Britain and Australia.

Two months earlier, Iran had looked in a very strong position. They had just made a successful test explosion of their first nuclear device, the development of a blue water navy and the purchase of long-range bombers from Russia had made it the most well-armed power in the region and their main enemy, the West, seemed at bay because of terrorist activity in its own backyard and the bitter memories of its interventions in Iraq and Afghanistan. But reckless over-confidence had led to an ill-advised decision to arrest and put on trial for spying members of the private navy sponsored by Western business interests to tackle piracy in the Indian Ocean.

The response of the USA, backed by the United Kingdom and Australia had been swift and brutal. In a two-week campaign named "Desert Anvil", they comprehensively destroyed the Iranian nuclear processing facilities, along with their air bases, the main naval facility at Bandar Khomeini, the barracks of the Revolutionary Guards and the headquarters of the feared VEVAK intelligence agency. Special forces from the Western allies pulled off a spectacular raid on Evin prison and rescued the prisoners held there.

Slowly, the members of the National Defence Council trooped into the briefing room. First to take his seat was Defence Minister, General Farzad Barkhorda who, after the debacle, was favourite to be dismissed. He was followed by the Interior Minister, Gholam Kashemi, the Energy Minister, Ali Moussavi and the Foreign Minister, Hamidreza Yazdani. Finally, the Director of VEVAK, Massoud Elmieh, joined the meeting.

"Gentlemen, I need no explaining of the circumstances we are in" said President Khoramzadeh as he opened the meeting. "The Islamic Republic of Iran has suffered grave humiliation at the hands of the Great Satan and its Zionist lackeys. The Supreme Council will want explanations of what went wrong and an assurance that immediate action will be taken to ensure that nothing like it ever happens again. If

1

they are in a forgiving mood, nothing more than dismissals will take place. But you need no explaining of what might happen if their Eminences are not so disposed. I think some explanations are in order for the dismal performance in the defence of the Islamic Republic."

General Barkhorda was the first to respond. A career soldier, he had cut his teeth in the war with Iraq in the 1980s and had risen through the ranks to command the army prior to his appointment as Defence Minister in 2010. "Mr President, before you meet their Eminences, you should consider the following. We managed to shoot down no less than 15 warplanes of the infidels and sink three of their ships. The reason we lost was due to the criminal failure of some of my commanders to follow orders. I will ensure they are subject to the most extreme penalties available for their wilful dereliction of duty. As for the future, the only option is to rebuild our armed forces. We have the revenue from our oil, and Russia and China are only too willing to sell equipment to us. Believe me Mr President, next time we will destroy the imperialists."

Interior Minister Kashemi and VEVAK Director Elmieh were shaking their heads. "If I remember correctly, Barkhorda", Kashemi said, "all but four of the planes shot down were transport or reconnaissance planes and two of the four warplanes were B-52s which first flew sixty years ago. And two of the ships sunk were supply vessels. Hardly a success story, more like shooting tethered game."

Elmieh was more forceful. "Mr President, we are not going to beat the infidels through conventional warfare. For the past fifteen years, our Muslim brothers have been taking the fight to them in their backyard. We've got active *hizbollah* cells in all the major countries in North America, Europe and Oceania who are working in partnership with Al-Q'aida and with radical Marxist organisations. All we need to do is to activate those cells and they can paralyse the infidels. We only have to be lucky once, they have to be lucky all the time. Their security services might catch one or two but they can't contain thousands."

Energy Minister Moussavi was the next to speak. "Have we all forgotten that the one major asset the Islamic world has and the infidels want is oil? If we persuade our Islamic neighbours to turn off the tap, we will have the Great Satan and its allies at our mercy."

"Have you forgotten Moussavi that the infidels are looking for oil in their own backyard?" Kashemi pointed out the Energy Minister's apparent over-optimism about the West's energy situation. "They've found oil in Australia and New Zealand and it looks like Britain might be next. Also, they've embarked on a programme of building nuclear power stations and it looks like they will have mastered fuel cell technology within the next 20 years. The infidels will no longer need our oil—explain that!"

"You haven't spoken yet Yazdani" interjected a rather jocular Elmieh. "Still thinking of that pretty secretary at the United Nations?"

This certainly drew a response from the Foreign Minister.

"I have not spoken yet Elmieh but this doesn't mean that I have no opinions on the issue. Frankly, in all my years, I've never heard such a load of self-serving drivel spoken as in the last ten minutes. None of you understand the real reason why we lost the war. You all believed your own propaganda that the infidels lacked the stomach for a fight and that Islam would prevail because there are more of us and that we wanted to win. What you have forgotten is that the Great Satan and its allies had the will to win and were backed by their own people. And all because we foolishly provoked them."

"Unlike any of you, I have lived in the USA and Britain and I know what the people are like. They may appear decadent and complacent but provoke them and they will be up for a fight. Germany and Japan made that mistake seventy years ago." Yazdani had been a student in the United Kingdom in the 1970s and had lived in New York in the late 1990s when part of the Iranian delegation at the United Nations. "We made the mistake of being a threat to their security and in trying to humiliate them. That's why they've turned to hard-line leaders who've promised to get tough with their enemies."

"Barkhorda, your idea of rebuilding the capacity of the Iranian armed forces is fantasy. It doesn't matter how many planes, ships, missiles and guns you buy from Russia and China, the infidels will always have more. And better trained men and women I must say. Elmieh, you appear to have forgotten that all the infidel countries have all strengthened their internal security and have tightened up their immigration laws. It's now barely possible for Muslims from *any* country to get in, legally or otherwise. Their security services have got spies into our ranks, as well as Al-Q'aida and they are their police are being supported by volunteer militias. And have you noticed that the USA, Britain and Australia have introduced laws which enable them to intern Muslims without trial and to deport them, even if they are born there and holding passports of those countries. Your idea of infiltrating *feyadeen* into the infidel countries just won't work. If by chance you get them in, they risk being found out and, if lucky, thrown out. If not, they will end up dead at the hands of the infidels."

"Mr President, I know that their Eminences will not like to hear anything which looks like surrender or capitulation to the Great Satan. But we need to be realistic. As long as the infidels have the stomach for a fight, we are not going to beat them. I am therefore suggesting that we stand down all military activity against the Great Satan and its allies for the next 3-4 years."

Barkhorda and Elmieh were incensed at this suggestion. "Yazdani, are you suggesting that we abdicate our responsibility as Muslims to continue the *jihad* against the imperialists and Zionists?" They were cut short by an irate Khoramzadeh who shouted "Barkhorda, Elmieh, QUIET! Both of you are walking on thin ice and it would be sensible to listen to Yazdani and let him finish."

Yazdani continued. "There are lessons from history. Just over 20 years ago, the Warsaw Pact and the Soviet Union collapsed. While the Cold War was on, the West turned to warlike leaders like Reagan and Thatcher who they felt would protect them against an enemy who wanted to impose an alien political system on them. But after the end of the Cold War, there was no enemy. Voters started demanding that their governments spent money on schools, hospitals and infrastructure rather than weapons of war. Under this climate, Clinton and Blair were elected and the armed forces were run down. If we suspend our struggle with the infidels, voters will cease to support their current Governments. They will start demanding better standards of living. Minority groups will start demanding rights. People will question expenditure

3

on the military and the size of the infidel forces will be run down. In a matter of a few years, they will not be in a position to respond to events in other countries. That is the time when we should make our move"

President Khoramzadeh was impressed with Yazdani's proposal. The Foreign Minister may have been a bit too cosmopolitan for some of his colleagues but Khoramzadeh knew that he was as committed as anyone in the room to the cause of Islam. His skill as Foreign Minister was beyond question; he had successfully defused the threat of co-ordinated action against Iran before through driving a wedge between the USA and Europe. And Khoramzadeh was a pragmatist at heart and recognised the futility of taking on the USA and its allies in either conventional or guerrilla warfare.

"Yazdani, you speak wisely. As much as it pains me, we have to recognise reality. The Great Satan and its Zionist lackeys currently have the upper hand. And you rightly say we have underestimated their will to fight. Victory will be ours but we can afford to bide our time until the balance of power is to our advantage. I will be commending your proposed course of action to their Eminences when I meet them in Qom tomorrow."

4 February 2014
Department for Trade and Enterprise
Victoria Street
London

"Secretary of State, your visitors have arrived."

"Thank you Lucy. Let Philip, Caroline and Dominic know that we are on the way down." Mark Hampson, Secretary of State for Trade and Enterprise was in a good mood as he collected his papers and joined his Principal Private Secretary, Lucy Alexander, to head for Conference Room 5 in the Department for Trade and Enterprise's Victoria Street headquarters. He was now 65 years old and was due to stand down as an MP in the forthcoming General Election which everyone now expected to take place in May or June. Four years earlier, shortly after the Conservatives regained power following 13 years of Labour rule, the Department for Trade and Enterprise had commissioned a survey of Britain's remaining oil resources as part of a programme to strengthen energy security and to reduce dependence on unstable and hostile parts of the world. The survey was carried out by multi-national mining giants Xstrata and it was accompanied by a financial survey by bankers Goldman Sachs. Early indications were highly promising and is looked likely that the United Kingdom still had significant oil reserves. If confirmed, the impact on the country's economy would be immense; oil prices were still at $200 per barrel following the previous year's war with Iran.

Hampson had first entered Parliament 35 years earlier as one of Mrs Thatcher's "Young Turks" and, apart from an eight-year absence after losing his seat in 1997, his career had been a distinguished one, having held Cabinet posts with four different portfolios. The news that the United Kingdom was sitting on a financial goldmine would be the best possible way to bow out of politics—he could imagine the reactions of his Cabinet colleagues to the news.

Mark Hampson and Lucy Alexander met their colleagues by the lifts reserved for Ministers. Sir Philip Stevens, the Department's Permanent Secretary was waiting there, along with Caroline Johnson, the Minister of State for Energy and Dominic Collins, Chief Political Adviser. Sir Philip was two years older than Hampson and was due to bring to a conclusion a 45-year Civil Service career later that year. In contrast, Johnson and Collins were both in the early stages of their careers. Johnson, blonde and attractive, was in her mid-30s and had been an MP for just 4 years, while Collins, the political adviser, had just turned 30 and had been selected as prospective Conservative candidate for the safe seat of Maidstone South.

"Ah, Philip, Caroline, Dominic, there you are. At last, the news of whether we've won the Lottery. About time too—any later and it would risk being caught up in purdah if the Election's called."

"Rumours sound good, Secretary of State" said Energy Minister Johnson. "Heard there might be a load more oil in the North Sea, as well as some in the Atlantic and the Channel."

Dominic Collins brought in his financial perspective. "If so, this could make the UK the wealthiest country in Europe. Just think what we could do—further tax cuts and at the same time spending more on defence and the police. Will make the PM's dream of the UK becoming the world centre for enterprise a reality."

Sir Philip Stevens was cagier. "I think we should wait until we've all seen the report. Also, I think a wash-up meeting is in order to discuss handling issues. After all, we don't want sensitive information to end up in the wrong hands."

The lift reached the basement and the Ministerial party made their way to Conference Room 5 where a PowerpointPlus presentation had been set up. Already waiting for them were the Programme Manager from Xstrata, Glen Mitchell and the investment analyst from Goldman Sachs, Sarah Maguire.

Glen Mitchell was a tall, raw-boned New Zealander with long straggly hair and stubbly beard which made him look more like a rock musician than the leading geologist whom Xstrata had headhunted from rivals Rio Tinto with a seven figure salary. He looked as out of place in this corporate environment as Hampson would have looked at a heavy metal concert. But Mitchell's record spoke for itself and he had been personally commended to Hampson by Xstrata's CEO.

In contrast, Sarah Maguire looked in her element. Only 26 years old, she had enjoyed meteoric career progress since being recruited by Goldman Sachs after leaving Harvard Business School with a Masters just four years earlier. Tall, dark-haired and very attractive, she looked the stereotypical New York businesswoman in her designer skirt and jacket and Jimmy Choo stilettos.

Lucy Alexander turned the lights to dim as Glen Mitchell started his PowerpointPlus presentation. A map of the United Kingdom came up on the screen with red circles marking the areas where Xstrata had surveyed for oil deposits. Mitchell also had the same presentation on his laptop and, by touching the screen, he was able to run the presentation.

"We carried out surveys in five areas where geological formations suggested there might be oil deposits. These were: fifty miles off the North-East coast of Scotland, which is close to a field the Norwegians opened five years ago; the North Atlantic approaches to the North Sea; the approach to the Irish Sea and two in the English Channel, one close to the Isle of Purbeck and the other near Hastings." Glen Mitchell continued. "Test borings were carried out and were supported by ultrasound equipment, which is a new technology but was proved effective when we discovered oil in Australia and New Zealand two years ago. I am confident that reliable estimates of the size of the oil reserves are available."

Mitchell touched the red circle off the North East coast of Scotland with his finger and "60bn" came up. "Finding new reserves in the Forties area was a surprise, considering that the existing fields there have nearly been worked out, but oil there is. 60 billion barrels worth of oil lies in British territorial waters. I'm afraid that the rest of the field belongs to Norway."

He then touched the red circle off Scotland's North West coast and "80bn" came up. "The North West approaches to the North Sea, one of the most inhospitable areas known to man. 100mph gales a daily occurrence in winter. But not impossible—with the new generation of rigs, it's possible to drill anywhere. We reckon there's 80 billion barrels of the black stuff there. Getting it out's no problem, it's getting it to the ships and refineries. The nearest port with suitable facilities is Aberdeen, 200 miles away. And the nearest refinery's at Grangemouth, another 100 miles on top of that. The Scottish lochs however are deep and should be able to take the big tankers, but you'll need to build road and rail links to it."

Mitchell then touched the red circle south of the Irish Sea, and a figure of "100bn" came up. "The Celtic Sea, the rumours were right all along. There's altogether 200 billion barrels of oil out there but half of that belongs to Ireland. That still leaves 100 billion barrels in British waters. And with the harbourage and refining capacity at Milford Haven, there's no problem with transporting and refining the stuff."

Mitchell then moved his finger to the English Channel and it alighted on the red circle off the Isle of Purbeck. A figure of "20bn" came up. "We were a bit disappointed with Purbeck because all the indications suggested there were large deposits of oil. Only other problem is that it's in a main shipping lane and it's close to a National Park. Otherwise, it's only 40 miles from Fawley and Southampton Water."

He ended his presentation by touching the red circle off Hastings where two figures came up. A black figure of "10bn" came up along with a blue figure of "75bn". Mitchell explained. "The field off the Sussex Coast has the smallest yield of oil of any of the fields surveyed—10 billion barrels. Also, it's close to a National Park. However, we also found a natural gas field with 75 billion cubic feet of the stuff. That may make it worth exploiting."

"In short, Secretary of State, the UK appears to be sitting on 270 billion barrels of oil. That should last you for the next 100 years and bring in a load of money. But I'll leave that part to Ms Maguire. Sarah, over to you."

Sarah Maguire took over the PowerpointPlus presentation from the New Zealander. "Secretary of State, Minister, you will be well aware that oil is a volatile commodity on the world markets. The spot price is currently $200 per barrel which is high by historical comparison. Four months ago, it was $250 per barrel. Yet it can fall dramatically; all it needs is for Russia, Saudi Arabia and Iran to start pumping out oil in bulk and the price could fall by half. My father remembers the 1980s when oil fell to $30 per barrel. You will appreciate this has made it difficult for me to forecast the expected fiscal benefit to the United Kingdom. I have therefore taken the median average price over the last 30 years and compared with the highest and lowest average. Are you content with this approach?"

Mark Hampson and Caroline Johnson indicated their approval.

Maguire continued. "The median average cost is $75 per barrel" and she touched the screen to bring up that figure. "From Mr Mitchell's report, it appears that annual output once all the new fields have been commissioned will be 2 billion barrels. On this cost basis alone, it should benefit the United Kingdom economy by an additional $150 billion each year which, in sterling terms, is about £100 billion at current exchange rates. Of course, if oil prices stay at or about their current level, the net benefit to the United Kingdom will be much higher"

"Jesus Christ" said Hampson. "This country's sitting on a fucking goldmine—scuse my French ladies and gentlemen!"

"This of course will need to be balanced against necessary investment costs. All the fields are offshore and the three largest are in locations renowned for their inclement weather. Furthermore, I've estimated that at least £100m will need to be spent in developing a deep water port in the North West of Scotland to handle the tankers and to build suitable road and rail links. There is also a time lag to consider: my estimate is that it will take until 2017 for the first oil to come out of the Forties, Celtic Sea and Channel field and until 2019 for oil to come out of the North Atlantic field. Existing oil producers may see the new fields as a threat and increase their own production. This could make it uneconomic to invest in the North Atlantic and Channel fields. But, to sum up, I think the most likely outcome will be highly favourable to the economy of the United Kingdom." With that, Sarah Maguire finished her presentation.

A short question and answer session followed before the meeting finished.

As Glen Mitchell and Sarah Maguire got up to leave, Mark Hampson shook them warmly by the hand. "Mr Mitchell, Ms Maguire, on behalf of Her Majesty's Government, I would like to thank you deeply for the excellent work you have done with this survey. You will understand that the contents are highly sensitive and, for this reason, we are going to have them classified. I should be grateful therefore that you do not disclose any of the contents to third parties unless I or my successor says so."

"No problem, Secretary of State. We've done surveys like this for other Governments and recognise the need for discretion." With this, Lucy Alexander escorted Glen Mitchell and Sarah Maguire to the door.

Ten minutes later, Lucy Alexander, along with Sir Philip Stevens, Caroline Johnson and Dominic Collins were with Mark Hampson in his office. Hampson reached for his drinks cabinet and drew out a bottle of Glenfiddich and a set of whisky glasses, and poured a celebratory drink for everyone. "To future economic prosperity—cheers" rang round the room.

Hampson then set out his proposals for handling the news. "I want to get this through Cabinet as quickly as possible so the Treasury can work out what scope we might have for tax cuts or for spending on defence and law and order. If we can get these into the Manifesto for the Election, we could be on for a record landslide."

Caroline Johnson and Dominic Collins both agreed with Hampson's approach and, with this, Hampson asked Lucy Alexander to check his diary for the next Cabinet meeting. "One's due on Friday Secretary of State" she replied.

"Excellent" replied Hampson. "The sooner we can get this out, the better."

Johnson and Collins both left for their own offices while Alexander returned to the outer office. However, the worried figure of the Permanent Secretary remained.

"Secretary of State, can I have a word?"

"Of course Philip. What's on your mind?"

With this, Stevens closed the door to ensure there was privacy. "Secretary of State, do you realise where most of that oil's located? 140 billion barrels off Scotland and 100 billion off Wales. That will set the Scottish and Welsh Nationalists off again about "their" oil. Especially as it would make Scotland and Wales amongst the wealthiest countries in Europe if they were independent."

"Philip, I think you're worrying too much" Hampson replied. "The campaign for independence is dead in the water now—the Scots and the Welsh are satisfied with having their toytown Parliaments and the events over the last few years—the recession five years ago and the threat from Islamic terrorism has driven most of their voters back to the comfort blanket of the Union. What's more, the SNP and Plaid Cymru are busted flushes now, split from top to bottom and voters haven't forgotten the cock-ups they made while in power. As for their new leaders, I've heard they've got some very dodgy friends—Communists, Trotskyists, Islamic radicals and some with a terrorist past. That won't go down well with voters there."

"Secretary of State, I think you've underestimated the impact of new oil reserves off Scotland and Wales" replied the Permanent Secretary. "Both countries have long memories and a sense of grievance towards England over the perceived theft of their wealth. When we first found oil in the North Sea forty years ago, it transformed the SNP from a fringe party that few Scots took seriously into the second strongest party there. There was real fear that the demand for independence would grow. In 1975 the Department of Energy suppressed a report which stated that Scotland would be the fifth wealthiest country in Europe if it was independent because of its oil reserves. I was one of the officials responsible for doing this. The danger is not so much this year. But in 2015 there are elections for the Scottish Parliament and Welsh Assembly. Do you really want to run the risk of the SNP and Plaid Cymru taking control?"

"Alright Philip". Mark Hampson knew that his Permanent Secretary had a valid point. "When I attend Cabinet on Friday, I will mention we need to be careful over the handling of the report. Maybe we can issue a limited statement about the existence of oil while keeping the specifics secret. But you realise the PM is keen to exploit any good news coming out with the Election on the horizon."

CHAPTER 1

8 May 2015, 8:30am
Sky News

"This is Adam Rennie on Sky News with this morning's main news headlines."

"The UK Government is having to face up to the prospect of dealing with nationalist governments in Scotland and Wales following the results of yesterday's elections for the Scottish Parliament and the Welsh Assembly. With two results still to come, the Scottish National Party has won an absolute majority in the Scottish Parliament taking 65 of the 129 seats and the new First Minister, Alastair Ferguson, expects to name his cabinet today. In Wales, Plaid Cymru have won 29 of the 60 seats in the Welsh Assembly and are the largest party, but they do not have an overall majority and will either have to govern as a minority government or find a coalition partner. Plaid Cymru leader Emyr Roderick is reported to have invited the four Independent Labour members for talks about forming a government."

"The potential impact on relations between Whitehall and the devolved governments is immense. Both the SNP and Plaid Cymru have been in Government before but never before have their policies been as radical as they are now. Both parties propose windfall taxes on oil companies using their devolved taxation powers which will fund regeneration of depressed areas and education and training for the unemployed. They also plan to set up national broadcasting networks for Scotland and Wales when the BBC is broken up. But the most contentious proposal is for both countries to seek independence from the United Kingdom. If the SNP and Plaid Cymru carry out their threatened policies, there will almost certainly be conflict with the UK Government."

The same day, 10am
Conservative Party Headquarters
Millbank
London

"Bloody hell Lyndon. I can't believe it. I thought that the Scots and Welsh voters had more sense than to fall for the old independence gambit again. Don't they realise how much it would cost them to go it alone?"

Sir Anthony Simmons, the tall, urbane Conservative Party Chairman, turned away from the television monitor in his office and pressed the mute button. With him was the party's main strategist, Lyndon Jefferies, a stocky, pugnacious Australian who had been hired two years previously after masterminding a comprehensive victory for the Liberal Party in Australia. Jefferies, a former journalist, was an earthy character who called a spade a spade and was not the sort of person who would fit into polite society. But his effectiveness was unquestioned; the previous year, he had been instrumental in steering the Tories to a 200-seat overall majority in the House of Commons.

When campaigning for the four-yearly elections to the Scottish Parliament and Welsh Assembly had started a month previously, there had been no indication that the status quo in either country would change. Since 2011, both Scotland and Wales had been ruled by coalitions of the Labour and Liberal Democrat parties and the Conservative Party had been the second strongest party. The party's strategy was entirely focused upon its traditional opponent, the Labour Party, and its Liberal Democrat allies. But barely a week of campaigning had passed when a highly classified report done by mining giants Xstrata and leading merchant bankers Goldman Sachs on the UK's oil reserves a year earlier was leaked. The report stated that the new oil reserves off the Scottish and Welsh coasts would last for most of the current century and that if Scotland and Wales were independent, they would be Europe's sixth and eighth wealthiest countries. Suddenly, the fortunes of the two nationalist parties, the Scottish National Party and Plaid Cymru, were transformed. From being seen as busted flushes with a poor record in power, divided and with suspect acquaintances, they suddenly became standard-bearers for their country against the perfidious English.

"Tony, how many times did I say it would be tough. Scotland and Wales has never been promising territory for the Tories—large numbers of people on benefits, most of those in work in the public sector and the fact they associate the Tories with England. But until that knobhead leaked the Mitchell-Maguire Report, we had a good chance of doing well. The Nats were a joke—cocked up last time they were in power, split from top to bottom over policy. But as soon as the Jocks and Taffs got a smell of black gold, it was manna from heaven for SNP and PC."

Jefferies continued. "We did all we could do Tony and more. We got our financial guys to cost the SNP and PC manifesto and what it would cost your average family. We flagged up the economic impact of the loss of overseas investment and the increased threat to security if the Army, Navy and RAF all pulled out. We also found out some very interesting background about Ferguson and Roderick and the people they've done business with in the past. Look at this."

Jefferies pulled out two election posters, one done for Scotland, the other for Wales. They showed seven-year old photographs of current leaders Alastair Ferguson and Emyr Roderick meeting the then Iranian Foreign Minister Mohammed Khoramzadeh at a function hosted the Communist and Green grouping in the European Parliament. Khoramzadeh was currently President of Iran. The straplines read 'A true friend of Scotland/Wales?'

"Tony, the problem is you guys don't understand the Jocks and the Taffs. I do. My dad came from Glasgow, my mum from Swansea. They've got memories like a fucking elephant and particularly where England's involved. The Highland Clearances, the Welsh Not. All remembered like it was yesterday, not hundreds of years ago. And the same with their industries—coal, steel, water. They think the English stole these from them and gave nothing in return. Complete bollocks of course. It's the same with oil—they think it's *their* oil, not the UK's."

"Point taken Lyndon" replied Simmons "but the key issue is what we do next. We've now got to manage relations with potentially hostile administrations in Edinburgh and Cardiff who've got the capacity to derail our flagship policies. We can't afford to let them get the upper hand—the PM won't tolerate it any more than Maggie did with the GLC thirty years ago. But I'm worried that if they decide to jump ship, they'll have foreign support. The EU would love to get one over on us for leaving, and that's before we consider what Russia and China will do."

Before Jefferies could reply, the phone rang. "Tony Simmons here. Hello Prime Minister."

On the other end of the line was Robert Delgado, Prime Minister of the United Kingdom for the past five years. He was displeased at the Scottish and Welsh election results to say the least. "Tony, not a very pretty sight. Two jokers like Ferguson and Roderick now in charge. What were you and Jefferies doing to stop this?"

"Prime Minister, virtually everything" Simmons replied. "We costed the SNP and PC manifesto commitments, including how much independence would cost. We also reminded the electorate of the type of company Ferguson and Roderick keep—you know, Communists, Trots, Islamic radicals. We had party workers and canvassers out on the stump in Scotland and Wales and ran wall-to-wall party political broadcasts. But Jefferies was explaining to me why it didn't work when you rang."

Delgado responded. "The leaking of the Xstrata-Goldman Sachs Report on our new oil reserves I suppose. We needed that like a hole in the head. Tony, I'm going to bring the issue of our relations with the devolved Governments up at Cabinet next Tuesday. Could be fireworks over the next four years. Can you attend?"

"Certainly, Prime Minister" said Simmons.

"I'm not proposing to play our hand yet Tony" said the Prime Minister. "But I and other Cabinet members are well aware that the new Governments in Edinburgh and Cardiff may well try to make mischief for us. They are talking about shaking down the oil companies for money, which is clearly in breach of legislation banning the devolved governments for carrying out policies adversely impacting on national interests. We introduced that after Megrahi—remember the Lockerbie bomber? Also, there is no way we will allow them to set up their own broadcasting corporations. When we sell off the BBC, what goes for England goes for the rest of the UK. And finally regarding independence, the United Kingdom remains united—Ferguson and Roderick can forget any idea of breaking away. If we have trouble from either government, I will have no hesitation in getting Cabinet approval to close them down. Remember Maggie did the same to the GLC 30 years ago."

The same day
Scottish Parliament
Edinburgh

A massive crowd had gathered outside the Scottish Parliament to wait for SNP leader and new First Minister Alastair Ferguson to speak. Many were waving the blue and white saltire, Scotland's national flag.

At 11am, Ferguson appeared on the steps. A chartered accountant by profession and just short of six feet tall, Ferguson was 50 years old and had been an MSP since 2007. He still had the trim physique he had over 30 years earlier when he had a trial with football club Dundee United, although his hair was now starting to turn grey.

"People of Scotland" began Ferguson. "Today marks a watershed in the history of Scotland. For the first time in over 300 years, you have voted for a Government that will act in the interests of Scotland and will put Scotland first. During that time, we have been a colony of England. Our resources have been plundered, asset-strippers have decimated our industries and have left our people without a decent living. Our young men and women have been sent to fight needless wars. Skilled and talented people have been forced to leave Scotland to find a living elsewhere. From 8 May 2015, this will end."

"From now on, the Government of Scotland will ensure that Scotland's resources and mineral wealth benefit the people of Scotland, not the faceless bankers and speculators in the City of London. We will regenerate Scotland's towns and cities. We will ensure there is work for everyone who wants it and we will encourage those Scots who have left to return home."

"Scotland is a generous, welcoming country. We do not seek conflict with the English, despite what some of the English press have said. We are prepared to work in partnership with the Government in Westminster—but only if they want it. If they try to coerce the Scottish people, my Government will not lack the will to defend the interests of the Scottish people."

This was followed with a massive cheer and the singing of the Scottish National Anthem, "Flower of Scotland".

The same day
Plaid Cymru headquarters
Cardiff

"Emyr, Jane Lewis is here to see you". The voice of Megan Rees, Personal Assistant to Plaid Cymru leader Emyr Roderick came over the intercom.

"Send her up Megan" replied Roderick.

A minute later, Jane Lewis, leader of the Independent Labour group in the Welsh Assembly was sitting opposite the man who was hoping to become First Minister of Wales. Roderick, now 49 years old, was of average height but powerfully built. As a younger man, he had played rugby as a centre threequarter for Carmarthen Quins and had had a trial with then Welsh champions Neath. A surveyor by profession, he had been an AM since 2007.

Mrs Lewis was in her mid-50s and, although plumpish and bespectacled, was not unattractive. She had been a member of the Labour Party from her teens until 2005 when she and several fellow party members in the Gwent Valleys left the party over the imposition of Parliamentary candidates by the Labour Party's central office. She had been elected AM for Torfaen, near Newport, in 2011 and headed a group of 4 AMs.

"Jane, you know why I've invited you here" started Roderick. "Plaid Cymru holds the largest numbers of seats in the Welsh Assembly but we don't quite have enough to govern by ourselves. You have seen our manifesto commitments—economic regeneration, using Welsh resources for the benefit of Wales, a referendum on independence. Independent Labour probably agree with most Plaid Cymru policy commitments—OK, maybe not all. But I think there is more common ground between us than with any of the other parties. For that reason, I would like to invite Independent Labour to become Plaid Cymru's coalition partners. Under the deal, I would like to offer you a post in the Cabinet as Minister for Social Affairs."

"Emyr, I'm most flattered by your offer." Mrs Lewis seemed delighted by the prospect of serving her country as a Minister. "But there are a couple of areas where I feel there may be difficulty. The first is on your policy of regeneration and retraining. The intent is admirable. But I don't think you fully understand the reality in the former mining valleys. Generations of people have been out of work. Many have suffered physical and mental health problems. It will take a lot of effort to get them looking for work again. All it will take is one rejection and they won't bother again. Your approach looks too much like compulsion. Also, I fear that new jobs might end up being filled by foreigners, which will give rise to racial tensions and be exploited by the BNP."

"The other is your pledge for a referendum on independence. Personally, I'm not against independence, providing it delivers greater prosperity for Wales and its people. But many of my constituents are sceptical Emyr. For them, Plaid Cymru is the party of Welsh-speaking Wales. They fear that if Wales becomes independent, money will only be spent on Welsh-speaking parts of Wales."

Roderick pondered Mrs Lewis's comments for a few seconds, then replied. "Jane, I'm well aware of the social problems stemming from worklessness. It's the same in some of the western valleys. Plaid Cymru's set up a working party to address this issue and one of the reasons I'd like to put you forward for Social Affairs is for your expertise in the matter. A lot of the people surveyed would jump at the chance of getting back into work. If we can give them the skills needed and, as you say, the confidence and self-worth, we should be able to get even the longest term unemployed back to work. Just for the record, we're getting a lot of co-operation from employers who are quite keen to offer work experience before taking people on."

"On the second point Jane, I think I need to make clear that Plaid Cymru is the Party of Wales. All Wales, not just the Welsh-speaking parts. If I become First Minister, I will ensure that the whole of Wales benefits from Government policies, whether English-speaking or Welsh-speaking. You will have noticed that we're now picking up seats outside our heartlands—we won in the Rhondda and the Vale of Clwyd."

"The decision whether to join us in a coalition is yours Jane—I can't force you. But if you stay out, you may regret it if the main Unionist parties are still able to call the shots and block policies you would have supported."

Mrs Lewis asked for a half an hour to consider. During that time, she conferred with her fellow Independent Labour AMs.

At 12:30pm, Emyr Roderick's intercom rang again. It was Megan. "Jane Lewis is back, Emyr."

"Emyr, good news" said Mrs Lewis. "All my fellow members agree to joining Plaid Cymru in a coalition government on the terms discussed."

"Excellent Jane. Would you like to join me in a celebratory drink?" With that, Roderick removed a bottle of Penderyn Gold whisky and filled two glasses to celebrate the formation of a government to take Wales forward, hopefully to independence.

9 June 2015
Cabinet Room
10 Downing Street
London

Members of the Cabinet trooped into the Cabinet Room for the routine Tuesday morning meeting. Coffee and pastries were available for those who wanted it.

Cabinet meetings were usually preoccupied with progress on formulation of policies and on legislation progressing through the Houses of Parliament, as well as reviewing budget outturns and expenditure forecasts and identifying and mitigating barriers to delivery of key policies and identifying potential elephant traps that could derail such policies. Members expected much of the meeting to be devoted to progress on the four flagship bills being enacted.

One was a Broadcasting Bill which would break up the BBC and sell off the constituent parts to private sector bidders. For over thirty years, the Conservative Party had considered the BBC to be a nest of left-wing and anti-British and anti-Conservative bias funded at public expense and was taking steps to bring this to an end. The second bill was a Local Government Bill which would amend the franchise in local government elections by increasing the minimum voting age to 25, by requiring all newly-settled immigrants to serve a probationary period of five years before being eligible to vote and by giving business owners an additional vote. The stated reason for this legislation was to ensure that local government reflected the interests of residents who made the greatest contribution to their community; in reality, the Tories saw the political advantage of maximising their core vote and diminishing that of the Labour Party. The third was a Higher Education Bill, under which Government funding was to be withdrawn for all university courses outside the elite Russell Group of universities that were not considered to be linked to the interests of commerce and industry. The Conservative Party considered this would bring an end to the hordes of students graduating with worthless degrees.

The last and most controversial bill was the Young Persons (National Service) Bill which was intended to reintroduce national service for all persons aged between 16 and 25 not in employment, further or higher education or training. Critics of the Bill described it as legalised slavery and there had been a series of violent demonstrations against the Bill, notably one less than two weeks earlier in London which had resulted in over 200 demonstrators and 70 police officers being injured and over £5m damage to property.

Robert Delgado took his customary place at the centre of the table. Now 61 years old, Delgado was a thirty year veteran of Westminster and had served in the Cabinets of both Margaret Thatcher and John Major. Tall and broad-shouldered, he still had a full head of dark hair which betrayed his Spanish ancestry. He had been leader of the Conservative Party for the past ten years and had not only steered it back to power in 2010 after thirteen long years in opposition, he had consolidated their position in power.

The first two years had been rough. An economic downturn, unemployment which rose to over 4 million and social unrest which gave rise to urban rioting of an unprecedented scale in the summer of 2011 had threatened to make him a one-term Prime Minister. But the Conservatives were a lucky party. The marriage of Prince William, son of the Prince of Wales and second in line to the throne that year took people's minds off the dire economic situation. The opposition Labour Party were in disarray following their defeat in the 2010 General Election. The 2012 Olympic Games was to prove a resounding success for the country, not only in competition where Great Britain took a record number of medals and was third overall behind China and the USA, but in terms of finances where it turned over record profits.

In the autumn of 2012, Al-Q'aida launched a massive terrorist attack on London, targeting the Stock Exchange, the finance houses in the City of London and Docklands and the offices of the main newspapers, killing over 200 people. This gave the Government the excuse to introduce the most draconian peacetime security legislation in history. The death penalty was restored for murder and treason, the police were routinely armed and immigration law was radically tightened with the right to remove British citizenship introduced, along with a ban on settlement from not only Muslim countries but also on Muslims from other countries. Al-Q'aida and other named radical Muslim organisations were outlawed, along with six ultra left-wing parties which had been held responsible for the riots in 2011 and had been found to be helping Muslim terrorists.

Finally, British participation in the third Gulf War in 2013, in which US, British and Australian forces destroyed Iran's nuclear and conventional weapons installation and eliminated the Islamic Republic as a threat to peace in the region all but guaranteed a landslide win for the Conservatives in the 2014 General Election.

To his right sat Chancellor of the Exchequer, Ed Villiers. Boyish looking and in his early forties, Villiers had been Chancellor since the start of the Tories' second term twelve months earlier. A graduate of Oxford University and Harvard Business School, Villiers was regarded as 'dry' on economic issues but liberal on social issues.

On the other side of the Prime Minister sat Foreign Secretary, Christian Vale. Tall, blond-haired and good-looking, Vale had been something of a pin-up boy for the party when he was younger. A former diplomat and well to the left of the party on both economic and social issues, he was not held in favour by many of his party colleagues who thought he was too soft in his dealings with other countries and with international bodies like the European Union, the United Nations and the Council of Europe, all of whom had been critical of the UK's domestic and foreign policies. But Delgado trusted Vale and recognised his immense contribution through the successful negotiation of the UK's withdrawal from the European Union which had resulted in minimal damage to UK interests.

Next to Vale sat the slim, bespectacled figure of Stephen Lansbury, the Attorney-General, Caroline Johnson, the Secretary of State for Environment and Local Government, James Berry, the Secretary of State for Education and Lord Manson, the Secretary of State for National Heritage. To the right of Villiers sat three of the most vociferous right-wingers in the cabinet, Deborah Pearson, the Home Secretary, Henry Arbuthnot, the Secretary of State for Defence and Jason Steer, the Secretary of State for Trade and Enterprise.

"Good morning Ladies and Gentlemen" began the Prime Minister. "We've got a lot of business to get through today so I should be grateful if everyone is brisk with their points. Firstly, you should note that a revised agenda was issued yesterday. We've had to introduce a last minute item to the agenda at Jason's request. Jason, can you please explain." Delgado motioned to the short, stocky figure of the Secretary of State for Trade and Enterprise.

Jason Steer was 1980s Thatcherism personified. An East Ender whose original vocation, after an unsuccessful trial as a footballer with West Ham United, was a motor mechanic, he had become a trader in the City of London following deregulation in 1986. The fortune he made on the City trading floors set him up for a financial services consultancy. He first became a Conservative councillor in Redbridge in 1998 and followed this up by winning his outer East London constituency from Labour in 2005. He had been in the cabinet for just one year.

"Prime Minister, thank you. Last Wednesday, I had a visit from the Chairmen of three leading US oil companies, Exxon, Texaco and Chevron. As you know, they are significant players in opening up the Cromarty, Fastnet and Hebrides fields and will be major contributors to the Exchequer. All of them told me that their companies had received tax demands from the Scottish and Welsh Governments for their on-shore installations, which they had not expected. They are threatening to pull out unless Edinburgh and Cardiff desist with their demands—I don't have to explain the impact that would have on both the development of the fields and the country's finances."

"You'll recall we discussed relations with the Scots and Welsh at Cabinet a month ago. We all feared they'd try something like this on. Looks like we've got them by the short and curlies over this though because the Scotland and Wales Acts as revised ban them from carrying out policies which impact on reserved areas of business. Such as using their taxation powers to tax oil by the back door. One of the first things we did after getting back in power five years ago to stop another Megrahi. Prime Minister, I feel we need to wave the big stick to the Scots and Welsh over this one. Show then who's boss."

Henry Arbuthnot, the Defence Secretary was the next to speak. A former colonel in the Grenadier Guards and a highly useful rugby player in his younger days, Arbuthnot towered over the dimunitive Trade and Enterprise Secretary. "Prime Minister, I'm absolutely with Jason on this. We're already having problems with Edinburgh and Cardiff over the MoD ranges in Scotland and Wales. Also, the SNP want to kick the Americans out of Faslane and Holy Loch and Plaid Cymru wants to close the UAV testing grounds at Aberporth. This will cause frightful problems with the Americans. If we don't read the Riot Act to Ferguson and Roderick now, they will get bolder. You realise the risk to British interests this may cause?"

Christian Vale, the Foreign Secretary, was the next to speak. "Jason, Henry, I think you're getting a bit carried away. We're not dealing with some rogue state, they're nothing more than a regional government. I know they're technically in breach of their brief on this but I can understand where they're coming from. Scotland and Wales have suffered disproportionately from high unemployment and the collapse of their traditional industries over the past 30-40 years. All that Ferguson and Roderick are doing is trying to use some of the benefit from oil to regenerate their economy and ensure their workforce have the skills that employers are looking for. Surely, that's in the interests of the likes of Exxon and Texaco?"

"If we go round wielding the big stick, it won't make the UK look good abroad. The EU's gone further left after last month's election results in Greece, Portugal and Sweden and all the indications are that France will go left when it votes this month. There are plenty of countries who want to make life difficult for us—why give them an opportunity?"

"For God's sake Christian, don't be so wet" boomed the Home Secretary, Deborah Pearson. A blonde Yorkshirewoman just turned 50, she epitomised 1980s Thatcherism as much as Jason Steer. The grammar school-educated daughter of a police inspector, she had been educated at Oxford University and Harvard Business School before being employed by Chase Manhattan where she met her husband. She had been elected as MP for Worcestershire North East in 2005 and had been Home Secretary since 2012. A fierce right winger on both economic and social issues, she was seen by many as a future Prime Minister and the heir to Margaret Thatcher.

"Christian, all Ferguson and Roderick want is to get their greedy hands on the oil and to grandstand on the world scene. They are like naughty children; give into them and they'll want more and continue to play up if they don't get their own way."

Pearson continued, directing her attention to the Prime Minister. "The prospect of Scotland and Wales becoming independent fills me with dread. Not only are the UK's economic and defence interests affected, national security would be affected too. We've already got enough problems in getting co-operation from our European neighbours in the fight against crime and terrorism. An independent Scotland and Wales would add to those problems and as long as the SNP and Plaid Cymru are in power, that is a realistic threat."

"We've spent the past five years tightening our borders and making the UK safe and secure for its citizens. Do we want to gamble that away by giving the SNP and Plaid Cymru a free hand to destroy the Union?"

Chancellor of the Exchequer Ed Villiers and Attorney-General Stephen Lansbury motioned to speak but before they could get a word in, the Prime Minister moved to conclude the issue. "It appears that our hopes that the new administrations in Edinburgh and Cardiff would water down their policies have not been fulfilled. What Jason said happened is a very serious breach of the devolution acts and, as Jason, Henry and Deborah have said, potentially damages national interests. Christian, we've given the Scottish and Welsh governments decent block grants for years to cover regeneration and training costs. A lot of English voters have complained, and with some justification, that the Scots and the Welsh are being treated more favourably. And yet they still have large numbers of economically inactive people. A waste of public money, don't you think?"

Delgado continued. "I completely agree that we must lay down the law to the First Ministers at this early stage. Scotland and Wales are both part of the United Kingdom and must therefore comply with UK law as passed by Her Majesty's Government."

He then turned to the Attorney-General. "Stephen, can I have a letter to go to each First Minister by Thursday reminding them of the scope of their powers under the Scotland and Wales Acts as amended, including what they are allowed to do and what they are not allowed to do. And give as an example of the latter their plans to levy tax on the oil industry. By the way, can you also ensure that the First Ministers are reminded that HMG has the power to suspend the devolved administrations in the event of non-compliance."

Lansbury replied "Certainly, Prime Minister. I'll ask for letters to First Ministers Ferguson and Roderick to be prepared for my signature to go as planned."

"No Stephen. The letters are to go under my signature." Delgado couldn't have been more emphatic.

15 June 2015
Office of the First Minister
Scottish Parliament
Edinburgh

"Duncan, am I right in what I'm hearing? You think we're in the right on this?"

Duncan McRae, Chief Legal Adviser to the Scottish Government had been summoned to advise First Minister Alastair Ferguson on the contents of a letter he had just received from the Prime Minister warning him that the Scottish Government was in breach of the terms of the Scotland Act because they had carried out domestic policies which were considered to be harmful to UK interests. This was related to the Scottish Government's decision to use their local powers of taxation to collect revenue from oil companies that were exploiting the newly-discovered Cromarty and Hebrides fields.

"Ally, the onus would be with the UK Government to prove that the acts of the Scottish Government were harmful to wider UK interests. That would effectively require the entire oil industry to unite and bring a formal complaint to the UK Government. So far, that has not happened."

"Aye Duncan" responded First Minister Ferguson. "We all know that the Chairmen of the three companies who went to see the Trade and Enterprise Secretary two weeks ago are known barking right neocons. The others I've met see much more reasonable and supportive of our plans for regeneration and building a skilled workforce. If they don't throw their lot in with Exxon, Chevron and Texaco, you're saying that Delgado won't have a leg to stand on?"

"Ally, yes. The Scotland (Amendment) Act was brought in back in 2011 to prevent a repeat of the Megrahi episode. Remember the Lockerbie bomber who former Justice Minister Kenny MacAskill had released on compassionate grounds as he was dying from cancer? He was perfectly within his powers to do so, but it had serious repercussions for Anglo-US relations. When the Tories got back in power, one of the first things they did was to amend the Scotland and Wales Acts to tie the hands of the devolved governments on issues impacting on UK national interests. But the way its worded puts the onus on the UK Government to prove that you have harmed national interests, not the other way round. And if any of the oil companies are prepared to accept the taxes the Scottish Government proposes to levy, it severely weakens the UK Government's case."

Ferguson was delighted. "Duncan, that's the best news I've heard all day. Like to see Delgado's smug face when he finds out he can't touch us."

After McRae had left, Ferguson reached for the telephone to contact his Welsh counterpart. The phone rang. "First Minister's Office" trilled a female voice. "Is First Minister Roderick available? Tell him it's First Minister Ferguson."

Ten seconds later, Emyr Roderick was on other end of the line. "Ally, I think I know what it's about. Guess you've had the same letter from Delgado?"

"Emyr, good news. I had our Chief Legal Adviser in today and he reckons that unless the entire oil industry threatens to walk out over our planned taxes, Delgado's got no grounds to claim that our actions have harmed UK national interests. So far, only three companies, Exxon, Chevron and Texaco are kicking up a fuss. I think we're on solid ground here."

"Ally, our legal advisers are looking at the issue right now. I'll let them know what you've told me but I would be surprised if they disagree. Looks like we're in the clear. Next steps—I think letters from us to Señor Delgado telling him politely to fuck off. Agree?"

"Absolutely." With that, First Ministers Ferguson and Roderick proceeded to ratchet up the temperature in the dispute with Her Majesty's Government.

19 June 2015
Prime Minister's Office
10 Downing Street
London

"Impertinence. Absolutely damned impertinence Stephen." Prime Minister Robert Delgado was furious. With him was Attorney-General Stephen Lansbury.

The reason for Delgado's anger was the two letters he had received from the First Ministers of Scotland and Wales in reply to his of 11 June reminding them of the limits of their jurisdiction. First Ministers Ferguson and Roderick basically questioned the Government's interpretation of the Scotland and Wales Acts and argued that unless Westminster could prove that the actions of the Scottish and Welsh governments had harmed wider United Kingdom interests, they were within their powers to decide where taxes should be levied.

"Prime Minister, I still stand by the legal advice I previously gave" said a worried looking Lansbury. He had every right to look worried; there was a feeling within the Cabinet that he was not up to scratch and the embarrassment caused by the

Scottish and Welsh governments was considered by many to be the final straw. "Even if only three oil companies pull out, I think we can still argue that the Scottish and Welsh governments have damaged UK interests. The fact the other companies have remained does not necessarily mean they have given consent. And there must be other investors who will have been put off."

"Stephen, its now time to get serious" barked Delgado. "Ferguson and Roderick think they've got the better of us. Well they haven't. My next step will be to summon them to a meeting here next week, which I intend to use to give them a final warning about undermining UK Government policy. Can you be present? If Ferguson and Roderick continue to defy us Stephen, I am fully prepared to get Cabinet approval to suspend the Scottish and Welsh governments. Stephen, this may be an opportune time to start a review of options for the future governance of Scotland and Wales."

"Prime Minister" exclaimed Lansbury, "Do you seriously mean that we're considering abolishing the devolved governments?"

"Yes Stephen. Absolutely" replied Delgado.

24 June 2015
Prime Minister's Office
10 Downing Street
London

"Mr Ferguson, Mr Roderick, good morning. Could you please follow me".

The Prime Minister's Principal Private Secretary, Lucy Alexander, led First Ministers Alastair Ferguson and Emyr Roderick to the outer office where they would wait until summoned to go into see the Prime Minister.

"Tea, coffee, gentlemen?" asked the pretty PPS. "Tea, one sugar" replied the Scottish First Minister. "White coffee, two sugars" replied his Welsh counterpart.

"The Prime Minister's been detailed at the House but he should be ready to see you in five minutes time".

As Lucy Alexander returned to her desk, the two First Ministers started discussing the forthcoming meeting. "Ally, I don't think even Alex Salmond or Rhodri Morgan ever got the privilege of a bilateral with the Prime Minister in their first month in office" said Roderick. "We must have made an impact on him".

Ferguson had a more worried look on his face. "Emyr, what worries me is what Delgado's got up his sleeve. You saw his letter and the veiled threat to suspend us. I wouldn't rule out him doing that."

"Delgado wouldn't dare try it on, surely Ally? He'd be risking possible civil war?"

"I think he would Emyr. Hesford's advising him." Ferguson was referring to Frank Hesford, the Security Adviser to the Prime Minister. He knew Hesford's views on tackling threats to not only national security but anything considered to be the Government's interests, and it included using the armed forces to support the police in suppressing civil disorder. "And don't forget Delgado got his break under Mrs Thatcher 30 years ago. He cut his political teeth on her wielding the big stick. The miners strike, the Greenham women, banning unions at GCHQ and abolishing the GLC. He wants to show us whose boss and to impress the Yanks and the oil industry."

The First Ministers were interrupted by a heavy footfall and they had sight of Prime Minister Robert Delgado as he entered his office. He was accompanied by the Attorney-General, Stephen Lansbury. Ferguson and Roderick were promptly invited to enter the Prime Minister's office and sit down in two chairs on the other side of a large oblong desk made of oak.

"Good morning gentlemen" said the Prime Minister. "So good of you to come to London."

Delgado continued. "You will be familiar with the reasons why I've invited you to this meeting. Your Governments have embarked upon policies which are harmful to UK national interests. I am referring to the levy of taxation on property owned by the oil industry. You will understand that the new oil reserves present an opportunity for the United Kingdom to develop energy security and to support economic growth for the entire United Kingdom. Including Scotland and Wales. Part of the deal for the oil companies was that the exploration sites would be designated enterprise zones under which they would be exempt from most UK taxes, whether national or local. The oil industry was not expecting to receive further tax demands from your Governments."

"Your action in using devolved powers of taxation has put that opportunity at risk. Already, three companies have threatened to pull out rather than pay tax."

"You realise that the Scotland and Wales Acts as amended prohibit your Governments from executing policies which have a harmful effect on wider UK policies or interests that are reserved by Her Majesty's Government. Even if your Governments have the power to carry out those policies."

Alastair Ferguson was the first to respond. "Prime Minister, you appear to have overlooked the fact that First Minister Roderick and I thoroughly checked the legality of our action. We both took legal advice before we decided to issue tax demands on the oil industry, and that advice unequivocally backed our legal rights under the Scotland and Wales Acts. Our replies of 18 June stated this."

"As our Legal Counsel explained, Prime Minister, for our Governments to have been in breach of the law, there would have had to be objections from the oil industry on a much greater level than has happened—in fact, there would have had to be a threat of a universal pullout. That has not taken place."

Roderick then joined the conversation. "Wales and Scotland has had little benefit from your Government Prime Minister, or indeed, any previous Tory government. We suffered the Great Depression in the 1930s, the virtual wipeout of our industrial base in the 1980s and further job losses after the 2008 banking collapse. Large numbers of our young men and women have had to leave to find work. Yet we had the resources which built the British Empire—Welsh coal and steel and Scottish engineering, plus the graduates of the most envied education systems in the British Isles. But where did the wealth created go Prime Minister? To your friends in the City, to robber barons and asset-strippers, not to the people who built that wealth. This time round, First Minister Ferguson and I intend to use the benefits of our mineral wealth for the benefit of our people."

"Spare me the class war rhetoric gentlemen" said an increasingly exasperated Delgado. "Apart from the fact you've both appeared to have forgotten that Scotland and Wales have been net beneficiaries at the expense of the English taxpayer for the past 40 years, the fact remains that you have both overstepped your powers under the devolution acts."

Ferguson and Roderick reacted angrily. "You've been cutting our grant for the past five years, Prime Minister."

Delgado resumed. "If you let me continue, I referred this to the Legal Secretary to the Law Officers, who is the highest legal authority in the land. Isn't that so Stephen?" The Prime Minister motioned to the Attorney-General who nodded his approval. "He said that there was a *prima facie* case that your activities were harmful to UK national interests and he had no doubt that you were in breach of the law."

Ferguson countered with a threat to take the matter to the European Court.

"Not a chance Mr Ferguson. Since the UK left the EU earlier this year, the EU or any of its institutions have no jurisdiction over UK law." Both Ferguson and Roderick came to the conclusion that the Prime Minister was not going to change his opinion.

Delgado moved to sum up. "Gentlemen, Her Majesty's Government wants to have cordial relations with the devolved governments, even when they are led by parties of different political persuasion like yours. But you have both taxed my patience, and that of the Attorney-General this morning. It is clear that you've got little desire to comply with the law of the land passed by the United Kingdom's democratically-elected Government. You have given me little option but to give your governments a final ultimatum. Within two weeks from today, I want to have a signed statement from both of you which should state that the devolved governments for Scotland and Wales will fully comply with the terms of the Scotland and Wales Acts 2011 as amended for the remainder of their term of office and desist from carrying out policies which have an adverse impact on United Kingdom national interests."

"And what if we don't?" snarled Roderick.

"Then I will seek Cabinet approval for the suspension of the Scottish and Welsh governments with a view to possible abolition and replacement with revised governance arrangements. Good day gentlemen."

9 July 2015
Cabinet Room
10 Downing Street
London

First item on the agenda for the Cabinet meeting was the issue of governance in Scotland and Wales. With the Prime Minister having given the First Ministers in Scotland and Wales two weeks to provide a statement agreeing to comply fully with the terms of devolution legislation over the issue of activities adversely affecting wider UK interests, the meeting had been held back two days. In the briefing packs were copies of the exchange of correspondence between the Prime Minister and the

Scottish and Welsh First Ministers and the minutes of the meeting the Prime Minister and Attorney-General had with the First Ministers.

Prime Minister Robert Delgado opened the proceedings. "Ladies and Gentlemen, may I first update you on the contretemps with the devolved governments over carrying out policies which damage national interests. You will have seen the minutes of the meeting I had on 24 June with First Ministers Ferguson and Roderick. Since that meeting, I have had no communication from either First Minister and enquiries made by my office suggest that no statements will be forthcoming. It is clear they have no intention to comply with devolution legislation and will continue to behave as if they are not part of the United Kingdom. I therefore regret we have no choice but to consider the immediate suspension of the Scottish and Welsh governments."

"The second issue we need to discuss is the future of governance in Scotland and Wales. I know many of you never supported devolution in Scotland and Wales right from the day that the Blair government held the referendums eighteen years ago. I have never seen the value of a further layer of government. It's expensive and is a godsent opportunity for mischief-makers and grandstanders to waste public money. The only reason we've tolerated it is because of the image problem our party has had there in the past. I think it is now reasonable to consider whether we want to continue with the Scottish and Welsh governments in their current form."

"I've asked Stephen to carry out a review of options for future governance in Scotland and Wales. He will report to Cabinet on 23 July, which will enable us to get the ball rolling before the recess. In the meantime, I intend to ask the Scotland and Wales Offices to appoint residuary bodies to run the affairs of the governments if suspension takes place."

There was only one dissenting voice to the proposed suspension of the Scottish and Welsh governments, and that was Foreign Secretary Christian Vale. "Prime Minister, don't you think that suspension is a provocative move? The public in Scotland and Wales broadly support the concept of devolved government. This will be seen as England imposing direct rule. I think the last person who tried that was Edward I."

Delgado was distinctly unimpressed with Vale's case. "Christian, may I remind you that this Government was elected on a plank of strong Government. This means being decisive, risking unpopularity and not being afraid of taking on special interests. Over the past five years, we've proved to the British public that we're prepared to be tough. We clamped down on the compensation racket that was costing British business, we took on the public sector unions and banned strikes in the public sector, when a lot of people said we could not do it. We weren't afraid to bring back the death penalty and to face down critics. We drove through reforms to the criminal justice system which made judges and magistrates accountable to the public. We backed the USA against Iran when most of the rest of the world stood on the sidelines keeping their head down. Everyone said we would face everything from economic collapse through sky-high oil prices through to a massive Islamic jihad against the West. Well, Christian, where is it?"

"The Scottish and Welsh governments are pushing their luck, just like Ken Livingstone and Derek Hatton did thirty years ago. On that occasion, Margaret

Thatcher showed she had the balls to get rid of the GLC and to cap local authority powers to stop the loony left frittering away ratepayers' hard earned money. Ferguson and Roderick are the same—give them an inch and they'll take a mile. Remember, their ultimate aim is to leave the United Kingdom. Deborah and Henry have amply spelled out the consequences of what would happen if that takes place. Quite simply, if we allow them to get away with flouting the law, our Government's credibility is at risk."

The Cabinet agreed by a majority of 19:1 to suspend the Scottish and Welsh governments. Christian Vale was the only dissenter.

10 July 2015
Sky News

"This is Adam Rennie on Sky News. The main news headline of today is the Government's decision to suspend the devolved Governments in Scotland and Wales. Mr Delgado made the announcement this morning at a special news conference outside 10 Downing Street."

"Relations between Westminster and the devolved governments in Edinburgh and Cardiff were always going to be difficult following the election of nationalist governments in May's elections. But few people expected that the SNP and Plaid Cymru to proceed with policies which brought them in direct conflict with Westminster. However, the Scottish and Welsh governments were determined to use their countries' recently found oil wealth for their own benefit. This meant in practice using their taxation powers on the oil industry which is currently drilling for oil in the Cromarty, Hebrides and Fastnet fields. The oil industry had been promised by the UK Government that they would be tax exempt in order to encourage inward investment. The actions of the devolved governments in Edinburgh and Cardiff has already led three major oil companies to reconsider their investment."

"Mr Delgado also announced that a review of governance for Scotland and Wales would be taking place. The potential key options are: replacing the Scottish Parliament and Welsh Assembly with elected assemblies with no tax raising powers but the right to decide how the delegated budgets for Scotland and Wales should be spent; the creation of Grand Committees for Scotland and Wales, comprising MPs from those countries who would have responsibility for policy decisions relating to them, and; reverting to the pre-1999 position where policy decision and laws are decided by the UK Parliament."

The same day
Cabinet Room
Scottish Parliament
Edinburgh

"Ladies and gentlemen, we've got just two choices open to us. We either capitulate to Westminster and allow them to close down Scotland's democratically-elected Government and lose face forever. Or we stand up and fight. And that means taking control of our destiny and walking tall as a proud nation." First Minister Alastair

Ferguson could not have been more emphatic about the choices facing his government in the face of the United Kingdom government's decision to suspend them.

"I take it you mean declaring independence Ally" said Home Affairs Minister Nicola Glennie.

"Absolutely, Nicola" replied the First Minister.

Exclamations of approval rung through the Cabinet Room. However, there was one dissenter, Finance Minister Stuart Purvis.

"Ally, have you thought through the implications of what you've just said" argued Purvis. "If we declare independence, I don't imagine for one minute that Delgado will take it lying down. As you've said before, we've got 100 years worth of oil and Delgado's got that lined up to pay for tax cuts and expansion of the police and armed services. That's a powerful motive for stopping us. What's more, we could all be up on treason charges and could be in jail for the next 20 years or so, if not worse." Purvis was referring to the fact that treason now carried the death penalty. "You realise what you're asking us to sign up to—do you really want to force us to tell our families that they might never see us again?"

Ferguson was distinctly unimpressed with his Finance Minister's lack of enthusiasm for independence. "Stuart, have you forgotten that it is our party's policy to seek independence from the United Kingdom? And has been since we were formed over eighty years ago. If you think we might persuade Delgado to compromise, you're living in cloud cuckoo land. He was elected on a platform of strong government and he's shown it in his dealings with the unions, the EU, the judges and the EU over the past five years. The Tories never accepted the idea of home rule for Scotland and they would relish the opportunity to take things back to what they were before 1999. Remember, that was how we got the poll tax first."

"If we make the break, I can guarantee we'll have international support. Delgado's not made Britain very popular over the past few years. For starters, the EU will back us and I reckon Russia and China will support us too. And don't forget the USA's got a lot of voters of Scottish descent. I doubt if President Whitney will want to piss them off by backing Delgado."

Health Minister Liz Turner was more forceful. "Stuart, I seriously wonder if you're really one of us or whether you've joined the SNP just to further your own career." Purvis had been a banker with the Royal Bank of Scotland before becoming an MSP in 2007. "The rest of us know what the risks are, but we're all prepared to go ahead and declare independence. The English have ripped our country off over the past 300 years, taken our natural resources, built their wealth on the back of our engineering skills, taken our most skilled and talented people and given us nothing in return apart from unemployment and the poll tax. Once we're free of England, we'll be the masters of our own destiny and Delgado won't be able to do anything about it. This is our chance Stuart—let's grasp it."

First Minister Ferguson moved the meeting towards a vote. "I would now like to move to a decision on whether we should declare independence now."

All but one Cabinet member raised their hands in favour of independence. With this, Alastair Ferguson announced that the Scottish Government would be issuing a declaration of independence from the United Kingdom.

The same day
First Minister's Office
Welsh Assembly Government
Cardiff

"I can't do this, Emyr. Independence? Wales isn't big enough to go it alone. What's more, have you thought of the risk to those AMs who vote for the break?" Social Affairs Minister, Jane Lewis had a worried look on her face.

"Jane, we've done our homework thoroughly on this" replied Welsh First Minister Emyr Roderick. "We're sitting on enough oil to last us for the rest of the century—that will pay all the bills. If the Americans leave, the Russians and Chinese are interested in investing. The other thing is that Delgado's already burnt a few bridges—the EU, the Islamic world—and he won't have the appetite for further conflict in his own backyard."

"If you refuse to back me Jane, you realise you'll be on your own." This startled Mrs Lewis. "On my own—what do you mean Emyr?"

The First Minister explained. "Jane, I've already spoken to your fellow group members. Peter Walsh is behind us on this, as is Jim Ruddock and Dai Bent."

Roderick continued. "Jane, this is a golden opportunity for Wales. We've been tacked onto England as an appendage for nearly 500 years. And that's how the English see us. We've got two choices—either give in and see England pillage yet another Welsh resource for their own benefit or be bold and make the break. With the oil resources under our control, it'll pay for all the social welfare policies you want to see implemented."

Roderick could see that Jane Lewis was still unconvinced about supporting a declaration of independence. "Jane, I don't think the Welsh people will ever forgive you if you vote against independence. Your political career will effectively be over. You can think on it and come back to me later."

Mrs Lewis realised that Roderick had backed her into a corner. "Can I have more time to think about this Emyr? And to confer with my Senedd colleagues?"

"Okay Jane" replied the First Minister. "But I want a reply tomorrow. I can't wait forever."

CHAPTER 2

13 July 2015
Sky News, 10:30am

Sky News was in the middle of an interview with Thames Valley Police who had made extensive use of the Special Constabulary in their fight against crime. Laura Hitchen, a sales manager with IBM who was a volunteer sergeant with Thames Valley Police was being interviewed about her role.

Suddenly, the interview was terminated for an important newsflash.

"This is Claire Egerton on Sky News. We are breaking off from our scheduled programmes for an important piece of breaking news. Scotland and Wales have just declared unilateral independence from the United Kingdom."

"In the past hour, the governments in Edinburgh and Cardiff have announced that they are leaving the United Kingdom and are seeking international recognition. Customs and immigration checkpoints have been set up on the borders with England and there are already reports of traffic queues building up as motorists are being asked to produce identity documents."

"This has effectively thrown down the gauntlet to the United Kingdom Government which, three days ago, suspended the devolved governments in Scotland and Wales after they refused to comply with the terms of devolution . . . ."

The same day
Cabinet Office Briefing Room (COBRA)
London

The Cabinet Office Briefing Room (COBRA) was a facility used if there was ever a domestic or international emergency. The Prime Minister attended, along with Ministers from the relevant Departments, along with representatives from the armed forces, the Security and Secret Intelligence Services and the Association of Chief Police Officers. It had last been used in 2012 following Al-Q'aida terrorist attacks on the City of London and Docklands.

COBRA was already filling up. Prime Minister Robert Delgado was there, along with Home Secretary Deborah Pearson, Secretary of State for Defence Henry Arbuthnot, Policing Minister Darren Bramble and Homeland Security Minister Mark Taylor. Also present was MI5 Director-General Nicola Martin, the Head of the Joint Chiefs of Staff for the Armed Forces, Sir Mike Woodcock and the Chairman of the Association of Chief Police Officers (ACPO), Dave Tanner. Finally, the Prime

Minister's Security Adviser, Frank Hesford, arrived. A video conference link ensured that Archie Patterson, Chairman of the Association of Chief Police Officers for Scotland (ACPOS) and Emlyn Crowley, Chairman of the Welsh Association of Chief Police Officers (WACPO) could participate in the meeting.

Once everyone present had taken their seat, the Prime Minister opened the meeting. "Ladies and gentlemen, thank you for attending COBRA at such short notice. You will be fully aware of the reasons I've asked you to be here. Earlier today, the devolved governments in Scotland and Wales made an illegal declaration of independence from the United Kingdom. It appears that many public servants are assisting the illegal administrations in breach of their oath of allegiance to Her Majesty the Queen." Delgado was referring to the civil servants, Customs and immigration officers and police officers who were helping to administer the declaration of independence.

"As I have said many times before, my Government is absolutely committed to the integrity of the United Kingdom and will not tolerate any secession from the United Kingdom without its permission. The devolved administrations in Scotland and Wales clearly have no intention to comply with UK law. We therefore have no option but to use force to ensure that the jurisdiction of the United Kingdom Government is restored."

Delgado continued. "My Security Adviser, Frank Hesford, will outline what resources are needed to restore order. Frank, over to you."

Frank Hesford was in his 50s and was average height. He was wearing a pinstripe suit from Gieves and Hawkes and his short hair was swept back. He was however built like a middleweight boxer and had been an officer in the Special Air Service. He immediately commanded the attention of other people in the room.

"Ladies and gentlemen, it is beyond doubt that we need to execute a military solution and the sooner the better. Any delay and Ferguson and Roderick may have set up their own armed forces and there's always the risk they'll get overseas support." Hesford was referring to the possibility of European Union forces being invited to defend the fledgling countries.

"The first step is to seize control of the capitals. First to go in would be the Special Services who will take the Parliament buildings in Edinburgh and Cardiff. Their role will be to take control of the secessionist governments and remove them to custody in England. Deborah, can you ensure there is secure custody accommodation for the Scottish and Welsh Cabinets."

The Home Secretary replied "No problem Frank. We'll make sure there are places in Woodhill and Whitemoor available." These were two of the country's most secure prisons, the former close to Milton Keynes, the latter in Cambridgeshire. Both were an encouragingly long distance from either Scotland or Wales.

Hesford continued. "We will also need to take control of the airports, seaports and radio and television stations. Mike" he motioned to the Head of the Joint Chiefs of Staff for the Armed Forces, "can you ensure that regular Army units are mobilised for this task."

Before Sir Mike Woodcock had a chance to reply, there was a protest from ACPOS Chairman Archie Patterson. "Colonel Hesford, why can't the police do this?

They are fully capable of responding to emergency situations. Using troops is overkill and might provoke public disorder."

"Chief Constable Patterson" Hesford replied, "what has happened is more than mere public disorder. It is an open challenge to the authority of the national Government. If facilities like air and seaports and broadcasting stations are not secured, it will make it more difficult for the Government to restore the rule of law. The armed forces have been used to support the police in previous situations, using lessons learned from the military engagements in Iraq and Afghanistan in the 2000s. The police will continue to play a major role in the maintenance of law and order."

General Woodcock then replied to Hesford's earlier question. "Frank, we'll be able to send as many troops as you need to secure key installations. Let me know when and where you need them."

Hesford continued. "Maintaining law and order could be a problem. No doubt nationalist sympathisers will aim to get as many people onto the streets as possible to cause disruption. English owned businesses and properties will be those most at risk. To ensure that public order is maintained, it will be necessary to augment Scottish and Welsh policing capacity with support from English forces. Dave, how soon can you send police reinforcements to Scotland and Wales?"

The big, burly figure of the ACPO Chairman replied "Providing that there's suitable accommodation ready, within three days. I've dusted off the old papers from the Miners Strike thirty years ago which show how quickly the police could be deployed in a national emergency."

This drew an objection from WACPO Chairman Emlyn Crowley. "Colonel Hesford, you appear to be suggesting that the Scottish and Welsh police are incapable of coping with a national emergency. I can assure you that my officers are fully capable of maintaining order and don't need any of the English forces to help them out."

"And the same for the Scottish police" growled ACPOS Chairman Patterson.

MI5 Director-General Nicola Martin was next to speak. "Gentlemen, we're not doubting the integrity of the majority of your officers. But we've had information that a minority of your officers are openly collaborating with the secessionist governments in clear breach of their oath of allegiance to the Crown. If we're to rely on your officers to maintain order, we've got to be confident that all of them will remain loyal. Sadly, we cannot be assured that is possible. In the circumstances, we've got no option but to send officers from English forces to assist in maintaining order."

"Ms Martin" replied a grave ACPOS Chairman, "you and Colonel Hesford clearly have no idea of how provocative it will be having English police officers on the streets of Scotland and Wales. Even people who did not support the nationalist governments will think that the UK Government has gone too far. Now would be a good time to let the Scots and the Welsh prove they can be trusted to act responsibly. Otherwise, you may risk having more disorder and those English officers sent in may end up being the target for people's discontent."

There was a knock on the door. "Prime Minister, Sir Jocelyn Blackmore and Sir Gerald Norton are here." The Prime Minister's Principal Private Secretary, Lucy Alexander, was escorting two retired former Permanent Secretaries to COBRA.

"Thank you Lucy. Jocelyn, Gerald, delighted to see you. Please come in."

29

The Prime Minister continued. "May I introduce Sir Jocelyn Blackmore and Sir Gerald Norton. Jocelyn and Gerald have been invited to chair the residuary bodies that will govern Scotland and Wales until we have decided on future governance arrangements. In effect, they will be the civil governors for Scotland and Wales."

15 July 2015, 10:25am
Scottish Parliament
Edinburgh

"Papa Alpha Bravo, do you read me?"

Flight Lieutenant Keir Redman, the pilot of the lead Boeing Chinook helicopter carrying an SAS squadron charged with taking control of the Scottish Parliament, replied. "Base, this is Papa Alpha Bravo. We're now about five minutes from target. E.T.A. 10:30 as planned."

"Roger. Keep us informed of developments Papa Alpha Bravo."

"Roger" replied Redman.

Five minutes later, the two helicopters landed on the lawn outside the Scottish Parliament building. Within seconds, a heavily-armed SAS squadron had exited and burst into the Parliament building. There was no resistance from either the stunned MSPs or the officials present and at 10:40 onlookers were greeted by the sight of First Minister Alastair Ferguson and the other MSPs being led out at gunpoint and forced to board the RAF Chinook helicopters which would fly them back to England.

The same day, 10:40am
Welsh Assembly
Cardiff

Nobody paid much attention to the fast launch which sailed into Cardiff Bay up to the waterfront by the Welsh Assembly, the Welsh National Assembly. But on board were 15 members of the Special Boat Service, the maritime equivalent of the feared Special Air Service. Their task was to take control of the Welsh Assembly and to take into Custody the AMs from Plaid Cymru and Independent Labour who had declared independence.

Barely seconds after drawing up to the Welsh Assembly, the SBS troops had disembarked and burst into the Welsh Assembly. Within ten minutes, they had control of the building and were leading First Minister Emyr Roderick and fellow AMs out of the building for a journey back over the Bristol Channel and into custody.

Later that day, 1pm
Sky News

"This is Claire Egerton on Sky News with the lunchtime headlines. There were dramatic scenes in Edinburgh and Cardiff this morning as special forces stormed the Scottish Parliament and the Welsh Assembly to take control and put an end to the declarations of independence. Latest reports state that Alastair Ferguson and Emyr Roderick, the First

Ministers of Scotland and Wales, their cabinets and MSPs and AMs from the Scottish National Party and Plaid Cymru have all been put under arrest and are being held at unspecified locations."

"Meanwhile, troops from the Blues and Royals, the Green Howards, the Royal Anglian Regiment and the Queen's Lancashire Regiment are moving in to secure air and seaports, radio and television stations and other critical installations . . . ."

The same day, 1:05pm
Cabinet Office Briefing Room (COBRA)
London

"Brilliant, absolutely bloody brilliant." Prime Minister Robert Delgado was ecstatic with the news. "Let that be a lesson for anyone who thinks they can mess with the UK Government."

Delgado continued. "Henry, Deborah, what's the latest with Ferguson and Roderick."

Defence Secretary Henry Arbuthnot was first to reply. "Prime Minister, Ferguson, Roderick and the Scottish and Welsh Cabinets are being held at RAF Boulmer and RAF Lyneham pending their transfer to Home Office custody. Were also holding MSPs from the SNP and AMs from Plaid Cymru and Independent Labour who were not in the Cabinets. See little point in holding onto them as they've had barely anything to do with the secessions. Is it OK to let them go?"

"Yes Henry" replied Delgado. "Deborah, how about their transfer to prison?"

"The Home Secretary replied "Prime Minister, I've arranged for a chartered plane to transport the Scottish prisoners from RAF Boulmer to Cambridge Airport. From there, Prison Service will transfer them to HMP Whitemoor. Further transport is already on the way to RAF Lyneham to pick up the Welsh prisoners. Oh and by the way, I've arranged with Dave to arrange for an armed police escort to make sure there's no attempts to spring them." She gave a nod to ACPO Chairman Dave Tanner.

Delgado then turned to General Sir Mike Woodcock. "Mike, what's the situation like in Edinburgh and Cardiff?"

"A few demonstrators on the street but nothing the police can't cope with. Otherwise, fairly quiet."

"So you think it will be OK for Blackmore and Norton to take up their office now?"

"Can't see why not Prime Minister."

"Good. By the way Mike, what's the situation like with the police there? Are they on our side?"

"Largely yes Prime Minister" said the Head of the Joint Chiefs of Staff. "I reckon no more than two percent of the police in Scotland and Wales have refused to work with us."

"I'll be contacting Patterson and Crowley" said Pearson who had now assumed responsibility for policing in Scotland and Wales under emergency powers enacted.

"And I'll be expecting them to take rigorous action against any officers found to be in breach of their oath to the Crown."

"Well done Deborah" replied Delgado.

There was a knock on the door and Attorney-General Stephen Lansbury and Foreign Secretary Christian Vale walked in.

"Stephen, Christian, good to see you" said the Prime Minister. "Stephen, can you give me an update on the review of governance."

The Attorney-General removed a sheath of papers from a locked case. "Prime Minister, ladies and gentlemen, the Working Group on Governance for Scotland and Wales has now been set up and we plan to have our first meeting tomorrow. Here's a list of members." Lansbury handed out a paper containing details of the members and their interests. There was a mixture of MPs, MSPs, AMs, businessmen and civic leaders, along with two constitutional lawyers. "For obvious reasons, we've excluded the SNP and Plaid Cymru but otherwise, there's a mix from all three main parties."

"Good progress Stephen" said the Prime Minister. "One thing I want you to bear in mind. After what the SNP and Plaid Cymru have done, I want no more talk of separate assemblies. From now on, Scotland and Wales are to be administered as constituent parts of the United Kingdom. There will be no more nonsense about home rule. Make that clear."

Lansbury was slightly put out by this. "Prime Minister, are you serious? What we've done is highly unpopular, even amongst the Scots and Welsh who disagreed with independence. If we give them elected assemblies with no more power than the average county council, most Scots and Welsh will be content and we'll probably hear nothing more from the SNP and Plaid. But impose direct rule from Westminster and it will look like the English oppressing their Celtic subjects. And that will make the nationalists more dangerous, not less."

Delgado's brow had furrowed. He was not impressed by this show of dissent from his Attorney-General. "Stephen, I've made myself clear. No assemblies. The SNP and Plaid Cymru have had their last chance. From now on, we run Scotland and Wales from London. Understand?"

He next turned to Vale. "Christian, what's been the world reaction?"

The Foreign Secretary had an ashen look on his face as it had been a torrid morning. "Not encouraging, Prime Minister. The EU's lodged a protest against us at the United Nations, Russia, China and Iran were not surprisingly critical. But what's worried me is that we've not got support from countries we'd thought would support us. Australia and New Zealand were lukewarm and some Commonwealth countries were hostile. South Africa's on the side of Scotland and Wales. Even Rose had reservations." The news that US Secretary of State Milton Rose was not unequivocally supporting the United Kingdom was a surprise.

Delgado however knew the solution. "Christian, leave it to me. Rose might be wet but I can assure you that the President won't be. I'll phone her after this meeting's over."

Half an hour later, Delgado was back in his office at 10 Downing Street. He had passed by the long gallery of photographs of previous Prime Ministers ranging from Sir Robert Walpole, through the Duke of Wellington, Sir Robert Peel, William

Gladstone, Benjamin Disraeli, David Lloyd George, Sir Winston Churchill, Harold Wilson, Margaret Thatcher and Tony Blair. At the end of the line was the photograph of himself—Robert Francis Delgado, Prime Minister from 2010.

Delgado picked up the telephone and rang the pre-programmed number.

"The President's Office. How can I help?" A pleasant female voice was on the line.

"Robert Delgado here. Can I speak to President Whitney?"

"Absolutely sir. I'll transfer you now."

"Bob, what a pleasure to hear from you." At the other end of the line was the first ever female President of the United States of America, Katherine Dale Whitney. A Republican from Texas, Whitney was 50 years old, tall and statuesque with jet black hair. The daughter of a wealthy Dallas businessman, she had followed her state's predecessor as President, George W Bush on a route to power by becoming a State senator first before becoming Governor of Texas. She had become president in 2012. Victory in the war with Iran in 2013 had resulted in sky-high popularity for her in the USA.

"Katherine, you'll know why I'm on the line."

"If you mean the military operation against Scotland and Wales, you've got nothing to worry about Bob. The rest of the world might be limp-wristed panty-waists but I'm not. You did the right thing. Ferguson and Roderick are about as trustworthy as a case of rattlesnakes—after all, look at the crazies they've shacked up with?" Amongst those she was referring to Iranian President Mohammed Khoramzadeh, whom the former First Ministers had met years earlier. "What's more, we need every drop of oil we can get our hands on and we can't afford to have a pair of jerks like them in charge of it."

"Great to hear that Katherine. But I've heard that Rose's less than enthusiastic."

"Milton?" replied the President. "He's always over-cautious. Don't worry. The Vice-President is behind you, as is Senate Majority Leader Burton." Whitney was referring to her Vice-President, Philip Odell, a one-time Democrat from Illinois and the abrasive Republican Leader of the Senate, Mississippi Senator Troy Burton. Both men were close to the oil industry.

"Katherine, you know that the EU's got a censure motion against us at the UN. I trust the USA will veto that."

"Absolutely Bob. As I've said, I fully support what you've done. With Philip and Congress also behind you, you've got nothing to worry about."

17 July 2015
Cabinet Office Briefing Room (COBRA)
London

"Jesus Christ, they're having trouble holding control. Deborah, Henry, looks like we'll need Plan B."

Robert Delgado had just finished a video conferenced discussion with Sir Jocelyn Blackmore and Sir Gerald Norton, the Chairmen of the Scottish and Welsh Residuary Bodies appointed to wind up the affairs of the former Scottish and

Welsh governments. The news had not been good. There had now been two nights of disturbances in the Scottish and Welsh capitals and these had spread to other cities, with Aberdeen, Dundee, Glasgow, Newport, Perth, Swansea and Wrexham all reporting trouble. English-owned businesses and properties had been targeted by mobs and the latest reports were of crowds massing by the now closed and cordoned-off Scottish Parliament and Welsh Assembly buildings.

Blackmore and Norton had more difficulties to contend with. The main civil service union, the Public and Commercial Services Union, had called for its staff to refuse to work with the Residuary Bodies, and it was estimated that over 50% of the civil service in Scotland and Wales had heeded the call.

"Prime Minister, we've got no choice but to send in police reinforcements now to maintain order" replied Home Secretary Deborah Pearson. She immediately turned to the ACPO Chairman, Dave Tanner. "Dave, how soon can you send them in?"

"They're all ready to go today Home Secretary" advised the ACPO chief. "Main issue is emergency accommodation but I understand that's been arranged by the Home Office. Isn't that so?"

"Absolutely, Dave. My Department's civil contingency people have already sorted that out. By the way, Prime Minister, shouldn't we notify Patterson and Crowley that they'll be having guests on their doorstep?"

"Yes Deborah" replied Delgado. "Call up Patterson and Crowley now."

Thirty seconds later, the ACPOS and WACPO Chairmen were on the video screen. "Archie, Emlyn, good morning. How are things at present?"

Patterson was the first to respond. "Home Secretary, things were a bit torrid last night. Mobs on the streets, damaging property and throwing things at my men and women. But I think we" be able to contain it."

Crowley then responded. "We've had much the same. Looks like English-owned property is being targeted. But we've got a good idea who's behind it and we expect to be making arrests shortly."

Pearson continued. "Gentlemen, 'torrid' was something of an understatement. From what Blackmore and Norton told me, there's a virtual breakdown of civil order. The Government's got no choice but to send reinforcements, and the only source is from English forces. ACPO Chairman Tanner will be sending in officers from English forces, including members of Territorial Support Groups who have experience in dealing with public order situations. I trust they will have you full co-operation."

"I guess we've got no choice" replied ACPOS Chairman Patterson.

Delgado next turned to the Secretary of State for Defence, Henry Arbuthnot. "Henry, are the troops you sent into Scotland and Wales still there? And how quickly can they be used to keep public order if the need arises?"

"Prime Minister, most of the troops are back in their barracks as the job they were required to do has been completed." Arbuthnot was referring to the securing of the air and sea ports and the television and radio stations. "But it should be possible to mobilise them quickly. Is that so Mike?"

General Woodcock replied "Secretary of State, there are still detachments controlling the main airports, so there's no problem with getting the men in. The Universals at Brize Norton should be able to transport troops into Wales in half an hour and to Scotland in just over an hour." Woodcock was referring to the massive Airbus-built transport planes delivered to the RAF earlier in the decade to replace the ageing Hercules dating from the 1960s. "On top of that" Woodcock continued, "Chinook and Merlin helos will be on hand to move the northern regiments into Scotland. Also, road and rail transport is ready to be mobilised to move further men and equipment in. We should be fully capable of supporting the police by tomorrow if things get worse. Hopefully, they won't be needed."

Delgado gave the response. "That's excellent news. Dave, can you activate plans for sending police from English forces to support their Scottish and Welsh counterparts. And Mike, can you activate plans for troops to be on hand to support the police if needed." Tanner and Woodcock nodded.

"Now all I have to do is notify Blackmore and Norton. Lucy" motioned Delgado to his Principal Private Secretary, "can you call up the Chairmen of the Scottish and Welsh Residuary Bodies."

19 July 2015
BBC News

"This is Asif Ahmed on BBC News with today's headlines. Nearly 400,000 people are taking part in demonstrations in Edinburgh and Cardiff to protest against the suspension of the Scottish and Welsh governments and the arrest of their cabinets following last Monday's declaration of unilateral independence by the two countries. So far, the demonstrations have been peaceful and so incidents have been reported. But the authorities are not taking any chances following four nights of disturbances across Scotland and Wales. Police reinforcements from England have been sent in to support the Scottish and Welsh forces, and it is reported that army regiments are being held as a contingency against deteriorating order."

The same day
MI5 Headquarters
Millbank
London

Thames House was very quiet on what was a warm and sunny summer Sunday. Only a few staff were in and most of these were either single or divorced and came in because their social calendar at the weekends was often empty. One of these was Richard Donovan, the Head of F6 Section which dealt with domestic terrorism and subversion other than high priority areas, which meant Al-Q'aida, Irish Republicans, Marxists and anarchists and animal rights activists. For over 30 years, this had been a backwater in MI5, nothing happening since the Free Wales Army's campaign of burning English-owned holiday homes in the early 1980s and the threat by the Scottish National Liberation Army to assassinate Mrs Thatcher.

Donovan was in his early 50s, a burly, balding man who had been a career civil servant who had joined MI5 from the Home Office six years earlier on the recommendation of MI5 Director-General Nicola Martin, for whom he had previously worked.

Having checked reports and filed them, Donovan had virtually nothing to do, and this gave him an opportunity to catch up with the news headlines online. He had just opened up the website of the *Mail on Sunday* when he was interrupted.

Sukhvinder 'Suki' Basra, a pretty Sikh girl, had been working for MI5 for just under a year since graduating from Nottingham University and was working in Richard Donovan's section. Unlike most of her colleagues who were working that Sunday, her motives for working were to obtain time off in lieu. She was engaged to her cousin in India who was a qualified accountant and she needed the time for her marriage.

"Richard, have you got a minute" said Suki. "Just had in some interesting developments reported by our field agents in Scotland and Wales."

Donovan walked over to Suki's workstation and her assessment was correct. Field agents had reported the theft of explosives, assault rifles and JCBs and there was speculation that they could be used in an assault on the Scottish Parliament and the Welsh Assembly. Agents had also intercepted telephone and e-mail traffic which suggested that there were plans to murder the Chairmen of the Residuary Bodies and senior officials working for them.

"Suki, thanks for pointing this out. Talk about ruining someone's weekend! Have you got the DG's private number?"

Suki Basra gave Donovan the top secret number for MI5 Director-General, Nicola Martin. Using the encryption to keep the message away from prying ears, Donovan rang the Director-General.

"01372 726124,"

"Nicola, Richard Donovan here. Got some very disturbing developments you might like to know of. There's been reported thefts of weapons, explosives and JCBs—you know, the mechanical diggers. Field staff reckon it might be used in connection with the troubles in Scotland and Wales. Do you want to report it to COBRA?"

Nicola Martin had been in the middle of a dinner party. "Richard, you certainly know how to spoil someone's Sunday afternoon. But thanks for spotting this. If it hadn't been reported, I'd probably end up before some Commons committee asking why MI5 failed to be on the ball."

"Not me Nicola" replied Donovan. If anyone needs thanking, it's Suki."

"Richard, you know she's engaged. And what's more, you're old enough to be her father!" Nicola Martin was being jocular about the fact it was known throughout Thames House that Donovan had a soft spot for Suki Basra. She then became more serious. "COBRA's largely closed today. But the PM will be dropping in. I'll let him know. I'll also notify General Woodcock, Frank Hesford, Jocelyn Blackmore and Gerald Norton. Can you stay onto 5pm in case anything arises?"

Donovan indicated he would.

The same day
Outside the Scottish Parliament
Edinburgh

A massive crowd had assembled outside the Scottish Parliament building at Holyrood. Many were waving the Scottish national flag, the blue and white saltire, and others were holding pictures of the imprisoned First Minister, Alastair Ferguson. Every now and again, the crowd burst into a chorus of 'Flower of Scotland' and 'Scotland the Brave'.

It was now 7pm and the sun was still beating down on what had been a warm day. Behind the sealed-off Scottish Parliament complex, a detachment of the Duke of Lancaster's Regiment were in position to defend it in the event that defences were breached.

There were now ominous signs that the mood of the crowd had changed. The originally peaceful crowd had been infiltrated by several militants who wanted confrontation with the forces of law and order, and they had been augmented by people who had spent much of the day drinking in the pubs in Rose Street and the Old Town who were now steaming drunk and ready for a fight. Word had got out that English police were manning the lines outside the Parliament and there had been several attempts to charge the line. Batons had been drawn and blood drawn. Before long, missiles started to rain down on the police lines, followed by flares and petrol bombs. Reports then came in that demonstrators had cut the barbed wire surrounding the Scottish Parliament and were heading for the buildings. The mood of the soldiers behind the cordon was now very itchy.

The Commanding Officer of the Duke of Lancaster's Regiment battalion, Colonel Tim Burnside, was in touch with Sir Jocelyn Blackmore. "Sir Jocelyn, the situation's starting to get ugly. The crowd's charging police lines and some of my men have apprehended demonstrators who've got into the ground. I'm worried we might not be able to hold them if they break through."

Blackmore was uncompromising in his response. "Colonel Burnside, if they get through, open fire over their heads. That will send a message that we mean business. If, and this is a last resort, they don't get the message, open fire on them. God knows how many times we've done that in the past—Palestine, Cyprus, Aden, Northern Ireland. We even did it in Wales a century ago. If people refuse to respect the law, we've got no option but to take tough action. And don't worry about the consequences—if there's any flak, I'll take full responsibility."

By 7:30pm, there were fierce clashes between police and demonstrators outside the main entrance to the parliament building. This however diverted police attention away from another contingent of demonstrators armed with bolt cutters who had managed to get into the grounds half a mile away. On patrol in that sector of the grounds was Captain Daniel Fairclough, accompanied by two sergeants, two corporals and twenty troopers. His attention was drawn to the intrusion by a shout from the unmistakeable Liverpudlian tones of Sergeant Kevin Rooney, "Sir, bandits have got into the grounds. Orders?"

Already, 100 demonstrators had managed to get through the hole in the barbed wire cordon. Fairclough realised he and his men were outnumbered. Hurriedly, he radioed his commanding officer, Major Doug Merrington. "Sir, bandits in the grounds. About 100 of them. Not believed to be armed—oh shit!" A missile had just whizzed past his head. "Instructions to deal."

Major Merrington replied "Dan, you have authority to fire over their heads. That should disperse them. If the lives of you and your men are at risk, you've got authority to shoot as a last resort. Over."

Fairclough replied "Roger that sir". He then relayed his orders to his men.

The demonstrators in the grounds of the Scottish Parliament were greeted by a volley of gunfire over their heads which stopped them in their tracks for a couple of seconds. Some of the more nervous demonstrators turned and fled but there was still a hardcore who continued to fling bricks and bottles at Captain Fairclough's unit. Suddenly a van outside backfired.

"Sir, we're under fire" shouted Sergeant Chris Lake. Captain Fairclough had been trained to respond quickly and firmly to any military challenge. He had cut his teeth against the Taliban in Afghanistan as a subaltern six years earlier, so was not unused to sneak attacks. The safety of his men was paramount, so the order came "Open fire". Several of the demonstrators fell to the ground, while others fled in terror.

The same day
Outside the Welsh Assembly
Cardiff

As with Edinburgh, Cardiff had been the scene of a massive demonstration demanding the release of the First Minister, Emyr Roderick, his Cabinet and the restoration of devolved government. The Welsh national flag was being waved in profusion while the demonstrators had been singing 'Land of My Fathers'.

At 8pm, the news came in that demonstrators in Edinburgh had been fired upon and that 17 were dead. The formerly good natured gathering turned ugly within barely a minute. Bricks and bottles started to rain down on the police guarding the Welsh Assembly as angry demonstrators charged police lines in a bid to force their way into the building. Chants of 'Murderers' and 'English scum go home' rang through the air.

Half a mile away from the Welsh Assembly, a breakaway group of demonstrators seized a 40-ton HGV from a lorry park. Driving down towards the east wing of the Welsh Assembly, they drove it at speed through the barbed wire cordon which they cut through with ease. Other demonstrators seeing the broken barrier poured through.

A detachment of the Royal Anglian Regiment was defending the Welsh Assembly following intelligence reports that armed extremists were going to attempt an assault on the building. They had been given orders to open fire over the heads of anyone who entered the Welsh Assembly site without permission and to use lethal force if their lives were at risk. Sergeant Wayne Turvey saw the stolen lorry smash its way through the cordon and it was already heading for his men. Turvey barked "Open fire" and the volley of shots which followed claimed the lives of the driver and two passengers in the stolen HGV.

Turvey, along with a corporal and ten troopers were now confronted with an angry mob which wanted to tear them limb from limb. Using a loudhailer, he shouted "Get back now of we'll open fire again." Still the mob advanced and Turvey and his men came under attack from a shower of bricks and bottles. A volley of gunfire over the demonstrators head failed to disperse them. By now, they were desperate. Turvey radioed his commanding officer, Major Tom Rideout, for advice.

"Sir, we've had to open fire to stop a lorry being driven into us. We're now facing the Indians and we're hopelessly outnumbered. Can we use lethal force?"

"Wayne, yes, if that's what needs doing to save lives. The Chairman of the Residuary Authority's with me and he agrees."

With that, Turvey shouted "Open fire" as the demonstrators advanced. Within less than a minute, a further ten dead bodies lay on the grounds of the Welsh Assembly as the horrified demonstrators dispersed.

CHAPTER 3

20 July 2015, 8:30am
Sky News

"This is Adam Rennie with this morning's news headlines. The death toll in last night's disturbances in Edinburgh and Cardiff is now confirmed at 30. Both cities are now quiet after a night of intense rioting which saw widespread damage to property. However, police and troops are patrolling the streets in case there is any repetition."

"Large demonstrations against the suspension of home rule and the arrest of the devolved government leaders following their attempted declaration of independence from the United Kingdom had largely been peaceful for most of the day but, about 7pm, they started to turn ugly as protestors clashed with the police defending the Scottish Parliament and Welsh Assembly buildings. At about 7:30pm, a group of demonstrators broke into the grounds of the Scottish Parliament and were confronted by soldiers from the Duke of Lancaster's Regiment. It is not certain what sparked the clash, but there were reports of gunfire being heard, which may have led the soldiers to believe they were under attack and led them to open fire. It is now known that 17 deaths occurred."

"The trouble in Cardiff began at just after 8pm when a stolen lorry was driven through the barriers outside the Welsh Assembly and driven towards soldiers from the Royal Anglian Regiment who were guarding the building. The defending troops opened fire on the lorry to stop it running them down. They were then confronted by further demonstrators and they again opened fire to prevent a life-threatening situation. A total of 13 demonstrators are now known to have been shot dead."

"The deaths are a major setback to the Government who were hoping there would be a peaceful transition to the return of direct rule from Westminster following the end of devolved rule. Some security experts fear that last night's tragic events might escalate towards terrorism. The United Kingdom has not suffered from domestic terrorism since the end of the IRA campaign nearly twenty years ago."

"I'm handing over to Sara Ratcliffe who will report on how last night's events have been reported across the world."

"Hello, this is Sara Ratcliffe on Sky News. There has been a violent response across the world to the news of the shooting of demonstrators in Edinburgh and Cardiff last night. The British Embassy in Washington was burned down by protestors and the High Commissions in Canberra, Ottawa, Pretoria and Wellington all suffered damage. The police used water cannon and tear gas to disperse demonstrations outside the embassies in Berlin, The Hague, Madrid, Paris and Rome, and there were clashes between the Garda and demonstrators in Dublin. Meanwhile, the action of the British Government has been

criticised by the President of France, Marie-Christine Dumas, the German Chancellor Roland Straub, the President of the EU, Emilio Santana and the Russian President Boris Cherenkov, while a motion censuring the United Kingdom is being prepared at the United Nations."

The same day, 10am
Prime Minister's Office
10 Downing Street
London

Monday was not a normal day for a full meeting of the Cabinet, but Robert Delgado had convened one in the wake of the Edinburgh and Cardiff shootings. As a career politician, he was well aware of the potential for events to get out of control. Prior to the Cabinet meeting, he had held a lengthy briefing with his Press Secretary, Andy Christie to ensure that media outlets favourable to the Government ran stories which emphasised the damage caused by the rioters, the targeting of English-owned properties, the involvement of criminal elements and that the soldiers defending the Parliament and Assembly buildings had opened fire to protect themselves. He could guarantee that the *Sun*, the *Daily Mail*, the *Daily Express* and the *Daily Telegraph* would run favourable stories, as would Sky News.

All of the Cabinet, except for Secretary of State for Defence, Henry Arbuthnot, were present. Arbuthnot had been delayed by an emergency and would join the meeting later.

"Good morning ladies and gentlemen" began Delgado. "You will be fully aware why I've convened an extraordinary meeting this morning. Last night, there was serious disorder in Edinburgh and Cardiff which ended with soldiers having to open fire on demonstrators who tried to attack them and the Scottish Parliament and Welsh Assembly buildings. Already, mischief-makers are trying to take advantage of the situation. The SNP and Plaid Cymru party chairmen have called it a declaration of war by England on Scotland and Wales. Jeremy Sanderson has called for me to be tried for war crimes." Sanderson, the Labour MP for Islington North was an extreme left-winger renowned for making inflammatory statements. "And the EU and UN want to censure us. For what? For defending the territorial integrity of the United Kingdom."

"Before this meeting started, I had a meeting with Andy Christie. At least the *Sun*, the *Mail*, the *Telegraph* and the *Express* will be putting out stories favourable to us. The first issue to discuss is what actions we need to do. Deborah, you first." Delgado motioned to the Home Secretary. "Have you done anything about long-term policing requirements in Scotland and Wales?"

Deborah Pearson realised that she hadn't. "Prime Minister, I'll need to raise this with Dave Tanner first. At the moment, English forces have been deployed to Scotland and Wales on a temporary basis. To have them there for a longer term will require having both resources and accommodation available and a satisfactory contingency for policing England. We don't want our criminals to take advantage of reduced policing levels. We may need to make more use of the specials. Tanner will

41

know what's needed. He's using the papers on policing the Miners Strike in 1984 as a precedent."

"Can you get in touch with Tanner immediately Deborah? Next, you Christian" as the Prime Minister turned to the Foreign Secretary. "France, Greece, Italy, Portugal, Spain and Sweden have tabled a hostile motion at the United Nations, and China, Russia and Iran have all indicated they will support it. If it goes through, we could have sanctions placed on us. In any case, it will adversely affect our international standing. Can you ensure it is shot down."

Christian Vale replied "There should be no problem in tackling the motion, Prime Minister. US Ambassador Drayton has assured me that the USA will veto it. But there's plenty of scope for trouble elsewhere. Left-wingers in the EU want them to impose trade sanctions on us and there's trouble also stirring in the Commonwealth. South Africa's sponsoring a motion to have the United Kingdom suspended for abuses of human rights."

"Christian, I want any hostile motion or act robustly attacked. The EU can be split—lobby the Eastern Europeans, they've got little time for the likes of France and Germany. As for the Commonwealth, remind them who pays the piper."

"Prime Minister, I'm not sure I can pull it off this time" replied Vale. It's not just the Left who are criticising us. A lot of centre and centre-right politicians abroad have criticised us for what happened last night. And frankly, I can't blame them. We've shut down the Scottish and Welsh governments, arrested their leaders, sent police and troops in from England and now shot unarmed demonstrators. This hardly looks like the activities of a democracy. And what for? So we can get our hands on their oil. I said before that we should have sought compromise with Ferguson and Roderick. Instead, we're now an international pariah."

It was already 11am when Henry Arbuthnot arrived at Cabinet. "Sorry for being late Prime Minister. You better hear what's happened first. I've had the Commanding Officers of the Royal Regiments of Scotland and Wales on the phone. Seems like some 30-40% of their men have deserted. What's worse, a load of weapons and explosives have gone too. A lot of those men served in Iraq and Afghanistan and are well versed in roadside bombs and guerrilla tactics. You don't need to be a rocket scientist to know that the lives of our troops could be at risk."

"I've forewarned the MOD Police and I've also let Darren Bramble and Mark Taylor know. Deborah, Bramble and Taylor are notifying ACPO and will brief you when you get back to the Home Office. Hope they're not too late."

The same day, 3:45pm
A1(M) near Darlington, County Durham

"Oh shit, it's the polis." Lance Corporal Stuart MacDougall recognised the unmistakeable two-tone siren and blue flashing lights of the Durham Constabulary patrol car following the 61-registered Ford Focus being driven by Sergeant Derek Milne.

"Stuart, Jim, leave the talking to me." Milne, a native of Edinburgh, was the oldest at 33 and the most senior in rank terms of the three Scots from the Royal Regiment who were in the car. He pressed the button to open the drivers side window and spoke to PC Chris Robson, one of two motorway patrol officers in the BMW 325 estate that had stopped them. "Afternoon officer. How can we help?"

"Can I see your papers sir" replied PC Robson. Milne withdrew his driving licence and insurance documents from his wallet. "Where are you heading for, Mr Milne?"

"Home" replied the Sergeant from the Royal Regiment of Scotland. "Me and the other lads have got some leave."

"Pull the other one mate" replied Robson. "I've got reason to believe that all three of you are deserters. Get out the car and open the boot. Laura, cover the other two." PC Laura Dinsdale drew her Heckler and Koch machine pistol and pointed it towards the Ford Focus where Lance Corporals Stuart MacDougall and Jim Loughlin were sitting.

Milne knew that he and Lance Corporals MacDougall and Loughlin would be in trouble. Not only were they absent without leave but in the boot of the Focus were ten assault rifles, ten machine pistols, two rocket launchers, two mortars and forty pounds of high explosive. He opened up the Focus's tailgate, knowing that he was covered by PC Robson's sidearm. As the officer moved to look in the Focus's boot, he seized his opportunity and brought the tailgate hard down on PC Robson's head. He followed this with a knee to the officer's kidneys, following which he fell to the ground writhing in agony.

PC Dinsdale, alerted by the commotion immediately reacted and turned to help her fellow officer. She took her eye off the other two soldiers in the car and that was to prove fatal. Loughlin drew his pistol and opened fire through the open window. A bullet ripped through PC Dinsdale's skull and she fell to the ground dead.

Milne realised the danger of the situation. One police officer lay dead and another was still alive and able to identify him, MacDougall and Loughlin. He had nothing personally against PC Robson but it was a case of either him or me. He drew one of the pistols from the boot and shot PC Robson dead.

"Now let's get the fuck out of here" he shouted to MacDougall and Loughlin as the Ford Focus sped off leaving the bodies of the two officers sprawled on the ground.

The same day, 6pm
BBC Evening News

"This is Asif Ahmed on BBC News with this evening's headlines."

"Firstly, the latest on the troubles in Scotland and Wales. Troops and police have been patrolling the streets of Edinburgh and Cardiff and there have been no further reports of trouble since last night's disturbances which ended with thirty demonstrators being shot dead. But tension is still high, and the authorities are taking no chances. Police patrols have been increased in Glasgow, Aberdeen, Dundee, Swansea and Newport."

"The Government's expectations of a return to order were not helped by reports that soldiers from the Royal Regiments of Scotland and Wales have deserted and that weapons and explosives have been stolen from military bases. The civilian and military police are searching for deserters before they can cause any harm."

"A motion criticising the United Kingdom for suppressing the national identity of Scotland and Wales failed to be passed at the United Nations following a US veto, but the country continues to face international disapproval for shutting down the devolved governments and for its robust handling of disorder."

"The troubles in Scotland and Wales have claimed their first Ministerial casualty. Foreign Secretary Christian Vale has resigned, stating that he cannot support the Government any more following last night's events. Mr Delgado has moved quickly to fill the vacancy. Defence Secretary Henry Arbuthnot has been appointed as the new Foreign Secretary, with Trade and Enterprise Secretary Jason Steer becoming the new Defence Secretary."

"News has just come in that two police officers have been shot dead in an incident near Darlington. The officers, who have been named as PC Christopher Robson and PC Laura Dinsdale, were from Durham Constabulary's motorway patrol, are believed to have stopped a car containing deserters from the Royal Regiment of Scotland and were fired upon by the suspects. An alert has gone out for a silver Ford Focus, registered SB61EVL which was seen driving away up the A1(M) towards Newcastle."

21 July 2015, 11am
The House of Commons
London

The House of Commons was packed to its limits as all 600 MPs were present. Following a motion from Scottish National Party and Plaid Cymru members, backed by twelve Labour backbenchers and the Sinn Fein and Respect members, the Prime Minister had agreed to make a statement on Sunday night's shootings in Edinburgh and Cardiff.

Robert Delgado rose from the Government front bench and made his way to the despatch box. The atmosphere was tense enough to cut with a knife.

Delgado began. "Following the tragic events in Edinburgh and Cardiff on Sunday evening, I have decided to give an official statement to the House on behalf of the Government."

He had barely started to speak when he was greeted with shouts of "Murderer" and "Butcher" from SNP and Plaid Cymru members on the Opposition benches. This was countered by shouts of "Disgraceful" and "Withdraw" from the Conservative benches.

"Order, order" boomed the Speaker, George Franklin. When some degree of decorum was restored, Delgado continued.

"The steps taken by the Government to restore order in Scotland and Wales following its decision on 9 July to suspend the Scottish Government and Welsh Assembly Government were not taken lightly and it is unfortunate that unpleasantness has resulted. But the Government had no alternative to act in the way it did."

"Like shooting unarmed demonstrators?" shouted the SNP member for Stirling, Greg McAllister. Once again, the Speaker called for order.

"I should remind the Right Honourable Member that the devolved governments have acted illegally twice" responded an increasingly exasperated Delgado. "Firstly by breaching the terms of the devolution legislation by proceeding with acts which were damaging to United Kingdom national interests. Then compounding this by their wholly illegal declarations of independence from the United Kingdom. There was no alternative left but to arrest them. It is for the judicial authorities, not me or any member of this Government, to decide what charges, if any, to lay before them."

"The Government's decision to deploy additional police officers and the armed forces to Scotland and Wales was taken at the request of the Chairmen of the Residuary Bodies following serious disorder which threatened both property and life. The armed forces were used to protect the Scottish Parliament and the Welsh Assembly buildings, which are under the control of the Residuary Bodies pending decisions on future governance for Scotland and Wales and their further use. During the course of the evening of Sunday, 19 July, demonstrators broke through the protective defences of the two buildings with the intention of either illegally occupying the premises or causing wilful damage in order to disrupt the business of the Residuary Bodies. When the troops defending the buildings attempted to remove the trespassers from the premises, they came under attack to the extent that they feared for their lives. Furthermore, there were reports that someone had opened fire on the soldiers guarding the Scottish Parliament."

"Liar" screamed the SNP MP for Perth and Kinross, Morag Stevenson. She leapt out of her seat and charged down the aisles to confront the Prime Minister. The Serjeant-at-Arms saw that a potentially violent clash could break out and sent two of his officials into the Chamber to restrain Stevenson. As they tried to seize her, she lashed out. Almost immediately, the other six SNP MPs and the four Plaid Cymru MPs to join the fray. Greg McAllister, who had heckled the Prime Minister earlier took a swing at him.

This was the green light for mayhem to break out. Tory backbenchers, outraged by the SNP man's assault on the Prime Minister, leapt out of their seats and charged into the SNP and Plaid Cymru MPs as if they were in a pub brawl. Then the fray was joined by Labour backbenchers and the MPs from Respect. The Serjeant-at-Arms immediately called for police presence to break up the brawl.

The Tories not only had numerical advantage, with 398 of the 600 MPs, they also had some formidable physical specimens in their ranks. Prominent was the bulky figure of David Pickavance, Conservative MP for Basildon South and a former light-heavyweight boxer. Although now more than six stones heavier than when he was in the ring, he could still pack a punch and, within a minute, three Labour MPs, two SNP MPs and one Plaid Cymru MP were flat out on their backs.

Jeremy Sanderson, the hard-left Labour MP for Islington North, was outraged by the sight of Pickavance decking several of his colleagues. He was a second Dan black belt in karate and launched a flying roundhouse kick at Pickavance which connected under his jaw. The Conservative MP for Basildon South fell to the ground.

Seconds later, a squad of policemen from the Response Squad based at Rochester Row police station burst into the House of Commons to restore order. Having seen Sanderson's assault on Pickavance, PC Jack Rayner drew his Taser and brought down Sanderson. Rayner's colleagues promptly moved into separate the other protagonists and clear the Chamber. Once all the MPs had been ushered out, the Speaker decided to suspend Parliamentary business for the rest of the day.

25 July 2015
Bridgend Farm near Callander
Perthshire
Scotland

Doug Paterson, the Chairman of the Scottish National Liberation Army's General Council could hardly believe his luck as a procession of cars and minibuses rolled into Bridgend Farm, which was owned by a sympathiser with the cause of Scottish independence. Callander also had the advantage of being relatively isolated from the main urban centres of Scotland and out of sight and mind of the authorities.

The Scottish National Liberation Army had up to that point been a small organisation with no more than 100 members and its activities had best been described as having nuisance value. MI5 had barely paid any attention to it since the 1980s when a plot to assassinate Margaret Thatcher was foiled. But "Bloody Sunday" six days earlier in Edinburgh had changed the political landscape in Scotland. When the SNLA's General Council advertised a meeting to discuss defending Scotland, they were overwhelmed by the interest.

Paterson could see that many of the volunteers were potentially high calibre fighters. Although there were many idealistic youths and yobs from the tough council estates of the main cities, there were also a large number who either had served, or were serving, in the armed forces, including several who had experience of fighting in Iraq and Afghanistan.

Paterson, along with his deputy, Charlie Renwick, took the stage to address the audience. Over a thousand were in attendance.

"Ladies and gentlemen, thank you very much for coming here today. We have all come for a common cause. To defend Scotland from the rapacity of the English and their friends in the City of London and international high finance."

"For over 300 years, the people of Scotland have been exploited in the cruellest way possible. Our natural resources have been stolen, our people were kicked off their land and our best and brightest were forced to emigrate. The English have now taken away our Parliament and showed their true colours in Edinburgh last Sunday. The patriotic men and women whose lives were taken away must not be forgotten. And to repay them, our option must be to fight for our right to be independent of the English for ever more."

"The struggle will not be an easy one" continued Paterson. "The English will do everything in their power to stop us. After all, they want to get their hands on our oil. We will face the full force of the polis, the courts, the armed forces, MI5. They will rely on the support of English living here. They will have the support of the USA.

But we can win. There may be only five million people in Scotland. But there are many more Scots living across the world. And they will support our cause. Finally, remember the words of Robert the Bruce. If at first you don't succeed, try, try and try again. And what did he do? He went onto beat the English at Bannockburn and sent Edward home to think again."

"If you are ready to join up, then now's the opportunity. Recruitment will take place here today. You will shortly receive instructions on targets to hit. Believe me, the English will regret the day they took on Scotland!"

3 August 2015
Edinburgh

August Bank Holiday in Edinburgh had dawned wet and windy. Two months of warm and sunny weather had come to a spectacular end two days earlier as a belt of violent thunderstorms had crossed Scotland and given the capital a sleepless and sodden Saturday night. Despite this the crowds were out in force in Princes Street and the shops anticipated bumper takings.

Since 1965, August Bank Holiday in Scotland had been on a different date to the rest of the United Kingdom. Until then, it had taken place in the first weekend in August across the whole of the United Kingdom but, after 1965, August Bank Holiday in England, Wales and Northern Ireland took place in the final week of August. This was not practicable for Scotland, where the schools went back before the end of August.

The Marks and Spencer store in Princes Street had been doing impressive business that day as shoppers flooded in. At 3:15pm, a phone call was received asking for the Branch Manager. "Alison, a call for you" said Kirsty Molloy, her Personal Assistant. Two seconds later, Alison Glennie, the Branch Manager was on the line.

"Alison Glennie, can I help?"

"Ms Glennie, this is the Scottish National Liberation Army. There is a bomb in your store that will go off in twenty minutes time. If you don't want to have a lot of dead bodies on your hands, I would suggest that you evacuate the building now." The line then went dead.

Glennie reacted immediately. Firstly she phoned the store's Security Officer, Davie McCormick, who advised her that an immediate evacuation should take place. Then she phoned the police who, within two minutes, had turned up to supervise the safe evacuation of the public away from the Marks and Spencer store and cordoned off the area.

3:35 pm approached and, at first, there was a sense that the call had been a hoax. But, as the clock struck 3:35pm, all suspicions of a hoax call were dispelled as a massive blast blew open the front of the Marks and Spencer store, leaving a trail of shattered mannequins and scorched clothes.

4 August 2015, 9:30am
MI5 Headquarters
Millbank
London

Suki Basra was working her last week before flying out to India for her wedding when her Section Head, Richard Donovan, came over to her desk.

"Suki, can you get me an intelligence report on the Scottish National Liberation Army. I've got a meeting with the DG in an hour's time."

"Richard, is it that urgent? I've got three other reports to complete before the end of this week."

"Afraid so, Suki. The SNLA blew up M&S in Edinburgh yesterday. The DG's worried that a terror campaign might be starting."

An hour later, Richard Donovan was in the office of MI5 Director-General, Nicola Martin, along with three field agents, Deputy Assistant Commissioner Darren Charnock, Head of the Metropolitan Police's Special Branch and Professor Robert Harrison, a counter-terrorism and security expert.

"Richard, can you summarise your report for the benefit of our guests?" said the Director-General.

Donovan opened up the report. "The Scottish National Liberation Army has been in existence since the late 1970s but the threat it has posed has been insignificant up to now. Apart from letter bombs sent to Mrs Thatcher and the Princess of Wales in 1983 and acid sent to Cherie Blair in 2002, their activity has been nothing more than nuisance value. Estimated membership before recent events in Scotland was no more than a hundred."

"There have been reports that the SNLA have embarked on a recruitment drive following Bloody Sunday and that some of the soldiers from the Royal Regiment of Scotland who deserted over the past week have joined up. But this is awaiting verification and I'm unable to provide concrete details at this point."

Professor Harrison was the next to contribute. "I'm afraid the SNLA will provide something of a challenge. As Mr Donovan has explained, many of its recent recruits will be "clean skins"—that is to say people for whom there is no previous record of terrorist activity. To gain human intelligence on the SNLA, we will need to start from scratch to build it up."

Peter Firth, a field agent was next to speak. "If I recall, we managed to build up extensive intelligence on the IRA and Al-Q'aida during their terror campaigns. There must surely be lessons learned from the past that can be repeated."

Last to contribute was DAC Charnock. "Madam Director-General, I think it would be sensible not to exaggerate the threat posed. A significant percentage of the recruits for both the IRA and Al-Q'aida were of low calibre. Either petty criminals, idealists or misfits. They will be more of a liability than an asset to the SNLA. There is a risk of harm being caused and we need to be live to that. But if we build up good human intelligence and manage to get some recruits to inform, we should be able to interdict anything the SNLA might be planning to do before it happens."

Nicola Martin was the last to comment. She had a reputation of being slow to decide but lightning-fast to act once she had decided. "Gentlemen, thank you for your helpful contributions. Yesterday's bombing in Edinburgh clearly confirms that the SNLA now poses a clear and present threat to security. However, as it is early days and, as you Darren has said, many of the recruits will be green and not battle-hardened, we have a window of opportunity to nip the SNLA in the bud before they become really dangerous."

"Richard, can you arrange for counter-SNLA activity to be stepped up. Peter, can you manage field intelligence on the SNLA. And Darren, can you liaise with Lothian and Borders Special Branch and arrange for surveillance on known SNLA members."

8 August 2015, 8:30pm
The Castle Hotel
Y Maes
Caernarfon, Wales

"Three pints of bitter please." Trevor Rees placed his order with the young barmaid with the strawberry dyed hair and pierced eyebrows.

Trevor Rees had been a regular at the Castle Hotel for over thirty five years, as had his friends, Dai Havard and Richard Thomas. All three men were in their early fifties and had been born and bred in the North Wales town famous for its castle where the Princes of Wales had been invested.

Rees, Havard and Thomas were treated with respect by the other patrons of the Castle Hotel, even by the small groups of lairy-looking youths who patronised the snooker table. Over three decades earlier, all three men had been part of the Free Wales Army and had been responsible for arson attacks against English-owned holiday homes in North Wales. They were regarded as local heroes by many locals.

Rees collected the three pints of M&B bitter he had ordered and placed them on the table where his friends were sitting. He then joined Havard and Thomas.

On most nights, their conversations were very predictable. Football, rugby and cricket took up much of their time, along with motorbikes, what was happening in at work and in their families and the dire straits of current rock and pop music compared to their youth. But tonight there was a new topic to discuss.

"Dai, Rich, did you hear about what's happened in Scotland?"

Thomas replied "Trev, if you mean the SNLA bombings in Edinburgh and Glasgow, yes. Good on them. It'd be great to see the English bastards on the run after what they did three weeks ago." He was referring to the shooting of demonstrators in Edinburgh and Cardiff on 19 July.

"Boys, I think we should be doing the same here" replied Rees. "After years of being run down and asset-stripped by the English, we're sitting on a golden opportunity for Wales to be a wealthy independent country. But once again, nobody here seems to be doing anything."

Havard had his doubts about the value of direct action. "If Wales is to achieve anything, we need the whole country to mobilise. When has that happened in the past? It always ends up with the western counties being the only ones who do anything. The English-speaking parts of Wales don't want to know."

Rees however was confident that the whole of Wales was ready to unite to fight for independence. "Dai, I met a couple of guys from Wrexham yesterday. They were asking if we were going to do anything to fight back against the English." Wrexham was some eighty miles to the east and virtually on the English border. "I reckon the whole country's up for a fight and I'm planning to call a meeting to find out if anyone will volunteer to take the battle to the English. Can you give me a hand?"

Havard and Thomas indicated they would.

31 August 2015
Cardiff

August Bank Holiday in the Welsh capital dawned cool and cloudy. People who had hoped that the month of unseasonable weather would end for the last major holiday before Christmas were to be disappointed as the temperature stubbornly refused to go above the 60 degree mark. However, Cardiff's retail trade were expecting good business.

The St David's Centre was doing brisk business and the Topshop branch was turning over well from young people from Cardiff, the Vale of Glamorgan and the Valleys who were buying clothes for their social life. The Branch Manager, Ceri Hughes was pleased with the day's business. She had given up her Bank Holiday in order to save money so she could visit her relatives in the USA the following year.

1pm approached and Hughes was about to clock of for lunch when the phone rang. Her Personal Assistant, Rosanna Solari, answered it.

"Topshop here, how can I help?"

"This is the Welsh Republican Army. A bomb has been planted in your shop and is set to go off at 1:30 this afternoon. If you value your lives and those of your customers, I would suggest you evacuate the premises immediately." He them rang off.

Rosanna Solari immediately alerted Ceri Hughes. "Ceri, I think we've got a nutter on the line. Claims to be from the Welsh Republican Army. Says they've planted a bomb in the store."

"Rosanna, we can't take chances. I've heard of the Welsh Republican Army—there was an article on them in the *Western Mail* a few days ago. We've got to evacuate the store. Call the police."

Solari immediately telephoned the Security Office for the St David's Centre and a message was broadcast immediately to evacuate the mall. Everyone was out within 20 minutes and the police cordoned off the site.

At 1:30pm, Cardiff was rocked by the sound of a massive blast as the WRA bomb ripped through the Topshop branch.

7 September 2015
Home Office
Marsham Street
London

The previous week had seen no less that eight bomb blasts. Two had taken place in Edinburgh and one apiece in Aberdeen, Cardiff, Dundee, Glasgow, Newport and Swansea. Five had been claimed by the SNLA and the other three by the WRA. In addition, there had been ongoing disturbances in towns and cities across Scotland and Wales and, in a disturbing new development, there had been reports of the police coming under small arms fire. Clearly, the SNLA and WRA had obtained guns and were prepared to use them.

Deborah Pearson, the Home Secretary, was worried that a mass terror campaign was starting on two fronts and had called in all her key officials. Darren Bramble and Mark Taylor, the Ministers responsible for policing and homeland security were present, along with the Permanent Secretary, Sir Derek Copperfield and the Director-General for Security and Counter-Terrorism, Richard Harbottle. From outside the Home Office, MI5's Director-General, Nicola Martin was present, along with the Chairman of ACPO, Dave Tanner, the Head of Metropolitan Police's Special Branch, Deputy Assistant Commissioner Darren Charnock, counter-terrorism expert, Professor Robert Harrison and the Prime Minister's security consultant, Frank Hesford.

Deborah Pearson opened the meeting. "Ladies and gentlemen, you will probably know why I've asked for you to be here today. Over the past month, there have been a series of bomb blasts targeted at British-owned businesses in Scotland. All have been claimed by the Scottish National Liberation Army. It now looks like the problem has spread to Wales as there have been explosions in their three main cities over the past week, all of which have been attributed to the Welsh Republican Army. And on top of this, there have been continued disturbances which have involved acts of civil disobedience, deliberate vandalism against property and infrastructure and attacks on the police."

"I don't have to emphasise how serious the problem might be. We spent almost 30 years dealing with the IRA and all because the politicians of the day failed to show resolve in nipping the problem in the bud during the early days. We don't want the same to happen in Scotland and Wales, especially as it might frighten off investors in the oil industry. Can I have your solutions please."

Nicola Martin was the first to speak. "Home Secretary, we've managed to gather some intelligence on the SNLA and WRA. Up to July, neither organisation warranted more than a glance because of the lack of numbers and expertise. But since the shootings on 19 July, both organisations have had success recruiting. What's worrying is that they've recruited deserting soldiers from the Army and many of them have taken weapons and explosives with them. However, F6 Section has stepped up field intelligence on the SNLA and will be doing the same on the WRA. And I understand from Darren that Special Branch has upped its surveillance of known nationalist sympathisers."

Dave Tanner was next. "We've deployed 5,000 officers from England to both Scotland and Wales, and this includes members of the Territorial Support Group from the Met, West Midlands, Greater Manchester and West Yorkshire. All have had extensive experience in tackling violent disturbances. NCA are working with MI5 in gathering intelligence on the SNLA and WRA—Nicola, Kevin Russell is in touch with Richard Donovan on this. We've also sent specialist SWAT squads to be trained by the SAS so if there is further terror acts, the police will be ready to counter it."

"Home Secretary, I fear you will have to use the armed forces to help the police if the situation continues to deteriorate" said Professor Harrison. "The fact that soldiers have deserted is most worrying because many of them have served in Iraq and Afghanistan and will have had experience in fighting terrorist warfare."

Frank Hesford was even more forthright. "If we'd had sent troops into Northern Ireland as far back as 1968 and given them a free reign to act against the IRA and its sympathisers, we would have ended the Troubles within three years. But the politicians of the day pussyfooted around, frightened that bloodied heads and dead bodies wouldn't look good on TV."

"Home Secretary, if you send the troops in against the SNLA and WRA and let them off the leash, I guarantee you that you'll bring the problem to and end within the next two years, if not earlier. Don't worry about hostile news media. All you need to do is to declare a State of Emergency and you can have hostile journalists arrested for jeopardising national security. The Americans did that in the last Gulf War—when CBS reported on the bombing of a children's hospital which was found to be cover for a weapons factory, the FBI arrested their chief reporter and her film crew when they got back to the USA. That stopped all further attempts to run knocking copy on the Gulf War. You can do the same here."

Deborah Pearson's body language clearly showed she liked what Hesford had to say. As the meeting drew to a close, she summed up. "Dave, I like what the police are doing with the SWAT squads. Why we haven't had them before, I don't know. As soon as they are ready, deploy them to Scotland and Wales immediately. Nicola, Darren, we need to improve our human intelligence on the SNLA and WRA—can you increase surveillance and report to me on progress each month."

"I am however tempted by Frank's suggestion. This country's used the armed forces to help the police maintain public order many times in the past. There is no good reason why they cannot do so again."

Dave Tanner murmured an oath beneath his breath as he knew the reaction of his fellow Chief Constables to losing their monopoly on law enforcement.

"Dave, I know what you're thinking. The police will continue to have primary responsibility for law enforcement in Scotland and Wales, and I will be making that clear to Archie Patterson and Emlyn Crowley. But the situation has now gone beyond keeping the peace. We are facing a potential insurrection and tough measures are needed to ensure it is eliminated."

CHAPTER 4

Bannerman's Bar was an ancient pub with stone floors and vaulted ceilings and was a popular venue with young residents of Edinburgh, particularly students at the University. It had also become popular with the detachments of police and soldiers from England who had been posted to Edinburgh to deal with the growing troubles in the Scottish capital. They were expecting bumper takings because it was Halloween Night, and a disco had been organised.

The previous month, the British Government had authorised the deployment of soldiers from the Army to support the police in tackling the growing levels of disorder and civil disobedience that had sprung up since the UDI bid had been crushed. There had been ongoing rent and tax strikes, buses had been set on fire and further bombings of commercial properties by the SNLA had continued. The use of the Army to support the police in breaking up riots and in arresting known troublemakers had only served to inflame the situation rather than calm it. Only the previous night, police and Army detachments had been pelted with stones, bottles and firebombs on the Wester Hailes estate when they had tried to execute an arrest warrant against a known nationalist agitator.

Edinburgh's Old Town was the centre of the city's night-time economy and, by as early as 7:30pm, the Grassmarket and Cowgate was thronging with young people, many in fancy dress. Many of the bars and clubs were operating an entrance by ticket system to avoid overcrowding.

By 8pm, Bannerman's Bar was already nearly bursting to capacity. The mixture of locals and students was reinforced by several off-duty policemen and soldiers, who were mainly from England. They had hired extra security for the night as several of the soldiers had already earned themselves a rowdy reputation and they feared there might be a confrontation with locals.

Not only additional doormen had been hired but, because of the large numbers of customers expected, additional bar staff were taken on for the night. One of these was Jason Kirwan, a local lad in his early 20s who hailed from the Craigmillar estate on the eastern side of the city.

During the day, Kirwan worked as a mobile phone salesman and his reason for taking the second job, namely to earn some additional money for his forthcoming marriage, seemed plausible. But what his colleagues did not know was that Jason Kirwan was a member of the Edinburgh brigade of the SNLA and that his mission was to bomb Bannerman's. The presence of military and police personnel from England made it a legitimate target for the SNLA.

Earlier that day, Kirwan had helped set up the "Cavern" area for the night's entertainment. It was customary to deploy used beer barrels as decorative features and this provided Kirwan with his opportunity to plant a bomb. Two former sappers with the Royal Regiment of Scotland with experience in Iraq ten years previously helped build the bomb, a mobile phone engineer helped install the detonator and all Kirwan had to do was to drive to Bannerman's and place it by the service entrance. Using a porter's trolley, he and Adrian Thompson, one of his colleagues, wheeled it into the pub and set it up close to the stage. When a signal from a remote mobile phone was punched in, the bomb would detonate.

By 11:30pm, Bannerman's had reached its capacity limit and no one else was being admitted. The dance floor was thronging with young people and several local girls and students had already made a beeline for the soldiers and policemen in the pub.

Jason Kirwan, who had just finished serving a large order of Tennant's Extra, Magners Cider and Bacardi Breezers to a soldier from the Royal Green Jackets, received a call on his mobile phone. "Lisa, sorry but I've got a call from home. It's my mum. Can I go outside and take it?"

Bannerman's manageress, Lisa Hastings, was not pleased. The bar was still three deep and the bar staff were struggling to cope with the demand. But Jason had already put in more than would have been asked of him, and he was only a part-timer. She felt he was better than many of the regular staff. "Okay Jason—but don't be long. We've got people queuing at the bar and we can't afford to be short-handed for too long."

Kirwan walked out into Cowgate through the staff exit. "Jason, how's it gone?" It was the voice of Mark Podborski, the Brigade Commander. "Mark, sweet as a nut—the device is in place. No one's the wiser—they think it's part of the décor. They even helped me wheel it into the bar."

"Well done Jason" replied Podborski. "Any Sassenach soldiers or polis in there?"
"Loads."
"Best get moving Jason. We're about to detonate."

Kirwan started to head towards the Grassmarket. Barely thirty seconds later, a massive blast ripped through Bannerman's, throwing masonry in all directions.

1 November 2015
Sky News, 9am

"This is Adam Rennie on Sky News with this morning's headlines."
"The death toll from the SNLA bombing of an Edinburgh pub has now risen to fourteen. A further 92 people were injured in the blast, of whom 41 are still in hospital."
"Revellers were celebrating Halloween at Bannerman's Bar in Edinburgh's Old Town when just after 11:30pm a bomb was detonated using a mobile phone signal. Forensic experts believe that the explosives were packed into a beer barrel which was used as part of the pub's décor and it was programmed to be detonated by a mobile phone signal."

"The SNLA were believed to have targeted Bannerman's because it was patronised by soldiers and police from England who have been deployed to Scotland to deal with the troubles which have occurred since the failed attempt to declare independence from the United Kingdom."

6 November 2015
Tiger Tiger
Greyfriars Road
Cardiff

Cerys Thomas and her friends Jane Goldsworthy and Bethan Lewis had been drinking in Tiger Tiger for the past half hour. Dressed in miniskirts, skimpy tops and high heels, it was obvious that they were out on the pull. All three of them hailed from the St Mellons estate to the east of the city and only Cerys Thomas, who had a job in a call centre, had a permanent job. Unusually for them, they were staying off the alcohol and had ordered three J2Os.

It was already 10pm and Tiger Tiger was starting to fill up. It was Bonfire Night and many of the customers had been to the fireworks display at Cardiff Castle before moving onto the numerous bars and clubs in the centre of the Welsh capital. The majority of the patrons of Cardiff's nightlife were Welsh, either from Cardiff itself or from the towns in the South Wales Valleys. But increasing numbers of English travelled across the border for one of the United Kingdom's most vibrant nightlife scenes. And the presence of several fit-looking young men with uniformly short haircuts betrayed the presence of soldiers from English regiments who had been sent in to help maintain order in the aftermath of the abortive UDI bid by the former Welsh Assembly Government.

Cerys noticed that several men eyeing them up were clearly soldiers. "Beth, looks like those guys giving us the eye are squaddies. Let's go for it."

Within a minute, a group of five soldiers from the Blues and Royals had joined them. Three of them, Darryl Canavan, Jason Pike and Dave Woodger were from the East End of London and were full of Cockney banter. The other two came from outside London; Simon Francome hailed from Chatham while Eddie Butcher came from Northampton. Darryl Canavan, recently promoted to sergeant, bought the girls Bacardi Breezers and before long the three cockney soldiers were dancing with the three girls from a Cardiff council estate.

Bethan Lewis was quite upfront about the plans for later that night. "Guys, how about coming back with us for the night?"

Canavan and Woodger were up for it but Pike raised the issue of the other two of their group. "Not sure Beth. We all came out as a group. If we go back, we'll be leaving Si and Ed out of the fun."

Butcher replied "Jase, don't worry about me and Si. The night's young and we'll be sure to find someone. Go ahead and enjoy yourselves."

Cerys Thomas butted in as she had a solution. "Guys, all five of you are welcome to come. I'll call up a couple of mates to ensure we're all matched." With that, the five Blues and Royals agreed to go back with Cerys, Jane and Bethan to St Mellons.

At 1am, the party took two taxis to St Mellons.

Had the soldiers known more about the background of Cerys Thomas and Bethan Lewis, they would have thought twice about accepting the offer of late night hospitality. Both girls had brothers who had joined the Cardiff brigade of the WRA and Garin Thomas had previously served in the Royal Regiment of Wales. But the thought of easy sex with three attractive Welsh girls caused all judgement to fly out of the window.

Twenty minutes later, they pulled up outside Cerys Thomas's flat. "Come in and make yourself comfortable lads" she said. The five soldiers from the Blues and Royals followed in.

Jane Goldsworthy put the kettle on in the kitchen and, with Bethan Lewis, helped serve up eight coffees. Fifteen minutes later, there was a knock on the door. Two more of Cerys's friends, Sue Alexander and Kirsty James, joined the party.

At 2am, Cerys said to the soldiers that she and the other girls would be heading into the bedrooms and they should head up in five minutes.

There were three bedrooms in Cerys Thomas's flat. Waiting for the soldiers were not the girls they had met and a promised night of passion, but three WRA terrorists, each holding an M16 assault rifle with a silencer fitted. As the soldiers went in, they were greeted with gunfire from the M16s. Barely fifteen seconds later, all five soldiers lay dead.

Garin Thomas turned to his sister and said "Nice work sis. We'll get rid of the bodies and ensure there's no trace of blood if the cops come calling."

8 November 2015
BBC Morning News

"This is Asif Ahmed with the BBC news headlines this Sunday morning."

"Five soldiers from the Blues and Royals were murdered in Cardiff last night after they were seen going off with some girls they met at a nightspot. The five men, whose names have yet to be disclosed, were reported to have met some local girls at Tiger Tiger in Greyfriars Road and were last seen catching a taxi with them. Their bodies were found on waste ground just outside the city and all had been shot."

"A police manhunt is on for the girls, who were captured on Tiger Tiger's CCTV cameras."

9 November 2015
Home Office
Marsham Street
London

Deborah Pearson was furious. Firstly, the SNLA Halloween bombing in Edinburgh, then the honeytrap murders of soldiers in Cardiff had given the impression that the Government was losing control of the situation in Scotland and Wales.

She had hurriedly called a meeting of the policing and homeland security Ministers, the Permanent Secretary, the Chairman of ACPO, the Director-General of

MI5, the Head of Special Branch at the Metropolitan Police and the Prime Minister's Security Advisor. On the video screen in her office was Sir Jocelyn Blackmore and Sir Gerald Norton, the Chairmen of the Scottish and Welsh Residuary Bodies, live from their offices in Edinburgh and Cardiff.

"When we met two months ago, didn't we agree actions to tackle the threat of the SNLA and WRA? And what has happened now—within a week, a fatal bomb blast and five of our soldiers murdered? I now want explanations. Nicola, what's been done to improve human intelligence on the SNLA and WRA?"

"We've now got field intelligence officers working in Scotland and Wales and a couple of them have now infiltrated both groups. It's taking time though Home Secretary" said Nicola Martin. "Both organisations are suspicious of outsiders and the only way we can get someone in is to recruit locals. We've had past problems with that approach—six years ago we found that more than one of our Muslim agents who infiltrated Al-Q'aida were double agents who betrayed us. It could take until March next year before we've got reliable human intelligence on the SNLA and WRA."

"Nicola, that's not quick enough. You've got to get someone in by the end of this year. What's more, I want reports from you every two weeks."

"Yes, Home Secretary" replied the MI5 Director-General.

Pearson next turned to the Chairman of ACPO. "Dave, have you deployed the SWAT teams yet?"

"Yes, Home Secretary" replied Tanner. "We've used them to suppress disorder and most effective they've been too. At this very moment, SWAT teams are working with the regular police in searching for the Bannerman's bombers and the mob who murdered those soldiers in Cardiff two nights ago."

"Any progress in arresting deserters?" The Home Secretary was aware that soldiers from the Royal Regiments of Scotland and Wales who had deserted following Black Sunday were providing the SNLA and WRA with a dangerous level of expertise.

"Already, we've nicked over 500 deserters. MoD gave us full lists." Deborah Pearson made a mental note to thank Jason Steer, the Secretary of State for Defence who had ordered his Department to compile this information for the police.

"Jocelyn, Gerald, thank you for giving us your time" said the Home Secretary. "What have you done or are proposing to do?"

Blackmore spoke. "Gerald and I have had a discussion about what to do next, Home Secretary. We've both agreed to declare a State of Emergency. This means that the police have the powers to search properties, to examine bank statements and internet accounts and make arrests with or without warrants, and that anyone who is considered to have obstructed the police, the army or the courts in the administration of justice can be arrested and charged under emergency powers. We can also ban critical articles in the press or on radio and TV and have anyone breaching such orders arrested and charged under Emergency Powers legislation. We can also extend the arm of the law to cover the internet and e-mails."

The Home Office's Permanent Secretary, Sir Derek Copperfield, was rather concerned about the legalities of the approach. "Home Secretary, I think it would be advisable to check with Counsel on the legality of what Jocelyn and Gerald are planning to do. If we get beaten in the courts, it will damage the Government's credibility and give aid and comfort to the SNLA and WRA."

"Derek, we're fighting a war" replied the Home Secretary. "There's no time for legal niceties."

19 December 2015
Bluewater Retail Park near Dartford, Kent

The last Saturday before Christmas was always a busy day for the retail trade and the massive Bluewater complex in North Kent was no exception. Since it had opened nearly 20 years earlier in a disused chalk quarry, it had attracted large numbers of shoppers from London and the South East, attracted by the wide range of shops and the ease of parking not available in traditional high streets.

Early that morning, Steve Clarke backed his 40-ton MAN artic against the Bluewater service bay and got ready to unload his cargo. He was relieved to have some rest, having driven down from Aberdeen.

However, restocking stores had not been the sole reason for Clarke's journey down to Bluewater. Hidden at the back of his artic was almost a ton of hydrogen peroxide, a volatile compound used in explosives. Once all the regular cargo had been despatched, he had instructions to liaise with two members of the SNLA who were temporarily working on maintaining the communications system at Bluewater.

By 10am, all of Clarke's regular cargo had been taken off the artic and was being delivered by fork-lift truck to the stores. Clarke himself had eaten breakfast at the truckers' cafeteria on site and was now taking a rest.

"Steve, there you are" said Craig Beattie, one of the SNLA operatives. Is the stuff still on board?"

"Aye" replied Clarke.

"I'll get Ormond so we can get the stuff off" replied Beattie.

Five minutes later, Tom Ormond, the second SNLA operative, had turned up. "Guess we better get the stuff off. Thanks Steve for bringing it down."

Clarke had shown the good sense to palletise the volatile cargo so it would not move around and Beattie and Ormond had it off the artic within three minutes.

Most of the warehouse staff were out of the loading area so Beattie and Ormond had it to themselves. Nevertheless, they had to move fast in priming the explosives because workers might enter the loading area or their absence might be noted. But they had expertise in handling explosives as Beattie had formerly been in the Royal Engineers and Ormond had formerly worked in a quarry.

Shoppers were already crowding into Bluewater, so Beattie and Ormond switched on the flashing orange light on their service vehicle so they could get through the crowds. There were a lot of decorative features in Bluewater so hiding the bomb would not be difficult. They selected a location where the crowds would be at their densest, which was close to the main entrance.

By 3:30pm, the crowds at Bluewater had reached their peak. The weak winter sun had just disappeared over the horizon and dusk was starting to set in. Many of the shoppers who had arrived earlier in the day were starting to go home, but there were still new arrivals even at this late hour.

The last Saturday before Christmas was also a busy day for Kent Police. Shoplifters were also out in force, while it was also a profitable day for car thieves who targeted electronic gadgets and high value goods in car boots. But for Sergeant Chris Jackson and his neighbourhood policing team, it had been a relatively quiet day.

Without warning, there was a massive explosion close to the entrance. Masonry was scattered over a wide area and everything went quiet before the air was rent by screaming of the injured and of people whose relatives were caught up in the blast. Within seconds, PC Jane Jordan was on the phone to the main North Kent police station a mile away and to police headquarters at Maidstone.

At 3:35pm, Reuters took a call from a man with a Scottish accent. "This is the SNLA. We were responsible for the Bluewater bombing. There will be more unless England gets out of Scotland."

23 December 2015, 7:45pm
MI5 Headquarters
Millbank
London

There was no Christmas party for staff in F6 Section this year. Two days earlier, a terse Director-General had made it clear that their first priority was to monitor intelligence traffic and to ensure that intelligence on the SNLA and WRA was improved. Staff from other sections had been temporarily deployed to help. With Christmas Eve only a day off and New Year's Eve to come, both presenting opportunities for terrorists to cause death and destruction, Thames House was eerily quiet and full of staff hunched over computer terminals.

Marcel Francois, the son of immigrants from St Lucia and one of Section Head Richard Donovan's Team Leaders, took an incoming call from the encrypted telephone on his workstation. "Snuffbox, this is Indigo Two." Francois knew this was a field agent phoning in from Scotland. "Indigo Two, I read you. Go ahead."

"Good news Snuffbox. We've got two agents into the Glasgow Brigade of the SNLA and am posting details of a future operation. SNLA plan to explode bombs in Trafalgar Square at midnight on 31 December."

"Jesus Christ" exclaimed Francois. "Any more details about who's involved? Otherwise, we'll be searching for a needle in a haystack."

"Affirmative Snuffbox" came the reply. "It's been established that the London Brigade of the SNLA will plant the explosives, but they will be transported down by the Glasgow Brigade."

"Any names or other details, like vehicles?"

"We've established that the SNLA's been using a safe house in Glasgow. 15 Kelso Street, Drumchapel. Owner is Allan Thompson Irvine, born 23 April 1981, occupation motor mechanic. Confirmed member of the SNLA. Owns a dark blue Ford Mondeo estate registration number SC16EXY. Shall we move in now or continue to keep tabs on Irvine?"

"I'll refer this to Richard Donovan" replied Francois. "Richard, Indigo Two on the line."

Donovan took the call transfer. "Richard Donovan here, Indigo Two. Well done."

"You've probably heard we've located another bomb plot and where it's being planned from. Shall we move in now?"

"Not yet Indigo Two" replied Donovan. "Keep The Glasgow Brigade under continued surveillance. At some point, they'll be moving the stuff to London. If we follow them, we'll find out who's working in the London Brigade. We can then get someone in down this end. Then we can arrange for the lot of them to be lifted. Keep up the Good Work Indigo Two and Merry Christmas."

Donovan then turned to Francois. "Good work Marcel. That's the Christmas present we've wanted. I'll let the DG know. Can you contact Special Branch and NCA?"

"Yeah, I'll do that now. By the way Richard, can I head off early tomorrow? I've promised to take my girlfriend out on Christmas Eve."

31 December 2015
Kentish Town
London

Craig Beattie swung his Ford Transit van out of Falkland Road into Kentish Town Road. Along with Tom Ormond and two newer recruits to the SNLA London Brigade, Alex Jardine and Kevin Gorman, they were on their way to Trafalgar Square. In the back of the van lay four high explosive devices they had assembled and which were going to be planted and timed to explode at midnight amongst the crowds gathered to welcome in the New Year.

The previous day, Beattie and Ormond had disguised the van with vinyls to show it as belonging to Veolia Environmental Services, the French company which held the contract for waste management for the City of Westminster. They had also obtained stolen high visibility jackets in Veolia markings in order to give the impression that they were employees of that company on business.

It was 5:45pm and traffic was light. "How long before we reach Trafalgar Square Craig" said Kevin Gorman, at 19, the youngest of the four men in the van.

"If traffic's like this, another ten minutes and we'll be there" replied Beattie.

Detective Sergeant Jack Bundred and Detective Constable Julie Pitcher of Special Branch had been waiting in their unmarked BMW 530 for over an hour before they saw the fake Veolia Transit turn into Kentish Town Road. "There's our baby, Julie" said Bundred as he hit the accelerator. Meanwhile, Pitcher radioed the Territorial Support Group team in a police Mercedes Sprinter Van and two marked BMW 530s to notify them that their target had been identified.

Painstaking work by MI5 field agents before and after Christmas had first identified the Glasgow Brigade of the SNLA who had obtained the explosives, prepared the devices and arranged for their transport south, then identified the

London Brigade who would plant the explosives. On MI5's advice, Special Branch and the Territorial Support Group had waited until the terrorists had moved off and were on the way before intercepting them.

As Kentish Town Road entered Euston, Bundred and Pitcher made their move. Bundred swerved in front of the Transit forcing it to screech to a halt. Suddenly, the Territorial Support Group put on their flashing lights and sirens as they kettled the van, preventing its escape. Twenty heavily-armed officers leapt out and surrounded the Transit. Using a loudhailer, Bundred shouted "Armed Police. Put your hands up and get out of the van now. No funny stuff or we'll open fire."

The four SNLA men got out of the van and, with Heckler & Koch machine guns trained on them, were forced to lie down while they were searched and handcuffed.

The same day
Sky News

"This is Sara Ratcliffe on Sky News with an important newsflash."

"An SNLA plot to bomb Trafalgar Square tonight has been thwarted. Police stopped a van near Euston Station fifteen minutes ago and arrested four suspected SNLA terrorists. It is reported that four explosive devices were found in the van. The men have been taken to Paddington Green Police Station for questioning."

"The arrests are an important breakthrough in the fight against the SNLA terrorist campaign which has already claimed over a hundred lives, including the 43 people killed in the Bluewater bombing just before Christmas."

The same day
Trocadero
Leicester Square
London

"Guys, tonight will be the busiest night of the year. Even though it's all ticket and a complete sellout, there will still be people trying to gain entry. You know the score, no ticket, no entry." Gary Demetriou, the short, stocky manager of one of London's leading nightclubs was briefing his doormen who would be responsible for controlling entry and in tackling any potential disorder which might break out.

Demetriou continued. "You know the code for entry. No trainers, no ripped jeans, no football tops and no entry to anyone who's already pissed. We're not expecting any VIPs tonight." These were mostly professional footballers who would not be attending as there was a full programme of games on New Year's Day.

The doormen ranged in age from early 20s to late 40s. They ranged in height from five feet six inches to six feet eight inches. But all were powerfully built with bodies honed by relentless weight training in the gym, and many held martial arts qualifications.

Gareth Carver, a former Welsh Guard who hailed from Swansea was one of the doormen. He knew that the fire exits, which had to be left open for health and safety reasons could be an opportunity for unauthorised entry. "Gary, what about the emergency exits? Shouldn't we have someone guarding those?"

Demetriou recognised there was a problem. "Thanks for pointing that out Gareth. The way to deal with it is to have a rota for policing the emergency exits. One man per exit for an hour at a time. Lucy, can you prepare a rota" said Demetriou to the attractive blonde Assistant Manager, Lucy Southerton.

Fifteen minutes later, Lucy Southerton had prepared the rota. She called over the big Welshman. "Gareth, we've got you down for exit duty between 10pm and 11pm. Okay for that?"

"No problem Lucy" replied Carver.

It was still a half an hour before the Trocadero's doors opened. Carver used the lull in proceedings go through an emergency exit to make a call on his mobile phone.

"Hello, Mickey Prosser here. Is that you Gar?"

"Yeah, Gar here Mickey. How's things going for tonight?"

"Great. We've got the bombs primed. All we need is to get in."

"That's where I come in boy" replied Carver. I'm guarding the emergency exit leading out onto Great Newport Street between 10 and 11. Make sure you, Billo and Del all dress smart. That way, you'll raise no suspicion here."

"Don't worry Gar" replied Prosser. We'll all have our top gear on. See you in four hours."

The same day, 11:58pm
West End Central Police Station
London

The mood at West End Central Police Station was one of jubilation as the New Year approached. Earlier that evening, the police had arrested four SNLA terrorists as they were on the way to plant bombs in Trafalgar Square. This had been followed by further arrests of SNLA suspects in Glasgow and Aberdeen.

Chief Superintendent Matthew Fisher, the Area Commander, emerged from his office to ask about how things were shaping up. Slim, athletic and good-looking, Fisher was relatively young for the post, being in his late 30s, but he was recognised as a high flier who many saw as potential Chief Officer material.

"Marianne, how's things been going tonight?" Chief Inspector Marianne Wood replied "Quieter than normal tonight sir. I wonder if the threat of terrorist bombs has put people off."

"Most unlikely Ma'am" replied Sergeant Kevin Reardon, a force veteran of 25 years. "One thing about the Brits is that they've got bottle when it comes to things like that. Remember when ETA bombed the Spanish Costas a few years back. All the Germans and Swedes fled the beaches but not us."

"All the same, we've had far fewer arrests tonight than in previous years. Hope it continues beyond midnight."

Their conversation was suddenly interrupted by the sounding of the emergency siren from the control room. Fisher had last remembered this going one July morning ten years previously when he was a young Sergeant in his first posting, when Al-Q'aida terrorists had let off bombs on the Underground and buses and killed 52 people. As he rushed in, he was greeted by one of the control room staff, Delores McKenzie with a panic-stricken expression across her face. "Sir, there's been a bombing at the Trocadero. They reckon there's many dead."

1 January 2016
Sky News

"This is Adam Rennie with this morning's headlines on Sky News. Fifty people are now known to have been killed in last night's terrorist bombing of the Trocadero nightclub in Leicester Square. Responsibility for the atrocity has been claimed by the Welsh Republican Army."

"Eyewitnesses reported that seconds after midnight, there were three separate explosions, one close to the bar and two by the dancefloor. The police are examining CCTV footage to try and find clues to the identity of the terrorists responsible for this outrage."

"Unlike its Scottish counterpart, the SNLA, the WRA has enjoyed a much smaller profile up to now. They have been responsible for several bombings in Wales, mainly against English-owned properties but the only fatalities were of five soldiers who were murdered in Cardiff two months ago after being picked up by three girls they had met in a nightclub."

3 January 2016
Dolphin Square
Pimlico
London

Deborah Pearson had invited Henry Arbuthnot, Jason Steer and the Prime Minister's Security Adviser, Frank Hesford over for Sunday lunch. The first Cabinet meeting of 2016 was due in two days time and she knew that the security situation in Scotland and Wales would be a prime issue for the agenda.

A State of Emergency had been declared in both Scotland and Wales and additional powers of search, entry and arrest had been given to the police and the Army. MI5 had at last been successful in inserting agents into the SNLA and the WRA and the first arrests had been made. But, if anything, the SNLA and WRA had become bolder. The terrorist bombings of Bluewater and the Trocadero nightclub had proved the ability of the SNLA and WRA to strike at will in England. Both organisations were behind growing public disorder in Scotland and Wales and news had come in that two soldiers on patrol in Aberdeen had been shot dead the previous night.

The three Ministers and the Prime Minister's Security Adviser retired to the lounge after finishing their coffees. Pearson's housekeeper then proceeded to clear the table in the dining room.

"Frank, any suggestions on what we can do next?" said the Home Secretary. "We've introduced a State of Emergency, increased police powers and at last MI5's starting to deliver. But it see it's having little effect."

"Could we try reintroducing internment without trial?" said Defence Secretary Steer. He was referring to the controversial policy used in Northern Ireland from 1971 after the Troubles escalated there.

"Just what I've been thinking" replied Hesford. "Half the problem in Northern Ireland had been the difficulty in getting witnesses to testify against the IRA. Known terrorists were walking free from the courts. It was an unpopular move and the Governments of the day suffered international criticism. But it successfully removed known terrorists from the streets and held back the IRA's capacity to commit acts of terror."

"If we were to reintroduce internment without trial in Scotland and Wales, I reckon we could break the SNLA and WRA fairly quickly. Both organisations are at a relatively early stage of development and the removal of key operatives should damage their capacity to function. I also think this presents an opportunity to open specialist interrogation centres like the one we had at Castlereagh. It had a mix of police, military and security service interrogators if you remember. Their methods weren't pretty and there were a lot of bleats from the human rights brigade. But we got invaluable intelligence from captured IRA oppos."

"Frank, I like that idea" said Pearson. "All we need to do now is to find secure accommodation to hold terror suspects and other troublemakers. Jason, do you have any possible sites? I'm afraid that prison capacity's almost full."

Steer replied "Two possible locations come to mind Deborah. Both are former training facilities. The first is near Brecon, the other near Stirling. Both are fairly close to the main population centres so problems with transit of prisoners should be minimised."

Pearson then turned to the Foreign Secretary. "Henry, how do you see it going down overseas?"

"We can expect the usual protests and bleats from EU countries. But I reckon Russia and China will be less vocal. After all, they've got their own problems with separatists. And now we've got more oil and our economy's booming, they'll want to keep in with us. What's most important Deborah is that the USA will be on our side. Rose might be lukewarm." Arbuthnot was referring to the US Secretary of State, Milton Rose who was less than enthusiastic about the robust line the UK Government had taken towards the attempted secession by Scotland and Wales. "But President Whitney's right behind us, as is Vice-President Odell. Remember that the USA effectively did the same as us with Guantanamo Bay. And Congress is on our side too—after all, no one's going to go against Troy Burton."

"Excellent" replied Pearson. "I therefore intend to bring this to Cabinet on Tuesday."

5 January 2016
Cabinet Room
10 Downing Street
London

The opening Cabinet meeting of 2016 was a solemn one. Prime Minister Robert Delgado had opened the meeting by mentioning that he had just written a letter of condolence to the mother of a soldier from the Rifles who had been shot dead the previous day while on patrol in Bangor, North Wales.

First item on the agenda was Deborah Pearson's proposal for the reintroduction of internment in Scotland and Wales.

Only one Cabinet member, Attorney-General Stephen Lansbury was less than enthusiastic about its introduction. "Prime Minister, Deborah, do you realise that imprisonment without trial goes against everything that the country stands for. We've rightly protested about other countries jailing political opponents. Do you realise the damage this will cause to the country's reputation abroad? Not only that, it'll give the SNLA and WRA a massive propaganda boost."

Delgado was distinctly unimpressed. "Stephen, there's a war on. The SNLA and WRA couldn't give a toss about human rights of their victims, so why should we be concerned about them. Do you realise I've spent the past hour writing letters of condolence to the widow and the mothers of soldiers who were shot dead by snipers during the past few days. Try telling them about the human rights of terrorists."

The vote to introduce internment was passed almost unanimously. There was one abstention, from Lansbury.

CHAPTER 5

24 March 2016
Fitzroy Avenue
Drumcondra
Dublin

The sound of two Ford Mondeos pulling up alerted Martin Hallinan to the fact that his guests had arrived. Out stepped two men whom he was meeting for the first time and, indeed, were meeting themselves for the first time. Former IRA commander and current Sinn Fein councillor for Drumcondra East ward on Dublin City Council, Hallinan was about to meet Doug Paterson and Trevor Rees, the Chairmen of the General Councils of the SNLA and the WRA who had been invited to attend the celebrations for the centenary of the Easter Uprising.

Anyone visiting Dublin could not help but notice that the centenary celebrations for the Easter Uprising of 1916 were about to be held. In two days time there was to be a parade through Dublin, down O'Connell Street, past the General Post Office building, round Pearse Street and past the Dail and finishing at Dublin Castle where the Taoiseach, Kevin Doyle, was to deliver a speech. Already, the world's leaders were arriving in Dublin. The President of France, Marie-Christine Dumas, had flown in, as had German Chancellor Roland Straub and Russian President Boris Cherenkov. EU President, Emilio Santana, Spanish Prime Minister Jose Ruiz and Chinese Prime Minister, Ho Chinzhou were on the way, as was one of the more controversial attendees, President Mohammed Khoramzadeh of Iran. The USA was to be represented by the Vice-President, Philip Odell, who was of Irish descent. However, a significant absentee was the United Kingdom, who had declined an invitation to attend.

Fitzroy Avenue was unlikely to be on many tourists' itinerary for visiting Dublin as it was located in the city's less prosperous and more crime-ridden Northside. The only attraction which brought people in was the massive concrete edifice of Croke Park, less than half a mile away, which was home to the Gaelic Athletic Association and, in addition to hurling and Gaelic Football, was also used for soccer and rugby internationals which the smaller Aviva Stadium in South Dublin could not accommodate.

"Gentlemen, failte, croeso. Come in." Hallinan welcomed his guests into the lounge of the terraced property which had once been an IRA safe house and was still owned by Sinn Fein, its political wing.

The men from the General Councils of the SNLA and WRA settled into the sofas in the lounge as Hallinan's wife, Maureen, brought in cups of tea and a tray of biscuits.

"Absolutely delighted that you guys could attend the Centenary celebrations" said Hallinan. "Any difficulties getting over?"

"No trouble" said Paterson. "I've got a passport issued in a false name and I was not challenged at Glasgow Airport."

"Same for me" said Rees.

"I've also heard that you guys are after our advice on sustaining your campaigns" said Hallinan. "I'm more than willing to offer it." Again, there were nods of approval from the SNLA and WRA men.

Hallinan continued. "There's no doubt you guys have made a great start. You've already done in less than a year what the IRA took four years to achieve. But the real challenge to you starts now. It's not taking the fight to the English—you've clearly done that. It is more about securing finances, obtaining a regular supply of weapons, strengthening your internal intelligence and extending political influence. Is that the kind of info you're after?"

"Dead right" replied Paterson and Rees.

"First question. How do you guys secure funding?"

"Collections in pubs and clubs" said Paterson. "The same" said Rees.

"Just like the IRA" said Hallinan. "Trouble is, we found it didn't raise that much. And the authorities were on to us quickly. A lot of pubs and clubs where we did our collecting got closed down. This led us to look further afield."

Hallinan continued. "We set up Noraid out in the USA. That raised millions for us and gave us a regular cashflow."

"Won't that run into problems with the Yanks?" asked Paterson. "They've been paranoid on security ever since 9/11."

"They tried Doug. On many occasions. Even when Ronald Reagan was President. But he can't control State law or even the Federal courts. And we had strong support in Congress. They were never able to prove Noraid had IRA links."

"The IRA also raised money through bootleg booze and ciggies and, in later years, through fake designer clothes, CDs and DVDs. Reckon you guys could shift the stuff?"

Rees's eyes lit up as he knew that Wales had a widespread network of workingmen's and social clubs. "No problem turning it around Martin. There's at least 2-3 clubs in every village."

"In our last years before the Good Friday Agreement, we ran a credit card scam" said Hallinan. "Nicked credit cards off wealthy businessmen and cloned them. Got others through hooky credit card terminals. Others have copied us. Al-Q'aida and ETA."

"Lastly, we raised money through the drugs trade" said Hallinan. "Heroin, cocaine, cannabis, you name it, we shifted it. We got the stuff from both crime cartels and other terrorist groups. Proved one of our best moneyspinners."

"Don't like it Martin" said Rees. "Nor me" added Paterson. "I've seen the damage drugs has caused and I don't want to do it to my people."

"I know what you guys are thinking" said Hallinan. "Believe me, the IRA had the same concerns when we started shifting drugs back in the 1970s. I for one was against it at the start, just like you are now. But it enabled us to expand our operations massively. Our guys had brand new weapons and we were able to take the fight right to the heart of the UK. And take on the Brits anywhere in the world. What's more, we targeted our operations carefully. Most of the gear we shifted was done on mainland Britain, not in our backyard. There was a double benefit for us—it tied up the Brit authorities in tackling all the fallout from the drugs trade—you know, crime, the cost of treating addicts."

"Also, we know plenty of people who can help you move your money out of harm's way where the British authorities will be unable to touch it."

The next item on the agenda was security. Paterson gave a rueful smile as he realised that MI5 had penetrated the SNLA. Their most notable success had been the arrest of the Glasgow and London brigades three months earlier before they could plant bombs in Trafalgar Square on New Year's Eve.

"I hear you guys have had a bit of local difficulties with MI5 and Special Branch" said Hallinan. Paterson and Rees both nodded. "Same happened with the IRA. Some of the plants were very difficult to find. But we were able to weed many of them out. First thing to remember is they are acting a lie. At some point, they will be indiscreet and betray their identity. Watch any new recruits closely or any who are not known well by colleagues. Also, build up your own intelligence network. Use local people's knowledge. We found that people in the Nationalist communities were only too happy to help us. They will unmask any spies planted by MI5 or Special Branch. And make an example of any traitor you find. As soon as the IRA left a few mutilated bodies of spies and snitches, others were reluctant to come forward and help the authorities."

Hallinan then moved to the subject of building political influence.

"Have you guys done anything about building links with potential allies?"

"Not yet" replied Rees.

"Worth doing" said Hallinan. "The IRA built links with almost every Marxist organisation in Europe and beyond. The 1970s were the golden age for terrorist organisations—we had the Red Brigades, the Baader-Meinhof Gang and the PLO. In Britain, hard left organisations supported our cause. Gave us safe houses and invaluable intelligence on the authorities and on spies and informers within our ranks. But we also built links with mainstream politicians. Particularly in the States. Several leading Irish-American senators and congressmen fought our corner. They stopped Noraid being shut down, they blocked arms sales to the RUC and the UDR and prevented the extradition of our men and women to the UK."

"We've got several other guests visiting at about lunchtime. The PLO rep in Dublin, Abu Jibril, will be calling in, as will the Iranian ambassador. We've also got Carlos Padilla of FARC, Mohammed Sarwar of Al-Q'aida and Tom Gleeson of Noraid. They'll be able to advise you about getting a solid cashflow in place. Heidi Kunz, who's worked for Bank Zwingli, will be able to advise you on hiding your assets out of reach of the British authorities. Jibril and Padilla will be able to advise you about strengthening your organisations against spies and informers and Sarwar can help with providing safe houses and false identities. So can Dave Newcombe of the Socialist Alliance."

"Senator Leahy's over later this afternoon. He's got with him a couple of Congressmen—Senator Brad McAllister and Representative Graydon Hopkins. Both have been vocal in their support for the Scottish and Welsh cause. Good idea if you guys find out how they can help you."

"It's also worth getting a few good lawyers on your side" continued Hallinan. "One will be over today. Justin Hemingway. He used to be with Birnberg Pierce before going it alone. Defended everyone from celebrities facing drugs or assault charges, through to Al-Q'aida. An expert on process and procedure. Justin's a legend for getting people off. The Brit authorities can't stand him—they call him 'Mr Loophole'."

"Last bit of advice fellas" said Hallinan. "Given any thought to joint operations? The two of you working together could potentially bring Britain to a halt."

15 April 2016
Highfield Avenue
Farington near Preston, Lancashire

Members of the SNLA and WRA General Councils had gathered at the suburban semi-detached house in the small Lancashire town just south of Preston. It had been bought at auction just two weeks earlier. Nobody knew that the buyer was acting on behalf of the SNLA.

Gathered round the 24-inch computer screen in the lounge were Doug Paterson and Trevor Rees, along with Charlie Renwick and Mike Grogan from the SNLA and Richard Thomas and Gethin Davies of the WRA. Earlier that day, they had been identifying the location of military bases, airports and railway stations. They had spent the last hour surfing listings sites giving details of major events taking place in the United Kingdom during the forthcoming summer. All were potential targets for the SNLA and WRA.

"I think we've got enough targets for tonight" said Paterson, as he suggested that the meeting should move to discussing the logistics of carrying out the attacks.

Renwick and Davies were both concerned about the high risks attached to attacking the same types of target in quick succession. "Guys, don't you realise that if we hit shopping centres once, the authorities will tighten up security elsewhere. This will make it more likely that we'll get picked up."

"Much the same for tourist attractions" said Davies. "What's more, there's a good chance some of them will pay for their own security. Like the Yanks did in Iraq."

Renwick was also concerned about plans to hit events where members of the Royal Family would be present. "I think we need to be cautious about going for the Derby, Royal Ascot or Wimbledon. The Royals will be present so security's going to be ultra tight."

Rees was unimpressed by the SNLA Deputy Chairman's reticence. "Charlie, every operation we do carries a risk. Just because the Royal Family might be present is no reason not to target an event. Quite the opposite. Just imagine the impact if we let off a bomb at something like the Derby or Royal Ascot. Even if we just leave one there and tell the authorities, it'll cause a lot of disruption. Remember when the IRA forced the evacuation of the Grand National back in the 1990s? No one was hurt but it cost the organisers and the economy a lot of money. Same if we ring in a threat to a shopping centre or an airport or railway station."

"Sorry Charlie, I agree with Trevor on this" said Paterson. "We're fighting a war and any target considered valid is reasonable to go for."

4 June 2016
Epsom Racecourse
Surrey

Chief Inspector Mark Clifford of Surrey Police was standing in front of a bank of monitor screens in the police post set up for the Derby. He was pleased that the day's events had passed off smoothly in the run-up to the big race. The day was gloriously sunny and record numbers of visitors were in attendance. The usual problems were drunkenness, disorder, theft and illegal bookmaking, but this year the incidence of crime was less than normal. Of course, there were security concerns because of the threat from the SNLA and WRA, but MI5 and Special Branch and the National Anti-Terror Squad which had been formed a month earlier had been in attendance from the first day of the race meeting to ensure that both the Royal Family and other VIPs were kept safe and there was no threat to the general public.

The Derby was more than just a day out for Londoners and the chance to make a financial windfall if they placed a bet on the winning horse. There was a massive corporate presence too and the Derby was an opportunity for businessmen to network and negotiate deals. Large sections of the prime viewing points were out of bounds to the public as they had been secured for corporate hospitality.

There was still an hour to go when Mandy Dent, who was working in the control room, took a call. The caller had a Scottish accent and said there was a bomb on the racecourse that would go off while the race was in progress. He then rang off.

Clifford had been familiarised with procedures in the event of an emergency. He immediately called Assistant Commissioner Darren Charnock, the recently appointed Head of the National Anti-Terror Squad, who was on site, along with the Head of F6 Section at MI5, Richard Donovan. "Sir, just had a call saying a bomb's been planted and will go off while the main race is on. Didn't say anything about location. What shall we do? Evacuate?"

Charnock feared something like this might happen. "Mark, absolutely. It might be a hoax, but we can't afford to take chances. Even if one or two people are killed, it is too many. The safety of the public is paramount. Richard, your views?"

Donovan agreed. "Chief Inspector, I'm with Assistant Commissioner Charnock on this. I don't imagine the owners will be too pleased. Or the sponsors or bookmakers. But human life must come first."

Two minutes later, an announcement came over the public address system.

"Ladies and gentlemen, there has been an unexpected emergency which has made it necessary to close the race meeting today. Can you please evacuate the venue immediately.

Stewards will show you the nearest exit. Please leave your cars behind. I am sorry for any inconvenience this might cause."

The same day
Sky News

"This is Claire Egerton with this afternoon's headlines on Sky News.

"For the first time ever, the Derby has had to be abandoned. Epsom Racecourse was evacuated after a call was received an hour ago from the SNLA saying that a bomb had been planted on the course. Racing for the day was brought to an end while the police and security services carry out a thorough inspection of the course."

"The Derby will of course be re-run a later date. But the economic damage caused by the bomb alert will be considerable. Apart from the lost business to the bookmaking industry, there will be compensation claims from visitors who were forced to leave and will be unable to attend the rescheduled race."

"Now for further news. Military police were called in to deal with disturbances at Thelwall Barracks in Cheshire after National Servicemen barricaded themselves in their barracks and refused to parade. This follows the death of a National Service recruit three days ago."

"The reintroduction of National Service has been unpopular with young people who feel it penalises those who have been unable to secure employment or further education at a time where access to both has been radically reduced. Already, there have been allegations that National Service recruits have been bullied and degraded by non-commissioned officers. But supporters of the scheme claim that National Service has given young people skills that will equip them for the jobs market and has reduced crime and anti-social behaviour by taking them off the streets. It has also been reported that the far-left Socialist Alliance is under investigation for inciting these disturbances, and those a week earlier at Chigwell Barracks in Essex."

10 June 2016
J D Wetherspoons
Barbould Street
Warrington, Cheshire

The Warrington branch of J D Wetherspoons was popular with young people from the area and, since the reintroduction of National Service, had been patronised by those stationed at Thelwall Barracks just over a mile away. Its main attraction was that drinks prices were low in comparison with other pubs and bars and the management were not too fussy about dress codes.

At the right hand end of the bar stood a group who were identifiable as National Service men and women from Thelwall. Friday was one of two nights that they were permitted to be off the base and, even then, they were expected to be back on the base by midnight. This was before most of the pubs and all of the clubs had closed.

The mood amongst the group of National Service trainees was morose to say the least. The experience had been everything they feared and none of them saw any benefit. The days had been composed of endless and repetitive drills and hard physical labour. Pay and remuneration was a pittance, they were subject to endless petty restrictions and they had been subjected to the bullying of NCOs who were seen to be setting almost impossible standards for them to meet.

Just over a week earlier, the trainees' anger boiled over after a trainee collapsed and died on a route march carried out on a searingly hot day. A riot had broken out, and military police had to be called in to quell it. Six trainees who had been regarded as the ringleaders behind the disturbances had been court-martialled and sentenced to two months in the "glasshouse", the military prison at Colchester. The rest had been summoned to a 6am parade in which the base's commanding officer had read the riot act and placed several more restrictions on the trainees, including bans on membership of political parties and in talking to the media.

Prominent in the group was Kevin Doherty, a Mancunian from the sprawling Wythenshawe estate on the city's south side. He was easily the best educated of the group, having obtained A-levels the previous year. He had been unsuccessful in getting into university, and had found similar barriers to finding work or training. He was convinced that as soon as employers or colleges saw his Wythenshawe address, his application was thrown in the bin.

"Fellas, I reckon that if we skip the UK, the bizzies won't be able to get us back. We'll be able to claim asylum. After all, all foreign governments are against the UK on many counts. Bringing back the death penalty, over Scotland and Wales, internment. And several foreign politicians have said that National Service is slave labour."

"Kev, there's one problem" said Mohammed Iqbal. "Our passports have been impounded by the military authorities so we can't skip the country. And we'll need them to travel abroad."

"Also, don't forget we now need to show passports to UK Borders when we leave the country" said Sam Crossthwaite. "As soon as they see who we are, we'll get pulled up."

"How about Ireland guys?" replied Doherty. We've still got the Common Travel Area. All we need to show is our ID card."

Steve Raybould had noticed the group of National Service trainees in J D Wetherspoons. He was a member of the WRA's Warrington Brigade and Thelwall Barracks was a prime target for them. A local member of the Socialist Alliance has tipped him off that large numbers of National Service trainees patronised J D Wetherspoons on Friday and Saturday nights and he knew from recent media coverage that a lot were discontented. The opportunity for some inside help in getting into the barracks beckoned.

Raybould headed over to the group of young trainees. "You lads from Thelwall?" asked Raybould. "How are you finding National Service?"

"Who the fuck are you pal?" snarled a sullen Crossthwaite. "Looking for something?"

Doherty and Iqbal moved in. "Sam, for fuck's sake, don't start something. Otherwise we'll all end up in the fucking glasshouse" shouted Doherty.

"Welsh are you mate?" asked Iqbal.

"Right first time butt" said Raybould.

"You're not WRA?" asked Doherty.

"Over there lads" said Raybould pointing to an alcove. "It's a bit quieter."

In the alcove, Raybould spoke. "For the record, the answer is 'yes'. I'm in the WRA. You lads fancy helping us get into Thelwall?"

"To do what" said Iqbal. "Not bomb the place?"

"That's right son. Me and my buddies intend to hit the officers and sergeants mess. That will send a message to the Brit government that they're not wanted in Wales. I can see you lads are pissed off with National Service."

"Too right" said Doherty. "Endless bull, crap pay and no freedom. And for what. Just because the fucking Government has cut university places and traineeships, and no one wants to offer us a job."

"Here's your chance to get some revenge" said Raybould. "If you guys could let me or a mate have a map of the barracks and information about guard points and rotas and details of contractors who've got access to the site, we'll give the officers and NCOs a present they won't forget."

Doherty's eyes lit up. He had visions of Colonel Bruce Field, the base's pompous Commanding Officer and the two most hated warrant officers, Sergeants Jim Carlin and Kevin Dooley being blown sky high. "Yeah, count me in mate. I'll help. By he way, what's your name?"

Raybould replied "Just call me Steve. When are you lads in next?"

Iqbal replied "Tomorrow night Steve. We'll have the stuff you want."

15 June 2016
Thelwall Barracks
Warrington, Cheshire

The Sergeants Mess at Thelwall Barracks was doing good business that evening. With the day's training and other duties over, the base's NCOs had retired to the bar for a few pints with their mates. On the television were the highlights of the second day of racing at Royal Ascot.

Sergeant Jim Carlin of the Mercian Regiment, a short, stocky Liverpudlian, was at the bar. "Two pints of Stella, Kayleigh" he asked the barmaid.

Carlin was in his mid-40s and had been a soldier since leaving school 30 years earlier. He had served in Northern Ireland, all three Gulf wars and Afghanistan.

"Ta, Jim." Fellow Sergeant Kevin Dooley, another Liverpudlian who was almost a full foot taller and towered over Carlin, gratefully accepted the pint his colleague had bought.

Carlin and Dooley's conversations were predictable. The fortunes of Liverpool FC, the racing form at Royal Ascot and the fortunes of the country's professional boxers formed the basis of most of their discussions. But that day's edition of the *Sun* had a feature on the campaign by Labour MP Geraldine Partington for a public inquiry into mistreatment of National Service trainees. Both Carlin and Dooley were hostile towards Partington; to them, she epitomised the do-gooders from well-off backgrounds who had no understanding of real life and failed to appreciate that most of the trainees were surly, truculent chavs who needed a good kick up the backside to knock them into shape.

"Kev, did you see today's *Sun*? That daft bitch Partington's calling for a public inquiry into the treatment of National Service trainees. Reckons we're being too hard on them."

"Typical lah-di-dah champagne socialist Jim" replied Dooley. "Thinks they're all poor dears. Little does she know what scumbags most of them really are and that all we're doing is trying to turn them into responsible citizens."

All of a sudden, everyone present was startled by the sound of a loud explosion coming from the direction of the Officers' Mess. "Jesus Christ!" exclaimed Dooley. "What the fuck was that?"

Before any of the NCOs had a chance to react, a second blast ripped through the Sergeant's Mess.

16 June 2016, 7:45am
Ascot Racecourse
Berkshire

Kyle Eastman had arrived early at Ascot Racecourse that morning. He was working as a waiter in the Pavilion Restaurant during the 2016 Royal Ascot race meeting, which had been hired out to merchant bankers Goldman Sachs for corporate hospitality, and had turned up to assist with a fresh delivery of food and drink. Although Thursday was regarded as the quietest day of Royal Ascot, it was nevertheless expected to be busy.

Eastman, a media studies graduate from London Metropolitan University twelve months earlier, had been forced to take temporary employment while looking for permanent and better-paid work. He had found his qualification of limited use and had already racked up forty rejections. Employers were only interested in graduates with traditional degrees and from prestigious universities. To avoid being drafted for National Service, he had been forced to find menial work, which did little to clear his sizeable debt incurred while at university.

Eastman found the job mind-numbingly boring, as well as being tiring, and he bridled against the dismissive attitude that the wealthy customers took towards him. The previous day he recognised a former girlfriend who was now working for a merchant bank. She was now arm candy for a wealthy merchant banker and had blanked him.

At 8am, a refrigerated truck turned up from Christian Salvesen. The driver and his mate presented their credentials to Eastman. The shorter of the two men, Jackie Lennox, was a Scot from Glasgow while the taller, Tony Smith, was a Brummie.

"Can ye lads give us a hand in unloading the food for today?" said Lennox.

"I'll give a hand" said Eastman. "Sam, Chris, can you help me?"

"Hang on Kyle" said Sam Elkoubi, "I'll get the trolleys."

Over the next half hour, the waiters helped the Christian Salvesen delivery men unload the truck and wheel in the food for the restaurant staff to prepare. By 9am, all the food had been handed over to the kitchen staff who were at work in preparing the gourmet spread for the corporate guests.

Eastman's last act was to sign for the delivery. He motioned Lennox and Smith to a quiet spot where they would not be disturbed. The two delivery men had with them what looked like a gigantic wine cooler. It was nothing of the sort; instead, it was a massive bomb that was to be detonated by mobile phone. The real names of "Lennox" and "Smith" were Dave Connolly and Iain Carmichael, and they were both members of the SNLA's London Brigade who were on a mission to bomb Royal Ascot. The SNLA had stolen the identity of two Christian Salvesen delivery men.

"Dave, Iain, I'll show you the best place to leave that wine cooler" whispered Eastman and pointed to a location close to the entrance to the Pavilion Restaurant. Eastman knew that later in the day, it would have a large footfall as guests moved in and out of the restaurant to see the races.

Eastman had been forced to undergo security and criminal record checks before he got the job at Royal Ascot. However, MI5 and the National Anti-Terror Squad had both managed to miss the fact that one of Eastman's flatmates was a member of the Socialist Alliance. On hearing Eastman's resentment about the fact he had failed to find regular work and was having to work as a flunky and be insulted by people who often had less of an education than himself, his flatmate had introduced him to the SNLA. They were delighted to find that Eastman was working inside Royal Ascot and was ready and willing to help them. For Eastman, he could not wait to see the bomb go off and blow those smug bankers and businessmen sky high.

16 June 2016, 11:30am
Ascot Racecourse
Berkshire

Assistant Commissioner Darren Charnock, Head of the National Anti-Terror Squad and Chief Constable Zoe Bridges of Thames Valley Police were looking pleased with the results of the first two days of Royal Ascot. Lessons had been learned from the alert which had caused the abandonment of the Derby less than two weeks earlier. Scanners similar to those used at airports had been installed to screen customers and all contractors had been required to provide the police with records of all staff who would have access to the racecourse. The opening day in which the Queen attended and Ladies Day had passed off without incident.

"So far so good, Zoe" said Charnock. "Make sure though that your officers don't drop their guard now there's no Royals. I've had to send some of my men up north today. The WRA bombed Thelwall Barracks last night. So there will be more for Thames Valley to take on."

"Don't worry Darren" said the Chief Constable. "I'll personally ensure that my officers are all on the ball today."

16 June 2016, 3:35pm
The Pavilion Restaurant
Ascot Racecourse
Berkshire

The 3:30 race had just finished. Sheikh Mohammed of the United Arab Emirates was leading his horse, *Wirewool*, through the paddock, having accepted the winning prize. Punters were collecting their winnings from the bookies.

Back in the Pavilion Restaurant, it was almost time for afternoon tea. Many of Goldman Sachs' wealthy clients were already well oiled from a considerable intake of champagne, fine wine, malt whisky and vintage brandy. A group of City brokers rolled in through the doors brandishing wads of money they had won on the 3:30.

Without warning, there was a massive blast in the Pavilion Restaurant. A gigantic fireball flung masonry, wood, glass, chinaware and bodies everywhere. For a moment, there was a deathly silence. Then the screaming and wailing of the grievously wounded began, followed by the sound of the fire alarm.

The same day
Sky News

"This is Claire Egerton with the latest headlines from Sky News."

"Enquiries are continuing following the WRA bombing at Thelwall Barracks near Warrington last night which killed ten soldiers from the Mercian Regiment. The atrocity has raised concerns about how secure military bases are, since they are guarded round the clock and are backed up with CCTV."

"One lead the police are following up is the possibility that the WRA had help from inside. Several National Service trainees are accommodated at Thelwall and it is believed that some may have collaborated with the WRA to give them access to the base. It is common knowledge that many National Service trainees are unwilling recruits and the disturbances at Thelwall two weeks ago may have radicalised them to the point of being prepared to help terrorists."

"We've got a newsflash coming through. There has just been a report of a bomb explosion in the grandstand at Ascot Racecourse. There are believed to be very high numbers of casualties. We are just getting an update . . . . the SNLA has just claimed responsibility for this bombing."

17 June 2016
Home Office
Marsham Street
London

Deborah Pearson had postponed plans to return to her Midlands constituency in order to convene an urgent meeting following the Warrington and Ascot bombings. She had summoned attendance from MI5 Director-General Nicola Martin, Head of the National Anti-Terror Squad Darren Charnock and ACPO Chairman Dave

Tanner, all of whom were present. Also attending the meeting were Sir Derek Copperfield, the Permanent Secretary, Richard Harbottle, the Director-General for Security and Counter-Terrorism and Frank Hesford, the Prime Minister's Security Adviser.

"Well ladies and gentlemen" said Pearson icily. "Another forty people dead. And this time several City bankers and businessmen. I thought you were supposed to have the matter under control."

"Home Secretary, we've at last made headway in getting agents into the SNLA and WRA" said Nicola Martin. "We've penetrated several of their largest cells and intelligence is now in the hands of the police and the National Anti-Terror Squad. Isn't that so Darren?" she asked the Head of the National Anti-Terror Squad.

"Most grateful for the intelligence Nicola" replied Charnock. "We've pulled in the suspects for Bluewater and the Trocadero bombings and we're close to making arrests for Warrington and Ascot."

Pearson's icy expression did not change. "Nicola, Darren, that's only a start. You realise there are plenty more terrorists out there who we haven't got sight of. They're the people we need to track down."

Pearson continued. "Darren, Dave, I want any person who might have the slightest connections to the SNLA or WRA, to be pulled in, no matter how tenuous. That means people involved in street disorder, running hostile or critical campaigns or inciting people to defy the law. That will include local politicians or journalists. Understand?"

"Home Secretary, you realise you are breaching habeas corpus if you go ahead with this" said a concerned Sir Derek Copperfield.

"Derek, sod habeas corpus" replied an irate Pearson. "The SNLA and WRA have declared war against the British people. We're entitled to protect ourselves. Anyone criticising what we're doing is by extension helping the SNLA and WRA. Let's show them we mean business."

"Nicola, I want MI5 to step up surveillance both in Scotland and Wales and against any Scots or Welsh working in England. Anyone considered subversive I want to see on your records. And keep an eye on all the Trot groups who might be helping them."

The same day
National Anti-Terror Squad
Spring Gardens
London

"Sir, we've got a lead." Chief Inspector Russell Colbourne had called into the office of the Head of the Squad, Assistant Commissioner Darren Charnock with the news that intelligence from MI5 field agents had identified possible leads to the Warrington and Ascot bombers.

"Fire away Russ" said Charnock.

"Firstly, we've got a trace on a red Vauxhall Insignia, registration number LX13 OBY. Registered to a Mr Glen McFarlane of 56 Avondale Road, Streatham, born 4

March 1989. He works in the construction industry. According to neighbours, he's due to travel home today for a long weekend. Been rumours that he's linked to the SNLA."

"Any CRB record against him?" said Charnock.

"Only two sir" replied Colbourne. "One for criminal damage in 2012, another for assault in 2013. Otherwise clean."

"Keep McFarlane under surveillance Russ. If he's found travelling to Scotland, lift him. What's the other lead?"

"Got a lead on an address in Warrington sir" said Colbourne. "10 Salisbury Street. Reckoned to be a bit of a doss-house. Neighbours have advised a field agent that a couple of dodgy-looking Welsh blokes have stayed there. We've got a name—Martyn Thomas, born 25 June 1992. Got a conviction two years ago for drug possession. He's reckoned to be sympathetic to the WRA."

"Good work Russ" said Charnock. "Wait until the house is fully occupied. Then go in. Okay?"

"Yes sir" replied Colbourne. "I'll get things moving now."

Later that day
Salisbury Street
Warrington, Cheshire

Friday night was usually a profitable night for Martyn Thomas. A small-time drug-dealer originally from Corwen in North Wales, he had been living in Warrington for the past two years. For a while, he had worked as a fork-lift driver on an industrial estate but he had found selling drugs a more profitable venture. In addition, he sold copies of a small Welsh nationalist newspaper in Warrington town centre to the town's significant number of Welsh exiles.

He was just preparing to go out when he was assailed by the sound of the front door being kicked in, followed by several heavily-armed policemen.

"Armed police!" shouted Sergeant Neil Baker of the National Anti-Terror Squad. "On the floor now!" Outnumbered, Thomas and his housemates had no option but to comply.

Approximately the same time
Knutsford Services, M6

Glen McFarlane steered his car into the car park at the motorway service station close to the Cheshire town of Knutsford. He had already been on the road for five hours in the heavy weekend traffic. With him as passengers were four of his workmates, also Scots, who had taken the opportunity of a free ride home.

Sergeant Jason Scholes of the National Anti-Terror Squad observed McFarlane's car as it drew in. Heading an eight-man squad, Scholes, said "There they are guys. Let's go."

The five Scots had barely got out of McFarlane's care when they were greeted with an Uzi submachine gun pointing in their face. "On the ground now!" snarled Scholes as handcuffs were applied.

Later that evening
Sky News

"This is Scott Parfitt with the late evening headlines on Sky News."

"There has just been an important breakthrough in the fight against terrorism. Officers from the National Anti-Terror Squad made dramatic arrests of five SNLA suspects at Knutsford Services just over half an hour ago. The five suspects were travelling in a red Vauxhall Insignia and were arrested in front of startled members of the public."

"In a second raid, officers arrested four suspected WRA terrorists in a raid at an address in Warrington."

CHAPTER 6

The Great Britain Athletics Squad was making its final preparations before flying out to Rio de Janeiro for the Olympic Games which would be starting in a month's time. The 2012 Olympics in London had been a glorious one for the British Team, in which they won the third highest number of medals behind the USA and China. Although the most successful medal hauls came on the cycling track, in rowing and in the boxing ring, the athletes had done far better than expected. For 2016, there were high hopes of gold medals from 100 metre sprinter Darren Mead, high hurdler Graeme Telfer, 400 metre runner Ieuan Thomas, triple jumper Duane Campbell, shot-putter Mike Rothwell, 800 metre runner Jenny Dent, high jumper Gail McCormick, javelin thrower Nicola Bevan and heptathlete Donna McGibbon.

Training for the day had finished at 6pm and the athletes were now changed, showered and were queuing up in the cafeteria for their dinner.

Graeme Telfer sat down to eat his dinner of grilled chicken breast, jacket potato and broccoli opposite Ieuan Thomas. The Scottish high hurdler and the Welsh 400m runner had been friends since first breaking into the Great Britain team five years earlier and were now both members of the London-based Newham and Essex Beagles athletics club, which was the leading club in the country.

Thomas could see that his clubmate was not his usual cheery self. "Gray, anything bothering you?"

"My brother got pulled in by the polis last night" replied the high hurdler. "He's been involved in the campaign against the State of Emergency and internment and that was seen as reason to nick him under the emergency powers laws."

"Adam?" Thomas knew Telfer's younger brother.

"Yeah. Not sure I want to run for Britain in the Olympics now."

"I know how you feel butt" replied Thomas. "I feel the same way now—the same happened to one of my cousins a couple of weeks ago. But we've spent the last four years training for this—are you sure you want to sacrifice going for gold?"

"Ieuan, the thought of standing on the medal rostrum hearing "God Save the Queen" being played and the Union Jack going up makes me want to throw up. I'd rather eat my own shit rather than allow fucking Delgado wallow in glory on the back of my efforts."

"Gray, if you're not going to go, the only way we'll get our message over is if we get a Scottish and Welsh boycott of the Olympics. And not just in the athletics team. The swimmers, cyclists and boxers too. Also competitors from other sports. Do it alone and you'll be picked off by the Establishment without any impact having been made. How about calling a meeting of the other Scottish and Welsh athletes first?"

"We've got some free time tonight Ieuan. I'll text the others and let them know we're discussing pulling out. Let's do it!"

12 July 2016
Lee Valley Athletics Centre
North London

Horace Moseley, the Manager of the Great Britain athletics team, was up early and ready for the last but one of the days for preparation before the team flew out to Miami to prepare for competition in the hot and humid conditions they would face in Brazil. He was meticulously prepared and, even while having breakfast, he had with him his laptop with which he was working on his pre-Olympics preparations. For Moseley, the son of Jamaican immigrants and a former Great Britain sprinter back in the 1980s, a successful Olympics would vindicate his selection as Manager and disprove the claims that he only got the post because of his colour.

At 8:30am, Moseley left the cafeteria and was ready to start his working day in full when he was greeted by the sight of eight of his athletes with their suitcases packed and ready to leave.

"Hey guys, what's going on here?" shouted Moseley.

Graeme Telfer was the first to respond. "Sorry Horace but the Scottish and Welsh athletes have decided to leave the training camp. We're not going to run for Great Britain in the Olympics."

Ieuan Thomas was next to speak. "I know this will have fucked your plans up Horace, but we all feel we've got to make a stand against the oppression of our countries by the British Government. There's no way we're prepared to stand to attention on the medal rostrum if the Union Jack is raised and "God Save the Queen" is played."

"Hold on" shouted Moseley. "Are you guys being serious? You've all spent the last four years training to get a gold medal and you're now planning to walk out? You will all regret doing this. For starters, it won't make an iota of difference to the Government's policy. And once you see the athletes from other countries on the rostrum, you'll all be thinking "I wish I was there"."

"We know that Horace" replied high jumper Gail McCormick. "But for us, this is bigger than anything. Even getting gold at Rio. The British Government has denied our countries the right to self-determination, it's stolen our oil and it's locking up our brothers and sisters. Everyone here thinks it's worth making a stand on this."

The Scottish and Welsh athletes walked out of the main accommodation block towards the car park leaving a stunned Horace Moseley to contemplate finding late replacements for the British Olympics athletics squad.

17 July 2016
Winthrop Manor
near Tetbury
Gloucestershire

The Secretary of State for National Heritage, Lord Manson, was enjoying his weekend break at his Gloucestershire home. The weather had been kind and the previous day he had attended a party thrown by Sir Joshua Brown, a well-known businessman who lived nearby. It had been a busy year as he had steered through a new Broadcasting Act into being against considerable opposition, not only from opposition parties and the arts and entertainment community, but from several members of the Conservative Party too. The new Act had broken up the constituent parts of the former British Broadcasting Corporation and sold off the radio stations and all the television channels apart from BBC1 and BBC2 to the private sector. It had also scrapped the television licence fee and the remaining parts of the BBC were now funded by Government grant and governed by a Board of Directors appointed by, and answerable to, the Government.

Lord and Lady Manson's housekeeper, Janice, had served breakfast in the conservatory and it was now time to relax before meeting the head gardener. The strawberry crop was about to be harvested and he was optimistic it would be a good one. Later that day, he would be returning to London as Parliament had still to rise.

"Darling, here's the latest edition of the Sunday Telegraph" said Felicity Manson as she passed the main pro-Government broadsheet.

"Thanks Felicity."

Lord Manson took one look at the front page of the Sunday Telegraph and that was enough to lose him his appetite for lunch. The front page headline read

British Olympic plans in chaos after athletes walk out

Manson read through the leading article and the more he read the worse it got. Five days earlier, Scottish and Welsh members of the Great Britain athletics team for the Olympics had walked out of the pre-Olympics training camp in protest against the British Government's suppression of the independence struggle in Scotland and Wales. The revolt had then mushroomed to the point that Scottish and Welsh members of the other British teams due to take part had also walked out. The Olympics was now less than a month away and Great Britain had lost no less than fifteen of its prime medal hopes for the Olympics and was faced with the prospect of having to find replacements at short notice.

Britain had hosted a glorious Olympics four years earlier in London which had delivered a record number of medals. It had not only been a boost to sport in the United Kingdom, it had also been a national morale-booster and had played a significant role in helping the Conservatives to be re-elected in 2014. Manson recognised the impact that a poor Olympics might have.

"I don't believe it. I just don't bloody believe it" spluttered Manson. "Why didn't those idiots at Cockspur Street let me know about this?"

"What's up Robert?" asked Lady Manson.

"Sorry darling. Read this" said Lord Manson, passing his wife a copy of the Sunday Telegraph. "Happened five days ago and no one's thought of telling me. It'll make us a laughing stock."

Manson immediately went to the telephone in the main hall and rang Dame Jill Caulfield, Permanent Secretary at the Department for National Heritage.

"743810" replied a female voice.

"Could I speak to Jill Caulfield? Tell her it's Lord Manson and it's urgent."

A few seconds later, Jill Caulfield was on the line.

"Good morning Secretary of State. What can I do for you?"

"Jill, have you read the Sunday Telegraph? Looks like all our Scottish and Welsh competitors have walked out of the Olympic team. It's been five days since this happened. Why didn't anyone think to tell me?"

"Very sorry about this, Secretary of State. No one told me either until I had journalists on my doorstep yesterday morning. Yet another cock-up by the Olympics Unit at Cockspur Street. I'll be demanding explanations from the officials responsible tomorrow."

"Never mind that Jill" said Manson. "We need to nip this problem in the bud, and sooner rather than later. Can you arrange for Giles Richardson of the BOA and David Moulton of Sport England to meet me this week."

"I'll do it first thing tomorrow morning" replied Caulfield.

"No Jill, tomorrow's too late" said Manson. "I want you to do it today. I'll be back in London this evening. Phone me at 8pm to let me know when the meeting will take place."

20 July 2016
Department for National Heritage
Cockspur Street
London

"Your visitors are here Secretary of State" said Lord Manson's Assistant Private Secretary, Alison Wainwright.

"Show them in Alison" replied Lord Manson.

Giles Richardson, the Chairman of the British Olympic Association and David Moulton, Chief Executive of Sport UK entered Lord Manson's office.

"Giles, David, thank you for coming in at such short notice" said Manson. "You'll guess why I've asked you to come in. Complete bloody impertinence I say. I remember when sportsmen and women saw it as a privilege to compete for Britain and minded their Ps and Qs. What's the latest position and what are you doing to mitigate it?"

Giles Richardson was first to reply. A portly man in his mid-50s, Richardson had been educated at Cranleigh School and had been a former leading yachtsman.

"We've managed to replace all the competitors who've walked out, Secretary of State. Problem is that, with barely a month before the Olympics start, we've got hardly any time to integrate the new team members. This is going to have a big impact in team events."

"Has everyone from Scotland or Wales walked out Giles?" asked Manson.

"Not everyone" replied Richardson. "We've still got about 25% of those originally selected. Problem is, I fear that some of those who are still in the squad might make a gesture if they're on the medal rostrum."

"You mean like Tommie Smith and John Carlos did nearly fifty years ago?" Manson was referring to two black American athletes who performed the Black Power salute on the medal rostrum after getting the gold and bronze medals in the 200 metres at the Mexico Olympics in 1968.

"Afraid so, Secretary of State. We've warned all squad members of the standards of behaviour we expect from them and we've told anyone who chooses to make a political gesture that we'll expel them from the Olympic squad."

"Thanks Giles" said Manson. "David, what has Sport UK done?"

David Moulton had been one of Britain's best middle-distance runners in the late 1970s and early 1980s. In most eras, he would have been the top runner at his distance in the United Kingdom and one of the world's best too. Unfortunately, he had been around at the same time as Seb Coe, Steve Ovett and Steve Cram.

"We've asked all the competitors who pulled out to attend a meeting to discuss their grievances" said Moulton. "We're hopeful that we can persuade some of the competitors to reconsider their decision."

"And what if they don't, David?" asked Manson.

"We've told them that it could damage their career prospects and that they risk not being selected for Great Britain in the future" replied Moulton.

"David, we need to go much further" said Manson. "I want you to tell every competitor who's pulled out of the Olympics for political reasons that they will never be selected for Great Britain ever again. And I mean ever. Understand?"

"Secretary of State, you need to realise that those competitors do not only compete for Great Britain. They also compete for the Scottish and Welsh national teams. If we ban them for competing from Great Britain, it will hardly be skin off their nose. A lot of the international sporting bodies are quite prepared to invite Scotland and Wales to compete as teams in their own right. And, in the case of the athletes, they can compete in competitions on their own."

Manson's face was becoming redder by the minute. "David" he thundered. "Get this straight. If any of the competitors who've walked out of the Olympics aren't suspended or banned from competition by their constituent bodies, I'll personally ensure that they will never receive any more Government funding. I want action on this—and now!"

5 August 2016
Olympic Stadium
Rio de Janeiro

The opening ceremony of the 2016 Olympic Games had been underway for an hour. Following the display of samba dancing, the national teams had been parading around the track of the Olympic Stadium. After the final team had paraded, there was to be a speech from President da Silva of Brazil and the President of the International Olympic Committee, following which the Olympic flame would be lit.

Keith Ridgeway, the Manager of the Great Britain Olympic Team, was pacing nervously through the undercroft in the stadium. It was already 1:30pm and the heat under the stadium was stifling. Outside, the sun was blazing down and the temperature was in the upper 80s. The British team would have to parade at the hottest time of the day.

"Gran Bretagna" cried out a steward. Ridgeway knew that it was a signal for the Great Britain team to be ready to march out into the stadium.

The past month had been a turbulent one for the Great Britain team. Three weeks earlier, most of the Scottish and Welsh competitors had walked out of the squad in protest against the Government's campaign to put down the insurgency in Scotland and Wales. Despite pleading and threats from the constituent sporting bodies and from the British Olympic Association itself, the rebels refused to back down, forcing the team to find replacement competitors late in the day.

Just before flying out, the Foreign & Commonwealth Office had summoned the team to attend a briefing before flying out. They were warned they would face considerable anti-British sentiment because there was widespread sympathy across the world for the Scottish and Welsh cause. They were also warned not to react to any provocation.

As Ridgeway led the British Olympic Team into the bright Rio de Janeiro sunlight, he soon found out what the FCO had meant. The British team was greeted with a chorus of jeering and derisive whistling and, while they were marching around the arena, several rotten oranges and tomatoes were thrown in their direction.

14 August 2016
Olympic Stadium
Rio de Janeiro

Darren Mead paced nervously behind the starting blocks in the Olympic Stadium. In little more than a minute, he would be running the most important race of his life in the final of the Olympic 100 metres.

Mead had qualified impressively for the final with the third fastest time. Only American Jermaine Foster and Jamaican Duane Gilchrist had run faster, and only just. So he was incensed that he had been given the inside lane for the final rather than one of the middle lanes.

The first week of the Olympics had been a catalogue of disasters for the British team. Early in the week, there had been a bout of food poisoning which had affected the swimmers and rowers. Medal prospects sank without trace as a result and the only medals they got were two bronzes, one from the men's rowing eight and the other from the coxless twins. The cyclists had suffered too. The fancied pursuit team crashed out in the quarter-final when Jason Rose fell over. Gold medal favourite Nicola Pemberton was disqualified after failing a drugs test. Colleagues suspected foul play in both cases. The athletes had also suffered setbacks. Jenny Dent had failed to qualify for the 800 metres final after falling in the semi-final. Many team colleagues thought she had been deliberately tripped. Duane Campbell had no-jumped in the Triple Jump qualification, controversially as television coverage had shown that a massive 18 metre jump had been legal. And the silver medal won by shot-putter Mike Rothwell had been taken away after another drug test failure. Again, team mates thought he had been set up.

Mead found himself running alongside Nigerian Samson Ojukwu and was even less pleased. The Nigerian had a reputation for being jittery on the starting blocks and for being pulled up for false starts.

"Will the runners take their marks" shouted an official. Mead knew this was the signal to get ready.

The eight athletes crouched, their feet pressing back against the starting blocks. The starter held the starting gun.

"On your marks. Get set." The gun sounded as the eight athletes got away.

A split second later, the gun sounded again for a false start. The electronic starter board showed that two athletes had false started. Lanes 1 and 2. "Oh shit" thought Mead. "That's me".

The eight athletes returned to the starting blocks and took up position again. Mead's concentration was even more intense than before. He knew that one more false start meant disqualification.

"On your marks. Get set." The starting gun sounded again.

For a second time, the gun was fired a split second later. As Mead walked back, he was stunned as the electronic starter board showed Lane 1 as the offender. He was facing disqualification from the Olympic 100 metres final.

Mead made directly for the starter. He was fuming. "You're having a laugh man" he yelled. "No fucking way I false started. Check the blocks first—they must be faulty."

The starter was apologetic but firm. "I'm sorry Mr Mead. You were recorded as making two false starts. I've got no option but to disqualify you."

Athletics Team Manager Horace Moseley saw the commotion and headed over. "Darren, what's up?"

"Horace, those starting blocks are faulty. No way I false started."

Moseley had seen the starts on the television screen and felt that Mead had a case. He sought out an Olympic official. "Can you check those blocks before restarting the race? I'm not satisfied they're working properly. I saw both starts and I felt that Darren got away fair and square."

The official was unmoved. "Mr Moseley, it is open to you to lodge an official protest which the International Olympic Committee will consider. But we're not able to reinstate your athlete at this point in time. We have to uphold the decisions of officials and, as Mead made two false starts, he was rightly disqualified."

20 August 2016
Olympic Village
Rio de Janeiro

The telephone by Keith Ridgeway's bed rang.

"Keith, is that you? Giles Richardson here." The Chairman of the British Olympic Committee was phoning from his home near Southampton.

"Giles, what can I do for you."

"Only phoning to find out how morale's holding up."

"Not well. Everyone's feeling depressed after the events of the past two weeks. Many feel there's been a conspiracy to sabotage Britain's chances of achieving medals. And I reckon it's because of Scotland and Wales."

Ridgeway's comment was no understatement. It had been the worst Olympics for Great Britain ever. The medal tally was six silver and nine bronze and, with three exceptions, all in minority sports. The bad luck of the first week continued into the second week. The top showjumper Diana Luxton had to pull out after her horse was bitten by a snake. The boxers, so successful in London four years previously, left Rio without a single medal. The two best hopes, light-welterweight Frankie Rawlings and super-heavyweight Tom Branch ended on the wrong end of controversial decisions in the quarter-finals. The athletics team continued to hit ill fortune which only ended when heptathlete Donna McGibbon won a bronze medal.

"What's the press coverage been like Giles?" asked Ridgeway.

"Mixed" relied Richardson. "The *Sun* and the *Daily Mirror* have been hostile, calling our competitors flops. But the *Daily Mail* and *Daily Express* have been on their side. Both papers have referred to the campaign of hatred against the British team, as has the *News of the World*. In fact, the *Express* was calling for the team to be recalled in protest against the gamesmanship used against them. By the way, I guess you're preparing for the closing ceremony?"

"Giles, we're not going to attend."

Richardson was aghast. "Keith, you can't do this. You've just got to attend. Don't you realise the damage you'll cause to Britain's position, not only in the Olympic movement but to its diplomatic standing? It will look like sour grapes."

Ridgeway was however adamant that his team would not attend the closing ceremony. "Giles, sod the bloody Olympic movement and its ideals. It's a complete load of bollocks. You saw the reception the team got at the opening ceremony. Jeering, whistling, chanting "SNLA" and "WRA", throwing rotten fruit and rubbish. I don't want to put the team through that, after what they've been through over the past two weeks. And if the IOC don't like it—tough. They can all piss off."

And with that message, Ridgeway put the phone down.

Later that evening
Sky News

"This is Scott Parfitt with the late night headlines on Sky News."

"The United Kingdom has been engulfed in a diplomatic storm following the decision by the Great Britain Olympic Team to boycott the closing ceremony of the Olympics. The International Olympic Committee has taken the unprecedented step of suspending the Brotish Olympic Association, pending a disciplinary hearing in Zurich in October and the Brazilian Foreign Minister called in the British Ambassador to register his displeasure at what he considered to be an act of discourtesy to his country."

"The Olympics has unfortunately been overshadowed by the Troubles in Scotland and Wales and the British team was subject to hostile protests for the whole two week period from people sympathetic to the Scottish and Welsh independence cause. Many competitors felt they were on the wrong end of hostile decisions for this reason, and there was also suspicion of deliberate attempts to sabotage the British team's efforts, particularly when there was a bout of food poisoning in the first week and when cyclist Nicola Pemberton and shot-putter Mike Rothwell failed drugs tests."

"At this stage, it is hard to gauge the extent to which the country's interests have been harmed. Brazil has become a trading partner of growing importance in recent years, and a falling out between the two countries could cause damage to the United Kingdom's economic interests. However, Foreign Office sources do not believe that discord between the two countries would last long. More serious is the long-term implications for British sport tht could arise from any suspention from the International Olympic Committee."

CHAPTER 7

Iain Murray and Gareth Evans followed Nasrul Miah into the lobby of the 19-floor tower block, one of several forming the Regent's Park Estate and all named after landmarks in the English Lake District. The flats had been built some sixty years earlier and had been one of London's first high rise estates when built. The first residents of the estate were white Londoners who had been rehoused following the Blitz. However, most of the estate's residents by now were of Bangladeshi origin.

The three men took the lift to the fifth floor where Al-Q'aida had a safe house which MI5 and the National Anti-Terror Squad had yet to be able to locate. The ring of the doorbell notified Shamsul Islam that his guests had arrived. "Mohammed, can you go to the door. Our guests have arrived."

The younger man opened the front door and beckoned in Iain Murray and Gareth Evans.

Murray, a Scot from Govan, Glasgow, was a blond-haired man in his late 30s, of average height but stockily built. Evans, who hailed from Gorseinon, a town between Swansea and Llanelli, was slightly younger and was dark-haired and was six feet tall and wirily-built. The two men were from the General Councils of the SNLA and WRA and had called into London to meet some Customs officers from HM Revenue and Customs who had indicated their willingness to co-operate with the SNLA and WRA in return for cash.

"Shamsul, many thanks for inviting Gareth and myself over" said Murray. "Heard you've found some guys at HMRC who are ready to help us."

"We're just about to get our drug trafficking and contraband goods operations going" said Evans. "The money we expect to raise will help us buy top-of the range weapons. The Brits won't know what's hit them. But we need some help from the inside if we're not going to get turned over."

Evans knew that the British Government had increased its expenditure on anti-drugs operations, and was using MI5, MI6 and the armed forces to help the police and the National Crime Agency to interdict traffickers. They were also using draconian measures under the Proceeds of Crime Act 2014 to confiscate the assets of anyone remotely involved with the trade, and were also using the powers against black marketers who were selling contraband alcohol and cigarettes and against fraudsters, forgers and counterfeiters. All had been identified as potential sources of income by the SNLA and the WRA.

"Gentlemen, we have three men who are working for HMRC over here tonight" said Islam. "You will be aware of the recent industrial dispute involving Customs officers." Murray and Evans nodded. Islam continued "We have three men who've used their knowledge to help us run drugs into the UK. They've said they're prepared to help you."

During the summer, Customs officers working at Britain's airports and seaports had gone on strike in a dispute with HM Revenue and Customs over proposed changes to shift patterns and working hours and the reduction of overtime payments, allowable expenses and uniform allowances. The management at HM Revenue and Customs felt that the changes were needed to make front-line Customs officers more efficient in order to meet budget constraints. But serving staff saw the move as another attack on their terms and conditions, following previous measures which had saw their pay slip behind the private sector and their generous final salary pension scheme scrapped.

The strike had been short but bitter. Timed in the last week of July and the first week in August, it had caused considerable disruption to the public's holiday plans. The Government had resorted to emergency powers legislation to bring the strike to an end, and there was considerable bad feeling within the service.

In the lounge of Islam's flat were seated three men and a woman. Kevin McNally, like Murray, was a fellow Glaswegian and had been working in Customs for 25 years. Vince Nichol, a Londoner, was some 20 years younger than McNally and had been a frontline Customs officer for just over a year. Mark Brennan, a Liverpudlian, was in his late 20s and had four years experience at the frontline. Finally, wearing a headscarf in deference to her Muslim hosts was Jane Furness, the youngest of the four officers and only three years out of university where she had graduated in English and Drama.

"Ladies and gentlemen, please meet Iain Murray and Gareth Evans. Mr Murray and Mr Evans are from, respectively, the General Councils of the SNLA and the WRA. As I explained to you earlier today, the SNLA and WRA are about to follow our lead and start up operations for importing and selling drugs, contraband goods, fake designer clothes and pirated DVDs. Your colleagues have been most helpful to us in everything from advice on how to avoid detection through to waving us through at air and seaports. You may wish to do the same for the SNLA and WRA."

"You guys are willing to help us?" asked Murray.

"Aye" replied McNally. "I can tell you this Mr Murray. Our members are totally pissed off at the way the Government has shat on us. On top of holding back our pay and scrapping our pensions, they're now requiring us to work longer and more frequent shifts. And all so the fucking bankers and businessmen can have bigger tax cuts and can buy a Porsche to go with the Roller. They've pushed us too far this time. A load of the boys and girls are now willing to take money and look the other way. How much will you give us?"

"We'll pay you well Mr McNally" said Murray. "A thousand pounds a month for each officer. How does that sound?"

"Bloody brilliant" replied McNally. "By the way, Mr Murray, who do you support?"

"Rangers. Are you Celtic by the way?"

"Aye. And I thought you were a bluenose."

Murray had a chuckle at the fact he had just signed a deal with a supporter of Rangers' sworn enemy.

"Mr McNally, can I trust that you and your colleagues will keep stchum if the plods start sniffing around?" asked Evans. "And also that you'll keep it hidden from any colleagues. One of my cousins was a Customs officer and I know what they're like. They love doing drugs busts—the instinct never goes away."

"Don't worry about someone grassing Mr Evans" said Mark Brennan. "As Kevin said, everyone in Customs is so pissed off that they would be prepared to work with the Devil to get back at the Government. By the way, what's the WRA rate?"

"Same as the SNLA" replied Evans.

"One final thing ladies and gentlemen" said Murray menacingly. "If anyone grasses on either the SNLA or WRA to the authorities, that will be their death warrant. Neither the SNLA nor the WRA tolerates grasses. Isn't that right Gareth?"

"Too right" said Evans.

Shamsul Islam reappeared in the lounge. "Can I take it Mr McNally that you and your colleagues are ready to accept the deal offered by these gentlemen."

"We are."

27 September 2016
Kelly, Gleeson and Partners
328 East 63rd Street
New York City

"Mr Gleeson, Messrs Fraser and Meredith are here to see you" trilled the voice of Donna Fruscante, the Personal Assistant to Thomas J Gleeson, Executive Partner of Kelly, Gleeson and Partners.

"Send them through Donna" replied Gleeson, a short, stocky and pugnacious New Yorker of fifth-generation Irish descent. "Could you also please bring through a pot of coffee and cookies."

"Will do, Mr Gleeson."

Three months earlier, Bill Fraser, a Scottish-American from Illinois and Ben Meredith, a Welsh-American from Ohio had helped start up Caledonian Aid and Cambrian Aid, fundraising operations, supposedly to help the Scottish and Welsh families suffering hardship as a result of the economic disruption arising from the unrest following the British government's suppression of their bid for independence. However, the reality was that the funds raised were being used to support the SNLA and the WRA.

Progress in raising funds had been slow because of the lack of organisation, the dispersed nature of the communities of Scottish and Welsh descent in the USA and the interest of the FBI. Ever since the terrorist attacks on the World Trade Center in New York City fifteen years earlier, the USA had been paranoid about anything related to terrorism. Furthermore, US interests were firmly tied up with the exploitation of Britain's offshore oil reserves and the SNLA and WRA were considered to be a threat to these. At the suggestion of Doug Paterson and Trevor Rees, the respective Chairmen of the General Councils of the SNLA and WRA, Fraser and Meredith had been advised to contact Gleeson.

Fraser and Meredith walked into Gleeson's office and were greeted by Gleeson. "Bill, Ben, great to meet you guys. I hear you're both planning to start fundraising to support the independence struggles in Scotland and Wales. Well you couldn't have come to a better place for advice. Take a seat. Coffee?"

Fraser and Meredith both indicated they would and Fruscante poured two cups of coffee.

Tom Gleeson was better-placed than most men or women to advise Fraser and Meredith on the intricacies of fundraising. Thirty years earlier, he had helped organise Noraid, the US-based funding operation which provided the IRA with much of their revenue. Noraid became a major thorn in the flesh of the British government, who saw massive amounts of money being raised with impunity and was being used to buy guns and explosives in order to kill British troops and innocent civilians. On several occasions, Mrs Thatcher's administration had asked President Reagan if he could do anything to close down Noraid. The FBI had it under constant investigation and several attempts were made in the courts to close it down. But none were successful as Noraid's board successfully argued that it was a charitable organisation, the Federal government had no jurisdiction over state courts and, as most of the litigation against Noraid took place in states with large Irish-American populations, juries took Noraid's side.

"How far have you guys got with fundraising?" asked Gleeson.

Fraser and Meredith both indicated the slow progress that had been made.

"Guys, the important think to remember is don't rush things" advised Gleeson. "Noraid started as a hole-and-corner operation in New York back in the 1970s. But we steadily expanded over the years into Boston, Chicago and Frisco. We registered as a charity early on. The authorities don't like crawling over charities unless they're Muslim for obvious reasons. We brought in bankers and investment experts from Wall Street who told us how to invest our money most effectively. Also, we built links with the police unions in New York and Boston and their Hibernian societies. Not only would the police not touch us but also they tipped us off about planned FBI raids."

"Looks like we've got the wrong side of Senator Burton" said Meredith. "He's called for us to be banned."

Troy Burton, a Republican senator from Mississippi, was the Senate majority leader and an aggressive advocate for Britain. He was also had friends in high places, including CEOs of oil companies and President Whitney.

"Ben, don't worry about Burton" said Gleeson. "He's a known blowhard and without Whitney's patronage he's nothing. Even many of his own party don't like him. What's more, he can't touch you under the First Amendment. He's got to prove you're actually funding a terrorist organisation. Finally, many ordinary Americans are sympathetic towards your fight for independence."

"Tom, any recommendations on banking and investments?" asked Fraser.

"Yep, I've arranged for Maureen O'Gara to come in. She works for Morgan Stanley on Wall Street. She's young but she really knows what she's doing. Also, one of my legal executives, Pat Dempsey, will be able to advise you on keeping the right side of the law. He used to be a detective with New York Police Department."

Gleeson rang his intercom. "Pat, could you come up for a minute. I've got the guys from Caledonian Aid and Cambrian Aid here, and they would like to pick your brains on avoiding getting busted by the law."

"I'm on my way up Tom" replied Dempsey.

Less than a minute later, the tall figure of former Police Lieutenant Pat Dempsey was in Gleeson's office and being introduced to Fraser and Meredith. Dempsey then began outlining how Caledonian Aid and Cambrian Aid should avoid coming to the notice of the authorities.

"Bill, Ben, remember this. There's probably quite a few cops out there who've got Scottish or Welsh blood in them. They may be cops but blood's thicker than water—after all, look at the Irish! Over 150 years in the US of A and we still go over for the annual parades." Earlier that year, the NYPD Band went over to Dublin for the centenary of the Easter Uprising.

Dempsey continued. "Many cities have already got social organisations for the Scots or Welsh. Get involved with those. If there are any cops, FBI, DAs, invite them in. They got Noraid out of some tight spots in the past and they'll do the same for you."

The final word was with Gleeson. "And also try to build contacts in Congress. Senator McAllister and Representative Hopkins are particularly vocal about your cause and would be good bets to approach." He was referring to Senator Brad McAllister from Washington State and Representative Graydon Hopkins from Pennsylvania. Both were Democrats and vocal critics of the British government.

"Finally guys, best of luck."

3 October 2016
near Corleone, Sicily

The silver Mercedes-Benz S-Type limousine swung off the road and into a long driveway. In the back were SNLA and WRA General Council members Iain Murray and Gareth Evans, who were on the way to a meeting with Mafia don Vincenzo Scifo.

"Gentlemen, Don Vincenzo is ready to see you" said Mafia underboss Marco Simeone as he opened the rear door of the Mercedes.

Murray and Evans, who had left a rainy London a day earlier, climbed out into the blazing Sicilian sun and followed Simeone into Scifo's large villa.

Scifo, who was casually-dressed in a designer polo shirt and slacks, was a short man and was dwarfed by the two visitors and, even more so, by Simeone. But even though he was now sixty-one years old, he was still muscular and powerfully-built and commanded instant respect. He had played a significant role in restoring the Mafia's reputation as the world's most feared organised crime syndicate over the past six years. He had heard that the SNLA and WRA were interested in shifting drugs and was interested in a deal.

"Good afternoon gentlemen" said Scifo, welcoming Murray and Evans into his lounge. "Anything to drink? Whisky? Brandy? How about trying the local *grappa*?"

The two visitors indicated they would try the fiery Italian licquer.

"Can we get down to business" said Scifo. "I hear you guys are shipping in drugs to the United Kingdom?"

"That's right Don Vincenzo" said Murray. "We've both signed deals with FARC, Hamas and Hizbollah to ship in cocaine, heroin and cannabis. Where does the Cosa Nostra fit in?"

"Signor Murray, we have extensive distribution networks across much of Europe and the USA" replied Scifo. "If you can get the drugs into the United Kingdom, we will look after their distribution."

"What's in it for us Don Vincenzo?" asked Murray.

"One third of total profit."

"That's a bit low Don Vincenzo" said Evans. "I recognise that Cosa Nostra have got the distribution networks we don't have. But we're doing the hard slog of getting the stuff into the country in the first place. I think we should be entitled to fifty percent."

"Gentlemen, as you said earlier, neither of your organisations have experience or expertise in shifting the stuff to dealer networks. We do. That is why I've suggested the two-thirds-one third split."

"Don Vincenzo, two weeks ago, we bought off several members of the Revenue and Customs Service in the UK" said Evans. "More have since come over. These guys will be instrumental in ensuring that no one interferes with this operation. Do you realise we will have to pay them off? If Iain and myself hadn't managed to turn the Customs guys, there wouldn't be anything for the Cosa Nostra to distribute. That's why we think we're due half shares."

Scifo was stunned. As a *capo*, he hadn't had his authority challenged in this way for years. But at the same time, he couldn't help but admire his visitors for their steely resolve. Although he knew that one word could have both Murray and Evans killed, he did not want to do that. Besides, he knew that if he did, he would be a marked man for the rest of his life. Scifo, like many fellow Mafia dons, knew that terrorist organisations like the SNLA and WRA were equally as ruthless as he was and had elephantine memories and a thirst for revenge. All they would need to do was to hire a rival don to do the dirty work. There were several rival *capo de capos* who would love to see him buried under tons of concrete. This was a time for discretion and compromise. After all, both his clan and the SNLA and WRA would benefit.

"Gentlemen, how about a sixty-forty split? The size of the expected turnover is so large that each of your organisations should be better off by over a million pounds a year. That's an offer you can't refuse."

"Looks a reasonable offer Don Vincenzo" said Murray. "Don't you agree Geraint?"

"I agree" said the Welshman. "Iain, I think it's time to agree on the deal and thank Don Vincenzo."

Murray and Evans agreed and shook hands with Scifo to confirm the deal.

22 November 2016
Rotterdam

Iain Murray and Gareth Evans disembarked from the Trans-Eurep-Express train at Rotterdam Station and made for the car hire point. They hired a VW Golf hatchback and, with Murray at the wheel, set off for Europoort.

The rain was falling steadily and the mid-afternoon gloom was descending fast. However, Murray and Evans barely noticed and were used to such inclement weather in their respective homelands.

"Europoort now only about two miles away Iain" said Evans. "Next turning on the right."

"Thanks Gareth."

Ten minutes later, Murray and Evans were in the middle of Europe's largest docks complex and headed for Quay No 7. As they pulled up, they noticed a large, meaty figure. Jan van Geloven was an arms dealer and the SNLA and WRA had paid him with the first of the proceeds from the drugs trade to buy weapons from the Middle East.

"Good afternoon, Mr van Geloven" said Murray. "Have you got the stuff?"

"Follow me" said the Dutchman as he led them to a container.

Van Geloven opened a large container containing pallets of food destined for the United Kingdom's supermarkets, switched on a powerful torch to show the way through the darkness and directed Murray and Evans towards the back of the container. He gestured to a cardboard box which, for all intents, looked destined for supermarket shelves.

"Open it."

Murray pulled back the sealing tape and could see inside a consignment of Kalashnikov AK-47 assault rifles.

"There are several more boxes of those" said van Geloven. Have a look at the boxes on your right.

Evans stripped off the sealing tape and found RPG-7 rocket launchers.

"Jesus Christ, with this stuff, we'll be able to take on the whole fucking British Army."

"Mr Evans, we've also supplied ammunition."

"Gareth, have a look at this" shouted Murray. "SA-15 missiles and launchers. We'll be able to down choppers with those."

"Finally, gentlemen, there's over 200 tons of Semtex in those boxes over there."

The three men walked out of the container having resealed the boxes. It was now starting to get dark.

"By the way gentlemen, that was only part of the consignment" said van Geloven. "There's another container with more weapons inside. In fact, the next one along."

Murray and Evans were virtually speechless.

"Mr van Geloven, when will this stuff be delivered to the UK?" asked Murray. "We need to get our distribution networks in place to receive and distribute it."

"It is going over to Felixstowe in two days time" said van Geloven.

Murray and Evans shook hands with van Geloven and returned to the car for the drive back to Rotterdam Station.

28 November 2016
Maida Vale
London

Rebecca Davison had endured a nightmare Monday. The 25-year old Executive Officer in the Home Office had received a humiliating dressing down from her line manager over work she had presented the previous Friday. She had foregone going out on Friday night and had stayed until 10pm to get the work done, yet all she had received was criticism for failing to comply with the prescribed format for presentation and for missing a couple of key facts that the Head of Unit had failed to communicate.

The rest of the afternoon had been spent dealing with work demands. She knew that she had two more pieces of work with deadlines looming and did not want to miss these. But she had found it almost impossible to collate the information because of colleagues either on leave, on detached duty or at the seemingly interminable meetings that took place. It was not helped that there had been a power cut that afternoon which had resulted in over half an hour of working time lost while the computers rebooted. Then at 5:15pm she had been lumbered with another urgent and unnegotiable request. The Director was meeting the Deputy Director-General of MI5 the following day and needed briefing on intelligence reports on the SNLA and WRA and known sympathisers.

The only way that Davison was going to complete the task was to borrow a laptop and work at home that evening. The remote media facility on Government laptops had been disabled to prevent the loss of sensitive information, but Davison knew how to connect her laptop to her home computer account. This would enable her to e-mail the completed work to her Home Office e-mail account, where she would save it onto the corporate file plan. All strictly a breach of departmental security procedures but it would enable her to complete the task without having to work at the Home Office until midnight. And what her employers didn't know could not harm her.

She exited from Warwick Avenue underground station and started walking up Shirland Road towards the flat she shared with three other girls. It had been dark for over an hour and steady rain was falling, which did not improve her mood. She could hardly believe it had just been three years since she had been a Modern Languages student at Nottingham University and had enjoyed a blissful period teaching English in Madrid.

As Davison wended her weary way home, Mohammed Boudiaf also walked into Shirland Road. Born 17 years earlier in London to Moroccan parents, Boudiaf already had a criminal record for burglary and robbery to his name and had spent two spells in Young Offenders' Institutions. There were hardly anyone else about and the side streets off Shirland Road offered a quick escape route. He noticed a lone woman carrying a shoulder bag. Surely it contained something of value.

Boudiaf stood little more than five foot five inches tall, but he was athletic and fast on his feet. Shod in designer trainers, he moved up on his quarry silently and, with a sharp tug, seized the shoulder bag, pulling a stunned Davison over onto the pavement. Before she could regain her senses, Boudiaf was sprinting down a side street with the bag containing the Home Office laptop.

Ten minutes later, Boudiaf had arrived at the flat of Samir Aboukass, like him, of Moroccan parentage. Aboukass was four years older that Boudiaf and was dressed in designer clothes he had funded from drug-dealing and fencing stolen goods.

"Hey Sam, look what I've just bagged. A brand-new Siemens laptop. Should make quite a bit?"

Aboukass had a look at the laptop. "Nice one Mo, except for one thing." He pointed to the label on the bottom of the laptop stating it was property of the Home Office. "It's a Government laptop. All are registered on a central database. Even if you pull the label off, its identity is microchipped. No one will touch those with a bargepole Mo, not unless you want MI5, NATS or NCA coming after you. Best thing you can do is bin it."

"Sam, you said it was a Home Office rig. Maybe worth seeing if there's documents that would be useful to sell." Boudiaf had heard from his older brother that there was a market for sensitive Government information.

"OK Mo. Fire it up and see what's on board" said Aboukass.

Boudiaf obtained a cable and connected the laptop to the mains electricity. Once open, he and Aboukass trawled the documents for anything that might be of value to the criminal underworld, a newspaper or a website.

Aboukass and Boudiaf spent a quarter of an hour trawling through what appeared to be dry-as-dust Government bureaucracy when they hit upon a file marked "Work 2016 11 28". When they opened it, it took less than two seconds for Aboukass to realise that they had stumbled on details of MI5 agents infiltrating the SNLA and WRA and of informers.

"Mo, you fucking genius. You've only nicked the details of a secret MI5 operation. I know just who will be interested in this."

Two minutes later, Aboukass and Boudiaf were at a fifth floor flat in the same block. A large, muscular man in his early thirties opened the door.

Barry Llewellyn knew Aboukass as the Moroccan had occasionally helped the WRA by selling counterfeit designer clothes and DVDs. But he had little regard for him as he saw him as nothing more than an opportunist and a small-time petty criminal.

"Hey Bar, my mate has just got something you might find useful. Are you interested?"

Llewellyn towered over the two Moroccans. "Sam, I hope you're being fucking serious. I haven't got time to waste."

Boudiaf was next to speak. "I've got a Home Office laptop. Contains details of MI5 double-agents who've infiltrated your lot and the SNLA, as well as informers. You interested?"

Llewellyn beckoned Aboukass and Boudiaf into the flat.

"How recent's this stuff? And how reliable? We don't want to be sent on a wild goose chase." Llewellyn had every right to be sceptical. As he saw it, two petty crims with no interest in his country's fight for self-determination and seeking to make money at their expense.

"I'll show you" said Boudiaf. "It's genuine stuff and up to date." He opened up the laptop and switched it on. A minute later, Llewellyn was looking at the details of double-agents and informers.

"Jesus Christ" swore Llewellyn. "Never realised it was this bad." He had just come to terms with the fact that MI5 had heavily infiltrated both the WRA and the SNLA. If action was not taken quickly, he and his comrades-in-arms could be behind bars.

"Okay, I'm interested. What's your price?"

"A thousand pounds man" said Boudiaf.

"Fuck off" said Llewellyn. "Five hundred at the most."

"Bar, would seven fifty be reasonable?" asked Aboukass.

"Hey Sam, you're selling me out" wailed Boudiaf.

"Mo, shut it" shouted Aboukass. "Don't push it with this guy. He's killed people before. And in any case the laptop's not even worth seven fifty."

"Yeah, I'll do seven fifty" said Boudiaf. "And how about an additional two fifty for delivery charges?" Boudiaf was referring to the way he obtained the laptop at the expense of Rebecca Davison.

By now Llewellyn was having difficulty in containing his temper. The big Welshman seized Boudiaf by the lapels of his leather jacket and lifted him clean off the floor before slamming him against the wall. "Listen, you little cunt. I decide the price. You're lucky to get anything off me. And one last warning Boudiaf, if you grass me up to the pigs or the spooks, our boys will blow your fucking kneecaps off. Understand?"

6 December 2016
Charrington Street
Somers Town
London

The General Councils of the SNLA and WRA had gathered in the council flat in Charrington Street that was used as a safe house for the SNLA in London. The location had two advantages. The first was its proximity to Euston and Kings Cross railway stations, which was the embarkation point for many Scots living in London. And secondly it was located in the heart of London's second "Bangla Town".

Four years earlier, Al-Q'aida had launched a spectacular assault on London. Suicide bombers drove lorries loaded with high explosive into the offices of News International, Associated Newspapers and the Daily Telegraph, while gunmen attacked the London Stock Exchange and several merchant banks. Over 400 people were killed. The Government's response was draconian. Under cover of a State of Emergency, new laws were rushed in, reintroducing the death penalty for murder and treason, enabling subversives and terrorist suspects to be interned without trial and giving the Government the power to summarily strip people of British citizenship and to deport them without the right of appeal.

Several residents from Somers Town were arrested and interned in the wake of the 2012 terror attacks and over fifty were expelled from the United Kingdom and forced to return to Bangladesh which, for some, was a country they had never lived in. Resentment against the British government still simmered in Somers Town and there were residents who were willing to help the SNLA and the WRA as an act of revenge.

Doug Paterson and Trevor Rees took their places at the head of the table in the lounge. Around them sat fellow General Council members Charlie Renwick, Mike Grogan, Mark Podborski and Iain Murray from the SNLA and Richard Thomas, Gethin Davies, Bob Ahern and Gareth Evans from the WRA.

"Gentlemen, firstly I think a big thank you is due to Iain and Gareth for sorting out our cashflow, for signing a deal with the Mafia and for purchasing a load of high grade weaponry" said Paterson.

"Hear, hear" echoed across the room.

Paterson continued. "And I think that thanks are in order to Bill Fraser and Ben Meredith over in the USA for getting Caledonian Aid and Cambrian Aid up and running."

"Got some further good news" said Richard Thomas. "Cerys Thomas, Jane Goldsworthy and Bethan Lewis were all cleared today. A combination of unreliable CCTV evidence and one of the prosecution witnesses found to be unsound helped." Thomas was referring to the three Cardiff girls who had been on trial for luring soldiers from the Royal Anglian Regiment to their deaths just over a year earlier.

"Before we proceed with the self-congratulations, fellers, I think you need to see the following" said WRA General Council Chairman Trevor Rees.

"One of our London Brigade has found out we've both been infiltrated by MI5. What's more, there's a chain of informers who've been recruited. Guys, we've got to move quickly on this, otherwise, we'll all end up in the clink. Or worse." Rees knew that no less than ten members of the SNLA and WRA had gone to the gallows that year.

"Where's the information from, Trev?" asked Podborski. "Can we trust it?"

"It's kosher" replied Rees. "Our man in the London Brigade bought it from a petty thief who swiped it from a Home Office official. The details are genuine Home Office."

"Look at the bright side" said Mike Grogan. "If we take out the spies and narks who've been listed, it'll set back MI5 at least a year."

"Quite agree Mike" said Paterson. "Trev, I think a further vote of thanks is in order for the guy from your London Brigade who got hold of the information. Can we now move onto next year's campaign?"

"We should now target the economy" said Rees. "The City of London's an obvious target, even though it's well-defended. But we can go further and wider. If we hit airports and road and rail communications and the main utilities, we could bring the country's economy to a halt. The tourist industry's another good target. All you need to do is let off a few bombs and foreign tourists and particularly the Americans will stop coming."

"I think the time's ready to start hitting British targets abroad" said Renwick. "That'll send a message that there's no hiding place."

"Anything particularly in mind Charlie" asked Evans.

"Holiday resorts" said Renwick. "We'll get help from ETA in Spain and ELAS in Greece."

"We need to start targeting the loudmouths and blowhards who are campaigning against us" said Murray. "Like the Tory backbenchers who've called for the RAF to be used against us and for us to be put on summary trials. Just imagine the impact of bagging one of those cunts."

Gethin Davies was the last to speak. "Does anyone realise how many English are actually resident in our countries? They reckon about a third in Wales and nearly a quarter in Scotland. That represents a sizeable potential fifth column to help the Brits. Get rid of them and we'll deny the authorities valuable intelligence and co-operation."

Paterson and Rees sat back to consider the suggestions made.

"I like the ideas of going after economic targets and spreading the campaign abroad" said Paterson. "We've now got the weaponry and the number of recruits is still growing. Not sure about the other ideas though. I'm sure we'd all like to see the back of wankers like Pickavance and Parmenter." Paterson was referring to two highly vocal Tory backbench MPs, David Pickavance and Spencer Parmenter. "But we have to consider whether it will further our cause and what risk it might present. As for kicking out the English, I think we have to be careful who we target. After all, there has been English support for us."

"We're meeting again just before Christmas" said Rees. "If everyone can think over these ideas and present plans for execution, we'll prepare an action plan for next year then."

CHAPTER 8

23 December 2016
MI5 Headquarters
Millbank
London

It was already 5:40pm and there was barely a handful of staff still on duty at Thames House. It was the last Friday before Christmas and most people had left for home.

Richard Donovan was still on duty. However, with nothing further happening and with all reports completed and future meetings scheduled, he was tidying up his desk and was about to depart from the Christmas break when the secure telephone rang.

"Richard, is that you? Peter Firth here."

Donovan knew that Firth was one of MI5's top field agents and had been active in the battle against the SNLA and WRA, so he recognised the call would be important.

"Peter, how's things out in the field?"

"Bad news Richard. It seems that the SNLA and WRA have got hold of top secret information about our agents who've infiltrated them, and about the informers recruited. Apparently, a Home Office laptop went astray. It's completely blown our intelligence operation against them sky high. We've had to pull our agents out for their own safety."

"Any casualties Peter?" asked Donovan.

"Afraid so. Three informers have already been murdered. We've had to give the others new identities but you now how easy it is to compromise them. At least we managed to get our agents out unscathed."

"What do you think the damage is Peter?"

"Pretty bad Richard" replied Firth. "Human Intelligence on the SNLA and WRA is now non-existent. It'll take over a year to rebuild it."

"Oh shit!" exclaimed Donovan.

Firth continued and the more he did, the worse it got. "On top of that, we've heard that the SNLA and WRA have just got their hands on high-grade weapons. Semtex, rocket launchers, SAM missiles and AK-47s."

"How the hell did they manage that?" asked Donovan.

"They've got involved in the drugs trade" said Firth. "Apparently, they've hooked up with FARC, Hamas, Hizbollah and the Mafia. You'll need to let NCA and NATS know. They're also running fake designer clothes, pirate DVDs and contraband booze and cigarettes."

"Surely HMRC should be going after them" said Donovan.

"There's another problem Richard" said Firth. "Looks like several Customs officers have been collaborating with the SNLA and WRA in return for money. Probably as payback for the dispute they had with HMRC over pay and conditions earlier in the year."

3 January 2017
Cabinet Room
10 Downing Street
London

The first Cabinet meeting of 2017 had been brought forward a week by Prime Minister Robert Delgado because of the security leak which had resulted in details of MI5 agents landing in the hands of the SNLA and WRA. Not surprisingly, Delgado was furious, not only at the leak but also because of the news that corrupt civil servants were helping the terrorists.

First to be questioned was the Home Secretary, Deborah Pearson.

"Deborah, this is the umpteenth time there has been a lapse of security at the Home Office. Only this time, it's potentially cost us a year's worth of human intelligence on the SNLA and WRA. What's being done to tighten things up—and please don't say shutting the stable door after the horse has bolted."

"Prime Minister, I've just launched a root-and-branch overhaul of the way the Home Office is structured and works to make it more responsive to our needs" replied Pearson. "Firstly, I've persuaded Derek Copperfield to take early retirement. He was always too fussy and a stickler for the rulebook. I'll be bringing in Richard Benson from GCHQ as the new Permanent Secretary. He's used to working in a security-minded environment and will give the place a thorough shake-up. I'm also upgrading departmental security into a directorate on its own and the new Director will have to have a security background as part of the job description. Finally, I've introduced a new rule prohibiting staff from taking laptops out of the building without the approval of departmental security at senior level. Currently, that's the Acting Director."

"Has there been any progress on finding how the information went missing?"

"Yes, Prime Minister. It appears that an EO in the Counter-Terrorism Branch was responsible. She took out a laptop to work at home and had it stolen. Because she didn't report it, the SNLA and WRA had time to move against agents and informers. She's being dealt with under normal disciplinary procedures."

"Thanks Deborah. For your sake, I hope the Home Office is sorted out, and the sooner the better."

Next up was the Paymaster General, Jennifer Chadwick.

"Jennifer, where do you stand on finding the corrupt Customs officers? You realise the damage it has caused to both the reputation of the service and to public confidence."

"Prime Minister, I've ordered our departmental security to launch an investigation, 'Operation Skylight'. They're getting help from the police, NCA, NATS and MI5. We've already caught twelve officers red handed and CPS and the Procurators-Fiscal are currently preparing prosecutions. We've offered a reward for officers to inform on colleagues suspected of wrongdoing and this has helped catch some of the rogue officers. Some of those caught have agreed to turn Queen's Evidence and we expect to catch further rogue officers shortly."

"Do you think you'll have the situation under control?"

Chadwick replied "Yes, we do Prime Minister. I think we've caught the bulk of the rogue officers already. There's still a few unaccounted for, but I think we'll mop them up within the next two months."

"Thank you Jennifer" replied the Prime Minister.

Foreign Secretary Henry Arbuthnot was next to be questioned.

"Henry, I'm very concerned to hear that the SNLA and WRA have teamed up with other terrorists and organised crime. What's being done?"

"Prime Minister, MI6 are active in gathering intelligence and on disrupting drugs and arms supplies routes. In the case of FARC, Hamas, Hizbollah and the Mafia, they're working closely with the CIA as we've got a common interest in squashing these organisations. I'm in Washington later this month for the inauguration of Katherine Whitney's second term and I'm planning to meet the new Secretary of State, Larry Horvath. He'll be much more robust than Milton Rose ever was." Arbuthnot was referring to the previous US Secretary of State whom President Whitney had replaced.

"I'm also pushing for further bilateral agreements. Looks like we'll have one with Colombia which reinforces the existing mutual assistance agreement. They will be able to extradite to us any British national suspected of terrorism with the minimum of bureaucracy."

"Thank you Henry" replied Delgado. "We'll revisit your last suggestion at the next Cabinet meeting."

Last to be questioned was Dominic Collins, Attorney-General since July 2016 when he had replaced the ineffective and out-of-favour Stephen Lansbury. Collins was still in his early 30s and had enjoyed a meteoric rise up the Ministerial ladder since entering Parliament less than three years previously.

"Dominic, I don't have to spell out my concern about the criminal justice system. Despite the measures we've taken over the past six years to make it more rigorous, we still get the situation where defendants who are guilty all the way through escape punishment on technicalities." Delgado was referring to the acquittal of three alleged female WRA terrorists a month earlier on charges of accessory to murder. He was also aware that a verdict on the trial of four suspected SNLA terrorists for the Bannerman's pub bombing in October 2015 was due shortly.

"Like you and other Cabinet members, Prime Minister, I'm concerned about the continuing lack of rigour in the criminal justice system. For this reason, I'm meeting the Lord Chief Justice, the Lord Advocate, the Director of Public Prosecutions and the Chief Executive of the Court Services for England and Wales, and for Scotland, next week. Amongst the measures I'm planning to put in place are a new Criminal

Law Bill to strengthen prosecution rights to challenge jurors, simpler Rules of Court which should be less open to challenge, the right to restart a trial in the event of a collapse on technical grounds and the right of the judge or the prosecution to challenge perverse jury verdicts. I intend to bring proposals with cost estimates back to the next Cabinet meeting."

"Thank you Dominic" said Delgado. "I look forward to seeing these."

20 January 2017
Edinburgh Sherriff Court
Chambers Street
Edinburgh

The trial of the "Bannerman's Four" was now drawing to a close. The proceedings against the four men suspected of bombing the pub in Edinburgh's Old Town on Halloween Night over a year earlier and killing 15 people, including soldiers and police officers seconded in from England had ended the previous day and the jury had been sent to deliberate on their decision.

The tension in the court was high. The prosecution felt they had a rock-solid case against the four defendants. However, the defence offered by the solicitor acting for the four men, Rosemary Baxter, had been robust, so much so that the prosecution raised no less than six objections about allegations that the defendants had been brutally treated by police and army interrogators. The temperature had not been helped by inflammatory newspaper articles in the *Sun* and the *Daily Mail* which had alleged that the SNLA had intimidated witnesses and the jury and had highlighted Mrs Baxter's past involvement with the Scottish Socialist Party and that her previous lovers had included a member of Hamas's high command and a well-known gangster.

The Bannerman's bombing had been a shock to the citizens of Scotland's capital city, particularly as the dead included two local girls who were on a night out and a member of the bar staff. But the army and the police from English forces had made themselves unpopular with their high-handed behaviour and many locals through they had got their just deserts for their role in suppressing Scotland's bid for independence.

The day before, there had been an article in the *Daily Record* which claimed that the United Kingdom government would be giving judges or the prosecution the right of appeal against acquittals and the right to challenge juries, as well as introducing juryless courts to try terrorist cases. This led many Scots to think it was a further attempt by the British authorities to subvert the criminal justice process just because it was not delivering the results they wanted.

At 2:30pm, the jury returned into the main courtroom. It was clear that they had finally reached a decision.

The High Sherriff, Alexander Johnstone, was seated to the left-hand side of the jury. Directly opposite the High Sheriff was the dock, where the four defendants, Derek Gillespie, Jason Kirwan, Bruce Moffat and Peter Smith were seated. Next to the defendants was their solicitor, Rosemary Baxter.

"Have the Members of the Jury reached a decision on which they are agreed?" said the Clerk to the Court.

Jury Foreman Sally Lamerton stood up. "Yes we have."

"How do you find the following defendants on the charges laid against them that, on 31 October 2015, they murdered 15 persons at Bannerman's Bar, Cowgate, Edinburgh through detonating an explosive device?"

"Derek Gillespie" continued the Clerk.

"Not guilty."

"Jason Kirwan."

"Not guilty."

"Bruce Moffat."

"Not guilty."

"Peter Smith."

"Not guilty."

A massive cheer went up from the public gallery.

The same day
Sky News

"This is Claire Egerton with this afternoon's headlines on Sky News."

"The four men accused of the Bannerman's pub bombing in Edinburgh in October 2015 have been acquitted of all charges against them. Derek Gillespie, Jason Kirwan, Bruce Moffat and Peter Smith were found not guilty of the charges of fifteen counts of murder and left the Sherriff Court to the cheers of their families and friends."

"This was another setback to the Government in their battle against Scottish and Welsh terrorism, following hot on the heels of the acquittal of three female WRA suspects a month ago on charges of accessory to murder and compromising of MI5's operations against the SNLA and WRA after they got hold of details of agents and informers. However, the Government is currently reviewing the handling of terrorist cases in the courts and it is expected that they will ensure that procedures are tightened up in the future."

4 February 2017
Lampeter Road
Tregaron
Ceredigion
Wales

Peter and Gail Winterton had been living in the small mid-Wales town of Tregaron for the past two years after they had both left their high-powered jobs in the City of London. Now in their mid-40s, they had decided to opt out of the rat race and run a small arts and crafts business.

The Wintertons had first met while studying at University of Wales Lampeter over a quarter of a century earlier and were familiar with the area. They had promised themselves that one day they would return there to live and had fulfilled that promise. Since moving to Tregaron, they had both become fluent in Welsh, which was the first language there and had made friends with local people. The Troubles which had started two years earlier had largely passed them by. None of the locals they knew held it against them that they were English.

At 10:30am, their doorbell rang. Gail Winterton went to answer it.

Waiting for her were three men, all of whom were wearing military fatigues. One was short and stocky, the second was of average height and the third was tall and ginger-haired. Initially, she thought they were from the British Army whose barracks were near Aberystwyth. A couple of local men had been arrested earlier that week for suspected WRA activity.

The tall man was first to speak and Gail Winterton suddenly realised they were not from the British Army but from the WRA.

"Mrs Winterton?"

"Yes, what can I do?"

"You and your husband have got 48 hours to leave your house. By order of the WRA. We don't want English round here—this is Wales and we're putting the Welsh people first. Too many of you have grassed on the authorities"

Peter Winterton heard the commotion and rushed to the front door.

"Who the hell do you think you are, telling us to leave. We've paid for this house and have every right to live here. If you don't bugger off, I'll call the police."

"Not very advisable Mr Winterton" said the short man. "You know what we do to narks and collaborators."

By now, Gail Winterton's face was red with anger. "And what if we don't leave?"

"That, Mrs Winterton, will be your death warrant" said the third man. "The WRA is clearing Wales of all the English living here."

21 February 2017
Ullapool
Ross & Cromarty
Scotland

The three years since oil had been discovered off Scotland's Atlantic coast had seen rapid change in the formerly quiet fishing town in Scotland's far North West. A massive oil terminal and deep-water port was emerging on the shores of Loch Broom, the A835 which ran south-eastwards to Inverness had been substantially widened and straightened so that heavy lorries could use it without difficulty. Finally, a new railway branch had been built from a junction at Garve on the Inverness-Kyle of Lochalsh line to serve Ullapool.

Not all the locals were happy about the changes brought about. The town's fishing fleet found that the movement of oil tankers interfered with their movements, and relations had not been helped by an oil leak the previous March which grounded the fleet for three months. House prices in Wester Ross had been sent soaring by the influx of high-earning oilmen. And there was resentment about how little the new arrivals contributed to the local economy. The Americans were the worst, living in a compound with food and supplies shipped in from the USA.

The SNLA had taken an interest in the oil terminal too. Oil revenues were vital to the British economy and any disruption would damage this vital cashflow. Also, the SNLA knew how nervous many Americans were about terrorism. They wouldn't have to kill anyone. A bomb blast and many would start to pack their bags.

Fraser McLeod had worked on the construction of the oil terminal until he had been sacked five months earlier following a strike over pay. Not only did he know where the oil was piped in, he also knew the security arrangements for the whole site. He was at the wheel of a Ford Transit van that he had driven from Inverness. With him were two fellow SNLA men, Jackie Thomson and Ross Dick, both like him from the Inverness Brigade.

It was now 8:30am and, as the sun started to rise, McLeod could see the massive oil terminal ahead of him as he drove into Ullapool. On him he had a forged identity pass in the name of Adam Longmuir of Ross Plumbers. To make his visit look even more bona fide, he had phoned the previous day to confirm his planned purpose of visit.

The period between 8am and 10am was generally the busiest for the arrival of contractor traffic arriving at the oil terminal. McLeod therefore drew no suspicion has he pulled up to the security gate.

"Can I see you site pass please sir" said the security guard.

McLeod presented the forged pass. "Adam Longmuir, Ross Plumbers. I've come to carry out routine maintenance on the pipework."

"Thank you Mr Longmuir" said the security guard. "Just drive straight through. You can park up near the Terminal Offices."

Two minutes later, McLeod parked the Transit near the location of the pipes where oil was pumped ashore. Some of it went into storage tanks for collection by the ranks of supertankers moored in Loch Broom. But the rest was pumped into the long pipelines which served the refineries at Cove and Grangemouth.

"Ross, Jackie, have you got the gear out?" said McLeod.

"Aye Frase" replied Dick.

"Let's get to it then guys."

No one else was on site and the three SNLA men had an uninterrupted two hours to prime explosive devices on the main oil terminal. They used Semtex plastic explosive as the main combustion agent. Since it looked like plumbers' putty, no one would have had need to question what they were doing. The detonator was primed to be started by a mobile phone signal.

By 11am, the explosive devices were in place. McLeod, Thomson and Dick got back into the Transit and headed for the site exit.

"Was there much needing fixing today laddies?" asked the security guard as they checked out.

"A bit of corrosion on a couple of pipes" replied McLeod. "Glad I fixed them now and not left them. Don't want a repeat of last year's oil leak. The fishermen were somewhat pissed off."

"Thank you Mr Longmuir. Look forward to seeing you again some time in the future" said the security guard.

Five minutes later, McLeod, Thomson and Dick were passing Beann Eilideach. McLeod slowed down the Transit and said to Thomson "Now Jackie."

Thomson dialled in a pre-set number into his mobile phone. Seconds later, a thunderous roar split the air as three massive explosions blew apart the Loch Broom oil terminal.

2 March 2017
Department for Trade and Enterprise
Victoria Street
London

"Secretary of State, your visitors are here." Harry Moulton, Principal Private Secretary to the Secretary of State for Trade and Enterprise, Cheryl Parkinson, led through three American visitors representing the oil industry to see her.

The three men were a contrast in appearance and physique. Bob Murdoch, the Chairman of Texaco was a towering silver-haired Texan now in his 60s and had been a career oilman, following his father and grandfather. Bruce Hellstrom, Chairman of Exxon, was a Minnesotan of Swedish background, blond-haired, much younger being only in his 40s and built like a linebacker. Milton Spector, a New York Jew and Chairman of Chevron was short, stocky and puglike.

"Thank you Harry" said Parkinson. At 47 years old, Cheryl Parkinson, a Lancastrian from Preston and a businesswoman prior to becoming an MP in 2010, was still attractive, having kept herself in shape by regular sessions at the gym. She had been Secretary of State for Trade and Enterprise for nearly two years.

The mission by Murdoch, Hellstrom and Spector to see the Secretary of State for Trade and Enterprise had been prompted by a spate of terrorist attacks on oil installations in Scotland and Wales over the previous week. Ten days earlier an SNLA bomb had blown up the Loch Broom oil terminal at Ullapool and had put it out of action. This had been followed by WRA sabotage of the cross-country oil pipeline between Abersoch and the refineries at Llandarcy and an unsuccessful attempted bombing by the SNLA at the Invergordon terminal.

Murdoch was first to speak. "Secretary of State, I and my fellow Chairmen are most concerned about recent events over here. Within one week, eighty million dollars of damage has been caused to installations. You guys have been at war with the SNLA and WRA for two years now and appear to have got nowhere."

Parkinson was somewhat put out by the towering American's implied criticism of the British Government's efforts to counter the SNLA and WRA. "I must disagree with you Mr Murdoch" she replied. "The British Government had made immense efforts to control the separatist insurgencies in Scotland and Wales. We've deployed troops and additional police officers to keep order. We've introduced internment for terrorist suspects, made the prosecution process more robust so suspects do not escape justice on technicalities. I think you'll find our new court procedures even more robust than those in the States."

"That's all very well Ms Parkinson" bellowed Hellstrom. "But you've got to catch the SOBs first. And stop them hitting our installations. So far they've only destroyed property. What happens when they start targeting our people here?"

Spector then joined the fray. "Ms Parkinson, your troops and police have frankly achieved diddly squat. From now on, we intend to hire our own security in the USA and use them to protect our oil installations. Castle Security have quoted us and can provide guys trained to Special Forces standard."

Parkinson was horrified at the suggestion. "Mr Spector, do you mean you're going to hire mercenaries? My Government and the people will never stand for that. Will they be armed?"

"Yes Ms Parkinson" replied Spector.

Cheryl Parkinson now looked flushed and angry. "Gentlemen" she spoke in a sharp tone, "May I remind you that your companies are guests of the United Kingdom and, while you're here, you will comply with the laws of the land. The United Kingdom police and armed forces are perfectly capable of guarding the oil installations and does not need an armed force of mercenaries to do this. I repeat what I said before—no way will my Government allow this."

"Then Ms Parkinson, me and my colleagues have no choice but to pull out from the United Kingdom unless your Government changes its mind" said Murdoch.

6 March 2017
Department for Justice
Petty France
London

The Press Suite at the Department for Justice's headquarters was packed with invited journalists. The Attorney-General, Dominic Collins, was due to make an announcement about the constitutional future of Scotland and Wales, which would be simultaneous with the publication of a report commissioned by his predecessor, Stephen Lansbury, two years earlier.

At 11am, Collins walked into the Press Suite. He was accompanied by the two men the Government had chosen to serve as Secretaries of State for Scotland and Wales. Although Stuart Grieve and Jonathan Morgan represented English constituencies, Grieve hailed from Glasgow and Morgan from Swansea and consequently had good credentials for their new posts.

Also present on the top table were Home Secretary Deborah Pearson, Secretary of State for Defence Jason Steer and the Chairmen of the Scottish and Welsh Residuary Bodies, Sir Jocelyn Blackmore and Sir Gerald Norton. Aides carried copy of the Department for Justice Report *Scotland and Wales: Towards Effective Governance* which was available free to invited guests.

Collins stood up before the microphone while cameras flashed. "Ladies and gentlemen, I am most grateful for your presence. Today marks a milestone in the history of Scotland and Wales, two proud countries within the United Kingdom who have been most unfortunate to suffer from the machinations of politicians falsely claiming to be acting in their best interests."

"Two years ago, the devolved governments then ruling Scotland and Wales made the ill-advised decision to try and break away from the United Kingdom on the false understanding that they would gain control of oil reserves off their coast. With the integrity of the United Kingdom at risk for the first time in over 300 years, Her Majesty's Government was forced to take decisive action. It was necessary to close down the devolved Governments for this foolhardy act."

"My honourable predecessor, Stephen Lansbury, commissioned a review of governance arrangements for Scotland and Wales in order to establish the most effective and cost-efficient arrangements for governing those countries. That review has now been completed and the findings are set out in the report, *Scotland and Wales: Towards Effective Governance*, which is available here."

"The report considered a range of options for the governance of Scotland and Wales and concluded that the best option was to return to direct rule by Her Majesty's Government, which as you may remember was the position before May 1999. Two new Departments of State, the Department for Scotland and the Department for Wales, are being set up and will be responsible for education, health, housing, local government, community cohesion, environmental matters, the arts, media and sport. However, they will not be responsible for defence, taxation, immigration and border security, crime and policing, justice, prisons, employment and transport, all of which remain reserved matters. The Government has invited Stuart Grieve, currently Minister of State for Aviation and Jonathan Morgan, currently Minister of State for Housing, to serve as Secretary of State for Scotland and Secretary of State for Wales respectively with effect from 1 April. I am pleased to say that Stuart and Jonathan have accepted."

The two new Cabinet members stood up to applause as camera flashes lit up the Department for Justice Press Suite.

"Finally" Collins continued, "I would like to pay special tribute to the following people. Firstly to Jocelyn Blackmore and Gerald Norton, who so capably chaired the Residuary Bodies for Scotland and Wales. Their work will finish when the Departments for Scotland and Wales come into force on 1 April. I would also like to pay tribute to the following members of the Working Group on Governance for Scotland and Wales, George Graham MP, Diana Riches MP, former MSPs Charles Alexander and Maria Laidlaw, former AMs Gerald Bowen and Alun Thompson, Andrew Carmody, David Price, Mary Kearney, Jim Murphy, Rupert Brooks QC and Alison Seaward QC. It was your hard work and dedication which made *Scotland and Wales: Towards Effective Governance* a reality."

After the meeting finished, Dominic Collins invited the new Cabinet members for a short talk in his office. Also joining them were Deborah Pearson and Jason Steer.

Collins' office had a glorious view of St James' Park. He asked his Principal Private Secretary, Laura Kessler, to arrange for five coffees to be prepared.

"Stuart, Jonathan, what's it like to be in the Cabinet?" asked Collins. The two men were barely two years older than Collins who was the youngest member of the cabinet.

"Absolutely delighted Dominic" said Grieve. "A challenge" said Morgan "but I'm up for it."

"Excellent guys" replied Collins. "You're probably wondering why I've invited Deborah and Jason over."

"I guess because of the security situation" replied Morgan.

"Quite right Jonathan" replied Pearson. "Even though your guys' brief is relatively low-level stuff in comparison—mainly education, health and housing, there's going to be information that will be of use to Dominic, Jason and myself. Can I rely on you to keep in touch?"

"Don't worry Deborah" replied Grieve. "Jon and I will make sure you are all informed first about relevant developments spilling into your briefs."

Pearson was disturbed by her Blackberry ringing. She picked it up.

"Home Secretary, Mark Taylor here." It was the Minister for Homeland Security, so she knew it had to be important.

"Go ahead Mark."

"Just seen a story from the *Daily Mail*. English residents in Scotland and Wales are being forced from their homes by the SNLA and WRA. Ethnic cleansing, you know, just like in Yugoslavia twenty five years ago. If they succeed, it'll make intelligence-gathering even more dangerous than it is at present. They'll have the local populations virtually in their pocket."

"Thanks for telling me Mark, I'll be over now" replied Pearson.

CHAPTER 9

22 March 2017
The Valentine
Perth Road
Ilford, Essex

The Valentine was a large 1930s roadhouse built on Eastern Avenue to cater for coach parties travelling between the East End of London and Southend for the day. It had several bars and a large function room normally used for live bands, discos and parties.

Many other pubs of its kind had been closed down after becoming a magnet for criminals. But the Valentine was still thriving over 80 years after being built.

The function room was seldom in use during the middle of the week. But on the night of 22 March it had been let for a public meeting.

The appearance of the attendees left no doubt about the motivation of the audience. Most were male, either in their 20s or 30s although several were in their 40s or 50s. But all seemed to be shaven-headed and were wearing England football or rugby shirts or T-shirts with English nationalist slogans.

At 8pm, the "Committee for the Defence of England" took the stage to raucous applause from the audience. First to speak was Phil Barden, a short, stocky, balding man in his 50s. Ten years earlier, he had been a local councillor for the British National Party.

"Ladies and gentlemen, thank you for coming tonight. It's encouraging to see so many of you committed to fighting for England."

Barden continued. "You will all be familiar with the disgusting reign of terror being waged by the SNLA and the WRA. For the last two years, our brave lads in the Army and the police have been shot and maimed by those murderous bastards. And to add insult to injury, they've also let off bombs down here. Remember Bluewater, the Trocadero, Royal Ascot?"

Many of the audience did. No less than seven of the audience present had close relatives who were killed in SNLA or WRA atrocities.

"And what has our so-called tough Government done?" bellowed Barden. "Sweet fuck all, that's what. They claim to have interned the terrorists. They claim to have put them on trial. Then why, Mr Delgado, do they repeatedly get off scot-free?" A chorus of cheers nearly raised the rafters in the Valentine.

"And why is it" shouted a now nearly hysterical Barden "that you go down the Caledonian Road or into Ealing and see the Jocks and Taffs strutting about boasting about their scum's exploits, and no one does anything about it? There are pubs where the SNLA and WRA raise money through collections. Celebrities give money to them under disguise of 'charitable donations'."

"If, Mr Delgado, you had any balls, you'd stop pussyfooting around, send in the police and army to carry out identity checks on all Jocks and Taffs and arrest any found to be sympathetic to the SNLA and the WRA. You'd put armed guards on the borders and stop any of them coming into England without good reason. And if you catch any gooks, put them on summary trial then hang them." Another roar of approval swept through the Valentine.

Next to speak was Glenn Nicholls, a tall, raw-boned former paratrooper in his early 40s.

"Ladies and gentlemen, the Committee for the Defence of England will be doing more than just talk. We intend to take action because the Government is showing no signs of doing so. The SNLA and WRA have been bombing and shooting our brave troops and police. They've killed innocent civilians here. And now they're driving our compatriots from their homes that they've paid for." Nicholls was referring to the growing so-called ethnic cleansing of English resident in Scotland and Wales.

"We will create an armed force that will defend the English anywhere in this country or abroad. We will fight fire with fire. Remember, an eye for an eye, a tooth for a tooth. That means, if the SNLA or WRA let off a bomb here, we'll do the same in Scotland and Wales. If they assassinate English businessmen, politicians or officials, we'll hit back at their officials. And if the SNLA and WRA continue to force the English from their homes, we'll do the same to the Scots and Welsh resident in England."

The cheering was by now reaching fever pitch.

Nicholls continued. "If any of you wish to join the army to defend England, I want you to come and see me at the end of the meeting. We need to start recruiting quickly as we've got the first training camp booked for next month."

Before the night was finished, no less than 300 expressions of interest had been made in joining an armed defence force for England.

9 May 2017, 9:30am
The Channel Tunnel
between Coquelles and Folkestone

Jan Grobbelaar had eased his Nedrail locomotive into the Channel Tunnel twenty minutes earlier and was on the way to the freight transfer yard near Ebbsfleet International Station to transfer his cargo of Volkswagen and Audi cars. It was a routine run for him, which he had done hundreds of times before. By 7pm, he expected to be back home in Tilburg.

The alarm on his locomotive suddenly sounded and Grobbelaar brought his train to a halt. He was about to radio the signals at Coquelles when his onboard closed circuit radio sounded too.

"Coquelles to India Alpha 66. You have a fire on your train. Evacuate immediately."

Grobbelaar knew that meant going into the service tunnel. That was sealed and he knew he would be safe there. But he thought back to the checks he did earlier that day. Surely he checked all the cars to make sure there were no fuel leaks? That was going to be the inevitable question he would be asked. If he had not been thorough in his checks, his employer would not be best pleased. There could be disciplinary action to follow.

After waiting five minutes in the service tunnel, a Eurotunnel Land Rover was on hand to pick him up and take him to the Cheriton terminal on the British side. When he got out, Grobbelaar was met by five police officers, which worried him.

The officers were however far from hostile. "No need to worry Mr Grobbelaar. We just need to ask a few questions" said the Sergeant Paul Robinson who accompanied him to the police station at the Eurotunnel terminal.

"What has happened?" asked Grobbelaar.

"Terrorists planted a bomb in one of the cars on your train" replied PC Dawn Lucas. "Probably did it before you started off. Doubt if you could have done anything to stop them."

"Are you certain of this?" asked Grobbelaar.

"Definitely" replied Sergeant Robinson. "The SNLA have claimed responsibility."

The same day, 5:15pm
Dartford Crossing, M25

The Dartford Crossing was the last point where the River Thames could be crossed before it reached the North Sea. The northbound crossing constituted two tunnels, the original built in the early 1960s and the second, built well over a decade later. The southbound crossing was the Queen Elizabeth II suspension bridge, which had opened in 1992. The volume of traffic using the Dartford Crossing was starting to reach a peak as the evening rush hour began. The M25, which for the past 30 years had served as London's orbital motorway, had earned an unenviable reputation as the world's largest car park as traffic using it far exceeded the original estimates made as far back as the 1970s. Traffic in weekday rush hours was slow-moving at the best of times and all it took was an accident or a broken-down vehicle to bring it grinding to a halt.

For the past seven years, the Kent and Essex police forces had shared many of their operational functions, and this included traffic control for the Dartford Crossing. Sergeant Sue Gosling, who was in charge of the control room, was optimistic that the first day back after the early May Bank Holiday, would be incident-free. The television monitors in the control room all showed traffic to be free-flowing.

Within two minutes, Sergeant Gosling's hopes of a quiet evening had been shattered. Ben Turner, a graduate in urban studies from the University of East London who had been recruited four months previously took a call.

"Kent and Essex Police Joint Control Centre" said Turner.

"This is the WRA" replied the caller who had a noticeable Welsh accent. "A bomb has been placed under the QE2 Bridge and is timed to go off at 6pm. If you don't want several hundred dead bodies on your hands, I would suggest you close the bridge and evacuate the whole area now."

10 May 2017
Sky News

"This is Adam Rennie with this morning's headlines on Sky News."

"The Government is counting the cost of the two terrorist incidents yesterday which closed the Channel Tunnel and the Dartford Crossing on the M25. The cost to the economy has been estimated at £2.5 billion."

"The National Anti-Terror Squad is working with Interpol to find out how the SNLA managed to plant a bomb in a Volkswagen Prinz. Although nobody was killed, the explosion caused a massive fire which has put the northbound tunnel out of use for the next nine months. The enforced closure of the tunnel has resulted in no less than five hundred lorries being stranded on either side of the English Channel. Eurotunnel anticipates significant compensation claims from hauliers and exporters who have suffered from delays."

"Bomb disposal experts from the Royal Engineers managed to defuse a twenty pound bomb under the Queen Elizabeth II Bridge at 8:30pm yesterday. But the WRA, who claimed responsibility for placing the bomb, managed to cause traffic chaos which lasted into the early hours of this morning as motorists were diverted via the Blackwall Tunnel."

29 May 2017
Thorpe Park near Chertsey
Surrey

The late May Bank Holiday had dawned fine and sunny, which was a relief for many people after the poor and unseasonable weather which had dogged all four Bank Holidays in 2016 and the Easter and early May Bank Holidays earlier in the year. Near record numbers of people headed out for the day, for whom a trip to the coast or to a theme park was their intended destination.

The amusement park at Thorpe Park had been a major attraction since opening nearly forty years earlier and the good weather brought out massive crowds. By midday, they were having to turn people away as there were already 50,000 people on the site.

Highlight of Thorpe Park were the 40 rollercoaster rides which were doing roaring business that day. Families were queuing for over an hour to get on the rides, and this was adding to the congestion within the site.

Four days earlier, a team of maintenance men had called to ensure that the rides were all in proper working order. The last thing Thorpe Park wanted was a breakdown or, worse, an accident.

What Thorpe Park's management had not realised was that two members of the WRA had infiltrated the maintenance team and had taken advantage of their access to the site to plant a bomb. One of the WRA men had been a former Army bomb disposal expert and knew about bomb making and concealment. No one would have suspected that anything untoward had happened.

Without warning, there was a massive explosion at 12:30pm.

The same day
Pleasure Beach
Blackpool
Lancashire

Blackpool's Pleasure Beach was one of the country's oldest amusement parks, having opened in 1896. Despite its age, Pleasure Beach had kept up to date with its attractions and over 6 million people visited it each year. The good weather had attracted massive numbers of visitors through its gates and it had been forced to close them after the 30,000 mark had been passed.

By 3:30pm, large queues had built up for the rides, including the flagship 'Pepsi Max' rollercoaster. No one would have been aware that, three hours earlier, a bomb had gone off at Thorpe Park, some 240 miles further south. However, visitors to the Pleasure Beach were in mortal danger as they had not been aware that the SNLA had planted a bomb in one of the busiest areas. As with Thorpe Park, they had infiltrated a maintenance crew and used the opportunity to plant and prime a Semtex device which would be detonated by mobile phone.

A minute later, a member of SNLA's Manchester Brigade dialled a number into a stolen mobile phone which had been reprogrammed. An immense blast ripped through the Pleasure Beach.

Later that evening
Sky News

"This is Sara Ratcliffe with an emergency news bulletin on Sky News."

"At least a hundred people are believed to have been killed in two terrorist bombings today. The first took place at Thorpe Park at about lunchtime, while the second took place at Blackpool Pleasure Beach later in the afternoon. The WRA have claimed responsibility for the Thorpe Park bombing, while the SNLA have claimed responsibility for the Pleasure Beach bombing."

"Unlike the bombs in the Channel Tunnel and the Dartford Crossing three weeks ago, there was no prior warning from either the SNLA or the WRA, which suggests that they are stepping up their operations in support of their campaign for independence from the United Kingdom."

"Surrey Police and Lancashire Constabulary have both issued emergency telephone numbers for people concerned about relatives who they think might have been caught up in either bombing. These are: 0845 5025 1790 for Surrey and 0845 5025 1791 for Lancashire."

8 June 2017
Hadley Wood
Hertfordshire

The green Mercedes Benz parcels van in the livery of City Link, one of the country's main mail and parcels courier firms, pulled up to the gatehouse at the entrance to Glebelands, an exclusive private estate.

"Delivery for Mr Andrew Gorvett of Newlands" said the driver.

"You're a bit late calling round" said the security guard. "It's already half past eight."

"I know" replied the driver. "It's been a long day. This is our final delivery."

The barrier across the entrance road to Glebelands was raised and the van proceeded through.

"Nice work Huw" said Mark Powell in the passenger seat. "First turn on the left and Gorvett's house is second on the right."

Andrew Gorvett was the Chairman of the British League of Freedom, a right-wing pressure group whose main interest was lobbying in favour of business and the free market. However, a week earlier, Gorvett had made a speech at London Guildhall in which he announced that the British League of Freedom would offer a reward to anyone who provided information to the authorities which helped convict an SNLA or WRA terrorist. This had made him a target for the SNLA and WRA.

Gorvett had been offered protection by the police but had turned it down. He lived on a very secure estate which was guarded and patrolled by a private security company and he had no reason to feel his life was at risk.

However, the SNLA and the WRA were both becoming extremely proficient at their craft. Even in the early days of the struggle back in 2015, they had benefited from the expertise of former soldiers. Two years on, they had learned from mistakes and were increasingly capable of carrying out operations and avoiding being caught. Both organisations were cash-rich from fund-raising donations in the USA and from the proceeds of drug trafficking, cigarette and alcohol smuggling and the vice trade. The money had bought Semtex explosive, guns and rocket launchers which increased their capacity to wage war against the British Government. Recruitment was high as repressive measures by the Army and police alienated increasing numbers of Scots and Welsh. Finally, they had scored a massive intelligence coup six months earlier when they got hold of critical information on MI5 operatives and informers after a petty thief stole a laptop from a Home Office official, which enabled them to cripple the British Government's intelligence operations against them.

Huw Davies, the driver of the van, personified the new approach by the SNLA and the WRA. An East Ender from Manor Park, Davies was the son of a Welshman who had moved to London and married a local and, to all intents and purposes, was a Cockney. He raised no suspicions at the security gate of Glebelands and had been waved through. But what the security guard did nor realise was that Davies, along with Mark Powell, were both members of the WRA. The van had been disguised in the identity of City Link to make them look legitimate. Their mission was to assassinate Andrew Gorvett.

Gorvett's house was a massive affair befitting the wealthy businessman that he was. After pulling up, Davies rang the entryphone.

"Good evening, can I help you." Davies recognised the voice. It was Gorvett.

"City Link here Mr Gorvett" replied Davies. "We've got a package for you."

"Are you sure?" asked Gorvett. "I wasn't expecting anything."

"It's definitely for you Mr Gorvett" said Davies. "If you don't sign for it now, you'll have to come down to our depot in Barnet."

"Okay, come on through."

The electronic front gate opened and Davies walked through with the fake package. Powell meanwhile kept the van's engine running.

Gorvett opened his front door. He was a large man in his late 50s, who had once been quite athletic in his younger days but had now run to fat.

"Here's the package Mr Gorvett" said Davies. "Would you kindly sign for it."

Gorvett reached for a pen. As he did, Davies withdrew an Uzi machine pistol with a silencer and shot Gorvett. As the Chairman of the British League of Freedom slumped to the ground, Davies sprinted away, jumped into the van and drove off. By the time the alarm was raised, Davies and Powell were on their way to the Somers Town safe house. On the way, they set light to the van to destroy the evidence of its use.

12 June 2017
Warrington Crown Court
Legh Street
Warrington, Cheshire

The trial of the so-called "Warrington Three", Martyn Thomas, Glyn Maddock and Carol Davies, was now in its fourth week. The three defendants had been charged with the murder of ten soldiers from the Mercian Regiment a year earlier after two bomb blasts ripped through the Officers Mess and Sergeants Mess at Thelwall Barracks.

The prosecution had finished giving its evidence and defence solicitor Jamie Pritchard stepped up to the bar to question witnesses.

Pritchard recognised that the defence faced a difficult challenge. Only two weeks earlier they had pulled off their largest atrocities ever when bombs at Thorpe Park and Blackpool Pleasure Beach on the Bank Holiday Monday killed over 150 people. And four days earlier, the Chairman of the British League of Freedom, Andrew Gorvett, had been murdered on his own doorstep. He knew this would be fresh in the minds of jurors.

Detective Chief Inspector Warren Duckworth took the witness stand. A member of Cheshire Constabulary's Murder Squad, he had led the interrogation of the suspects. A big, broad-shouldered man in his 40s, Duckworth had made his name as a tough operational policeman. He was not averse to roughing up suspects and the three defendants had told Pritchard that they had suffered ill-treatment during their interrogation.

"Detective Chief Inspector Duckworth" started Pritchard, "you previously told this court about your interviews with Mr Thomas, Mr Maddock and Ms Davies. In addition, your colleagues, Detective Inspector Tilsley and Detective Sergeant Caplin also gave evidence about their interviews with my clients."

"That is correct sir" replied Duckworth.

"What methods did you use to interrogate my clients?" asked Pritchard.

"Standard police procedures, as prescribed under PACE as revised" replied DCI Duckworth.

"Then why did committal proceedings have to be delayed while Mr Thomas and Ms Davies underwent medical treatment for injuries Detective Chief Inspector Duckworth? My clients allege that they were assaulted by your officers from arrest through to questioning."

"That is a false and malicious allegation sir" growled Duckworth.

"May I continue Detective Chief Inspector Duckworth" said Pritchard. "My client Ms Davies alleges that, with you present, Detective Inspector Tilsley and Detective Sergeant Caplin threatened her with rape unless she co-operated and named Mr Thomas and Mr Maddock as having been responsible for the Thelwall bombing."

"That is totally false sir and a slur on the reputation of two of my officers" said Duckworth.

"Furthermore, Detective Chief Inspector Duckworth, it appears that officers' electronic notebooks used to make a record of the interview were changed after the interviews had taken place. That is a serious breach of police procedure, isn't it Detective Chief Inspector Duckworth?"

"Mr Pritchard, may I make it totally clear that I supervised the interviews of the suspects from start to finish" said an increasingly exasperated Duckworth. "I am 100% satisfied that I and my officers conducted them in a professional manner."

"I understand you have had dealings with Mr Thomas before Detective Chief Inspector Duckworth. You used to be in the Drugs Squad three years ago."

"That is right" replied Duckworth.

"I put it to you Detective Chief Inspector Duckworth that you wanted to get your own back on Mr Thomas because he twice walked free when you tried to fit him up on a drugs charge."

"Objection, your Honour" shrieked prosecuting counsel Debbie Crowe.

"Objection upheld" said the judge, Mr Justice Penfold. A known hard-liner, he had been recommended to be the trial judge by the Attorney-General.

Penfold continued. "Mr Pritchard, I must warn you to stick to the facts. You have made scurrilous and unwarranted slurs against serving police officers. If I have to warn you again, I will consider disqualifying you from the rest of this trial."

18 July 2017
House of Commons
London

"Can I call on the Right Honourable Member for Basildon South?" said the Speaker, George Franklin.

David Pickavance, the Conservative MP for Basildon South, stood up on the Government back benches to present the Private Member's Bill he was introducing. The Seditious Communications Bill would make criticism of the conduct of the police, the armed forces or the security services in the fight against the SNLA and WRA a criminal offence, whether in a public speech, in print, on the Internet or through broadcast media. The Bill would carry a penalty of either a fine of £20,000 or 18 months in prison.

Public disquiet about the way the authorities were pursuing the battle against terrorism was growing in the United Kingdom. Suspects had complained of being beaten up in custody by the police and prison officers and stories were coming out about the use of torture at the Brecon and Stirling interrogation centres. But to other Britons, the human rights campaigners were unpatriotic mischief-makers who were giving aid and comfort to the SNLA and WRA, and MPs like Pickavance articulated their view.

"Thank you Mr Speaker" replied Pickavance in his characteristically blunt Yorkshire tones. "May I introduce the Seditious Communications Bill?"

"My Right Honourable ladies and gentlemen, I do not have to illustrate the sterling work that the police, the armed forces and the security services have been doing over the last two years to combat the menace of the SNLA and the WRA. They have put their lives on the line to make the country safe for law-abiding taxpayers and, indeed, many have paid with their lives."

Pickavance continued. "Unfortunately, not all our citizens share this view. All too often, we hear scurrilous stories about alleged torture and brutality towards prisoners and suspects, often with very little foundation. For example, this."

Pickavance held up a copy of *Socialist Challenge*, the newspaper of the Socialist Alliance, along with extracts from online blogs.

"Do the people who are responsible for this seditious rubbish realise the pressure our brave policemen, soldiers and security service agents are working under to keep the country's law-abiding citizens safe? Do they realise they are undermining the war against terror and are giving aid and comfort to the thugs and murderers from the SNLA and WRA? Do they not realise they are undermining the country's security by slandering and libelling the security forces?"

On the Opposition benches, Geraldine Partington, the Labour MP for Bradford North, was on her feet.

"May I remind the Right Honourable Member for Basildon South that the evidence of maltreatment of prisoners did not come from some supposedly subversive political group as he and other members of his party believe. It came from the Human Rights Committee of the Council of Europe . . . ."

Partington was drowned out by a chorus of jeers and catcalls from the Conservative benches.

She resumed her speech. "The Council of Europe, and has been endorsed by Member governments from the European Union. The Bill proposed by the Right Honourable gentleman would be more at home in apartheid-era South Africa or a military dictatorship than a country with our long history of democratic rule with a tradition of respecting people's rights."

Pickavance was back on his feet. "The Right Honourable lady epitomises all that is wrong with the Labour Party and why it should never be allowed to rule the United Kingdom ever again." Conservative MPs waved their order papers in support of the belligerent backbencher. "The Council of Europe have no right to interfere in the United Kingdom's domestic affairs and I trust that my Right Honourable ladies and gentlemen will agree. Remember this was the reason we left the European Union."

"May I return to the Bill I am placing before this House. This country is at war. Whenever there is a war on, all citizens are expected to rally behind the forces defending it. Anyone who undermines that fight is acting against the national interest. To put it bluntly, they are traitors. And traitors need to be punished."

Shouts of "disgraceful" and "withdraw" came from the Labour benches.

"This Bill will ensure that those persons who choose to undermine the struggle against terrorism by acts of seditious slander and libel are brought to account for their actions and do not have the freedom to insult the forces protecting our freedom and security. I trust you will support it."

20 July 2017
House of Commons
London

Fionnuala Gray was coming to the end of her six month stint working as a barmaid at the House of Commons. A Glaswegian, she had graduated a year earlier from South Bank University with an upper second class degree in Sociology and Politics, and had been unable to find a permanent job. She had taken on bar work to pay off her debts and to avoid being conscripted under National Service, but she had found the work boring and she hated the boorish and self-important attitude of many of the MPs.

20 July was the last day Parliament met before the summer recess, and the MPs had been engaged in the Adjournment Debate. Custom at the Terrace Bar was therefore very quiet. The calm before the storm before the demob-happy MPs took over the bar and got pissed.

"Ryan, is it all right to have a ciggy break now?" said Gray.

"Yeah, Fionnuala" replied the Bar Manager, Ryan Parkes. "Be back by one though. The MPs may be out by then."

Gray headed down to the House of Commons car park. No one was around. She knew there were CCTV cameras, but they had to scan a large area and there were periods when parts of the car park were out of focus.

From her shoulder bag, Gray removed a silvery grey box. At the base, four powerful magnets had been welded on. Inside was two kilos of Semtex with a detonator which was programmed to be set off by a signal from a mobile phone. Gray had collected it from a fellow member of the SNLA's London Brigade the previous day. Her objective was to fix it to the underside of David Pickavance's car.

Pickavance's Mercedes-Benz M430 was not difficult to find. The large black 4x4 had a personalised number plate, DP 1956. Gray removed a tube of adhesive from her handbag and applied it to the metal casing of the device in four places. She then fixed it underneath the fuel tank of the Mercedes. The adhesive would make sure the bomb did not fall off.

Two hours later, David Pickavance climbed into his car for the journey back to his home near Billericay. He was feeling pleased with himself as his Private Member's Bill had been passed. In two weeks, he and his wife would be sunning themselves at their luxury villa near Marbella.

Pickavance headed for the Victoria Embankment, from which he would head through Upper and Lower Thames Street, Tower Hill, East Smithfield and the Limehouse Link to reach the A13 to take him back to Essex.

Back at the House of Commons, Gray rang Joey Wallace on her mobile phone. "Joey, Pickavance left the Commons about twenty minutes ago. He'll probably be near the City of London now."

"Good work Fi" replied Wallace.

Thirty seconds later, Wallace dialled a pre-set number into his mobile phone. At the same moment, Pickavance was in East Smithfield. He stood no chance of survival as his car exploded in a massive fireball.

21 July 2017
Reading Crown Court
The Old Shire Hall
Reading
Berkshire

The prosecution and defence counsels had finished their summing up for the jury in the case of *R v Allan, Banahan, Eadie, McFarlane and Shepherd*, five suspected SNLA terrorists who had been charged with the murders of thirty-nine racegoers and a member of staff at Royal Ascot a year earlier. The jury was led to their room to deliberate on the verdict.

The murder of Tory backbencher David Pickavance was fresh in the minds of the jurors as they sat down to discuss their verdict. It had dominated the news of the previous evening and that morning, along with reports on a parallel trial taking place in Warrington of three WRA suspects for the Thelwall Barracks bombing.

Linda Jessop, a schoolteacher in her mid-40s, voiced her doubts that the right men had been caught. "Something doesn't seem right about this trial. None of the men seem to act like terrorists. I wonder if they just happened to be in the wrong place at the wrong time."

Dennis Pleat, an IT executive in his late 50s, disagreed. "Sorry, Linda, but I can't agree with you on that. The prosecution's evidence looked pretty sound and there's forensic evidence to back it up. They're guilty all right."

Pleat was backed up by Samantha Reynolds, an attractive blonde businesswoman in her late 30s. "I too think they're guilty. Look at the evidence of their backgrounds. None of them are of good character. All of them were found with pro-independence material on them. You can only draw one conclusion from that."

Wayne Cockerill, a plasterer, was even more forthright. "Those bastards are all fucking guilty. They were all trying to hide something. I hope they take 'em all outside and hang the lot of them straight after the trial. Look what happened to that MP yesterday."

Thirty-five minutes later, Linda Jessop reluctantly conceded that the five defendants were probably guilty.

Forty minutes later, a court official opened the door.

"Has the jury reached a verdict yet?"

"Yes" replied Reynolds, who had been nominated to speak for the jury.

The jury trooped back into the court room and took their place.

"Has the jury arrived at a verdict that they are all agreed on?" asked the Clerk to the Court.

"They have" replied Reynolds.

"How you find the following defendants to the charges of murder laid against them?"

"Robert Leslie Allan."

"Guilty."

"Kevin James Banahan."

"Guilty."

"James Irvine Eadie."

"Guilty."

"Glen Fraser McFarlane."

"Guilty."

"Rory Malcolm Shepherd."

"Guilty."

There were gasps from the public gallery at the verdicts. Next, McFarlane shouted out "That's a travesty of justice. We're all innocent!"

"Silence in court!" shouted the Clerk.

The trial judge, Mr Justice May, then proceeded to pass sentence.

"Robert Leslie Allan, Kevin James Banahan, James Irvine Eadie, Glen Fraser McFarlane and Rory Malcolm Shepherd, you have been found guilty of the most heinous murders of forty innocent members of the public who had every expectation that they would return to their loved ones at the end of the day. At no time during this trial have you shown remorse for these crimes. I have no alternative but to pass the most severe penalty available to me, and that is death." May then put on the black cap to signal the passing of the ultimate penalty.

"You will be taken from this courtroom to a place appointed, where you will be hung by the neck until you are dead."

Dennis Pleat and Samantha Reynolds were glad that the trial was over. They could get back to their jobs and families with whom they had little contact with over the previous two months. As they walked back towards the town centre car park to collect their cars for the journey home, they passed a news stand where free copies of the *London Evening Standard* were available.

"Sam, like a copy of the Standard?" asked Pleat.

"Oh, go on, Dennis."

Pleat and Reynolds saw the front page headline on the Evening Standard, which read

WARRINGTON THREE TO HANG AFTER GUILTY VERDICT

"Looks like great minds think alike" said Reynolds.

CHAPTER 10

30 July 2017
Cardigan
Wales

The oil industry had transformed Cardigan. Once a sleepy fishing port and market town, it had been rejuvenated by the construction of a massive oil terminal to serve the Fastnet oilfield. Along the banks of the River Teifi, there were oil storage tanks, heavy duty pumps to service the pipeline which ran to the Milford Haven and Swansea refineries and lorry parks. A new dual-carriageway road connected Cardigan to Carmarthen, from where it led to the M4 and the railway link to the town, closed over 50 years earlier, had been rebuilt.

Not everyone was happy with the changes. The conservative West Wales community had to cope with an influx of workers from the oil industry. Prostitutes and drug dealers had followed in their wake and crime had gone up. Many of the oil industry staff were Americans who did very little to mix with the locals. They lived in their own gated communities where they shopped at stores which sold American groceries rather than use facilities in the town. Particularly unpopular were the security guards from Castle Security who policed the terminal and who were notoriously boorish and offensive.

Garin Davies and Stuart Williams were both bored. They had left school a year earlier and had dropped out of college. Neither had a job.

Breaking into the terminal and stealing metal pipes to sell on looked an attractive proposition. It was Sunday evening and the hated "goons" from Castle would be thin on the ground.

"Gar, we can get in here" said Williams, who had spotted a slack section of boundary fence. The two teenagers crawled under the fence and made their way towards a pile of metal pipes and copper wire. The latter looked particularly attractive as it was easy to hide and commanded high prices.

Davies and Williams started loading up copper wire into a supermarket carrier bag when they were disturbed by a floodlight pointing in their direction, followed by the stentorian tones of Castle security guard Jay Werner, a former corporal in the US Marines.

"Hey you! Put your hands in the air and no sudden movements."

"Shit Gar, we've been caught" said Williams.

Werner approached the two local lads, smirking.

"Look what we've got here tonight. Do your parents know you're here? You're messing with the big boys here."

Davies started to raise his arms when suddenly he remembered he had a weapon. Two coils of copper wire. Without warning, he flung it at Werner.

"Run for it Stu" shouted Davies.

The two Welsh lads were fast runners and had taken the opportunity to make some seventy metres on the American security guard. The boundary fence was invitingly close. But Werner was boiling with rage and was armed. He pulled out his M16 rifle, took aim at Davies and Williams and opened fire. The two Welsh lads took a brace of bullets clean through their vital organs and were dead before they reached the fence.

31 July 2017
Sky News

"This is Adam Rennie with this morning's headlines on Sky News."

"Police reinforcements have been deployed to Cardigan following violent clashes last night after the fatal shootings of two local youths by a security guard employed to guard the oil terminal. The two youths, Stuart Williams, 18 and Garin Davies, 17, were reported to have broken into the oil terminal, where it is believed they were trying to steal copper wire. They were challenged by a security guard employed by Castle Security and were shot when attempting to flee."

"During last night's disturbances, several properties were damaged in arson attacks and cars belonging to oil company employees were attacked. The latest reports say that all is calm at present, although the oil companies have warned their staff to be vigilant."

"Last night's shootings were the latest in a series of incidents involving personnel employed by the American security company to protect oil installations in Wales and Scotland. This is bound to put pressure on the Government to impose restrictions on the use of private security by the oil industry."

4 August 2017
Cardigan
Wales

The eastern sky was beginning to lighten as the Cambrian Travel coach pulled into the compound to the north of Cardigan where the security staff employed by Castle lived. The thirty men and women who were to form the day shift were already waiting and, as soon as the coach pulled up, boarded it. Within two minutes, the driver, David Jenkins, was back on the A487 and was heading back towards Cardigan.

The coach had just passed the sign indicating that Cardigan was a mile away and the incandescent glow of the remaining street lights indicated that they were approaching the town. The next second, the coach was blown apart as a massive fireball erupted.

KINGDOM COME

Two minutes later
Dyfed-Powys Police Headquarters
Carmarthen
Wales

The control room at Dyfed-Powys Police Headquarters was only at half-strength. Early mornings were usually quite times for the police.

Gemma Lewis, a member of the police staff manning the control room took a 999 call. It was unusual to have such calls early in the morning, but the caller seemed to be in a state of some distress.

"There's been an explosion on board a coach. It's serious, there's bodies in the road."

"Where are you calling from sir" asked Lewis.

"Just north of Cardigan. On the A487."

"Someone will be with you shortly."

Lewis put out an immediate alert, after which she phoned Inspector Graham Evans, who was in charge of the control room.

"Gemma, what's happened? Unusual for an alert at this time of the day."

"There's been an explosion on board a coach near Cardigan sir" said Lewis. "There's reckoned to be fatalities."

"Cardigan eh" relied Evans. "We had a lot of trouble there last weekend. Wonder if the WRA are involved."

Evans' query was answered two seconds later. Another member of the police staff manning the phones, Kate Williams, took a call.

"Dyfed-Powys Police. How can we help you?"

"This is the WRA. We were responsible for the bomb on the coach north of Cardigan. That was our payback to Castle for the murders of Garin Davies and Stuart Williams."

8 August 2017
London

The first influx of foreign tourists visiting London had already arrived. About half of them were from the USA, Japan and China. Predominantly middle-aged, their aim was to visit venues associated with Britain's past and were redolent with pomp and tradition. This meant visiting Buckingham Palace, the Tower of London, the Houses of Parliament and Trafalgar Square.

The other half were generally younger and were predominantly from Europe, although a significant share of Australians and New Zealanders who were doing a world tour made up the numbers. They generally headed for the symbols of a trendier London—Carnaby Street, Camden Market and Brick Lane—even though Britain's pre-eminence in the fields of rock music, fashion, film and art had faded since the recessions of 2008-09 and 2010-12.

Security in London was tight—memories of the Bluewater and Trocadero bombings little more than a year and a half previously were still raw. The Metropolitan

127

and City of London police forces were augmented in their search duties by volunteer members of the Special Constabulary, while the City of Westminster used its street wardens to assist the police. In addition, the Government had introduced an amendment to the Terrorism Act which placed a duty on all employers to carry out a criminal record check through the Home Office and a security check through MI5 on all employees it wished to take on. It was backed up by a requirement for all central and local government staff to robustly scrutinise any requests for identity documents, such as passports or birth certificates which looked suspect.

However, such systems were only as strong as the commitment of the people running them. All it needed was a small number of staff who were either disaffected or open to compromise to undermine their effectiveness.

The public sector had not fared well under the Conservative government since its election seven years previously. Swingeing cuts in public expenditure, required according to the Government to reduce the country's massive budget deficit, had resulted in compulsory redundancies, not only for local government staff but also for civil servants who had previously thought their jobs were safe. For those left in post, their pay had been frozen for three years, final salary pensions were withdrawn at a stroke and training and development programmes were drastically scaled back.

As the decade advanced, further changes were imposed on an unwilling workforce. On the advice of business consultants brought in at great expense, radical changes were made to the workforce. Staff who previously had a high level of responsibility in their work found themselves relegated to being call centre drones. Middle managers responsible for drafting policy and for executing programmes found themselves turned into glorified supervisors. External recruitment to the Civil Service at senior grades was extended to middle grades. For most staff below senior ranks, the opportunity for career advancement had finished as the de-skilling of their work meant they no longer had the skills and competencies needed to advance.

The majority of public servants knuckled down and got on with the job in hand, even if they disagreed with the Government's policy towards them. But a minority were tempted by the opportunity to enrich themselves by providing services to criminals and terrorists in return for money. Or simply getting revenge on the Government, their backers and the people who voted for them.

A month earlier, a former junior official at the Department for Employment had met a couple of SNLA members in a Westminster pub when he and former friends from university had a reunion. A deal had been struck; he and several colleagues would help the SNLA obtain false identities through obtaining birth certificates for people born 25-30 years previously who had died in childhood. Any Criminal Record Bureau or MI5 check on them would be negative and they would be free to work anywhere.

A week later, the Department for Employment official was introduced to a member of the WRA and he agreed to do the same.

The SNLA and WRA had promised to damage the United Kingdom's economic base and that Tuesday, they fulfilled that promise.

The same day, 9am
London Stock Exchange
Paternoster Square
City of London

Activity at the London Stock Exchange was frenetic. With the holiday season coming up, businesses were trying to conclude deals and shares were exchanging hands at breakneck speed.

Half a mile away in Gracechurch Street was the main broadband junction box which controlled the high-speed broadband connections to the telescreens which supported the Stock Exchange's business. Half an hour earlier, British Telecom workers had carried out apparently routine maintenance work on the junction box. However, no one realised that the two workers were SNLA members on a mission to cripple the City of London's business communications. Davie Graham and Gavin Kerr had obtained employment with British Telecom through using the birth certificates of children who had died in infancy almost thirty years previously, obtained through the services of a corrupt official in the Department for Employment. They had planted a Semtex device and primed it to be detonated by mobile phone signal.

At 9am, Graham and Kerr pulled up the British Telecom van in a side street close to London Bridge station.

"Okay Gav" said Graham.

Kerr dialled a number into his mobile phone. A mile away, the bomb attached to the broadband junction box blew it apart. All the telescreens in the Stock Exchange suddenly went blank.

Ten minutes later
Heathrow Airport

The two hours between 8am and 10am were normally the busiest at London's main airport as no less than fifteen long-haul flights from the USA and the Far East arrived. Most of the burden fell on Air Traffic Control who had to handle an extremely congested airspace. All it took was for one flight to be overdue and they would have planes, in many cases low on fuel, stacked up over London.

Emma Leeson at the reception Desk at Air Traffic Control took what initially seemed a routine telephone call. She noted that the caller had a Welsh accent and initially she thought it might be ATC at Cardiff International requesting permission to divert a plane. What followed was more chilling,

"This is the WRA here. A bomb has been placed in the Air Traffic Control building and will be detonated in thirty minutes time. If you don't want to have blood on your hands, I would suggest you evacuate the building now." With that, the caller rang off.

Leeson immediately rang Tony Hayward, the Chief Air Traffic Controller to alert him. Within seconds, a full evacuation of the building was in progress.

Hayward realised the severity of the problem. With his deputy Rob Angelis, he contacted their counterparts at Gatwick, Stansted and Luton to request authority to divert all incoming flights. He also contacted the pilots of flights about to leave to ask them to suspend takeoff. Then he and Angelis evacuated the building.

British Transport Police had sealed off the Air Traffic Control building by the time the promised explosion was due to take place. Chief Superintendent Gary Holden initially thought the call had been a hoax.

But a mile away, parked up in Harmondsworth, were two WRA members, Gary Budgen and Wyn Pritchard. It was Budgen who had successfully breached security at the airport by obtaining a job as a security guard under a false identity. An official at the Department for Employment had assisted in setting up that identity which belonged to a child who had died at the age of three a quarter of a century before, and had been rewarded for his enterprise.

Budgen gave a nod to Pritchard, who took out his mobile phone and dialled a number. Barely a second later, a massive blast ripped through the Air Traffic Control Centre.

The same day, 2pm

Queues were building up at London's chief tourist attractions. Buckingham Palace, the Tower of London and Madame Tussaud's were all doing excellent business, while Harrods had one of its busiest days outside Christmas.

Many of the tourists were rather perturbed to see armed police on patrol at the main railway stations, key road junctions like Hyde Park Corner, the bridges over the River Thames and the main Government buildings in Whitehall. But they were aware of the cause for concern by reading the lunchtime edition of the *Evening Standard*, which had reports on the bombing attacks on the City of London's broadband communications system and Heathrow's Air Traffic Control.

The SNLA and WRA had however not finished their day's work. More targets had been planned and, this time, they had lethal intent. As with the City of London and Heathrow bombings, they had inserted active service personnel into the staff of the Tower of London, Madame Tussaud's and Harrods using false identity documents.

Within the space of five minutes, three massive blasts ripped through the Tower of London, Madame Tussaud's and Harrods.

9 August 2017
near Granada, Spain

Robert and Sarah Delgado were into the third day of their summer holiday at the large villa they owned nine kilometres from the historic city of Granada in Andalusia. Delgado had a strong emotional attachment to Spain's southernmost province for family reasons. His father had hailed from Lanjaron, a village in the shadow of the Sierra Nevada, and one of his earliest memories had been going on holiday to his father's home village in the early 1960s, long before the development of the Costa del Sol became reality.

The Delgados were both early risers and breakfasted on coffee, rolls and fruit prepared by their housekeeper Maria. Later that day, they would be travelling to the holiday villa owned by Jose Ramos, the Partido Popular leader. Their social calendar was already full.

Delgado switched on Sky News to keep in touch with events at home.

"Darling, how about relaxing a bit more? Ed's in charge of things while we're out here and I'm sure he can cope" said Sarah Delgado, a blonde woman in her mid-50s. She was referring to Chancellor of the Exchequer, Ed Villiers, who was acting leader in Delgado's absence.

"Come on Sarah" replied the Prime Minister. "Just want to keep in touch with events at home. No worries about Ed. But remember what Harold Macmillan said, old girl. 'Events, dear boy'. All it takes is a couple of pieces of bad news and people start questioning your competence. Very wise to be on top of things."

The news that followed was Delgado's worst nightmare come true.

"This is Adam Rennie with this morning's headlines on Sky News."

"London was left reeling after five terrorist bomb blasts which killed over seventy people yesterday. The SNLA and WRA have both claimed responsibility."

"Just after 2pm yesterday, bombs ripped through the Tower of London, Madame Tussaud's and Harrods which were packed with foreign tourists. It was here that all the fatalities occurred. In addition, over 200 people were injured, of whom 34 are in intensive care."

"The Metropolitan Police and City of London Police have set up a combined helpline for people concerned about relatives. It is 0845 000 5018."

"This followed two bomb blasts earlier in the day. One was in the City of London and knocked out broadband communications for the Stock Exchange and the leading merchant banks, bringing the day's trading to an unplanned end."

"The other blast was at the Air Traffic Control centre at Heathrow Airport, which resulted in all flights to and from Heathrow being suspended. Air Traffic Control coverage has now been provided by using RAF Northolt, but its capacity is little more than half that of Heathrow. It is estimated that Heathrow's Air Traffic Control facility will not be restored for another six months."

"The concern for the Government is the impact on the economy. Financial services and tourism are major contributors to the exchequer. The disabling of the broadband communications for the City of London is estimated to have cost £2bn on one day alone. The closure of Heathrow is believed to have cost another £1.5bn. There are also reports from hotels of cancellations of travel plans by potential visitors to the United Kingdom following today's bombings."

Delgado switched the television of and walked into the hallway of his villa. He phoned Ed Villiers to get an update on what has happening. An emergency Cabinet meeting seemed inevitable.

"Chancellor of the Exchequer's Office" replied the receptionist.

"Is the Chancellor there? Tell him it's the Prime Minister and it's very urgent" said Delgado.

15 August 2017
Cabinet Room
10 Downing Street
London

A full Cabinet meeting in August was unprecedented, but Delgado considered there was a national emergency which warranted cutting short people's holidays. Losses to the economy from the damage to the City of London's broadband facilities and to Heathrow Airport's Air Traffic Control were now in the region of £10bn. On top of that, the bombings of the Tower of London, Madame Tussaud's and Harrods, which had now claimed the lives of nearly 90 victims, had resulted in a rash of cancellations of hotel bookings by overseas tourists.

The final straw had been the threat by Chevron and Texaco to pull out of the United Kingdom because of the perceived threat to the safety of their staff. This had been precipitated by the sudden withdrawal of Castle Security following the WRA coach bombing at Cardigan just over a week earlier which had killed twelve security guards.

Delgado called the meeting to order.

"I am sorry that it's been necessary to interrupt your holiday plans, but the severity of the situation has made it necessary to recall the Cabinet. If you must know, I've cut short my holiday to be here."

"The SNLA and WRA terrorist campaign has entered a new and threatening phase. They have now moved beyond threatening life and limb of innocent civilians. They are now openly targeting Britain's economy."

"During the course of this year, we have seen attacks on the Wester Ross oil terminal, the Channel Tunnel, the Dartford Crossing and, most recently on the City of London and Heathrow. In addition, the SNLA and WRA are now targeting the country's tourist industry, as shown by the attacks on the Tower of London, Madame Tussauds and Harrods last week."

"I do not need to spell out the impact on the country's economy. Already, we've had Chevron and Texaco threatening to pull out. Last week's bombs in the City and at Heathrow have cost the country £10 billion alone. And I understand that hoteliers across the country have reported mass cancellations of bookings by overseas visitors. Ed, can you spell out the potential loss of revenue and the consequences."

The Chancellor of the Exchequer laid out a sheath of papers in front of him and started to speak.

"Thank you Prime Minister. Ladies and gentlemen, the withdrawal of Chevron and Texaco could cut oil production by almost two-thirds. They are two of the world's largest oil producers and there is no one who could step in and make up the difference. This could cost the economy between £25 billion and £30 billion a year in lost income."

"The Prime Minister has outlined the cost of last week's attacks on the City of London and Heathrow Airport. If there are further attacks on the country's infrastructure, the economy could face an additional annual loss of income amounting to £12bn."

"Lastly, the Treasury has calculated that the loss to the economy from cancelled visits from abroad has cost the economy overall another £4bn. If there are further terrorist atrocities, this figure could grow."

"The consequence of such losses for the economy are serious. We were planning to go to the country next year and, under normal circumstances, we would have been able to offer tax cuts. That will not be possible. Furthermore, we may have to consider cuts to public expenditure. Hardly the sort of approach we would want in an election year."

Deborah Pearson, the Home Secretary, was next to speak. "All we need to do is to increase the size of the police and put more resources into the National Anti-Terror Squad, and back it up with CCTV coverage at all sensitive installations. On top of that, we should have specially-trained police teams guarding places like oil terminals."

"Have you costed this Deborah?" asked Villiers. "If I recall, the police budget is running at record levels."

Cheryl Parkinson, Secretary of State for Trade and Enterprise followed up Villiers' point. "Deborah, have you forgotten that there are record numbers of police, all armed and with draconian powers of arrest? We've got internment without trial and require employers to carry out CRB and security checks on new staff. And they're still unable to protect the public. I think some scrutiny of the police and MI5 might be in order before giving them extra resources."

Pearson gave the Secretary of State for Trade and Enterprise an angry glare.

Jason Steer, the Defence Secretary then joined the conversation. "May I suggest as an alternative that we use the armed forces to assist the police on counter-terror duties? We've got some spare capacity."

"That is a preposterous idea Jason" replied Parkinson. "That will hardly give the business community a vote of confidence in the country's ability to protect its citizens."

Delgado rapped his gavel on the desk to call for order. "Alright, I think that's enough. We'll get nowhere if we all start blaming each other."

"We need to focus on the main issue. Doing nothing is not an option. The country will start leaking money like a sieve and we'll be forced into unpopular decisions in advance of an election. Do you really want Labour to come back? Squabble like children and that's what will happen."

"Deborah, you are right to say that we need more police to maintain order and I'm pleased to see you haven't suggested more powers. But if I give you the money, I want to see more value for money from them. Some of them seem to like appearing on TV more than actually going out after the bad guys. Can you start an audit of the police's effectiveness in counter-terror operations and report back to me in three months."

"Jason, I like the idea of using the armed forces, but only up to a limit. Cheryl's got a valid point—visitors to the United Kingdom will be put off by seeing soldiers in uniform patrolling the streets. However, there's no reasons why regular soldiers cannot guard vital installations. Can you prepare a plan and bring it back to Cabinet when we resume next month."

"Any other business?" added Delgado.

Dominic Collins, the Attorney-General, indicated he had.

"Some good news on the legal front, Prime Minister. The defendants responsible for the Royal Ascot and Warrington bombings last year were all found guilty of murder three weeks ago and sentenced to death. They've all appealed, but the appeals will be heard by Mr Justice Oldham and Mr Justice Woolgar at the end of next month." Both judges were regarded as highly conservative and unlikely to show any leniency.

"At least there's some good news on the horizon" replied the Prime Minister.

7 September 2017
Richmond
Surrey

The MAN delivery lorry in the livery of John Smith's crossed Kew Bridge for the final leg of its journey. On board were two large orders for draught beer for delivery to London Welsh Rugby Club and London Scottish Rugby Club. The new rugby season would be starting in two days time and both clubs anticipated large numbers of players and supporters turning up, all seeking liquid refreshment.

At the wheel of the lorry was Mick Green, a burly, shaven-headed East Ender 40 years old. He had worked as a driver for most of his working life and had been employed by John Smith's for the past ten years.

Alongside Green was the driver's mate, Craig Short, another East Londoner, some 15 years younger and who had joined after a spell in the Army. He was slimmer than Green but looked fit and muscular from his work and from regular use of a gym.

"Next right Mick" said Short as they approached the junction between Kew Road and Mortlake Road. "London Welsh's about a mile down on the right hand side."

On the dashboard of the lorry was a copy of the *Sun*. The headline story was on the unsuccessful appeal by the five suspected SNLA terrorists convicted of the Royal Ascot bombing a year earlier. Both men had voiced their approval of the fact the five suspects now faced the gallows.

Five minutes later, the lorry pulled up at London Welsh where they were greeted by the bar steward.

"Glad to see you boys arrived on time" said the steward. "We've got a big party here on Saturday. First game of the season."

"Where do you want the beer to go mate?" asked Green.

"In the cellar" replied the steward. "We'll open the hatch for you."

Over the next half hour, Green and Short unloaded 100 kegs of beer and, with the assistance of the steward and club volunteers, moved them into the cellar.

After the steward signed for their delivery, Green and Short headed off to London Scottish Rugby Club, which was barely half a mile round the block.

London Scottish shared the Richmond Athletic Ground with Richmond Rugby Club, an arrangement which had been in place for over a hundred years. One end of the clubhouse was occupied by Richmond. The eastern end was occupied by London Scottish, and that is where Green and Short found the London Scottish bar steward.

"We've got your order for beer, mate" said Green. "Where do you want it to go?"

"I'll open up the cellar for you laddies" replied the steward.

Green and Short then unloaded another 100 kegs of beer which went into the cellar, all ready for the start of season function which was advertised all over the clubhouse.

After the steward signed for delivery, Green and Short got back into their lorry for the return journey to Romford.

On their return to the depot, Short said that he wanted to call his girlfriend.

"Okay Craig" said Green. But be quick. The guvnor will wanna see our delivery records before he goes tonight. And he usually leaves about now."

"Ta Mick" replied the younger man.

Short headed to a secluded spot round the back of the depot to make his call. Only that he did not call his girlfriend. He was calling Glenn Nicholls, the Deputy Commander of the English Volunteer Force to report back on the placing of bombs disguised as beer kegs at London Scottish and London Welsh Rugby Clubs. The EVF had been formed six months earlier but, apart from a large demonstration in London on St George's Day, little had been heard about them. But they had recruited volunteers and given them training and explosives, so there was little doubt about their lethal intent.

"Glenn, is that you?"

"Yeah, how did it go Craig?"

"Sweet as a nut. The kegs are in the cellars below the main bars at both London Scottish and London Welsh. When they go off, they'll put both fucking clubs into orbit, along with the Jock and Taff scum who drink there."

"Good work Craig" replied Nicholls. "Only thing to remember is that we're not aiming for loss of life at this stage. We're going to detonate them overnight. The police will probably think local kids did it. But it will send a message out to the Jocks and Taffs that England's fighting back."

8 September 2017
Richmond
Surrey

Chief Inspector Donna Atkinson looked up at the clock in her office. It was 2:45am and nothing appeared to be happening. She had used the quiet period to catch up on paperwork.

The reform of the licensing laws seven years earlier had been a godsend for the police who beforehand had faced three nights of mayhem between Thursday and Saturday when the pubs shut at 1am, followed by the nightclubs two hours later, disgorging drunk and often aggressive customers onto the streets in search of transport home. However, many people thought the Government had gone too far the other way and were unfairly penalising low-income groups and young people. In parts of London, cheap contraband booze had become a problem, as had unlicensed bars, many of which were fronts for organised crime. There had been stories that the SNLA and WRA had muscled in on the trade. But this was not a problem for Richmond.

Chief Inspector Atkinson was alerted by a knock on the door.

"Come in" she said. It was Inspector Matt Lawrence.

"Ma'am, we've just had reports of fires at the Athletic Ground and Old Deer Park. The Response Team's on the way but there's only one car available. Can we get help from Hounslow, Kingston or Wandsworth?"

"I'll try Matt. By the way, do you mean the rugby grounds?"

"Yes Ma'am" replied Lawrence.

By 8am, the Chairmen of London Scottish, London Welsh and Richmond rugby clubs were surveying the burnt-out remains of what had been their clubhouses for over a century. Not only had the bars and changing rooms been burnt down, but all three clubs had lost priceless and irreplaceable memorabilia.

The three men then headed to Richmond Police Station for a meeting with the Borough Commander, Chief Superintendent Mike Barnes.

Barnes was the first to speak. "Gentlemen, many thanks for coming out here so early. I am really sorry to learn what happened last night but, at the moment, we've got no idea how the two blazes started. Our forensic teams are down there and, once we know a bit more, we'll let you know."

"The first thing I would like to ask is could the fires have started accidentally? I know it would be an unfortunate coincidence but all it takes is for someone to be a bit careless, like not turning a cooker off or worn electrics. I've seen it happen before."

"Absolutely not" replied London Scottish Chairman Norrie Macpherson. "I spoke to our bar steward and he assured me he made a thorough check of the clubhouse before locking up last night. We've had Jimmy in this job for twenty years now—I would trust him with my life."

"I bet it's kids mucking about" said Richmond Chairman Charles Beevor.

"Have any of you had any problems with vandalism and anti-social behaviour before" asked Barnes. "From our reports, we don't appear to have heard anything previously. What's more, they're now back at school"

"Do you think it's connected in anyway to the troubles in Scotland and Wales?" asked London Welsh Chairman Gerald Pugh. "I've head that some English nationalist group is talking about seeking revenge on us and the Scots for what the WRA and SNLA have done."

Before Barnes could reply, there was a knock at the door of his office. It was Chief Inspector Atkinson.

"Sir, have you got a minute?"

"Is it urgent Donna?" replied Barnes. "I'm rather tied up at the moment."

"Yes it is sir" replied the Chief Inspector. "We've got a firm lead on the arson attacks at the Athletic Ground and Old Deer Park. An organisation called the English Volunteer Force has claimed responsibility."

The same day
MI5 Headquarters
Millbank
London

"The DG wishes to see you immediately Richard."

Richard Donovan found Shazia Hussein, PA to the MI5 Director-General Nicola Martin, on the other end of the line.

"Any idea why Nicola wants to see me Shaz?" asked Donovan. There had been no significant SNLA or WRA activity since the London bombings back in August.

"Sorry Richard, no idea" replied the PA. "Guess you'll just have to find out."

Donovan walked through to the Director-General's office where she was seated behind a large oak desk.

"Thanks for coming in Richard, I'm afraid I'm going to be adding to your work."

"What's happened Nicola?"

"Have you heard of the English Volunteer Force Richard?" asked Martin.

"No, not yet. What have they supposed to have done?"

"They burned down London Scottish and London Welsh rugby clubs with incendiary bombs last night. A message to Reuters states this is the start of the 'fightback against Scotland and Wales'."

Donovan was sceptical about the threat posed by the EVF. "Nicola, it sounds like common or garden arson. The sort of things bored kids do over the summer holiday. There's been a few instances of petty vandalism directed against anything associated with Scotland or Wales but nothing more. One incident was claimed by the 'English Defence Army' but it comprised nothing more than a gang of yobs from South London. I think this should be left to the police."

"Richard, this incident is far more serious than anti-social behaviour" replied Martin. "The police forensic team that's gone in were horrified by the professionalism of the guys responsible. Fuel air devices were used and were primed to be detonated by mobile phone. They reckon whoever made the bombs had expertise."

"Was anyone killed or injured?" asked Donovan.

"Fortunately, not on this occasion" replied Martin. But the English Volunteer Force made it clear that this was a first warning and that next time they won't hesitate to kill. Can you prepare me an intelligence report on the English Volunteer Force and try and insert someone inside."

"I'll aim to get a report to you by the end of the month. Is that okay? You realise we have hardly any human intelligence on them to start, so I'll be starting with a clean sheet."

"End of the month is okay Richard" replied the Director-General. "But we need to get cracking. If the English Volunteer Force carry out what they've threatened, we'll have a full-scale civil war on our hands. It'll make what happened in Northern Ireland in the 1970s and 1980s look like a tea party."

Chapter 11

27 October 2017
Department for Justice
Petty France
London

During the past month, the Department for Justice had been swamped by letters, e-mails and petitions from both the United Kingdom and other parts of the world calling for the Attorney-General to commute the death sentences passed on eight defendants who had been found guilty of murder following two terrorist incidents in June 2016. The first had claimed the lives of ten soldiers from the Mercian Regiment at Thelwall Barracks, Warrington, the second had claimed the lives of thirty nine racegoers at Royal Ascot and a waitress.

It was not just members of the public who had written to appeal for clemency. The Presidents of Argentina, Brazil, France, Germany, Italy, Poland, Russia, South Africa and the European Union, the King of Spain and the Prime Ministers of Australia and New Zealand had all appealed for commutation of the death sentences, as had petitions signed by thirty US senators and 75 members of the House of Representatives. Numerous celebrities including actors, sportsmen and women and rock and pop stars had also appealed.

The eight defendants, Robert Allan, Kevin Banahan, Carol Davies, James Eadie, Glen McFarlane, Glyn Maddock, Rory Shepherd and Martyn Thomas, had appealed to the Court of Appeal against their convictions the previous month, but these had been unsuccessful. Their last recourse to avoid the gallows was to appeal to the Attorney-General for commutation.

Many people had serious doubts about the guilt of the seven men and one woman facing execution. Although none of them could be regarded as persons of good character and several of them had expressed sympathy for the SNLA and WRA, the evidence linking them to the Warrington and Ascot bombings was circumstantial at best. There was disquiet about the alleged methods the police had used to extract confessions from the defendants and of the way the trials had been conducted, in particular, the intimidation of the defence solicitors by both the trial judges and the prosecution. It seemed that the British Establishment had made up its mind that the defendants had to be found guilty to be an example to others and to regain public confidence that it was winning the war against the SNLA and WRA.

Department for Justice had a Review Team in place to consider final appeals to the Attorney-General against capital sentences, and they had spent the past week preparing a submission for the Attorney-General's attention. The Head of the Team, Samantha Honeyman, had sent the submission to the Attorney-General the previous day, using the secure e-mail system for highly-classified documents. It was marked SECRET.

Matthew Elkington, Principal Private Secretary to the Attorney-General, brought in a paper copy of the Capital Sentences Review Team in its sealed envelope and passed it to Dominic Collins.

"Attorney-General, here is the review report on the appeal by the Warrington and Ascot bombers."

"Thank you Matthew" said Collins as he took the envelope and opened it.

An hour later, a visibly angry Collins was not far from boiling point. The Capital Sentences Review Team had recommended commuting the death sentence in all eight cases. They felt that the possibility of a miscarriage of justice was high, noting that there was limited evidence to link the defendants to the two bombings, that four of the eight defendants had seemingly credible alibis and that new evidence was emerging that linked the bombings to active SNLA and WRA cells. The submissions also referred back to the precedents of the Guildford Four and Birmingham Six from the 1970s and the Tottenham Three from the 1980s, where defendants convicted of murder and sentenced to life imprisonment had subsequently been cleared and released after the discovery of new evidence.

For Collins, the issue was a no-brainer. The SNLA and WRA were starting to run rings round the Government and needed to be stopped by whatever means possible. For Collins, the trouble with the Civil Service was that there were too many wet liberals who were all too prepared to listen to the other chap's point of view and shied away from tough action when it was needed.

Collins reached for his telephone and rang his Principal Private Secretary.

"Matthew, can you ask Samantha Honeyman to come up. Now."

Two minutes later, the Head of the Capital Sentences Review Team was sitting opposite the Attorney-General. She was 40 years old, a brunette and not bad-looking, and had risen through the fast stream entrance scheme.

"Samantha" started the Attorney-General, "I'm not at all pleased with the recommendation you've put up to me on the defendants from the Warrington and Ascot trials. I've made it clear in the past that the Capital Sentences Review Team makes its judgements in accordance with the guidance on grounds for commutation. In serious murders and terrorist cases, there are expected to be none. What you have put up effectively accuses this country of running kangaroo courts. I expect better from my officials."

"Attorney-General, this is hardly a routine cut-and-dried case" replied Honeyman. "There are genuine doubts about the guilt of the eight defendants in these two cases. Many people consider the case against them to be circumstantial at best. There's new evidence emerging which points to active service units from the SNLA and WRA. To many people, these guys appear to be guilty of nothing more than being in the wrong place at the wrong time."

Honeyman continued. "I know it's not my place to comment on the conduct of the trials and I've reflected that in my submission. But I think it's relevant to point out that the Council of Europe and the United Nations have both been critical of the conduct of the trials and . . . ."

"I will not be lectured to on judicial propriety by a bunch of limp-wristed liberals and corrupt failed states" shouted Collins as he cut Honeyman short. "We left the EU precisely to get away from meddling busybodies who want to stick their noses in our affairs. I expected better of you Samantha."

"Attorney-General" cried an increasingly tremulous Honeyman "there have also been pleas for clemency from over twenty world leaders. I think it is relevant . . . ."

"Samantha, do I make myself clear" roared Collins. "Those men and women were tried and found guilty by due process of law. There is no reason why we should show any leniency to them, after what they did. And I don't care what the Presidents of France, Germany or anywhere else for that matter think. Her Majesty's Government rules the United Kingdom, not them."

30 October 2017
Sky News

"This is Sara Ratcliffe with this evening's headlines on Sky News."

"There have been violent demonstrations across the United Kingdom today following this morning's execution of eight suspected SNLA and WRA terrorists for the fatal bombings at Warrington and Royal Ascot last year. For the past two days, there had been peaceful vigils outside the prisons at Belmarsh, Holloway, Strangeways and Wandsworth where the eight condemned prisoners were being held. However, as soon as the announcement that the executions had taken place, the mood turned ugly. Bricks and bottles were thrown at police officers as scuffles broke out, and a total of sixty people were arrested."

"There were also disturbances reported in Scotland and Wales. Anti-English demonstrations took place in Cardiff, Edinburgh and Glasgow, while English-owned businesses were damaged in Aberdeen and Wrexham.

Police are currently investigating whether the extreme left-wing Socialist Alliance played a role in inciting the disturbances and is considering whether charges should be laid."

"The United Kingdom's decision to execute the eight suspected terrorists was condemned by the European Union, the Presidents of France, Russia and South Africa, the Chancellor of Germany and the Prime Ministers of Italy, the Netherlands, Spain and Sweden, all of whom had appealed for clemency. The Prime Ministers of Australia and New Zealand expressed their disappointment that the seven men and one woman had been hanged."

"It is difficult to gauge the impact that today's executions will have for the United Kingdom. However, there are fears that the numbers of countries refusing to co-operate with the United Kingdom on judicial matters, such as the extradition of terrorist suspects may grow. Already, the European Union has refused to extradite SNLA and WRA suspects and there is now pressure for Australia, Canada, New Zealand and South Africa to follow."

14 November 2017
The Old Bailey
London

The Old Bailey was London's Central Criminal Court, and had been ever since it had been built on the site of the former Newgate Prison over a century earlier. In Court Number 1, the trial of the so-called 'Dalston Ten' was in progress.

Two months earlier, the National Anti-Terror Squad had arrested eight men and two women at an address in Dalston on charges of murder, attempted murder, conspiracy to murder and membership of proscribed organisation after several months of surveillance by MI5. During a search of the house, NATS officers had found stocks of plastic explosives, detonators, rifles, ammunition, building plans, maps showing strategic targets like bridges, tunnels, road and railway junctions, electricity sub-stations, gas storage facilities, sewage farms and broadband junction boxes, and biographies of businessmen, military leaders, senior policemen and leading politicians. For MI5 and NATS, it represented a massive coup in the fight against the two terrorist organisations as it effectively crippled their London-based operations.

The Crown was being represented by Chris Morrison QC, who was recognised as one of the leading barristers in the country. His services came at a price but the Crown Prosecution Service considered it worthwhile if it secured convictions. The previous day, he had finished his presentation of the prosecution case.

The defence counsel was Justin Hemingway. In his early 50s, Hemingway was still as slim as he was in his 20s and stood over six feet tall. He had long hair down to his shoulders which made him look more like an ageing rock star than one of the country's leading counsels. But, like Morrison, Hemingway was recognised as one of the most effective briefs in the country.

Hemingway was not popular with many of the country's political establishment. He was a master of process and procedure and had first come to notice nearly 20 years earlier when the Labour government of the day had introduced the Human Rights Act. His roll-call of clients had included gangsters, drug traffickers, celebrities and Al-Q'aida terrorists, and the high rate of acquittals he had achieved had earned him the nickname of 'Mr Loophole'. The SNLA and WRA, now awash with cash earned through drugs, contraband alcohol and cigarettes, prostitution, fake designer clothes and DVDs, credit card scams and income raised in the USA by Caledonian Aid and Cambrian Aid, were able to hire Hemingway to defend their members.

Hemingway was fully aware that the Government's decision to allow the execution of the Warrington Three and the Ascot Five two weeks earlier had given the defence a strong hand. He knew that the recent executions of men and women widely believed to be innocent would make the jury think hard whether they were making the right decision in delivering a guilty verdict.

Hemingway also knew how to play dirty if he looked likely to lose a verdict. The Government had tightened the rules of court in favour of the prosecution under the Criminal Law Act, which made it easier for the prosecution to withhold evidence. But that was an obstacle easily overcome. He would despatch one of his attractive female junior solicitors to inveigle her way into the prosecution's offices, where she would use her camera phone to record confidential prosecution documents. Hemingway also obtained information of the whereabouts of prosecution witnesses and had passed this to friends and relatives of defendants. Where he could not secure an acquittal on a technicality, he had managed to cause trials to collapse through prosecution witnesses absconding or changing their story.

Hemingway had already questioned the defence witnesses earlier that morning. He was building a case on the fact that the guns found had been left by previous residents who had been involved in the drugs trade, and that the plastic explosives were used by one of the defendants as tools for his job.

"May I call Chief Inspector Toby Headford" said Hemingway.

Hemingway was surprised when a slim, good looking young man in his early 30s took the stand. Most Chief Inspectors in "sharp end" operations were usually about ten years older, hard-faced and built like rugby forwards.

"Chief Inspector Headford, I understand you were the officer in charge of the operation at 53 Malvern Road, Dalston on 6 September which resulted in the arrests of my clients. Is that right?"

"Yes sir, that is right" replied Headford.

"You have already described to this court the circumstances which led to that raid and of what you and your officers found when you searched the premises. Can you say with any authority how long you think the guns you found had been left on the premises?"

"I have no idea sir" replied the Chief Inspector.

Hemingway continued. "No idea Chief Inspector Headford? For an officer of your rank, don't you think that's a bit sloppy? Particularly as the police had evidence that prior to my clients taking up residence there, 53 Malvern Road had been occupied by drug dealers who were well-known to them. Didn't it occur to you that the guns might have been left there by previous residents as they fled to avoid arrest?"

"I very much doubt it sir" replied Headford. "For a start, the weapons we found were M16 rifles. An American make and which have been found on SNLA and WRA members arrested elsewhere in the country. Drug dealers tend to go for AK-47s or Uzis."

"May I next turn to the stock of Semtex your officers found. Did you find anything unusual in the way it was stored?"

"It was stored in the shed in the back garden. A lot of care had been taken to ensure it did not deteriorate."

"Chief Inspector, my client, Mr Griffiths, works as a demolition contractor. What are the main tools of his trade?" asked Hemingway.

"Explosives, I guess" replied Headford.

"Exactly, Chief Inspector Headford. Yet you appear to have jumped to the conclusion that my client was a terrorist because he was in possession of tools for his job."

Hemingway then turned to the question of the maps found at 53 Malvern Road.

"Chief Inspector Headford, your officers found maps and diagrams of road and rail junctions and utility installations at 53 Malvern Road."

"Yes sir" replied Headford.

"Did it occur to you that my clients, Mr Gunn, who is studying to become a civil engineer and Mr Laird, who is a maintenance engineer for Veolia, had good reason to have those maps and diagrams in their possession?"

"Sir, we had good reason to raid those premises. They had been under surveillance for three months and there was good reason to believe that they were being used for terrorist activity."

"And finally, Chief Inspector, you are telling me that the biographies you found of leading businessmen, politicians and public officials was evidence that my client, Ms Price, was plotting to murder them."

"Sir" replied Headford, "don't you think it see rather suspicious if you were to find in a house a stock of plastic explosives, guns, diagrams of road and rail communication and utility installations, and details of political and business leaders? Not the normal stuff you would expect to find?"

"I was just about to add that my client, Ms Price, is studying for her PhD in modern political history" added Hemingway.

"Chief Inspector Headford" said Hemingway, summing up, "I don't doubt for a minute that you and your officers have a difficult job to do. But on this occasion, I think you and your officers allowed their enthusiasm to run away with them and have added two and two and arrived at seven and a half. To the untrained eye, finding a combination of plastic explosives, guns, maps, diagrams and biographies of important people might look very suspicious. But I put it to you that you and your officers did not bother to investigate my clients' occupations before you charged in and arrested them."

It was a dejected Chief Inspector Headford who left the witness box. He had been warned about Hemingway, yet had been powerless to prevent him undermining the prosecution case.

19 December 2017
Sky News

"This is Sara Ratcliffe with this evening's headlines on Sky News."

"There were scenes of jubilation outside the High Court today after the Crown's appeal against the acquittal of ten suspected SNLA and WRA terrorists arrested in North London in September was unsuccessful. The ten men and women, who had faced possible death sentences, are now free."

"The case marked another triumph for defence solicitor Justin Hemingway, who took his place with the freed defendants when they held a press conference after the decision was announced."

The same day
Valance Way
Langdon Hills
Basildon, Essex

The General Council of the English Volunteer Force was gathered in the lounge of Barry Pickett, one of the Council members. Alongside Pickett were the other five members, Phil Barden, the Chairman, Glenn Nicholls, the Deputy Chairman, Mark Stubbs, Darren Finnerty and Alan Wilkinson. They had just heard the news about the acquittal of the Dalston Ten.

The EVF had come to notice nationally three months earlier when they burned down London Scottish and London Welsh rugby clubs. Since then, they had engaged in relatively low-level activity. The London Scottish Territorial Army Regiment headquarters in Victoria had been badly damaged in an arson attack, as had the Caledonian Club near Hyde Park Corner and two Welsh churches in London. There had been a campaign of intimidation against known sympathisers with the nationalist cause living in London and one, Neil McDonald, had been badly injured when his car crashed after being tampered with. But, to-date, the EVF had not been responsible for any deaths. That was about to change.

It was Phil Barden who called the meeting to attention.

"Gentlemen, you saw today's news. Once again, the SNLA and WRA have made monkeys of our so-called criminal justice system and are free to continue with their campaign of murder and violence against the English. And what have we done in return? Burn down a few meeting places."

"No gentlemen, now is the time that we take the fight directly to the Scots and the Welsh. Not just the SNLA and the WRA. But also those who give them aid and comfort and the English traitors who help their cause. It will be their turn to bury their dead. Glenn, I believe you've got something to say about possible targets."

"Yes Phil. We've identified two potential targets in London. Both are pubs. One is the Rob Roy, near Paddington Station. It is the main Scottish pub in London and loads of the Jocks go there. The other is the Famous Three Kings in Kensington, which is near West Kensington Tube. This is the main Welsh pub for London."

"Before anyone thinks they are non-military targets, I've found out that both pubs have been carrying out collections for the SNLA and the WRA. Also, on Thursday night, they're both holding big pre-Christmas parties and will be celebrating the acquittal of the Dalston Ten. There's good reason to believe that both pubs will be packed with SNLA and WRA. Mark, I believe you've been planning something."

Nicholls handed over to Stubbs, a burly, thickset man in his early 40s.

"We've already done some preliminary reconnaissance of the two pubs" said Stubbs. "Not without a great deal of personal risk. These days, the boozers at the Rob Roy are nearly all Jocks and those at the Three Kings are nearly all Taffs. Hardly any English go there anymore cos they'll probably get beaten up. They've got security goons on the door and it's an even bet they're SNLA and WRA."

"Things is, on Thursday, a lot of them will have their guard down, particularly once they've got a few pints of beer down their neck. It should be easier to get in. Only thing is that most of us will stick out like a bacon roll at a barmitzvah."

"How do you plan to get round that Mark?" asked Wilkinson.

"We've got some female recruits" replied Stubbs. "Rather attractive too. No one's going to stop them going in. Also, the Jocks and Taffs will all be too busy staring at their tits to pay any attention to what they're doing."

"A couple of our lads in South-West London are going to build the bombs. Both are former Army bomb-disposal guys. Another of our lads, who is an electronics student, will prepare the detonators, which will be triggered by mobile phone. The bombs will be light enough to be carried in a woman's handbag. The girls we've recruited will go into the Rob Roy and the Famous Three Kings on Thursday night. One will distract the punters while the other will plant the bombs. After leaving, they will key in the code on their mobiles and the rest will be history."

"As will a load of Jocks and Taffs hopefully" added Finnerty.

21 December 2017
Central Line
London

Shanelle Bryan, Rachel Emerson, Heidi Luff and Danielle Temple looked indistinguishable from other girls in their late teens or early 20s out for the night. The week before Christmas was always busy for the night-time economy and the Central line was full of young people out on the town.

All four girls were very attractive and, dressed in miniskirts and low-cut tops and wearing high-heeled shoes or boots, were getting a lot of admiring glances from male passengers. Few would have guessed they were on a deadly mission on behalf of the EVF.

At Notting Hill Gate, the girls all disembarked from the Central Line train. At this point, they were going to split up. Bryan and Luff would be taking the Circle Line to Paddington, then heading for the Rob Roy. Emerson and Temple were taking the train in the opposite direction to Gloucester Road, where they would change for West Kensington and then walk to the Famous Three Kings.

As they parted company, they hugged each other and said "Good luck girls. Remember, it's for England."

The same evening, 8pm
The Rob Roy
Sale Place
Paddington
London

Glen Alexander and Ross Burns could not believe their eyes as Shanelle Bryan and Heidi Luff walked into the Rob Roy.

146

"Jesus Christ Ross, you seen those two babes who've just walked in?" said Alexander.

"Aye" replied Burns. "But I bet they've got fellas in tow. Don't think we'll get anywhere with them."

Alexander was more optimistic, probably the result of the copious amounts of Tennants Extra he'd been drinking. "Worth trying though. You know what they say—nothing ventured nothing gained."

The Rob Roy was already heaving with customers, many of whom were having a final celebration in London before travelling home to Scotland for Christmas. A double cause for celebration was the acquittal of the 'Dalston Ten' two days earlier. There was a rumour that Bruce Gunn, one of the acquitted defendants, was going to be present that night.

Bryan and Luff made their way to the bar with some difficulty through the crowds, where Bryan bought two Bacardi Breezers. As they moved away, Alexander made his move.

"How yer lasses doing? Last night before travelling home?"

Bryan replied "Yeah, we're travelling home alright? To Wembley."

"You're English then?" asked Alexander. "Strange you should come to the Rob Roy. You know it's London's main Scottish pub?"

"Actually, we didn't" replied Luff. "But it's convenient for us. We're going clubbing later."

"By the name, what's your name?" asked Alexander. "Mine's Glen. This is my mate Ross" pointing to Burns.

"Heidi. And my mate's name is Shanelle. By the way, Glen, what are you and your mate doing over Christmas?"

"Afraid we're both back in Scotland" replied Alexander. "I've got to go to Aberdeen, Ross's from Dundee."

"A long way to go then?" said Bryan. "Bet it's cold up there."

"Shanelle, Heidi, would you like to join me and Ross for a dance?" asked Alexander.

"Yeah, but the only problem is that we don't want to leave our bags unguarded. Mine got nicked in a pub last year" said Heidi.

Burnside saw there was space under a table at the edge of the dance floor. "Ladies, put your bags there. They should be safe."

Jesus Christ, thought Bryan. Those pissed Jocks are making it easier for us already.

Ten minutes later
The Famous Three Kings
North End Road
Kensington
London

At the same time as Heidi Luff and Glen Alexander went for a dance in the Rob Roy, Rachel Emerson and Danielle Temple walked into the Famous Three Kings.

Like the Rob Roy, it was crowded with punters who were having a final celebration in London before travelling home for Christmas.

At the bar, Temple ordered a Bacardi and Coke for herself and a glass of Chardonnay for Emerson. When the barman called out "that will be six pounds fifty love", Temple pulled the gambit that had earned her free drinks before.

"I'm awfully sorry, I seem to have left my purse at home. Guess you don't take credit cards?"

"Afraid not, love" replied the barman.

At this point, Gareth Ellison, a North Walian from Rhyl, stepped in and offered to buy the girls a round.

"I'm really grateful for you stepping in and helping me out" said Temple. "By the way, what's your name?"

"Gareth. And this is my mate Paul" pointing to Paul Owen. "How about you?"

"Danielle. And this is Rachel."

"I take it you girls are English" asked Owen.

"Yeah, from Acton" replied Emerson. "Guess you're surprised to see us here."

"You could say that" said Ellison. "This pub's the main Welsh drinking hole for London. The English aren't normally welcome here."

"But we'll make an exception for you" said Owen.

"Girls, fancy joining me and Paul for a dance?" asked Ellison.

"We'd love to" replied Emerson. "But we're worried about leaving our bags."

"You won't need to worry about them being nicked here Rachel" said Ellison. "The Welsh are honest people."

"Put them over there" said Owen, pointing to underneath a table near the dance floor. "They'll be safe."

By 9:30pm, both the Rob Roy and the Famous Three Kings had filled to near bursting point. Most of the customers had already threequarters the way to being drunk. The four girls explained to the men they had met that they were leaving to go nightclubbing in Central London and thanked the men they had met for their company. No one in the demob-happy crowds noticed that, in both cases, the girls had left one handbag behind.

Heidi Luff and Shanelle Bryan were walking up Edgware Road when Luff removed a mobile phone from her handbag and dialled in a preset number. Barely a second later, there was the muffled sound of an explosion. For Luff, it was personal. Her brother, Darren, a corporal in the Rifles, had been shot dead on patrol in Glasgow the previous year. Revenge was sweet.

At the same time, Rachel Emerson and Danielle Temple were walking towards Earls Court Underground Station. They heard a low rumble in the distance.

"Looks like Shanelle and Heidi have done their job" said Emerson. "Our turn now Danni."

Temple repeated the same procedure that Luff had done barely a minute earlier. Within seconds, they heard a distant boom.

22 December 2017
Sky News

"This is Adam Rennie with this morning's headlines on Sky News."

"The death toll in last night's bombing attacks on two West London pubs has now risen to twenty five. Just after half past nine last night, bombs exploded in the Rob Roy at Paddington and the Famous Three Kings at West Kensington, both of which were packed with pre-Christmas revellers. The English Volunteer Force has claimed responsibility and has stated that 'further bombings against Scottish and Welsh targets will continue until the SNLA and WRA cease their terrorist campaign against England'."

"Little has been known about the EVF and, up to now, their activities have focused primarily on attacks on property. Three months ago, they were responsible for arson attacks which gutted London Scottish and London Welsh rugby clubs. But this is the first incident involving the EVF which has cost lives."

"It is believed that the Rob Roy and Famous Three Kings were targeted because they were heavily used by Scottish and Welsh expatriates."

"The bombings were condemned by the Prime Minister, by the Labour Party leader Iain Turner and by the Liberal Democrat leader Julia Goldwater. The Commissioner of the Metropolitan Police issued a statement saying that all efforts would be made to bring the perpetrators to justice."

"Fears that last night's attacks might lead to an escalation of the troubles intensified after the SNLA and the WRA issued a joint statement promising that the deaths last night would be avenged."

CHAPTER 12

1 January 2018, 6am
A former gas rig off the Dutch coast

"Good morning, this is Nicky Weaver on Radio Free Britain, 127.5 FM. The alternative music station, playing the music the mainstream stations don't want to know about. No adverts, no game shows, no bullshit, just unbroken rock music.

To kick off the breakfast show this morning, here is "Warchild" by Full Metal Jacket."

With that announcement, Europe's newest radio station hit the airwaves.

Radio Free Britain promised to be an alternative to the commercial radio stations which dominated the airwaves in the United Kingdom, particularly after the break-up of the BBC and the selling off of its stations the previous year. The mainstream stations focused their efforts on either bland commercial pop music or antiseptic adult-orientated rock music which had dominated the music charts for most of the previous decade. Radio Free Britain promised to play nothing but genuine and cutting-edge rock music which the mainstream stations shunned.

However, Radio Free Britain had not gone to the trouble of obtaining a licence to broadcast. It had secured the ownership of a former gas drilling rig in international waters off the Dutch coast. It was therefore in breach of United Kingdom law and its staff faced arrest if they set foot in the United Kingdom. For the record, Radio Free Britain was also breaking the law of other European countries. However, EU countries did not see the pursuit of 'pirate' broadcasters as a major priority and the Dutch government, a coalition of Socialists, Greens and Islamists was not unsympathetic to a station which did not hide its hostility to the British government.

What many people did not know was that Radio Free Britain had been set up to launder money raised illegally by the SNLA and the WRA through drug trafficking. The solid cashflow enabled the station to be able to shun advertising and sponsorship. The station also had a secondary purpose. The SNLA and WRA knew that the station would gain a sizeable audience from young people in the United Kingdom because they were playing alternative rock music that the mainstream stations did not play, and that it could be used as a tool to sow disaffection amongst the country's youth.

9 January 2018
Cabinet Room
10 Downing Street
London

Plans for a forthcoming General Election were on the agenda as the Cabinet held its first meeting of 2018.

Five months earlier, the Government had faced the unwelcome prospect of having to cancel proposed tax cuts and slashing public spending after SNLA and WRA terror attacks had crippled the City of London's broadband cables and air traffic control at Heathrow Airport and scared off tourists following fatal bombings at the Tower of London, Madame Tussaud's and Harrods. Chevron and Texaco were threatening to pull out of the lucrative oil industry.

However, in the intervening period, the Government had taken action to reassure both business and tourists that the United Kingdom was safe. Soldiers from the SAS and SBS had been deployed to guard economically vital sites, such as oil installations, airports, the main financial centres in the City of London and Docklands and road and rail bridges and tunnels. The National Anti-Terror Squad had received an increase to their budget, which had enabled them to take on 100 further officers, while digital CCTV cameras, including some with infra-red low-light capacity had been installed in business-critical sites to improve surveillance and gather evidence on terrorist suspects. Chevron and Texaco changed their mind.

First to speak was the Chancellor of the Exchequer, Ed Villiers. What he had to say was waited with barely-concealed anticipation as it would decide whether the country's economy was in a sound enough state for the Government to call a General Election.

"Prime Minister, ladies and gentlemen, I will summarise the latest economic report. In the three months to September, economic growth was 0.7% compared with the same period twelve months earlier and the budget deficit stood at £14 billion. This figure may sound disappointing but, if you recall, economic activity had been damaged by the SNLA and WRA bombings. Because of this, I have asked my economists and the Bank of England to carry out an unaudited survey of the economic performance in the three months to December. The full report will be due later this month, but the provisional report suggests that growth has risen to 2.5% and the budget is in surplus to the tune of £5.7 billion."

"Ed, what scope have we got to cut taxes?" asked Conservative Party Chairman, Sir Anthony Simmons.

"Things are still a bit tight Tony" replied Villiers. "However, the main thing is that we're out of the woods over the risk of public spending cuts."

"Tony, how are the polls going?" asked Robert Delgado.

"Pretty good Prime Minister" said Simmons. "We've got a five percent lead over Labour according to YouGov and ComRes. We've got over the blip which occurred back in October when the Warrington Three and the Ascot Five were hanged."

"Providing we hold this lead and don't slip up, I see no reason why we shouldn't go to the country this May" said Delgado. "Does everyone agree?"

The Cabinet indicated their approval.

Home affairs was next on the agenda. Deborah Pearson awaited the Prime Minister's question.

"Deborah" said the Prime Minister, "I and Cabinet colleagues are most concerned about the English Volunteer Force. We've had our hands full with the SNLA and WRA over the past two years and now we've got another organisation killing people. I guess you've heard that the SNLA and WRA have sworn revenge. If we're not careful, we could risk having a full-blown civil war on our doorstep."

Delgado was referring to the English nationalist terrorist organisation which had killed 25 people just before Christmas when they bombed two London pubs popular with Scottish and Welsh exiles.

"I'm meeting MI5 and NATS later this week Prime Minister" replied Pearson. "Top on the agenda is the EVF. By the way, do you want me to invite Frank Hesford?" The former SAS colonel was Delgado's security adviser.

"Good idea Deborah" replied the Prime Minister.

This was followed by criminal justice. Dominic Collins was ready to field questions.

"Dominic, it appears that, despite the Criminal Law Act, there are still terrorist suspects escaping justice. We have really got to go further to ensure that the SNLA and WRA do not run rings round us in court."

Delgado was referring to the ten SNLA and WRA terrorist suspects who had been acquitted at the Old Bailey the previous month.

"I know Prime Minister" replied Collins. I think this case was swayed by the Warrington Three and Ascot Five. Left-wing politicians and campaigners have been making out that they were all innocent and that there's been a miscarriage of justice. It must have affected the way the jury made its decision. Also, they had Justin Hemingway defending them. He's well-known as a master of procedure and has got a reputation for securing acquittals. He rang rings round high-ranking police officers and forensic experts at the trial."

Collins continued. "There's also been rumours that the jury and key witnesses were nobbled. We weren't able to prove them, hence the fact the prosecution lost the appeal against acquittal. I fear this could happen again."

"Prime Minister, I would like to seek approval to bring to Cabinet for approval plans for a special criminal court to try the so-called 'untouchables'. A kind of Star Chamber. Such a court would have no jury, with decisions being taken by a panel of judges. It would be closed to the public and journalists would be subject to tight reporting restrictions. Defence solicitors would be required to submit their papers for scrutiny and all prosecution papers would be highly classified. Finally, there would be armed escorts for defendants to ensure there are no escape attempts."

"Have you costed it Dominic?" asked Ed Villiers. "Whatever its merits, it looks like it could be rather expensive."

"Dominic, the main concern I've got is that it breaches habeas corpus" said Sir Anthony Simmons. "Not that I care anything about the SNLA or WRA, but it drives a coach and horses through the concept of trial by jury, which dates back to the Magna Carta. You might have some difficulty in getting that past some of our backbenchers, let alone the civil liberties lobby."

"Ed" replied Collins, "I accept it will be an expensive option. Unfortunately, a necessary one. If we can break the SNLA and WRA and put their men and women either behind bars or on the gallows, it will be worth any additional expense. Tony, likewise, you've made a fair point. But I think that our backbenchers will bite the bullet on this one. All we have to do is ask them to remember David Pickavance. They will accept that tough measures are necessary to break the SNLA and WRA, even if it runs against their principles."

"I like the idea Dominic" said Delgado. "Can you cost your proposals and bring them back to the next Cabinet meeting."

Later that day
Home Office
Marsham Street
London

Deborah Pearson had invited Jason Steer, to attend a short meeting, along with MI5 Director-General Nicola Martin, the Head of the National Anti-Terror Squad, Darren Charnock, the Head of the Joint Chiefs of Staff for the Armed Forces, Sir Mike Woodcock and the Prime Minister's security adviser, Frank Hesford.

Pearson opened the meeting.

"Thank you for coming here at such short notice. You will be aware why I've asked you to attend. The SNLA and WRA still present clear and present danger to the United Kingdom, despite the hard work by the police, army and security services which has put many of their number behind bars and, in the most serious cases, sent them to the gallows. We cannot afford to be complacent about them."

"However, we now have a new threat to security in the form of the English Volunteer Force. My concern is not that they might bump off a few SNLA or WRA members. It's more that they'll kick start a civil war. Already, the SNLA and WRA have sworn vengeance for the pre-Christmas bombings of the Rob Roy and Famous Three Kings."

"Home Secretary, the reason for that is that both the SNLA and WRA lost some of their fundraisers in the bombings. Those pubs had been under surveillance for terrorist fundraising activities for several months" said NATS chief Charnock.

"Nicola, has MI5 made any headway in establishing intelligence on the EVF?" asked Pearson.

"Yes, Home Secretary" replied the MI5 Director-General. "We've managed to insert a couple of agents into the EVF and have steadily built up intelligence on them. It appears a lot of their leading figures used to be involved with the BNP. Their Commander-in-Chief, Phil Barden and two other General Council members, Barry Pickett and Alan Wilkinson, were former BNP councillors." The British National Party had been an extreme right-wing party which a decade previously had won over fifty council seats by exploiting public anxiety about rising immigration and, in particular, about Muslim immigration following the terrorist attacks on New York City on 11 September 2001.

"However" continued Martin, "the EVF has been successful in recruiting former soldiers. Their Deputy-Commander, Glenn Nicholls, used to be a sergeant in the Paratroop Regiment. They've also managed to recruit several IT specialists. For a relatively new organisation, they've got a worryingly high level of expertise."

"The real problem" said General Woodcock "is that the SNLA and WRA have been so successful in avoiding justice. All the hard work that our boys and Darren's guys have been doing in capturing these bastards—sorry ladies—and they end up walking free." Woodcock was referring to the Dalston Ten whose acquittal on terror charges shortly before Christmas 2017 had been headline news.

"Mike, the Government's acting on the problem" said Pearson. "Dominic Collins is going to bring in a Star Chamber to try the so-called untouchables. It will have no jury."

"Home Secretary" continued Woodcock "I think now is the time for a reappraisal of tactics. The days of fighting with one hand tied behind our back needs to end. If the SNLA and WRA are found in the course of committing terrorist acts, we must be prepared to open fire."

"You don't mean a 'shoot-to-kill' policy, do you General?" asked Martin.

"Yes I do" replied Woodcock.

"Do you realise the impact such a policy will have General? We get precious little co-operation from the international community now. Start a 'shoot-to-kill' policy and that will shrink to nothing."

"Ladies and gentlemen, I think we've strayed from the main issue which was the EVF" said Pearson.

"Actually Debbie, I wonder if we need to spend time and money chasing the EVF" said Steer. "They could be useful to us."

"How do you mean, Jason?" asked Hesford.

"They could do our dirty work for us. If the police and armed forces were to leak information about SNLA and WRA terrorists to the EVF, I'm sure they'd be delighted to have an opportunity to waste a few SNLA and WRA. Remember, we did the same in Northern Ireland forty years ago and the Prods got rid of several leading IRA terrorists that the armed forces had been trying to capture."

30 January 2018
British Embassy
35 Rue de Fauberg St Honore
Paris

"Monsieur, we have the Ambassador's car back."

François Renard, a representative for Transauto, the company which had serviced the Ambassador's official car, a Rolls-Royce Ghost, had pulled up at the Embassy's gatehouse.

"Can you please show your identity" said the security guard.

Renard pulled out his driving licence and Transauto identity card.

"That's fine Monsieur Renard" replied the guard. "Leave the car by the Ambassador's regular parking slot."

Renard drove the Rolls-Royce through the courtyard and left it in a parking space specifically reserved for the official car. After disembarking, he headed for the exit where a Transauto colleague would pick him up for the drive back to Nanterre.

"Au revoir" said Renard to the guard at the gatehouse.

"Au revoir Monsieur Renard" replied the guard.

The Rolls-Royce Ghost was not the company's largest car but, at over 17 feet long, it was hardly small. It had been in for its periodical service and had been fully valeted, and looked immaculate.

What Renard or the Embassy security staff did not know was that the Ambassador's life was in danger. Two days earlier, a young Welshman, Gareth Vaughan, had been at the Nanterre service facility, supposedly to collect a Renault Trafic van that had been serviced. Although Vaughan was a foreigner, no one questioned his right to be on the premises. The Troubles in Scotland and Wales had resulted in a large number of young Scots and Welsh coming to live in Paris to stay out of the way of the British authorities, and their numbers had been reinforced by several English who were avoiding National Service.

Vaughan was however a member of the WRA. On finding that the British Ambassador's car was in for service, he took the opportunity to attach an explosive device to be triggered by a signal from a mobile phone while the car was unattended.

The same evening
Paris

Sir Charles Richardson, the British Ambassador and his wife, Carolyn, were dressed formally for a function at the Elysee Palace being hosted by President Dumas and her husband. Although Anglo-French relations were frosty, and had been since the United Kingdom's departure from the European Union and Marie-Christine Dumas, a former human rights lawyer, had had some harsh words for the British Government, Richardson saw the event as an important opportunity to network with representatives from Europe. The US Ambassador, Hank Crosby, would also be present.

The Elysee Palace was little more than a stone's throw from the British Embassy but, because of Paris's one-way system, it involved a drive of over a mile. At 8pm, the Richardsons got into the back of the Ambassador's official car. Their chauffeur, Henri Besson, was already in the driver's seat.

Besson headed down the Rue de Fauberg St Honore before turning into the Rue Royale. The next junction was by the Place de la Concorde where Besson turned the Rolls-Royce into Avenue Gabriel which led into the Champs-Elysees.

Gareth Vaughan was walking past the US Embassy when he saw the British Ambassador's car pass. He withdrew a mobile phone from his jacket pocket and started to dial in a number. Seconds later, the British Ambassador's Rolls-Royce was blown to smithereens as the bomb planted was detonated.

1 February 2018
Foreign and Commonwealth Office
Whitehall
London

Sir James Beveridge, the Director-General of the Secret Intelligence Service, MI6, was feeling most uncomfortable. He was facing a full-blooded grilling from the Foreign Secretary, Henry Arbuthnot about the gaps in intelligence which, two nights earlier, had allowed the WRA to assassinate the British Ambassador to France and his wife with a bomb which blew their car apart. Matters had been made worse by an article in that morning's *Daily Mail* about the large numbers of young people from the United Kingdom who were living illegally in EU countries and the many who were sympathetic to the SNLA and WRA.

"Foreign Secretary, I'll assure you that we'll give maximum priority to obtaining intelligence on SNLA and WRA operations in Paris. I knew Charles Richardson well—he used to work for us."

"James, the SIS is not looking very good" replied Arbuthnot. "Hordes of Brits living in Paris. Many of them from Scotland and Wales. And you've got no idea how or who killed Charles Richardson."

"Foreign Secretary, I know you're angry" said Beveridge. "As are many people. But SIS is doing its best to find out who killed Richardson. I've already got our Western European Section trying to insert agents into the Paris cells. Problem is that the SNLA and WRA are both getting help. There's loads of National Service evaders living illegally in France. A lot of them are pretty left-wing in their views and support the aims of the SNLA and WRA. Also, they're getting help from Trotskyists and radical Islamists. The risk of agents getting their cover blown is high."

Arbuthnot was unimpressed. "James, I don't want problems. I want solutions and results" he thundered. "I want to see the bastards who got Richardson in chains. And don't forget to spread the net wider into other European cities. You saw today's *Daily Mail* article, didn't you?"

5 February 2018
Department for National Heritage
Cockspur Street
London

Lord Manson, Secretary of State for National Heritage, was facing a difficult meeting with five Chief Executives from the United Kingdom's leading radio stations. They had called in to ask him what action the Government was taking against Radio Free Britain.

Radio Free Britain had come on air just under a month earlier, broadcasting from a disused gas rig off the Dutch coast. They were not only broadcasting illegally without a licence but they were also using a powerful transmitter which was overpowering the signals of the legitimate radio stations. In addition, the station was quite blatant with its anti-capitalist and anti-British bias. Most of the radio stations were owned by corporate business interests who were furious that this unlicensed station was slandering them.

"Ladies and gentlemen" said Manson "we have the power to prosecute Radio Free Britain under the Marine Offences Act 1967. If anyone involved with the station, whether broadcasters, technicians, suppliers or funders sets foot in the United Kingdom, I'll ensure they are arrested and put on trial."

"Secretary of State, you don't understand it's unlikely that anyone from Radio Free Britain will set foot inside the United Kingdom" said Jane Allison, Chief Executive of Radio 1, the former BBC channel that was now owned by venture capitalists Orion. "Their base is off the Dutch coast and, from what I've heard, they go ashore to Groningen. If you need to put pressure on anyone, it should be the Dutch government."

"You realise this is something I can't do by myself" said Manson. "But the Foreign Secretary can, and I'll speak to him."

"I don't want talk, Secretary of State, I want results" said Wayne Finnigan, Chief Executive of Sunrise Radio. "Radio Free Britain is costing us money through lost coverage and revenue. If nothing is done, we won't hesitate to take legal action against the British government to compensate us for lost income."

Later that day
Foreign and Commonwealth Office
Whitehall
London

"Robert, are you being serious?" asked Foreign Secretary Henry Arbuthnot. "You've got the Marine Offences Act to nail illegal radio stations offshore."

"Henry, these guys appear to be operating from the Netherlands" said Lord Manson, Secretary of State for National Heritage. "The Marine Offences Act is useless against them. You'll have to press the Dutch government."

"Right now Robert, I've got more pressing matters on my mind than pirate radio" replied Arbuthnot. "Like overseas cells of the SNLA and WRA."

Manson fell silent. He was fully aware of the murder the previous week of Sir Charles Richardson, the British Ambassador in Paris.

A few seconds later, Manson felt it safe to speak. "Henry, I know how serious the consequences of having active SNLA and WRA cells abroad is to our national security. But the radio companies are threatening to sue the Government if we don't put Radio Free Britain off the air. They're losing money."

At that moment, Arbuthnot's Principal Private Secretary, Kate Lowes, rushed into the office in a state of some agitation.

"Foreign Secretary, sorry to interrupt you, but there's been another murder abroad."

"Sorry Robert" said Arbuthnot. "You see what's been happening. Kate, can you tell me the details."

"Chris Moorhouse, the Chief Executive of BP Europe. He's just been shot dead in Paris. A van cut him up and gunmen opened fire. SNLA have claimed responsibility."

8 February 2018
Foreign & Commonwealth Office
Whitehall
London

"I don't think you understand or are listening to what I'm saying Mr Rensenbrink."

Foreign Secretary Henry Arbuthnot was a forceful man at the best of times, and now he was in a bad mood at what he saw as prevarication by the Dutch government over taking action against Radio Free Britain. Arbuthnot towered over the Dutch Ambassador by over six inches and was over seventy pounds heavier. The former British Army rugby player carried a presence that intimidated his opponents.

Arbuthnot had not planned to give priority to the request by the Secretary of State for National Heritage, Lord Manson, to put pressure on the Dutch government to take action against Radio Free Britain. But the day after Manson, he received a report from MI6 which suggested that Radio Free Britain's income was from laundering the proceeds from drug trafficking by the SNLA and WRA. With the murders of Sir Charles Richardson and Chris Moorhouse still fresh in the mind, he had decided to summon the Dutch Ambassador to explain the reasons for his country's inaction.

"Can I repeat myself" said Arbuthnot. "Radio Free Britain are broadcasting to the United Kingdom without a licence. They have repeatedly made slanderous allegations about public figures here and are inciting its listeners to break the law. Reports from our intelligence agencies suggest that they have received funds from the SNLA and WRA. We have enough evidence to put them on trial for broadcasting offences, let alone incitement to disorder and money laundering. The United Kingdom may no longer be part of the EU. But your Government is a signatory to the Europe-wide extradition and mutual assistance treaty. You should therefore be taking action to arrest anyone involved with Radio Free Britain and extradite them to the United Kingdom to face justice."

Wim Rensenbrink, the Dutch Ambassador, had up to now been calm and composed in the face of Arbuthnot's blustering. But he had by now had enough.

"Foreign Secretary" he shouted "Radio Free Britain has not committed any offences against Dutch law. Their officials pay Dutch taxes. Furthermore, my Government was elected on a platform of fair play and respecting diversity and the rights of national minorities. Something your Government does not do. I will not allow you to bully my Government into becoming a poodle for the British Government in prosecuting an organisation which does nothing more than oppose its policies."

Arbuthnot's face was white with fury. "How dare you slander my Government" he thundered. "Remember this, Mr Rensenbrink. We are the elected Government of the United Kingdom and we have the mandate to govern. We don't take instructions from other countries, least of all one ruled by a bunch of old hippies and drug users who are in bed with a load of Islamist thugs. Good day to you."

13 February 2018
Cabinet Room
10 Downing Street
London

"Henry, has there been any developments on the Richardson and Moorhouse murders?" The Prime Minister, Robert Delgado was concerned that no progress had been made in arresting the perpetrators.

"Nothing yet, Prime Minister" replied Arbuthnot. "But the French Ambassador has assured me that the Sûreté are doing their best to find the suspects and Deborah has advised me that officers from NATS and Interpol are out in France and working with them. I'll keep you posted on developments."

"Thank you Henry" replied Delgado. By the way, anything else to report?"

"Yes, Prime Minister" replied Arbuthnot. "I met the Dutch Ambassador last Thursday to ask him what his Government were doing about Radio Free Britain. You know that Robert came to see me a week ago. Appears that some of the commercial stations are upset about being blocked out by Radio Free Britain's signal."

"Not only that Henry" said the Secretary of State for Trade and Enterprise, Cheryl Parkinson. "They've repeatedly slandered businesses and the business community is livid that nothing's been done about them."

"On top of that—and this is not for the minutes—SIS think they're laundering dirty money for the SNLA and WRA."

"So that's how they've been so successful" said Home Secretary Deborah Pearson.

"When I asked the Ambassador if his Government could arrest and extradite the owners and staff from Radio Free Britain, he effectively told me to bugger off. We're going to get no co-operation from the Dutch."

"How do you propose that we handle this Henry?" asked Chancellor of the Exchequer Ed Villiers.

"Impose trade and travel sanctions on them" replied Arbuthnot.

28 February 2018
Wembley Stadium
London

England's national football team was playing its final qualifying match for the World Cup due to take place in Russia later that year. They had won their qualifying group convincingly with eight wins and a draw, and had booked their place in the finals.

There was just ten minutes left to play in the match against group runners-up Portugal and England were already 3-0 up through goals from striker Vic Egbunike, winger Wayne Russell and midfielder Gary Coleman. The England side, based around the team which had won the Junior World Cup two years earlier was outplaying a highly competent Portuguese side.

The past eight years had not been a happy one for the England national side, and they had failed to qualify for the European Championships in 2012 and 2016 and the World Cup in 2014. These failings had been rubbed in by the success of the Scotland and Wales national sides who had qualified for all the tournaments which England had failed to do and had reached the semi-finals of the European Championships six years earlier. Four managers had come and gone. But the current incumbent, Stuart Holden, had taken advantage of what appeared to be a new "Golden Generation" of players and had welded a winning side.

Central defender and captain Anton McKenzie easily cut out a cross from the Portugal right-winger Simoes and England's main holding midfielder, Matt Schofield, picked the ball up and started to move forward. Seeing winger Wayne Russell free on the left, he passed the ball to the dimunitive winger who turned Portugal's right-back Silva first one way, then the other, before crossing the ball into the Portuguese penalty area where Vic Egbunike outleapt the Portuguese defence to head the ball decisively past goalkeeper Pereira. Four-nil.

Even with the match decisively won, England were looking to score again. Manager Holden was on the touchline frantically shouting orders to his players.

One minute to go. Gary Coleman, a tall, elegant midfielder with a superb passing game, planted an inch-perfect pass into the path of right-back Glen Cannon who hammered a long cross towards the far post where the second England striker, Kevin Marquis, was moving in. A collective groan went up as Cannon's cross forced the short, wiry Marquis to turn his back to the goal. Two seconds later, the groans had turned to cheers as Marquis let fly with an overhead bicycle kick to score England's fifth.

1 March 2018
Conservative Party Headquarters
Millbank
London

Copies of the *Sun*, *Daily Mail*, *Daily Express*, *Daily Telegraph* and the *Financial Times* were set out on the desk in the office of Conservative Party Chairman, Sir Anthony Simmons. Two main stories dominated the papers. One was the spectacular 5-0 win by the England football team over Portugal, which had confirmed their appearance in that summer's World Cup. The other was speculation that the Government would call a General Election in the light of favourable poll ratings.

Simmons was joined by Lyndon Jefferies, the aggressive Australian who had been the party's chief strategist and had masterminded the previous General Election victory.

"Lyndon, we need to decide whether to go for a General Election this year or to leave it until 2019. Can I have your views."

"Tony, we should go for it this year" replied Jefferies. "The way I see it, the economy's doing OK and has picked up now we've tightened up on security. We're back into a surplus, growth's back up to 2.5% and there's scope for some small-scale tax cuts. Also, public approval of tackling the SNLA and WRA's still high. The last lot of polls have got us between six and eight percent ahead of Labour."

"We need to be vigilant Lyndon" said Simmons. "Iain Turner's quite popular and he's seen as the sensible face of Labour. Also, Labour's vote tends to be concentrated in urban areas. Even with boundary changes, they're still getting proportionately more seats for their votes than we do."

"Tony, don't worry about Turner" replied Jefferies. "He may be sensible. But a lot of Labour aren't. The likes of Geraldine Partington and Jeremy Sanderson for example. Play on some of the things they've said and you'll frighten Middle England back into our camp."

Geraldine Partington and Jeremy Sanderson were two left-wing Labour MPs who had been highly critical of the Government's human rights record in pursuing the fight against SNLA and WRA terrorism. Consequently, may people thought that they and, by extension, the Labour Party, were sympathetic to the terrorists' cause.

"I think you're thinking what I'm thinking Lyndon" said Simmons. "That we should go for an election this year."

"You're dead right Tony" replied Jefferies.

10 March 2018
The Woodrow Wilson
Botchergate
Carlisle, Cumbria

Marcus Benton ordered three lagers, one for himself and two for his friends, Ben Cousins and Gordon English. "That'll be seven pounds fifty" said the barmaid.

Benton handed over a ten pound note and collected his change before returning to the table where his mates were sitting.

"Ere Marc" said Cousins, "yer man over there's giving you funny looks. What's he after?"

"Dunno Ben" replied Benton.

"He looks like someone official" said English.

Major Julian Potter of The Rifles walked over to the table. "Marcus Benton?" he asked.

"Yeah, that's right" replied Benton in a defiant tone. "What's it got to do with you pal?"

Potter showed his credentials. "Major Julian Potter, Army Intelligence. Have you got a minute Mr Benton?"

"Can you hang on here lads" said Benton.

Potter and Benton headed round the corner into a back street.

Benton was a big man, six feet three inches tall and had a height advantage of two inches over the Army man. But he could see that Potter was extremely fit and saw little value in starting a fight.

"Alright, Major. Tell me what you want."

"I understand you are the EVF brigade commander round here, Mr Benton" said Potter.

"That's right" replied Benton.

"The EVF could be very useful to us. The Army's had a lot of difficulty in bringing the SNLA to justice. We've pulled in known terrorists and had them put on trial, only for them to walk free. They've got the locals in a grip of fear so no one will go against them and give evidence. Nearly all the English who used to live north of the border have left after being driven from their homes. We reckon some of the local police are helping them too. However, if a few of them had a nasty accident?"

"You mean, bump them off?" asked Benton.

"Exactly Mr Benton" replied Potter. "And this is where the EVF come in. We know where these guys live, where they work, what pubs and clubs they drink in. We give you photos of them, addresses and car registration numbers and you do the rest."

"Can I ask you one thing Major Potter" asked Benton. "This is not a set up, is it? Several of our guys are already behind bars."

"I can guarantee that Mr Benton" said Potter. "After all, I don't think that anyone who bumps off an SNLA is going to be a priority for the authorities."

"Okay Major, we're on" replied Benton.

16 March 2018
Harbour Street
Irvine, Ayrshire

Sam Lauder acknowledged the thumbs-up sign from four youths in a Vauxhall Astra. The Commander of the Irvine Brigade of the SNLA was both feared and respected in his hometown.

Lauder locked the doors of his car, an Audi A4 and started to walk towards the Ship Inn which was his local pub.

Parked close to the Ship Inn was a silver Citroen C5. Inside it were two men, one tall, one shorter, both with shaven heads. Lauder took no notice. The car had a Scottish registration and therefore did not stand out.

What Sam Lauder did not know was that the two men in the Citroen were both from the EVF and both were armed. The taller of the two men, Luke Benton, was the younger brother of the Commander of the Carlisle Brigade of the EVF. The shorter man, Matt Fowler, was a former soldier from the Duke of Lancaster's Regiment. The day before, Benton's older brother, Marcus, had collected a set of papers from a military intelligence officer with details of Lauder, a photograph, his address, car registration details and the places where he socialised. They had bought a Citroen from a Carlisle dealer and fitted false Scottish registration plates to ensure they would not be recognised as English.

Their mission was to kill Lauder.

"Luke, that's Lauder over there" said Fowler.

"Okay Matt, take aim now. I'll fire up the car for a getaway" said Benton.

Lauder was now walking past the Citroen. He had not noticed that the window was down. After all, who would be so foolish to try and take out an SNLA hardman in his home town?

Fowler lifted the Heckler and Koch sidearm out of its holster and, as Lauder walked past, opened fire. Lauder fell to the pavement, already dead.

Benton hit the accelerator and headed out of town as quickly as possible. Once they were on the M74, it would be an hour back to Carlisle.

4 May 2018
Sky News

"This is Adam Rennie with this morning's headlines on Sky News."

"The Conservative Party has won its third General Election in a row after securing 319 of the 600 seats. Robert Delgado therefore joins Margaret Thatcher and Tony Blair in securing three terms of office."

"The Conservatives knew it would be difficult to repeat the scale of the victory in 2014 against a resurgent Labour Party. Although Labour won back seats in the North of England and in the big urban conurbations of London and Birmingham, they made only limited inroads into the Conservative vote in the south of England outside London."

"The General Election was once again disappointing for the Liberal Democrats who managed to win only seventeen seats. Party leader Julia Goldwater has announced that she will resign."

"There was success for the Scottish National Party and Plaid Cymru who won respectively fourteen and eleven seats. It is however unlikely that the MPs elected from either party will be able to take up their seats in Parliament unless they are prepared to sign an oath of allegiance to the Queen. This will effectively require them to abandon the main planks of their policy, namely full independence from the United Kingdom."

"And now for further headlines. The EVF have claimed responsibility for last night's murder in Swansea of suspected WRA member Gerald Evans. Evans, who was wanted for the authorities for his part in several shootings of British soldiers, was shot dead while on his way home from the pub. He is the seventh suspected member of the SNLA and the WRA to have been murdered by the EVF over the past two months. The six previous murders have all provoked tit-for-tat killings by the SNLA and WRA, and the police and Army are being vigilant in case of reprisals by the WRA."

The same day
Conservative Party Headquarters
Millbank
London

Robert Delgado was bleary-eyed after a long day but delighted at the same time. He had just joined Margaret Thatcher in winning a third term of office and would be guaranteed immortality in the history of the Conservative Party. However, he wanted to leave a legacy to the United Kingdom to match that left by the "Iron Lady". Helping to defeat Iran in the Third Gulf War had been one achievement. Having the guts to take the United Kingdom out of the European Union was another. As was tackling the culture of indolence which many people felt had gripped the United Kingdom since the 1990s. This was why the Government had reformed local government and higher education and had reintroduced National Service. The changes to the criminal justice system had swung the scales of justice back in favour of the law-abiding citizen. But the SNLA and WRA remained a running sore. Delgado felt that all the Government needed to do was to persist in the battle to suppress the dealers of death and destruction. Eventually, the people in Europe and across the world would come to their senses and support the United Kingdom.

In two hours time, Delgado would be on his way to Buckingham Palace to see the Queen and accept her invitation to form a Government. This was the third time he had made such a journey. The first had been in 2010 after he had led the Conservatives back to power after thirteen years in the wilderness. The second had been four years earlier after a landslide win on the back of the Gulf War. But now was a crossroads for Delgado. He was now 64 years old and there was speculation that it would be his last term in office before handing over. Like all leaders, he wanted to go out on a high note, and he was aware that Margaret Thatcher and Tony Blair had failed to do so.

With Delgado was Sir Anthony Simmons, the Party Chairman and Lyndon Jefferies, the chief strategist, both of whom had convinced the Prime Minister of the need to go to the country in 2018 rather than wait another year.

"Tony, Lyndon, we've done it again" said a beaming Delgado. "Good thing that I listen to your advice. Only regret is that we've lost some good people." Delgado was referring to the 79 outgoing MPs who had lost their seats.

"Think nothing of it Bob" said Simmons. "You are the reason we've won again. The country likes someone who's straight-talking and means what he says."

"And has got the balls to back it up" added Jefferies.

"Thanks guys. I think I should let you know that this coming term might be my last. There's one thing I want to achieve above everything else before I go."

"What's that Bob?" asked Simmons.

"To rid the country of the cancer of terrorism by destroying the SNLA and WRA once and for all."

CHAPTER 13

7 May 2018
Crowne Plaza Hotel
Badenerstrasse
Zurich

Graeme Wilson, the Scottish Football Association representative on FIFA, ordered a Dortmunder lager at the hotel bar. He had flown out to Zurich from Glasgow earlier that day for a FIFA meeting. It would be the last meeting of Congress before the World Cup due to take place in Russia the following month.

Wilson looked around and found five other FIFA representatives already staying in the hotel. Ruud Viljoen, the Dutch representative was already sitting at a table along with Michel Renault, the French representative, Diego Marotta, the Argentinian representative, Edward Radebe, the South African representative and Ruslan Karimov, the Kazahkstani representative. He motioned to the group and joined them.

"Graeme, delighted to see you again" said Renault. "How are you keeping?"

"Personally fine Michel" replied Wilson. "But there's been some bad news on the family front. My nephew's been arrested by the National Anti-Terror Squad and has been interned. All he did was help make a satirical video which lampooned the armed forces and the police."

"Graeme, you might wish to know that there are many in FIFA who want to throw England out of the World Cup" said Viljoen. "My Government has asked me to find out if other national representatives are in favour. You know we've had trade sanctions imposed."

"No I didn't" said Wilson. "What was that for?"

"Because we refused to close down Radio Free Britain" said Viljoen.

"Alan Freeth's here" said Karimov, noting the arrival of the Football Association of Wales representative.

Freeth had just bought a stein of Hurlimann, a Swiss lager, at the bar and made his way over to join his fellow FIFA representatives.

"See to be quite an animated discussion going on here" said Freeth. "Have I missed anything?"

"We've been talking about the possibility of expelling England from the World Cup Alan" replied Marotta. "Because of the British Government's human rights record and its denial of rights to national minorities."

"There's more to come" said Freeth. "You already know that the British Government is going to try terrorist cases in a juryless court. Well, on top of that, a report's been leaked which says that the British Army's adopting a 'shoot-to-kill' policy and that the British Army's also collaborating with the English Volunteer Force and using them to carry out murders. Effectively, the British Government's been implicated in extra-judicial murder."

"I agree Alan" said Renault. "I think we have a very strong case for expelling England from the World Cup. After all, UEFA did the same to Yugoslavia in 1992."

8 May 2018
FIFA Headquarters
Zurich

FIFA Chairman Juan Miguel Ayala had worked his way through the agenda for the FIFA Congress meeting. He reached Item 17. It read:-

"The Government of the United Kingdom has, for the past three years, been in breach of the United Nations' conventions on Human Rights and the Rights of Minority Peoples through its repressive actions against the campaign by the Scottish and Welsh people for independence. They have failed to respect habeas corpus through imprisonment without trial, their security forces have used torture to extract confessions from suspects and have carried out extra-judicial murders and they are now proposing to introduce juryless trials. They have denied the rights of freedom of movement to opponents of Government policy and have carried out acts of aggression against another member country, namely the Netherlands, who have been subjected to sanctions because of their refusal to close down an anti-Government radio station.

We, the undersigned, consider that the presence of the England national football team at the World Cup taking place in Russia this year is undesirable because of the failure of the United Kingdom Government to comply with the principles of the United Nations Charter. We therefore invite Congress to withdraw the invitation for England to attend and, instead, offer it to Ukraine, who finished third in Group Ten."

Mehrdad Bazargan (Iran)	Edward Radebe (South Africa)
Alan Freeth (Wales)	Fernando Ramos (Spain)
Dinos Karagounis (Greece)	Michel Renault (France)
Ruslan Karimov (Kazakhstan)	Edilson dos Santos (Brazil)
Diego Marotta (Argentina)	Ruud Viljoen (Netherlands)
Vladimir Mazarov (Russia)	Graeme Wilson (Scotland)

"Mr Viljoen, can you please take to the floor to explain your motion" said FIFA Chairman Ayala.

"Gentlemen, the motion that Edward Radebe and I have proposed may seem extreme. But the repressive conduct of the United Kingdom government towards their national minorities in Scotland and Wales and the blatant breaches of the United Nations Charter on Human Rights must bring into question the participation of the England team in next month's World Cup."

The England representative on FIFA's Governing Council, Sir David Johnson, leapt to his feet, his face puce with anger.

"Mr Chairman, you're surely not going to allow this motion to proceed? My country qualified for the World Cup legitimately and it is not in FIFA's remit to play politics. This motion has been motivated by pure malice and should be thrown out without further delay."

"Sir David, sit down and wait to be called" said a stern Ayala. "Let FIFA Congress decide that."

"Can I repeat myself?" shouted Johnson. "FIFA has no authority to take decisions on the basis of a member state's politics."

"You are quite wrong Sir David" replied Radebe, a one-time African National Congress activist who had spent time in prison during Apartheid-era South Africa. "Remember that South Africa was suspended from FIFA between 1964 and 1994 because of its Apartheid policy. FIFA has the right to take action against countries if their political activities offend basic human decency, and I and my fellow signatories all believe this is the case with the United Kingdom."

This made Johnson even more irate. "May I remind members that my Government is having to defend its citizens against brutal and vicious terrorists who have been murdering innocent civilians without remorse. And that they were given a popular mandate for their third time a week ago. What mandate have the SNLA and WRA got?"

This drew an acidic response from the Scottish representative. "Like my nephew who's been banged up for nothing more than poking fun at the security forces in a video."

The US representative, Bryce Dempsey, was next to speak. "Gentlemen, don't you think you're being a bit hasty? Surely we can defer the matter until after the World Cup? And I think that Sir David's got a very good point. It's not the role of FIFA to bring politics into sport."

Juan Miguel Ayala was not used to seeing his authority as Chairman being challenged. He angrily rapped his gavel in his desk to call the Congress meeting to order.

"Gentlemen, will you kindly keep order. You're supposed to be representatives of your country's Federations. Behave as such."

Fifteen minutes later, there was a vote on the motion to expel England from the World Cup. It was carried by 27 votes to two, with 15 abstentions.

9 May 2018
Department for National Heritage
Cockspur Street, London

Secretary of State for National Heritage, Cheryl Parkinson and Minister for Sport, Sebastian Shaw sat glassy-eyed as they read the national newspapers sitting on her office desk. **BOOTED OUT** read the headline on the *Sun*. **KICKED OUT** read the *Daily Mirror's* headline. The *Daily Mail* headline read **FIFA'S REVENGE** while that on the *Daily Express* read **SPITEFUL FIFA END ENGLAND'S WORLD CUP DREAM**.

Cheryl Parkinson was just about accepting that her ascent up the greasy pole of Ministerial advancement had stalled. Under Robert Delgado's second term, she had been promoted to the prestigious Trade and Enterprise brief, but her performance in office had been rather lacklustre. She had appeared out of her depth when three leading American oil companies threatened to withdraw following terrorist attacks a year earlier and she had fallen out with two leading Tory grandees, Home Secretary Deborah Pearson and Secretary of State for Defence Jason Steer over their plans to use additional police and the military to defend key strategic industrial installations.

Following the Conservatives' third election victory a week earlier, Robert Delgado had offered her the National Heritage brief. Darren Bramble, the former Policing Minister and a protégé of Deborah Pearson took her old job at Trade and Enterprise and she had only held her Cabinet position because Delgado had wanted Lord Manson to lead the Tories in the House of Lords.

"Seb, I can't believe it. I just can't fucking believe it" said Parkinson. "The best England team we've had for years and we're kicked out. Just what I fucking needed." She knew that the Prime Minister and her Cabinet colleagues would expect tough and decisive action. And as her remit for sport was for England only, she was powerless to take action against those treacherous snakes from the SFA and FAW who had put their names to the motion.

"Secretary of State, I'm sure that Stuart Grieve and Jonathan Morgan will be in favour of action against the SFA and FAW" said Shaw, one of the 2014 intake and now on the second rung of Ministerial office. Stuart Grieve and Jonathan Morgan held Cabinet portfolios for Scotland and Wales. "Probably stop their grant" added Shaw.

"But there's still FIFA to deal with Seb" said Parkinson. "My instinct is to tell the Football Association to leave FIFA. But if they do, we will be more likely to suffer than the other members. Our top football sides will be banned from lucrative tournaments like the European Champions League. This could tip some clubs into bankruptcy."

15 May 2018
Cabinet Room
10 Downing Street
London

The first Cabinet meeting of Robert Delgado's third term as Prime Minister began with a welcome to new Cabinet members. There were just three newcomers: Darren Bramble as Secretary of State for Trade and Enterprise, Angela Woolliscroft, who had become Secretary of State for Employment and Mark Taylor, who had become Chief Secretary to the Treasury. Otherwise, all Cabinet members had already served.

Second item on the agenda was the expulsion of the England football team from the World Cup. The Prime Minister asked Cheryl Parkinson to address the meeting.

"Ladies and gentlemen, you will all be aware of the disgraceful and politically-motivated decision by FIFA to expel England from the 2018 World Cup" said Parkinson. "I spoke to FIFA's Chairman, Juan Miguel Ayala on Friday to ask for an explanation. He told me that twelve FIFA Congress members had signed a motion calling for England's expulsion on the grounds of "the United Kingdom Government's repression in Scotland and Wales and denial of human rights to persons opposed to the Government's policy". I told him forcefully that FIFA had no right to either pass judgement on the policies of a member state or to expel a country from a tournament on political grounds."

"What was Ayala's response?" asked Chancellor of the Exchequer Ed Villiers.

"This is the same as the Left did over South Africa back in the 70s and 80s" exclaimed Foreign Secretary Henry Arbuthnot.

Cheryl Parkinson resumed where she had left off. "I've obtained advice from our Senior Legal Officers. We've got excellent grounds to sue FIFA for loss of income. If you agree, I propose to go ahead with this."

She then turned to Secretary of State for Scotland, Stuart Grieve and Secretary of State for Wales, Jonathan Morgan. "Stuart, Jonathan, you know that Graeme Wilson and Alan Freeth put their names to the motion. What action are you taking?"

Grieve replied "I've written to the Chairman of the SFA to demand an explanation and for disciplinary action to be taken against Wilson. If they fail to comply, I propose to withdraw all Government financial support for the SFA."

"Thank you Stuart" replied Parkinson. "Jonathan?"

"Exactly the same Cheryl" replied Morgan. Like Stuart, I propose to withdraw Government support for the FAW if they fail to take action against Freeth."

18 May 2018
Residence Inn
East 4th Street
Cincinnati
Ohio

"Mr Stevenson, there's a Mr Fraser and a Mr Meredith for you in reception."

"Thank you. Tell them I'm on the way down."

Neil Telfer put down the telephone in his bedroom and walked out into the corridor towards the lifts. He knocked on the door of the third room down.

"Tony, Bill and Ben are here. Are you ready?"

Tony Edwards opened the door and joined Telfer.

To the unknowing, Neil Telfer and Tony Edwards were Hamish Stevenson and Gary Pritchard, British businessmen who were in Cincinnati on business. But the false identities, obtained for money through the corrupt services of officials at the Identity and Passport Agency, disguised the fact that both Telfer and Edwards were terrorists, Telfer from the SNLA and Edwards from the WRA. Their business in the USA was to meet Caledonian Aid and Cambrian Aid, the two charities set up to raise funds for the Scots and Welsh affected by the troubles in their homeland. The meeting would be about securing transfers of money that would be used to buy arms.

Telfer and Edwards walked up to the reception desk to be greeted by Bill Fraser of Caledonian Aid and Ben Meredith of Cambrian Aid.

"Hey Neil, Tony, great to see you guys again. How's tricks over the pond?"

Telfer was first to speak. "Good news and bad Bill. Good news was that we bagged the British Ambassador in Paris and WRA bagged BP's European CEO. And FIFA have kicked England out of the 2018 World Cup."

Edwards then spoke. "Bad news was the re-election of the Tories. And the EVF have started to waste both our guys and Neil's. We reckon the Army's tipping them off."

"We've booked a meeting room guys" said Meredith. "Coffee and donuts provided."

The four men headed off to one of the Residence Inn's meeting rooms where they could discuss their business behind closed doors.

The smartly-dressed couple at the Residence Inn's bar were probably mistaken for a husband and wife on vacation. But Curtis Miller and Lauren Davenport were anything but. Both were FBI agents and were on the tail of Bill Fraser and Ben Meredith for suspected terrorist funding. Their suspicions had been confirmed by the presence of Telfer and Edwards. Bureau headquarters had confirmed their identity.

Davenport felt her Blackberry vibrate. She knew there was a call on the line. She headed for the Ladies toilet where she took the call.

On the other end of the line was Carl Roeder, the Precinct Captain for downtown Cincinnati.

"Carl Roeder, Cincinnati Police Department."

"Carl, Lauren Davenport here. We've got a biggy to report. Fraser and Meredith are here and meeting two Brits, one from the SNLA and one from the WRA. We reckon they're talking about money for arms. Miller and I are going to bust them. Can you provide backup?"

"No problem Lauren" replied Roeder. "They'll be over in two minutes."

Lauren Davenport emerged from the Ladies to find Miller waiting for her and ready. "Lauren, what's the dope?"

"Curt, Roeder's sent back-up on the way. Let's bust these guys."

Neil Telfer and Tony Edwards had just learned that over $2 million was on the way to the SNLA and WRA when the two FBI agents burst into the room brandishing Uzi pistols.

"Freeze" yelled Miller. "You're all under arrest."

"On the floor now" shouted Davenport as Cincinnati Police Department's Tactical Support Team followed in. Bill Fraser, Ben Meredith, Neil Telfer and Tony Edwards were all put in handcuffs and led to a waiting GMC van of the Cincinnati Police Department.

22 May 2018
Portcullis House
Westminster
London

The telephone in the office of Jeremy Sanderson MP rang. His secretary, Isabella Ramirez, picked it up.

"It's Reception for you Jeremy. Your guests have arrived."

"Can you collect them please Isabella."

Isabella Ramirez was a Spanish girl from Seville and the daughter of a politician from Spain's Socialist party. Although her hair was short, her smooth olive skin and dark brown eyes gave her the stunning look of a Latin beauty. She had been Sanderson's secretary for the past two years and it was no secret that they were an item as Sanderson was now living apart from his wife.

A minute later, Ramirez escorted in Glen Johnstone and Mark Howell. Both men were in their early 30s. Johnstone was the taller of the two men at six feet tall and was sandy-haired while Howell was some four inches shorter and dark-haired.

To say that Sanderson's choice of guests for a visit to the House of Commons was controversial was an understatement. Johnstone was Chairman of the SNLA's political wing, Clann na h-Albann, while Howell was Chairmen of the WRA, equivalent, Meibion Cymru.

Ten minutes later, Sanderson was in the House of Commons with Johnstone and Howell and holding a press conference. The only newspapers and magazines invited were the *Guardian*, *Morning Star* and the *New Statesman*.

Sanderson read out a statement.

"Today, I have done what no one else in the British political establishment has been prepared to do and that is to engage with the voices of Scottish and Welsh nationalism as represented by my guests, Glen Johnstone from Clann na h-Albann and Mark Howell from Meibion Cymru."

"For the past three years, the British government has refused self-determination for the Scottish and Welsh people and suppressed its fight for freedom so it can reward its friends in the oil industry and the City of London. Prime responsibility for the thousand deaths that have occurred lie squarely with the British Government."

"The people of Scotland and Wales do not want war with either the British Government or with the English people. But they want to have control over their own destiny, something that has been denied to Wales since 1536 and to Scotland since 1707. If the British Government wants to bring the sad catalogue of death and injury to an end, they will have to find a political solution to Scotland and Wales. This means removing troops and non-local police from the streets of Scotland and Wales. It means the British Government talking to the SNLA and WRA and to Clann na h-Albann and Meibion Cymru."

23 May 2018
Labour Party Headquarters
Victoria Street
London

Jeremy Sanderson knew he would be in for a grilling as he entered the Labour Party Headquarters. Less than an hour earlier, he had received a terse telephone call from the party's Chief Whip, Jane Duffy, ordering him to report to the Whips' Office.

He was not surprised to find copies of the leading newspapers on Jane Duffy's desk as he walked in to her office. The front page on all the papers were focused on Sanderson's invitation for Clann na h-Albann and Meibion Cymru to attend a meeting at the House of Commons. **MADNESS** screamed the headline in the *Sun*. **INSULT TO THE VICTIMS OF TERROR** read the *Daily Mail*. **MPs SAFETY PUT AT RISK** read the headline in the *Daily Express*. Even the *Guardian*, regarded as many as being the conscience of liberals and the left wing, had a headline reading **SANDERSON INVITE TO CLANN NA H-ALBANN AND MEIBION CYMRU MAY BACKFIRE ON LABOUR.**

"Sit down Jeremy" commanded Jane Duffy. A Liverpudlian woman who had just turned fifty, Duffy was still an attractive woman. Her glossy dark hair was shaped into a bob and she still retained a relatively youthful figure. But she was renowned as being a tough cookie and had done a lot to knock the Labour Party back into shape after a disastrous five years following the loss of power in 2010.

"What the hell did you think you were doing in inviting the political wings of the SNLA and WRA to the House, Jeremy? You must have known what the Press reaction would be?" Duffy held up copies of the *Sun* and the *Daily Mail* to illustrate her point.

Sanderson was in no mood to apologise. "The only way we'll ever get peace in Scotland and Wales is to talk to the SNLA and the WRA. If we address their grievances, chances are that they'll lay down their arms. That's why I invited Glen Johnstone and Mark Howell to the House yesterday."

Duffy continued. "I hope you realise the damage you've caused the Labour Party, Jeremy. We've sweated blood and tears into making the party electable again over the past three years and there you go and screw it all up by cosying up to terrorists. Haven't you thought of the impact it will have on potential voters? It'll turn the clock back five years and allow the Tories to portray us as the friend of Britain's enemies." Duffy was referring to the rebellion within the party in 2013 when backbenchers, party activists and trade unions opposed the Third Gulf War shortly before the alliance of British, US and Australian forces destroyed Iran's capacity to wage war. Support for the Labour Party collapsed to a record low as voters saw them as friends of Britain's enemies.

"You've effectively ruined our chances of ever getting back into power, Jeremy. I hope you're proud of yourself."

"Jane, has it ever entered your head that it's been people on the Party's left that has revived its fortunes? We've been doing all the campaigning against the repressive and unfair Government policies like the death penalty, National Service, arming the police, the privatisation of local government and the removal of the vote from young people. And what have you and Iain Turner been doing? Trying to cosy up to business fat cats and getting the vote of *Sun* and *Daily Mail*-reading tossers from Middle England."

Jane Duffy was now incandescent with rage at the defiant attitude of the MP for Islington North. "Jeremy, how dare you refer to decent, hard working people like that. That confirms what I've always thought about the left. That they've got contempt for decent ordinary people who are patriotic, work hard, pay taxes and obey the law. I'm not going to let the likes of you spoil all the work that Iain and others in the Party have done to make it electable again. Or to let down those people whose lives have been blighted by the Tory government. I am withdrawing the Party whip from you Jeremy. You will not be allowed back until you prove to the National Executive Committee that you've changed your attitude."

8 June 2018
HMP Whitemoor
Cambridgeshire

The prison farm was one of HMP Whitemoor's jewels in the crown. Located in the fens, one of England's most fertile regions, Whitemoor grew fruit and vegetables and had the contract to supply HM Prison Service. To many people both within and outside the Prison Service, it was a positive enterprise which engaged the prisoners in productive activity and which went some way to atoning to society for their crimes.

HMP Whitemoor had been built just over 20 years earlier on the site of a former railway marshalling yard, and was a Category A prison which housed some of the country's most dangerous inmates. Murderers, armed robbers, drug traffickers and organised crime syndicates were all held there, as were terrorists from Al-Q'aida, the SNLA and the WRA. HM Prison Service and its staff were under no illusion about how dangerous the men in their custody were.

The first eight days of June had been gloriously sunny and the prisoners had been active in harvesting the crops of lettuces, cucumbers, tomatoes, new potatoes and strawberries. The milking parlours, sheep shearers and the slaughterhouse had all been busy too. The Farm Manager, David Burwell, looked pleased as he saw new contracts coming his way.

It was no secret that disproportionately large numbers of SNLA and WRA prisoners had volunteered for farm work. Several of the prisoners came from farming backgrounds and had the necessary farm husbandry skills. It was also a relief for the prison staff as it reduced the scope for clashes with other prisoners. Indeed, since they had started arriving at Whitemoor, the SNLA and WRA prisoners had earned a fearsome reputation and many of the country's most hardened criminals were frightened of taking them on.

Most of the agricultural tools were stored in a concrete breeze-block building and was supposed to have a prison officer routinely on duty to ensure that all tools were returned to the store. The risk of them being used in an escape attempt or as weapons in battle for jail supremacy was high.

However, even a maximum security prison like Whitemoor suffered from staffing shortages, something which the Prison Officers Association routinely raised with the prison management. But the POA was not held in high favour by HM Prison Service management or by Government Ministers as they were regarded as Luddite in their practices and an obstacle to efficiency. Prison Service therefore relied on an external CCTV camera to provide security for the agricultural store.

Underneath HMP Whitemoor, Shaun McRae and Matt Probert, unbeknown to the authorities, were digging an escape tunnel. McRae, a Glaswegian and Probert, who hailed from Swansea, were both short, stocky men, ideally suited to the role of digging tunnels. McRae's maternal grandfather and Probert's father and paternal grandfather had all been miners and so they had acquired some knowledge through their family.

McRae and Probert had found the soft Fenland soil easy to tunnel through. The biggest challenge had been to reinforce the tunnel ceiling with wooden planks to ensure it did not collapse. They had been digging for a week and they estimated that they should be beyond the boundary fence.

"Reckon about here Matty" asked McRae.

"Yeah, this should do Shaun" replied Probert. "Let's start digging upwards."

Fifteen minutes later, McRae and Probert felt the earth give way as they broke through and found daylight. The two men emerged from the tunnel and had a look around.

McRae and Probert found themselves close to a copse. An unmetalled track, presumably used for farm vehicles, was nearby. There was no sight of the boundary fence.

"Jeez Shaun. We couldn't have done better if we tried" said Probert.

"Better get back Matty" said McRae. "Otherwise our absence will be noted and this whole operation will go tits up."

McRae and Probert descended back into the tunnel and crawled back to HMP Whitemoor.

9 June 2018
HMP Whitemoor
Cambridgeshire

Weekends were usually the quietest time at HMP Whitemoor. It was the time that relatives visited the prisoners and prison staff were normally on high alert to ensure that contraband articles like drugs and mobile phones were not passed to prisoners. Consequently, the staff presence on the prison farm was less than it should have been. Reliance was placed on the CCTV system to prevent anything untoward happening.

"Morning, Mr Burwell. Bet you're well-pleased with the early harvest this year." Mel Jones, the most senior-ranked WRA prisoner greeted the Farm Manager.

"Absolutely delighted Jones" replied Burwell. "Keep up the good work."

As Burwell headed off to his office, Jones headed towards Iain Hunter, his SNLA counterpart.

"Iain, the tunnel's ready. Reckon we should start sending the men through from about five o'clock. Any earlier and we'll arouse suspicions and give the police the time to pick them up."

"Mel, I'd prefer an earlier start" said Hunter. "Four o'clock start. That way, we could send them out in relays of two at a time every five minutes. If they all go at once, it might raise the alarm."

"Do you reckon all the men will be out by the time of lockdown?" asked Jones.

"Should be."

"Then four o'clock it is" said Jones.

The sun was still shining brightly over the Fens as the late afternoon beckoned. Prison Land Rovers rolled back from the farm laden with boxes of fruit and vegetables. For David Burwell, it had been a profitable day.

Gareth Moore and Tom Beattie had been amongst the first prisoners out in the fields that day and had been allowed to finish early. They took the collection of scythes, hoes, spades and forks back to the store and hung them up in their allotted space. They noticed that there were no prison officers on duty.

"Alright Gar, the coast's clear" said Beattie.

The WRA man lifted a hatch on the floor. It was where the electrics for the building were housed.

"Let's go Tom" whispered Moore.

The two prisoners descended through the hatch and Beattie closed it behind him. If any prison officer or staff member called in for a check, nothing would look out of place.

Moore pulled out a small pocket torch he had secreted and switched it on. The two men searched for the tunnel in the half-light.

"Here it is Tom. Let's go." The two men crawled into the narrow tunnel and started to make their way to freedom.

10 June 2018
"Windermere"
Gerrards Cross
Buckinghamshire

Deborah Pearson had already been up for four hours working on the contents of her red Ministerial box. Like her heroine, Margaret Thatcher, Pearson possessed extraordinary reserves of energy and could function on little more than four hours sleep a night. The previous day, she had been staying in her constituency home while she held a surgery for her North Worcestershire constituents. She had them driven the 120 miles south to the massive detached home she shared with her husband in Gerrards Cross.

Later that day, she and her husband, Henry, would be having lunch with her daughter, Lucy and her son, Ben, both of whom would be accompanied by their partners. Both Lucy and Ben had followed their parents' career path into investment banking.

At 10am, the telephone rang. Henry went to answer it.

"324125."

"Is that you Henry?" On the other end of the line was Sir Richard Benson, Permanent Secretary at the Home Office.

"Certainly is Richard. I need to speak to Deborah rather urgently."

"Darling, it's Richard Benson for you."

"Good god Henry. Wonder what Benson wants. After all, it's Sunday."

Deborah Pearson walked into the hallway to answer the phone.

"Richard, what brings you here? Anything important?"

"I'm afraid so Home Secretary" replied Benson. "There's been a prison escape. 43 SNLA and WRA prisoners have got out of Whitemoor."

"Whitemoor! That's a Cat A prison. How the hell did that happen Richard?"

"I don't know Home Secretary. But we've got a border lockdown in place and a police manhunt for the prisoners is also taking place."

"Thanks Richard. Can you keep me posted about what's happening. And I want to see Phil Webley first thing tomorrow morning. He's got some explaining to do."

11 June 2018
Sky News

"This is Claire Egerton with the lunchtime headlines on Sky News."

"Firstly, an update on the jailbreak by SNLA and WRA prisoners from Whitemoor. The police have managed to arrest eight prisoners, but the remaining thirty five who escaped from Whitemoor on Saturday are still reported to be at large. There are fears that some of the men may have fled the country, despite the lockdown at all air and seaports put in place by the National Border Police Force. Descriptions of the escaped prisoners are being place in all newspapers and are being made available on the Internet. For details, go to www.nbp.pnn.police.uk. The National Border Police and the National Anti-Terror Squad have both advised the public not to approach any of these men and instead to telephone the following emergency number 0845 72000 150."

"The consequences of the escape have been felt most acutely at Prison Service. Earlier today the Director-General, Phil Webley, was dismissed from his post by the Home Secretary, and it has been reported that the Governor at Whitemoor Prison and three other key officials may also face the sack. The Deputy Director-General, Maureen Callaghan, will take charge until a successor to Mr Webley is appointed."

"The Government has suffered a further setback in its fight against terrorism. Earlier today, the District Court in Nanterre released on bail five Britons, Rob Burnside, Mark Davies, Kirsty Ingram, Jack Lawrence and Gareth Vaughan, who are suspected of being part of SNLA and WRA cells which murdered the British Ambassador, Sir Charles Richardson and the Chief Executive of BP Europe, Chris Moorhouse earlier this year. The authorities here fear that the suspects will abscond before they are due to face trial."

12 June 2018
Foreign and Commonwealth Office
Whitehall
London

Roland Collombin, the French Ambassador, was looking very uneasy. A small, slim man of no more than five feet six inches, he was sitting opposite the very angry figure of the United Kingdom's Foreign Secretary, Henry Arbuthnot. Arbuthnot was a good foot taller and, with his broad shoulders, looked very intimidating.

"Monsieur Arbuthnot, I understand why you are angry. But I repeat what I've said before. There is nothing that my Government can do to force the courts to reverse their decision. They are fully independent of both the government and Parliament and it is for them to decide whether or not to charge or bail suspects on the basis of the evidence they have."

"That Monsieur Collombin is complete rubbish" shouted Arbuthnot. "Your country's laws are quite specific on what courts should do when dealing with murder suspects. There is no way that those five should have been given bail. Over here, we routinely remand in custody anyone suspected of a crime carrying a prison sentence. We learnt our lesson from suspects absconding."

Arbuthnot continued. "Those suspects are responsible for murdering our Ambassador and one of our leading businessmen. If your Government is not prepared to take that seriously Mr Collombin, my Government will have no choice but to seek their extradition to stand trial in the United Kingdom. May I remind you that our Governments are party to a treaty on the extradition of fugitive offenders and I expect your co-operation."

"I regret that my Government will be unable to comply with any request for extradition Monsieur Arbuthnot" replied Collombin. "They do not extradite anyone, French nationals or others, to a country which has the death penalty. Nor do they extradite anyone to a country who have abandoned the concept of judicial fairness." Collombin was referring by implication to the special criminal court to try so-called "untouchables", for which legislation was passing through Parliament.

Later that day
Dolphin Square
Pimlico
London

Deborah Pearson had invited Henry Arbuthnot, Dominic Collins and Jason Steer round to her London flat for an evening drink. However, the meeting was anything but social and, instead, focused on the events of the past few days.

"Did you get any joy out of Collombin, Henry?" asked Pearson.

"Nothing Deborah" replied Arbuthnot. "Came up with the usual lame excuse that you have to allow the courts to make their own decision. What's more, he's said that we're wasting our time with applying for extradition."

"Why Henry?" asked Collins.

"Because we've got the death penalty and have suspended *habeas corpus*, Dominic" replied the Foreign Secretary.

"What next?" asked Pearson.

"Put out a reward for their capture and return" said Collins. "There's bound to be some ex-soldiers or mercenaries who would be tempted."

"Don't think that would work Dom" said Steer. "Firstly, they've got to know what they're doing. Chances are we'll get some cowboys who'll fuck up the whole operation. And don't forget that anyone trying it will be on their own with no co-operation from the Frogs."

Steer continued. "However, I like the idea of extraordinary rendition. The Yanks pulled it off several times with success. They caught everyone from drug lords, Somali pirates and Al-Q'aida leaders and ensured they faced US justice. I think those that weren't topped face another 30-40 years behind bars."

"What are you thinking of Jason?" asked Pearson.

"MI6 probably know where the five suspects live and where they socialise. In partnership with the SAS, they could arrange for them to be seized. It would then be arranged for an RAF Diplomatic Flight to be on hand at Le Bourget to fly them back here. The first the French authorities will know anything about this is when they hear that they've gone on trial. Do you like it Debbie?"

"Absolutely Jason, I'm in" said Arbuthnot. "I'll let Beveridge know."

"I'm in too" said Pearson.

"And me" said Collins.

"By the way, Deborah, what's the latest on the prison break?" asked Arbuthnot.

"At least something positive to report" said Pearson. "Eleven of the escapees are back in custody. You'll know I've sacked the Director-General of HM Prison Service and the Governor of HMP Whitemoor. Well, this time, I'll be looking to the private sector for replacements. And possibly from outside the United Kingdom. An advertisement for the Director-General post goes out tomorrow."

Pearson continued. "I've also called in Black Prince to do a study on bringing in a Supermax prison. Biggest problem is finding a secure site."

"Anywhere in particular being considered?" asked Collins.

"The three favoured sites are in the Outer Hebrides, the Cambrian Mountains near the Elan Valley Dam and a refurbished Dartmoor."

"Don't like the first two" said Arbuthnot. "Isolated islands are always going to be at risk of a seaborne or airborne assault. You'll need a large military detachment there just to protect the island. And don't forget that the Highlands and Islands are hotbeds of support for the SNLA. Same with mid-Wales and the WRA. There's going to be locals who will shelter any escaped prisoners."

"Not keen on Dartmoor either" said Steer. "No longer isolated. With the A38 nearby, anyone escaping could be into a car and be well over 100 miles away in barely two hours."

"Well, what do you suggest?" asked Pearson.

"The MoD might have a suitable site Debbie" said Steer. "Foulness. About ten miles east of Southend. It's currently a military firing range, and a top security one with armed guards patrolling the place. Anyone there with no authority is likely to be shot. There's only one road in and out, and the beaches are protected with stakes and razor wire so a seaborne escape is virtually impossible."

"I like the idea, Jason" said the Home Secretary. "Can you let Black Prince know if Foulness is available."

CHAPTER 14

12 July 2018
The Frog and Rosbif
116 Rue St Denis
3me Arrondisement
Paris

The Frog and Rosbif was already crowded by 8pm. The themed British pub was popular with the large numbers of expatriate Britons living in the French capital. However, in recent years, it had obtained a somewhat notorious reputation. A sizeable part of its clientele were either members or supporters of the SNLA and the WRA, while many others were deserters from National Service or draft dodgers. All around the pub were posters advertising political meetings and demonstrations against the British Government, and it was no secret that collections for the SNLA and WRA were being made.

Rob Burnside was bringing a tray of drinks back to the table he was sharing with the other members of the so-called "Paris Five". Kirsty Ingram, his girlfriend and a fellow defendant was also present, as were the girlfriends of the two WRA men, Mark Davies and Gareth Vaughan, and of Jack Lawrence, an Englishman who was a National Service deserter. They were all in a good mood as their lawyer had told them earlier that day that the French authorities were considering dropping proceedings against them for lack of evidence.

On the small stage, a band was setting up their PA equipment. Shakin' Solution were a French band but they knew the kind of music which went down well with the Frog and Rosbif regulars. Songs by the Beatles, the Rolling Stones, U2 and Oasis were always well-received.

At 8:10pm, a couple in their early to mid-20s walked into the Frog and Rosbif. Casually dressed in jeans and t-shirts, they looked little different from the other drinkers. But Steve Castle and Ali Hewitt were both members of MI6 and were on a mission. To track down the five suspects wanted for the murders of Sir Charles Richardson and Chris Moorhouse earlier that year.

Ali Hewitt nudged Steve Castle and whispered "Steve, there they are."

"Good spotting Ali" replied Castle. "We'll play it cool for the first hour, then we'll make our move."

At 10pm, Shakin' Solution took a 20 minute break, having just done a cover of "Brown Sugar". Gareth Vaughan was heading for the bar to buy a round of drinks.

Seeing Castle and Hewitt blocking his way, he asked "Scuse me butt, any chance of getting to the bar?"

"Sorry mate" replied Castle. "Didn't realise I was blocking your way."

Vaughan noticed that both Castle and Hewitt were wearing a badge with the peace symbol and another with the words "Don't blame me—I voted Labour" on it. He assumed they would be sympathetic.

"I see you don't think much of the British Government" said Vaughan. "By the way, what's your name?"

"Alex" replied Castle. "And this is my girlfriend, Emma. And you're right—we can't stand Delgado and his crew. We're not going back to Britain until they've gone."

"Fancy joining us at our table Alex?" said Vaughan. Castle and Hewitt indicated they would.

Later that night

Shakin' Solution had just finished their set with an enthusiastic, if limited cover of the old Oasis song "Cigarettes and Alcohol". Castle and Hewitt had become friendly with Vaughan, Burnside and their friends.

At 2am, the lights came on, signalling that the Frog and Rosbif would be closing. As the five wanted suspects were about to leave, Ali Hewitt threw open a question to them. "Guys, do any of you fancy coming back with me and Alex for a few late night drinks?"

Normally, the five suspects would have been suspicious about offers from strangers they had never met before. They were all aware that MI6 were active in surveillance against the SNLA, the WRA and draft evaders. But the drink had taken effect and Alex and Emma seemed a genuine couple.

"Love to, Emma" said Davies.

"Where's Alex?" asked Ingram.

"Oh, he's trying to arrange taxis" replied Hewitt.

Out in the Rue St Denis, Castle withdrew his encrypted mobile phone and rang.

"Catnap here." Castle recognised the voice of Captain Roly Patrick of 2SAS.

"Catnap, this is Doghouse. I'm outside the Frog and Rosbif. The targets should be out in just over a minute."

"Brilliant Doghouse. We'll be there."

Thirty seconds later, Hewitt emerged from the Frog and Rosbif with Burnside, Davies, Ingram, Lawrence and Vaughan, along with the three girlfriends of the two WRA men and the National Service deserter.

"Alex, any luck with taxis?"

"Half hour wait I'm afraid. Tonight see somewhat busy. Hope that's not a problem with you guys."

"No problem Alex" said Burnside.

Rob Burnside barely knew what had hit him as he was seized from behind. A sharp dig to the kidneys followed by a blow to the solar plexus and he was helpless on the ground. A split second later, all his friends were similarly disabled and were being tied up. The SAS had struck.

"Steve, Ali, many thanks for what you've done tonight" said Captain Patrick as the wanted fugitives were bundled into a van. "At last we've brought the killers of Charles Richardson and Chris Moorhouse to justice."

13 July 2018, 6:30am
Le Bourget Airport
Paris

Le Bourget Airport had once been Paris's main international airport. It had lost this title to Orly after just 13 years of existence and the opening of Charles de Gaulle Airport, some two kilometres up the road at Roissy in 1974 pushed Le Bourget further down the pecking order. The airport was now used almost exclusively for general aviation and business flights.

One of the regular users of Le Bourget was the Royal Air Force, whose Communications Flight of British Aerospace 125 business jets serviced the British Embassy by flying in personnel, mail and packages. A BAe 125 was standing inside Hangar B, which was reserved for the RAF flights.

An unmarked Citroen Berlingo van pulled up inside Hangar B. The van's doors were opened and four men and a woman stepped out under armed guard.

Group Captain Robert Arnold of the RAF was on hand to receive the prisoners from the MI6 Paris Station Chief, Jonathan Barclay. Arnold had an escort of three armed RAF policemen to accompany the prisoners.

"Well done Jon" said Arnold. "Have you had any trouble with the prisoners?"

"None Bob" replied Barclay. "Mind, having a couple of SAS riding shotgun helped, I think. Is everything planned at your end?"

"It is" replied Arnold. "National Anti-Terror Squad will be waiting for us at Northolt to formally charge the prisoners and escort them to prison. I've arranged for a total news blackout until the prisoners are all behind bars. That way, we'll avoid any embarrassing questions from the French authorities."

"All right you lot" snapped Sergeant Dean Woodgate of the RAF Police. "On board now, and no funny stuff. Otherwise you get both barrels. Understand?"

Less than twelve hours earlier, Rob Burnside, Mark Davies, Kirsty Ingram, Jack Lawrence and Gareth Vaughan had been enjoying a night out at the Frog and Rosbif in the centre of Paris. The last thing they remembered was meeting a couple called Alex and Emma. After that, they remembered nothing until being woken up at dawn at gunpoint and being herded into a van.

All five prisoners were still handcuffed and Woodgate and his two colleagues all had semi-automatics trained on them. They were clearly taking no chances.

The BAe 125 began to taxi out to get ready for take-off for the flight back to Northolt. Group Captain Arnold stood up at the front of the plane to address the prisoners.

"You may be wondering where you are and what's going to happen. Well, I will give an explanation. All of you are being held in British military custody on suspicion of having been involved in the murders of Sir Charles Richardson and Mr Christopher Moorhouse in Paris earlier this year. Under the Murder Act of 1861, any British citizen who commits a murder outside the jurisdiction of the United Kingdom is still liable to be tried in the United Kingdom for that act."

Kirsty Ingram was in the mood for a confrontation and shouted out "That's complete bollocks. You've basically by-passed agreed mutual assistance procedures and fucking kidnapped us."

"Silence" roared Woodgate.

Group Captain Arnold continued. "On arrival in the United Kingdom, you will be handed over to the police who will formally charge you and escort you to prison, where you will be held prior to being tried. I would strongly advise you to be co-operative during this flight. Sergeant Woodgate and Corporals Bryden and Harris are all armed and have orders to shoot if you attempt to resist or interfere with this flight."

The BAe 125 was now positioned at the end of the runway at Le Bourget, waiting for clearance from Air Traffic Control to take off. Within seconds the small business jet started to rev up its engines, then began to roll. Its speed rapidly increased before it finally lifted off the ground and started a steep climb.

For Gareth Vaughan, there seemed little choice. Either go back to the United Kingdom tamely and face a virtual show trial at the new Special Criminal Court and a certain death sentence. Or go out in a blaze of glory.

Now was the best opportunity. The plane was still climbing and the police guards had been forced to take a seated position. The pilot was sitting only ten feet away. If he could knock the yoke out of his grasp, the plane would lose control.

Vaughan decided to make his move. He was athletic and sprung out of his seat like a panther. Before the military police guards could react, he dived on top of the pilot and knocked him out of his seat.

Pandemonium followed. Corporal Rick Bryden pulled out his semi-automatic and opened fire, killing Vaughan immediately. But a split second later, the gun was lying on the floor as Burnside kicked it clear from his grasp. As Davies and Lawrence rushed the other two guards, Burnside dived for the yoke. Even though he was handcuffed, he managed to cause the plane to lose control. Group Captain Arnold pulled out his sidearm but, before he could use it, the plane violently spun round to the left before tumbling into a spiralling dive as control was lost.

The same time
Air Traffic Control
Charles de Gaulle Airport
Paris

Françoise Menetrey had been delighted to obtain a job in what had once been a male-dominated profession. An attractive blonde of 25 years old, she was now in her second year of employment at Charles de Gaulle's Air Traffic Control.

The early part of her shift promised to be quiet but it was after 7am that things would get lively. Three pan-Atlantic jumbos would be arriving in quick succession, along with a flight from the Ivory Coast, and there would be departures in the opposite direction. In addition, business flights from Le Bourget two kilometres down the road would be starting up.

Menetrey had just cleared the first flight out of Le Bourget, GB274, the 6:45 RAF diplomatic flight to London Northolt and was ready to accept Flight AA101, the American Airlines overnight flight from Chicago which was now less than 30 miles from Paris.

"Charles de Gaulle to Flight AA101. Do you read me?"

"Roger" replied Captain Brad Summers of American Airlines.

"You have clearance to land."

Suddenly, Menetrey's attention was drawn to what appeared to be an unauthorised plane which was on direct collision course with the American Airlines jumbo. It was Flight GB274.

"Gemini Bravo 274, do you read me? You are heading into the flightpath of Alpha Alpha 101. Please take immediate evasive action."

There was no reply from GB274. All she heard was shouting which suggested that not all was well on board.

The same time
Onboard American Airlines Flight AA101

Flight AA101 had left Chicago just over eight hours earlier and was on course to land at Paris Charles de Gaulle on time. The plane, an Airbus A380, was holding 550 passengers. Most of these were Americans and were a mixture of middle-aged couples taking their annual vacation to Europe and students whose college year had just finished.

"Ladies and gentlemen, will you please fasten your seat belts and turn off all electronic equipment. We are preparing to land at Charles de Gaulle in fifteen minutes." The honeyed tones of Chief Stewadess Sherilyn McGuire advised the 550 passengers on board that their journey was nearly over.

On board the flight deck, the two pilots, Captain Brad Summers and Captain David Jelinek prepared for the descent before landing. The engine tone on the massive A380 quietened and the nose began to tilt downwards. Beneath them, they could see the green fields of the French countryside which would shortly give way to the urban sprawl of Paris. Both men were looking forward to a night in the French capital before flying back to Chicago, but for different reasons. Summers, at 50 the older man, had promised his wife that he'd buy her some Chanel perfume and a box of chocolates. Jelinek, the younger man in his mid-30s and single, was looking forward to a night out on the town.

Suddenly, there was an emergency message from Air Traffic Control.

"Flight AA101, do you read me. Take immediate evasive action to the right, there's an unauthorized flying object heading into your path."

"Roger" replied Summers. "Dave, stick hard to right, now."

184

Summers and Jelinek both grabbed the control sticks of the A380 and put it into a hard 90 degree turn. The big plane's fly-by-wire controls meant it was surprisingly manoeuvrable, but there was simply too much of the A380 to avoid the stricken BAe 125 of the RAF. The out-of-control business jet smashed into the port wing of the massive airliner. As fuel lines were ruptured, there was a massive explosion. Both planes plummeted towards the ground, out of control.

"Mayday, Mayday. This is flight AA101. Unidentified plane has collided with us and we've lost all control."

The same time
Avenue Maurice Thorez
St Denis

St Denis was not one of Paris's more salubrious areas. It had a long history of being a working-class district and for years had been run by the Communist Party. The main thoroughfares were named after past French Communist functionaries, including the notoriously Stalinist party leader Maurice Thorez who ruled it with a rod of iron for over thirty years.

In recent years, St Denis had become home to mainly immigrant families from North and West Africa and the Caribbean. Most of the families were now rising in order to go to work of school, and the smell of flatbread and falafel came out of the municipal flats as wives prepared breakfasts for their menfolk and children.

None of the residents would have realised the mortal danger their were in as, above them, the stricken American Airlines jumbo jet of Flight AA101 was plummeting earthbound after a collision with an RAF jet. It was totally without warning when the Airbus A380, streaming flames and fuel, plunged into the Residence de L'Ermitage complex of municipal flats.

The impact of the massive jet smashed a hole through no less than five floors before it exploded in a massive ball of flame. Within minutes, almost the whole of the upper five storeys were on fire.

The same day, 9:30am
Foreign and Commonwealth Office
Whitehall
London

Staff at the Foreign and Commonwealth Office were routinely instructed not to raise important issues with Ministers after the final Ministerial box closed on Thursday afternoon. Friday was always the day that Ministers headed back to their constituencies for the weekend.

Henry Arbuthnot was present at his desk because he had a relatively short journey to his constituency of Hertfordshire South West. He had issued his Diary Secretary with orders not to be disturbed. That came to an end as his Principal Private Secretary, Kate Lowes, came into his office.

"Foreign Secretary, can I disturb you for a minute?"

"Is it urgent Kate?" asked the Foreign Secretary. "You know that I've got to head off to my constituency today."

"I'm afraid so" replied Lowes. "One of the diplomatic flights has crashed just outside Paris. All on board are dead."

"Look Kate, sad though it is for the families of those concerned, it's not exactly world-stopping news. Can you find out the names of the deceased and prepare letters of condolence for me to send to their next of kin."

"It's a lot more serious that that Foreign Secretary" said Lowes. "The plane crashed into an American Airlines jumbo coming into Charles de Gaulle and that in turn has crashed into an apartment block in Saint Denis. There were over 500 passengers on the jumbo and god knows how many in the apartment block that's been hit."

In the outer office, there was television coverage and the Paris air crash was headline news.

"This is Jason Keegan of Sky News reporting from Paris."

"More than two hours after American Airlines flight AA101 crashed into the Residence de L'Ermitage complex of municipal apartments, the fires are still burning fiercely. Residents on the lower floors have all now been evacuated safely but, despite the best efforts of the Paris and Saint Denis fire service, there appears to be no hope for the residents of the top five storeys."

"Local accident investigators are trying to establish the reason why an RAF BAe 125 business jet on a routine diplomatic flight lost control on take off and flew into the path of the incoming American Airlines flight."

Within a minute, Arbuthnot was on the phone to the British Ambassador in Paris.

"Good morning Foreign Secretary. Jeremy Porter here."

"Jeremy, what the hell happened?" asked Arbuthnot. "How come a routine diplomatic flight lost control? We've had the 125s in service for over thirty years and they've never given any problems before." Arbuthnot had been at one point in his career a military attaché and had used the Communications Flight.

"There's something you should know Foreign Secretary" said Porter. "Last night, a joint operation between MI6 and the SAS successfully apprehended five suspected SNLA and WRA terrorists suspected of the murders of Charles Richardson and Chris Moorhouse earlier this year. Flight GB274 was being used to transport them back to the United Kingdom to face trial."

Arbuthnot remembered the offer by his Defence counterpart, Jason Steer to deploy the SAS and the RAF to bypass an obstructive French judiciary.

"Then what happened, Jeremy? Why did Flight GB274 lose control?"

"I've got no idea Foreign Secretary" replied Porter. "All I can guess is that the prisoners put up some resistance and may have incapacitated the pilot."

"For God's sake Jeremy, weren't the prisoners handcuffed of anything? And weren't the escorts armed? We weren't dealing with gas meter bandits you know."

"As far as I understand Foreign Secretary, the prisoners were handcuffed and under armed guard. It's possible that the plane developed a fault."

"Not the 125 Jeremy" replied Arbuthnot. "Those planes have had over thirty years trouble-free service. I used them when I was an staff officer."

"I guess we'll have to wait until the inquest takes place" said Porter.

"No Jeremy, I've got no intention in letting the Frogs crawl all over our business. If Dumas finds out we've used diplomatic flights to bypass extradition agreements, there'll be hell to pay. Not only from her but from the rest of the EU too. We're going to have to remove all evidence of the purpose of Flight GB274. And Jeremy, I want a total news blackout on the flight until I advise you further."

Arbuthnot next phoned Sir James Beveridge, Director-General of MI6.

"Good morning James, Henry Arbuthnot here."

"Good morning Foreign Secretary, what can I do for you?"

"Firstly, can I pass on my gratitude to the agents who helped secure the capture of Burnside, Davies, Ingram, Lawrence and Vaughan last night. That was an outstanding example of a well-worked operation."

"I couldn't agree more" said Beveridge. "I'll ensure that the agents involved are suitably rewarded."

"The next issue is the crash of Flight GB274 earlier today. I don't know what happened but you don't need to be a rocket scientist to know that, if the French find out we've used diplomatic flights for rendition of prisoners, we're in for big trouble. And I don't think the Americans will be too pleased either as over five hundred of their nationals have been killed. There's Congressional elections this autumn in the States and I don't think Katherine Whitney will be too pleased in finding the Democrats back in control."

"James, it is therefore important that MI6 remove all evidence of the purpose of Flight GB274 before the French Accident and Investigation Team get hold of it."

"Very well Foreign Secretary" said Beveridge. "We'll send agents out to remove the bodies of the five prisoners and the flight recorder. All that will be found are the bodies of the pilots and the officials on board."

CHAPTER 15

3 August 2018
Gatika
Basque Region
Spain

Rob Douglas pulled up the hired Renault Trafic panel van outside the unprepossessing terraced house in Barrio de Sertuxta. With him were two SNLA colleagues, Greg Laird and Alison Sutherland.

Gaizko Orzebal had been expecting their arrival and was at the door to greet them. Twenty years earlier, Orzebal had been a leading member of Euskadi ta Askatasuna, better known as ETA, which had been involved in a struggle for independence for the Basque homeland from Spain since the late 1960s. But, three years earlier, the armed struggle had come to an end after the government of Jose Ruiz had signed an historic agreement for the full devolution of domestic affairs for the Basque region and Catalonia. ETA and its political wing, Batasuna, laid down their arms and focused their efforts in fighting for the Basque people's interests through the Basque parliament.

Orzebal was now a town councillor in Gatika but, although their struggle against Spain was now over, it did not prevent Batasuna or former ETA members from maintaining their support for national minorities in other countries that were seeking independence. It was no secret that Batasuna was maintaining close links with the SNLA and the WRA, and the immigration authorities at Bilbao Airport were paying close attention to British nationals entering the country.

In order to avoid coming to attention, Douglas, Laird and Sutherland had all flown to Madrid and hired the van there. A Madrid registration was unlikely to draw the notice of the Guardia Civil in another part of Spain.

"Good to see you, Señor Orzebal" said Douglas as the two men greeted each other. "I understand you may be able to help us."

"Please come through" replied Orzebal. "Anything to drink?"

"No thanks" replied Douglas. "We've got to keep our heads clear."

"What is it you need, Señor?" asked the former ETA man.

"Enough Semtex to make three anti-personnel bombs, along with detonators and primers" said Laird.

"We have just what you need" said Orzebal. "Come with me. By the way, where are you heading for?"

"Benidorm" replied Sutherland. "Schools broke up two weeks ago. The place will be heaving with British holidaymakers. The English think they'll be safe from us while abroad on holiday. Tomorrow, they learn otherwise."

"I believe ETA tried to bomb Benidorm about twenty years ago" said Laird.

"We did" replied Orzebal. "But a traitor in our ranks tipped off the Guardia Civil. I think you should have less trouble with them."

"I sincerely hope so" commented Douglas as they boarded Orzebal's SEAT Almeria for the journey to ETA's secret arms dump.

4 August 2018
Benidorm
Spain

The Costa Blanca resort of Benidorm, midway down Spain's Mediterranean coast, was now full with holidaymakers, the majority of whom were from the United Kingdom. Two weeks earlier, the schools had broken up, and this had precipitated a massive rush of holidaymakers from the United Kingdom to sunnier climes.

It was hard to believe that sixty years earlier Benidorm had been a sleepy fishing village. The seafront skyline was filled with skyscraper hotels. The fortunes of Benidorm had been transformed when it was found that the attraction of guaranteed sunshine and high temperatures with low prices made it attractive to holidaymakers from more northern climes. Hotels sprung up along the seafront, followed by the development of bars and nightclubs to cater for tourists.

Over the previous 20 years, Benidorm, in common with the rest of the Mediterranean, had started to face competition. Cheap, long-haul flights made the USA and the Caribbean affordable to British holidaymakers, and the fact that the USA and much of the Caribbean spoke English was an added attraction. Turkey had emerged as a competitor and offered cheaper prices. The recession in the earlier part of the decade had resulted in many Britons being unable to afford foreign holidays, and custom temporarily dropped. But better economic fortunes in the previous four years had resulted in a return of customers.

At 7am, Rob Douglas pulled the Renault Trafic van up to the Santa Margarita apartments by Levante Beach and parked it in the car park. They had driven overnight from the Basque Country, taking the E804 to Zaragoza, the A23 to Sagunto, then the E15 to Benidorm. The three SNLA members disembarked and headed for the entrance to the apartment block.

"Apartment number seven" replied a female Scottish voice.

"Margaret, it's Rob" replied Douglas.

The catch to the door was released.

Margaret Stanton, Rob Douglas's partner, had rented the self-catering apartment for a week. Enough time for it to be used as a base for the SNLA to start their terror campaign against the English abroad. She had also laid out a tourist map of Benidorm to help find the best targets.

"Alright, Greg, Ali, listen up." Douglas was a former corporal in the Argyll and Sutherland Highlanders and had fought in the first Gulf War 27 years previously. Picking up a marker pen, he highlighted potential targets.

"The busiest site is likely to be the Playa de Levante. Margaret, that was heaving yesterday, wasn't it?"

Stanton nodded her agreement.

"The coolbags we bought should provide adequate cover. No one will suspect anything untoward. Greg, could you deal with the Playa de Levante."

"The next most profitable target is the Old Town. There's loads of English pubs in the Calle sant Vicent area. From previous visits, they've all be busy. Ali, can you look after the Old Town."

"Finally, there's the Playa de Poniente. I'll look after that."

"What's our escape plan Rob?" asked Sutherland.

"At 1pm sharp, we're making our getaway. We've got tickets for the midnight flight from Madrid to Glasgow. When we get back to Madrid, we'll return the van to Hertz. No one will link us to the bombs. Margaret."

"Yes Rob."

"Can you have the van ready to go at 1pm."

By 2pm, both the Playa de Levante and the Playa de Poniente were busy with sunbathing holidaymakers. Meanwhile, the pubs and bars in the Old Town were also doing good business as English holidaymakers flocked in for both lunch and liquid refreshment. No one paid any attention to the coolbags which appeared to have been left by their owners. Mishaps of this kind often occurred.

Without warning, the bag left on the Playa de Levante exploded in a massive fireball. Less than a minute later, there were two similar blasts in the Old Town and on the Playa de Poniente.

The same day
Comisaría de Policía
Benidorm
Spain

Sergeant Mañuel Ortiz of the Policia Municipal had so far found Saturday quiet after the usual hive of activity on Friday night. He was on the day shift and would be having dinner with his wife and family when his colleagues arrived to take on the night shift. Here's to you dealing with the lager louts, he thought.

Ortiz was shaken out of his torpor a split second later. It was Officer Ana Maria Rodriguez, who was helping on the control desk.

"Sir, there's a report of three bomb blasts. One on each of the playas and the third in the Old Town."

"Thanks Ana." Ortiz reached for the emergency button and followed it with an announcement. "This is an emergency, can all officers report to the control room now."

There were just six officers on duty. Ortiz despatched them in twos to the Playa de Levante, the Playa de Poniente and the Old Town. He knew he needed reinforcements and rushed up to the office of his boss, Captain Emilio Canizares.

"Come in Mañuel" said Canizares.

"Sir, there's been three bomb blasts reported. One on each of the Playas and the third in the Old Town. We've only got eight officers on duty. Can you ask Alicante for reinforcements."

"Bomb blasts? I thought that had all stopped after ETA signed the peace agreement three years ago. Okay Manuel, I'll put a call through to Alicante. But they'll want to send the Guardia Civil down to investigate. Please be co-operative with them." Canizares knew that several of the officers in the Policia Municipal resented intrusions by the more prestigious Guardia Civil.

Later that evening
Sky News

"This is Scott Parfitt with this evening's headlines on Sky News."

"The death toll from the SNLA terrorist bombings in Benidorm has now risen to ninety two. Just after 2pm today, there were three bomb blasts in the popular Spanish holiday resort, two on the main beaches and the third in the Old Town where there are several pubs and bars. The carnage on the packed beaches and in the narrow streets of the Old Town was devastating."

"The bombing has been condemned by the Prime Minister, who is currently on holiday in Spain, the Leader of the Opposition and the Prime Minister of Spain, Jose Ruiz, who has promised to make every effort to hunt down those responsible."

"The latest atrocity marks a dangerous new twist in the SNLA's war of terror in support of Scottish independence, as it is the first time they have targeted the general public outside the United Kingdom. It has exposed how vulnerable members of the general public are in countries which are not prepared for terrorist activity."

21 August 2018
The Cabinet Room
10 Downing Street
London

For the second year running, Ministers had found their summer holidays interrupted by an emergency Cabinet meeting. The previous year, it had been the result of SNLA and WRA attacks on vital infrastructure and on tourist attractions. This time it had been due to the escalation of the SNLA and WRA terrorist campaigns to outside the United Kingdom.

Just over two weeks earlier, 92 people had been killed in a triple bombing attach by the SNLA on Benidorm. The SNLA had followed this up with a nightclub bombing in Arenal, Majorca which had claimed thirty more lives. Then the WRA had got in on the act with the bombing of the beach at Agios Nikalaos in Crete and of a bar in Faliraki in Rhodes. Eighty more lives had been lost.

Robert Delgado called the meeting to order.

"I am most sorry that, for the second year in succession, it's been necessary to recall you for an emergency session of the full Cabinet. But it appears that the SNLA and WRA terrorist campaign has now spread to our European neighbours. Clearly we need to take immediate action to avoid harm to the reputation of this Government and of the country as a whole."

Deborah Pearson immediately responded. "Perhaps our European neighbours will now wake up to the threat posed by the SNLA and the WRA, and start giving us some help."

"Fair point Deborah, but we've got to look at the wider picture and the impact on our national interests."

Darren Bramble was next to speak.

"Prime Minister, thought I'd better report on the meeting I had with ABTA last week. They're claiming that the terror attacks in Spain and Greece has hurt their trade and that members are facing potential bankruptcy. I think there's a load of shroud-waving going on. According to the papers, tourist numbers are still high and only a few people have been put off."

"Precisely what today's edition of the *Sun* says" said Jason Steer.

"However, I think you'll agree that I'm right in letting you and colleagues know" continued Bramble. "The last thing we want is for travel companies to go bust without warning. All we'll end up with is a load of whinges from the proles who've been left out of pocket."

"Thank you Darren, I quite agree" said Delgado. "Ed, can you make sure that the Treasury check national statistics for the overseas tourist trade when they come through to see if the industry's claims are verified."

"I'll ensure that's done" replied Ed Villiers.

Delgado then turned to the Foreign Secretary.

"Henry, what's been the response of the Spanish and Greek governments?"

"Not helpful, Prime Minister. They're blaming us for what's happened and asking for us to prevent further occurrences. When I put it to them that it was the failure of European Union governments to co-operate with us on fighting terrorism that had given rise to the bombings, they became almost hysterical. Same when I suggested putting British police and security personnel on patrol overseas. I think I've done everything reasonable to help them."

"My earlier point precisely" added Pearson.

"Henry, continue to maintain dialogue with the governments in Madrid and Athens. But I agree that, until they agree to provide mutual assistance in our fight against terrorism, there's little more we can do."

There was a knock on the door. It was Jenny Mitchell, the Prime Minister's Principal Private Secretary.

"Sorry to interrupt the meeting Prime Minister. There's an extremely urgent call for the Foreign Secretary. It's from the Spanish Ambassador."

"Oh God, don't tell me there's been another bombing" said the Foreign Secretary as he hurried out of the Cabinet Room.

"Jesus Christ, it's going to get hot now" said Jason Steer as he saw the television screen in the outer office. The reason for the Foreign Secretary's sudden departure was clear to see.

"This is Aidan O'Brien reporting for Sky News from Marbella."

"The death toll from last night's shooting at McLintock's Bar in Marbella now stands at fifteen. At about 11:30 last night, two gunmen burst into the bar and opened fire on the customers in a random attack. It is now known that the gunmen were both from the EVF which had threatened revenge for the terrorist murders of English holidaymakers earlier this month, and it is believed that McLintock's Bar was targeted because its clientele were mainly from Scotland."

4 September 2018
United States Supreme Court
Washington DC

"Will Mr Anthony Glyn Edwards and Mr Neil Archibald Telfer follow me this way." The Court Clerk's request signalled that the Supreme Court hearing of the appeals by Tony Edwards and Neil Telfer against the decision of the US Immigration Tribunal that they should be deported to the United Kingdom on account of illegal entry was about to start.

Accompanied by their lawyer, Debra Kelly of Kelly, Gleeson and Partners of New York, Tony Edwards and Neil Telfer walked into the chamber of the highest judicial authority in the USA.

Edwards and Telfer had both been arrested in Cincinnati back in May along with Bill Fraser of Caledonian Aid and Ben Meredith of Cambrian Aid, and had faced charges of arms trafficking, money laundering and conspiracy to commit terrorist acts. All four men had faced potential prison sentences of fifty years to life. But Fraser and Meredith were extremely well-connected, having influence in both Congress and the Ohio State Legislature. Charges were dropped.

However, Edwards and Telfer still faced deportation back to the United Kingdom because they had entered the USA using false passports. The US Immigration Appeals Tribunal had upheld the decision by Immigration and Naturalisation Service. Their last recourse was to the Supreme Court.

Edwards and Telfer were however not without their supporters. Their argument that they would face an unfair trial back in the United Kingdom and disproportionate punishment was persuasive. A large group of Congressmen, mainly from the Democrats and led by Senator for Washington State, Brad McAllister and Pennsylvania Representative Graydon Hopkins, was lobbying for Edwards and Telfer to be allowed to stay. Several Hollywood actors and rock musicians were also prominent in the campaign.

Debra Kelly took to the stand to put the case for Edwards and Telfer.

"Your honours, may I present the case in support of the appeal by my clients, Anthony Glyn Edwards and Neil Archibald Telfer against the decision by Immigration and Naturalisation Service that they should be deported from the United States of America to the United Kingdom of Great Britain and Northern Ireland."

"Both Mr Edwards and Mr Telfer admit that they have been active in support of the campaign for the independence of their countries, Wales and Scotland, from the United Kingdom. They also accept that they used false passports to enter the USA. But please consider this. The purpose of their visit was to secure the transfer of monies raised through charitable donations to help people in Wales and Scotland who have been suffering privation as a result of the troubles which have taken place there. Mr Edwards and Mr Telfer have no quarrel with the American people, nor do their activities present any threat to the USA."

"It was not possible for Mr Edwards and Mr Telfer to travel to the USA on their own passports. Because of their activities in support of independence for their countries, the United Kingdom government has put them on a list of people to be challenged if they travel outside the country. They will face almost certain arrest and prosecution if they are forced to return."

"The United States is a signatory to the United Nations Convention on Human Rights, which binds it to prevent anyone from being subject to cruel or unusual punishment. It is my opinion that, if you agree to the deportation of Mr Edwards and Mr Telfer, they will face a significant risk of such punishment on their return to the United Kingdom. The current government of the United Kingdom has abolished many of the legal protections which ensure that prosecutions are carried out in a fair way. They have introduced internment without trial for anyone considered to be a terrorist suspect. This has been interpreted so widely that simply being active in the campaign for independence has been sufficient reason to intern people. There has been reliable evidence that torture has been used at the interrogation centres at Brecon and Stirling. The Government is now bringing in legislation to allow terrorist cases to go before juryless trials. And the media in the United Kingdom is notoriously partisan and defendants in terror cases have to contend with relentless 24/7 media coverage which aims to intimidate judges and juries into passing guilty verdicts and the most severe punishments."

"Nearly twelve months ago, eight suspected terrorists were hanged for terrorist bombings at Warrington Barracks and Royal Ascot. Increasing numbers of people believe they were all innocent and were set up by the British Government and Establishment who were determined that someone should take the rap. There was evidence that none of these men and women were anywhere near the venues which were bombed, yet during the trial, it is believed that evidence which would have freed them was deliberately suppressed. Their defence attorneys were threatened with suspension from the trial when they questioned prosecution witnesses too rigorously. And there was evidence that they were mistreated by the police and prison officers while they were in custody."

"The government of the United Kingdom is at best only democratic in name. Freedoms and protections from excess of official process have been scrapped, and the government panders to the most illiberal public attitudes in order to garner support. I therefore urge you to allow this appeal."

7 September 2018
Radio Free Britain

The newsroom at Radio Free Britain could barely contain their excitement. They had just come into the possession of a top secret memo from the British Embassy in Paris. It was from First Secretary, Anne Calcott, and was addressed to Colonel Adam Ryder, the Military Attaché. It read:

From:	Anne Calcott	cc:	Jeremy Porter
	First Secretary		James Beveridge
	British Embassy		Simon Marshall
	Paris		Mike Woodcock

15 June 2018

Adam

The French authorities are still refusing to return the five suspects in the murder cases of Sir Charles Richardson and Christopher Moorhouse (Robert Burnside, Mark Davies, Kirsty Ingram, Jack Lawrence and Gareth Vaughan) to custody, and it looks unlikely that they will agree to their extradition. The Government has agreed that extraordinary rendition should be used to bring the suspects into British custody. A joint operation between MI6 and the SAS should achieve this objective. We will make available diplomatic flight GB274 from Le Bourget to transport the suspects back to the United Kingdom.

Grateful if you could liaise with MI6 and with Mike Woodcock to take this forward.

Regards

Anne

Newsroom Manager Sarah Atkins called the room to order.

"This is probably the most explosive leak for years. Not only does it confirm that the British Government has engaged in extraordinary rendition but the plane used was the one which caused the Paris air crash. The British government is going to have to do some explaining, particularly to France and the USA."

10 September 2018
Foreign Ministry of France
Champs-Elysees
Paris

Sir Jeremy Porter, the British Ambassador, feared the worst as he was escorted into the office of France's Foreign Minister, Jean-Michel Betancourt.

"Good morning Sir Jeremy" said Betancourt, a tall man in his mid-50s with an aristocratic manner. "Take a seat. Coffee?"

"No thanks Monsieur Betancourt" replied the Ambassador.

"I am afraid I've got an unpleasant duty to perform" continued Betancourt. "The conduct of certain members of the Embassy staff was in contravention of how diplomatic staff are expected to behave. Let us not get drawn on the views my Government has about the policies of your Government in relation to independence for Scotland and Wales or on its internal judicial and security policies. They are not relevant. But what is relevant is the way your officials conduct themselves while they are guests of my country."

"Firstly, you arranged for the kidnap and forced transportation against their will of five of your nationals, in complete contravention of all international agreements."

"All of them were terrorist suspects who were responsible for two murders on your soil, Monsieur Betancourt" said Porter. "One of the victims was my predecessor. Your Government was doing nothing to ensure they stood trial."

"That did not justify kidnapping them Sir Jeremy" replied Betancourt. "There are international agreements for extradition of criminal suspects, which you did not even bother to use."

"Your Government has not been very co-operative with extradition requests" said Porter.

Betancourt continued. "Furthermore, Sir Jeremy, you used a diplomatic flight to transport the five people you seized. With tragic consequences. You know the conventions for diplomatic transport, don't you?"

"I've spent over thirty years in the diplomatic service Monsieur Betancourt" replied Porter.

"There is an international convention that protects the contents of diplomatic bags Sir Jeremy. We trust that all countries abide by it. On this occasion, the United Kingdom has been in breach of that convention by using the cover of a diplomatic flight to by-pass international agreements. My Government takes a most serious view of this transgression. And furthermore, the flight recorder from flight GB274 was missing. I am not saying that you were responsible for this going missing, but I should remind you that is a serious breach of international aviation conventions."

"My Government has decided to remove diplomatic accreditation from six of your officials. Here is the list." Betancourt passed it to Porter. On it was Anne Calcott, Adam Ryder, James Preston, a Second Secretary, Sara Romney, a Third Secretary, Dan Crosby, another Military Attaché and Luke Morris, an MI6 operative.

"Your officials have a week to leave Paris Sir Jeremy. I trust you will co-operate with this distasteful task."

14 September 2018
United States Supreme Court
Washington DC

The Supreme Court had spent the past week and a half listening to the evidence presented by the attorneys for appellants Tony Edwards and Neil Telfer, and for the US Immigration and Naturalisation Service, along with the cross-examination of all parties involved. The panel of judges emerged from their chambers and it was evident that they were either ready, or close to, announcing their decision.

When the appeal began, few people in the USA believed that either Edwards or Telfer stood a realistic chance of escaping deportation to the United Kingdom. Both men had entered the USA on false passports, and intelligence records had them down as members of terrorist organisations. The United Kingdom was the USA's closest ally and, although there were many Americans who were sympathetic to the Scottish and Welsh campaigns for independence, the vast majority recognised the United Kingdom's long history of support for the USA and felt that the USA should help its ally. Finally, the composition of the Supreme Court was conservative, reflecting the fact that the Republicans had been incumbent in the White House for 26 of the previous 38 years.

However, there had been some disquiet in the USA about the lack of information from the British government about the circumstances surrounding the diplomatic flight which had collided with an incoming American Airlines flight and resulted in the world's worst air disaster. Over 500 Americans had perished as Flight AA101 crashed into Residence de L'Ermitage flats in Saint Denis on 13 July. The leaking of an Embassy document earlier that week which claimed that the flight had been used for the extraordinary rendition of terrorist suspects, combined with the fact that the bodies of the suspects and the flight recorder from the HS125 had gone missing had led to a campaign for the British government to compensate the bereaved relatives of the passengers who had died aboard Flight AA101.

Alex Rodriguez, the Director-General of the Immigration and Naturalisation Service, had a pensive look as he conferred with the INS attorney, Tim Landon.

"Tim, I'm worried we could lose this as a result of the British Embassy leak earlier in the week. What Edwards and Telfer say about facing extra-judicial process if they are returned now looks credible in the light of what happened in Paris two months ago. Not only that, there's growing anger that over 500 American lives were sacrificed."

Landon was more relaxed about the issue. "Relax Alex" he said. "I can't see the Supreme Court letting those guys stay. All the legal arguments are in our favour. And what's more, the Brits are doing only what we did a decade ago in Afghanistan and Iraq."

Chief Justice Warren Berenson, a severe-looking man in his late 50s, rose from his seat to speak.

"With my fellow justices, the Supreme Court has considered the case for the appellants, Anthony Glyn Edwards and Neil Archibald Telfer, against the decision by the United States Immigration and Naturalisation Service that they should be forcibly removed from the United States of America and returned to their country of origin, the United Kingdom of Great Britain and Northern Ireland."

"Anthony Glyn Edwards and Neil Archibald Telfer, there is no question that your method of entry to the United States of America was not legal. You both used false identities to secure entry and to disguise the fact that you both hold membership of the Welsh Republican Army and the Scottish National Liberation Army, both of whom are classified as terrorist organisations by the State Department. There was little doubt that the motive of your visit was to advance the cause of the Welsh Republican Army and the Scottish National Liberation Army. Had information about your membership of these organisations and the purpose of your visit been known, you would not have been granted visas to visit the United States of America."

"However, I along with my fellow justices recognise that you both have a real and justified concern about the possibility of facing ill-treatment and unfair judicial process in the United Kingdom. The United States of America had a precedent of granting sanctuary to overseas nationals who have proved they face the risk of persecution, ill-treatment or unfair judicial process if they were returned to their country of origin, even if our Government does not approve of their cause."

"Anthony Glyn Edwards and Neil Archibald Telfer, your appeal is allowed."

The same day
Home Office
Marsham Street
London

"Home Secretary, have you got a minute? Afraid it's urgent." Sir Richard Benson, the Permanent Secretary, was on the other end of the line.

"What's it about Richard?" replied Deborah Pearson, who was clearing her desk before making the journey to her Midlands constituency.

"Just heard on the news that the US Supreme Court have allowed the appeals of the SNLA and WRA men against deportation."

"Oh God!" exclaimed the Home Secretary. "Who were they?"

"Tony Edwards and Neil Telfer" replied Benson. "They were on an arms purchasing mission."

"Richard, can you set up a meeting for me with Henry Arbuthnot and Jason Steer. This morning. Sorry for the short notice, but it's urgent."

Later that morning

"The Embassygate affair's been an absolute disaster for the country" said Henry Arbuthnot. "The Frogs have kicked out six of our Embassy staff. Other EU countries have tightened restrictions on our diplomatic staff. And in the USA, relatives of passengers on board the flight that crashed are seeking millions from us."

"And now the US Supreme Court has let two terrorists stay because they would face torture or persecution over here" added Deborah Pearson. "And all because some squealer leaked a top secret document to that poxy radio station Radio Free Britain. Henry, I take you've had no more success with the Dutch government?"

"A complete no-go Deborah" replied Arbuthnot. "The Dutch have done bugger all and other EU countries are supporting them."

"We need to do something about Radio Free Britain" said Pearson. "They've now gone beyond being a nuisance. They're openly engaged in sedition and espionage. What they've done has caused incalculable damage to the country's reputation and interests."

"Perhaps it's time for direct action" said Jason Steer.

"What are you thinking of Jason" asked the Home Secretary.

"A military operation to seize their base and arrest everyone on board, Debbie" replied Steer. "Then for the base to be destroyed so it can't be reused."

16 September 2018, 6am
Radio Free Britain

"This is Rob Pearce on Radio Free Britain for the final hour of the Night Owl. And now for "Ignoreland" by R.E.M. from their 1992 album, "Automatic for the People". Sums up the present state of the United Kingdom."

Rob Pearce, the self-styled "Night Owl", had one more hour of his show before handing over to Safiya Hussein, who presented the breakfast show on Sundays. He devoted this section to lower tempo records and called this the "chill-out zone.

In the murky half-light before dawn, a grey shape approached at speed out of the gloom. A fast Vosper Thorneycroft naval launch carrying twenty men of the Special Boat Service under the command of Major Rupert Thornley.

Meanwhile, in the sky, a Royal Navy Merlin helicopter carrying 25 Royal Marines approached the former gas rig, escorted by a Royal Navy Lynx helicopter which was armed in case there was any resistance which put the operation in danger.

As the launch pulled up alongside Radio Free Britain, Sergeant Alex Kirwan and Corporal Dave Meacher fired grappelling hooks up to the main platform. This suspended a pair of Kevlar ladders, up which the SBS men ascended rapidly.

At the same time, ropes descended from the Merlin hovering above the platform and the Royal Marines quickly abseiled onto the platform.

Rob Pearce was just about to select his next record when a pair of SBS men pointing guns burst into the studio.

"Freeze. On the floor now" they shouted. A stunned Pearce could do nothing more than comply.

The other SBS men rapidly took control of the station's administration office and the accommodation block. The Royal Marines swept the converted rig to make sure that no one was hiding ready to spring and ambush. Within five minutes, the entire station staff were in custody.

A second Merlin helicopter came into view, and Flight Lieutenant Mark Warner lowered it onto the platform. The staff of Radio Free Britain were transferred to the second Merlin, with ten of the 25 Royal Marines providing an armed guard. After the fiasco of Paris two months earlier, no chances were being taken. The three helicopters and the naval launch departed from the now empty Radio Free Britain.

Five minutes later, Flight Lieutenant Gary Oldfield and Flight Lieutenant Wayne Goody, flying an RAF Tornado GR4 from RAF Marham, were twenty miles from the abandoned base of Radio Free Britain, flying at 500 miles per hour. They were carrying two 2,000 pound JDAM guided bombs.

"Two minutes to target nav" said Oldfield. "Ready to fire?"

"Roger" replied Goody.

Goody obtained radar co-ordinates for the former gas rig, primed the bombs and pressed the release button. The two bombs, guided by radar, glided on a trajectory towards the former base of Radio Free Britain and hit home. As 4,000 pounds of high explosive detonated, the former gas rig dissolved in a massive ball of flame.

"Target destroyed" said Oldfield into his radio to notify the base commander that the primary objective had been achieved. "Alright Wayne" he said to his backseater, "let's head for home and breakfast."

CHAPTER 16

27 September 2018
House of Lords
London

"Ever since the Magna Carta was signed in 1215, the concept of trial by jury has been one of the bedrocks of British justice. It has distinguished the United Kingdom from countries where justice is arbitrary, subordinate to the governing party and where judgement is at the whim of the executive rather than the views of fellow man, and is a reason why the United Kingdom has been admired across the world for having a fair and balanced justice system."

Lord Lane of Eastwick, a Conservative peer, was speaking in the debate of the Criminal Justice Bill which the Government was introducing. The main plank of the Bill was the introduction of a special criminal court to try terrorists and organised criminals who the Government considered were escaping justice through the clever manipulation of procedure by defence solicitors and by intimidation of juries and witnesses. The proposed court would have simplified procedures to prevent defendants being acquitted on technicalities, and would have no jury, with the decision instead being delivered by a panel of three judges.

The Bill was a controversial one. Although it had passed through its first reading in the House of Commons with ease, it had faced stiffer opposition in the House of Lords. Not only were Opposition members opposed, but several Government peers also disliked the Bill's provisions, which they regarded as alien to British judicial principles. Amongst these were Lord Lane of Eastwick, a moderate Conservative, now 71 years old and who had been ennobled back in 1997 after losing his seat in the Labour landslide that year.

Lord Lane continued.

"The proposed Bill goes against all concepts of natural justice and it is for this reason that I cannot support it. It is to our eternal regret that we allowed juryless trials to be introduced in Northern Ireland in the 1980s. There is little doubt that this move helped the IRA rather than helped defeat it. I accept that we have introduced juryless trials for complex fraud cases, but this was because of the difficulty that lay juries might have in understanding complicated issues. Which would have made miscarriages of justice more, not less, likely."

"My noble Lords will be aware that, with the ultimate penalty available to the judiciary, utmost care must be taken with judicial process to ensure that wrong decisions are not made. You will be aware of the Ascot Five and the Warrington Three who went to the gallows last year. There is now significant reason to believe that they may have been innocent of all charges against them. Unfortunately, it's now too late to reverse that decision."

Lord Manson, the Government leader in the House of Lords, was next to speak.

"I appreciate the thoughtful contribution of my noble Lord. It is, with great regret, that the Government is considering changes that will, as my noble Lord says, throw away principles which have stood since 1215. But I regret there is no alternative course of action. I do not have to explain how ruthless the Scottish National Liberation Army and the Welsh Republican Army are. Less than a month ago, over 200 innocent people were killed in bombing attacks in Spain and Greece. They are continuing to murder members of the police service and the armed forces while they are trying to maintain public order. They are evading justice through using unscrupulous defence solicitors to secure their release on technical points of law rather than the evidence presented before the courts and by intimidation of witnesses and juries. The only way to ensure that we bring the Scottish National Liberation Army and the Welsh Republican Army to justice for their heinous crimes will be, my noble Lords, if you vote for the motion before you."

Two hours later, the debates had finished. It was time for the House of Lords to vote. Lord Manson was uneasy and, not without justification. The queue in the "non-contents" lobby was long.

After fifteen minutes, the Speaker in the House of Lords, Lord Maxwell, was ready to announce the results.

"The result of the House of Lords vote on the first reading of the Criminal Justice Bill is as follows. The contents, 240 votes. The non-contents 262 votes."

Later that evening
Members' Bar
House of Commons
London

Dominic Collins' the Attorney-General, was not in a good mood. The defeat of the Criminal Justice Bill in the House of Lords meant it would be referred back to the House of Commons. And that would now not take place until after the Party conferences had finished.

"Jesus Christ Deborah, I just don't believe it. That old fool Lane rambled on about the Magna Carta for god knows how long. Don't some of those senile idiots know there's a war on?"

"Relax Dominic" said Deborah Pearson. "We got a solid majority in the Commons and I think we'll do so again. Who knows, the SNLA or the WRA might get us out of jail if they let off a bomb or shoot someone before the next Lords vote."

"Next time round Dominic, I'm thinking of getting some of the backwoodsmen down from the Shires" said the Government's leader in the House of Lords, Lord

Manson. "Maggie did it on the Poll Tax nearly thirty years ago. It worked then and it'll work now. I guarantee we'll get the Bill through."

"I hope you're right Robert" said Collins.

6 October 2018
Ty Mawr near Caernarfon
Wales

The General Councils of the SNLA and the WRA were holding their periodical bilateral meeting at a WRA safe house just outside Caernarfon. Trevor Rees, the Chairman of the WRA General Council reckoned it would be safe to hold the meeting at Ty Mawr. The security forces were focused on protecting the three main Party conferences. The Liberal Democrats had just finished their conference in Blackpool, Labour was about to start its conference in Brighton and the Conservative conference would follow a week later in Bournemouth. They would be paying less attention to events in North Wales some 300 miles away from England's South Coast.

In addition, the WRA had several members of North Wales Police on their payroll. They had provided valuable intelligence.

The SNLA and WRA leaders were discussing the next big target to hit. Doug Paterson, the Chairman of the SNLA General Council was in favour of bombing London on Remembrance Sunday, 11 November. It would be particularly symbolic as it would be exactly 100 years since the end of the First World War. As Paterson said, London would be packed.

"Doug, bombing Remembrance Sunday would be a big mistake." The Deputy Chairman of the SNLA General Council, Charlie Renwick, was less enthusiastic about the proposed mission. "Haven't you forgotten that most world leaders will be in London for the ceremony? Many of them have supported our cause. If we kill any of them, we'll lose overseas support for our struggle. And we cannot afford to kill President Whitney under any circumstances, even though I can't stand the bitch. Most of our funding comes from the USA. If Whitney was to cop it, Caledonian Aid and Cambrian Aid would be shut down overnight. And what's more, there's mid-term Congressional elections next month. We can't afford to lose the likes of McAllister and Hopkins."

"We're not planning to bomb the Cenotaph, Charlie" said Rees. "The idea is that we plant bombs on the Underground and by the queues for the buses. Security round the world leaders will be tight as a drum, so there's no point in even trying, apart from the fact that we don't want to lose friends. But the English can't be everywhere. If we hit public transport as everyone's leaving, the carnage will be enormous. Far in excess of anything else either of us has done."

"One thing I can probably guarantee is that most of the public present will be Government supporters and will support repressive measures against us" said Paterson. "Most of the public attending Remembrance Sunday in the past were generally strongly Conservative in their opinions—it attracts that type of person. For that reason, I think they form a legitimate target."

13 October 2018
Bradford Labour Party Offices
Kirkgate
Bradford

Geraldine Partington, the MP for Bradford North, was holding her regular weekly surgery for constituents on the second floor of the party's offices in Bradford. Even though Parliament was in recess and she had been at the Labour Party conference in Brighton earlier in the week, she was diligent when it came to holding her surgeries for constituents.

Partington had not been a popular choice for the constituency when first selected. A Londoner and a strident feminist, she grated with many of the more traditionally-minded northern Labour Party members and also with the city's large Asian community who had hoped that one of their number would be selected. But by sheer effort and bloody-mindedness, Geraldine Partington had won over both local Labour Party members and the Asian community, and had increased her majority in both the 2014 and 2018 General Elections.

It would have been pushing it to suggest that Partington was popular with the Party leadership. A fiery left-winger who championed minority causes, she was a thorn in the side of Labour leader, Iain Turner, who was trying to make Labour electable again after the ineffectual leadership of Harriet Walker between 2010 and 2014, during which left-wingers in the Party were in the ascendant and made it unelectable outside its traditional strongholds of Scotland, Wales, the North of England and the deprived inner cities, many of which had large immigrant communities.

Most of her surgery visits were from people of Pakistani origin who formed a massive proportion of her constituents, particularly around Manningham. It was therefore a surprise when she found three white people waiting to see her.

A young man in his mid-20s introduced himself. "Good morning Ms Partington. My name is Tim Palmer. I am a qualified solicitor and I'm working for Fair Trials UK, a not-for-profit organisation which seeks to tackle miscarriages of justice. With me are Mairi McDonald and Nerys Thomas. Mairi's boyfriend, Rob Allan and Nerys's brother, Martyn Thomas were, as you may remember, executed a year ago for their part in the bombings of Royal Ascot and Thelwall Barracks. They have been campaigning with the families of the other members of the Ascot Five and the Warrington Three for a pardon. Sadly, a posthumous one."

Partington acknowledged that she knew about the case of the Ascot Five and the Warrington Three. She had been one of eight MPs who had laid a motion condemning the Government's decision not to commute the sentences.

Palmer continued. "You will be aware Ms Partington that there were several discrepancies and contradictions in the prosecution's evidence for both trials. Furthermore, it was clear that the police subjected the defendants to sustained ill-treatment in order to force confessions and the defence were obstructed by the trial judges and the prosecution in their attempts to question prosecution witnesses. We at Fair Trials UK believe there is a prima facie case for a full review of the verdicts.

204

We want to see justice done for the Ascot Five and the Warrington Three and their families. Can you help in any way?"

"Tim, I would be delighted to help" replied Partington. "I'll try to secure a debate on the issue in the House. Also can you let me know if I can help with a press campaign. I've got contacts at the *Guardian* and the *Daily Mirror*. And by the way, call me Geri."

24 October 2018
MI5 Headquarters
Millbank
London

"Richard, I've got Peter Firth on the line" shouted an excited Marcel Francois. "Looks like he's got some hot news."

"Thanks Marcel" said Richard Donovan.

"Hi Peter" said Donovan. "Heard something big's cooking. Let's have it."

"Richard, we've made a breakthrough with the SNLA. They've got a highly-placed mole who advised me that they and the WRA are planning a joint operation for Remembrance Sunday."

"Bloody hell Peter, that's serious. You know that most of the world's leaders will be in London."

"Richard, fortunately they're not the target, nor is the Government" replied Firth. "Instead, the SNLA and WRA are planning to plant bombs on the Underground and by the bus queues. With the crowds present, there'll be carnage. The death toll will go way past anything they've done before."

"Thanks Peter" replied Donovan. "I'll let the DG know. I'll also alert NCA and NATS."

30 October 2018
Dolphin Square
Pimlico
London

"Mr Collins at reception to see you Ms Pearson."

"Thank you George" replied the Home Secretary. "Let him come up."

A minute later, Dominic Collins was sitting on the sofa inside Deborah Pearson's London flat.

"Bet you're pleased that the second reading of the Criminal Justice Bill passed through the Commons with no trouble, Dominic."

"Absolutely delighted Deborah" replied the Attorney-General. "Now the real struggle begins with the Lords. How can we get the backwoodsmen down to vote?"

"I may have the solution Dominic" said Pearson. "The second reading in the Lords starts on 14 November. Three days after the Centenary Remembrance Sunday. I've been advised by MI5 that the SNLA and the WRA are planning a joint bombing operation on that day. Not against the Government—they're too scared of killing

ROB MURPHY

foreign leaders and losing money and support. But against the general public. They're planning to plant bombs on the Tube and buses."

"Bloody hell" exclaimed Collins. "The country will be livid if the SNLA and WRA do that. Besmirching the most sacred ceremony this country has."

"Precisely, Dominic" replied Pearson. "The second reading is three days afterwards. Many of the peers who opposed the first reading will be so angry that they'll probably fall in line behind us. And the backwoodsmen will turn up by the busload to vote the Bill through."

"Deborah, you genius" exclaimed Collins. "How about toasting the Criminal Justice Bill?"

"Couldn't agree more" said Pearson as she opened the antique drinks cabinet and withdrew two brandy glasses and a bottle of Courvoisier.

"By the way Deborah, there will be another benefit. Geraldine Partington has been planning to arrange a press conference on 12 November to launch the campaign to clear the names of the Ascot Five and the Warrington Three. She'll be lucky not to get lynched if she goes ahead."

11 November 2018
Whitehall
London

The Government had wasted no expense in ensuring that the centenary Remembrance Day ceremony was going to be one to remember. The whole of Whitehall had been cordoned off for the benefit of invited guests. Opposite the Cenotaph a large grandstand had been erected for the world leaders who had been invited.

Seats in the front row of the grandstand had been allocated to the Queen, the Prince of Wales and the Duchess of Cornwall. Also present in the front row were the Prime Minister and his wife, the US President, Katherine Whitney and her husband, Jaroslaw Boniek, the Prime Minister of Poland, Karel Dvorak, the Prime Minister of the Czech Republic and Laszlo Nemeth, the Prime Minister of Hungary. Also seated in the front row were Bob Challenor, the Prime Minister of Australia, Stephen Gilbert, the Prime Minister of Canada and Doug McKinnon, Prime Minister of New Zealand. Robert Delgado, the Prime Minister, had made sure that the United Kingdom's friends had been rewarded.

Consequently, the French President, Marie-Christine Dumas, the Russian President, Boris Cherenkov and the Chinese President, Li Zhaobang, all found themselves in the second row.

The back row of the grandstand was where the Opposition politicians were seated. Iain Turner, the Labour Party leader was there with his wife, as was the Liberal Democrat leader, Nick Moss.

At 10:30am, Queen Elizabeth II, now 92 years old, stood up at the podium and gave an address. She recalled her own service in the Second World War and paid tribute to the soldiers who had fought in the two World Wars in the previous century, and in the major conflicts since. She also paid tribute to the efforts of world leaders to secure peace.

206

At 11am, exactly a century from when the guns in the First World War fell silent, the sound of cannons from the Royal Artillery positioned in Horse Guards Parade, provided the signal for five minutes of silence, which was repeated at ceremonies across the country. Above Whitehall, there was a flypast by the Royal Air Force, led by a Spitfire, a Hurricane and a Lancaster from the Battle of Britain Memorial Flight and followed by a procession representing the current air arm. Firstly came six Typhoons, the RAF's current principal fighter, six Lightning fighter-bombers and six Tornado bombers. This was followed by the "heavy" brigade—an example each of the Poseidon maritime patroller, the Globemaster and Universal transport planes, an Airbus Voyager aerial tanker and a Sentry airborne radar picket. This was followed by twelve trainers—six Hawks and six Tucanos. Finally at the rear flew a mix of helicopters from the Royal Navy and the Army—Chinook and Merlin transporters, Apache gunship helicopters and Lynx armed reconnaissance helicopters.

Jamie Boyd could hardly believe his luck. Along with Allan McRae, Kirsty Baird and Siobhan Morton, he had walked into Charing Cross Station on the London Underground unchallenged and had managed to leave a black case close to the barriers which, in a few minutes time, would be thronging with people returning from the Cenotaph. To dispel suspicion, a Transport for London roundel had been applied to the case, which made it look like it was a toolkit.

The four Scots then headed for Embankment Station, less than half a mile away. This too would be crowded as spectators from the Remembrance Day ceremony headed home. Siobhan Morton left another almost identical case, again close to the ticket machines.

"We better get going" said Boyd. "Kirsty, you know the drill. At quarter past eleven, you dial 666."

"Aye Jamie. Will do."

At the same time, Micky Davies and Eddie Prosser were driving down Charing Cross Road in a red Ford Focus van, to which they had applied a Transport for London roundel. Prosser, in the passenger seat, noticed an AA sign directing the public to the bus stands where special services put on for the Remembrance Day ceremony would be waiting to transport them home.

"Next turning on the right Micky" said Prosser.

Davies swung the van off Charing Cross Road into Orange Street, then into Whitcomb Street where they came out into Trafalgar Square. Already parked up were no less than 100 buses which were to carry spectators from Remembrance Day home. He pulled up opposite the row of parked buses where he and Prosser got out.

Kevin Dean, an inspector from Transport for London, was supervising the departures. Davies went up to him.

"Good morning mate. Is it OK to park there? We're on hand to monitor traffic."

"Can I see your ID?" asked Dean.

"No problem" said Davies, who pulled out a forged Transport for London ID card in the name of Ryan Jones.

"Yeah, should be OK Mr Jones. It's going to get hectic in the next few minutes."

Charing Cross Underground Station was heaving with passengers by 11:15am. No one had paid any attention to the black case left near the barriers. It had a Transport for London logo on it and was assumed to be official. It was the same at Embankment Station.

Meanwhile, at Trafalgar Square, passengers were queuing up to board the special bus services laid on. A few passengers commented about the Transport for London van parked on a double yellow line but, otherwise, paid no attention.

Jamie Boyd's Vauxhall Astra had now crossed the Euston Road and was now heading up the Hampstead Road towards Camden Town. In the front passenger seat, Kirsty Baird withdrew her mobile phone from her handbag and dialled in 666.

Almost simultaneously, massive blasts ripped through Charing Cross and Embankment stations. With both stations packed with returning passengers, the consequences were horrendous.

As the sirens from police cars and ambulances started to blare, the van parked in Trafalgar Square exploded in a massive fireball next to the queue of passengers waiting to board for their return journeys.

Later that day
Sky News

"This is Scott Parfitt with the latest news headlines on Sky News."

"London has been left reeling after yet another terrorist atrocity in which the SNLA and the WRA have claimed joint responsibility. Bombs planted in Charing Cross and Embankment underground stations and a car bomb in Trafalgar Square went off shortly after the end of the centenary Remembrance Day ceremony at the Cenotaph as crowds were leaving to go home. The death toll is known to be widespread and sources claim it may be as much as two hundred."

"The atrocity has been condemned by the Prime Minister, the Leader of the Opposition and by the leaders of other world governments who were present in London for Remembrance Day. The Prime Minister, when interviewed this afternoon, described the perpetrators as cowards who had insulted the memory of those who had given their lives for the country in past conflicts, and added that no effort would be spared to ensure they were brought to justice."

12 November 2018
MI5 Headquarters
Millbank
London

Richard Donovan was in at his desk early to ensure that he caught Superintendent Russell Colbourne at the National Anti-Terror Squad before he disappeared into meetings for the day. He was furious that his warning about the planned SNLA and WRA terrorist bombing in London on Remembrance Sunday had been ignored.

He rang Colbourne's number. His Staff Officer answered it.

"Richard Donovan, Security Services. Is Superintendent Colbourne available?"

"He's just coming back to his desk, Mr Donovan. I'll hand him over."

"Russ Colbourne here."

"Russ, it's Richard. Can you tell me what the hell happened? I let both you and Dawn Butler at NCS know about the SNLA and WRA's plans to bomb London yesterday. And I turn on the news yesterday and find out that over 200 people are dead. You guys have always acted quickly on any intelligence we've given you—why not now?"

"I'm sorry you had to find out this way Richard" replied Colbourne. "You'll hear sooner or later."

"What do you mean Russ?" asked Donovan.

"We had orders from above to stand down any surveillance, apart from around Whitehall itself" replied Colbourne. "By the way Richard, don't bother phoning Dawn. NCA were told to do the same thing."

"Why?" asked Donovan. "You're not seriously saying that you got orders from Nicola or Darren to ignore a warning of clear and present danger. You've seen today's papers, haven't you? The *Telegraph* and the *Mail* are calling for heads to roll at MI5 and NATS. And I wouldn't rule out the Government taking such action."

"I am, Richard" said Colbourne. "There's strong speculation that the order to do nothing came from the Government. They've got a debate on the Criminal Justice Bill in Parliament in two days time. You know, the one to introduce a juryless court for terror trials. It's had difficulty in getting through, but after yesterday, I reckon it'll sail through."

"So you're saying that the Government deliberately let the SNLA and WRA bomb Remembrance Day so they could get a Bill through Parliament?" asked Donovan.

"Afraid that's right, Richard" replied Colbourne. "By the way, can you keep this quiet and to yourself. Don't even tell colleagues at Five about it. It could land both of us, and a lot of other people, in serious trouble."

The same day
Conway Hall
Red Lion Square
London

Conway Hall was packed for the meeting to launch the campaign for a judicial review of the guilty verdicts in the case of the Ascot Five and the Warrington Three, all of whom had been hanged a year earlier for terrorist atrocities at Royal Ascot and the Royal Mercian Regiment's barracks at Thelwall, near Warrington, in 2016. The audience consisted mainly of left-wing activists, trade unionists and Scots and Welsh who were sympathetic to the independence cause. Most of the remaining members of the audience were journalists, with preferential slots being given to those from the *Guardian*, the *New Statesman* and *Time Out*.

On the top table were Geraldine Partington, the MP for Bradford North, Tim Palmer from Fair Trials UK which was co-ordinating the campaign, Justin Hemingway, the well-known defence solicitor who had secured acquittals for several SNLA and WRA terror suspects and Mairi McDonald and Nerys Thomas, the girlfriend and the sister respectively of two of the executed men. Also present were David McLagan from the Scottish National Party and Rhys Price from Plaid Cymru.

Palmer signalled that it was time to address the meeting.

"Ladies and gentlemen, I am most grateful for you giving up your time to attend today. Just over twelve months ago, British justice took the lives of Robert Allan, Kevin Banahan, Carol Davies, James Eadie, Glen McFarlane, Glyn Maddock, Rory Shepherd and Martyn Thomas because it believed they had been responsible for two separate terrorist bombings, one at Royal Ascot and the other at Thelwall Barracks in Warrington."

"It was clear from the outset that the British Government had no intention that there should be a fair trial. They basically wanted the authorities to seize the first people they could find who looked like they would fit the stereotype of a terrorist and then subvert the process of justice to produce the result they wanted. So Robert, Kevin, Carol, James, Glen, Glyn, Rory and Martyn were subjected to brutal, gratuitous violence by the police and prison officers from the moment they were taken into custody. The Government ensured that judges with a reputation for harshness were selected to preside and that the most aggressive prosecuting counsels were selected. Defence solicitors were repeatedly obstructed during the course of the trials and repeated and hostile media coverage which made lurid and unfounded allegations about their lifestyles put pressure on the jury to return a guilty verdict."

"The Attorney-General had the opportunity to commute the sentences to life imprisonment and there is evidence that he was advised to do so by his civil servants. There were also requests for clemency from foreign governments, including friendly governments like Australia and New Zealand. Yet the Attorney-General refused to do so."

"In the past twelve months, there has been increasing evidence that Robert, Kevin, Carol, James, Glen, Glyn, Rory and Martyn were all innocent. We recognise there is nothing that can bring them back. But the least the Government can do is to reopen the investigation into the Royal Ascot and Thelwall bombings and, if Kevin, Carol, James, Glen, Glyn, Rory and Martyn are found to have played no part in them, to issue a pardon."

"Geraldine Partington has very kindly accepted an offer to support our campaign and to use her position as a Member of Parliament to drive it forward. Geri, you may wish to speak."

Outside Conway Hall, a crowd had gathered to protest against the meeting, angered by what they saw as blatant SNLA and WRA propaganda only two days after the Remembrance Day bombings. A large proportion were young and male, but the crowd also contained young mothers who had attended with their children in pushchairs and some older people, including military veterans who were wearing their campaign medals from previous wars. All the demonstrators were waving St

George's Crosses and chanting "No surrender to the SNLA, no surrender to the WRA".

The police were aware that the presence of the demonstration could give rise to trouble and ten officers blocked the way into Conway Hall. However, they were unaware that about forty protestors were already inside, having gained entry through using false identities.

Geraldine Partington had started her speech when the first interruption took place.

"You're a fucking traitor, Partington" screamed a fat, shaven-headed man in his late 20s. "You should be strung up. Who've you been sleeping with from the SNLA and WRA?"

Stewards rapidly moved in to remove the protestor. The protestor immediately tried to head-butt the first steward but his blow was blocked by a well-placed forearm. All the stewards had martial arts training.

This prompted his colleagues to leap from their seats. Chants of "EVF, EVF" rang round Conway Hall as a hail of missiles flew towards the stage. Pitched battles between protestors and stewards broke out when suddenly a brick flew through one of the windows, sending shards of glass showering on the audience.

PC Ben Rooney, on duty outside Conway Hall, immediately radioed his station. "Charlie 234 Rooney here. Can we have reinforcements to Conway Hall. Trouble's broken out."

14 November 2018
House of Lords
London

The House of Lords was packed for the second reading of the Criminal Justice Bill. Many peers who had been conspicuous by their absence from the House had responded to the call from the Government whips and, motivated by anger arising from the SNLA and WRA Remembrance Day bombings in London, turned up in their droves with the intention of voting through the controversial bill.

Nevertheless, Lord Manson, the Government's Leader in the House of Lords, found he still had a lot of work to do to ensure there was a Government majority vote for the Bill. Lord Lane of Eastwick was maintaining his opposition to the Bill and Manson feared that there would still be enough Tory peers opposed to the Bill to arrest its progress.

Following Lord Lane, Lord Barker was the next Peer who indicated that he wished to speak. In the debate on the first reading, Barker had voted against the Bill.

"When the first reading of the Bill was debated in this House on 27 September, I was not convinced that the creation of a special court with no jury was the best way to tackle terrorism. For me, the principle that people should be tried by their peers was the right way that justice should be dispensed."

"Three days ago, my noble Lords and Ladies will be aware that the Scottish National Liberation Army and the Welsh Republican Army perpetrated the most heinous atrocity seen in this country, possibly ever. As people gathered to pay tribute to the brave men and women who have given their lives in defending this country's freedom, they were attacked by an enemy which knows no degree of human decency whatsoever."

"After I heard the news and saw the pictures of people who had been killed or maimed being carried away, I thought to myself 'why should we grant the people who are responsible for such a merciless act enjoy the same privileges as the common man and woman'. It is for that reason that I am now prepared to support the Government's proposals as they stand."

Manson sensed that the tide of opinion was swinging the Government's way.

At the end of the debate, the Lords queued up to pass through the "contents" and "non-contents" lobbies. The queue through the "contents" lobby was long.

After 20 minutes, the Speaker, Lord Maxwell, announced the result.

"The result of the House of Lords vote on the second reading of the Criminal Justice Bill is as follows. The contents, 341 votes. The non-contents 259 votes."

**Later that evening
Members' Bar
House of Commons
London**

Deborah Pearson, Dominic Collins and Lord Manson were in a jubilant mood as they celebrated the Government's victory in the House of Lords vote on the Criminal Justice Bill. They were somewhat surprised when they saw a glum-looking Henry Arbuthnot and Jason Steer come in.

"Henry, Jason, how about joining us for a drink to celebrate?" said Pearson. "We've got the Criminal Justice Bill through."

"Have a look at this" said Arbuthnot, dropping a copy of that day's *Daily Telegraph* onto the table.

The leading article on Page 2 of the *Daily Telegraph* read:

Whitney faces battle with Congress as new leaders flex their muscles
The consequences of the resounding Democrat victory in the Congressional elections on 6 November are already being felt by US President Katherine Whitney. The Democrat leaders in the Senate and the House of Representatives, Senator Brad McAllister and Representative Graydon Hopkins, made clear in victory speeches their intention to challenge the President on several key areas of policy.

Both McAllister and Hopkins have been vociferous critics of the Pentagon and will press for reduced spending on defence and its diversion to housing, transport, education, regeneration and retraining of workers. They argue that the absence of military opposition to the USA has created a peace dividend which should be used for the benefit of ordinary people in the USA. Potential casualties may be the proposed new aircraft carrier, USS George W Bush, the A-22 strike bomber and the B-3 long-range strategic bomber.

A further area of conflict may be over the United States' relations with the United Kingdom. Whitney has regarded the United Kingdom as the United States' most valuable military ally ever since the United Kingdom helped the USA in the Third Gulf War back in 2013. But McAllister and Hopkins are less favourably disposed towards the United Kingdom. Both men have been strong supporters of independence for Scotland and Wales, and it is believed may use their position to block the sale of military equipment. Particularly vulnerable is the F-35 Lightning fighter-bomber, which is currently on order for the RAF and the Royal Navy.

CHAPTER 17

7 January 2019
The White House
Washington DC

The US President, Katherine Whitney, was not looking forward to her meeting with the Democrat leaders in Congress. For most of her political life, first as Governor of Texas and, since 2012, as President of the United States, she had been used to dealing with a Republican-run legislature. Not only that, both Senator Brad McAllister from Washington State and Representative Graydon Hopkins from Pennsylvania, had reputations for being prickly and combative.

During the previous sessions of Congress, McAllister and Hopkins had clashed with Whitney's administration on several occasions. The most recent had been back in September over the appeals against deportation of two men, one from the SNLA and one from the WRA, who had entered the United States on false passports to arrange the transfer of cash raised by Caledonian Aid and Cambrian Aid. McAllister and Hopkins had previously helped thwart an attempt by the State Department to have Caledonian Aid and Cambrian Aid classified as terrorist organisations.

"Senator McAllister and Representative Hopkins are here to see you, Madam President" said Jeb Russell, President Whitney's Chief of Staff.

"Send them through Jeb" replied the President. "We'll meet in the Oval Office."

A minute later, McAllister and Hopkins were seated opposite the President.

"Senator McAllister, Representative Hopkins, good morning. Shall we get down to business?"

"As soon as you are ready Madam President" replied McAllister.

The first item on the agenda was defence. Or rather the transfer of a sizeable chunk of the Department of Defense's budget to housing, transport, education, regeneration and re-skilling the workforce. All had been neglected under eight years of Republican administration in the White House and control of Congress.

The proposals put forward by McAllister and Hopkins were for the cancellation of three flagship programmes which they considered were no longer needed in a world where there were no enemies with the capacity to threaten the security of the United States. The first was the planned new aircraft carrier, *USS George W Bush*. This was the first in a new class of aircraft carrier with low observable features which made them harder for enemy radars to detect. The second was the A-22 strike bomber. A development of the F-22 fighter, this plane had the combination of low observability

214

and high speed, aligned to an internally-carried payload which would give the US armed forces superiority over the battlefield. The last was the B-3 bomber, which combined Mach 2 speed, a weapons payload of over 30 tons and a 7,500 mile range to take the battle into the enemy's heartland. The money saved would be diverted to domestic programmes.

The President was in no mood for compromise and she knew the high regard that many Americans had for their armed forces.

"Gentlemen, the fact that the United States has not had to deploy its armed forces since 2013 does not mean that threats to its security have gone away. Both Russia and China have drastically increased the size of their military over the past ten years. Both countries now have powerful blue water navy fleets with aircraft carriers and nuclear submarines, backed up with long range aerial maritime patrol capability. They have also increased the size and capability of their air interception, interdiction and air mobility assets and, next year, they expect to put into service a new long-range bomber which will have the capacity to threaten the US homeland. And Iran, although defeated six years go, will be looking to use their oil revenues to strengthen their armed forces again. So please don't lecture me about a peace dividend."

"You don't get it, Madam President" replied McAllister. "Have you forgotten that Russia and China both offered to help you take on the pirates off the Somali coast? Hardly the act of countries wanting to destroy the United States? As I've said many times before, neither Russia nor China present a threat to the United States. Both countries are arming for the same reason—to defend themselves rather than attack other countries. The United States armed forces are stronger than the rest of the world's military assets put together. We don't need to upgrade them."

Hopkins was next to speak. "You seem to have forgotten, Madam President, that Joe and Joanna Ordinary in Main Street USA want to see their taxes spent on things that will benefit them. Like decent schools and colleges and prospects for their kids. Like decent and affordable housing. Like decent public roads and transport. Like having towns and cities that are not left to rot. And like being trained for skills that will give them a chance to live a decent life and support their families. All of which have been unaffordable luxuries under Republican rule."

Next on the agenda was foreign policy. Or rather that towards the United Kingdom.

McAllister was descended from Scottish Highlanders displaced by the clearances in the 19th century and, although his family was prosperous from business interests in lumber and brewing, the story of the injustices heaped upon his ancestors had been passed down from father to son. It had coloured his view towards the English.

Hopkins' ancestors had been slate miners in North Wales who had emigrated to the United States in the late 19th century to escape grinding poverty. They had been Welsh speakers and great-great-great grandfather Hopkins had been subjected to the indignity of the 'Welsh Not' which was used to force Welsh-speaking schoolchildren to speak English. Like his Senate counterpart, Hopkins had a low opinion of the English.

McAllister was the first to speak.

"Madam President, during the early years of your Presidency, you famously stated that you were a fighter for freedom and the rights of self-determination, and that the United States would support people anywhere in the world who wanted to achieve this."

"Indeed I did, Senator" replied Whitney.

"Then why has your administration repeatedly refused to do anything to support the rights of the Scottish and Welsh people to self-determination? Ever since the British government shut down the devolved governments in Scotland and Wales four years ago and launched a campaign to oppress those people supporting independence, I don't recall you doing anything to dissuade the British government" continued McAllister.

Representative Hopkins was next to join the argument. "Not only that, Madam President, your administration has done everything possible to obstruct people campaigning for Scotland and Wales. You've declared the SNLA and WRA and their political wings terrorist organisations, you've tried to prosecute Caledonian Aid and Cambrian Aid for money laundering and you've repeatedly blocked moves to censure Britain at the United Nations."

"If you were to threaten to withdraw favoured nation status from Britain or to impose trade sanctions" continued Senator McAllister, "Delgado would soon pull his troops out of Scotland and Wales. Why aren't you even considering doing anything, Madam President? All you need to do is shout "jump" and Delgado will say "how high?""

If President Whitney had any goodwill towards the two Democrat Congressional leaders at the start of the meeting, it had totally evaporated by now.

"Senator McAllister, Representative Hopkins" she said with a glacial stare, "you both appear to have forgotten two things. Firstly Robert Delgado is a good friend of the United States and one of the few in the world who is. Six years ago, he sent his armed forces to fight alongside with us when Iran threatened global war in the Gulf. More than most people in the world, he is deserving of my support. And, secondly, gentlemen, have you forgotten that the SNLA and the WRA are both organisations with blood on their hands from over 1,000 murders in the past four years, including a number of US citizens. They are not concerned with freedom and democracy. They want to break up the United Kingdom by armed force and use the control of a precious natural resource to hold the free world to ransom. The United Kingdom government is engaged in a battle to defend its territorial integrity, and I consider it to be fully justified. Prime Minister Delgado therefore has my full and unqualified support."

"Very well Madam President" responded McAllister, "you've made your position perfectly clear. As will Representative Hopkins and I. Understand this. Congress is no longer a poodle of your administration. We have the power to approve legislation, control taxation and to approve export sales. If you defy the wishes of Congress, we will not hesitate to use the powers we have to block your policies."

10 February 2019
Delmonico Restaurant
Marsham Street
London

The Delmonico was one of London's smartest restaurants, and its price list reflected the selective clientele who used it. It was popular with MPs and Government Ministers, many of whom lived nearby.

The Delmonico was relatively quite that Sunday evening, which suited Stuart Grieve and Jonathan Morgan. The Secretaries of State for Scotland and Wales had agreed to meet after returning home from their constituencies.

Both Grieve and Morgan were well known to Head Waiter Benito Castellini, and it was Castellini who directed them to a secluded part of the restaurant where they could discuss sensitive business without prying eyes seeing what was going on.

The two men ordered their meal. For Grieve, it was a starter of Parma Ham with a melon, followed by fillet of seabass with leeks and porcini mushrooms. For Morgan, it was a starter of grilled prawns with garlic mayonnaise, followed by escalope of veal with tomatoes and mushrooms.

"Stu, it sounds like you've got something important to tell me" said Morgan.

"Absolutely right, Jon" replied Grieve. "I've been thinking about devolving some of the powers currently held by the Department for Scotland to local government and removing the dead hand of Whitehall. Obviously, you would want to consider the position in Wales."

"Don't you think that's rather high-risk Stu?" asked Morgan. "What if the SNP win control of councils? We've got similar issues with Plaid Cymru in Wales." The SNP and Plaid Cymru were still committed to full independence for Scotland and Wales and the 14 SNP MPs and 11 Plaid Cymru MPs had not been permitted to take up their seats until their parties renounced support for independence.

"Also, Stu, you've got to consider the possibility of Clann na h-Albann and Meibion Cymru winning council seats" continued Morgan. He was well aware of the threat posed by the political wings of the SNLA and the WRA.

"I know that Jon" replied Grieve. "But I've heard that there's a split emerging in the SNP. Conservatives and moderates in the party are annoyed that the extremist wing has taken Scotland down the road of conflict and terror, has wasted the oil legacy and has kept them out of political power. The new SNP Chairman, Russell Paton, appears to be amenable to compromise which might allow the SNP back into the corridors of power. Exercising power in local government might be a way forward."

"What benefit might there be for us, Stu?" asked Morgan. "After all, there's not much of a vote for the Conservatives in either Scotland or Wales these days."

"Jon, if we manage to successfully re-establish strong local government in Scotland and Wales, just think of the damage it will do to the SNLA and WRA. It will show that normality has returned and, what's more, if we get both the SNP and Plaid Cymru on board, it will give local government some legitimacy. And finally, the

SNP and Plaid Cymru will take votes from Labour and deny them the opportunity of re-establishing their old fiefdoms."

"I like the idea Stu. What happens next?" asked Morgan.

"I'm planning to put it up to Cabinet next week" replied Grieve. "If we get the go ahead, we can then start talks with the SNP and Plaid. Are you interested in backing me Jon?"

"Definitely" replied Morgan.

28 February 2019
Department for Scotland
Dover House
Whitehall
London

"The Secretaries of State for Scotland and Wales are ready to see you gentlemen" said Iain Bryce, Private Secretary to Stuart Grieve, the Secretary of State for Scotland. "Come this way."

Russell Paton, the Chairman of the Scottish National Party and Brynmor Jones, the Chairman of Plaid Cymru followed Bryce into Grieve's office.

Waiting there was Stuart Grieve and Jonathan Morgan.

Grieve opened the meeting.

"Mr Jones, Mr Paton, good morning to the both of you. Firstly, both I and the Secretary of State for Wales will explain the reasons for inviting you here."

"The events of the past four years in Scotland and Wales are most regrettable and I will not dwell on them. However, both I and the Secretary of State for Wales are keen to see normality return to the political and social life of Scotland and Wales, and I think you will agree that you would like to see that too."

"Aye" replied Paton.

Jones indicated his agreement by nodding.

Grieve continued. "Her Majesty's Government is ready to offer Scotland and Wales a fresh start. In just over two months time there are local government elections due. We recognise this could be an opportunity for the Scots and the Welsh to take charge of local affairs once more. This could be the first building block in rebuilding civic society and removing the cancer that is driving support for the SNLA and WRA."

"For the past four years, local government in Scotland and Wales has been subject to constraints by central government. This was unfortunately necessary to prevent the risk of public assets falling under the control of extremists or separatists. But Her Majesty's Government is ready to remove these restrictions and allow democratically-elected representatives to decide how best to deliver services to the people who voted for them. As part of this initiative, we would like to invite the SNP and Plaid Cymru to participate in these elections."

Morgan then took over.

"Mr Jones, Mr Paton, the reason why we've invited you here today and to a further meeting at Department for Wales at Gwydir House in a week's time, is that the Secretary of State for Scotland and I both see the political rehabilitation of the SNP and Plaid Cymru as an important part of the return to normality. We both recognise that you are sensible men who see no value in meaningless conflict or pointless gestures. What we are offering today is a first step in a return to peace and security in Scotland and Wales, and I hope you will be prepared to accept the invitation to participate."

Brynmor Jones was first to respond.

"Mr Grieve, Mr Morgan, many thanks for inviting both Russell Paton and myself here today. We are both grateful that Her Majesty's Government is now prepared to talk to us and you are right to say that we do not see any value in prolonging conflict between the peoples of our countries and Her Majesty's Government. However, there is one barrier to us having a working relationship. Currently, there are 14 SNP MPs and 11 from Plaid Cymru, all democratically elected to the UK Parliament. Yet they are not permitted to take up their seats unless they renounce support for independence. That, gentlemen, remains the overriding objective of both our parties. I am sure that Mr Paton wishes to agree with me."

"Mr Jones, I am afraid this is something I cannot resolve myself" replied Grieve. "Parliamentary rules require that Members of Parliament swear an oath of allegiance to Her Majesty the Queen. And this requires that Members support the territorial integrity of the United Kingdom. It is not therefore possible for either I or the Secretary of State for Wales to waive this requirement."

"However, both I and Mr Morgan would be most disappointed if you did not accept this olive branch just over this one issue. Remember, gentlemen, that we are talking about local government, not national. The participation of the Scottish National Party and Plaid Cymru in local government and, in some cases, possibly running councils, will be a big step back for your parties in political participation. It will also be a big step back for Scotland and Wales and a sign of rejection of the men and women of terror. This is a golden opportunity for you. Do you really want to spurn it and allow the shooting and bombing to continue?"

"Can Brynmor and I have a few minutes to consider your offer?" asked Paton.

"There should be no problem with that, Mr Paton" replied Morgan. "But don't be too long."

Ten minutes later, Jones and Paton both returned to Grieve's Ministerial office.

"We've got our answer" said Jones. "Plaid Cymru and the SNP are both ready to co-operate. We'll accept your offer."

30 March 2019
Bridgend Farm near Callander
Perthshire
Scotland

The heavy snow which had fallen over the past few days in the Trossachs was ideal as far as the SNLA's General Council was concerned. It meant that communication in the area was disrupted and that the bilateral meeting they were having with their WRA counterparts could proceed without prying eyes noticing.

The ten men from the two terrorist group's General Councils were gathered round the dining room at Bridgend Farm. On the agenda was the two groups' planned campaigns for 2019 and first on the list was the local government elections due on 2 May.

Doug Paterson, who shared the duty of chairing the meeting with Trevor Rees, called the meeting to order.

"Gentlemen, you will have seen that the English government has arranged for local elections to take place on 2 May. They have bribed the SNP and Plaid Cymru with offers of devolution of responsibilities to local government to obtain their co-operation and agreement to take part. And the SNP and Plaid Cymru have sold out the people of Scotland and Wales and have agreed to trade independence for a few crumbs from the master's table."

"If we allow these treasonous elections to go through unmolested, we will see the struggle for national liberation of our countries fall by the wayside. It will allow the English government to claim that normality has returned and that the Scots and the Welsh have turned their back on independence. I am sorry to say that there are too many of my compatriots who would be content with the easy life as a subject of English rule."

"And I'm afraid that the same goes for the Welsh, Doug" said Rees. "And don't forget that there's still significant numbers of English resident in both Wales and Scotland."

"We should do everything in our power to disrupt the elections if we are going to maintain our battle for independence" said Paterson. "Anyone who stands for office, acts as an election official or provides policing or security is a legitimate target. Campaigning begins on 11 April."

The Deputy Chairman of the SNLA's General Council, Charlie Renwick, was less convinced. "I don't like this idea Doug. We'll be killing our own people. And it'll be the same for the WRA. We've both now got political wings. Shouldn't Clann na h-Albann and Meibion Cymru be contesting seats?"

"Charlie, we won't be killing 'our' people" shouted an agitated Trevor Rees. "As Doug said, they're traitors. They've sold our two countries down the river to an enemy in return for personal gain. They don't deserve any mercy."

"Sometimes Charlie" said Paterson "I wonder if your heart is really in the cause of Scottish independence."

8 April 2019
MI5 Headquarters
Millbank
London

MI5 had arranged a joint briefing session with the National Crime Agency and the National Anti-Terror Squad to brief teams of MI5 and NCA agents and NATS officers on maintaining security during the forthcoming local government elections in Scotland and Wales. On the platform in the main briefing room was

Richard Donovan from MI5, Dawn Butler from the NCA and Russell Colbourne from NATS.

Field intelligence reports from MI5 agents suggested that the SNLA and the WRA were planning to disrupt the forthcoming elections. MI5 Director-General, Dame Nicola Martin, had communicated to Donovan the importance of ensuring that the elections took place without incident. The Government had placed a lot of faith in the restoration of full local democracy in Scotland and Wales as a sign that the people not only rejected the men and women of terror but they were reconciled to remaining part of the United Kingdom.

Dame Nicola, who had gained her 'gong' in the New Year Honours List, was well aware that Donovan was still seething about the Government's role in the Remembrance Day bombing, when intelligence he had passed onto NATS had been deliberately ignored on order from higher authority. Which, as far as he was concerned, was the Home Secretary. But the hint that he might be on course for an OBE for his services had persuaded Donovan to stay on.

It was Donovan who opened the meeting.

"Ladies and gentlemen, many thanks to you for attending this meeting today."

"Our Director-General and the Director-General of the National Crime Agency and the Head of the National Anti-Terror Squad have all felt that our three organisations need to work more closely together in order to combat the menace of the SNLA and the WRA. In just under a month's time, this will be put to the test as local elections take place in Scotland and Wales."

"You will be aware that the Government reached an agreement with the Scottish National Party and Plaid Cymru that they would be allowed to participate in these elections. This marks the rehabilitation of the two mainstream nationalist parties. Furthermore, they have agreed to devolve to local government several functions which were previously vested in Whitehall. Not surprisingly, these elections are seen as a flagship initiative by the Government and Ministers want them to succeed. If successful local government is re-established in Scotland and Wales, it will strike a massive blow against the SNLA and the WRA by showing that Scotland and Wales want peace."

"Not surprisingly, the SNLA and the WRA both want the local elections to fail. We have received intelligence reports which suggest that both organisations will seek to disrupt the local elections. One method will be using gangs of hooligans to heckle and disrupt meetings and to throw missiles at candidates. But more ominous is the likelihood that they will try to bomb polling stations and meetings and to target candidates for assassinations. Leaflets have already appeared accusing the SNP and Plaid Cymru of being traitors."

"All of us can bring different skills and competencies to ensuring that the SNLA and the WRA do not succeed in disrupting the local government elections. There are three strands to this work. One is to observe. This means gathering and using intelligence. The second is prevention. Ensuring that lawful activity is protected from hostile acts. And the last is interdiction. Arresting and charging the bad guys. If we successfully ensure the re-establishment of local democracy in Scotland and Wales, the local people will forever be grateful to us."

"I would now like to hand over to Dawn Butler of the NCA."

9 April 2019
Cumbria Constabulary Headquarters
Penrith
Cumbria

Charlie Renwick had set off from Dundee in the early hours of the morning and, having driven down the A9, the M80 and the M74, he was now in England and nearing his destination. The sun was starting to rise in the east as he left the M6 at Junction 40 and took the A66 to Kemplay Bank Roundabout. Then it was a 400 metre drive drive up Carleton Avenue to the junction with Carleton Hall, where Renwick made a right turn. He parked his car and headed for Cumbria Constabulary Headquarters on foot.

Zoe Westgarth, a civilian worker with the police, was on desk duty at headquarters. Renwick walked up to the desk.

"Good morning sir" said Westgarth. "Can I help you at all?"

"Is there anyone from NATS or Special Branch around?" asked Renwick.

"I'm not sure sir" replied Westgarth. "I'll need to check. By the way, what's your name and the nature of your enquiry?"

"Charles Renwick. You'll see a picture of me on that notice over there" said Renwick, pointing to a notice with pictures of wanted SNLA and WRA terrorists. "I'm handing myself in."

Later that day
MI5 Headquarters
Millbank
London

Marcel Francois took the call on Richard Donovan's phone. Donovan was at a meeting. On the other end of the line was Superintendent Russell Colbourne of NATS.

"Marcel Francois, Security Services."

"Hi Marcel, it's Russ Colbourne. Is Richard there?"

"He's at a meeting Russ. Is it important?"

"That's an understatement, Marcel. Tell him that Charlie Renwick, the SNLA's Deputy has turned himself in. And ask him to ring me immediately."

10 April 2019
An MI5 safe house
near Cheltenham
Gloucestershire

The former Deputy Chairman of the SNLA's General Council was being questioned by MI5 about the SNLA and WRA plans to disrupt the local government elections due in Scotland and Wales the following month. He had been flown down to Slade Hall from Penrith the previous day.

"So, Mr Renwick, you are definite that the SNLA and the WRA will attempt to disrupt the forthcoming local elections in Scotland and Wales by violent means." Fiona Hammond, one of MI5's officers responsible for debriefing the former Deputy Chairman of the SNLA's General Council, was continuing to probe for information to prevent terrorist disruption of the elections.

"I am. I was at a meeting of the joint SNLA and WRA General Councils late in March, and they were pretty emphatic that the elections represented a sell-out of both Scotland and Wales. Both Doug Paterson and Trevor Rees said they wanted to see SNP and Plaid Cymru candidates dead as well as those from the Unionist parties, as they regard them as having sold out."

"What do you think they'll try and do Mr Renwick?" asked Peter Firth, another MI5 agent.

"Everything from using local neds to heckle and break up meetings through to bombing polling stations and shooting candidates and election officials" replied Renwick.

"What are "neds" Mr Renwick?" asked Hammond.

"Hooligans, yobs, what are referred to as "chavs" down in England."

"Where do you think that the SNLA and the WRA will base their operations Mr Renwick?" asked Firth.

"I've given you the details of the SNLA safe houses" replied Renwick. "All of them are likely to be used as campaign bases. Bridgend Farm is being used as the main base so you'll probably find guns and explosives there. But don't waste time looking for Paterson—he's always on the move."

"Anything on the WRA Mr Renwick?" asked Hammond.

"Very little" replied Renwick. "However, I do know two of the bases they may be using as I've been there for meetings. The SNLA and WRA held meetings frequently to discuss joining up their campaigns and about buying arms and raising money."

"One is a farm near Caernarfon, Ty Mawr. The old boy who owns it is a veteran Welsh nationalist who's done time for bombing water pipelines years ago. The other's in Swansea—Morriston I think. It's on the main road and on the top of a hill. Not far from a girls school."

"Thank you Mr Renwick" said Firth. "You have been most helpful. Is there anything we can do for you?"

"Yes, Mr Firth. My wife and kids. Can you make sure they're safe. Paterson and the rest of the SNLA will be after my blood and, if they can't get me, they'll go for Morag and wee Jimmy and Sheena. And if they can't get me, they'll ask the WRA to do their dirty work."

"Don't worry Mr Renwick" said Hammond. "We'll ensure your wife and kids are OK."

11 April 2019
Bridgend Farm near Callander
Perthshire
Scotland

Susie Baird, Andy Campbell and Jem McDonald had all got up long before sunrise to start preparing for the SNLA's assault on the local government elections. Later that day, campaigning would begin. They had a list of addresses for polling stations, venues for public meetings and private addresses of election officers and candidates from all the main parties.

In the former milking shed, Campbell and McDonald began to collect and load into a Transit van several M16 and AK-47 rifles. They then had the delicate task of moving an explosive device that would be destined for Dundee Guildhall where a debate between the main parties was due to take place.

"Susie, time to wake the others up" shouted McDonald. "We've got a long day ahead of us."

Outside Bridgend Farm, several unmarked Mercedes-Benz Sprinter vans were parked. Overhead, a helicopter from the National Police Air Service hovered over the farm. In the Command and Control BMW 530 estate, Inspector Luke Jaffray of the National Anti-Terror Squad was seated, directing operations. Two black-painted Range Rovers then pulled up.

"Alright, let's go" said Jaffray.

The two Range Rovers drove up to the track to the farm when, suddenly, eight heavily armed officers leapt out. The lead officer, Sergeant Mick O'Neill, gave the front door an almighty kick. As it flew open, the other officers piled through the front door, guns cocked.

Susie Baird, Andy Campbell and Jem McDonald had no time to react before they were surrounded by three heavily-armed policemen.

"On the floor, face down, now" barked Sergeant O'Neill. "Rob, Dennis, can you search them. Terry, Sam, can you search the rest of the house."

A few minutes later
Ty Mawr near Caernarfon
Wales

Kieron Ellis and Phil Hughes were busy loading up a Vauxhall Mevira panel van parked in the yard. The cargo was not the usual one of grain or potatoes, but was instead rifles and explosives. They were part of a WRA cell that was due to target Bangor and Caernarfon on the first day of campaigning in the Welsh local government elections. They had not noticed either the helicopter hovering over the farm or the unmarked Land Rovers or Volkswagen vans that were moving up the track.

Sergeant Bryan Barrett of the National Anti-Terror Squad led a team of seven armed policemen into Ty Mawr and Ellis and Hughes found themselves surrounded by policemen brandishing guns. They had no option but to surrender.

Later that morning
Sky News

"This is Adam Rennie with this morning's headlines on Sky News."

"Earlier this morning, officers from the National Anti-Terror Squad raided several addresses in Scotland and Wales and arrested more than fifty members of the SNLA and WRA who were planning to carry out attacks to disrupt the local elections in Scotland and Wales, where campaigning starts today. A spokesman for the National Anti-Terror Squad said that the raids have removed several experienced and dangerous terrorists from the streets and have severely disrupted the capacity of the SNLA and WRA to carry out further acts of terror."

3 May 2019
Prime Minister's Office
10 Downing Street
London

The television monitor in the Prime Minister's outer office was tuned into Sky News. Adam Rennie, the regular Sky News anchorman for the morning, was in the chair and talking about the local government elections in Scotland and Wales.

"Yesterday's local government elections in Scotland and Wales have been hailed by the Government as a success. Despite threats from the SNLA and the WRA to disrupt the elections, no incidents were recorded and an unprecedented 70% of those eligible to vote turned out to vote. A Government spokesman said 'The high turnout by voters in Scotland and Wales, in the face of terrorist intimidation, represents a full endorsement of the democratic process by the Scottish and Welsh people and a resounding rejection of violence and terror. We are optimistic that this represents the beginning of the road to normality in Scotland and Wales'."

"The Government was also encouraged by the performance of the Conservative Party which secured 22% of the vote in Wales and 21% of the vote in Scotland. Although the largest shares of the vote went to Labour and the two nationalist parties, the Tories took control of five councils in Scotland—Dumfries and Galloway, East Renfrewshire, Perth and Kinross, South Ayrshire and Stirling, and four councils in Wales—Conwy, Monmouthshire, Pembrokeshire and the Vale of Glamorgan."

At 8:30am, Robert Delgado walked into his office, where his Principal Private Secretary, Jenny Mitchell, was waiting for him.

"Good morning Prime Minister. Can you ring Anthony Simmons as soon as possible."

Delgado didn't need to ask what it was about. "Jenny, I guess Tony's ringing about yesterday's local elections in Scotland and Wales. Afraid I didn't have time to catch up on them." He had returned from a visit to the USA only the day before.

Delgado reached for his telephone and rang Simmons' number at Central Office.

Simmons' PA took the call. "Chairman's Office. Can I help you?"

"Yes please. Robert Delgado here. Can I speak to Anthony Simmons? I'm returning his earlier call."

A few seconds later, Simmons was on the phone.

"Is that you, Bob? Bet you're delighted with the results from Scotland and Wales."

"Tony, I got back at midnight last night. For much of the day, I was engaged in talks with Katherine Whitney and Larry Horvath. Congress are trying to put a block on sale of arms and helicopters to the police. I think we've found a way out of that one. Troy Burton, the Republican minority leader's a master of procedure and should be able to block it. Unfortunately, I'm out of touch about the local elections. How did they go?"

"Excellent on all counts, Bob" replied Simmons. "No terrorist incidents, a seventy percent turnout, twenty two percent of the vote in Wales and twenty one percent in Scotland and we've got control of five councils in Scotland and four in Wales. The party's back in business there."

"Tony, I couldn't agree more" replied the Prime Minister. "Do you realise that the success of the elections will send a message to the SNLA and WRA that they're not wanted in Scotland and Wales. And it will send a message to the rest of the world that they're wasting their time backing the independence cause. The people have sent a clear message that they're content with staying part of the United Kingdom."

"Bob, I think a special world of thanks is due to Stuart Grieve and Jonathan Morgan. It was their idea to give more powers to Scottish and Welsh local authorities and to bring the SNP and Plaid Cymru back in from the cold."

"I agree Tony" replied Delgado. "I will be raising this at Cabinet next Tuesday. But I also think praise is due to Nicola Martin at MI5 and Darren Charnock at NATS. It was due to their diligence that the election campaign passed off without any significant disruption by the SNLA and WRA."

"I hear that Charnock's being lined up as the Met's next Deputy Commissioner" said Simmons.

CHAPTER 18

15 June 2019
Waterstones Bookstore
Charing Cross Road
London

Security at Waterstones flagship central London store was tight for the launch of Rupert Holland's book, *Inside the Enemy*. Over the past three years, Holland, a freelance investigative journalist, had managed to penetrate the SNLA and the WRA right up to its upper echelons and find out the details of how the two terrorist organisations operated and, in particular, how they raised money, how they bought support and the people they consorted with. Not surprisingly, both the SNLA and the WRA were furious and had issued a £200,000 bounty on Holland's life. Holland was now in hiding in fear of his life, but Random House, the publishers, were continuing with the launch. There was a sizeable presence from the Metropolitan Police outside the bookstore and Random House had augmented this inside by hiring security personnel from Carlton Protective Services, a security company run by a former officer in the SAS.

Holland's book made uncomfortable reading for both members of the Government and the security forces, as well as Government opponents and supporters of the independence cause for Scotland and Wales. It gave details of the ruthless reign of terror that the two organisations had imposed within their strongholds, which had been reinforced by punishment beatings and murders of anyone who displeased them. This ranged from anti-social youths through to anyone seen helping the police or the armed forces. It also gave details of the ethnic cleansing of English residents from Scotland and Wales, on the grounds that they were seen as a fifth column.

Holland had also given details of the fund-raising and money-laundering activities carried out by the SNLA and the WRA. It confirmed many people's suspicions that Caledonian Aid and Cambrian Aid were funding terrorist activity rather than charitable activities. But its other fund-raising activities were much more chilling. Both the SNLA and the WRA, it was claimed, was responsible for nearly two-thirds of the drug-trafficking trade in the United Kingdom, and they were working with the Mafia and with drug gangs from Jamaica, Mexico and Turkey. The SNLA and the WRA were also involved in credit card fraud, production and distribution of forged currency, counterfeit goods, prostitution and vice which frequently operated under the guise of massage parlours, people trafficking and the operation of unlicensed bars and clubs and taxi services.

The revelations were to come as a shock to many people who considered themselves as law-abiding, patriotic Britons and would discover that they had been inadvertently funding terrorists. But it was even more of a shock that many people were openly assisting the SNLA and the WRA. A sizeable proportion of these were people who had been made unemployed in the recession between 2010 and 2014 which had been made a lot worse when the Government savagely cut its spending by 40%. People who had been thrown on the scrapheap and denied a living due to the contraction of the welfare state had little inhibition about working in illegal enterprises if it paid the bills.

The money-laundering arrangements for the SNLA and the WRA were also described. They had used traditional money-laundering techniques through using Swiss banks and investing in property, works of art, classic cars and precious metals like gold and platinum. But they had also laundered money through investment in community amenities, and not only in Scotland and Wales. Government expenditure cuts in the earlier part of the decade had led to community centres and affordable sports and leisure centres being closed and sports pitches being sold off for development. The Government's line had been that the voluntary and charitable sector should provide such facilities rather than the taxpayer. The SNLA and WRA had willingly filled the gap.

The final section of Holland's book concentrated on the role of the political wings of the SNLA and the WRA, Clann na h-Albann and Meibion Cymru, in winning support for their cause within the United Kingdom and abroad. Clann na h-Albann and Meibion Cymru had already built close links with the extreme left Socialist Alliance and the anarchist organisation, Class War, and this had provided not only a useful 'rent-a-mob' for street demonstrations. It had also enabled them to penetrate the banks, the civil service and local government and provide the SNLA and WRA with valuable intelligence on everything from potential targets to moves by the authorities to either arrest members or freeze bank accounts. Clann na h-Albann and Meibion Cymru had also close links with four MPs—Labour MP Geraldine Partington, Independent Labour MP Jeremy Sanderson, who had invited party leaders Glen Johnstone and Mark Howell to the House of Commons the previous year, and Sinn Fein MPs Pat Devlin and Mairead Donachy.

Outside the United Kingdom, Clann na h-Albann and Meibion Cymru had influence in the European Parliament through its Left group headed by French Trotskyist Hervé Emmanuelli and in the United States Congress where Senate Leader Brad McAllister and House of Representatives Leader Graydon Hopkins were both sympathetic to the independence cause. But Clann na h-Albann and Meibion Cymru had also built links with less savoury individuals. They had formed an alliance with the remnants of Al-Q'aida, and also had close links to FARC in Colombia and Hamas and Hizbollah in the Middle East. Finally, Holland reported that both Johnstone and Howell had met the Iranian Foreign Minister, Hamidreza Yazdani to discuss arms purchases.

17 June 2019
Home Office
Marsham Street
London

Deborah Pearson had wasted no time in calling a high level meeting to discuss the Government's response to the revelations in Rupert Holland's book. Present at the meeting were the Chief Secretary to the Treasury, Mark Taylor, who had been a former Home Office Minister under Pearson, the Paymaster General, Jennifer Chadwick, the Secretaries of State for Scotland and Wales, Stuart Grieve and Jonathan Morgan, the Home Office Ministers of State for Policing and Homeland Security, Luke Outram and Baroness Hornby, the Chairman of the Association of Chief Police Officers, Roy Plummer, the MI5 Director-General, Dame Nicola Martin and the outgoing Head of the National Anti-Terror Squad, Darren Charnock. Also in attendance were the Permanent Secretary at the Home Office, Sir Richard Benson and the Director-Generals of the National Crime Agency and the Serious Fraud Office, Wayne Hapgood and Emma Morris.

Pearson gave the opening address to the meeting.

"I don't know if all of you have had the opportunity to read *Inside the Enemy*. But if you have, you will understand the magnitude of the threat that the SNLA and WRA pose to the national security of the United Kingdom. The SNLA and WRA, to put it bluntly, are undermining the very foundations of society in the country. They have virtually established gangland rule in large parts of Scotland and Wales. They are undermining the economy through forgery, counterfeiting and contraband goods. They have undermined social stability through drug trafficking, prostitution and vice. They have undermined the country's financial institutions and public administration through bribery. They are working with organised crime, with Marxists and Islamic extremists and the country's enemies. They have suborned whole sections of the country by buying their support. If we do nothing about it, we risk losing the battle to maintain the integrity of the United Kingdom."

"I will not deny there have been successes. The local government elections in Scotland and Wales a month ago were a resounding success as they showed that the majority of people reject the message of terror. Credit must go to Stuart and Jonathan for persevering with the idea." Pearson glanced over to Grieve and Morgan.

"Furthermore, the recent intelligence breakthroughs by MI5 and NATS have had an impact on the ability of the SNLA and WRA to wage terror. Nicola, I have been critical of MI5 in the past but, on this occasion, congratulations are due. And to you Darren."

"But the fact remains that *Inside the Enemy* came as a nasty surprise. How come a journalist has managed to obtain more information on terrorist organisations than Government agencies?"

"To get the upper hand over the SNLA and WRA, we need to strike at their sources of revenue, both here and abroad. And to cut off the funding they provide to other bodies which buys their support."

"The Home Office proposes to use mutual assistance procedures to ask the Swiss government to freeze SNLA and WRA-controlled accounts at Bank Zwingli in Zurich. Luke, how's that progressing?"

"A formal request has been prepared and will be sent out tomorrow, Home Secretary" replied Outram.

"Excellent work Luke" said Pearson. "I hope the Swiss don't prove too awkward. Our next step will be to crack down on the SNLA and WRA's criminal activities in the United Kingdom. This will mean disrupting their drug-trafficking, money-laundering, fraud and vice-related activities. The police cannot do this alone. We need the assistance of other agencies like Revenue and Customs, and the Serious Fraud Office. Mark, Jennifer, this is why I've invited you here today. Do we have sufficient powers of search, seizure and confiscation of assets against anyone suspected of helping the SNLA and WRA?"

"Yes we do Deborah" replied Taylor. "Section 50 of the Criminal Justice Act 2018 contains provision for investigating officers working on the Government's behalf, accompanied by a constable, to enter, search and seize property if he or she has reason to believe it has either been used in the commission of criminal activity or is being traded in order to raise revenue for criminal purposes. Section 51 contains provision to seize assets of any kind if there is reason to believe that it is the proceeds of criminal activity. And the Notes to the Act make clear that the provisions cover terrorist activity as defined under the Terrorism Act 2012."

"In short, it means that the police and Revenue and Customs working together have almost a free hand to enter, search and seize assets or property they think is being used to fund terrorist activity or if it has been purchased or funded by terrorist activity. They will be able to seize all contraband and counterfeit goods, close down taxi firms and dodgy massage parlours, illegal bars and clubs and anything that has been funded by such money."

"If HMRC, the SFO, MI5 and the NCS start working together now to identify irregular or suspect transactions, we should be able to start finding where the SNLA and WRA are getting their money from and what they are doing with it. And then, Deborah, it is up to the police to go in and nick those responsible."

"Excellent" said the Home Secretary. "I think that constitutes the green light for us to go forward and turn off the tap that's feeding the SNLA and WRA. Nicola, Wayne, can you let me know in two weeks time how things have progressed. And one last thing, ladies and gentlemen. I think congratulations are in order to Darren for being appointed as Deputy Commissioner of the Metropolitan Police."

"Hear hear" was the response across the room.

11 July 2019, 10am
Express Taxis
Main Street
Cumbernauld
Scotland

"Express Taxis, can I help?" Morag Shaw, the receptionist at Express Taxis, took a call from a customer in the outlying part of Cumbernauld who wanted to go shopping at the Easterhouse Shopping Centre.

"Thank you madam, a cab will be with you in ten minutes."

Express Taxis had been founded two years earlier by Willie Duncan, a former council maintenance worker who had been made redundant earlier in the decade when Government cuts to public expenditure had resulted in mass public sector job losses. Duncan was one of several men and women across Scotland who had received money from the SNLA to start up businesses or to invest in social enterprises. The conditions were that the SNLA received a tithe of 10% of the profits.

Local people were delighted with the taxi companies set up. Cheaper than the rival bus operations of Stagecoach and First Group, they offered door-to-door service at very low fares. It was well-known locally that they were SNLA-funded and, in addition, bought the co-operation of local people with the SNLA.

Not everyone was supportive of the taxi firm. The main bus operators, Stagecoach and First Group, were angry that what were effectively 'pirate' operators were taking their business away.

As Shaw put the phone down, three police cars and a van pulled up outside Express Taxis. She was startled as ten heavily-armed officers burst into the premises, guns cocked.

Inspector Paul Kirby of the National Anti-Terror Squad walked up to the desk. "Sorry for the way we've come in miss, but we're from NATS. Is the proprietor around?"

"I'm afraid not" replied Shaw. "He's out working."

"Then tell him that we've got a search and seizure order to execute under the Criminal Justice Act 2018. We suspect that this company is being funded by the SNLA. If it is, we've got no option but to seize its assets."

The same day, a few minutes later
Megan's Hair and Nail Studio
St Teilo Street
Pontardulais
Wales

Megan Williams had started her beautician's business eighteen months ago. Formerly employed at a local factory, Williams had undergone retraining as a hairdresser and beautician after being made redundant. The business had done well by offering low prices, yet it seemed that Williams had been able to pay her staff reasonable wages. The reason was that she had agreed to launder money for the WRA.

Business always started to pick up towards the end of the week as customers came in to prepare themselves for the weekend. Megan Williams was certainly not expecting a visit from the police, but that is what she got. Without warning, three police cars and van pulled up outside her business and armed officers burst in.

"Is the owner around?" shouted Inspector Alan Dear of the National Anti-Terror Squad. "We've got a warrant to search this place under Section 50 of the Criminal Justice Act."

Williams appeared from the back office.

"What are you doing here, gentlemen? Do you realise you've frightened my customers?"

"Ms Williams, we're here because we've got reason to believe you've been laundering terrorist funds."

An hour later
Royston Sports and Social Club
Oakwood Road
Royston
Yorkshire

Bryan Schofield, the Secretary of Royston Sports and Social Club was astounded to find ten armed police officers from the National Anti-Terror Squad calling to see him. He could not understand why a warrant for search and seizure was being executed.

"Inspector, I can assure you that all our business is totally above board. If you want evidence, I can arrange for our accountants, Goldthorpe and Wainwright, to be present."

"Look, Mr Schofield, we've got a job to do" replied Inspector Julie Bright of the National Anti-Terror Squad. "We've got evidence that your association took money from the Scottish National Liberation Army. You should know that taking money from terrorist organisations is an offence, whether you know about it or not."

23 July 2019
Cabinet Room
10 Downing Street
London

The final Cabinet meeting of 2019 before the summer recess had an upbeat note. At long last, the Government appeared to be making inroads into the SNLA and the WRA. The local government elections had been a success. Following Charlie Renwick's defection, no less than ten other senior SNLA and WRA commanders had surrendered to the authorities. The number of terrorist murders and incidents was down compared with 2018. And Deborah Pearson was about to report progress on shutting down the SNLA's and WRA's sources of funding.

The subject was the first item on the agenda and a beaming Home Secretary opened her papers.

"Deborah, what progress has been made in searching and seizing terrorist assets?" asked the Prime Minister.

"Excellent progress, Prime Minister" replied Pearson. "Following initial investigations by HM Revenue and Customs, MI5, the National Crime Agency and the Serious Fraud Office, we've found no less than five hundred organisations which have either acted as a front for the SNLA and the WRA or have laundered terrorist money. Their accounts have been frozen pending criminal charges being levied. The National Anti-Terror Squad, working in partnership with NCA, have arrested no less than twenty SNLA or WRA members involved in drug trafficking, protection racketeering, contraband and vice, along with members of the criminal underworld who have been working with them. The Swiss authorities have acted on a request for assistance and have frozen SNLA and WRA accounts at the Bank Zwingli and have arrested one of their bankers on suspicion of money laundering."

"I can't promise that the SNLA and the WRA will disappear. But I think they will experience great difficulty in funding their campaign of terror."

"What are MI5 doing with the former terrorists who surrendered Debbie?" asked Secretary of State for Defence, Jason Steer. "Any information they get will surely lead us to the General Councils."

"I can assure you Jason that MI5 are debriefing the SNLA and WRA members who came over" replied the Home Secretary. "It's early days yet, but I am confident they will obtain enough information to lead us to the SNLA and WRA leadership."

"Deborah, I would like to thank you for your leadership in co-ordinating action in shutting down the SNLA's and WRA's sources of funding" said Delgado. "Rupert Holland's book could have put us in a bad light and, instead, you used it to turn the tables on the SNLA and the WRA. With a bit of luck, we may have turned the corner in our fight to protect the integrity of the United Kingdom and the safety of its people."

The same day
Home Office
Marsham Street
London

Opposite the Home Office, a noisy demonstration had gathered to protest against the Government's decision to freeze assets of organisations who had been suspected of laundering terrorist money. The demonstrators did not see the Home Secretary's official car, which entered by the rear of the building.

Most of the demonstrators were either proprietors of small businesses or from community groups, sports and leisure organisations or workingmen's clubs, all of whom had accepted SNLA or WRA money because they needed it and legitimate sources like banks were unwilling to lend money to businesses or organisations which were unlikely to make much profit. But the demonstration had been infiltrated by members of the Socialist Alliance and Class War, who were hell bent on confrontation with the police.

By 12pm, Superintendent Barry Caswell at Rochester Row Police Station has received several complaints about the noise and inconvenience from residents of Romney House, a former Government building which had been converted into luxury flats. This was the excuse the police needed to break up the demonstration.

Caswell radioed Inspector Kate Parsons, who was in charge of the police detachment outside the Home Office.

"Kate, Barry Caswell here at Rochester Row. How's things at the Home Office?"

ROB MURPHY

"Getting rather noisy sir. Looks like we've got the Socialist Alliance and Class War out in force."

"We've had complaints from local residents Kate. Can you disperse the demonstration."

"We may need backup sir" replied Inspector Parsons.

"I'll send over the TSG to help" said Superintendent Caswell.

Inspector Parsons took a police loudhailer to address the demonstrators.

"Will you please disperse and go home now. We've had complaints from local residents about the noise and, under the terms of the Public Order Act, we have the right to stop demonstrations in such circumstances."

Within seconds, Inspector Parsons realised that the demonstrators would not be going quietly. Shouts of "fuck the rich" started to come from the crowd, followed by "we shall not be moved". Missiles started to be thrown.

Inspector Parsons realised she had a potentially serious public order incident on her hands right outside the Government department responsible for law and order. She turned to her two sergeants, Eric Wright, a veteran policeman with 28 years service and Richard Perry, a young sergeant who had just been promoted after just four years in the service.

"Eric, Richard, get the officers ready to disperse the demonstrators and to make arrests. We've got trouble on our hands."

"Have we got any backup, Ma'am" asked Wright.

"We have Eric. The TSG are on their way."

Wright and Perry shouted instructions to the constables to draw their batons and prepare to disperse the demonstration. As the officers advanced on the crowd, it was the signal for militants in the crowd to start trouble. A crash barrier was thrown at the officers. Wright, along with two constables, advanced on the miscreant. A heavy blow from a police baton felled the thrower of the crash barrier, while Wright and another constable forced the demonstrator to the ground and handcuffed him.

Barely seconds later, the Territorial Support Group arrived with response backup. The TSG squad leapt out of their van and piled into the demonstrators, batons swinging indiscriminately. Not only were troublemakers hit and arrested, but many people who had come to demonstrate peacefully were also caught up. As was Miles Chaucer, a freelance photographer who took several photos of the mayhem before he was felled by a well-aimed blow from a TSG baton and thrown into the back of a Mercedes Sprinter van.

3 August 2019
Roger Street
Mynyddbach
Swansea

The General Councils of the SNLA and the WRA had gathered for a crisis meeting at a recently-acquired safe house in the northern suburbs of Swansea. Gethin Davies from the WRA's General Council had acquired the property at 44 Roger Street some three months earlier. With Ty Mawr now seized following a raid by the

234

National Anti-Terror Squad back in April, the modest property in Mynyddbach was now one of the few WRA safe houses that were not known to the authorities. With many people now away on their summer holidays and the authorities concerned with preventing repetitions of the bombings in Benidorm, Majorca and the Greek Islands the previous year, the WRA were confident that the use of their latest safe house would not attract undue attention.

The mood inside 44 Roger Street was pessimistic. Over the past four months, everything which could go wrong for the terrorists had done so. The former Deputy-Chairman of the SNLA General Council, Charlie Renwick, had handed himself into the authorities, and had been followed by several senior commanders from both the SNLA and the WRA. Local government elections in Scotland and Wales in May had been a resounding success. The publication of Rupert Holland's book, *Inside the Enemy*, blew open the details of how the SNLA and the WRA got their money to fund terrorist activities. Police raids made possible by the intelligence supplied by turncoats like Renwick and from Holland's investigative journalism had netted many experienced terrorists. Their sources of revenue had been cut off—now, they had to reply on donations from Caledonian Aid and Cambrian Aid in the USA and the Whitney administration was continuing to look for ways to suspend their operation. More worrying was the fall in recruitment as the acceptance of local government rule and the backlash against the extortion, racketeering and intimidation that the SNLA and WRA were practising in their strongholds was eroding support.

Doug Paterson, the Chairman of the SNLA's General Council, was desperately trying to lift the mood of despondency. He had just introduced Gordon Ross who had been appointed to the General Council. Iain Murray was the new Deputy Chairman.

"Gentlemen, we canna afford to throw in the towel after what we've achieved over the past four years. I know things have been tough of late, what with Renwick betraying us, the bizzies seizing our accounts and the SNP and Plaid Cymru selling out. But we've got to continue with the fight for independence. Otherwise, Scotland and Wales will end up as English colonies for ever more."

"Doug, we're not saying 'give up the struggle'" said Mike Grogan. "But we've got to face reality. All our money's now under lock and key. Our intelligence has been blown. A lot of our best men and women are behind bars and they're not being replaced quickly enough. I think we should take a break, regroup and then come back more strongly than ever."

"We can't afford to 'take a break' Mike" replied the Chairman of the WRA's General Council, Trevor Rees. "You know the English are dusting off plans to colonise Wales by homesteading. This will make the Welsh a minority in their own country. They'll try to do the same for Scotland. Doug's right. We need to keep the struggle for independence going."

The Deputy Chairman of the WRA's General Council, Richard Thomas, picked up a copy of the *Daily Telegraph* which was lying on the coffee table in the lounge. He pointed to an article which expected a large influx of wealthy visitors to Scotland for the grouse-shooting season which would be starting in little more than a week.

"Fellas, there may be an opportunity heading your way" said Thomas. "Just over a week's time and the 'Glorious Twelfth' begins. Looks like a few wealthy bigwigs will be heading up to Scotland this year."

"Have we thought about a kidnap and holding one of these wealthy bods to ransom?" asked Mark Podborski. "I recall the IRA did this on several occasions and with a fair bit of success."

**12 August 2019
Gleneagles Hotel
Perthshire
Scotland**

Roger Day, the Chief Executive of Incorpsys, was ready to depart for the first day of the grouse-shooting season. Every year, he and his wife Caroline made a weekly pilgrimage to the Scottish Highlands for the 'Glorious Twelfth'.

"Goodbye darling" said Day to his wife. "Hope you enjoy today in Edinburgh. See you for dinner this evening."

"I hope you bring back some grouse for dinner Roger" said Mrs Day.

Caroline Day was an attractive blonde in her late 30s. A former Personal Assistant, she had married Roger Day, who had been her boss, ten years previously. They had two young children, Toby and Samantha. She was not a great enthusiast for grouse shooting. But she liked Scotland and was looking forward to a day shopping in Edinburgh.

The Days had hired a BMW 535 during their visit and, with her husband not using the car, Mrs Day had full use of it. She unlocked the driver's door, got in, started the engine and pulled out of Gleneagles.

Some twenty minutes later, Mrs Day was approaching Dunblane after which the A9 would give way to the M9. She anticipated being in Edinburgh within the hour.

Caroline Day was startled to see a police car behind her with lights flashing and the siren blaring. Instinctively, she pulled into the side of the road.

A traffic officer from Central Police walked up to Mrs Day's BMW as she lowered the driver's side window.

"Good morning officer. Can I help you with anything?"

"Madam, it appears that your brake lights aren't working" replied the officer. "I'm afraid we need to check your licence and insurance details and the vehicle registration. Just as a precaution—there's been a lot of vehicle thefts by the SNLA for use in their terrorist campaign. Can you please step out of the vehicle?"

"Okay, if you insist" replied Mrs Day.

Caroline Day got out of her car just in time to feel a pistol pointed against the side of her head.

"Alright, Mrs Day" said the second officer. Hands behind your back and no tricks. If you do what we say, you'll come to no harm."

Later that day
Sky News

"This is Scott Parfitt with this evening's headlines on Sky News."

"Caroline Day, the wife of a leading London businessman, was kidnapped earlier today by the SNLA. A ransom of £30 million is being demanded for her release."

"Mrs Day was driving along the A9 near Dunblane at 10am this morning when she was stopped by a fake police patrol who were SNLA terrorists in disguise. Her car was left abandoned by the side of the A9 and the alert was not raised until Central Police found her abandoned car."

"This is the first time that the SNLA has resorted to kidnap, and counter-terrorism experts believe this may be an attempt to replenish their coffers after a joint operation between the police and HM Revenue and Customs in July sequestrated their assets."

"Central Police, in partnership with the Army and the National Anti-Terror Squad, are carrying out an exhaustive search of the Scottish countryside in order to find Mrs Day."

17 August 2019
Highlights Nightclub
Castle Square
Caernarfon
Wales

Being the son of the Chairman of the WRA's General Council gave Darren Rees a lot of power and influence in his home town. He was in charge of the WRA's punishment squads who handed out beatings to anyone who offended the WRA's code of conduct. Most of its victims were juvenile delinquents who were responsible for much of the petty crime and anti-social behaviour in Caernarfon. Many of the beatings were brutal, involving the use of baseball bats and metal bars and left victims requiring hospital treatment and, in some cases, permanent damage. But many of the local residents supported the WRA's activities as they were sick and tired of the sight of serial young offenders laughing at the courts.

Rees's punishment squad had also been responsible for punishing informers and traitors within the WRA's ranks. The outcome for these unfortunates was more lethal, with a bullet to the side of the head being the favoured way of dispatching traitors, with their bodies being left by the side of the road. Again, there was local support from a fiercely-nationalist part of Wales.

Saturday nights usually saw Rees and his cronies in Highlights, the sole nightclub in Caernarfon. Because of his status in the town, Rees was allowed to jump the queue and get in without paying by the bouncers. He also used that status to get hold of any woman whom he fancied. Most complied; they either fancied being the object of attention of a local WRA kingpin or did it out of fear that they or their families might face reprisals from the WRA.

It was also an unwritten word in Highlights than no man should date approach any woman seen as part of Darren Rees's entourage. To do so risked a beating.

By 11:30pm, Rees was already on his fifth pint of Carlsberg of the night and was eyeing round the club for women to approach. He noticed a stunning blonde in a miniskirt close to the bar, and decided to make a move.

"Hi there darling" said Rees. "Looking for a drink?"

Debbie Morgan, a receptionist at a garage, was not interested. "Piss off, creep."

Darren Rees was not used to being spoken to like that. "Don't you know who you're talking to darling? I'd advise you to wash your mouth out first."

Morgan was however determined to hold her ground. "You think youse fucking own this town cos your dad's head of the WRA. Well, you don't."

A short but wiry, dark-haired man returned from the bar with two drinks, a pint of lager for himself and a Bacardi Breezer for Morgan. It was her boyfriend, Mark Owen.

"Mark, sort this creep out" said Morgan. "He's annoying me."

Owen was shorter than Rees, but he had been a useful amateur boxer and could look after himself.

"Oi, you heard, butt. That's my woman. Piss off while you're still in one piece."

Rees seized the smaller man by the lapels of his shirt. "Listen, shorty, don't you know who I am? One word from me and you'll be eating hospital food for the next year."

Owen was alert to the threat he faced. He saw no point in a toe-to-toe slugging match against Rees as the WRA man was bigger and stronger. Instead, he dipped his right shoulder and brought up a right uppercut to the side of Rees's jaw. The bigger man went down.

Rees was however not out. He leapt to his feet and charged at Owen hurling a fierce overarm right which Owen ducked inside. He was not quick enough to dodge the follow-up left hook which went into his solar plexus and temporarily winded him. But Owen used his boxing skills to roll with Rees's punches and landed another fierce right hand on the bridge of Rees's nose.

The bouncers, who had been alerted to the disturbance, arrived to break up the fight. The two men were pulled apart and led to the door.

19 August 2019
Maes Meddyg
Caernarfon
Wales

Derek Price and Glyn Roberts, two of Darren Rees's best friends and fellow members of the Caernarfon Brigade of the WRA, had called round to discuss with Rees an appropriate retaliation against Mark Owen for breaking his nose in a fight at Highlights the previous night.

"Boys, we're all agreed that we need to sort out that cunt who whacked me last night" said Rees. "If we let him get away with this, other tossers will fancy taking us on and the WRA will lose credibility. We need to send out the message that no one fucks with us. Problem is, how, when and where do we find him?"

"I know who you mean Dar" said Roberts. "The guy's name is Mark Owen. Works as a car mechanic in a garage on Fford Bangor. Used to be an amateur boxer and fancies himself as a bit tasty, both with the birds and with his fists. Also plays footie for Palace Athletic."

"Palace Athletic eh" said Rees. "No doubt he boozes in the Palace Vaults on Sundays? Don't think he'll look so cool to the babes after we've done him over."

"Don't think it'll be a good idea to take him on at the Vaults, Dar" said Price. "He'll have all his mates from footie there and I've heard they're all a bit tasty with their fists."

"How about going further?" said Roberts. "Like shooting the bastard?"

"I like it" said Rees. "That'll send out a message not to fuck with the WRA. Can't see any comeback from the Palace Athletic mob after that."

18 August 2019
The Palace Vaults
Palace Street
Caernarfon
Wales

The Palace Vaults was doing good business that Sunday lunchtime. Members of Palace Athletic Amateur Football Club were in the bar, following their pre-season trials. Amongst the players was Mark Owen, a car mechanic, who played on the right wing for Athletic.

The previous night, Owen had been thrown out of Highlights following an altercation with Darren Rees, the son of the Chairman of the WRA's General Council. Rees had threatened to get him, but Owen was confident that he did not have the bottle to follow it up.

At 1pm, three men in paramilitary fatigues walked into the Palace Vaults. No one paid much attention as there was a general high level of support for the independence cause in Caernarfon. One of them called out "Mark Owen."

Owen turned round. "Yeah, that's me."

Without warning, two of the men in paramilitary gear withdrew Uzi machine pistols and opened fire. Owen fell dead as the three men sprinted out of the pub.

Later that evening
BBC Wales News

"This is Sian Hughes with this evening's headlines on BBC Wales."

"A 21-year old man was shot dead in by the WRA in a pub in Caernarfon earlier today. Mark Owen, a motor mechanic, was drinking in the Palace Vaults in the town centre when three gunmen in paramilitary fatigues burst in and opened fire."

"The WRA later issued a statement saying that they had executed Mr Owen because of his 'repeated and violent criminal activity'. However, local people who knew Mr Owen have expressed their surprise as they do not recall him being involved in any kind of

criminal activity. This has been backed up by North Wales Police, who confirmed that Mr Owen had no criminal record at all."

"There are reports that Mr Owen had been involved in an altercation with a member of the WRA in a Caernarfon nightclub the night before, and police are keeping an open mind over whether this had been the trigger for his murder."

19 August 2019
Central Scotland Police Headquarters
Randolphsfield House
Stirling
Scotland

A worried and distraught Roger Day was ushered into the office of Chief Superintendent Gavin Armstrong of Central Scotland Police, who was leading the search for his wife.

"How's the search for Caroline progressing, Chief Superintendent Armstrong?"

"We may have some leads Mr Day" replied Armstrong. "We've managed to establish the make and registration of the fake police car that was used from CCTV footage. A process of elimination as all other police cars photographed were the genuine article. We've also been able to track part of its progress. We know that it turned off onto the A84 at Stirling, heading for Callander. The only problem is that we've not got CCTV or ANPR cameras on the A84 as it's comparatively empty. But we've alerted our officers in the north west of the force area, along with Strathclyde Police who border us."

"Wouldn't it be easier if I paid the ransom and got Caroline back?" asked Day. "My company's got the money."

"Mr Day, I can understand how you feel" said Chief Superintendent Armstrong. "I am a married man too and I would feel the same if my wife had been kidnapped. But I would not advise you do so. We believe that the SNLA unit that's holding your wife are not very experienced. We've got trained negotiators who are trying to secure her release, and we're also receiving help from the National Crime Agency and MI5. I've got good reason to believe that they will lose their nerve and agree to releasing your wife without the need to pay a ransom. If you pay them, it will only embolden them and they will kidnap someone else."

23 August 2019
The Church of St David and St Helen
Twthill East
Caernarfon
Wales

The Church of St David and St Helen was packed for the funeral of Mark Owen. Despite warnings from the local battalion of the WRA for people not to attend, large numbers of local people turned out.

Steady rain was falling as the funeral cortege arrived at the church at 11am. Owen's coffin, draped with the Welsh national flag, was borne by his father, brother, uncle and five of his team mates from Palace Athletic FC. Behind them followed Owen's mother, sister and girlfriend Debbie Morgan. Several policemen were on duty in order to prevent any disruption of the funeral by the WRA or sympathisers.

The vicar of St David and St Helen, the Reverend Emrys Davies, gave a lengthy sermon which not only celebrated the life of the talented amateur boxer and football player, but condemned the violence that had swept Wales over the past four years.

Once the service was over, Owen's coffin was borne into the cemetery and lowered into the family grave to rest alongside previous generations of Owens. As a parting gesture, a Palace Athletic shirt with a Number 7 on the back was thrown into the grave before it was covered.

26 August 2019
near Firbush Point Field Centre
2 miles east of Killin
Perthshire
Scotland

The SNLA had deliberately chosen a remote location to hold Caroline Day. East of the village of Killin ran a narrow road which skirted Loch Tay. At Firbush Point was Edinburgh University's Field Centre but, on the other side of the road was dense woodland where it was possible to hide a large caravan in a clearing.

Craig Anderson, the SNLA commander in charge of the kidnap, was starting to get impatient. It was now two weeks since they had captured Mrs Day and there was no sign of any ransom. What was worse for Anderson to bear was the news that there was considerable public sympathy to Mrs Day's plight in Scotland. His chief lieutenant, Gavin Horsburgh, had reported the previous day that yellow ribbons had been tied to trees in Edinburgh in support of Mrs Day's release.

What Anderson and Horsburgh did not know was that, twenty years earlier, Mrs Day had been a student at Edinburgh University where she graduated in Modern Languages. Also, while she was there, she had earned considerable local popularity by raising money for a hospice for sick children by running in the Edinburgh Marathon in 2000.

Anderson and Horsburgh were away from the caravan that day, because they were having a clandestine meeting with a negotiator from Central Scotland Police to discuss a possible release. Just two members of the SNLA cell were left to guard Mrs Day at the caravan, Jason McGill and Kirsty Robertson. Both were inexperienced recruits to the SNLA.

Caroline Day was a resourceful woman and had remembered the lessons from a course she had been sent on eleven years before on personal safety and security. She was then engaged to Roger Day and was about to be posted to Colombia. The trainers were former SAS men who taught her how to escape from locked car boots and to release handcuffs. She was also a black belt in tae-kwan-do and perfectly capable of looking after herself.

Mrs Day had noticed there was a sharp edge to the bed in the berth where she was being held. She had steadily been rubbing the PVC hand restraints against the edge and weakening them. Suddenly, she felt them give way. Freedom at last!

The only problem was that she had to get past the two SNLA guards left behind at the caravan. And she was still wearing the pair of high heeled boots that she was to wear for the shopping trip. Not only highly unsuitable for possible a long walk, but they would alert her guards to the fact she was no longer tied up.

Robertson was in the next berth of the caravan watching daytime television. For Mrs Day, this was her opportunity. She crept up behind Robertson, yanked her head back and laid her out with a well-timed blow to the throat.

McGill was returning to the caravan when he heard movement. "Kirsty, is that you? Any idea how long before Craig and Gav get back?"

When he opened the door, he got a shock as he encountered Mrs Day. Before he could react, he was disabled by a fierce blow from Mrs Day's knee to his private parts, followed by an open-handed blow to the side of the neck. McGill was out cold.

Caroline Day did not know where she was, but she reckoned that if she followed the road adjacent to where the caravan was parked, she would find civilisation shortly. Unfortunately, she took the eastbound direction rather than the westbound. Had she gone to the west, Killin would have been four miles distant. But eastward there was no human settlement for another ten miles.

Craig Anderson was furious when he got back to the caravan and found that Mrs Day had escaped.

"What the fuck were you two jokers playing at?" shouted Anderson at the hapless McGill and Robertson. "Leave you for two hours with a captive tied up and you manage to lose her. Do you realise you've made the SNLA a laughing stock?"

"Sorry Craig" replied McGill. "We had her tied up and under guard. I went out to check gas and water levels and when I got back, I found that she had struggled free."

"Didn't ye try to stop her Jason?" said Horsburgh.

"I had no chance Gav. What she did to me and Kirsty, I reckon she must be a martial arts expert."

"Never mind that" said Anderson, "we've got to stop her getting away. Let's take the car."

"Where do we look for her Craig?" asked Horsburgh.

"It's obvious Gav. She'll be heading for Killin—its only four miles away" replied Anderson.

As the Land Rover Freelander pulled out of the clearing onto the main road, Horsburgh saw two men and a woman. Probably students from Edinburgh University staying at Firbush Point Field Centre.

"Craig, let's pull up and ask these people."

Horsburgh lowered the passenger side window and spoke to the three students.

"Scuse me, have you seen a woman round these parts? Blonde, attractive, late 30s, black T-shirt, black jeans, boots."

"We have" replied one of the students. Saw her walking to the east. Couldn't understand why—there's nothing for ten miles."

"Thanks pal" replied Anderson. With that, Anderson headed eastwards along the unclassified road.

Caroline Day had managed to walk three miles along the unclassified road skirting the southern edge of Loch Tay. She had been walking for nearly three hours without seeing a single sign of habitation. She had not even seen a single car or other vehicle pass in either direction.

The sun was now starting to lower on the western horizon. Mrs Day knew it would soon be dark. She had to keep going until she found either human habitation or a vehicle. She then heard the distant sound of a car coming along the road behind her. Her spirits rose.

Within a second, her mood switched from elation to despair as the blue Freelander screeched to a halt and two men leapt out. It was two members of the gang that had kidnapped her and their faces were contorted with fury.

Both Craig Anderson and Gavin Horsburgh were brandishing M16s as they closed in on Mrs Day.

"Thought you could get one over on the SNLA, you bitch" shouted Anderson as he struck Mrs Day in the face with the butt of his M16. She fell to the ground as blood started to trickle from her face.

"Look, I've got nothing against you guys" cried a desperate Mrs Day. "All I want you to do is release me and let me see my husband and children again."

"Don't buy it Craig" said Horsburgh. "She recognises who we are. If we let her go, she'll identify us to the police and testify in court against us. We're looking at up to 30 years in Barlinnie."

"Aye, you're right, Gav" replied Anderson. "Let's finish her off."

Caroline Day realised the mortal danger she was in and started screaming hysterically. "Please please, don't kill me. I'll come back with you to the caravan and wait for my release to be negotiated."

"You've gone too far this time, love" snickered Anderson. He raised his M16 and opened fire. A second burst of fire from Horsburgh finished off Mrs Day.

27 August 2019
Sky News

"This is Adam Rennie with this morning's headlines on Sky News."

"Police in Central Scotland have confirmed that the body found in a clearing by the southern shore of Loch Tay is that of Caroline Day, the wife of a London businessman who was kidnapped by the SNLA two weeks ago."

"The Prime Minister, the Leader of the Opposition and the leaders of the Liberal Democrats and the Scottish National Party all joined forces to condemn the murder and the Chief Constable of Central Scotland Police, Alfred Gemmill and the Head of the

National Anti-Terror Squad, Kevin Lazenby, have pledged that no stone will be left unturned in the quest to find Mrs Day's murderers. In addition, Incorpsys, the company for which Mrs Day's husband is Chief Executive, have offered a reward of £8 million for information leading to the arrest and conviction of her murderers."

CHAPTER 19

**27 August 2019
Staff Cafeteria
Driver & Vehicle Licensing Agency
Swansea**

Liz Church paid for her lunch of tuna salad and a yoghurt and headed for the table where three of her work colleagues, Sally Brennan, Glenda Davies and Tracy Nicholas were sitting.

Liz Church was now 47 years old, married with two children and a grandmother to one. She had originally worked in an insurance office for seven years from leaving school until having her first child, and had taken the job on the customer contact desk in the Driver & Vehicle Licensing Agency eight years earlier.

As the four DVLA employees ate their lunch, they discussed the main headline on the front page of the South Wales Morning Post. This was about the murder just over a week earlier of Mark Owen in Caernarfon. The headline read

Mourners defy WRA threats to say farewell to Mark

"Absolutely disgraceful what the WRA did. That poor boy was not involved in any trouble at all and they go and shoot him." Tracy Nicholas was emphatic in her views on the subject.

"The WRA are getting too big for their boots" said Sally Brennan, an attractive divorcee in her early 40s. "Some of them think they've got the right to chat any woman up, whether or not they're married."

"I know Sally" replied Glenda Davies. "One of them was after me in Chicago Rock Café a couple of months ago. Wouldn't take no for an answer. Good job my Gareth wasn't there. He'd have whacked him."

"Some of my neighbours have been saying what you girls have just said" said Liz Church. "Would you be interested in attending a public meeting if I call one?"

"Whereabouts do you plan to hold it Liz?" asked Sally Brennan.

"Should be able to get my old school at Mynyddbach. Malcolm's a governor there."

30 August 2019
Mynyddbach Girls School
Mynyddbach
Swansea

Even though the meeting had been arranged at short notice and was on a Friday evening, Liz Church was pleasantly surprised at the size of the turnout. Some 300 people had assembled in the school hall.

At 7pm, Mrs Church moved to the main stand to address the meeting.

"Ladies and gentlemen, I am most grateful for you giving up your Friday evening to come here for the first meeting of the 'Peace Now' campaign."

"For four years, we have had to put up with bombings and shootings as a fact of everyday life as the WRA claim to be fighting for an independent Wales. And has it achieved that? No! Instead, all it's done is to scare off businesses from investing in Wales, cause more job losses and make everyone's lives more miserable. And it has made it much more difficult for anyone from Wales to travel abroad. Every time we now enter another country, we are subjected to full security checks because they fear we might be terrorists."

"The only way that Wales will regain its self-respect and the respect of the rest of the world will be if we look to a peaceful solution to the country's identity. That will mean standing up to the men and women of terror. But if we do, I feel we will have the support of all right-thinking men and women in Wales."

"Believe me, I am not proposing surrender of the ideal of an independent Wales. But I believe this goal can only be achieved if peace and order returns to Wales. Where people can go to work without wondering if a bomb will go off. Or being able to go out for a drink without the fear that someone will open fire on you."

"What has started here tonight can, I believe, grow and be expanded to all of Wales. But it is a task I cannot deal with alone. So, if any of you are interested in helping me start the All-Wales Peace Movement, can you please stay behind after the meeting."

2 September 2019
Costa Coffee
St Enoch Centre
Glasgow

Sheena Lang returned from the counter with two flat whites, a cappuccino, three sandwiches and three cherry muffins, and joined her friends Isobel Scott and Maureen Geraghty.

On the table was a copy of the *Daily Record*, Scotland's main tabloid newspaper. The headline story was the funeral of Caroline Day, the wife of a London businessman who had been kidnapped and murdered by the SNLA. The article made clear the revulsion most people in Scotland felt for the murder.

"Disgusting, absolutely disgusting" said Isobel Scott. "They claim to be acting for Scotland and they kill that poor lassie and leave her bairns without a mother. Well, their no' having my support."

"It's time someone stood up to the SNLA" said Maureen Geraghty. "They've now gone beyond being the defenders of the Scottish people. I've heard they've been running protection rackets on pubs, clubs and businesses. You should see the money they've got—they all go round in flash cars and their wives and girlfriends all have designer clothes and jewellery."

"If some of us got together and started a peace movement, I reckon it would get a lot of support. People are sick and tired of the shootings and bombings, and of the Scots now being seen as violent outlaws" added Isobel Scott.

What Isobel Scott said suddenly jogged Sheena Lang's memory. "Girls, I think there's something in the *Record*. I'll have a look."

She found it on page 6. Under the headline **BIG TURNOUT FOR PEACE MEETING**, it read:-

"Over 300 people turned out for a meeting held last Friday in Swansea to support a peace campaign.

The meeting, organised by Liz Church, a DVLA employee, has pledged to campaign for an end to the violence which has occurred in Wales since the British Government ended home rule four years ago, and to seek a peaceful solution to the issue of Welsh sovereignty. Mrs Church told reporters present that she would be organising further meetings, firstly in the Welsh capital, Cardiff, and subsequently in towns across Wales."

"We need to get something similar going for Scotland" said Sheena Lang.

4 September 2019
Highfield Road
Kirkintilloch
Dunbartonshire
Scotland

"751382." The voice at the end of the phone clearly had a Welsh accent.

"Is that Liz Church?" asked Sheena Lang.

"It is. How can I help you?"

"My name is Sheena Lang. As you might guess, I'm from Scotland. I'm trying to start a peace campaign up here in Scotland and I read in the *Daily Record* two days ago that you've got one going in Wales. I'd like some advice on getting something similar going here."

"Have you had any meetings yet Sheena?" asked Church.

"No, not yet Liz" replied Lang. "We've got a first meeting next Friday in the Public Hall at Kirkintilloch. From that, I'll be able to work out the level of interest."

"What's the level of interest in Scotland?"

"I think it should be high" replied Lang. "There's a lot of public anger about the murder of that poor lassie a week ago. The SNLA should have let her go. How's it been in Wales?"

"So far, so good, Sheena" replied Church. "There's strong interest for the meetings we're having in Cardiff, Newport and Wrexham. The acid test will be further meetings we've got planned for Aberystwyth, Bangor and Carmarthen, because they're right in the middle of WRA strongholds. But you saw the big turnout for the funeral of the boy the WRA murdered in Caernarfon two weeks back."

"Afraid I didn't" said Lang.

"Well, there's a big backlash against the WRA in a town considered to be one of their main strongholds. The signs are that there's a groundswell of public opinion in favour of peace."

"That's great. Good luck with the further meetings Liz. I'll let you know how things are shaping up after the first meeting."

28 September 2019
Cardiff International Airport

Stuart and Sheena Lang's flight from Glasgow had landed half an hour previously and the Langs were retrieving their baggage from the carousel. As they walked towards the exit, they saw a man and a woman holding up a card with their names on it. It was Malcolm and Liz Church.

"Stuart, Sheena, great to see you" said Liz Church. "This is my husband, Malcolm." Malcolm Church introduced himself and shook the hands of both Stuart and Sheena Lang.

"Should only be fifteen minutes to Cardiff International Arena" said Malcolm Church.

The same day
Cardiff International Arena

Support for the All-Wales Peace Movement had grown massively in the month since it had been launched. Following successful meetings, firstly in Wales's main cities and then in the principal towns, the All-Wales Peace Movement had found it necessary to hire the Cardiff International Arena for its first national rally. Several special trains had been put on from Aberystwyth and Holyhead to Cardiff, while cars and coaches from all corners of Wales rolled into the Welsh capital.

Several speakers had been booked. Amongst them were three MPs, Emma Goldstone, the Liberal Democrat MP for Cardiff North, Sally Richards, the Labour MP for Rhymney Valley and David Williams, the Conservative MP for Monmouthshire, Brynmor Jones, the Chairman of Plaid Cymru and a well-known actor, Eddie Griffiths.

Sheena Lang was the fifth speaker on the agenda. She took to the rostrum to applause from the audience.

"Ladies and gentlemen, it is a pleasure to be invited to address the All-Wales Peace Movement today. You may or may not know that I am the Chair of Peace 4 Scotland. I helped start the movement after hearing what Liz Church had been doing in Wales and I felt that something similar should be done for Scotland."

"Both Scotland and Wales share a common Celtic heritage and a proud history. I will not dwell on the fact that we were both absorbed into the United Kingdom because we both played our part in developing the British Empire. Scottish engineers built the roads and railways and the machinery that drove the industrial effort behind the empire. The Welsh extracted minerals from the earth and taught the children how to read and write. But recent years have not been kind to either country. The 1980s were a disaster as our traditional industries closed down one by one and were not replaced. Our best and brightest young men and women left to seek employment elsewhere. Twenty years ago, we received at long last our own government, only for that to be taken away."

"However, the path of violence is the wrong path for either of us to take. It only offers succour to those who wish to denigrate us as savages who cannot be trusted to run their own affairs. It frightens off people who might bring wealth and employment to our countries. It needlessly wastes taxpayers' money on security and protective services, on repairing damage caused by explosions and on treating innocent people who get caught up in acts of terror. It stores up hatred between near neighbours which will sustain a continuing cycle of conflict for future years."

"I ask you this, ladies and gentlemen. We both have to share this island with the English. Very few of them wish any harm on either of us and would prefer to have a relationship of co-operation. If either Scotland or Wales is to thrive and prosper, we will have to build a relationship with England as a friend and a neighbour. This is something that the men and women of terror do not recognise. If we let them win, we will be doing our countries a disservice. It is time for the people of Scotland and Wales to take a stand."

Sheena Lang left the platform to a standing ovation.

22 October 2019
Cabinet Room
10 Downing Street
London

The Conservative Party had enjoyed a successful conference in Brighton the previous week. The party's policy on Scotland and Wales appeared to be delivering dividends as the rate of violence appeared to be falling, local government had successfully been re-established and significant inroads had been made by the security forces into the membership of the SNLA and the WRA. In addition, there was economic good news as the financial proceeds from the oilfields off Scotland and Wales and in the English Channel started to swell the Treasury's coffers. This made possible scope for tax cuts in the run up to the next General Election in 2022. This would surely deliver a fourth victory for the Tories and make Robert Delgado the first Prime Minister to serve four consecutive terms in the post.

Delgado had discussed substantive items of business first. These included a new Finance Bill which would reduce the level of corporate taxes on business and would make the United Kingdom the low tax haven for business that Margaret Thatcher had first envisaged forty years earlier. He had also given Jason Steer, authority to place an order for the delivery of the Lockheed Martin A-22 strike bomber to replace the elderly Tornado which had served since the 1980s.

The agenda now came to Any Other Business. Jonathan Morgan and Stuart Grieve indicated they did.

Morgan was first to speak.

"I would like to bring colleagues' notice to another encouraging development. Over the past two months, an All-Wales Peace Movement has been set up by a group of women. By all accounts, interest has taken off massively. They had a huge rally in Cardiff a month ago with nearly 4,000 people in attendance. There's going to be a march through London on Sunday with a rally in Hyde Park, which is jointly being organised with Peace 4 Scotland. For that, I will hand you over to Stuart."

Grieve then followed.

"As with Wales, there is now a peace campaign in Scotland and, once again, it is led by women. It's called Peace 4 Scotland and they too have had a large national rally at the Glasgow International Conference Centre, as well as several smaller rallies round Scotland. By all counts, their membership is growing very fast like their Welsh counterparts."

"What effect is it having on the SNLA and the WRA?" asked Home Secretary Deborah Pearson.

"I think they're both running scared Deborah" replied Morgan. "Media reports suggest they're suffering drastic falls in recruitment. Isn't that so Stuart?"

"Yesterday's edition of the *Scotsman* said as much" said Grieve.

"If you've got doubts Deborah, have a word with Nicola Martin" said Morgan. "She may be able to confirm."

"This may be the best piece of news we've received in a long time" said Delgado. "If this peace movement weakens the hand of the SNLA and the WRA, I think we should encourage it. By the way, who are the leaders? I would like to meet them."

"Liz Church and Sheena Lang" replied Morgan. "By the way, Prime Minister, a word of caution. Both women support independence for their countries."

"I think we can handle that little problem" said Delgado. "Jonathan, Stuart, keep me posted on developments."

24 October 2019
Treharne Street
Morriston
Swansea

Liz Church had been busy making final arrangements for the peace rally in London the following Sunday. Coaches had been booked and parking spaces arranged. Speakers had been booked and both she and Sheena Lang were delighted that the Leader of the Opposition, Iain Turner and former Foreign Secretary, Christian Vale, had agreed to speak.

At 9pm, she received a call. She was hoping it was not bad news.

On the other end of the line was a woman with a Cockney accent.

"Is that Liz Church?"

"Speaking. How can I help?"

"I'm head of a group called English Women's Peace Campaign. Is it OK to join the rally on Sunday?"

Liz Church was worried that this might be a 'false flag' call. She had never heard of the group and was well aware that, east of London, there was strong support for the EVF and they might be planning to cause trouble."

"Can I have your name and a contact number?"

"Yeah OK. It's Sharon Barden. Thurrock 351814."

Barden. That name seemed familiar to Liz Church.

"In case you're wondering, I'm the ex-missus of Phil Barden. You know, the EVF leader. He's a complete arsehole and I want nothing to do with his hate-filled, evil views anymore. I'm in support of what you and Sheena is doing."

"Thank you Sharon" said Liz Church. "Look forward to seeing you on Sunday."

27 October 2019
London

The Rally for Peace in Scotland and Wales was one of the largest ever seen in London. An estimated 200,000 people had gathered on the Albert Embankment where the march through London was due to start. Not only had people come down from Scotland and Wales, but there was also considerable support from across England. Scottish saltires and Welsh dragons could be seen flying alongside Union Jacks and St George's flags. The late autumn sunshine provided a perfect backdrop for the march.

The march began at 12pm. From Albert Embankment, they crossed Lambeth Bridge to proceed up Millbank, past the Houses of Parliament and Parliament Square, up Whitehall to Trafalgar Square, then via Pall Mall, St James's Street and Piccadilly to Hyde Park Corner and, finally, up Park Lane to Speakers Corner.

The Metropolitan Police were out in force to escort the march, but many officers believed they could have stayed at home, such was the good nature of the march. The only flashpoint was at Trafalgar Square where a counter-demonstration organised by Clann na h-Albann, Meibion Cymru and the Socialist Alliance took place. A solid barrier of policemen ensured that the counter-demonstrators were unable to get near the main peace rally, and the only arrests that day were of twelve counter-demonstrators on public order charges as, frustrated in being unable to get near the main march, they resorted to throwing missiles.

By 3pm, all the marchers were in Hyde Park by Speakers Corner. Speeches were made by Labour Party leader, Iain Turner, former Foreign Secretary Christian Vale, the EU President, Poul Rasmussen, actors Tom Carmichael and Ben Griffith, actresses Julia Bevan and Lindsey McDonald, footballer Andy Munro and rock musician Brian Thomas. The closing speeches were made by Liz Church and Sheena Lang.

The same day
Chequers near Wendover
Buckinghamshire

Robert Delgado was spending the weekend at the official Prime Minister's country residence of Chequers, set deep in the Chilterns. He had been catching up on his official papers when his wife, Sarah, came into the study.

"Darling, have you seen Sky News today? The peace march in London's attracted some 200,000."

"I'm coming dear" replied the Prime Minister.

The 42-inch television monitor in the main lounge was switched onto Sky News. The main topic of their coverage had been the peace march through London that afternoon.

"This is Helen Warner with this afternoon's headlines on Sky News."

"An estimated 200,000 people marched through London today to support the call for peace in Scotland and Wales. The march proceeded peacefully and without incident, apart from a few missiles that were thrown by supporters of a counter-demonstration in support of the SNLA and WRA at Trafalgar Square. The marchers finally assembled in Hyde Park where speeches were made by the Leader of the Opposition, Iain Turner and by the former Foreign Secretary, Christian Vale, as well as Poul Rasmussen, the recently-elected President of the European Union and by several celebrities from the sporting, film and music world."

"The impact of the mainly female-led peace movement in Scotland and Wales has been considerable since it was set up less than two months ago. It has been estimated that nearly a million people have now joined the two peace organisations, Peace 4 Scotland and the All-Wales Peace Movement. At the same time, there have been reports that recruitment to the SNLA and WRA have dropped by up to 50%. With the numbers of terrorist incidents this year having fallen by over a third and the high profile defections of several leading SNLA and WRA commanders, there is now optimism in Government and security circles that the SNLA and WRA may now be beaten."

"The events of the past two months have catapulted the peace movement's leaders, Liz Church and Sheena Lang into the public spotlight. From being middle-aged housewives in humdrum jobs, they are now seen as national leaders with a much influence as leading politicians. There are reports that Mrs Church and Mrs Lang are to be recommended for the Nobel Peace Prize next year."

"Well Robert, looks like women have come up with a solution once again" said Sarah Delgado.

"Yes, Sarah" replied the Prime Minister. "All the same, it looks like good news all round. The popularity of the SNLA and WRA are falling and I think all we need is one final push against them next year and they'll be throwing the towel in. Considering that the oil's now coming on tap at full production, that's the best news we've received for a long time. Just think, darling. We'll be able to cut business taxes and still fund all spending commitments. We'll make the United Kingdom the enterprise capital of the world. And we'll be able to cut taxes before 2022 and be in for a fourth term."

"Haven't you thought about retiring, Robert?" asked Sarah Delgado. "You'll be 66 next year."

"Not a bit, Sarah" replied the Prime Minister. "I've got more energy than most men half my age. I feel I can go on for another ten years."

20 November 2019
Cornwall Street
Oldham

The SNLA and the WRA had agreed to hold crisis talks at an equidistant venue. Through their links with Al-Q'aida, they had managed to secure the use of a safe house in Werneth, to the south west of the town centre. It had the advantage of being a venue that neither the SNLA nor the WRA had used before, and would not attract undue attention from the authorities. Furthermore, Werneth was almost now almost wholly Pakistani in its demographic makeup. Many still harboured a grudge against the authorities for the round of internments and deportations which followed Al-Q'aida's assault on London seven years earlier. Mohammed Aslam, the property's owner, assured Doug Paterson and Trevor Rees that there were unlikely to be any snoopers around who might give away their identity to the authorities.

The General Councils of the SNLA and WRA were gathered round a table in the lounge of the safe house. The mood was grim to say the least. Having to put up with the success of the local elections and the impact of the defection of several senior commanders was bad enough. But the peace movement was the rancid turd which capped it all. Since Peace 4 Scotland and the All-Wales Peace Movement had started two months previously, recruitment of new volunteers had fallen by half. Many of the new recruits were inadequate and replacement was below the attrition rate of volunteers being either killed in action or arrested by the authorities.

"How the hell do we stop the peace movement in its tracks?" asked the newest member of the SNLA's General Council, Gordon Ross.

"It certainly won't be by shooting Liz Church or Sheena Lang" said Richard Thomas. "I think we've both learned the lessons of the events of last August." Thomas was referring to the WRA shooting of Mark Owen, a Caernarfon man who had been involved in a nightclub altercation with the son of Trevor Rees and the SNLA kidnap and murder of Caroline Day, the wife of a London businessman.

"I see Delgado's invited Church and Lang to a meeting at 10 Downing Street" said Iain Murray. "That surely will be the kiss of death for them. We'll be able to portray them as lackeys of the British government. That will result in their popularity dropping like a stone."

"Not so sure Iain" said Gareth Evans. "Both Church and Lang are supporters of independence. They've still got credibility."

At that moment, the two General Councils heard the front door open. It was Mohammed Aslam.

"Good afternoon gentlemen, how's things progressing?" asked Aslam.

"Not well, Mo" replied Doug Paterson. "Those two women who started the peace movement seem on a roll, and we can't do anything about it. We're losing volunteers hand over fist and are unable to replace them."

"Killing them or carrying out another major bombing will only make things worse for us" said Trevor Rees. "We're basically snookered."

"Guys, how about doing what Al-Q'aida has done over the past six years?" said Aslam.

"Doesn't appear to be much from what I've read, Mo" said Mark Podborski.

"Mark, listen to what Mo's got to say" said Paterson.

"You are right, it appears that Al-Q'aida has done very little in recent years" continued Aslam. "But we've changed our focus. We are continuing to campaign, but in the community at local level and taking on people's grievances. About everything from schools, employment and unfair dismissal, social services, immigration, police harassment and wrongful arrest. We've also provided community amenities like drop-in centres and helped run football and cricket teams and provide support for arts and music projects."

"All this time, we've kept our noses clean and not come to the notice of the authorities. For us, that's critical. You will know that the authorities can take our passports away and deport us if they have evidence of involvement in terrorist activity. But, over the past six years, we have successfully bought the support of all the people we have helped. Basically, we've copied what Gramsci recommended—you know, building hegemony in civil society."

"Mo, where the hell did you learn about Gramsci?" asked Gethin Davies.

"When I was at university twenty years ago. Sooner or later, the Government will make the wrong move. Or find itself on the ropes. We have not given up the struggle—the *jihad*. Through building hegemony in civil society, as Gramsci would have said, we are in a strong position to strike when the enemy is at its weakest."

"If the SNLA and WRA were to concentrate its efforts on addressing community grievances and build support that way, I can assure you that you will both be in a position to continue your struggle for independence. And win."

The same day
Werneth Park
Oldham

There were few people in Werneth Park that Wednesday afternoon. A steady drizzle was falling and it was already starting to get dark.

Asif Mahmood was seated in the public shelter in the park. The son of second generation Pakistani immigrants from the city of Jhelum, he had grown up in Birmingham. However, he knew Oldham well because an aunt and an uncle lived there.

Mahmood had studied politics at Hull University and, on graduation four years previously, had joined MI5. This caused some consternation to his friends, but not to his family. His mother was a Conservative councillor and the family considered themselves loyal British subjects.

Mahmood had been dispatched to Oldham by his employers to keep tabs on Al-Q'aida. The organisation had been quiet for too long and there was concern they might have something planned.

He had rented a property in the next road, Worcester Street under the name of Sarfraz Butt and he bought a secondhand Ford Mondeo, which he had fitted out as a taxi. This provided an ideal cover for his surveillance activities. He also joined the Werneth Sports and Social Club and it was through games of snooker that he found out valuable intelligence on his quarry.

Three days earlier, Mahmood took a call to pick up four men from Manchester Piccadilly to take them to Cornwall Street in Oldham. His first reaction was it was it was probably a family returning from a holiday in Pakistan. Mahmood was very surprised to find that the four men he picked up were white. While driving up the East Lancashire Road, he heard them talking in the back. None of the men had local accents; two were Scottish and the other two were Welsh. The other issue which grabbed his notice was the fact they asked to be dropped off in Werneth. Mahmood regarded that as most odd as there were few white families living there.

Mahmood probed deeper. At Werneth Sports and Social Club, he found out that 24 Cornwall Street was an Al-Q'aida safe house. What were Scots and Welsh doing there? Then he remembered that there was evidence that Al-Q'aida had been helping the SNLA and the WRA.

Mahmood had a digital personal data assistant on him which combined the functions of mobile phone, camera and personal computer. He used his work as a taxi driver to cover Cornwall Street. All he needed was for someone to come out the front door. The previous day, he had success. Two men came out of No 24 and he managed to obtain good quality photographs of them. He e-mailed them off to MI5 headquarters for a check. Earlier that day, they came back with a positive identification. Gordon Ross and Gethin Davies. Both members of the General Councils for the SNLA and WRA. If they were there, it was a good bet that other members were there too.

He dialled an encrypted number into his personal data assistant in order to reach his boss, Peter Firth.

"Big Fry here. Please identify yourself."

"Latic here, Big Fry. Got some good news. Reason to believe that General Councils of SNLA and WRA have been traced to address in Oldham. 24 Cornwall Street, Werneth. Have definite identifications for Gordon Ross and Gethin Davies. Also, I picked up four men at Manchester Piccadilly on Sunday and took them to Cornwall Street. White, age between late 30s and mid-40s. Two had Scottish accents, two Welsh. Very unusual for anyone who's white to go to Werneth. Would not be surprised if they are also SNLA and WRA."

"Excellent work Latic" replied Firth. "Now make yourself scarce before anyone starts asking questions."

"Roger, Big Fry" replied Mahmood.

21 November 2019, 6:30am
Cornwall Street
Oldham

Chief Inspector Suzanne Cross of the National Anti-Terror Squad was in the back seat of the lead police car of eight as it pulled up to the northern entrance to Cornwall Street. She started issuing orders.

"Darren, Mark, seal off both ends of Cornwall Street. Leanne, seal off Ely Street. Jon, Simon, seal off Worcester Street. We don't want chummy escaping through the back exit."

Sergeants Darren Morley, Mark Featherstone, Leanne Blake, Jon Ridgeley and Simon Mather took their squads of constables to close off the escape routes from 24 Cornwall Street.

Overhead, two helicopters from the National Police Air Service hovered.

Once the police roadblocks were in place, Chief Inspector Cross issued the critical order.

"Alright, let's go in."

Eight officers from the National Anti-Terror Squad leapt out of the BMW 535 estate cars, charged up to 24 Cornwall Street and kicked down the front door. Shouting "Armed police, put your hands up", they burst into the lounge where four of the SNLA and WRA men were asleep in sleeping bags. Another eight officers followed, charging up the stairs and into the bedrooms. Before they could offer any resistance, the entire General Councils of the SNLA and WRA were in police custody.

Later that morning
10 Downing Street
London

Robert Delgado was in the middle of a meeting with the Australian Prime Minister, Bob Challenor to discuss trade and mutual co-operation.

Challenor had been re-elected for a fourth term earlier that year and had equalled the achievement of the previous Liberal Prime Minister, John Howard. The Australian economy had been booming for the past ten years on the basis of its mineral wealth, which now included oil. Challenor had been a steadfast supporter of the western world, which had been shown by his commitment of the Australian armed forces to the Third Gulf War six years earlier. However, the troubles in Scotland and Wales had spilled over into Australian domestic politics. There were large numbers of Australians who were either emigrants from Scotland and Wales or were of Scottish or Welsh descent. After Bloody Sunday four years earlier, demonstrators had badly damaged the British High Commission in Canberra. And Challenor had faced demands from MPs, not only from the opposition Labor Party but also from his own Liberal party, for the Government to lean on the United Kingdom over its policies for Scotland and Wales.

The meeting with Challenor had been a cordial one; after the United States, Australia was the United Kingdom's most favoured partner country. There was still business to discuss on reciprocal pension agreements for the citizens of respective countries who lived in the other, when there was a knock on the door. It was Delgado's Principal Private Secretary, Jenny Mitchell.

"Prime Minister, sorry to disturb you, but I've got Kevin Lazenby on the line. He says it's urgent." Lazenby was the new Head of the National Anti-Terror Squad following the promotion of his predecessor, Darren Charnock, to the post of Deputy Commissioner for the Metropolitan Police.

Delgado offered his apologies to Challenor. "Sorry Bob, we get a lot of this. I'll be back in a minute."

Delgado picked up the telephone in his office.

"Hello, Prime Minister, Kevin Lazenby here."

"Kevin, I hear you've got some news for me" said Delgado.

"Certainly have, Prime Minister. Earlier this morning, we nicked the entire General Councils of the SNLA and the WRA. All together at a house in Oldham."

"Oldham!" exclaimed the Prime Minister. "What the hell were they doing there?"

"It was an Al-Q'aida safe house, loaned to the SNLA and WRA for their General Councils to meet. It proves one thing, Prime Minister. Al-Q'aida are helping the SNLA and WRA. They're not as quiet as we thought."

"How did you find out that the SNLA and WRA were holed up there?" asked Delgado.

"Nothing to do with us, Prime Minister" replied Lazenby. "You need to thank MI5. Or rather one of their agents who found out by accident after keeping Al-Q'aida under surveillance. Nicola Martin has the details if you want to reward him."

CHAPTER 20

12 January 2020
The Sunday Express

TERROR LAGS' LIFE OF LUXURY
Supermax prison 'like holiday camp'

Terrorists, drug traffickers and armed robbers are living in conditions almost akin to a five-star hotel, an exclusive investigation by the Sunday Express has found.

A reporter from the Sunday Express managed to obtain access to Britain's first 'supermax' prison, HMP Foulness, which opened two months ago. The prison, which was designed to be escape-proof, houses some of the country's most dangerous terrorists and criminals, all of whom have either escaped from custody before or who are considered to be a high escape risk. These include members of the SNLA, the WRA, the Real IRA, Al-Q'aida and the EVF.

Our reporter found that

- Cells were unlocked for most of the day and prisoners were allowed to wander round the prison and associate freely.
- Prisoners were allowed to have mobile phones, iPads and MP3 players in their cells.
- The prison has a TV lounge with a 50-inch flat-screen TV.
- Prisoners have access to a gym and a games room with snooker tables and computer games.
- Prisoners are allowed conjugal visits from wives, girlfriends and families every weekend without supervision.
- Prisoners were free to order takeaways from the Indian and Chinese restaurants in the village of Great Wakering, four miles away from the prison.

A prison officer who did not wish to be named spoke of his disgust that prisoners who had killed and maimed innocent people were enjoying luxury which would have put many five-star hotels to shame.

These revelations will be a serious embarrassment to the Government, which had pledged it would spare no effort in its battle to defeat the SNLA and the WRA.

(continues on pages 4 and 5)

The Sunday Express had been the only one of the United Kingdom's Sunday newspapers to run the story on HMP Foulness. All the other papers had focused their headline story on the decision to award the Nobel Peace Prize to Liz Church and Sheena Lang, the two peace campaigners who had done much to reduce the level of violence in Wales and Scotland and reduce the influence of the WRA and SNLA.

More than fifty years earlier, the Daily Express and its Sunday partner, the Sunday Express, had been the country's leading newspapers with a circulation of four million. Owned by Lord Beaverbrook, both papers had a reputation for lively, pungent journalism and, although generally supporting the Conservative Party, it employed several left-wing journalists. Its sports coverage was regarded as amongst the best in the country and the Sunday Express had been one of the first papers to include a colour supplement.

In the intervening years, the Express lost its market leadership position. Seen as 'fuddy-duddy' and old-fashioned, it lost circulation to both the mass-market Sun and to its main middle-market rival, the Daily Mail. Many of its top journalists moved to rival papers. Not surprisingly, it was desperate to land a 'blockbuster' story. A decade earlier, the Daily Telegraph had virtually doubled its circulation after exposing MPs expenses fiddles. The Sunday Express was hopeful that the Foulness story would achieve similar results.

**The same day
"Windermere"
Gerrards Cross
Buckinghamshire**

The Home Secretary, Deborah Pearson, was not expecting any telephone calls that morning. The Christmas and New Year had been a quiet period. The SNLA and WRA were losing both manpower and influence, and there had been no significant bombing or shooting outrages for some months. The leadership of both the SNLA and the WRA were now in prison and would be facing the special criminal court that had been set up to try the so-called 'untouchables'—terrorists and criminals whose use of fear and manipulation had made impossible to try them in a normal court.

She was therefore surprised when the Permanent Secretary at the Home Office, Sir Richard Benson, was on the phone.

"Home Secretary, sorry to trouble you at the weekend. Have you read today's *Sunday Express*?"

"No I haven't Richard" replied the Home Secretary. "You know that Henry and I always take the *Telegraph*."

"I think you better" said Benson. "There's an explosive story about the new prison at Foulness. Claims that it's being run like a holiday camp."

Pearson was aghast. Foulness was the new ultra-high security prison the Government had built to house the most dangerous terrorists and criminals.

"Thank you for letting me know, Richard. I'll be seeking an explanation from David Rimington."

Later that day
Heath Drive
Sutton
Surrey

"Darling, it's the Home Secretary for you. Says it's urgent."

Anna Rimington, a redhead in her early 40s handed the telephone over to her husband.

David Rimington had been a senior executive for a media company when, eighteen months earlier, he had been headhunted for the job of Director-General of the Prison Service. He was well aware of the risky nature of the job and the high public profile it would carry, and knew that his predecessor, Phil Webley, had been sacked after a highly embarrassing escape by SNLA and WRA prisoners from HMP Whitemoor.

"David, what the hell's going on at HMP Foulness? According to today's *Sunday Express*, prisoners are leading a life of luxury and it's being run more like a holiday camp than the most secure prison in the country."

Rimington could tell from the sharp, clipped tone of the Home Secretary's voice that she was angry.

"Home Secretary, this is the first I've heard of this. What has the *Express* said?"

"That prisoners are allowed to roam the prison at will during the day, have mobile phones and iPads and have been allowed conjugal visits from wives and girlfriends. Also that they've got a plasma screen TV, a games room, a gym and have been allowed to order takeaway meals. Makes a complete mockery of our policy of getting tough with criminals and terrorists."

"Home Secretary, there is nothing in Prison Service rules and regulations which says that prisoners should be denied recreational facilities. Most other prisons have gyms, games rooms and TV lounges. As regards association during the day, we've always followed Council of Europe guidelines. You know that we're supposed to give prisoners classified as 'political' special category status. But I'll contact James Pocock tomorrow and tell him he needs to clamp down on illicit mobile phone use and will need to keep a tighter grip on prisoner movements."

"David, the Government is not—I repeat, not, bound by anything the Council of Europe says. Don't you remember that we left the EU to get away from interfering busybodies like that."

Pearson continued. "From now on, I want the prisons run my way. No special category status for so-called 'political' prisoners. No lavish leisure facilities. Routine cell-by-cell searches for prohibited items like mobile phones and summary punishments for any prisoners who break the rules. And I don't want to see of hear of prisoners wandering around the prison like it's a hotel. These are the most dangerous people in the country. If they go anywhere, it'll be with an armed escort. Understand?"

**14 January 2020
HMP Foulness
near Southend-on-Sea
Essex**

HMP Foulness had been formally opened by the Prince of Wales two months earlier. It was the United Kingdom's first ultra-high security prison and had been purposefully located on an island, only ten miles to the east of the bustling seaside resort of Southend-on-Sea but in the middle of a military firing range. The island was patrolled by armed members of the Ministry of Defence Police and there was only two means of access. One was by the single road which led to the island and was controlled by an Army checkpoint. The other was a pier on the northern side of the island, again, controlled by armed military police. Beaches on the island's shoreline had been fitted out with sharp stakes to prevent any marine-based unauthorised landings.

The new prison had been designed to be escape-proof. A twelve foot high inner fence surrounded the prison and its grounds, and watchtowers and digital CCTV cameras were mounted on top of the walls. Airspace around the prison was designated as a 'no-fly zone' and radar and anti-aircraft guns were installed to deter any heliborne escape attempt. Finally, the inner walls of the prison were surrounded by a 200 metre ring of bleached shingle which, at night, was floodlit. Anyone who managed to get through the inner wall would have to cross this shingle barrier. Apart from being highly visible against the background, it was impossible to avoid making a noise.

Most of the inmates at HMP Foulness were either terrorists or serious criminals with convictions for drug trafficking or serious violent crimes like murder, armed robbery or kidnapping. These included members of the SNLA and the WRA, but there were also members of Al-Q'aida, the Real IRA and the EVF held there.

From the day it opened, the prison regime at Foulness had been fairly relaxed, but that was about to change. Two days earlier, there had been a story in the *Sunday Express* alleging that the prison was more like a holiday camp. Orders had come from on high that this must stop.

Earlier that day, inmates had been summoned to the canteen to be advised that a stricter regime was to be implemented on Government orders. Prisoners would no longer have the right of free movement around the prison and would be escorted by prison officers everywhere they went. They were to be restricted to three hours of television in the evening and access to pay-per-view channels would be denied. Unless they were working, studying, eating or watching television, they were to be confined to their cells, and it had been made clear that any inmate found with a mobile phone or personal data device in their possession would be punished for breach of prison rules. The gym and the games room were to be removed and, finally, prisoners were to be confined behind a glass screen when receiving visits from families.

James Pocock, the Governor of HMP Foulness was a worried man. The liberal regime he had instituted at the prison had made the inmates relatively easy to manage. There had been no disturbances, no assaults on staff and no escape attempts. But a muck-raking journalist, with the help of a couple of prison officers, had run a story claiming that some of the country's most dangerous terrorists and criminals were living a life of luxury at the taxpayer's expense. A lot of what the *Sunday Express* had said was a load of bollocks but it had sold the paper a record number of sales over the previous weekend. And the readers believed everything that was written.

The previous day, Pocock had experienced an uncomfortable meeting with David Rimington, the Prison Service's Director-General. He had been told in no uncertain terms of the embarrassment caused to the Home Secretary and that he was effectively on probation. Pocock was a career Prison Service official and had little time for a jumped-up media whizzkid like Rimington. But he knew he had no choice but to knuckle down to what his superiors wanted. Or have to find a new career. He was now 48 years old, had a daughter at university, a mortgage and knew he was unlikely to find a job as well paid.

Pocock's worst fears were confirmed when Chief Officer Gregory came in at 2pm.

"Sir, two of the prisoners have requested to see you" said Gregory, a short, stocky man in his early 50s.

"Who are they, Tom?" asked Pocock. "And what do they want?"

"Prisoner 5610 Davies and Prisoner 7035 Murray" replied Gregory. "They want to know what are the reasons for the change of regime, sir. They don't think they or any of the prisoners have done anything to warrant it."

Pocock knew who the prisoners were. Gethin Davies and Iain Murray. Formerly on the General Councils of the WRA and the SNLA until their arrest in Oldham back in November.

"Okay Tom, bring them in."

Two minutes later, Davies and Murray were in the Governor's office.

"Davies, Murray, good afternoon. I understand you have asked to see me about the regime changes."

"That's right sir" replied Murray. "We cannot understand why the regime has been made harsher and facilities like the gym, the games room and satellite TV have been taken away."

"There's been no misconduct on the part of any of our men, sir" said Davies. "I think you'll agree on that."

"Davies, Murray, I can understand that you and many of the inmates are upset at having lost many of the amenities provided. You are indeed right that no one detained here has committed any acts of misconduct. But I think you will agree that providing prisoners with lavish amenities is likely to anger the taxpayer. You and your colleagues are being held here because you have committed heinous acts of terror. The public has a reasonable expectation that people who commit serious offences receive appropriate punishment. I however do not see my purpose in life as delivering the public's retribution on anyone in my charge. I see rehabilitation as being just as, if not more, important. But I have to realise that the public's taxes is paying my salary and that I am therefore accountable to them."

"You are effectively saying, sir, that you have caved into the *Sunday Express*" said Murray. The contents of the previous Sunday's edition was common knowledge amongst the prisoners at HMP Foulness.

"That is unfair, Murray" replied Pocock. "You cannot deny that I have been concerned about the welfare of the prisoners being held here. But I cannot thumb my nose at the taxpaying public—as I've already said, they are our stakeholders. Do you or Davies have anything else to say?"

"No sir" said Murray.

"No sir" said Davies.

"Tom, escort prisoners Murray and Davies back to their cells." With that command, Chief Officer Gregory led the two terrorists back to their cells.

18 January 2020
Fitzroy Avenue
Drumcondra
Dublin

The doorbell at Martin Hallinan's house rang. Hallinan's son, Brendan, went to open it. At the door were Adam Lamont and Rob Mathias, the Acting Chairmen of the General Councils of the SNLA and the WRA.

Martin Hallinan had been expecting the arrival of Lamont and Mathias. Until two months earlier, they had been the Commanders of the Dunfermline Brigade of the SNLA and the Llanelli Brigade of the WRA. But with the arrest of the two General Councils, they had found themselves projected to the top of both organisations.

Hallinan noticed that both Lamont and Mathias, both in their early 30s, were comparatively youthful compared to the now imprisoned members of the General Councils. But their youth did not hide their ability or their sheer ruthlessness. Both Lamont and Mathias had blood on their hands, not only British soldiers and policemen but also innocent civilians caught up in bomb explosions and suspected informers who had been tortured and murdered to set an example.

"Adam, Rob, good afternoon" said Hallinan. "Any problems in getting here?"

"None Martin" replied Mathias.

"Same with me" said Lamont.

"Come through to the lounge. Tea, coffee?"

"Tea" replied the two visitors.

Lamont and Mathias settled into the sofa in the Hallinan's lounge as Maureen Hallinan brought in tea and biscuits. The conversation quickly turned to business.

"How are the SNLA and WRA coping with the loss of your General Councils?" asked Hallinan.

"The SNLA's appointed temporary General Council to run things while Doug and the boys are inside" said Lamont. "Hear it's the same for the WRA—is that right Rob?"

"Yep, dead right" said Mathias.

"There's no lack of enthusiasm in the acting leadership" continued Lamont. "But we've lost the expertise that Iain brought to the finance side. And Mark's expertise in military matters was also invaluable."

"Similar issues for the WRA" said Mathias. "Twms used to be a quarry foreman. Knew everything about explosives back to front. And Gar was good on finance too and helped Iain."

"The Women's Peace Movement has been a pain in the backside" said Lamont. "Made a big dent into our recruitment. For the first time ever, it's fallen below replacement levels."

"On top of that, those two old bats have been put forward for the Nobel Peace Prize" added Mathias.

"What's galling is that people are starting to come to terms with English rule" continued Mathias. He was referring to the local government elections that had taken place the previous year. "And the SNP and Plaid Cymru have sold both our countries down the river in exchange for crumbs from the English."

Hallinan motioned that he wanted to speak.

"Fellas, all is not lost" said the Irishman. "The IRA was in the same position in the late 1970s. British intelligence had penetrated us right through to the top ranks. We were losing men and women daily to arrests and we couldn't replace them fast enough. Support for our cause was falling and, like you, we were beset with a women's peace movement."

"The turning point was when Margaret Thatcher became Prime Minister in the UK. She decided to take a hard line against us from the start, and withdrew privileges that our prisoners of war had. That, if you remember, triggered the hunger strikes in 1981, which was the turning point for us. Recruitment soared, we started to get overseas support and the UK found people less willing to do business with them. Extradition of our freedom fighters was blocked. The US Senate blocked arms sales to the RUC. Contributions to Noraid went up. We were once again awash with both money and new fighters and we were able to launch a highly effective mainland campaign, culminating in the bombing of the Conservative Party Conference in 1984. The following year, Thatcher was allowing the Irish Republic to have an advisory role in the governance of the Six Counties. They called her the 'Iron Lady' but everyone knew the real reason for the Anglo-Irish Agreement was that she was losing the battle against us and had no choice but to offer concessions to the Irish Republic to get them to help."

"Hey Ad, there may be a parallel with what Martin's told us" said Mathias. "The Brits have done the same to our guys. All because of the article in last weekend's *Sunday Express*."

"Rob, this could be our opportunity to turn the corner" said Lamont. "Let's see how the Brit government copes with a hunger strike."

23 January 2020
HMP Foulness
near Southend-on-Sea
Essex

The Governor of HMP Foulness, James Pocock, was working late, when he received a knock on his office door. It was Chief Officer Gregory.

"Sir, can I have a word?"

"Is it urgent, Tom?" replied Pocock. "Afraid I'm rather busy."

"Unfortunately yes, sir" said Gregory. "Six of the prisoners have started a hunger strike."

"Good god" exclaimed Pocock. "That's all we need. Who are they, Tom?"

"Prisoners 799 Allan, 1250 Davies, 2388 Lloyd, 2841 McLeish, 3993 Sutherland and 4068 Thomas."

"By the names, I take it they are all SNLA and WRA?"

"That's right, sir" replied Gregory.

27 January 2020
Home Office
Marsham Street
London

Deborah Pearson had convened a meeting in her office to discuss tackling the issue of the SNLA and WRA hunger strikes. The protest had now spread to Long Lartin and Woodhill prisons and to the detention centres at Brecon and Stirling. Present were the Prisons Minister, Carla Dean, the Permanent Secretary, Sir Richard Benson, the Director-General of the Prison Service, David Rimington, the Home Secretary's Chief Political Adviser, Ben Staines and the Home Office's Chief Legal Officer, Chris Rhodes and Chief Information Officer, Lisa Patrick.

"David, precisely what are the prisoners complaining about?" asked the Home Secretary.

"They claim that they should be treated as political prisoners rather than criminals" replied Rimington.

"Isn't that just what the IRA hunger strikers said nearly forty years ago?" asked Dean.

"Quite right Minister" said Benson. "I reckon the SNLA and the WRA have taken a leaf out of the IRA's books."

"What are the risks we face?" asked Pearson.

"If any of the hunger strikers die, the Government will be seen as heartless and callous" said Patrick. "It could kick-start the SNLA's and WRA's recruitment. The same happened with the IRA back in 1981."

"But surely, if we give in, the Government will be seen as capitulating to the SNLA and the WRA?" said Dean. "If we do that, won't we risk encouraging the SNLA and the WRA?"

"I'm with the Minister on this one" said Staines. "If we give into the SNLA and the WRA over the status of their prisoners, we'll only be encouraging their campaign to break up the United Kingdom."

"I think you need to remember that there's considerable sympathy for the Scottish and Welsh independence cause abroad" said Rimington. "The hunger strikers are quoting a Council of Europe convention which, to my knowledge, the Government is still signed up to. That is that prisoners being held in custody because their offences are of a political nature, should not be subject to the same sanctions as ordinary criminals. If we take a hard line on this, we may end up losing friends and emboldening our enemies."

"Chris, where do we stand legally?" asked Pearson.

"The previous Labour government did indeed sign up to the Council of Europe Convention in 1999" replied Rhodes. "However, it is not legally binding upon the United Kingdom government. It is perfectly open to us to withdraw from the convention. There are likely to be protests from the civil liberties lobby and European governments but, as we are no longer part of the European Union, it will be impossible for any overseas government or international body to impose legal sanctions upon us."

"Thank you Chris" said the Home Secretary. "My mind is made up on this. I have no intention of capitulating to the emotional blackmail of two terrorist organisations. I have therefore got no plans to grant political prisoner status to either convicted or remanded prisoners from the SNLA and the WRA. I will be asking Henry Arbuthnot to take steps to renounce the Council of Europe Convention relating to political prisoners. If any of the prisoners die—tough. They knew the risks of getting involved in terrorism. I am ready to face down the SNLA and the WRA over this and I can assure you that the Government will back me."

25 March 2020
Claremont Parish Church
High Common Road
East Kilbride
Scotland

The funeral cortege bringing Rob Sutherland to be buried in his hometown was massive. At the front was a horse-drawn carriage bearing his coffin, which was draped in the Scottish saltire, and a Scottish piper, dressed in a kilt, led the way. Behind them was a fleet of Jaguar saloons carrying Sutherland's family and friends and members of the SNLA and Clann na h-Albann, including party leader Glen Johnstone. From the Sutherland family home in East Mains Road, the procession moved down Kingsway, then turned into Calderwood Road and St Leonard's Road, before arriving at High Common Road.

Sutherland had been a member of the SNLA's East Kilbride Brigade and a year earlier had been sentenced to twenty years imprisonment for his role in the bombing of the main London to Glasgow railway line. Following an attempted escape from Barlinnie, he had been moved to the new 'supermax' prison at Foulness the previous

September. Two months previously, he had been one of six SNLA and WRA prisoners held in Foulness who had started a hunger strike in protest at having special privileges reserved for political prisoners removed. The previous Friday, he had become the first hunger striker to die.

The weather was atrocious. Steady rain, driven by high winds, was falling but, despite this, crowds turned out to line the streets of East Kilbride. Many held up Scottish flags to show their support.

Inside Claremont Parish Church, Reverend James Maxwell conducted the service. After singing "The Lord is My Shepherd", Maxwell began his speech.

"We are gathered here today to celebrate the life of Robert Fearns Sutherland."

"Robert was a devoted son to Thomas and Isobel, brother to Gordon, Ross and Sheena, uncle to Ruari and Siobhan and fiancé to Claire. He will be remembered round East Kilbride, not only for being a talented footballer with Claremont Rangers, a highly capable golfer and a keen motorcycle scrambler, but also for giving up his spare time to coach children. I first came across Robert nearly twenty years ago when he was a little boy, when he first played football for the juniors at Claremont Rangers. I always remember him with a great smile on his face and I think that is how you all wish to remember Robert."

"For many people, Robert will be judged by the act which led him to be incarcerated in one of Her Majesty's prisons. As a man of the cloth, I cannot condone violence. But Robert felt he had a cause worth fighting for. To defend the honour of his country. That is a sentiment which, no matter what he did, is a noble one. A sentiment which, over the years, has been expressed by William Wallace, Robert the Bruce and Prince Charles Edward Stuart. Robert may be no longer physically with us. But in spirit, he will always be in the minds of the family he loved and the friends he had in East Kilbride and Scotland."

"Let us pray and remember Robert."

After the service, Sutherland's coffin was borne by his father, brothers and cousins to be laid to rest. As they moved into the cemetery, they were escorted by eight men dressed in black and wearing balaclavas. They were from the East Kilbride brigade of the SNLA. All were bearing AK-47 assault rifles. As Sutherland's coffin was lowered into his grave and the first sod of earth was thrown to cover it, the SNLA men fired a final salute to their dead comrade.

26 March 2020
Isle of Anglesey County Council
Llangefni
Anglesey
Wales

The Chief Executive's Department at the Isle of Anglesey County Council was making the final preparations for the by-election that was due to take place the following Thursday. The Ynys Mon constituency had become vacant two months previously following the death of its Plaid Cymru MP, Hywel Ellis. Nominations had been submitted by the Conservative, Labour and Liberal Democrat parties and Plaid Cymru. Also standing were the Progressive Party and two independents.

Today was the deadline for getting nominations submitted. Dafydd Edwards, the Team Leader, was not expecting any further nominations to arrive when his deputy, Debbie Lewis, rang to say that three men had arrived to submit a late nomination.

"Debbie, what's the panic" asked Edwards. "You know that we can accept nominations that come in before 5pm today."

"Dafydd, the candidate's address is HMP Brecon. He's one of the WRA prisoners on hunger strike."

"You know the law on prisoners, Debbie" replied Edwards. "No one with a conviction is allowed to stand for Parliament."

"Problem is Dafydd is that the candidate they want to nominate has no conviction" said Mrs Lewis. "He's been interned under national security laws."

"Alright, Debbie. Send them through."

Five minutes later, Gareth Morgan, Kevin Richards and Alun Thomas were sitting in Dafydd Edwards' office.

"Gentlemen, I'm not trying to be obstructive" said Edwards. "You do understand that anyone who has been imprisoned for a criminal office is ineligible to stand for election to Parliament."

"You don't understand, Mr Edwards" said Thomas. "Emyr Ruddock has never been convicted of any criminal offence. He is being held in HMP Brecon under internment regulations that have been regarded as illegal under international law. It is our argument that he is perfectly eligible to stand for Parliament."

"If Mr Ruddock is representing Meibion Cymru, he won't be permitted to stand" said Edwards. He was well aware that the political wing of the WRA would relish the opportunity to win a Parliamentary seat.

"Mr Ruddock will be standing as an independent Welsh nationalist" said Morgan.

Edwards fully knew that, if he allowed a member of the WRA to stand for Parliament, his career in local government would effectively be over. He phoned the Chief Executive's office.

"Mike, is that you? We've got a potential problem. Three blokes want to put up a WRA hunger striker as a candidate in next week's by-election. The thing is, he's totally clean as regards eligibility to stand. But you know what the repercussions will be."

Mike Tucker, a Yorkshireman who had taken the Chief Executive's job three years earlier, was on the other end of the line.

"Have you checked legal precedents Dafydd?"

"The only one we've got is Bobby Sands and that's now nearly 40 years old."

Sands was a member of the IRA who had been interned in the Maze Prison at Long Kesh, who was one of several internees who went on a hunger strike early in 1981. He was nominated for the vacant seat of Fermanagh and South Tyrone and won the by-election. 27 days after being elected, Sands died.

"Sands had a conviction for possessing a firearm, but the law as it stood then did not prevent him being nominated to stand for Parliament. Although the law now prevents anyone with a criminal conviction from standing, it would not apply in this case. Emyr Ruddock, the man who the gentlemen who have come to see me wish to nominate has no criminal record. He's an internee, being held without charge in HMP Brecon. Technically, we can't stop him being nominated. Also, he's being nominated as an independent candidate."

"Oh shit!" said Tucker. "Dafydd, I'll call our solicitor to see what he thinks. But I fear that we're going to have to accept this."

27 March 2020
Sky News

"This is Sara Ratcliffe with this morning's headlines on Sky News."

"Edinburgh and Glasgow are clearing up after the second night of disturbances following the death of SNLA hunger striker Rob Sutherland. The police and Army came under attack from organised groups of rioters who threw stones, bricks and petrol bombs, and there are reports that snipers opened fire on them. Properties and businesses were looted and set on fire."

"There were anti-British demonstrations in Washington DC, New York, Paris, Berlin, Madrid, Rome, Amsterdam, Sydney and Auckland following Sutherland's death. There was some damage to the British Deputy High Commission in Sydney and slogans spray-painted on the British Embassy in Berlin but otherwise there was little trouble."

"The Government appears to be holding firm over the issue of Special Category Status for SNLA and WRA prisoners. A Home Office spokesman said that there are no plans to review the status of prisoners convicted of politically-motivated offences and emphasised that all SNLA and WRA prisoners are being held for committing criminal acts."

"One of the hunger strikers, Emyr Ruddock, is to stand as an independent Welsh nationalist in next Thursday's by-election in Ynys Mon. There are concerns that Ruddock may get a high share of the vote because of the highly-charged emotions generated by the hunger strikes."

The same day
Department for Justice
Petty France
London

Dominic Collins, the Attorney-General, was about to depart for his constituency for the weekend when the phone rang. It was Dame Catherine Anderson, the Permanent Secretary.

"Sorry to disturb you Attorney-General. Just heard something you need to be aware of."

"What is it Catherine? I'm a busy man."

"A WRA hunger striker has been nominated to stand in the Ynys Mon by-election. We've checked the legal position with Treasury Solicitors. Looks like we can't stop him because he's not been convicted of an offence yet."

31 March 2020
Cabinet Room
10 Downing Street
London

"Dominic, can you arrange for Regulations to be made that will prevent this happening again."

The Prime Minister, Robert Delgado, had just heard from the Attorney-General, Dominic Collins, that Emyr Ruddock, an internee at HMP Brecon, had been nominated to stand in the Ynys Mon by-election in two days time, and could not be debarred on account of the fact he had no criminal conviction. Delgado had asked Collins to amend the law to close this loophole.

"Yes, Prime Minister" replied Collins. "It will be taken forward as a matter of priority."

Next on the agenda was the SNLA and WRA hunger strikes. Following the death of Rob Sutherland a week earlier, three more hunger strikers had died.

"Can you give an update on the hunger strikes Deborah" asked Robert Delgado.

The Home Secretary responded.

"Four hunger strikers have died to-date. Thomas Allan, Edward Lloyd, Robert Sutherland and Gethin Thomas. Two more, Alastair Beagrie and Garin Jones are reported to be close to death."

"Is there any signs of the prisoners' resolve faltering?" asked the Secretary of State for National Heritage, Cheryl Parkinson.

"I'm afraid not Cheryl" replied Pearson. "But we cannot afford to give into the demands of the SNLA and the WRA at this stage. It'll only embolden them."

"Have there been any repercussions internationally?" asked Delgado. "Henry."

"I'm afraid there's been a series of noisy demonstrations outside our embassies abroad" replied Henry Arbuthnot. "Also, there's been reports of British—or rather English—tourists and residents abroad being verbally abused in the street. Very unpleasant. But I think Deborah's right. We cannot afford to give into the SNLA and WRA and reintroduce Special Category Status for their prisoners."

"Deborah, it would have been very helpful to have contacted me first" said the Secretary of State for Scotland, Stuart Grieve. "I've spent the last year trying to engage with the mainstream nationalists in order to normalise political life in Scotland. I hope you realise you've given the SNLA a massive propaganda boost."

"Before you removed Special Category Status for WRA and SNLA prisoners, you should have spoken to Stuart and I first" added Secretary of State for Wales, Jonathan Morgan. "This has undermined our efforts to rebuild normal political life there."

"Stuart, Jonathan, am I hearing you correctly?" said the Home Secretary in her most magisterial voice. "It sounds like you're both advocating that the Government should give into the demands of two terrorist organisations. Have you forgotten that this Government was elected on a policy of implacable opposition to the men and women who kill and maim innocent people and try to hold this country to ransom?

If we allow the SNLA and the WRA to have Special Category Status, it will allow them the freedom to plan further acts of death and destruction from behind bars. It will also be a slap in the face to the victims of terrorism over the past five years and their families. As long as I'm Home Secretary, there is no way that I am going to give into demands to organisations that live and die by the barrel of a gun."

"I agree with Deborah" said Delgado. "Stuart, Jonathan, I am appreciative of the work you've both done to normalise political life in Scotland and Wales over the past year. But I am not prepared to see the reputation of this Government destroyed by giving into threats and intimidation, no matter how expedient it might appear in the short term. Give them Special Category Status and they will abuse it and start conducting their campaigns from behind bars. I recognise the risks the Government faces by standing firm. In the short term, the SNLA and WRA will regain some of its operational capacity through recruitment of new members. We risk facing increased terrorist activity. We will lose international support. But we faced the same challenges in the 2010s from Al-Q'aida and Iran. But by standing firm, we overcame them. We will do so again."

There was one remaining agenda item. Foreign Secretary Henry Arbuthnot and Secretary of State for Defence, Jason Steer were due to fly to Washington the following day to conclude a deal with the US government to buy the Strike Raptor bomber to replace the Tornado in the RAF.

<h2 style="text-align:center">2 April 2020
Isle of Anglesey County Council
Llangefni
Anglesey
Wales</h2>

It was now close to midnight. Counting in the Ynys Mon by-election had been in progress for the past two hours since the poling stations closed. It had been a fine, sunny day, the first after nearly three weeks of wet, windy weather, and the turnout had been good.

The Returning Officer, Dennis Evans, signalled that the counting had been completed and that it was time to announce the result.

Eight candidates had stood in the by-election. In addition to the Conservative, Labour and Liberal Democrat parties, Plaid Cymru and the Progressive parties fielded candidates. The remaining three candidates were all independents. Two were nothing more than 'joke' candidates who stood more for the publicity than any hope of being elected. But the third candidate and the only one not present, on account of the fact he was on a hunger strike at HMP Brecon, was a serious candidate. Emyr Ruddock, a former maintenance engineer at Anglesey Airport, was standing as an independent Welsh nationalist.

"Polling for the Ynys Mon by-election has now been completed and I am now ready to announce the results. Candidates' surnames will be read in alphabetical order."

"Alderman, Felicity Ruth, Progressive Party. Nine hundred and forty one."

"Davies, Alun Gerald, Labour Party. Eight thousand, seven hundred and sixty."

"Davies, Roderick Charles, Conservative Party. Six thousand, three hundred and sixteen."

"Davies, Megan Teresa, Liberal Democrat Party. One thousand, seven hundred and fifty five."

"Gutbucket, Dai, Independent Alcoholic. Forty five."

Laughter rang out through the council offices.

"Price, Gethin Daniel, Plaid Cymru. Nine thousand, four hundred and twenty."

There was a hushed murmur. Plaid Cymru had been expecting to get more votes.

"Ruddock, Emyr Thomas, Independent Welsh Nationalist. Ten thousand and seventy one."

A massive roar of victory swept across the room as Ruddock's supporters punched the air to celebrate victory.

When the pandemonium finally died down, Evans moved back to the microphone to announce the final result.

"Zebedee, Florence Dougal Dylan, Magic Roundabout. Twenty."

CHAPTER 21

5 April 2020
Delmonico Restaurant
Marsham Street
London

The Secretaries of State for Scotland and Wales, Stuart Grieve and Jonathan Morgan, were regular customers of the Delmonico and had booked the restaurant for a meal after returning from their constituencies. They were joined by the Secretary of State for National Heritage, Cheryl Parkinson. The table was booked in one of the most discreet parts of the restaurant so that no one could listen in on their discussion.

The weekend had brought more bad news for the Government. Over the past week, five more hunger strikers had died, bringing the toll up to nine. Three more, including the newly-elected MP for Ynys Mon, Emyr Ruddock, were in a coma and were not expected to last the night. That afternoon, Clann na h-Albann and Meibion Cymru had held a joint rally in support of the hunger strikers in Trafalgar Square which more than five thousand people attended.

The weekend had brought more disturbances in towns and cities in Scotland and Wales. Overseas, there were anti-British demonstrations across Europe and in the USA, Canada, Australia and New Zealand. More worryingly, the United Kingdom was starting to lose trade as a boycott of British goods was being organised and several foreign companies were starting to withdraw investments in the United Kingdom under pressure from both campaigners and nervous shareholders.

During the previous twelve months, Grieve and Morgan had achieved considerable success with their efforts to normalise political life in Scotland and Wales. Their strategy of engaging the moderate wings of the Scottish National Party and Plaid Cymru had succeeded and they had restored effective local government to both countries. During the latter part of 2019, support for the SNLA and WRA appeared to be waning. But the Government's decision to withdraw Special Category Status from SNLA and WRA prisoners after newspaper reports suggested it was being abused had badly backfired. There were now nearly forty prisoners on hunger strike and recruitment to the SNLA and WRA had risen sharply over the two previous months, as had unrest and terrorist activity.

"Grim news over the weekend" said Grieve as the three Cabinet Ministers as starters were served. "You heard that police and troops came under fire in Edinburgh and Dundee last night? Three months ago we appeared to have the situation under control and now it's like being back in 2015 or 2016 all over again."

"If only Deborah had swallowed her pride and had stood up to the *Sunday Express* rather than trying to posture as the new Iron Lady before the press" said Morgan. "There would have been no hunger strikes, no renewed disturbances and SNLA and WRA membership would have been falling rather than going up."

"I'm concerned about the effect of the hunger strikes on the country's economy" said Parkinson. "There's a campaign abroad to boycott the United Kingdom and I'm worried that it will hit tourist numbers. Also, several artists and musicians are refusing to play over here. Manuel Cardoza's the latest to pull out."

Cardoza was a renowned tenor and was regarded as having taken the mantle of past classical singing greats like Caruso and Pavarotti.

"And Sincronicity have cancelled their planned dates at the O2." Parkinson was referring to the female Nu-Soul artists from New York who were now the world's biggest-selling pop group.

"But what's more serious is the potential impact on inward investment and on the United Kingdom's export trade." As a former Secretary of State for Trade and Enterprise, Parkinson knew how dependent the country was on both trade and investment.

"Reminds me of South Africa in the last years of Apartheid before they let Mandela out" said Morgan.

"Jon, Cheryl, I've got an idea I want to discuss with you" said Grieve. "I want to open secret talks with the SNLA and WRA and find out if they'll call off the hunger strikes if the Government partially reintroduced Special Category Status."

There was a stunned silence for several seconds from Morgan and Parkinson as they tried to take in what their Ministerial colleague had said.

"Stu, you realise we haven't got the power to reintroduce Special Category Status" said Morgan. "It's Deborah who's got that. And can you see her giving in? What's more, I doubt if the SNLA and WRA will play ball unless they are promised full restoration of Special Category Status. And the risks for us are immense. If anyone finds out what we're doing, the least we'll get is the sack from Delgado."

"Jon, I know it carries a high risk" said Grieve. "But if we sit back and do nothing, all the work we've done over the past year to normalise political life in Scotland and Wales will be wasted. The SNLA and the WRA are winning the propaganda war with us over the hunger strikes. They are gaining new recruits and new money. The Government and the United Kingdom is being seen as a heartless oppressor and our friends are running scared. As Cheryl said, we risk losing trade and investment, and if the economy slows down it could damage our chances of re-election in two years time."

"If we can persuade the SNLA and the WRA to accept only a partial restoration of Special Category Status and to call off the hunger strikes, we will not be causing the Government to lose face. We will still have sufficient control over prisons, but we will show the world that we can be humane. That way, we can revive our joint strategy of supporting mainstream political life and, hopefully, allowing the SNP and Plaid Cymru to stand in the next General Election. We need to save Deborah from herself. She's a strong and resolute woman but I think her judgement is wrong this time, and I hope we can persuade her that, by bringing a voluntary end to the hunger strikes, we are strengthening the Government's hand in the fight against terrorism."

"I'll back you on this Stuart" said Parkinson. "If you and Jon were to get a deal from the SNLA and WRA and end the hunger strikes, it could deliver benefits all round. The threat to our economy removed, continued moves towards peace in Scotland and Wales and a greater chance that we will win the next General Election. Jon?"

"Alright Stu" said the Secretary of State for Wales. "Let's give it a go."

10 April 2020
Fitzroy Avenue
Drumcondra
Dublin

Good Friday was one of the few days that Dublin was quiet. The pubs of Temple Bar, normally thronging with customers, were all closed. The same scene was repeated across cities, towns and villages in Ireland. The Republic of Ireland was still a nominally Roman Catholic country and observance of the anniversary of the crucifixion of Jesus Christ was still regarded as an important duty.

It also provided ideal cover for Stuart Grieve and Jonathan Morgan on their clandestine mission to open unofficial talks with the SNLA and the WRA about possible terms for ending the hunger strikes. The Secretaries of State for Scotland and Wales had flown into Dublin that morning, and had met their intermediaries from Sinn Fein, who had driven them to Martin Hallinan's house in the Northside suburb of Drumcondra.

At 11:50am, a silver Vauxhall Insignia pulled up outside Number 50. Two men got out of the driver's and front passenger's doors and opened the back doors. Out stepped Grieve and Morgan to be escorted up to the front door.

Brendan Hallinan, Martin Hallinan's youngest son, was on hand to welcome the guests. "Gentlemen, we're absolutely delighted to see you. Come through to the lounge. Mr Lamont and Mr Mathias are already waiting for you."

The Acting Chairmen of the SNLA and WRA General Councils shook the hands of the British Ministers.

Stuart Grieve started by outlining the purpose of the mission.

"Mr Lamont, Mr Mathias, Jonathan Morgan and I are here today to discuss with you possible terms for the SNLA and the WRA to call off the hunger strikes."

"Are you here in an official capacity, Mr Grieve?" asked Mathias.

"We're not" replied Grieve. "This is being done on our own initiative to find out if there is any way of breaking the deadlock."

"So, you've got no guarantee that the UK government will agree to anything discussed here today" said Lamont.

"I'm afraid that's true, Mr Lamont" said Morgan. "But if Mr Grieve and myself manage to establish there is a basis for further negotiation and a possible way out of this sorry situation, we can present it to the Government for agreement."

"Mr Morgan, do you really believe you will convince Deborah Pearson to reintroduce Special Category Status?" said Mathias.

Lamont was even more emphatic. "I'm sorry gentlemen. If you think you can ask us to call off the hunger strikes on the remote possibility that your Government will grant Special Category Status to our men and women being held by you, well there's no chance. The way I see it, it's you who are desperate for the hunger strikes to end. Your economy is suffering, you're losing friends internationally and that's going to force you to the negotiating table."

"Mr Lamont, Mr Mathias, can I ask you this?" said Grieve. "Is it really going to benefit you? And going to benefit the people of Scotland and Wales, who you claim to support if many more young men and women give their lives needlessly? And furthermore, are you able to look the relatives of those men and women who have starved themselves to death in the eye and say that their deaths were worthwhile?"

"What myself and Mr Grieve are here to ask you, gentlemen" said Morgan "is whether the SNLA and WRA would be prepared to accept a partial restoration of Special Category Status as a condition of ending the hunger strikes?"

"What do you mean by 'partial restoration', Mr Morgan?" asked Mathias.

"Prisoners being allowed to wear their own clothes, being exempted from forced labour and being allowed to associate freely while not locked in their cells. But we cannot allow exemption from censorship of correspondence, for prisoners to be allowed to have mobile telephony in their cells or to be allowed unmonitored visits by friends and relatives."

"You must agree, gentlemen, this is a very generous offer" added Grieve. If you agree to call off the hunger strikes on the basis of such an offer, we can present it to the Home Secretary as an option to bring to Cabinet for approval. Believe me, despite what many people think, Her Majesty's Government sees no benefit in allowing more men and women to give up their lives. As both Mr Morgan and I have said, we cannot promise that it will be adopted. The Home Secretary is a very resolute woman. But your agreement could be a start."

"Mr Grieve, Mr Morgan, I never thought I would find myself saying this" said Lamont. "Considering you are both Ministers in the British Government, you are both very reasonable and humane men and I think I can do business with you. Don't you agree Rob?"

"Definitely" said the Acting Chairman of the WRA's General Council.

"But I think you'll agree it's premature to ask us to make such a commitment on the basis of an offer that does not have any official status" continued Lamont. "I'm prepared to discuss the matter with fellow acting members of the General Council. Mr Mathias will presumably be doing the same with the WRA. But until we've got a firm guarantee from your Government about a partial reintroduction of Special Category Status, the hunger strikes continue."

"We'll communicate the Government's position to you through the usual channels once it has been considered further" said Grieve. "Is that satisfactory?"

"It is, Mr Grieve" said Mathias. "We will do the same once we have discussed the matter with our General Councils."

Not many people paid attention to the black 15-registered Ford Mondeo parked in Fitzroy Avenue. The Mondeo was a popular choice as a minicab in Ireland's capital city.

Inside the Mondeo sat Simon Leech and Anne-Marie Penfold. Both were MI6 agents attached to the British Embassy. They had been tasked with surveillance of Hallinan's house as MI6 had received a tip-off that Adam Lamont and Rob Mathias might be there. If they obtained evidence that Sinn Fein were helping the SNLA and the WRA, it would give the authorities in the United Kingdom the green light to move against Sinn Fein under the Terrorism Act.

"Simon, looks like something's happening at No 50" said Penfold, an attractive brunette in her late 20s.

"Get the camera ready, Anne-Marie" said Leech.

Two men exited No 50, one tall and one much shorter.

"Conal Geraghty and Paul Ryan" said Leech. Both Sinn Fein. Their fathers did time in the Maze."

Next out came two men, both late 30s or early 40s, one dark-haired, one fair-haired. Anne-Marie Penfold gasped.

"I don't believe this, Simon. That's Stuart Grieve and Jonathan Morgan."

Grieve and Morgan got into a silver Vauxhall Insignia which drove away.

Within a minute, two more men emerged.

"That's Lamont and Mathias, Anne-Marie" said Leech.

"So it seems that the Secretaries of State for Scotland and Wales have been meeting the SNLA and WRA" said Penfold. "I wonder if the Prime Minister knows of this."

14 April 2020
10 Downing Street
London

Stuart Grieve and Jonathan Morgan were puzzled by the request they had both received the previous evening to report to the Prime Minister's office at 9am sharp the following morning. A Cabinet meeting was scheduled for 11am that day, so surely any business for Scotland and Wales would be raised at Cabinet. Then they wondered. Had there been a leak about their unofficial mission to meet the SNLA and WRA on Good Friday?

"Mr Grieve, Mr Morgan, the Prime Minister is now ready to see you." Jenny Mitchell, the Prime Minister's Private Secretary, led them through to his office.

Grieve and Morgan could tell by the expression on Robert Delgado's face that he was not in a good mood.

"Good morning Stuart, good morning Jonathan" said the Prime Minister. "No doubt you're both wondering why I've asked you to come in to see me at this early hour."

"I understand you've both been going behind the backs of Cabinet colleagues and having clandestine meetings with the SNLA and the WRA" continued Delgado. "Explain this." Delgado slapped down on the desk pictures of Grieve and Morgan emerging from a house in Dublin that was owned by a Sinn Fein councillor, closely followed by Adam Lamont and Rob Mathias, the Acting Chairmen of the General Councils of the SNLA and the WRA.

"Prime Minister, I know we both acted without your consent, or Deborah's, and that we have broken Cabinet rules" replied Grieve. "But Jonathan and I both felt that it was worth putting out feelers about what terms the SNLA and WRA might accept for ending the hunger strikes."

"Prime Minister, you must be aware that the hunger strikes are damaging the country's interests" said Morgan. "Never mind the anti-British demonstrations abroad. What I'm talking about is the loss of inward investment and trade as companies are being put under pressure not to invest here and foreign consumers are refusing to buy British. Also, there are campaigns for tourists to boycott the United Kingdom. All this is going to put the economy under pressure and make it harder for us to win in 2022."

"I don't care" replied Delgado. "You both acted without consent in carrying out this venture. It is Deborah as Home Secretary who is responsible for the Government's policy on security and prisons. Not you."

The Prime Minister continued. "I hope you realise that you've both made the Government look weak and divided. We haven't been elected on three successive occasions on a platform of caving into demands by anyone, whether it be trade unions, pressure groups or terrorists. And I repeat what I said at Cabinet two weeks ago. There is no way that this Government will concede to the SNLA and WRA on Special Category Status. All SNLA and WRA prisoners are behind bars because they committed criminal offences."

"Look Prime Minister, Jonathan and I am sorry for the embarrassment we've caused" said Grieve. "We both thought we were doing the right thing to get the Government out of a pickle. We promise that we won't do it again."

"You certainly won't, Stuart" said Delgado. "I want the resignations of you and Jonathan as Secretaries of State for Scotland and Wales to be on my desk by close of play today."

"And if we don't" said Morgan.

"I will have no option but to dismiss you both."

The same day
Sky News

"This is Daniel Merryfield with this afternoon's headlines on Sky News."

"We have just received reports that Stuart Grieve, the Secretary of State for Scotland and Jonathan Morgan, the Secretary of State for Wales, have been dismissed from the Cabinet for undisclosed reasons, but it is believed to be because of a breach of Cabinet discipline."

The departure of Grieve and Morgan will be a significant setback for the Government at a time of renewed tension arising from the SNLA and WRA hunger strikes. Both men are held in high regard on both sides of the House of Commons for the painstaking work they did in restoring local democracy to Scotland and Wales a year ago which did a lot to undermine the popularity of the SNLA and the WRA."

"It is expected that their successors as Secretaries of State for Scotland and Wales will be announced tomorrow."

22 April 2020
Capitol Building
Washington DC

"Those in favour of ratification—two hundred and nineteen. Those against ratification—two hundred and eleven. I therefore declare that the House of Representatives has agreed to ratify the contract for the sale of the A-22 Strike Raptor bomber to the government of the United Kingdom, and therefore agree that this motion should proceed to the Senate for final ratification."

The voice of the Speaker of the House of Representatives, Steve Ricardo, confirmed that the lower house of the US Congress had ratified the proposed sale of one of the country's most potent weapons of war to a foreign Government for the first time ever.

The A-22 was a dedicated strike variant of the US Air Force's main fighter, the Lockheed Martin F-22 Raptor, and had first flown six years earlier. It was capable of flying 2,000 miles with a 15,000 pound weaponload carried internally, yet could fly at twice the speed of sound and had the ability to fly at Mach 1.6 without its afterburners on. The A-22 also had stealth features built in and was almost impossible to track on radar before it hit you.

The downside of the A-22 was its cost and Congress had ratified its purchase for the US Air Force four months earlier only after a struggle.

The United Kingdom government had shown interest in becoming the first export customer for the A-22. Its main strike bomber, the Panavia Tornado, had now been in service for over forty years and was due for replacement. When the fighter version, the F-22 had first entered US Air Force service in 2005, the administration of George W Bush had forbidden its sale to overseas governments and, consequently, it had served solely for the US Air Force. But the United Kingdom was a different matter for the administration of Katherine Whitney. They had been the USA's closest ally and had played a significant part in the defeat of Iran in the Third Gulf War seven years earlier. Whitney said that the sale of the A-22 to the United Kingdom could go ahead.

Ratification of the deal by Congress was by no means a certainty. In 2018, the Democrats had ended eight years of Republican control of both houses. It was a well-known fact that Irish-American congressmen were often antipathetic to the United Kingdom on account of the past unhappy history of conflict in the Emerald Isle. But they had now been joined by an increasingly vocal cabal of Scottish-American and Welsh-American congressmen who were hostile to the United Kingdom on account of their denial of independence to Scotland and Wales. The majority were Democrats but there were a few Republican congressmen who were hostile to the United Kingdom.

The leader of the majority Democrat group in the House of Representatives was a 49-year old Welsh-American, Graydon Hopkins, who came from the steelmaking town of Scranton in Pennsylvania. First elected to the House of Representatives in 2009, Hopkins had made his mark as a vociferous opponent of the White House and, four years earlier, had become leader of the Democrat group in the House of Representatives.

Hopkins was a committed opponent of the United Kingdom government and had attempted to secure a refusal to ratify the sale of the A-22 to the United Kingdom. He had pinned his hopes on the Democrat group remaining cohesive and to pick up support from the small number of Republicans who had reservations about the sale, But his plans had been undermined by five conservative Democrats and three Democrats whose districts stood to gain from the A-22 contract.

Representatives Wayne Harland from Texas, Bob Vermuelen from California and Steve Pietrowski from Michigan were leaving the Capitol Building when they were confronted by an angry Graydon Hopkins.

"What the fuck were you guys playing at?" raged Hopkins. "We had that vote in the bag. What were you thinking by voting to ratify the sale of the A-22 to the UK?"

"Gray, I'm sorry we let you down" said Vermuelen. "But we had little choice. If the A-22 sale goes ahead, it means that the contracts for the work will take place in the districts we represent. If any of us had voted against, we would risk losing our seats in the next Congressional elections. Which take place later this year."

Later that evening
Bullfeathers Bar
First Street SE
Washington DC

Representative Graydon Hopkins found Senate leader, Senator Brad McAllister with a scotch in his hand at the far corner of the Bullfeathers.

Senator McAllister was 54 years old, a two-term Senator from Washington State. A Scottish-American, McAllister was, like Hopkins, a fierce supporter of independence for Scotland and Wales and had clashed with the Whitney administration on several occasions. As leader of the majority Democrat group in the Senate, he was the final hope of derailing the sale of the A-22 to the United Kingdom.

"Hi there, Gray" said McAllister. "Sorry to hear about the Reps' vote. What caused it to fail?"

"A combination of things, Brad" replied Hopkins. "The usual 'blue dog' Democrats who are Republicans in all but name. Consider the UK to be an ally and should be allowed to do what they like in Scotland and Wales. And Harland, Pietrowski and Vermuelen who bottled it because of jobs in their districts. By the way, how do you think the vote will go in the Senate?"

"Hopefully better, Gray" replied McAllister. "The main contract for the A-22 is likely to be in Texas. Both Senators there are Republican. I'm confident that the

Democrat group will stay firm and oppose the sale. And if we can get Pat O'Leary and Jim McDonald to vote with us, we're home and dry."

29 April 2020
Capitol Building
Washington DC

The debate in the US Senate on whether to approve the sale of the A-22 strike bomber to the United Kingdom had been in progress since the morning.

"Senator Troy Burton, you wish to speak in favour of ratifying the contract." The voice of Senate Speaker, Nancy O'Brien, gave the green light for the Mississippi Senator to speak on the debate.

Troy Burton took to the floor to speak. A Senator who had represented Mississippi for the previous sixteen years and had been Leader of the Republicans in the Senate for the previous ten years, Burton was now 58 years old. He was six feet one inch tall and, although good living had given him a paunch, he still had the powerful, broad shoulders of the college linebacker he had once been.

Burton was a combative right-winger and a renowned hawk on military matters. He had been close to President Whitney and had trenchantly supported her by driving her measures through the Senate. Since 2018, the Republicans had been in a minority in the Senate but, as the Democrats did not have the necessary two-thirds majority to avoid a filibuster, Burton had a critical role of preventing the Democrats from undermining the will of the President. Lengthy filibusters from Burton and from fellow Republican Senators Byron Mitchell and Phil Scholtz and the offer of defence contracts in the home states of Democrat waverers had ensured that a US Air Force contract for the A-22, along with equally contentious contracts for the USS George W Bush aircraft carrier and the B-3 strategic bomber had been ratified.

"Madam Speaker, thank you for the honour of letting me speak" said Burton.

"Ladies and gentlemen of the Senate, you are being asked to ratify what will be the first overseas sale of one of the country's most potent weapons of war, the A-22 Strike Raptor bomber. The recipient of this plane will be the United Kingdom of Great Britain and Northern Ireland."

"I do not need to remind you of the immense contribution that the United Kingdom has made to the defence of the western world over the past 75 years. Since the end of the Second World War, United Kingdom military forces fought communism in Malaya, Kenya, Cyprus and Aden. They stood shoulder to shoulder with the United States during the Cold War and it was through the shared resolution shown by former President Ronald Reagan and the British Prime Minister Margaret Thatcher that we were finally victorious and brought the evil empire of the Soviet Union to an end."

"Since the end of the Cold War, the United Kingdom has, with the exception of Australia, been our only true and reliable ally in a world beset by the new evils of religiously-motivated terrorism, supported by unstable rogue states and, in many cases, by the proceeds of the illegal trade in narcotic drugs. The United Kingdom military played a highly important role in all three Gulf Wars—in 1991, to drive

281

Saddam Hussein out of Kuwait, in 2003, to overthrow Saddam Hussein before he started to launch weapons of mass destruction and in 2013 to put a stop to the Ayatollahs of Iran before they started a nuclear conflagration in the Middle East."

"The United Kingdom has the fourth largest combined military force in the world, after the USA, China and Russia. Some might say this is excessive for a small country. But the United Kingdom is an island country, separate from the continent of Europe both physically and, for the past five years, politically. It is a country which has historically relied on overseas trade for its wealth. For it to trade effectively without impediment from hostile states or criminal acts of piracy, it needs a strong military which can intervene outside its borders to defend its interests."

"The United Kingdom has modernised its airborne combat capacity over the past ten years. For air superiority, it depends on the Eurofighter Typhoon, of which there are 160 in service. For battlefield interdiction, it uses the Lockheed Martin F-35 Lightning, of which there are 130 in service, plus another twenty four in Royal Navy service on board the aircraft carriers *HMS Queen Elizabeth* and *HMS Prince of Wales*. There are twenty Boeing P-8 Poseidon anti-submarine and maritime patrollers in service. All these aircraft have been brought into service over the past ten years."

"The final component of the United Kingdom armed aerial force is the Panavia Tornado, of which sixty-five are still in service. The Tornado is a venerable and highly capable warplane which has served in all three Gulf Wars. But it first appeared in service forty years ago and is now due for replacement."

"The United Kingdom's case for the purchase of the A-22 is compelling. As I said earlier, it is a nation which subsists by trade and to protect its interests overseas, it needs to be capable of striking an enemy a long way away. Furthermore, the sale of the A-22 to the United Kingdom will remove some of the burden on the United States of maintaining a military presence in Europe to counter the threat of an incursion by Russia. It is clearly in our interests to have a well-armed ally on Europe's northern frontier."

"Earlier today, Senator Drummond said that the United Kingdom was an unfit country for the United States to be selling military weaponry to. He stated that the United Kingdom was denying self-determination to Scotland and Wales and was repressing its peoples. That is complete nonsense. I had the pleasure of going on a fact-finding mission to Scotland and Wales last year. They had local government elections and there was an overwhelming vote in favour of political parties who were committed to remaining within the United Kingdom. That, ladies and gentlemen, is called democracy."

"Let me tell you, and everyone who thinks that the Scottish National Liberation Army and the Welsh Republican Army are the legitimate voice of their people, that the SNLA and the WRA are violent, ruthless terrorists who have no compunction about killing innocent people. They have known Marxists amongst their leadership, their friends include the likes of FARC, Hamas, Hizbollah and President Khoramzadeh of Iran and they have raised money through the trafficking of narcotics and extortion. They are no friends of the USA and, ladies and gentlemen, you should not be giving them aid and comfort by voting against ratification of the sale of the A-22 to the United Kingdom. I urge you to vote in favour of the sale."

"Senator Brad McAllister, you wish to speak against ratification" said Speaker O'Brien.

Senator McAllister took to the floor.

"Ladies and gentlemen, you have heard at length why Senator Burton considers you should ratify the sale of the A-22 to the United Kingdom. Will you now please listen to the reasons why you should not."

"I accept that the United Kingdom has been an ally to the United States for many years. And that it has assisted us in military action in the Middle East on no less than three occasions. But that alone is no reason to accept the sale of what is one of the world's most sophisticated warplanes to a country which, over the past five years, has denied human rights to its national minorities. You will remember the words of former President, George W Bush, that the United States must stand up for freedom and democracy wherever it may be. If you approve the sale of the A-22 to the United Kingdom, you will be breaching this principle."

"Let me enlighten you about the recent political history of Scotland and Wales, something that Senator Burton has overlooked. Unlike Ireland, the demand for independence from the United Kingdom was never strong in either Scotland or Wales. But the discovery of oil off the coast of Scotland in 1974 changed that. And after their core industries of coalmining, steelmaking and heavy engineering were destroyed under the government of Margaret Thatcher in the 1980s, the demand for independence grew in both countries. The arrival of Tony Blair as Prime Minister in 1997 led to the creation of self-government for both Scotland and Wales. But I will now turn to the reason behind the insurgency which has sadly scarred the land of my forefathers and that of the forefathers of my counterpart in the House of Representatives, Graydon Hopkins."

"Five years ago, it was announced that substantial oil deposits had been found off the coast of Scotland and Wales. The two devolved governments had a reasonable expectation that Scotland and Wales would be able to share in the considerable wealth that would be created, which would help attract new investment and train their workforce so they could benefit from the wealth. But the United Kingdom government made it clear that they had no interest in allowing the devolved governments to benefit from this bounty, and when they used legitimate powers to raise revenues, the response from the United Kingdom government was to close them down. Hardly the act of democracy?"

"When the two devolved governments decided—perhaps ill-advisedly—to declare independence, the response of the United Kingdom government was to take military action. The First Ministers of Scotland and Wales, Alastair Ferguson and Emyr Roderick, are serving thirty year prison sentences for 'treason'."

"I do not need to elaborate on what has happened since. I accept that the SNLA and the WRA have, as Senator Burton has said, committed some atrocious acts of violence. Some of their allies are not exactly the kind of people you would want to invite home to dinner. But, ladies and gentlemen, what would you have done in the same position? The democratic voice of the country silenced. Their natural resources being exploited but receiving no benefit themselves. Armed police and soldiers sent in as an occupying army. Internment without trial. Torture of anyone considered to be a terrorist suspect, whether or not there is sufficient proof. A criminal justice system that has been criticised internationally for failing to give adequate protection to defendants. And the United Kingdom is in the international dock over a serious miscarriage of justice which led to the wrongful execution of eight men and women."

"When people face injustice and have no legitimate way of articulating their grievances, they resort to violence. None less than the founders of the United States, George Washington and Thomas Jefferson, did this. That is how our great country was formed. The Irish people rose up in 1916 and eventually got their independence from the United Kingdom. The French Resistance did in the Second World War and helped defeat the worst tyranny known to mankind. The SNLA and the WRA are only following these examples."

"If we vote to ratify the sale of the A-22 to the United Kingdom, can we rest on our conscience about selling such a potent weapon to a country which is denying national minorities the rights of nationhood, which has been criticised by almost every civilised country in the world and is breaching all the principles that we as Americans hold dear? If, like me, you cannot, then I ask you to join me in voting against ratification of the sale."

The Speaker of the Senate, Nancy O'Brien, stood up to announce the vote.

"Those in favour of ratification—twenty eight. Those against ratification—sixty two. Those abstaining—ten. I therefore declare that the Senate has not agreed to ratify the contract for the sale of the A-22 Strike Raptor bomber to the government of the United Kingdom."

The same day
Cureton Street
Pimlico
London

Jason Steer was working through his boxes when the telephone rang.

Steer's wife, Miranda, went to answer it.

"Is the Secretary of State around?" It was Sir Hugh Wiseman, the Permanent Secretary at the Ministry of Defence.

"He is" replied Mrs Steer. "Darling, it's Hugh."

"Thanks, love" replied the Defence Secretary.

"Hugh, what time do you call this?" It was nearly midnight.

"Thank god I've found you, Secretary of State. Bad news from the USA."

Steer remembered. The US Senate would be voting on the sale of the A-22.

"Don't tell me that the Yanks have voted against selling us the Strike Raptor?"

"I'm afraid they have."

CHAPTER 22

5 May 2020
Kelly, Gleeson and Partners
328 East 63rd Street
New York City

BOYCOTT BRITAIN!

Many of you will be considering visiting Britain this year. The image their Government likes to present is of it being the USA's closest ally, and of being a country steeped in history, pomp and circumstance while, at the same time, being a modern democracy. To many Americans, it is a country of smiling bobbies, red post boxes, pleasant rural pubs and one that speaks the same language as us. But what the British government wants to hide from you is the repression it is carrying out in Scotland and Wales.

Five years ago, the people of Scotland and Wales voted in favour of independence. The response of the British government was to send troops into Scotland and Wales, close down the governing bodies and arrest and imprison their leaders. Why? Because Scotland and Wales had supplies of oil in their territorial waters.

Since then, the British Government has

- Shot dead unarmed demonstrators;
- Introduced internment without trial;
- Tortured suspected freedom fighters in the notorious Brecon and Stirling interrogation centres;
- Introduced trial without jury;
- Kidnapped their own nationals in other countries in order to by-pass extradition procedures;
- Arrested and intimidated journalists who tried to uncover the truth;
- Approved the police, security services and armed forces to carry out extrajudicial executions; and
- Colluded with the terrorist English Volunteer Force in the murder of Scottish and Welsh patriots.

The United Nations, the Council of Europe and the European Union have all condemned the British government for having breached conventions on human rights, national minorities, the use of torture, fair trials, freedom of the Press and extrajudicial murder. Yet the United States Government still regards it as a trusted partner.

Before you visit Britain this summer, consider whether you want to support a country which has little respect for rights of the citizens of two of its constituent countries, Scotland and Wales. You may find Britain rather less palatable than you first thought.

Britain is a country which depends on trade and tourism for its wealth. If you stop buying British goods and refuse to travel there, you may help make the British government understand that it must listen to the voice of the people of Scotland and Wales.

Clann na h-Albann
www.clannnahalbann.com

Meibion Cymru
www.meibioncymru.net

Scott Drummond and Greg Roberts were standing under a giant banner outside the New York offices of Kelly, Gleeson and Partners to launch the joint campaign of Clann na h-Albann and Meibion Cymru for a trade and travel boycott of the United Kingdom.

The leaders of Clann na h-Albann and Meibion Cymru, Glen Johnstone and Mark Howell, were unable to be present as the US government had denied them visas. But branches of the political wings of the SNLA and the WRA had been set up in the USA and Drummond and Roberts, as leaders of the Stateside branches of the party, were launching the campaign.

Camera crews from Fox, CNN, CBS and NBC were present, along with journalists from the Washington Post, the New York Times and the New York Post.

At 10am, Drummond and Roberts took to the makeshift stage set up outside Kelly, Gleeson and Partners' office ready to launch the campaign.

Drummond was first to speak. A tall, blond Californian, he worked as a lawyer.

"Ladies and gentlemen, thank you for attending this morning."

"Today marks the launch by Clann na h-Albann and our partners, Meibion Cymru, of a worldwide campaign for a boycott of Great Britain. Many of you buy British goods like Jaguar or Land Rover cars or intend to travel there as a tourist. Before you do so, think again. They may appear to be a charming olde-world country with much history. They may have been the United States' most loyal partner in the past forty years. But they are viciously denying nationhood to Scotland and Wales and resorting to methods more at home in Latin American dictatorships or Saddam Hussein-era Iraq to deny the Scots and the Welsh their will, which is to be separate nations."

Roberts then took the microphone. Dark-haired and broad-shouldered, Roberts was an accountant and hailed from Pennsylvania.

"Many people think that consumer boycotts are a waste of time and effort. Meibion Cymru and Clann na h-Albann beg to differ. It is well over thirty years since South Africa had apartheid. The white minority government believed they would rule forever and that protests against the regime would fail. Remember, they had the tacit support of both our government and Great Britain. But the opponents of the regime targeted its weak spot. Its heavy dependence on export trade and on tourism. When shoppers started to boycott South African fruit and wine, the country's exports began to suffer from reduced turnover. This spread to other South African goods like gold and diamonds. Their tourist trade began to suffer as visitors stayed away. The final blow came when investors began to take their money elsewhere. By 1990, the apartheid regime was facing economic collapse. They had no choice but to give up the fight against majority rule."

"If the boycott we are launching across the world today is successful, we may succeed in bringing the British government to the negotiating table. We hope you will support us."

12 May 2020
Cabinet Room
10 Downing Street
London

The economy was the first agenda item for the day's business, and it had been raised by the Chancellor of the Exchequer, Ed Villiers. Increased policing and security costs for Scotland and Wales to deal with a renewed outbreak of disorder since the SNLA and WRA hunger strikes had led to a downward revision on the forecast for economic growth. But more worrying was the news over the previous week that Ford, IBM and Microsoft had all cancelled plans to invest in the United Kingdom following pressure from the Scottish and Welsh lobbies in the USA. And this was being compounded by news that hotel bookings were down by 15% compared with the same time 12 months earlier.

Villiers read out the report prepared for him by economists at the Treasury.

"I'm afraid that the news from this Report is not encouraging. Forecasts for growth have been downgraded from 2.0% to 0.7%. The reasons have been disruption to the oil industry due to increased levels of disorder in Scotland and Wales over the past four months which have adversely affected output. The budget surplus of £5bn we had twelve months ago has been replaced by a deficit of £29bn. The need for additional security in Scotland and Wales has contributed additional cost demands, which have been compounded by a decline in business activity."

"The news that three US companies have cancelled their proposed investment here and the fall in hotel bookings is the last news we want. A loss of foreign currency coming in and the need to make more benefit payments to the unemployed will lead to a growing deficit and a fall in the value of the pound. We are planning to hold a General Election in two years time. Having to cut public spending in advance is hardly going to win votes."

"Ed, you are aware that Clann na h-Albann and Meibion Cymru are trying to organise a worldwide boycott of the United Kingdom" said Secretary of State for National Heritage, Cheryl Parkinson.

"No, I wasn't, Cheryl" replied Villiers. "Is it having any impact?"

"Hard to say so far" said Foreign Secretary, Henry Arbuthnot. "It was launched a week ago. Problem is that it's got some high profile support. Several celebrities are backing the campaign. And it's got the support of the Leaders of the Senate and the House of Representatives. Looks like they've been tapping up shareholders and hedge funds to frighten them off."

"This is outrageous" said Secretary of State for Trade and Enterprise, Darren Bramble. "Clann na h-Albann and Meibion Cymru are effectively engaged in economic sabotage of this country. Henry, why aren't we taking them to court?"

"Darren, I don't think court action would work" said Attorney-General Dominic Collins. "The US courts haven't exactly been our friends up to now."

Collins was referring to the decision in 2018 to allow Tony Edwards and Neil Telfer, both from the WRA and the SNLA respectively, to stay in the United States, despite having entered illegally on an arms-buying mission.

The Prime Minister, Robert Delgado, was next to speak.

"It is clear that the SNLA and the WRA are running rings round us. The threat to our economy is clear and present, and is something we need to act on now. If we leave it, we are, as you have said Ed, facing the prospect of going into the General Election on the back of a recession and having to carry out unpopular measures. There is a real risk that we could lose."

"We need to come up with a strategy to counter this campaign."

Delgado turned to Party Chairman, Sir Anthony Simmons.

"Tony, we need a publicity campaign, not just to sell the benefits of doing business with the United Kingdom but also to aggressively rebut the claims that Clann na h-Albann and Meibion Cymru are making. And don't be shy of playing dirty. Find out if Clann na h-Albann and Meibion Cymru have got any suspect allies or friends. You know, rogue states, Islamic radicals, drug traffickers and gangsters. Also, dig into the background of those politicians and celebrities who are backing the boycott. MI5, MI6 and the NCA should be able to help. A lot of them are bound to have skeletons in their closet, like sex and drugs. If that gets relayed over Fox News, it could ruin them."

The same day
I H Horwood and Sons (Hauliers)
Eastern Road
Bracknell
Berkshire

"Gentlemen, I think a loyal toast is in order. Raise your glasses."

Carol James, the Managing Director of haulage company, I H Horwood and Sons, raised a glass of Veuve Cliquot champagne and invited her fellow directors to toast the company's success in landing, in the face of strong competition, a lucrative contract from the Ministry of Defence to transport supplies for the Army from Aldershot to Wales.

The six directors, who included her husband, Doug, and her brother, Stephen Rouse, dutifully followed.

"To I H Horwood and Sons" they chorused.

It was an irony that no one bearing the family name sat on the company board. It had been formed back in 1962 by Ivor Horwood, a former sergeant in the Army Logistical Corps. Horwood had been dead for fifteen years and would have been horrified to find out that no one with the family name on the company board.

It was unusual for a woman to be the Managing Director of a haulage company as the industry was male-dominated. But Carol James was no ordinary woman. Ruthlessly ambitious, she had begun her working life as a secretary at Horwood's and had married Ivor Horwood's ineffectual younger son, Richard. When the couple divorced, Carol drove for, and got, a twelfth of the company shares. When the elder Horwood brother, Michael, got into financial difficulties, she bought out half of his shareholding which gave her nearly 30% control of the company. After the death of Ivor Horwood, Carol moved to outmanoeuvre both her ex-husband and her former brother-in-law by bringing in new shareholders from outside. Her brother became one of the shareholders, as did her new husband, Doug James.

Carol James was a tough boss towards her staff as she expected nothing less than 100% commitment at work. She was also notoriously tough in dealing with business rivals. It helped considerably that her current husband was a former professional boxer and was not averse to using his fists against anyone who he considered had upset his wife.

James's robust approach not surprisingly made many enemies, not just business rivals but also in the workfore. The previous year, Horwood's had been hit by a strike by the drivers over pay and conditions. Carol James's response had been robust. She sacked all the strikers and hired new drivers on lower wages and longer working hours.

Bitterness from the strike still lingered a year later. Several of the sacked drivers found themselves up in court on charges of affray and common assault and had their HGV licences withdrawn, which meant they lost their livelihood. There had been several instances of vandalism at the company premises and Carol James believed that former workers had been involved.

Later that day
A WRA safe house
Grange Road
Ealing
London

Ryan Prosser was reading the *London Evening Standard* when he came across an article which grabbed his attention. It concerned a Bracknell-based haulage company, I H Horwood and Sons, which had been awarded a contract to carry supplies for the

Army down to Wales. It was of interest to the WRA who were engaged in a campaign of sabotage against businesses who were trading with the Army and police.

"Hey, Gar, read this" shouted Prosser. "Company down Bracknell's just got a haulage contract for the Army."

"Anyone well known?" asked Gareth Thomas, a commander in the WRA's London Brigade.

"I H Horwood and Sons. Not a household name."

"Hey guys, that was the company that was in the news last year" said Mickey Evans. "Load of their drivers went on strike. There was a lot of aggro and the cops were called in."

"Boys, this is a golden opportunity to send a message to English companies helping the Army and police repress our brothers and sisters" said Thomas. "We're going to do a hit on Horwood's. Mickey, I want you and Ben Grabowski to carry out a reconnaissance trip to Horwood's tonight. Suss out the security they've got in place, where the lights and CCTV cameras are located, whether they use dogs. Ryan, can you find out more about the strike at Horwood's. Sounds like there'll be a load of embittered former workers who'd only be too happy to help us. Report back to me tomorrow."

13 May 2020
The Old Manor
Grenville Place
Bracknell
Berkshire

Ryan Prosser found Tony Brophy and Rick Hazard drinking in one of the snugs in the Old Manor. It was a Wetherspoons pub which meant low prices. With Brophy and Hazard both out of work since they had been sacked by I H Horwood and Sons, they didn't have much spare money.

"Tony Brophy? Rick Hazard?" asked the young Welshman.

"Yeah, that's us" replied Brophy. "By the way, who are you, mate?"

"Ryan Prosser. I believe you guys worked for Horwood's?"

"That's right" said Hazard. "Until that bitch sacked us."

"You guys might be able to offer me and my mates some help" said Prosser.

"How?" asked Brophy.

"Horwood's have just got a contract to transport supplies for the Army down to Wales" said Prosser. "We're going to send them, and other businesses profiting from helping the Brits to repress our country, a blunt message."

"So you're WRA?" said Hazard. "Look, mate, Tone and I are in enough trouble as it is. No job, lost our licences, blacklisted by employers. I don't fancy spending the next 30 years in Foulness."

"There's no risk on your part, Rick" said Prosser. "All we want you do do is to come with us to Horwood's tonight and point out the internal security arrangements. We'll do all the heavy lifting."

"What's in it for us if we help?" asked Brophy.

"Five grand each"

"Rick, I reckon it's worth it" said Brophy. "It'll help clear our debts. And just think how Carol fucking James will react when she finds her shiny new fleet of lorries torched."

15 May 2020, 8pm
I H Horwood and Sons (Hauliers)
Eastern Road
Bracknell
Berkshire

The last drivers who were arriving back from jobs were clocking out and heading home. Shane Barker and Jason Meadows, the two security guards who would be guarding Horwood's during the night shift, were in the gate office and staring at the CCTV monitors installed.

Barker and Meadows knew that Friday and Saturday nights were peak times for trouble. It was still light and the industrial estates across Bracknell were magnets for bored youths who held car races round the estate, sprayed graffiti over property and looked for goods to steal.

A beat-up Vauxhall Astra screamed round the corner into Eastern Road. Inside it were four scrofulous local youths. Within minutes, another car, a Ford Focus, pulled up. All were wearing hooded tops, which were in breach of the law, but they figured that no one would stop them.

"Jase, looks like we've got trouble brewing" said Barker.

As dusk began to settle, four more cars drove onto the estate and began a road race. The peace outside Horwood's premises was briefly disturbed by a twelve-year old Ford Focus doing a handbrake turn. As far as Barker and Meadows were concerned, as long as the scrotes stayed in their cars, they couldn't care less what they did.

A blue Ford Transit van drove into Eastern Road and parked fifty yards away from Horwood's depot. On board were Mickey Evans and Ben Grabowski.

The two WRA men saw a green Astra and a red Focus pull up to a halt outside Horwood's.

"Look's like it's mischief time, Mickey" said Grabowski. "Just as Brophy said. Time for us to get to work, boyo."

Evans started the Transit's engine and drove further down Eastern Road before pulling up.

Barker and Meadows knew that trouble was brewing when several hooded figures leapt out of the beat-up cars. Within seconds, there was a loud **SPLAT** as a hail of eggs hit the plate glass front door, followed by the sound of shattering glass as a brick flew through an office window.

Meadows responded immediately and charged out to confront the troublemakers. He was not a tall man, standing no more than five feet eight inches tall, but he was stockily-built and capable of handling himself in a fight.

291

He seized the nearest youth, a lanky, smirking individual and lifted him bodily up with his powerful forearms.

"Listen, you little fucker" shouted Meadows. "What part of 'private property' don't you understand?"

"Oi, put me down" gasped the youth, struggling in Meadows' powerful grip.

Two of the youth's mates edged menacingly towards the two guards. Barker, a taller man at six foot one inches, withdrew his polycarbonate truncheon, ready to defend himself.

"Don't even think of it, son" snarled Barker. "Make one more step and you'll get this round your fucking head. And don't bother phoning your mates. We've got reinforcements on the way."

The youths backed off. Meadows put down the leader, who was now whimpering.

"If I see you or your mates round here again" shouted Meadows, "they'll need a fucking hoover to sweep up what's left of you. Now fuck off and don't come back."

The youths got back into their cars and sped off. As they left, one of them leaned out of the window and gave Barker and Meadows a raised finger. Another youth shouted out "Wanker!" as the cars drove out of Eastern Road.

Evans and Grabowski had done their homework thoroughly. They had made several reconnaissance missions and had taken photographs of the depot. The assistance of Brophy and Hazard had been invaluable, helping them find the locations of the CCTV cameras and the floodlights. On finding out that the site was protected by guard dogs, they acquired sonars. The local yobs also had their purpose, as they diverted the attention of the security guards.

Evans and Grabowski used bolt-cutters to cut through several lengths of chain-link fencing which protected Horwood's lorry park. They were wearing dark, light-absorbent clothing which made them hard to spot. Twilight was now setting in and the floodlights had yet to come on, which was ideal to work in as it would conceal them more effectively that full darkness.

As soon as Evans and Grabowski had cut a sufficient length of fencing, they slipped into the lorry park. They encountered the first pair of of Rottweilers.

"Ben, put the sonars on now" said Evans.

The sonars emitted a high-pitched squeal, inaudible to the human ear but dogs could hear it and found it extremely painful. The two Rottweilers retreated.

"Okay, Mickey, the coast's clear" said Grabowski.

Evans crawled under the chassis of a Mercedes-Benz artic parked in the middle of a row of five and found the fuel tank. He fixed to its underside a small but highly explosive charge. When it was detonated, the diesel fuel in the tank would explode in a massive fireball. To aid the spread of the fire, Grabowski scattered incendiary devices around the park. Evans primed the charge to detonate at 2am. That was the quietest time of the night and would given them plenty of time to get away. They would both be back in Wales by then.

Evans and Grabowski slipped unseen out of the Horwood's site as twilight started to turn to dusk. Fifty yards away, they heard a lot of commotion. They saw two men in uniform confronting a gang of local youths. This meant there was probably no one watching the monitors so they wouldn't have been noticed. They got back into the Transit and drove out of Eastern Road, unnoticed.

16 May 2020
I H Horwood and Sons (Hauliers)
Eastern Road
Bracknell
Berkshire

Carol James was close to tears. She was standing beside the charred remains of forty articulated lorries which had been destroyed in the inferno which followed the explosion of the device planted nearly twelve hours earlier by Mickey Evans.

Standing next to her was her husband, Doug James and Inspector Jamie Perkins of Thames Valley Police. He had just advised Mrs James that the WRA had claimed responsibility for the attack.

"Inspector, are you sure that it was the WRA who did this?" asked Mrs James. "It could have been local kids doing it for a laugh. You know there's been constant trouble on this estate at weekends."

"Or some of the workers we sacked last year after the strike" added her husband. "Some of them have threatened to get even with us."

"Mrs James, that was definitely the work of the WRA" said Perkins. "Have you got any contracts with the armed forces?"

Mrs James indicated that they had.

"I'm afraid you are not the only company to be attacked by the WRA. They've done the same to other companies with military contracts."

"Inspector, how the hell did anyone get through?" asked Doug James. "You've seen how tight our security is."

"Mr James, I'm afraid that no security system is 100% effective" said Perkins. "It'll deter most opportunist criminals. But these guys had most probably trained for the mission. They've probably been staking this site out, noting the strengths and weaknesses in your security and went equipped with specialist equipment."

"I'd also like to ask what the hell those useless sods on security were doing" said Doug James. "How in God's name did they fail to see someone breaking into the site?"

"One of my PCs spoke to them earlier" replied Perkins. "The security guys were dealing with a bunch of yobboes who were vandalising property on the estate. One of them threw a brick through the window of one of your offices, and they went outside to challenge them. We're investigating the possibility that the WRA used that as a window of opportunity to break into your site."

"Are you going to let us know the outcome of your enquiries, Inspector?" asked Mrs James.

"We will, Mrs James" replied Perkins. "In the meantime, we'll keep you advised of how our investigation is progressing and will let you know if you need to give evidence in court."

"Thank you, Inspector" replied Mrs James.

17 May 2020
London Stock Exchange
Paternoster Square
City of London

Paolo Vaccari was concentrating heavily on the task of servicing the main motherboard of the computer system supporting the London Stock Exchange. Maintenance work always took place on Sundays and had to be ready in time for trading to start early on Monday.

Vaccari hailed from Birmingham and had graduated in computer science from Salford University two years earlier. His cheeky charm and Italian good looks made him a popular member of the Siemens service team which looked after the computers of the London Stock Exchange and several leading merchant banks in the City of London. He had also earned considerable respect for his hard work and energy since joining Siemens after graduation.

"How's it going, Paolo?" asked Team Leader, Ed Simpson.

"Better than expected, Ed" replied Vaccari. "Should be done by late this afternoon."

"Excellent!" said Simpson. "Let me know if there are any problems."

"No worries" said Vaccari.

By late Sunday afternoon, the service was fully complete. All that the Siemens team needed to do was a test run. Simpson was content to leave that to Vaccari.

Vaccari was now alone in the London Stock Exchange building. From his jacket pocket, he extracted a memory stick and plugged it into the main terminal. It contained the Bot. Fly virus, perhaps the most lethal and contagious virus known in the world of computing. Within minutes of being activated, Bot. Fly would paralyse not only the main London Stock Exchange computer but also the computers of any other organisations receiving electronic communication from the affected computer. The United Kingdom's financial markets would be in meltdown.

What Vaccari's employers and workmates did not know was that his parents came from Scotland. Vaccari had spent part of his childhood living at Dunoon and he had a strong emotional attachment to the homeland of his parents.

18 May 2020
London Stock Exchange
Paternoster Square
City of London

Trading on the London stock market that morning was brisk, with the price of futures in oil, copper and cotton all rising.

At 9am, the computer screens suddenly flickered, then went blank. There was a collective gasp from the traders. When the screens did not come back on within the next minute, they knew there was a major problem.

An hour later
Sky News

"This is Emma Bulstrode with breaking news on Sky News."

"Trading at the London Stock Exchange was brought to a complete standstill earlier this morning when a virus crippled its computer system. The SNLA has claimed responsibility for the attack which has cost the City of London over a billion pounds."

"This is the latest in a series of attacks by the SNLA and the WRA on economic targets in their battle to force the United Kingdom to grant Scotland and Wales independence. All previous attacks have been on companies with contracts with the military and the attack on the Stock Exchange is a worrying new development and suggests that the SNLA and the WRA are now targeting the British economy in order to force the hand of the Government. The City of London Police and the National Anti-Terror Squad are jointly investigating this latest incident and they are following up on a lead that the SNLA managed to infiltrate the Stock Exchange before the attack took place."

20 May 2020
MI5 Headquarters
Millbank
London

Richard Donovan was about to depart for a meeting when Marcel Francois shouted for his attention.

"Richard, can you hold on. I've got Peter Firth on the phone. It's extremely important."

"Hello Peter. What's the news?"

"We've made a breakthrough against the SNLA and WRA. Two of our agents have infiltrated into their General Councils."

"Wow, that's great!" said Donovan.

"There's more to come, Richard" replied Firth. "The SNLA and WRA are planning a joint operation to bomb the Changing of the Guard at Whitehall next Saturday. The whole area is going to be packed with tourists because it's the Bank Holiday weekend. If they succeed, there will be carnage."

"Not only that, Peter" said Donovan. "It'll frighten off tourists. We've already got problems with their political wings running a campaign to boycott Britain. It's starting to affect inward investment and the tourist trade, and there's speculation that we're heading for another recession. Which is the last thing the Government wants before the next General Election."

"Richard, I'll send through details of the cells we've identified as active and planning the bombing. Names, dates of birth, addresses, known associates."

"Peter, once again, you field boys and girls have saved the day. By the way, is there any truth in the claim that the SNLA and WRA are using a load of 'clean skins' who've got no previous record?"

"Richard, if you want to thank anyone, it's Claire Gosling, Asif Mahmood and Luke Wainwright. They did the hard and dangerous work to penetrate the SNLA and WRA. And the answer to your query is 'yes'. You'll find that the cells responsible have got no record of previous involvement."

"So that's why it's been so hard to track them."

23 May 2020
Brownhill Road
Catford
London

The sun was starting to rise above the eastern horizon as the six-person joint team from the SNLA and the WRA rose from their slumbers. They had rented the Victorian house in one of London's less salubrious suburbs two weeks earlier, and had been preparing for this day since them. In six hours time, crowds would be assembling outside Whitehall for the Changing of the Guard. Their mission was to detonate a bomb. Apart from killing and wounding members of the armed forces, it would have a secondary effect of frightening off tourists and denting the Government's coffers.

For the past four months, the SNLA and the WRA had changed their tactics. Capitalising on the wave of sympathy generated by the hunger strikes, they had switched their focus to economic targets rather than innocent civilians. The 'Boycott Britain' campaign by their political wings, Clann na h-Albann and Meibion Cymru, had resulted in a downturn in both overseas investment in the United Kingdom and in tourism. It was starting to hurt the Government in the pocket. Both the SNLA and the WRA had begun to target businesses supplying the armed forces and the police, and it was starting to yield dividends as nervous business owners were starting to turn down military or police contracts for fear that their businesses might become terrorist targets. But it was the SNLA cyber attack on the London Stock Exchange earlier in the week had driven home how vulnerable the country was to economic warfare.

Another consequence of the hunger strikes was that recruitment of new members to the SNLA and the WRA had surged. Amongst the new members were the four men and two women loading up supplies into the back of a Vauxhall Movano van.

The joint cell came from diverse backgrounds. Hamish Stuart and Hywel Williams were from farming backgrounds. Pat Gallacher and Charlotte Bevan both came from tough inner-city council estates. While Ben Summerill and Chloe Brown came from well-off professional families and had been university-educated.

In the back of the van were two explosive devices which the cell had assembled over the previous few days. Through the assistance of local Muslim radicals, they had obtained fifty kilos of hydrogen peroxide. Stuart and Williams had prepared the detonators from a pair of cheap digital clocks which they had bought at B&Q. Gallacher and Bevan had bought the batteries separately in Tesco to avoid drawing suspicion. And Brown, a physics graduate and Summerill, a chemistry graduate, supervised the assembly of the explosive devices and obtained a contractors' pass from a disgruntled official employed on a low-wage temporary contract. Finally, a reconnaissance trip to Whitehall identified an ideal location where to plant the explosives.

The plan was to detonate the bombs as the troops emerged from the Palace for the ceremony. The Household Cavalry were considered a legitimate target as they had been deployed to Scotland and Wales.

At 5:30am, the van moved off. None of the SNLA and WRA members inside noticed a blue Ford Mondeo parked on the other side of Brownhill Road.

Inside the car were Claire Gosling and Asif Mahmood, both MI5 agents.

Gosling had a long-lens camera poised and took photographs of the SNLA and WRA members as they boarded the van.

Mahmood reached for his encrypted personal data assistant and rang Peter Firth.

"Big Fry, Latic here. Chummy has just moved off. Red Vauxhall Movano, registration LB18EAY. Travelling west along Brownhill Road."

"Big Fry here, read you Latic. Start heading for base. NATS will deal with Chummy now."

The same day
Albert Embankment
London

"Only about another ten minutes to go. How is everyone back there?" shouted Pat Gallacher, who was at the wheel of the Movano.

"Fine."

The joint SNLA and WRA cell had enjoyed an unobstructed journey into the heart of London. Another ten minutes and their destination would be reached.

"Hey, Pat, looks like we've got company ahead" said Charlotte Bevan, who was in the passenger seat.

Indeed, she was right. The road onto Lambeth Bridge had been sealed off by the police. Four Mercedes-Benz vans and four BMW 5-series estates were blocking the way and a phalanx of armed police were in place.

Gallacher slammed on the brakes and did a high-speed U-turn across the road.

Inspector Dave Brough of the National Anti-Terror Squad reached for his radio.

"Victor Alpha Bravo to all cars. Chummy's making a run for it. Red Vauxhall Movano, registration LB18 EAY, heading south along Albert Embankment."

Within a minute, the southern end of Albert Embankment had been sealed off by the police. Gallacher saw the second roadblock before he reached the junction with Vauxhall Walk.

"Pat, take the next left" screamed Bevan.

Gallacher swung the Movano into Vauxhall Walk.

High above London, Sergeant Neil Pike was piloting a Bell Jetranger helicopter of the National Police Air Service. He saw the terrorists' van heading up Vauxhall Walk.

"Gold Commander, suspects now heading north along Vauxhall Walk. Probably heading for Black Prince Road. Will continue to update."

"Roger, Batman."

Superintendent Russell Colbourne, the Silver Commander, ordered his command to block the junction of Black Prince Road and Vauxhall Walk.

In the Movano, Gallacher now had the feeling of being a trapped rat. Ahead of him, a roadblock sealed off access into Black Prince Road. Behind him, he could hear the sirens of pursuing police cars.

"Pat, let's cut our losses and make a run for it on foot" said Stuart.

"Don't think we've got much choice" said Williams.

The six terrorists abandoned their van outside a parade of shops halfway up Vauxhall Walk and decided to make a run for it. Only that the police had caught up with them.

"Armed police! Surrender now." It was Brough, whose voice was amplified through a loudhailer.

Stuart and Williams responded with a volley of gunfire from their M-18 rifles. Officers from the National Anti-Terror Squad took cover.

The six terrorists ran round the back of Baddeley House when Summerill had an idea.

"Let's take cover in here."

"Good idea, Ben" said Chloe Brown. "How do we get in?"

"Just shoot the fucking lock off" shouted Gallacher.

Inside Baddeley House, Ray and Judy Langley were about to head out of No 16 for their Saturday shopping trip. Ray Langley was 61 years old and a postman. His wife, three years younger, worked as a receptionist for Lambeth council. Their two children were now grown up and had moved away.

As Judy Langley was about to close the front door of her flat, she and her husband were suddenly disturbed by four men and two women in a state of high agitation. Before they knew what had hit them, they were facing down the barrel of three Uzi machine pistols.

"Put your hands up and get inside" shouted Williams. "Do what we say and you won't get hurt."

The same day
Sky News

"This is Daniel Merryfield with the lunchtime headlines on Sky News."

"Terrorists from the SNLA and the WRA have taken hostage a middle-aged couple in their South London flat. Raymond and Judith Langley were about to set out on a shopping trip when six terrorists on the run from the police burst into their flat and took them hostage."

"Armed police have sealed off Vauxhall Walk while negotiators have been brought in in an attempt to obtain the couple's release."

The same day
Outside Baddeley House
Vauxhall Walk
London

Superintendent Russell Colbourne of the National Anti-Terror Squad had taken every precaution possible. Residents of Baddeley House and neighbouring buildings had all been evacuated. Armed police had sealed off the area around Baddeley House.

Pauline Bird, an Inspector in the Metropolitan Police who was a trained negotiator, arrived at Vauxhall Walk shortly after 12pm. Colbourne knew her and greeted her.

"See what you can do, Pauline."

Colbourne then headed for his command vehicle. Using an encrypted number, he rang MI5 on his personal data assistant. He was delighted to find Richard Donovan on the other end of the line.

"Richard, have you got any information on the terrorists?"

"Yes, Russ. All six are recent recruits to the SNLA and the WRA. Joined between February and April this year. Bevan and Gallacher are the only ones with any previous, and it's for petty offences, drunken disorderly, shoplifting and common assault."

"Jeez, Rich. Clean skins. No wonder it's been so hard to track them."

Inspector Bird walked up to the front of Baddeley House. At the window were Hamish Stuart and Hywel Williams.

"Hamish, Hywel, my name is Pauline Bird. I have come here to negotiate with you and to ask you your terms for releasing Ray and Judy Langley. They have done nothing to harm you. You should let them go."

"We want free passage from the UK" shouted Stuart. "That's when Mr and Mrs Langley will be released."

"Hamish, you know we can't agree to that" said Inspector Bird. "You tried to blow up the Changing of the Guard."

"Then we won't release Mr and Mrs Langley" shouted Hywel Williams.

Later that day
Home Office
Marsham Street
London

Deborah Pearson had cancelled her weekend surgery in her constituency and returned to London after hearing about the siege in Vauxhall Walk.

Gathered in her office were the Policing Minister, Luke Outram, the Homeland Security Minister, Baroness Hornby, the Chairman of the Association of Chief Police Officers, Roy Plummer, the MI5 Director-General, Dame Nicola Martin, the Head of the National Anti-Terror Squad, Kevin Lazenby and the Prime Minister's Security Adviser, Frank Hesford. Jason Steer, the Secretary of State for Defence, was to join them by video conference.

"Roy, Kevin, what is the latest position on the siege?" asked the Home Secretary.

"The six terrorists are still holed up in 16 Baddeley House, Home Secretary" said Lazenby. "We've got a trained negotiator there trying to persuade them to release Mr and Mrs Langley."

"Any success?" asked Pearson.

"Not yet" replied Lazenby. "They're insisting on free passage out of the country as the terms for releasing their hostages."

"That is totally unacceptable" said Baroness Hornby, who was Nicola Martin's predecessor as Director-General of MI5.

"Any idea who the terrorists are?" asked ACPO chief Plummer.

"Yes, all six are recent recruits Roy" said Dame Nicola. "I reckon they lack experience and they'll crack after a couple of days."

"We can't bank on that, Nicola" said Hesford. The least we should do is have the SAS on standby."

"Frank, don't you realise that'll make it more likely that Mr and Mrs Langley will be killed" said Plummer. "Either by the terrorists or accidentally by the SAS. What Kevin and I are doing at least stands a chance of getting them out safely. They're only kids out of their depth. You want the SAS for hardened terrorists."

Pearson signalled she was ready to take a decision.

"Ladies and gentlemen, we must realise who we're dealing with. They may be 'little more than kids' but SNLA and WRA terrorists, whether new or highly experienced are just as dangerous as each other. We cannot afford to be seen as treating them with kid gloves. Roy, Kevin, keep your negotiator talking with them. But we've got to have a contingency if negotiation fails, and I agree with Frank that we need to have the SAS ready to go in."

On the other end of the television screen was Jason Steer.

"Hi Debbie. Hear you want my services."

"Indeed we do, Jason" replied the Home Secretary. "How quickly can you get the SAS out? We might need them to break a siege in Vauxhall. SNLA and WRA."

"Tomorrow morning, Debbie" relied the Defence Secretary. "Soon enough for you?"

25 May 2020
16 Baddeley House
Vauxhall Walk
London

Ray Langley was a worried man. His wife's prescription for angina was running low and he was concerned that she was going to have an attack. The third day of being held hostage by armed terrorists was about to start.

Langley looked wistfully at the large framed photograph of he and his wife on their wedding day thirty six years before. He had a then-fashionable mullet haircut, Judy, much younger and prettier, had hers in a feather cut.

"Fellas, I know you think I'm looking for a chance to escape. But my wife needs her prescription pretty soon. You realise that, if she doesn't, you might have a death on your hands."

"Mr Langley, we could ask for a prescription to be sent up" said Chloe Brown.

"Chloe, be careful" said Gallacher. "It could be a ploy to let the rozzers in."

"And, even if not, give them an opportunity" added Williams.

The same time
Outside Baddeley House
Vauxhall Walk
London

"Jesus, that's all we need" said Superintendent Russell Colbourne of the National Anti-Terror Squad. He had just been told that Mrs Langley suffered from angina and needed a repeat prescription.

Colbourne turned to Pauline Bird.

"Pauline, any sign of the hostage-takers' resolve flagging?"

"I'm afraid not, sir" replied Inspector Bird. "I can't understand it. They're first-timers and I thought they'd be cracking by now. After all, they won't have had much food or sleep since Saturday."

"Pauline, the situation's critical now" said Colbourne. "Mrs Langley suffers from angina and if we don't get prescription drugs to her, there's a risk of her dying. Imagine the newspaper headlines if that happens. I'll give you another chance to negotiate a peaceful end to the siege this morning. But, if nothing else happens, we may need to go in."

"Sir, you realise that risks the lives of Mr and Mrs Langley" said Inspector Bird forcefully.

"I do, Pauline" replied Colbourne. "But we may have to do it. The matter's now out of policing hands. The Government's got an interest."

Later that day
Outside Baddeley House
Vauxhall Walk
London

"Sir, it's the boss for you." Sergeant Deon McKenzie called out to Superintendent Colbourne who headed over to the command post.

"Superintendent Colbourne here, sir." On the other end of the line was the Head of the National Anti-Terror Squad, Kevin Lazenby.

"Any progress, Russ? The Home Secretary's getting a bit twitchy."

"Afraid not, sir" replied Colbourne. "We've had a negotiator speaking to the captors all morning, but there's been no progress. They still insist on free passage out of the country."

"Russ, if there's been no progress in the next hour, the SAS are going in. The Government's now setting the agenda."

An hour later, an unmarked personnel carrier pulled up just short of Baddeley House. A squad of ten men, all dressed in black fatigues with balaclava hoods hiding their faces embarked. All were armed. 2 and 3 SAS were ready to go in.

The first that Ray and Judy Langley's captors knew there was a raid on was when the front door to the flat came flying off its hinges, followed by a smoke bomb. Six members of 2 and 3 SAS burst in, followed by the other four, who smashed their way in through the front window after firing grappling hooks at the window sill and climbing up.

Although the SNLA and WRA terrorists were losing some of their alertness through a lack of sleep, they soon snapped into action. Stuart and Williams were familiar with firearms due to their farming backgrounds and opened fire on the raiders, felling two of them. But the SAS were ready and a return burst of fire ended the lives of the two farmers' boys who had chosen the life of violence.

Gallacher and Bevan hustled Mr and Mrs Langley into the kitchen and slammed the door shut.

Gallacher yelled out "Come in and Mr and Mrs Langley get it."

Captain Daniel Holmes of 2 SAS shouted to his men. "Fan out, men. Ryan, Steve, check out the bedrooms. There's two of them loose somewhere in here. Tom, Jack, Harry, follow me."

Holmes and Sergeant Tom Weston crawled on their bellies towards the kitchen door, then, using a pole, nudged it open. Gallacher and Bevan returned fire just as Weston lobbed another smoke grenade into the kitchen. Holmes and Weston, followed by Corporal Jack Stanley and Private Harry Pearce, burst in. A volley of gunfire from Pearce's Heckler and Koch sidearm felled Gallacher, while a similar burst from Stanley's sidearm saw off Charlotte Bevan.

Seconds later, there were two more bursts of gunfire. Corporal Ryan Dempsey and Private Steve Moore had finished off Chloe Brown and Ben Summerill.

"Mr Langley, Mrs Langley, are you alright?" Captain Holmes shouted out as the smoke cleared. There was no reply.

"Oh shit!" Sergeant Weston was ashen-faced.

"What's up Tom?" said Captain Holmes.

He pointed to the dead bodies of Ray and Judy Langley.

CHAPTER 23

7 June 2020
Courtland Drive
Chigwell
Essex

Phil Barden had arranged a barbecue that afternoon. The Chairman of the EVF's General Council had invited fellow members of the Council, along with EVF senior commanders. Also present were Eddie Barrett and Dave Shrimpton, expats living in Spain who were planning to set up an EVF brigade there, and two Americans, Curtis Blackstone and Harvey Treadwell, who were planning to set up the EVF in the USA.

Barden and the EVF's Deputy Chairman, Glenn Nicholls, were delighted to have overseas interest. They saw potential in targeting the SNLA, the WRA and their supporters and sympathisers outside the United Kingdom.

"Curt, what level of interest have you got for the EVF in the States?" asked Barden.

"Massive, Phil" replied Blackstone. "The combination of the SNLA and WRA attacks and the denigration of Britain and England has reminded a lot of Americans of their English ancestry and heritage. There's big interest right across the USA."

Treadwell then joined the conversation. "It's strongest in the South, Phil and particularly Florida." A lot of British expats lived there. "But there's also support in the North East, the Mid-West and on the West Coast."

"Have any of your guys got military expertise?" asked Barden.

"Plenty, Phil" replied Blackstone. "Several of the guys we've signed up have fought in each of the three Gulf Wars."

"And how about funding?" added Barden.

"We've got several guys on board who've worked as Wall Street traders or in merchant banks. Plus there's several hard-right businessmen and women who are prepared to back us."

"Any political support?" asked Barden.

"Senator Byron Mitchell, Republican, Alabama" said Blackstone. "Harvey and I met him three weeks ago. He's sympathetic to the English cause. What's more, he's well-connected. He's buddies with the Republican minority leader in the Senate, Troy Burton."

"Phil, that could be a masterstroke" said fellow General Council member Darren Finnerty. "If I recall right, Burton's good friends with our own Home Secretary."

"Our new Iron Lady – I think not" commented another General Council member, Alan Wilkinson.

"Curt, Harvey, have you guys identified any potential targets yet?" asked Barden.

"We have, Phil" replied Treadwell. "The US leaders of Clann na h-Albann and Meibion Cymru, plus Bill Fraser and Ben Meredith. They run Caledonian Aid and Cambrian Aid."

"How about that loudmouth Senator and his sidekick?" asked Wilkinson.

"Senator McAllister and Representative Hopkins" said Blackstone. "We have. But security at Capitol Hill is rather tight. We haven't forgotten the Al-Q'aida attacks on Congress eight years ago."

A few feet away, Nicholls was deep in conversation with Barrett and Shrimpton.

"Good to hear that there's a high level of interest" said Nicholls. "The only thing that worries me is the age of your guys. It appears that most of you are over fifty."

"I know that, Glenn" replied Barrett. An East Ender who had made his wealth in office equipment, he was a short, stocky man in late middle age. "But there's no shortage of quality. Many of the lads served in the army or the police and have got the expertise. I served in the Royal Engineers first—that's where I learned about electronics."

"This is no 'Dad's Army' Glenn" said Shrimpton, a tall, broad-shouldered man who had just turned fifty. "A lot of the lads still go down the gym and are probably fitter than most men half their age."

"I don't deny that, Dave" replied Nicholls. "But you guys need to realise this. You won't be fighting against callow, pimply youths. You're up against hardened terrorists who've been trained by the IRA and Hezbollah. And many like yourself with military experience."

"Point taken" said a resigned Barrett.

"Tell you what we could do" said Nicholls. "We're planning to send some of our men and women over. You know what they say about team effort."

Gail Barden emerged from the kitchen with several baked potatoes to go with the hamburgers and sausages her husband was grilling on the barbecue. An attractive blonde in her 30s, she was Phil Barden's second wife.

She was also holding a copy of that day's *News of the World*.

"Today's headline might interest you, darling."

"Thanks babe" said Barden.

The headline story on front page of the *News of the World* certainly grabbed Barden's attention.

POP LEGEND CAUGHT BANKROLLING TERRORISTS

Controversial pop star Sara Greenfield is facing a police investigation and possible prosecution after allegations that she has provided funding for the SNLA and WRA.

Eyewitnesses at the fashionable Elephant Trap club in London saw Greenfield, 38, introduced to two men in the club's VIP suite who the News of the World have been since identified as Ruaridh McLaren and Rhys Phillips, both leading members of the SNLA and WRA political wings Clann na h-Albann and Meibion Cymru. During the meeting, Greenfield, who first came to fame with 'Green and Black' fourteen years ago, negotiated an agreement with McLaren and Phillips for a total of £500,000 to be transferred to Caledonian Aid and Cambrian Aid, both organisations that are regarded as fronts for the SNLA and the WRA.

Sara has been no stranger to controversy during her long career at the top. Despite the brilliance of her songwriting and the double platinum success of 'Green and Black', she dissipated much of her talent through a booze and drug-fuelled lifestyle, which has seen her go through two husbands and a spell in prison for assault. Last year, she returned to the top with her best album for years, 'I Survivor' and she has recently acquired a younger lover in actor Ben Reed.

A spokesman for the Metropolitan Police said that the allegations against Greenfield were under investigation.

"See this Glenn" shouted Barden. "Another fucking celeb getting in bed with the SNLA and WRA."

Nicholls had a look at the copy of the *News of the World.*

"So the plods think they can do something about it by prosecuting her?" said Nicholls. "What a laugh. You know what will happen. Greenfield will get some slimeball lawyer to defend her, get a load of the lefty luvvies out in force to support her, someone will leak the name of the prosecution witnesses onto Facebook and put the frighteners on them and she'll get off. Seen it all before."

"Not this time, Glenn" replied Barden. "There won't be any fucking trial. The EVF will be judge, jury and executioner."

9 June 2020
The Elephant Trap
Wardour Street
London

Sara Greenfield was downing her eighth Tequila slammer of the night as she held court in the VIP area of the Elephant Trap. Earlier that night, she had done a spot of DJing and had followed that by joining a promising new band, the Ginger Toms, on stage. By her side was her current boyfriend, Ben Reed, an up-an-coming actor in his early twenties.

Greenfield was now 38 years old and had been on the music scene since the mid-2000s. Five feet five inches tall and dark haired, she had once been attractive, but years of boozing and drug-taking had ruined her looks. Nevertheless, she was charismatic and still attracted attention.

She had been in a good mood earlier in the evening but, as the Tequilas and cocaine began to kick in, it began to change for the worse. She was particularly angry about the story in the previous weekend's *News of the World* which alleged that she had funded the SNLA and WRA. Another prosecution was the last thing she needed with a US tour on the horizon.

"Fucking arseholes, that's what they are" she slurred. "Why doesn't someone go and wipe them off the face of the earth?"

"Don't worry, babe" said Kate Regan, a leading model and one of Greenfield's celebrity friends. "Most of their readers are fat, stupid losers. Your fans still love you." Regan had no love for the country's tabloid press, having been victim of a sting by the *Sun* a year earlier. A photograph of her allegedly snorting cocaine had resulted in the loss of modelling contracts.

"Tell you what you should do, Sara" said Johnny Bassett, the Ginger Toms' guitarist. "Sue those cunts for every fucking penny. Get Justin Hemingway to represent you. He did a great job for Dougie Simpson and Alan Watkins." Bassett was referring to lawsuits brought two years before by the lead vocalists from two of the country's leading bands, Ringer and the Everlasting, when the *Daily Mail* claimed they had raised money for the SNLA and WRA.

Standing a few feet away from Greenfield and her acolytes were another group of people who had managed to obtain entry into the VIP suite that night. Most were hangers-on, ranging from up-and-coming artists who wanted to associate themselves with stars, wannabe actors, actresses and models and starstruck punters. Amongst them were two girls, one mixed-race, one blonde. Both were dressed in mini-skirts and stiletto heels.

Shanelle Bryan and Heidi Luff excused themselves and headed to the ladies' toilets. So far, so good, they thought.

Bryan and Luff were both members of the EVF and already had blood on their hands. Two and a half years earlier, with two of their friends, they had planted bombs in the Rob Roy and the Famous Three Kings, London pubs popular with expat Scots and Welsh, which had killed 25 people. Their friends, Rachel Emerson and Danielle Temple, were now behind bars for their role in the murders of Clann na h-Albann and Meibion Cymru activists in London.

Luff dialled a number into her Personal Data Assistant.

"Is that you, Mickey?" she asked.

"Yeah. How's things going Heidi?" On the other end of the line was Mickey Gladwell. He and three EVF colleagues were parked round the corner in Dean Street.

"I reckon Greenfield will be on her way in the next 10-15 minutes" replied Luff. "She's pissed as a fucking arsehole."

Suddenly, Bryan motioned to Luff. "Heidi, quick. Looks like Greenfield's leaving."

The two girls from the EVF left the toilets just in time to see Sara Greenfield stagger out of the Elephant Trap on the arm of Ben Reed.

Outside the Elephant Trap was a phalanx of reporters and paparazzi ready to take photos of Greenfield.

"Sara, have you got anything to say about the *News of the World's* claim that you gave money to the SNLA and WRA?" shouted one reporter.

"Piss off!" shouted back Greenfield.

Greenfield's minder, Craig Sutton, appeared on the scene. A big man at six foot three inches and nineteen stones, he snarled "If you tossers don't get the fuck out of here, you'll be eating hospital food for the next six months."

Greenfield's boyfriend helped her into the back of the dark green Bentley Continental which Sutton would drive back to her home at Hadley Wood.

As Greenfield's car pulled away, few people noticed a dark-skinned girl making a call on her personal data assistant. It was Shanelle Bryan.

"Mickey, Greenfield's on her way. Dark green Bentley Continental, registered 82 SMG. Heading towards Dean Street and Charing Cross Road."

"Thanks, Shan" replied Gladwell.

An hour later
Cockfosters Road
near Hadley Wood
Hertfordshire

Sara Greenfield was now almost home. Her car, in the hands of her minder, Craig Sutton, was now passing Beech Hill golf course. There was hardly any other traffic about. Sutton had not even noticed the fact that they had been followed all the way by a blue Ford Mondeo.

As Greenfield's car approached the northern edge of the golf course, a white panel van suddenly pulled out without warning. Sutton slammed on the brakes in the Bentley and swore.

"You fucking knobhead. You left your white stick behind?"

The white van pulled across in front of the Bentley and blocked the road. Before Sutton had an opportunity to reverse and make an escape, the Mondeo pulled up behind the Bentley to close off the other way out.

Sutton leapt out of the Bentley to confront the four men in the Mondeo who had also leapt out. He was ready for a fight.

"You fuckers better have a good excuse, cos you're all in for it" shouted the hulking minder. Sutton however failed to see that Mickey Gladwell and Sean Parkin were both holding AK-47assault rifles. The two EVF men opened fire on Sutton, who fell to the ground, dead.

"Gary, Lee. Let's do the business" shouted Gladwell. Gary Carpenter and Lee Rogers uncocked their AK-47s and followed Gladwell and Parkin towards the Bentley.

Sara Greenfield realised something was wrong when she heard gunfire, followed by an anguished shout from Ben Reed.

"Sara, Craig's been shot."

"Ben, for fuck's sake, get in the driver's seat and make a run for it" shouted Greenfield.

Reed scrambled into the driver's seat but, before he could start driving the Bentley away, a burst of gunfire from Carpenter's and Parkin's AK-47s ripped through his body.

"You bastard!" screamed a near-hysterical Greenfield. It was to be the last words she said as a further volley of gunfire extinguished her life.

"That, Sara, is the EVF's calling card" said a smirking Gladwell.

10 June 2020
Sky News

"This is Daniel Merryfield with the lunchtime headlines on Sky News."

"The entertainment world is trying to come to terms with last night's murder of pop legend Sara Greenfield. Ms Greenfield, 38, was shot dead along with her boyfriend, Ben Reed and her driver, Craig Sutton, close to Beech Hill golf course in the early hours of this morning after being ambushed by the EVF. Their bodies were not found until an hour later when a Post Office van passed the scene of the shooting."

"Sara Greenfield had a highly controversial career since her first album, 'Rays of the Sun' charted sixteen years ago. Her most successful album by far was 'Green and Black' from 2006 which spent six years in the music charts and went double platinum in sales on both sides of the Atlantic. But Ms Greenfield wasted her considerable talent with a dissolute lifestyle of drinking and drug-taking. She has been twice-married and spent two months in prison in 2012 after being convicted of assault. In recent years, it looked like she was getting her life together. She had a new boyfriend in actor Ben Reed, some sixteen years her junior, and her album, 'I Survivor' released last year propelled her back into the limelight. But two weeks ago, it appeared that her life had once again taken a wrong turn when she was seen by a journalist from the News of the World passing money to the SNLA and the WRA."

"It is strongly believed that Ms Greenfield was targeted by the EVF for this reason."

"Crowds of mourners have gathered by both the scene of the shooting and Ms Greenfield's house in Hadley Wood to lay flowers. There was also an angry demonstration by some of Ms Greenfield's fans outside the offices of News International at Wapping this morning, in which damage was caused to property. The police were called and seven arrests have been made. In addition, there are reports that death threats have been made against the editor of the News of the World, Veronica Dunham."

The same day
Cazenove Road
Stoke Newington
London

The entrycom buzzer sounded at Ben Greenfield's townhouse.
"Who is it?"
"Jake Branning."

"Come in, Jake."

Branning, a Londoner in his early 30s, stepped inside and was warmly greeted by Greenfield. Dressed casually in black jeans, a checked Ben Sherman shirt and a leather jacket, he was not a tall man at five foot eight inches. But he was built like a welterweight boxer and was more than capable of using his fists to reinforce an argument, so people didn't mess with him.

Branning's late father, Dudley, had been a longstanding friend of Ben and Rachel Greenfield. On hearing about the death of Sara, he felt duty-bound to drop over and offer his condolences.

"Sorry to hear about Sara" said Branning. "How are you and Aunt Rachel shaping up?"

"I'm holding up, Jake" replied Greenfield. "But Rachel isn't. She's been put on tranquilisers."

Greenfield then asked Branning about the EVF.

"I know very little about the EVF, Uncle Ben. There's not many around here, but I understand they're well organised in outer East London. Places like Barking, Dagenham and Romford. And also Essex. It seems their main beef is with the Jocks and the Taffs, not the Jews. Remind me, why did they go for Sara?"

"This" said Greenfield, pointing to a copy of the *News of the World*.

Branning read the paper before throwing it down in disgust.

"Jesus Christ, Uncle Ben. A classic *News of the World* hatchet job. I wouldn't be surprised if they planted those guys there to stitch up Sara."

"Jake, can do me a favour?" asked Greenfield. "I'm not a vengeful man but I want to see that bitch of an editor wasted. Sara was my only daughter."

"That's a tough call, Uncle Ben" replied Branning. "News International protect their top execs more tightly than the Royal Family. Their bodyguards are ex-SAS. But I'll see what can be done."

"Thanks, Jake" said Greenfield.

Later that afternoon
Roman Road
Bethnal Green
London

Jake Branning picked up a copy of the *Evening Standard* on the way back to his flat. The front page and the first five inside pages were all devoted to the murder of Sara Greenfield. On page 5, he saw the following article which concerned the editor of the *News of the World*.

NOW EDITOR READY TO FACE THE FLAK

Veronica Dunham the editor of the News of the World, is no shrinking violet as one might guess from her flame-red hair, her attire of short skirts, high heels and low-cut tops and her forthright opinions on everything from the economy, trade unions, crime and terrorism. Tomorrow, she faces another daunting challenge as she appears on the BBC programme, 'Question Time' which is taking place at Television Centre at Salford Quays.

Last Sunday, rock legend Sara Greenfield was murdered by the EVF following an article in last Sunday's News of the World which alleged she was providing funds to the SNLA and the WRA. Many people believe that Greenfield was set up. Already, Dunham has received death threats and Greater Manchester Police have arranged for reinforcements to be on hand tomorrow to deal with the threat of public disorder. However, Dunham is unrepentant about the article . . . .

So Dunham's going to be up in Manchester tomorrow, thought Branning. She'll be a tough target. She'll have a bodyguard with her. And GMP will be providing protection at Salford Quays.

Branning suddenly remembered there were two SNLA guys living in Manchester he knew. Graeme Cuthbertson and Allan Ritchie. One ex-Para, the other an ex-Marine. Both hard as nails. If anyone was capable of taking out Dunham, it was them.

He got out a personal data assistant and dialled. He heard it ring, then a voice came up.

"Allan Ritchie."

"Hi Al, Jake Branning here. Got something that might interest you. Veronica Dunham's up in Manchester tomorrow. Taking part in 'Question Time' at the BBC. If you take her out, there's twenty five thousand for you and your mate. Interested?"

"Yeah."

11 June 2020
BBC Television Centre
Salford Quays

The edition of 'Question Time' was going to be a controversial one. The panel consisted of Geraldine Partington, the Labour MP for Bradford North who had been active in the campaign for a posthumous pardon for the Ascot Five and the Warrington Three, Mike Ward, the Conservative Chief Whip, Julia Goldwater, the former leader of the Liberal Democrats and Veronica Dunham, the editor of the *News of the World*.

The BBC was a much-diminished organisation compared to what it had been up to four years earlier when the Broadcasting Act had been brought in. The Act had forced the BBC to sell off its national and local radio stations and its digital channels. Its national television service was reduced to a rump of two channels. The Broadcasting Act also abolished the requirement to have a licence to use a television set, which meant that the BBC would henceforth be funded from general taxation. The impact on the Corporation's programme-making was considerable; with the Government holding the purse-strings, the BBC had to be careful not to offend its main paymaster. This meant taking care to ensure that programme content was as anodyne and uncontroversial as possible.

'Question Time' was a prime example of how the BBC had changed its emphasis in recent years. Prior to 2016, there was considerable anger from Conservative MPs, business leaders and many of the public about what was considered to be left-wing bias in the BBC's current affairs and drama output. 'Question Time' was a particular target, as it was commonly felt that the BBC chose panellists and selected audiences from people known to be hostile towards conservatism and capitalism. The current producers of the programme had taken care to ensure a balanced panel had been invited and took care to minimise invitations to trade unions and known pressure groups hostile to the Government.

The first part of the debate covered the Government's proposals for public spending cuts affecting education, health, housing and transport which were being brought in because of the deteriorating public finances. But, before long, questions were being asked about Scotland and Wales. It was the combination of policing and security costs and the fall in revenues arising from the Troubles and from reduced business investment and tourism that had taken its toll on the economy.

Josh Houghton, an Economics student at Manchester University then asked a question aimed at the editor of the *News of the World*.

"I have a question for Veronica Dunham. Two nights ago, Sara Greenfield was murdered by the EVF. Doesn't she show any remorse for the groundless claim in the *News of the World* on 7 June that Sara was providing funding for the SNLA and the WRA, which almost certainly resulted in her murder?"

Dunham was 35 years old, an attractive redhead who had been editor of *News of the World* for the past year. Since starting her career on the *Bolton Evening Chronicle* on graduating fourteen years earlier, she had enjoyed a meteoric rise and was expected to move into corporate management at News International.

"Like many people in this room, I was sorry to hear of Sara Greenfield's death. She was an extremely talented performer and I recognise that many people present were fans of her. But the fact remains that journalists working for the *News of the World* have categoric evidence that Ms Greenfield met members of the SNLA and the WRA and arranged for bankers' drafts to be provided to them. That surely is sufficient evidence that Ms Greenfield has provided funding for terrorist organisations."

There were cries of "Rubbish" from the audience.

"May I continue" said Dunham. "Whatever Sara Greenfield achieved during her singing career, she was prepared to support organisations which have ruthlessly murdered innocent civilians over the past five years. These are inconvenient facts which many people would like to sweep under the carpet. But the *News of the World* is ready to tell the truth and stand by what it says. That is why so many of the left-wing dislike us so much and, as some of the audience is showing, tries to use mob tactics to silence us. But as long as I am editor of the *News of the World*, I will not bow to mob rule and allow it to be silenced."

Veronica Dunham had taken no chances following reports that death threats had been made against her. She had arranged for a private jet owned by News

International to fly her direct from London City Airport and for an SAS-trained News International driver to drive her from the airport.

On her arrival at Television Centre, Ms Dunham had been greeted by a hostile demonstration protesting about the previous Sunday's *News of the World* article which they considered had contributed to the Sara Greenfield's murder by the EVF. Many were fans of the deceased singer. But there was also a core of professional demonstrators, including many from the Socialist Alliance and Class War. Fortunately, there was a strong police presence to contain them.

At 11:30pm, Veronica Dunham emerged from the BBC studios. Her car was ready to take her back to Manchester Airport for the return flight to London.

The demonstrators who had given Dunham a noisy and hostile welcome had now dispersed, but one of them was still loitering close to the television studios. Kate Pilcher was 24 years old, a former languages student at Salford University and a member of Class War. She was living in a squat in Salford and already had two convictions for public order offences.

The silver Mercedes-Benz E300 pulled out of the BBC television studios into Trafford Road. Pilcher saw it depart, then removed a personal data assistant from her bag and dialled a number. A Scottish voice answered it.

"Hi Al, it's Kate. Dunham's just left. She's in the back of a silver Mercedes-Benz E300, registration MA69 XBY. Heading south along Trafford Road. Probably on her way to the airport."

"Thanks Kate. We'll tail her. Andy and Bruce are ready to close off the Chester Road."

Graeme Cuthbertson and Allan Ritchie were seated on a Suzuki ZX500 motorbike parked in White City Way, just off the junction where Chester Road, Trafford Road and Bridgewater Way all met.

They saw Dunham's car round the junction into Chester Road. Cuthbertson, the taller of the two men, rang a number on his personal data assistant.

"Andy, Dunham's on her way. You know what to do."

Two miles down Chester Road in Stretford, close to the junction with Radnor Street, a Ford Transit van in the markings of McNicholas was parked. Seated inside were Andy Gray and Bruce Ingham. Wearing high visibility jackets, they switched on the van's orange warning lights to signify that roadworks would be starting. They carried out a set of polycarbonate barriers to close off a section of the inside lane and installed a set of traffic lights. There was still a significant amount of traffic using Chester Road and the installation of the lights would cause minor traffic jams. Enough to hold up Veronica Dunham for just a couple of minutes.

Dunham's chauffeur, Shane Holton, had served in the SAS and was now employed by News International as a driver and bodyguard to protect their top executives. The fact that News International enjoyed a near monopoly position in the British media, coupled to its aggressive pro-Government stance, had made it, its senior executives and its leading journalists prime targets for politically-motivated violence. The owners took no chances and security within the organisation was tight.

As Holton approached the junction with Raleigh Street, he noticed the traffic slowing down.

"Sorry, Ms Dunham. Probably another bloody set of roadworks. Afraid it's going to make us late."

"Don't worry, Shane" replied the *News of the World* editor. "I'll phone Dave Crossland at the airport to let him know. And I'll ensure that something goes in the next edition of the *News of the World* about the roadworks racket. It'll go down well with our readers."

Ritchie and Cuthbertson had followed Dunham at a discreet distance to avoid raising any suspicions. The traffic jam caused no problem to them; the Suzuki motorbike was nimble enough for them to go round the outside of the line of cars to the front of the traffic jam.

"There she is, Gray" said Ritchie. "Ready?"

"Certainly am, Al. Here's the SNLA's payback to the *News of the World*."

Cuthbertson withdrew an Uzi machine pistol from a holster in the pocket of his motorcycling leathers. As Ritchie pulled up alongside the Mercedes on the Suzuki, Cuthbertson could clearly see Dunham seated in the back of the Mercedes.

Cuthbertson took aim and opened fire. His first burst of fire took out Holton. Before Veronica Dunham could react, a second burst of fire from Cuthbertson's Uzi ripped through her, killing her instantly. Before stunned motorists and passers-by could react, Cuthbertson and Ritchie were racing down Chester Road away from the scene.

12 June 2020
Hayes Community College
Coldharbour Lane
Hayes
Middlesex

Janine Brooks was in a foul mood. The previous night, she had got into a row with her stepfather when she came in late. The ugly bruise she had across her face was the result of receiving a backhander from him.

Brooks was pretty but her mouth was pulled into a sullen pout and the hard glare she gave showed she was someone you didn't mess with. The 17-year old student studying for an NVQ in hairdressing, having left school the previous year.

Many of the students were discussing the murder the previous night of the *News of the World* editor, Veronica Dunham. It was front page news in all the paper and the *Sun* had a black typeface instead of its normal red. A picture of Dunham, edged in black, graced its front page. Below, its headline read

VERONICA DUNHAM 1985-2020
A FIGHTER FOR THE TRUTH

Brooks ordered a coffee and a Kit Kat and sat down next to Dave Igglesden.

Igglesden was long-haired, scruffily-dressed and his denim jacket was festooned with badges. A year older than Brooks, he was on the Student Union Committee and was a member of the Socialist Alliance. He was something of a legend to fellow students, having been involved in several violent demonstrations and obtained two convictions for public order offences.

"Hi Jan, anything I can help you with?" asked Igglesden. "God, what happened to you?"

"My stepdad did that, Dave" replied Brooks. "Fucking arsehole, one of these days I'm gonna shank him."

"Thought of reporting him to the police?"

"What's the point, Dave" said Brooks. "They'll probably sympathise with him. Fucking pillar of the community he's supposed to be."

Most of the students were talking about the murder of the *News of the World* editor, Veronica Dunham, the previous night at the hands of the SNLA. With few exceptions, most of the students were hostile to the *Sun* and the *News of the World* and felt that Dunham had it coming to her because of her perceived role in the death of Sara Greenfield. But Brooks was thumbing through some flyers for a meeting.

"Dave, this might interest you" said Brooks. "The EVF are going to be holding a meeting at the Grapes in Uxbridge Road on Saturday night. Trying to recruit new members from round here."

"Christ, Jan, how do you know that?" asked Igglesden.

"My stepdad's a member. In fact, more than just a member. He's the commander of the local brigade round here."

"That will be of interest to the comrades" said Igglesden.

"Better still Dave" continued Brooks, "I've heard that some of the EVF bigwigs from the General Council will be in attendance."

Igglesden's ears pricked up. "Any names, Jan?"

"Phil Barden, Barry Pickett and Alan Wilkinson."

"Thanks, Jan."

After Brooks went off to her next class, Igglesden headed for the car park. Students weren't supposed to bring mobile phones or personal data assistants in with them as they were considered to be disruptive to education. But Igglesden was someone who saw rules as bourgeois oppression and flouted them at will. He withdrew his personal data assistant and made a call.

Igglesden had no intention of contacting his fellow Socialist Alliance party members. The best they could achieve was a noisy demonstration and probably get beaten up by the EVF's minders. Instead, he was getting in touch with the London Brigade of the WRA.

"Hello." A Welsh voice answered the phone.

"Is that Gareth Thomas?" asked Igglesden.

"It is. And who are you, butt?" asked the Welshman.

"Dave Igglesden, Socialist Alliance. You might be interested to know that the EVF are holding a meeting and recruitment drive at the Grapes in Hayes on Saturday evening. From what I've heard, Phil Barden, Barry Pickett and Alan Wilkinson from the EVF General Council will be there."

13 June 2020
The Grapes
Uxbridge Road
Hayes
Middlesex

The Grapes was a large town pub in the middle of Hayes. Formerly a Beefeater pub, it was now owned by the Big Steak company and it continued to offer the same formula. The restaurant attached to the pub mainly traded on lower middle-class couples with traditional tastes, which meant meals like steak and chips. It had also added a function room and, that evening, a private booking had been made. The pub's management had not known until too late that it had been booked for an EVF meeting.

Brian Halfyard, the Commander of the EVF's West London Brigade, was a happy man. The recruitment night had passed off as an enormous success. Over 200 young men and women had signed up to join the EVF that evening. A barbecue had been arranged and large numbers of the recruits were still milling around the pub forecourt.

"Been a good night tonight, Brian" said the Chairman of the EVF's General Council, Phil Barden, who came over to join Halfyard. He was accompanied by fellow General Council members Barry Pickett and Alan Wilkinson.

"Couldn't have gone better, Phil" said Halfyard. "I reckon we've got over two hundred more members tonight alone."

"We're planning to hold similar recruitment events across London this summer" said Wilkinson, a lean, bespectacled Yorkshireman. "Can you give us a hand, Brian?"

"Love to, Alan" replied Halfyard.

The same time
Yeading Lane
Hayes
Middlesex

Gareth Thomas and Eddie Dacey had turned off Western Avenue five minutes earlier and were heading down Yeading Lane on a Yamaha M500 motorcycle.

"How far to go, Ed?" asked Thomas, the bigger of the two men.

"About a mile, Gar" replied Dacey.

"Better check where our quarry is" said Thomas. "I'll ring Stacey."

Thomas removed his personal data assistant from a jacket pocket and rang his girlfriend, Stacey Moore, who was working as a waitress at the Grapes.

"Hi Stacey, Gar here. Are Barden and the rest of the EVF here?"

"Out the front in the forecourt, babe" replied Moore. "Here, have a look at the CCTV screen."

Thomas could clearly see Phil Barden, Barry Pickett, Alan Wilkinson and two other unknown men who he assumed were EVF members from the local brigade.

"Have a look, Ed" said Thomas. "The last sight of Barden, Pickett and Wilkinson alive."

Ten minutes later
The Grapes
Uxbridge Road
Hayes
Middlesex

Gareth Thomas swung the Yamaha out of Yeading Lane into Uxbridge Road. Straight ahead was the Grapes.

"Ready, Ed" said Thomas.

Dacey withdrew an Uzi machine pistol from a holster on his jacket as Thomas slowed down. It was still light and the fine day had attracted a large turnout at the Grapes. He could clearly see the table occupied by Barden, Pickett and Wilkinson. He raised the Uzi, took aim and opened fire.

Dacey couldn't have wished for better luck. His first burst of fire cut down Phil Barden and Brian Halfyard, the EVF's West London brigade commander. His second burst accounted for Barry Pickett, Alan Wilkinson and two more men he assumed to be from the EVF. Job done, he hastily shoved the Uzi back into its holster as Thomas hit the accelerator and sped away at top speed, leaving six dead bodies on the forecourt of the Grapes.

19 June 2020
Courtland Drive
Chigwell
Essex

The EVF had spared no expense in ensuring that Phil Barden, Barry Pickett and Alan Wilkinson all had a spectacular send-off. Their coffins were hauled through the streets of Chigwell in horse-drawn hearses, each draped with a massive St George's flag. Crowds of people, both local and EVF members and sympathisers from round the country, lined the streets of the Essex town, while a guard of honour drawn from the EVF, dressed in paramilitary fatigues, escorted the hearses all the way to St Mary's Church. After the service was over, the EVF escorts fired volleys of blanks as the coffins of the former General Council members were laid to rest.

Back at Phil Barden's house, his widow, Gail, had arranged a reception for EVF brigade commanders from round the country. Neil Malkin was down from Stoke-on-Trent. Eddie Greenhalgh from Blackburn was present, as was Howard Tomlinson from Bradford, Mickey Robson from Sunderland, Dave Dixon from Birmingham and Doug Tremlett from Bristol. In addition, Eddie Barrett had flown over from Spain and Harvey Treadwell had flown in from the USA.

Glenn Nicholls and Mark Stubbs each took bottles of lager from a bin filled with ice and walked across the back garden to join the brigade commanders. Many of those present were looking to the big former paratrooper to take over the leadership of the EVF.

Eddie Greenhalgh was getting quite animated about what the EVF should do to avenge the deaths of three of their leaders.

"Look fellas" said Greenhalgh, "if we want to maintain any credibility, we've got to hit back at the SNLA and WRA soon and big time. It's no use bumping off some pimply kid who's just joined up. We need to go for the big shots."

"If you mean Doug Paterson and Trevor Rees, Eddie, they're both locked up in Belmarsh awaiting trial, along with the other members of the SNLA and WRA General Council" said Dixon.

"How about their stand-ins?" asked Robson. "Adam Lamont and Rob Mathias. Nasty fuckers, the pair of them"

"Lamont and Mathias are difficult to track down, Mickey" said Tomlinson. "Always on the move, them two. And protected by an inner circle of bodyguards. If one of us got remotely close, we'd get wasted."

"Forget trying to whack their leaders, fellas" said Tremlett. "We should copy what the SNLA and WRA do. A pair of fucking great bombs in Glasgow and Cardiff over the Bank Holidays should send the Jocks and Taffs the message that what they do to the English they'll get back."

"Not a great idea, guys" said Treadwell. "There's a lot of American tourists over at that time. Kill any of them and the EVF's toast in the States."

"Has anyone thought of bombing a rock festival?" asked Tomlinson.

"Why, Howard?" enquired Greenhalgh.

"It's common knowledge that the SNLA and WRA both recruit new members and fundraise at them" said Tomlinson. "And I reckon that many other rock artists have given money to the SNLA and WRA, just like Greenfield did."

"I'll back that up, Howie" said Malkin. "Our Ryan was out at Benicassim last year. Told me that the SNLA and WRA were openly fundraising and recruiting and that the festival organisers were turning a blind eye to it. What's more, a lot of the fans who go are openly sympathetic to the SNLA and WRA cause."

"Where's Benicassim?" asked Dixon.

"Spain" replied Barrett. "Where I now live, Dave."

Nicholls motioned to the brigade commanders to listen.

"Fellas, I don't know if anyone's thought of it but the idea of letting off a bomb at Benicassim rather appeals to me. It sounds like from what's being said that the SNLA and WRA use it for both recruiting and fundraising. Not only that, rock festivals always attract hippies, druggies, drop-outs and other scrotes. I bet there'll be a load of National Service deserters there as well as commie students from all over Europe. They need to be taught a lesson as much as the SNLA and the WRA. And it will send a message that England isn't to be messed with."

"Glenn, there's a couple of guys who might be able to help" said Malkin. "We've recruited a group of students at Keele University. If they go to Benicassim, no one will suspect them. They will fit in with the other fans easily."

"How are they going to smuggle a bomb through Spanish customs?" asked Greenhalgh.

"They won't have to, Eddie" replied Nicholls. "Our Spanish Brigade will build the bombs for them. That's right, Eddie?" turning to Barrett.

"You can rely on that, Glenn" replied Barrett.

14 July 2020
Calle de Wilkinson
Guadalmar near Malaga
Spain

Danny Pike felt a bit self-conscious as he drove the hired Seat Brava into Guadalmar. It was evident from both the size of the houses and the fact that most of the cars were Mercedes-Benzes, Ferraris and Bentleys that this was a wealthy area.

"Calle de Wilkinson next on the right, Dan" said Luke Chilvers in the front passenger seat. "Dave Shrimpton's gaff is at number six."

Pike drew the Brava to a halt outside 6 Calle de Wilkinson.

Dave Shrimpton was expecting them. Dressed in a navy blue Pierre Cardin shirt and white trousers and wearing a massive gold medallion, Shrimpton looked the caricature of the British expatriate and contrasted massively with the two engineering students from Keele University who were scruffily dressed in T-shirts and cut-off jeans.

"Come in lads" said Shrimpton. "Fancy a beer?"

"Love one" said Pike.

Chilvers and Pike were both members of the EVF's West Midlands Brigade and their expertise in electronics had helped the EVF kill and maim several SNLA and WRA suspects and sympathisers. They had been recommended to the EVF's General Council by the West Midlands brigade commander, Dave Dixon, and had volunteered to carry out what would be the EVF's most audacious bomb plot yet. They were going to bomb the Benicassim Rock Festival.

Shrimpton had managed to obtain thirty kilogrammes of PECT, probably the most lethal explosive in existence. The two Keele University students were to prime an explosive device which would be carried in a rucksack and detonated in the middle of the main arena through a signal from a personal data assistant. The expected carnage would be immense.

Shrimpton knew that he and his fellow expatriates would look as out of place at a rock festival as would the average rock fan in their expat community. In contrast, Chilvers and Pike would fit in at Benicassim without any problem.

"Are you lads ready" said Shrimpton.

"We are" chorused Chilvers and Pike.

"Follow me. The stuff's in the garage."

Chilvers and Pike followed Shrimpton into the massive garage. Parked inside was a Bentley Continental and a Range Rover.

"Luke, Danny, what do you think?" Shrimpton pointed to packs containing thirty kilos of PECT.

"Sweet, Dave" replied Pike.

"OK to start working now?" asked Chilvers.

"Fine, lads. Just let me know if you need anything."

18 July 2020
Benicassim
Spain

The 2020 Benicassim Festival was now into its second full day. Glorious sunshine dappled the festival site. For many young people, Benicassim was the curtain-raiser of the summer entertainment scene as schools and universities had just broken up for the year.

The first festival at Benicassim had been held back in 1994. Between the mid-1990s and 2010, the leading festivals had been in the United Kingdom, with Glastonbury, Leeds and Reading leading the way. But the United Kingdom's pre-eminence in the rock festival scene had faded over the previous ten years. The Government, pandering to the views of local residents who disliked the noise and influx of what they saw as an anti-social rabble, had imposed severe restrictions on festival organisers. The other factor was the unreliable British weather. The appeal of standing around in the mud and rain faded when there was an option of going to a country where rock fans were welcomed and where there was an excellent chance of sunshine. Consequently, the leading European festivals were now in southern Europe—Benicassim, Mont-de-Marsan in France and Novi Sad in Serbia.

Luke Chilvers and Danny Pike worked their way towards the front of the main arena and set their pitch in a location where they would have a good view of the bands playing without being subjected to the massive crush and 'moshing' closer to the front. They had remembered the advice that Glenn Nicholls, the new Chairman of the EVF's General Council had given them before setting off. Stay cool, don't get into any arguments and don't draw attention to yourselves.

On arriving at Benicassim, they saw what Nicholls meant. There were stalls set up by Clann na h-Albann and Meibion Cymru and they were openly soliciting money and support for the SNLA and WRA. Trotskyist and anarchist organisations from Europe were also in evidence and they were offering advice to young Britons on how to avoid National Service. On the first day, Chilvers and Pike had spoken to some fellow Britons who were festival veterans who advised them that, in the current climate, it was unadvisable to fly the Union Jack or the St George's flag. In the arena, they saw the flags of other countries and, significantly, large numbers of Scottish and Welsh flags. Further investigation found that many were being flown either by Australians, New Zealanders or South Africans of Scottish or Welsh descent or by European nationals sympathetic to the Scottish or Welsh cause.

During the afternoon, Chilvers and Pike made friends with a group of Sussex University students sitting next to them. There were two girls in the group, Bethany and Cheryl, both very pretty. They had just finished their degree in Modern Languages and were worried about the future. Both girls were however very left-wing in their views and felt that the SNLA and the WRA had just causes.

On stage were a London band, the Ginger Toms, whose first album was selling well in both the United Kingdom and in Europe. Their style was described as being something of a hybrid between Britpop and the Wall of Sound that Phil Spector had pioneered over half a century earlier.

The Ginger Toms were coming to the end of their set. For their last number, lead vocalist Matt Brazier made an announcement.

"Our final song will be one by Sara Greenfield, 'Don't you Remember Me'. Sara was a good friend to us and I'm sure you will all like to remember her."

A massive roar of approval rang across the main arena.

The main arena was still buzzing from the climax of the Ginger Toms' set when the next band, the Gars, came on. They hailed from Cleveland in the USA and played fast, thrashy garage rock. They were followed on stage by White Valiant, an Australian band which played melodic rock.

As the evening progressed to night and darkness set in, Chilvers and Pike had made friends with four more groups of rock fans close to them. One was a group of Australians who were backpacking their way round Europe, another were a group of French fans from Clermont-Ferrand and the third were a group of Spanish fans from the University of Madrid. The last group were composed of Scottish and Welsh fans. There were nine of them, and all were supporters of the SNLA and WRA.

"Dan, I think it's time for some nosebag" said Chilvers. "Fancy a beer or some grub?"

Pike looked back towards the bars and food stalls. It would take about twenty minutes just to get back before being served. He saw people struggling back with food and drink.

"Reckon you'll need a hand, Luke?" asked Pike.

"Yeah, probably will."

"Dan, we're going to have to leave our stuff here" said Chilvers.

"Luke, we'll ask someone to look over the stuff for us. Incidentally, we could offer to but them a beer."

Pike turned to the rock fans he and Chilvers had met.

"Anyone fancy a beer?"

"I'm interested" said Jim McRae, a Scot from Dumbarton.

"So am I" added Sarah Lewis, a Welsh girl from Caerphilly.

"Don't worry about your bag, mate" said McRae. We'll look after it."

Chilvers and Pike were back at the campsite. The bomb was being guarded by, of all people, Scots and Welsh. The two EVF men chuckled at the irony.

"Dan, so far, so good" said Chilvers. "What time should we leave?"

"Not before the end of the concert. We'll draw notice to ourselves. Remember what Glenn told us?"

They noticed large numbers of fans heading into the concert arena. The headline act for Saturday, Red When Angry, an American metal/funk crossover band, would be on stage shortly. They at least had an alibi if the crowd looking after their rucksack became suspicious, as they could argue that the crowds buying food and drink slowed them up.

In the background, they heard the compere announce "Benicassim, I want you to give a massive welcome for tonight's headliner, Red When Angry."

A deafening cheer rose from the main arena.

"Alright, Luke, here we go" said Pike.

Pike withdrew his personal data assistant from his shirt pocket and dialled in a number, then pressed ENTER.

A split second later, there was a flash of light from the arena followed by a thunderous boom.

19 July 2020
Sky News

"This is Sara Ratcliffe with this morning's headlines on Sky News."

"The death toll in the bombing at the Benicassim Festival has now risen to eighty four. A further three hundred and five people have been injured, fifty five seriously."

"The bomb exploded without warning just before 9pm as the headlining band, Red When Angry, was about to start its set. The main arena was packed with fans and the bomb, which was believed to contain the explosive PECT, caused damage on a massive scale. The organisers of the festival have decided to cancel the rest of the bill out of respect for the dead and injured."

"Responsibility for the bombing has been claimed by the EVF who, in a statement received by Reuters, said that the Benicassim Festival was a legitimate target because of its tolerance of fundraising and recruitment by the SNLA and the WRA and its promotion of anti-English sentiments."

"The police in the United Kingdom and Spain are co-operating in an attempt to find the perpetrators of the bombing. There is speculation that the EVF ordered the bombing in retaliation for the murder of three members of its General Council by the WRA a month ago."

20 July 2020
Spanish Ministry of Foreign Affairs
Palacio de Santa Cruz
Madrid

The British Ambassador to Spain, Sir Robin Perkins, was sitting opposite an extremely irate Spanish Foreign Minister, Ana Maria Cisñeros.

"Madam Foreign Minister, I have already said that our Government and authorities will offer yours full and unqualified co-operation in finding the perpetrators of the dreadful atrocity last Saturday. What more can I do?"

"Sir Robin, my Government has categoric evidence before it that the British government has colluded with the EVF in running a 'dirty war' against the SNLA and the WRA. This has included passing information to the EVF about suspected SNLA or WRA members and letting them do the dirty work. That is extrajudicial murder, something which the Council or Europe and United Nations Conventions on Human Rights specifically prohibit."

"Madam Foreign Minister, I completely reject that slur against my Government. The United Kingdom regards the activities of the EVF as no different to those of the SNLA and WRA. And may I remind you that the SNLA and the WRA are both ruthless terrorist organisations which have the blood of thousands of innocent people on their hands. They have been responsible for drug trafficking and other crime which has created misery for ordinary people. They are prescribed organisations, not only in the United Kingdom, but also in the United States, Australia and New Zealand. And you, Madam, should be aware from your own country's history of the misery that terrorism can cause."

Perkins was referring to ETA.

"Sir Robin, your country is exporting its problems to Spain" continued Cisñeros. "Firstly there was Benidorm and Arenal two years ago. Then the McLintock's Bar shooting. Now this. My government has a responsibility to its people to keep them safe. From today, we will be requiring all citizens of the United Kingdom to have a visa if they wish to enter Spain."

Perkins was well aware of the inconvenience this would cause. Not only did large numbers of Britons visit Spain on holiday but there were now significant numbers of permanent residents.

"Madam Foreign Minister, don't you think you have acted rather hastily?" asked Perkins.

"Not at all, Sir Robin" replied Cisñeros. "My Government means what it says."

CHAPTER 24

27 July 2020
Woolwich Crown Court
Belmarsh Road
Thamesmead
London

"The defendants are here, Ms Rowell." Sergeant Chris Denman notified the administration clerk, Jacqui Rowell, that the ten members of the General Councils of the SNLA and the WRA due to face trial on terrorism charges were ready to be escorted to the dock.

"Names please, Sergeant" asked Rowell.

"Here they are" replied Denman, handing Ms Rowell a sheet of paper.

"Thank you. You can escort the defendants into the courtroom."

The largest and costliest trial to be held under British law was about to start. It was also the first trial to be held under the provisions of the Criminal Justice Act 2018 which allowed for high-risk defendants to be tried without a jury.

Eight months earlier, the National Anti-Terror Squad had arrested the entire General Councils of the SNLA and the WRA at a house in Oldham that was owned by a member of Al-Q'aida following surveillance by an MI5 officer. At the time, the Government had thought it would be the death blow to the terrorist organisations that had been fighting the British government over the previous four years in order to force them to recognise independence for Scotland and Wales. The people of Scotland and Wales were starting to tire of the relentless bombings and shootings disrupting their lives, and burgeoning peace movements were growing. But the fortunes of the SNLA and the WRA had been revived after the withdrawal of Special Category Status for claimed political prisoners earlier in 2020 sparked a series of hunger strikes which led to renewed recruitment. The SNLA's and WRA's campaigns of terror were in full flow again and, to make matters worse, their political wings, Clann na h-Albann and Meibion Cymru, were having success in persuading foreign investors and tourists to boycott the United Kingdom.

For the Government, successful convictions of the General Councils were needed if they were to regain credibility.

Woolwich Crown Court had been opened twenty-seven years earlier and was the most secure in the country. It was adjacent to the maximum-security prison at Belmarsh and a tunnel between the prison and the court enabled the defendants to be transferred between the two venues without the risk of them being sprung in transit. Unlike ordinary prisoners, who were escorted by private security companies, the ten defendants were escorted by armed policemen. The authorities were taking no chances with ten men who were considered to be the most dangerous inmates in the country's prisons.

The ten defendants took their place in the dock. A reinforced glass screen was placed in front of the dock to prevent the possibility of any of the defendants escaping from the dock. To reinforce security, the dock was guarded by three armed policemen.

Justin Hemingway arrived at Woolwich Crown Court in his Audi S7 coupe, accompanied by his assistant, Maxine Joseph, a tall, statuesque black girl in her early 20s. He was already well-known to both the judicial establishment and the public through previous defences of defendants ranging from organised criminals and terrorists through to celebrities. Hemingway was regarded as a warrior for justice by his supporters but he was heartily disliked by the judicial establishment, the police, Tory MPs and many of the public because of his reputation for exploiting procedure to secure acquittals for his clients.

"Put your case on the table, Mr Hemingway" snapped PC Nathan Strange.

"Do we really have to go through this rigmarole, officer?" asked Hemingway. "These are my defence papers. I thought it was supposed to be a fair trial."

"Do as you're told, Mr Hemingway" repeated PC Strange. "I haven't got all day. And you, Miss", pointing to Joseph.

Hemingway and Joseph submitted their papers for examination.

PC Strange sullenly worked his way through the contents of Hemingway's and Joseph's briefcases before returning them.

"Okay, go through" said PC Strange.

"Be upstanding in Court." The severe tones of Raymond Fenwick, the Clerk to the Court, rapped out across the courtroom.

The three judges who would decide on the verdict in the absence of a jury entered the courtroom. At the front was the most senior of the three judges, Mr Justice Oldham, who would chair the panel. At sixty years of age, he was the most senior of the three judges. He was regarded as a strong conservative and likely to deliver a guilty verdict.

Following Oldham were the other two judges, Mr Justice Carrington and Mr Justice Sellers. Carrington was short, plumpish and in his early 50s and was looking to establish himself in the 'Premier League' of circuit judges, having been mainly confined to the provincial circuit during his career. Sellers was much taller, dark-haired and, at 46, the youngest of the trio. He was regarded as a high-flyer and a potential future Lord Chief Justice.

Once the three judges were settled, the Clerk to the Court began reading out the charges.

"Robert Daniel Ahern, Gethin Emlyn Davies, Gareth Dafydd Evans, Michael Francis Grogan, Iain Baird Murray, Douglas Robert Paterson, Mark Podborski, Trevor Owen Rees, Gordon Iain Ross and Richard Barrie Thomas, you all stand charged with the following offence."

"That, between 3 August 2015 and 21 November 2019, you engaged in action which caused the loss or endangerment of life, involved serious violence against a person, serious damage to property and interference or disruption to electronic systems for the purpose of advancing a political cause, all of which are defined as offences under Section 1 of the Terrorism Act 2012."

"Robert Daniel Ahern, Gethin Emlyn Davies, Gareth Dafydd Evans, Trevor Owen Rees and Richard Barrie Thomas, you all stand charged with the following offence. That, between 3 August 2015 and 21 November 2019, you held membership of the Welsh Republican Army, which is defined as a proscribed organisation under Section 3 of the Terrorism Act 2012."

"Michael Francis Grogan, Iain Baird Murray, Douglas Robert Paterson, Mark Podborski and Gordon Iain Ross, you all stand charged with the following offence. That, between 3 August 2015 and 21 November 2019, you held membership of the Scottish National Liberation Army, which is defined as a proscribed organisation under Section 3 of the Terrorism Act 2012."

"How do you plead?"

"Robert Daniel Ahern."

"Not guilty to the first charge. Guilty to the second charge."

"Gethin Emlyn Davies."

"Not guilty to the first charge. Guilty to the second charge."

"Gareth Dafydd Evans."

"Not guilty to the first charge. Guilty to the second charge."

"Michael Francis Grogan."

"Not guilty to the first charge. Guilty to the second charge."

"Iain Baird Murray."

"Not guilty to the first charge. Guilty to the second charge."

"Douglas Robert Paterson."

"Not guilty to the first charge. Guilty to the second charge."

"Mark Podborski."

"Not guilty to the first charge. Guilty to the second charge."

"Trevor Owen Rees."

"Not guilty to the first charge. Guilty to the second charge."

"Gordon Iain Ross."

"Not guilty to the first charge. Guilty to the second charge."

"Richard Barrie Thomas."

"Not guilty to the first charge. Guilty to the second charge."

The same day
Braganza Street
Kennington
London

Geraldine Partington was working on several papers. Although Parliament had risen the previous week, she still had plenty of papers to work through. She was aiming to have them cleared by Friday, as she and her partner, Mohammed Bourguiba, were due to go on holiday to Morocco for three weeks from Saturday.

Prominent amongst her work was the ongoing campaign for a pardon for the Ascot Five and the Warrington Three and compensation for their families for the wrongful execution. The campaign had gained interest abroad and the leader of the Left group in the European Parliament, Hervé Emmanuelli, had been successful with a motion to refer the case to the European Court of Human Rights. The campaign had been stonewalled by the political and judicial authorities in the United Kingdom, who had been aggressively supported by the media, notably the *Sun* and the *Daily Mail* who accused Partington of giving aid and comfort to terrorists. But if the case was referred to the highest judicial authority in Europe and, better still, subject to a favourable verdict, the United Kingdom government would be boxed into a corner. To defy the European Court of Human Rights, as many Tory MPs and pro-Government newspapers wanted them to do, would damage the country's reputation internationally and leave it further isolated.

At 5pm, the phone rang. It was Emmanuelli.

"Geri, is that you? Hervé here. I've got some good news."

"Is it about the Ascot Five and the Warrington Three, Hervé?" asked Partington.

"It is. The European Parliament has voted to refer the Ascot Five and Warrington Three cases to the European Court of Human Rights. The hearing's due on 3 September."

"That is brilliant, Hervé" replied Partington. "I can't thank you enough for what you and your colleagues have done."

"A pleasure to help you anytime, Geri" said Emmanuelli. "By the way, how's thing's going over in the Third Reich?"

"Getting very rough, Hervé" said Partington. "The EVF's become active again. I've had a death threat from them. It's real—they murdered Sara Greenfield six weeks ago and you're aware what they did at Benicassim. A lot of people reckon the police and security services are passing information to the EVF. Mo and I have got bodyguards though so hopefully we'll be safe."

"When's the trial of the SNLA and WRA General Councils due to start, Geri?"

"Today, Hervé. Would you believe it? A so-called democracy holding a secret trial without a jury."

After Emmanuelli rang off, Partington dialled in another number. A male voice was on the end of the line.

"Tim Palmer here."

"Hi, Tim, it's Geri. Got some good news. The Ascot Five and the Warrington Three cases are to be referred to the European Court of Human Rights. The hearing takes place on 3 September. Better start preparing now."

19 August 2020
Woolwich Crown Court
Belmarsh Road
Thamesmead, London

A furious Justin Hemingway stormed into the Clerk of the Court's office.

"Mr Fenwick, I want a word with you. Now."

"I'm a busy man, Mr Hemingway" replied Fenwick. "If you don't mind, it's normal courtesy for anyone wishing to see me to make a prior appointment."

"You don't get it, do you?" raged Hemingway. "This court's being run like a kangaroo court in the Deep South or in a military dictatorship. I was prevented from raising a perfectly valid point in defence of my clients."

The previous day, the Department for Justice had signed Public Immunity Interest certificates to cover several key items of prosecution evidence. These included transcripts of telephone intercepts and statements from prosecution witnesses. Hemingway then clashed with the panel of judges when he demanded the right to cross-question MI5 agents. The final straw came that day when Mr Justice Oldham stopped the trial when Hemingway presented as evidence information about the unreliability of some of the prosecution witnesses. The prosecuting counsel, Nicola Sawyer, realising that sensitive information about vulnerable witnesses had fallen into the hands of the defence, mounted an objection, which the panel of judges upheld. Hemingway had been given a reprimand with the threat that a repeat performance of obtaining and using confidential prosecution evidence would result in his disqualification from the trial.

"Mr Hemingway, if you continue to behave in a threatening way, I'll call Court security and have you removed from the premises."

"Haven't you got a conscience, Mr Fenwick?" shouted Hemingway. "Do you realise that those men are on trial for their lives? It is iniquitous that you are prepared to tolerate the withholding of evidence that will result in my clients either going to the gallows or spending the rest of their lives in prison. Is it any wonder that the rest of the world considers this fucking country to be a fascist dictatorship?"

Hemingway's diatribe finally tipped Fenwick over the edge as his anger too boiled over. "You, Mr Hemingway, appear to have forgotten the innocent victims of the bombings and shootings done by those bastards. Like all the other fucking champagne socialists. Remember this. My sister and her husband were killed in the Remembrance Day bombings two years ago. I haven't forgotten and I won't forgive."

At that moment, PC Strange burst into the office, in response to the commotion taking place.

"Anything up, gentlemen?"

"Nothing, officer" replied Fenwick.

Later that day
Hemingway and Partners
Upper Street
Islington
London

Justin Hemingway was still furious at the way he had been treated at Woolwich Crown Court. With him was his assistant, Maxine Joseph.

"Maxine, today you have seen the death of the concept of a fair trial. What's happening is nothing short of a Government-run kangaroo court."

"I know how you feel, Justin" said Joseph. "Reminds me of what happened to my granddad." Joseph was referring to the prosecution of her grandfather, Constantine Joseph, back in 1970 on conspiracy and incitement to riot charges after a police raid on a black-run café in Notting Hill led to a violent demonstration outside the nearby police station.

Hemingway remembered that he needed some important legal documents for another case.

"Maxine, could you go over to Temple tomorrow and collect the documents I need for the Ahmed case. I'll be able to cope at Woolwich, providing they don't suspend me."

"No problems, Justin" said Joseph. "By the way, one of my cousins works over there. A junior barrister. Is it OK if I stay over and have lunch with her?"

"Consider it done, Maxine" replied Hemingway.

20 August 2020
Middle Temple
London

"Is that you, Maxi? Wow! Been years since I last saw you. Come on through."

Dionne McKenzie, a junior barrister working in the bar practice of Lord Stern, was delighted to hear that her cousin was over at the Temple.

Maxine Joseph met her cousin at reception and followed her through to the small office which she shared with another junior barrister.

"Wow, Di, not a very big office for you. There's barely room to swing a cat."

"That's one of the drawbacks of being a junior barrister, Maxi" replied McKenzie. "But when you get to the top, the rewards are great. Have a look at Stern's office—you came past it on the way in."

A tall blonde in her late 20s came into the office. It was Catherine de Burgh, another junior barrister who shared the office with McKenzie. She made no effort to acknowledge Joseph.

"Catherine, this is my cousin, Maxine" said McKenzie. "She's training to be a solicitor."

"Really" said a disinterested de Burgh. "Dionne, I've got a lot of work to do, so I'd be grateful if you wouldn't use the office like the common room."

"Don't worry, Catherine. We're going for lunch now."

Joseph and McKenzie chose the Thai Square restaurant to have lunch. They had a starter of crab cakes with sweet chilli dipping sauce, followed by green chicken curry with steamed jasmine rice and Thai salad.

Having spent the first part of the lunch date catching up with family gossip, the topic of the conversation moved onto their careers.

"So, Di, you're going to be a top brief" said Joseph.

"Hopefully, Maxi" said McKenzie. "It's still difficult to get up the ladder if you're black. Until you start getting cases of your own, the pay's not good."

"What's Stern like to work for, Di?"

"Old Gideon's OK, provided you work hard and don't fuck up" said McKenzie. "He's been like a second dad to me."

"Who's that blonde bird you share an office with?" asked Joseph. "Got the impression she doesn't like us much."

"Catherine de Burgh" replied McKenzie. "Like me, a junior barrister. But went to Cheltenham Ladies College and Cambridge. Probably destined for the top. Yes, she's a right snooty cow as you've found out. But everyone's scared of offending her."

"Any particular reason, Di?" asked Joseph.

McKenzie lowered her voice. "Maxi, can you keep a secret? She's having an affair with a leading judge."

There was a stunned silence for a few seconds. Then Joseph asked "Anyone famous?"

"Yeah" replied McKenzie. "Mr Justice Sellers."

Jesus Christ, thought Joseph. He's one of the judges in the current terrorist trial at Woolwich that Justin's involved with.

21 August 2020
Rydal Water
Robert Street
Camden
London

Miles Chaucer had slept in late when the telephone rang.

"Miles, is that you? Justin Hemingway here."

"Hi, Justin, what can I do for you?"

"Have you heard of Mr Justice Sellers?"

"Yeah, I have. Supposed to be the golden boy of the legal establishment. Tipped as a future Lord Chief Justice. Isn't he on the terror trial at Woolwich at the moment?"

"Absolutely right, Miles" replied Hemingway. "He's one of three judges forming a panel. You know this is the first juryless trial."

Hemingway continued. "I, or rather, one of my staff, has just found out that Sellers is having an affair with a tasty young junior barrister working at the Middle Temple. Reckon you can get some shots of Sellers and his paramour?"

"Shouldn't be too difficult, Justin" replied Chaucer.

For Chaucer, revenge upon the Establishment, whether they were the Government, the judiciary, the police or business leaders, was the driving force which motivated him. A graduate in film and drama from Goldsmiths College four years earlier, Chaucer failed to break into the film or broadcasting industry and was reduced to working as a freelance photographer. A year earlier, he had been arrested on a charge of obstructing the police when covering a demonstration outside the Home Office opposed to the use of anti-terrorist legislation to freeze bank accounts of organisations suspected of receiving funding from the SNLA and the WRA. Chaucer had been doing nothing more than photographing the Territorial Support Group hitting demonstrators with batons when he too had been hit, then arrested. The charges against him were not proved but the Stipendiary Magistrate at Westminster Magistrates Court assumed he had been involved in some capacity with the disorder and gave him a conditional discharge.

Since his court appearance, Chaucer found the conditional discharge a barrier to obtaining employment from the mainstream media. Needing money to live, he turned his attention to the illegal underground economy. He earned commissions for photographing the rich and powerful in compromising situations. And he had a retainer from the website Whistleblower.com which published embarrassing disclosures about Government and corporate abuses of office. Finally, Chaucer made a sizeable amount of money from making pornographic films which was one of the main revenue raisers for both organised crime and terrorist and extremist organisations.

To Chaucer, Sellers was a smug, rich embodiment of the Establishment who needed to be brought down a rung or two. He had no regrets about the task he had agreed to take on.

24 August 2020
Middle Temple
London

Mr Justice Sellers had taken advantage of a break in the *R v Paterson, Rees and others* trial to catch up with some paperwork at his chambers when the phone rang. It was Catherine de Burgh.

"Hi Robert, it's Kate here. Fancy a spot of lunch?"

"Sorry, darling, I'm a bit busy" replied Sellers. "Only chance to catch up on paperwork because of that blasted trial."

"Oh go on, Robert." De Burgh was persistent. "I haven't seen you much over the past month. Let's go to the Old Bank."

"Okay, Kate. You win. Sounds like a good idea though. See you outside in a minute."

As Sellers left his chambers, he met his younger lover. The couple embraced and kissed. They had been in a relationship for the past three months and, so far, Sellers had managed to keep the affair hidden from his wife. There was the usual gossip going across the Inner and Middle Temple. But that was as far as it went. As one of the most senior High Court judges in the country, Sellers wielded a lot of power and influence. Junior staff depended upon the goodwill of senior judges and barristers for their career and an indiscreet word could jeopardise it.

As they walked up Middle Temple towards Fleet Street, neither Sellers nor de Burgh noticed a green Peugeot 311 parked halfway along. Nor did they pay any attention to the fact that the driver had on him a long-lens camera. Miles Chaucer had been snapping away since Sellers and de Burgh had met outside his chambers and had got several incriminating photographs of his target.

A few minutes later
Hemingway and Partners
Upper Street
Islington
London

"Justin, it's for you" said Maxine Joseph. "Miles Chaucer."

"Thanks Maxine." Hemingway took the phone.

"Miles, how did it go?"

"Absolutely brilliant, Justin" said Chaucer. "Got ten snaps of Sellers and his lover. Won't look good before the Lord Chief Justice, or in the papers."

"Miles, I don't want them to go there" said Hemingway. "All that will do is result in Sellers being taken off the case and replaced with another judge. Remember, we want to force him to return a favourable verdict. Can you send the photos in. I know who to use to put pressure on Sellers."

"Look, Justin, I went to a lot of trouble to get those photos" said Chaucer. I was expecting to make some money from this."

"Miles, you will get paid. And paid well."

25 August 2020
Middle Temple
London

Mr Justice Sellers had called into his chambers to pick up some legal papers before heading of for Woolwich Crown Court. He found a message for him to phone a Mr Cookson urgently. Sellers was slightly bemused as he did not know of any Mr Cookson.

He rang the number which, because of its five figure prefix, he knew was a mobile phone.

"371618."

"Is that Mr Cookson? Robert Sellers here."

"Hello, Sir Robert. I've been waiting to hear from you." The speaker had a Cockney accent.

"How can I help you, Mr Cookson?"

"Sir Robert, does Catherine de Burgh mean anything to you?"

Sellers suddenly went pale.

"My God, has anything happened to her?"

The speaker on the phone continued.

"No, Sir Robert. Ms de Burgh is fine and well. However, it appears you and her have been having a little relationship."

Sellers was by now looking flushed.

"I don't know who the hell you are, Mr Cookson. But it's none of your bloody business. Get off this phone at once!"

"You don't understand, Sir Robert. We've got photographs of you and Ms de Burgh in, dare I say it, a rather intimate embrace. I don't think that Lady Sarah would be too happy if she found out." The caller was referring to Sellers' wife of twenty years.

"Nor do I think the Lord Chief Justice or the Attorney-General would be too happy. One of the leading justices in the land showing gross moral turpitude by snogging a pretty young junior barrister."

"If you think you can blackmail me, Mr Cookson, you've got another think coming" shouted Sellers. Don't forget, I can trace your call. And I'll then go to the police. They'll come down on you so fast, sonny, that your feet won't touch the ground."

"I don't think so, Sir Robert" replied the caller. The phone I'm using was stolen in a street robbery a week ago. The owner thinks he's had it disconnected, but I've had it reprogrammed. You go to the police and the poor sod who owned that phone in the first place will get a battalion of London's finest on his doorstep. Not me. Let's face it, Sir Robert, you're over a barrel over this."

Sellers by now was close to panicking.

"What do you want from me, Mr Cookson? Maybe we can come to a deal."

"What I want, Sir Robert, is the following. You, along with Sir Stephen Oldham and Sir Dennis Carrington are judges in the trial of Doug Paterson, Trevor Rees and eight others at Woolwich Crown Court. If you return a 'not guilty' verdict in that trial, I will guarantee that all evidence of your relationship with Ms de Burgh will be destroyed."

27 August 2020
Rydal Water
Robert Street
Camden
London

"Miles, is that you? Anneli here. Got something that might interest you."

Miles Chaucer recognised the voice of Anneli Beckford and let her in.

Beckford was a prostitute who worked the streets of Camden Town. The daughter of a Jamaican father and Irish mother, she had left home at fifteen and had worked the streets for half her life. She had supplemented her work with some income from pornographic films, which is how she had met Chaucer.

"Hi, Anneli, come in. What have you got?"

"Have a look at this, Miles."

Chaucer found himself looking at a classified report from the Metropolitan Police's Child Protection Squad on Operation Pan, a massive investigation into child pornography.

"How did you get hold of this, Anneli?" asked Chaucer.

"A punter left it behind by mistake" said Beckford. "Must have been a copper."

Chaucer looked through the annexes. It listed the names and addresses of subscribers to child pornography websites. There were apparently respectable people listed, business executives, solicitors, police officers, civil servants.

Beckford may have been a prostitute but she had two children of her own and thoroughly loathed anyone involved in child pornography. "Miles, can you do anything to bring this to public notice? People who abuse kiddies are the lowest of the low. Worse than scum. They should all be fucking hanged."

"I'll have a go, Anneli. There seems to be several establishment figures named. No good returning this to the police—they were probably going to make an example of the small fry and leave Establishment figures alone. They've done it before. I think Whistleblower will be interested. By the way, how much do you want for this?"

"A grand" replied Beckford.

"Consider it done, Anneli" said Chaucer.

After Beckford had gone, Chaucer sat down to run through the report. He saw the list of well-placed figures, pillars of the community who would be ruined when Whistleblower ran the leaked story on Operation Pan.

There was a name in the report which looked vaguely familiar. Chaucer went back to the Annex to confirm his suspicions. He saw it. Sir Dennis Carrington, Nether Lypiatt, Hampshire. He checked with 'Who's Who' and his suspicions were confirmed. That's the High Court judge. Mr Justice Carrington. Who's currently officiating in *R v Paterson, Rees and others* at Woolwich Crown Court.

Chaucer picked up the telephone.

"Hello, Justin Hemingway here."

"Justin, you're not going to believe your luck. Listen to this."

2 September 2020
Woolwich Crown Court
Belmarsh Road
Thamesmead
London

"Will the Court please rise." The voice of Raymond Fenwick, the Clerk to the Court announced that the Court would adjourn while the judges considered their verdict.

Armed police officers escorted the ten defendants to the holding cells while Nicola Sawyer, the Prosecuting Counsel and Justin Hemingway, the Defence Counsel, returned to their respective waiting rooms.

Inside the judges' chambers, the three trial judges who would deliver both the verdict and the sentence began to evaluate the evidence presented.

The Chairman of the panel, Mr Justice Oldham, was convinced of the defendants' guilt. However, his colleagues, Mr Justice Carrington and Mr Justice Sellers, seemed less convinced. This surprised Oldham who regarded his judicial colleagues as men who took a robust view towards law-breakers and looked kindly on the forces of law and order.

"I didn't think the prosecution made a very good case" said Carrington. "They relied too heavily on circumstantial evidence, phone taps and testimonies of frankly unreliable witnesses. There was nothing that gave concrete evidence that any of the defendants planned or carried out acts of terror."

"I'm inclined to agree, Dennis" added Sellers. "Yes, those men are all members of the SNLA and WRA. But the prosecution appeared to assume that, because there was no jury, there would be an automatic conviction, and they failed to do their homework properly. The use of PII was cack-handed and withholding evidence was hardly a clever move. Suggests they rather than the defence have something to hide."

Oldham was aghast at the apparent soft-headedness of his judicial colleagues.

"Dennis, Robert, what the hell's come over you? Those men are as guilty as hell. They were all on the SNLA and WRA General Councils and it was those Councils which ordered and planned all the bombings and shootings over the past five years. Remember that the Attorney-General commended us to ensure that the SNLA and WRA were brought to justice."

"I'm sorry, Stephen" said Sellers. "You appear to have forgotten what our role is. We're here as judges for the Crown, not employees of the Government. Our job is to make an objective analysis of the evidence, arrive at a verdict and pass sentence. Not deliver the verdict the Government wants."

Carrington then added his view to the argument. "Stephen, if we find the defendants guilty, I can assure you that Robert and I will join you in pressing for the severest penalty. But, before doing so, we have to remember that those men are innocent until proven guilty. We all know what an obnoxious sod Hemingway is. But he may have a point. Unless we can satisfy ourselves beyond reasonable doubt that the defendants were involved in terrorist activity and there is reliable evidence to support this, we cannot pass a verdict just because the Government or public opinion expects it."

3 September 2020
European Court of Human Rights
Strasbourg
France

The 17 members of the Grand Chamber had spent the best part of a week considering the evidence in the case brought by Fair Trials UK and supported by Labour MP Geraldine Partington on what it considered to be the wrongful conviction and execution of Robert Allan, Kevin Banahan, Carol Davies, James Eadie, Glen McFarlane, Glyn Maddock, Rory Shepherd and Martyn Thomas three years earlier for their part in terrorist bombings at Royal Ascot and the Royal Mercian Regiment barracks at Warrington.

There had been no co-operation in the proceedings from the British Government, who considered the case to be politically-motivated meddling in their sovereign affairs. Requests by the court for judicial documents had been refused by the Department for Justice in the United Kingdom.

Shortly after 11am, the members of the Grand Chamber, headed by the President of the Court, Rafael Santana, filed into the main courtroom.

Santana, a Spanish judge from Badajoz, had been a thorn in the side of the British authorities for several years since being elected as President of the Court in 2010. His twelve-year term was due to end in 2022. He was ready to speak.

"Ladies and gentlemen, the European Court of Human Rights is ready to deliver its verdict in the case of *Fair Trials UK v the Government of the United Kingdom of Great Britain and Northern Ireland.*"

"Over the past week, we have considered evidence submitted by Fair Trials UK. It was very disappointing that the Government of the United Kingdom of Great Britain and Northern Ireland has refused to participate, bearing in mind that they are members of the Council of Europe."

"We firstly examined the evidence produced by the prosecution in the cases of *R v Allan, Banahan, Eadie, McFarlane and Shepherd* at Reading Crown Court and *R v Davies, Maddock and Thomas* at Warrington Crown Court, both in 2017. The evidence to link the subjects with the terrorist acts at Thelwall Barracks on 15 June 2016 and at Ascot racecourse on 16 June 2016 was based heavily on circumstance. It was claimed that the subjects were in possession of pro-independence literature, an act which was not an offence under the law of the United Kingdom. It was claimed that the subjects were sympathetic to the SNLA and the WRA, but it was based on statements given to security services agents by unreliable witnesses. The Court takes the view that insufficient rigour was given to gathering evidence."

"We next examined the process of questioning the subjects by Cheshire Constabulary and Thames Valley Police. There was categoric evidence that police officers involved in the investigations assaulted the subjects and made threats in order to secure confessions. There was also evidence that police officers altered the evidence in their notebooks. In both cases, this contravened the United Kingdom's Police and Criminal Evidence Act 1984."

"We then reviewed the conduct of the trials which took place at Reading Crown Court between 8 May 2017 and 21 July 2017 and at Warrington Crown Court between 15 May 2017 and 21 July 2017. Our expectation is that there should be a balanced hearing of evidence, that neither side should be allowed to withhold evidence and that the prosecution and defence should be allowed equal opportunity to question witnesses. We were not satisfied that, in either trial, the defence were permitted to question prosecution witnesses to the extent to which the prosecution were allowed to with the subjects or defence witnesses. In both trials, there was evidence that defence solicitors were threatened with disqualification for breach of rules of court when there was nothing to suggest that judicial rules had been breached."

"Finally, we reviewed the handling by the United Kingdom Department for Justice of the subjects' appeals against the death sentences imposed by the courts between 29 September and 27 October 2017. Evidence submitted by a former official at the Department for Justice, Ms Samantha Honeyman, has proved that the Attorney-General of the United Kingdom failed to follow Departmental guidelines in arriving at his decision to overturn the recommendation made by his officials."

"To summarise, we consider that the whole process under which Robert Allan, Kevin Banahan, Carol Davies, James Eadie, Glen McFarlane, Glyn Maddock, Rory Shepherd and Martyn Thomas were investigated, questioned, tried and punished under United Kingdom law failed to meet the standards expected of a member of the Council of Europe. The United Kingdom government allowed there to be interference with the judicial process in order to secure a favourable verdict. Because of verdicts passed and the sentences of death carried out, none of the subjects are able to be here today."

"We therefore find in favour of the case brought by Fair Trials UK and direct that the United Kingdom government should pardon the eight named subjects and offer compensation to their next of kin."

Later that day
Woolwich Crown Court
Belmarsh Road
Thamesmead
London

"Will the court please rise." Clerk to the Court, Raymond Fenwick's call meant that the panel of judges were about to deliver their decision.

Mr Justice Oldham, followed by Mr Justice Carrington and Mr Justice Sellers, took their place. The tension in the court was so high that it could be cut with a knife. The eight defendants knew that the next few minutes could decide whether they would be facing the rest of their lives in jail. Or worse.

Oldham indicated that he was ready to speak.

"Ladies and gentlemen, I along with my learned colleagues, have considered the evidence presented by both the prosecution and the defence and through the cross-examination of witnesses from both sides."

"That all the defendants are the members of proscribed organisations involved in acts of violence designed to separate Scotland and Wales from the United Kingdom cannot be denied. Indeed, all the defendants have pleaded guilty to membership of the Scottish National Liberation Army or the Welsh Republican Army. But, in order to be guilty of the first charge against them, we need to be satisfied beyond reasonable doubt that the defendants have engaged in action which has caused the loss or endangerment of life, involved serious violence against a person, serious damage to property and interference or disruption to electronic systems for the purpose of advancing a political cause, as defined under Section 1 of the Terrorism Act 2012."

"There is no doubt that the prosecution have been most thorough in their investigation and presentation of evidence. Similarly, the defence have been equally thorough in their collation and presentation of evidence in favour of their clients."

Superintendent Russell Colbourne of the National Anti-Terror Squad and the lead prosecuting counsel, Nicola Sawyer, looked askance at each other. It didn't sound like the real Justice Oldham, the fearsome hard-liner who was the scourge of criminals and terrorists and of smug defence briefs.

"However, I and my fellow learned colleagues, were not wholly convinced that the evidence submitted by the prosecution proves the guilt of the defendants on charges under Section 1 of the Terrorism Act 2012. There is strong reason to believe that the defendants have been involved in offences under the aforesaid act. But without undisputed proof, I and my learned colleagues are unable to conclude that the defendants before you have been guilty of the aforesaid offences beyond reasonable doubt."

"Robert Daniel Ahern, Gethin Emlyn Davies, Gareth Dafydd Evans, Michael Francis Grogan, Iain Baird Murray, Douglas Robert Paterson, Mark Podborski, Trevor Owen Rees, Gordon Iain Ross and Richard Barrie Thomas, we therefore find you not guilty of the charge of having engaged in action which caused the loss or endangerment of life, involved serious violence against a person, serious damage to property and interference or disruption to electronic systems for the purpose of advancing a political cause, all of which are defined as offences under Section 1 of the Terrorism Act 2012."

Shocked gasps went across the court as the decision was announced. Oldham continued.

"Robert Daniel Ahern, Gethin Emlyn Davies, Gareth Dafydd Evans, Michael Francis Grogan, Iain Baird Murray, Douglas Robert Paterson, Mark Podborski, Trevor Owen Rees, Gordon Iain Ross and Richard Barrie Thomas, you have already pleaded guilty to the charge that you held membership of a proscribed organisation. This Court takes a serious view of anyone who holds membership of an organisation which seeks to bring about political goals by violent means and causes death and injury to persons unconnected and damage to property. However, this Court acknowledges that you pleaded guilty to this charge and have not sought to waste the Court's time."

"The maximum penalty we can impose for membership of a proscribed organisation is five years imprisonment. However, in deciding an appropriate sentence, we have had regard to judges rules. We have therefore had regard to your plea of guilty and the fact that none of you have appeared before the courts before on terror-related charges. We are therefore sentencing you to six months imprisonment each. As you have served this time in custody on remand, we have no choice but to release you from this Court."

That evening
Sky News

"This is Scott Parfitt with this evening's headlines on Sky News."

"The Government suffered two major setbacks in the courts today. Firstly, ten leading members of the SNLA and the WRA walked free from Woolwich Crown Court after being found not guilty of charges under the Terrorism Act. The shock of this verdict has been compounded by the fact this was the first trial held under new legal provisions where there was no jury."

"The second setback was a judgement in the European Court of Human Rights which ruled that the Ascot Five and the Warrington Three, all of whom were hanged for terrorist murders three years ago, had been subjected to a miscarriage of justice. The Court also called upon the Government to exonerate all eight defendants and to pay compensation to their next of kin."

CHAPTER 25

8 September 2020
Cabinet Room
10 Downing Street
London

"Prime Minister, I've got no idea whatever possessed Oldham, Carrington and Sellers to clear the SNLA and WRA leadership of the terrorism charges" said Attorney-General Dominic Collins. "I asked for them to be chosen as the panel of judges as I thought they could be trusted to deliver a favourable verdict."

"But they didn't, Dominic" replied Robert Delgado. "Instead, they've made the United Kingdom a laughing stock. I hope you're going to take appropriate action."

"I can assure you of that" replied Collins. "Neither Oldham, Carrington or Sellers will ever again be given a high profile criminal case."

"On top of that" added the Prime Minister, "there was the judgement of the European Court of Human Rights. Bloody impertinent, sticking their nose in our domestic affairs. Henry, I trust you will take a robust line."

"Absolutely, Prime Minister" replied Foreign Secretary Henry Arbuthnot. "I will advise the ECHR that their judgement has no standing under UK law and we will not be either reviewing the case nor giving the relatives of the Ascot Five and the Warrington Three a penny. They were terrorists rightly convicted of murder."

"How do you think the Council of Europe will react, Henry?" asked Home Secretary Deborah Pearson.

"They will probably suspend us" replied Arbuthnot. "This may be an opportunity to leave."

Delgado noticed that the Secretary of State for Trade and Enterprise, Darren Bramble, was missing.

"Where's Darren?"

"He's got a meeting with the Chief Executives of the utility companies" said Pearson. "The meeting arose at short notice. It appears that the SNLA and WRA have been reconnecting gas, electricity and water to people who've been cut off for non-payment and threatening company employees. It's paid off as it's made them popular with locals in many of the more deprived areas and has boosted their recruitment and intelligence against the troops and the police. Not surprisingly, the utility companies are pissed off at this racket."

"As are many English voters, judging by yesterday's *Daily Mail*" said Chief Secretary to the Treasury, Mark Taylor.

There was a knock at the door. It was the Prime Minister's Assistant Private Secretary, Emma Robinson.

"Prime Minister, the Secretary of State for Trade and Enterprise has arrived."

"Thanks, Emma" replied Delgado. "Darren, what the hell delayed you? You know there was a Cabinet meeting on."

"Sorry Prime Minister" said Bramble. "The meeting with the utility chiefs went on longer than planned. I left a message for you yesterday."

Bramble continued. "The SNLA and WRA have been illegally reconnecting households which have been disconnected for non-payment. They've also been . . . ."

"We know, Darren" said the Prime Minister. "Deborah told us."

"Prime Minister, you ought to know that the utility companies are threatening to get heavy. They've given us an ultimatum that if the army and police don't put a stop to the organised theft of their electricity, gas and water within the next month, they're threatening to bring in private security."

"Darren, thought you should know that me and Debbie are meeting Frank Hesford this afternoon to discuss the security situation in Scotland and Wales" said the Secretary of State for Defence, Jason Steer. "If I remember rightly, you carried out a study into the possible use of private security as police auxiliaries when you were a Home Office Minister."

"That's right, Jason. I recall we dropped the idea because of accountability issues and potential opposition from the police."

"We're ready to consider it again" said Steer. "How about coming along?"

Later that afternoon
Home Office
Marsham Street
London

The Ministerial Conference Room on the third floor of the Home Office was once again in use. At the head of the table was seated Deborah Pearson, while Cabinet colleagues Darren Bramble and Jason Steer sat down the left hand side. Also present were the Home Office Ministers of State, Luke Outram, responsible for policing and Baroness Hornby, responsible for homeland security, the MI5 Director-General, Dame Nicola Martin, the Chairman of ACPO, Sir Roy Plummer, the Head of the Joint Chiefs of Staff for the Armed Forces, Sir Mike Woodcock the Head of the National Anti-Terror Squad, Kevin Lazenby, the Home Office's Permanent Secretary, Sir Richard Benson, the Home Secretary's Chief Political Adviser, Ben Staines and the Prime Minister's Security Adviser, Frank Hesford.

"Thank you for attending at such short notice" said Pearson. "I've called this meeting to discuss the situation in Scotland and Wales and the need to reconsider our tactics. You will all be aware that the SNLA and WRA have enjoyed a revival in their fortunes during the year. I do not have to explain the roll call of horrendous atrocities they've carried out. What is more worrying is the economic war the SNLA and WRA, and their political wings, Clann na h-Albann and Meibion Cymru, are waging against the United Kingdom."

"The SNLA and WRA are increasingly targeting business and commerce. Back in May, the SNLA crippled the Stock Exchange with a cyber attack. Both organisations have targeted businesses providing outsourced services for the armed forces and the police in Scotland and Wales. Clann na h-Albann and Meibion Cymru have organised an overseas trade and tourism boycott of the United Kingdom which is hitting our trade—isn't that right, Darren?"

"I'm afraid so, Deborah" replied Bramble.

"Most recently, the SNLA and WRA have been reconnecting households which have had their electricity, gas and water cut off for non-payment and have threatened utility company staff trying to carry out their duty. This act of organised theft is costing both the utility companies and the law-abiding public who have to pay higher charges in order to cover the losses."

"Last week's judgement at Woolwich Crown Court was the last thing we wanted to hear. Ten of the country's most dangerous men are now free to wage war against law-abiding Britain. Ladies and gentlemen, we now have to consider what to do to regain the initiative in our fight to defeat the men and women of terror and to protect the law-abiding people of this country."

"Firstly, we cannot but pay tribute to the wonderful work done by the armed forces and the police under most difficult circumstances and in the face of repeated criticism of the less patriotic members of Opposition parties." Pearson motioned to Plummer and Woodcock. "However, despite the provision of record levels of funding for policing and national security, they have not been able to contain the men and women of terror. This is no criticism of our troops and police officers, but a reflection of the scale of the task they face."

"Three years ago, the Home Office commissioned a study on the scope for the private security industry to provide an auxiliary presence to supplement the police and the armed forces in fighting terrorism. The Secretary of State for Trade and Enterprise, who is present today, was then one of my Ministers and reported on this study. At the time, we rejected the idea of using the private security industry to supplement the armed forces and the police because of concerns about accountability. But recent events have led us to reconsider the idea."

The faces of ACPO Chairman Plummer and NATS Chief Lazenby darkened.

"Home Secretary, neither ACPO nor most serving officers consider the idea of private security carrying out police functions to be a sensible idea in any circumstances" said Plummer. "If you're short of numbers, how about calling on the police reserve?"

"From an Army point of view, I too have my doubts" said Woodcock. "We always lose a lot of our guys to the private security industry because of the pay they can offer."

"Roy, Mike, I can assure you that, if we use the private security industry, they would be under police or military command and subject to police or military discipline" replied Pearson.

The Home Secretary then handed over to Hesford.

"Although we've done a good containing job, we haven't netted too many SNLA or WRA terrorists. We need to change our tactics and become the aggressor and go looking for the bad guys and, when we find them, pull them in. We need to put an immediate stop to the nonsense they are perpetrating in stealing electricity, gas and water and send a message to the local people that if they commit crime, they will be punished. Also, we shouldn't be confined to our borders. We should be ready to pursue the SNLA and WRA and their supporters overseas."

Pearson then resumed.

"Something I've learned from the United States is that they offer bounties for the capture of fugitive offenders. It has brought to justice several criminals and terrorists who otherwise would escape justice. We're getting no help from other countries. If we do this, other Governments will be unable to point the blame at us for infringing their territorial rights."

"We also need to target the supporters and sympathisers who give them aid and comfort. We're at war with the SNLA and the WRA and anyone who helps them should be regarded as a traitor. Kevin did a report in which he highlighted the difficulties in bringing such people to justice. The damage they can do to this country's interests is considerable—look what Geraldine Partington managed to pull off last week. If necessary, carry out dirty tricks. Nicola, MI5 could help with discrediting a few of the irritants who make our job so much harder, can't you?"

"Indeed we can, Home Secretary" replied Martin. "We've got records on a lot of the left-wing Labour MPs and so-called human rights activists going back into the 1980s. All we need to do is to get a friendly media source to leak a story, particularly if sex or drugs is involved. Or links with enemy regimes."

After the majority of the meeting attendees, there were just four left. Pearson and Steer were joined by Woodcock and Hesford.

"Home Secretary, the reason I waited for the others to leave was because of the sensitivity of what I am going to suggest" said Hesford.

"What is that, Frank?" asked the Home Secretary.

"We're not going to get a lot of the SNLA or WRA big shots to trial. But the country has a resource which we should consider using. The EVF."

"In what capacity, Frank?" asked Steer.

"The way I see it, the armed forces, the police, MI5 all know who the bad guys are. Trouble is, it's a waste of time trying to bring them to account. But if we were to tip off the EVF and let them do the rest. We did it in Northern Ireland back in the 1980s."

"There's a big risk with this approach, Frank" said Pearson. "If we get found out, we could lose our last friends we've got abroad. But otherwise, I like it. Give it a go."

9 September 2020
MI5 Headquarters
Millbank
London

"Have you got a minute, James?" Claire Armitage, head of Section F2 was at the entrance door to the office of MI5's Deputy Director-General, James Furnival.

"Is it important, Claire?" asked Furnival.

"It is."

Armitage, an attractive blonde in her mid-30s, was a high flyer, the daughter of a leading corporate lawyer who had attended Roedean and Somerville College at Oxford University. She was tipped to be future leadership material.

"James, my field team has found some interesting information about Geraldine Partington. Have a look."

Furnival picked up the material. There were several photographs of a younger Partington, taken during her days as a student a quarter of a century earlier. Three photographs particularly caught Furnival's attention. The first showed Partington rolling what looked like white crystals into a Rizla paper, the second and third pictures showed her smoking them.

"So Partington was a druggie during her student days" said Furnival.

"More than just being a "druggie", James. That's crack cocaine she was smoking."

Furnival then looked at the remaining sheaf of photographs.

"Jesus Christ, Claire. Partington, not only a crack user but friends with a nefarious bunch of people. That's Luis Alcazar" said Furnival, pointing to a swarthy man of South American appearance. "Colombian. Deported from the United Kingdom in 1996 as an undesirable. Last I heard a leading light in FARC and reckoned to be the lynchpin behind the cocaine trade."

Furnival continued to browse through the photographs. "Looks like Partington was the squeeze of several of the world's most wanted terror chieftains. Abu Jibril of Hamas and Khaled el-Nasri of Hezbollah."

Jibril was now a member of Hamas's Ruling Council for the Palestinian Authority and el-Nasri was a leading figure in the Hezbollah-run authority in Southern Lebanon.

"What do you want me do now, James?" asked Armitage. "Go to the papers? I take it the usual. The *Sun*, *Daily Mail* and *Daily Express*?"

"Not yet, Claire" replied Furnival. "The DG would like to have a look. So would the Home Secretary. But, once they're in the loop, then full speed ahead."

"Do you reckon they'll have much of an impact?" asked Armitage.

"They will, Claire" replied Furnival. "Partington's been a thorn in the side of the Government and has used the power and influence that goes with being an MP to advance the SNLA and WRA cause through her support for the Ascot Five and Warrington Three campaign. Once the story that she was a crack user and terrorist's moll breaks in the papers, she'll be toast. Labour will be under pressure to drop her as the next General Election draws closer."

10 September 2020
Rydal Water
Robert Street
Camden
London

"That's Chaucer's address" said Detective Inspector Aaron Franks of the National Anti-Terror Squad. "Dougal, Ryan, ready to go in."

Detective Constable Dougal Pearce was a big man, at six foot six inches tall and over eighteen stones, built like a rugby second row forward. A thunderous kick from DC Pearce loosened the door and fellow Detective Constable Ryan Smart followed up with a jemmy to force the door off its hinges.

Miles Chaucer was rudely awoken to find five large and menacing-looking men standing over him. He was roughly gabbed by DC Pearce and Detective Sergeant Dave Austin. A vicious punch to the solar plexus from DI Franks winded him.

As Chaucer recovered his breath, he shouted "What do you guys want with me?"

DI Franks snarled "We're the police, sonny. Hear you've been blackmailing High Court judges. Get your clothes on—you're nicked."

Later that morning
National Anti-Terror Squad Headquarters
Nine Elms Lane
Battersea
London

The headquarters of the National Anti-Terror Squad had been opened by the Prince of Wales two years earlier. A state-of-the-art building, built on a brownfield site close to the old Battersea Power Station, it had enabled the squad, set up four years earlier, to transfer out of the now outmoded Paddington Green Police Station. It was equipped with holding cells, interview suites and computer access to the National Crime Agency and MI5.

In Interview Room 2, a frightened Miles Chaucer was being interviewed by Detective Inspector Aaron Franks and Detective Inspector Emma Pascoe. They were using the well tried "hard cop and soft cop" technique to try and break Chaucer.

"You, Mr Chaucer, are in deep shit" said DI Franks. Although dwarfed by the hulking DC Dougal Pearce, Franks was a big man himself at six foot two inches tall. "We've got evidence from scans of e-mails and telephone records that you were in contact with a certain "Mr Cookson". Better known as Massoud Berishian, Iranian, born 29 December 1989, criminal record for theft, fraud, assault and demanding money with menaces."

"We've got Berishian in custody, Mr Chaucer. He's admitted to blackmailing Mr Justice Carrington and Mr Justice Sellers. We've also found the e-mail of the photos you sent to Berishian. On top of that, we've traced your DNA on the Operation Pan papers you sent to Berishian."

Franks seized the photographer by the lapels of his jacket. "Listen, you little cunt. You were set up to do this by Hemingway and by the SNLA and WRA. To get their top oppos let off. If you don't sign that fucking statement saying you were involved in blackmailing high court judges, I'll personally see you get charged under the Terrorism Act and go before a juryless court. You're talking about going down for twenty years. You'll be an old man by the time you come out. And by then, the photography business will have changed. There'll be no needs for the likes of you."

DI Franks brought his knee up sharply into Chaucer's groin. Chaucer fell to the ground, writhing in agony.

Once Chaucer had recovered, the interview continued. DI Pascoe took over.

"Look Mr Chaucer, I imagine you want to get home" said DI Pascoe. "So do I. If you co-operate, there's a good chance that any charges against you might be dropped. Berishian doesn't care about you. He's a chancer who's got his comeuppance. Neither does Hemingway. If you go on trial, they'll lie and see you go down. Why cover up for them, Mr Chaucer?"

"Okay, I'll admit I took the job from Hemingway and I gave the photos of Sellers and the papers on Operation Pan to Berishian" said Chaucer. Now can I go?"

"No" replied DI Franks. There's others involved with this, Mr Chaucer. SNLA and WRA. We want names."

"Honestly, I don't know any SNLA or WRA members at all, let alone involved with this" cried Chaucer.

"Then go and find them" growled DI Franks. "Otherwise, see you in court."

11 September 2020
Lakeside Convention Centre
Chicago

The Democratic Party National Convention was coming to its climax after five days of intense debate. By the end of the day, either Senator Jeremiah Gould of North Carolina or Governor Richard Williams of New York would become the party's candidate for the 2020 US Presidential Election.

The 2020 Democratic primaries had been the longest in history, with recounts taking place in no less than four states. Jeremiah Gould had been the favourite to win the Presidential nomination when the primaries started. He was a conservative Democrat, who had a military background and was regarded as pro-business. But, as the campaign unfolded, Richard Williams became the strongest challenger. Being black, he won a massive vote from the black, Hispanic and Asian delegates in the party, but had fared less well in the South and the West. Until he championed the Scottish and Welsh cause which resulted in him picking up support from Scottish-Americans and Welsh-Americans.

The Republicans had the luxury of sitting back and watching their opponents tear themselves apart. Katherine Whitney was coming to the end of her second term as President and could not stand again, but the Vice-President, Philip Odell, sealed victory as early as March. The Republicans were confident that Odell would win.

Although lacking Whitney's charisma, he was a highly effective administrator and was regarded by many commentators as the most effective Vice-President in US history.

The Democratic candidate the Republicans most feared was Gould because, as a Southerner with past experience of service in the first Gulf War, he would be a threat in the South. Williams, in contrast, was on the Left of the party and, allied to his racial origin, it was considered he would have difficulty in picking up votes from whites in the Bible Belt.

Earlier that week, Williams had been in close discussion with Senate Leader, Brad McAllister and House of Representatives Leader, Graydon Hopkins about his proposed platform. Also present were Bill Fraser, the Chairman of Caledonian Aid and Ben Meredith, the Chairman of Cambrian Aid. McAllister and Hopkins had convinced Williams that support for a political solution to Scotland and Wales would deliver votes from southern whites of Scottish or Welsh origin.

The climax to the Convention was now approaching. Senator Pat Walsh, the Party Chairman, took to the rostrum to announce the results.

"Ladies and gentlemen, I am now ready to announce the outcome of the votes that will decide who will stand for the Democratic Party as their candidate for the Presidential election on 3 November."

"Jeremiah Russell Gould, two thousand and fifteen delegate votes."

Groans went up from Gould's supporters. He had not achieved the 2,208 delegate votes necessary to win the nomination.

"Richard Franklin Williams, two thousand, two hundred and forty nine delegate votes."

A massive cheer from Williams' supporters rippled through the Lakeside Convention Centre.

"I declare that Richard Franklin Williams will be the candidate of the Democratic Party for the 2020 United States Presidential Election."

15 September 2020
Labour Party Headquarters
Victoria Street
London

The weekend had been a nightmare for Geraldine Partington. The previous Sunday, she had received a telephone call from her constituency party secretary, Mo Akbar, warning her there were stories about her in the *News of the World*, the *Mail on Sunday* and the *Sunday Express*. It was not in Partington's nature to read newspapers she considered to be fascist bile; her preferred reading was the *Observer*. But she broke a habit of a lifetime and bought all three papers.

What she saw horrified her. The front page headline of the *News of the World* read **RED GERI IN CRACK SHAME**. The *Mail on Sunday's* read **THE SHAMEFUL PAST OF LABOUR MP**. The *Sunday Express's* read **LABOUR MP WAS CRACK USER**.

Worse was to follow on her return to London on Monday. The headlines were still there in the *Sun*, the *Daily Mail* and the *Daily Express*. Only they had moved onto her past love life. Pictures of Luiz Alcazar, now Deputy Commandant of FARC, Abu Jibril, now on Hamas's Ruling Council and Khaled el-Nasri, effectively in charge of the terrorist state being run in Southern Lebanon, stared out of the newspapers. Her secretary, Sue Maplin, reported there had been a series of abusive phone calls and e-mails received. There was also a call for her to go to Party Headquarters for a meeting with Jane Duffy immediately. Partington feared the worst. She was well aware that Labour had withdrawn the whip from fellow left-wing MP Jeremy Sanderson two years previously after he had invited representatives from Clann na h-Albann and Meibion Cymru into the House of Commons.

"Come in Geraldine." Partington recognised the Liverpudlian tones of the Chief Whip. She entered Duffy's office and sat down on the chair opposite her.

On the table was a pile of newspapers. It was obvious why she had been asked to see Duffy.

"Geraldine, you will have seen the allegations made against you" said Duffy. "The party takes them very seriously. We expect exemplary conduct and rectitude from our representatives, whether in Parliament or at local authority level. I am most disappointed that you did not make these clear when you accepted the nomination to stand for Labour in Parliament."

"Jane, those photographs all date from twenty five years ago" said Partington. "I was a student then. We all did irresponsible things when we were younger—I bet you did. Like a lot of young people at that time, we all experimented in drugs. I can guarantee you that several fellow Labour members did, and Tory members. No one's squeaky clean on this."

"Geraldine, you've missed the point. What you were doing wasn't just having the odd cannabis joint. You were seen taking one of the most dangerous Category A drugs around."

Duffy continued. "The Party is also concerned that you never disclosed the fact you had relationships with terrorists and drug traffickers."

"Jane, I only knew Luiz Alcazar and Abu Jibril as acquaintances. I never went out with them. I'll admit I went out with Khaled, but there's no law preventing you from dating foreign nationals."

"Geraldine, Khaled el-Nasri is no ordinary foreign national. He is a leading light in a ruthless and vicious terrorist organisation which is a sworn enemy of the United Kingdom. Having a former girlfriend of his as one of our MPs hardly gives Middle England the confidence that the Labour Party has its best interests at heart."

"I have spent the past five years trying to make the Labour Party electable again, Geraldine. I recognise what you've done was long in the past and, even if we disagree on policy, I recognise you have been a good constituency MP. But we've got a General Election in just over eighteen months time and we can't afford to have headlines like those in today's papers. This allow the Tories to portray us as a party that can't be trusted to defend the national interest."

"I've got no issue about the fact you used drugs in the past or were in a relationship with a man who is now a wanted terrorist. But your failure to disclose these matters before you applied to become a Labour Party candidate is a disciplinary offence, Geraldine. These are matters which require further investigation by the Party and I am afraid I have no choice but to suspend the Party whip until these investigations have been completed and there has been a satisfactory outcome."

"Jane, get this straight" said Partington. "If you take the party whip away from me, I will stand for re-election in Bradford North as an independent."

"Do that, Geraldine, and I'll personally ensure you'll never stand for Labour ever again."

16 September 2020
Arlington Road
Camden
London

Miles Chaucer was putting the finishing touches to *Francine's Night In*, a pornographic film he had produced, when a tall, blond-haired man walked into the studio. Chaucer recognised him immediately; it was Adam Gilchrist, the Deputy Commander of the SNLA's London Brigade. The penny soon dropped as Chaucer realised who had funded production of the film.

"Good morning, Miles" said Gilchrist. "Is the film ready yet?"

"Nearly, Adam" replied Chaucer. "Should be ready this afternoon."

"When I meant 'ready' I was meaning ready for distribution" said Gilchrist.

"Monday, 28 September" replied Chaucer.

"Not soon enough, Miles" said Gilchrist. "There's an SNLA General Council meeting a week Friday and they want to see what the product looks like. Also, we've got Trevor Rees coming up over that weekend to discuss distribution."

So the WRA are also involved, thought Chaucer.

"Look, Adam, I'll do my best" said Chaucer. "Getting films like this produced in a hurry isn't easy. Finding a supplier who will do a good job and won't shop us to the cops is difficult."

"Miles" said an exasperated Gilchrist, "I want it ready by 25 September without fail. Or we'll be taking our business elsewhere."

Later that day
The Queen Anne
Spring Gardens
Vauxhall
London

Miles Chaucer hated what he was doing. Acting as a copper's snout. He knew full well that if Gilchrist found out, he would be toast. Most likely tortured by the SNLA before getting a bullet in the back of the head. But that was only a possibility. Whereas, the prospect of facing trial for perverting the course of justice was real. DI Franks had said as much a week earlier.

On stage, a stripper was gyrating to loud dance music. The Queen Anne was famous, if not notorious, for its 'adult entertainment' and it was well patronised by members of the National Crime Agency and the National Anti-Terror Squad, both of whom were based nearby.

"Ello, ello, ello, if we haven't got our favourite dirty pics snapper here." Detective Sergeant Dave Austin was wearing a leather jacket, a checked Ben Sherman shirt and Wrangler jeans and had a pint of beer in his right hand. If his hair had been longer, he would not have looked out of place in a remake of the 1970s police drama, *The Sweeney*.

"DS Austin, I've got something that might interest you" said the photographer. "Over there" he said, pointing to a marginally quieter part of the pub.

"Okay, Chaucer, spit it out" said Austin.

"There's going to be a meeting of the SNLA's General Council in Inverness a week tomorrow. I'm working on a film and found out today that the SNLA's funded it and will be collecting profits from its distribution."

DS Austin's eyes lit up. "Good stuff, Miles. Have you got an address for any of the SNLA guys in Inverness?"

"Yes, I have" replied Chaucer. "30 Blackwell Avenue, Culloden, Inverness. A Mr Baillie."

"Thank you for that, Miles. Sounds like an alias for Paterson." Austin was referring to the Chairman of the SNLA's General Council.

"One more interesting fact, DS Austin" said Chaucer. "Trevor Rees will be in Inverness on the Saturday."

"Rees, eh?" replied Austin. "No doubt looking after the Welsh end of the distribution."

"One more thing" asked Chaucer. "Any chance of dropping charges against me?"

"We'll have to see what the guvnor thinks" replied Austin. "And if he's in a good mood."

Later that evening
National Anti-Terror Squad
Victoria Quay
Edinburgh

The National Anti-Terror Squad's headquarters for Scotland was adjacent to the Department for Scotland's extensive offices which had been built some twenty years earlier during the heady days of devolution. High security gates and barbed wire protected it from unwanted visitors.

Detective Inspector Warren Yeo was on duty when his telephone rang. It was fellow DI Aaron Franks ringing from Nine Elms. Franks and Yeo were old mates, having served together during their early days of service in the Territorial Support Group of the Metropolitan Police and subsequently as Detective Sergeants in the Flying Squad.

"Aaron, how are you doing, mate?" asked Yeo. "Haven't heard from you for a while."

"Been busy, Wozza" replied Franks. "The Jocks and Taffs have kept us preoccupied. We're currently investigating a blackmail case against two of the judges from the Special Criminal Court."

"Anything to do with the SNLA or WRA, Aaron?" asked Yeo.

"Dead right, mate. You know their leaders got off terrorism charges earlier that month? We've got a lead on the defence brief. Justin Hemingway."

"Hemingway? Isn't he the guy who got a load of celebrities off charges on technicalities?"

"The same" replied Franks. "Only, it looks like he hired a photographer to take compromising photos and used a local crim to blackmail two of the judges."

"Any chance of Hemingway going down for this, Aaron?"

"If he's found guilty. Now, Wozza, the main reason for my call. A snout has just advised one of my sergeants that the SNLA General Council will be meeting on 25 September. At Doug Paterson's house, 30 Blackwell Avenue, Culloden. Not only that, Trevor Rees will be in town over the weekend. If you want to lift those guys, here's your chance."

"Thanks, Aaron."

Yeo then buzzed Detective Sergeant Michelle Preston.

"Can you come through, Michelle."

Thirty seconds later, Preston was in Yeo's office.

"Michelle, can you set up a squad briefing for nine o'clock tomorrow morning."

"I'll do that now, sir" replied Preston. "Anything important?"

"Yes, Michelle. Looks like we've got SNLA and WRA bigshots in town in just over a week's time."

"Are we planning to pull them in, sir? If we are, we'll need armed backup."

"Michelle, can you keep this to yourself?" asked Yeo. "We're not planning to arrest and charge them. They got off charges at the top court in the land. No, this time, we're aiming to take them out, once and for all. Tomorrow, we've got two guys from the EVF, Tony Buck and Howard Rolfe, coming in to see us. They will do the dirty work for us. Can you notify security that they'll be calling in. Only that they'll be using the names Dougie Bell and Hugh Muir."

18 September 2020
Dunsinane Drive
Letham
Perth
Scotland

Donnie Gillespie had been out of work for over eight years and was now regarded to too sick to work. His wife, Sheena, brought in a little money from a cleaning job but, otherwise, their only income was his incapacity benefit.

Earlier that year, the gas, electricity and water had been disconnected for being in arrears of payment. The local SNLA brigade had heard of the Gillespie's straightened circumstances and arranged for them to be reconnected to these services. Which they had been using free of charge and totally illegally.

The utility companies were reluctant to send their employees onto the Letham estate without protection from the police or Army because of the threats they faced. But the deployment of police auxiliaries provided by Trident Security a week earlier now made it possible for there to be a stronger presence of the forces of law and order in previously lawless areas.

At 7am, a Mercedes Sprinter van in Trident's livery pulled up outside Donnie Gillespie's house. Auxiliary officers Dave Prowse, a Londoner and Tony Spencer, a Yorkshireman, got out and walked up to Gillespie's front door.

"Mr Donald Gillespie, this is the police" shouted Prowse. "Open up."

Thirty seconds later, the door opened. Gillespie, in his mid-50s, a short, thickset and somewhat overweight man, was at the door. He realised that Prowse and Spencer were not regular officers and were English.

"What the fuck do you want, you Sassenach bastards?"

"Mr Gillespie, we have reason to believe that you have been stealing supplies of electricity, gas and water, the property of Scottish Energy and Scottish Water. This is a warrant to search this house."

"If you fucking take one step further, pal, I'll deck yer" shouted Gillespie.

"You obstruct us, sunshine and you're nicked" said Spencer.

Gillespie took a swing at Prowse who blocked the punch.

"Tony, the cuffs. Quick" shouted Prowse.

Spencer pulled out the handcuffs and tried to put them on Gillespie. Overweight and unfit he might have been, but he was struggling with the strength of ten men.

Without warning, Gillespie caught his breath and fell to the floor clutching his chest.

"Oh shit!" said Spencer. "Looks like he's having a heart attack."

19 September 2020
Sky News

"This is Sameera Ahmed with this evening's headlines on Sky News."

"There were further clashes between protestors and the police in Perth today following the death of a local man, Donald Gillespie yesterday while being arrested by auxiliary police officers from Trident Security. Businesses, including Tesco, HSBC, Halfords, Boots and WH Smith were set on fire and officers came under attack from a hail of stones, bricks and petrol bombs. There are unconfirmed reports that gunshots were fired at officers. Thirty eight police officers, including auxiliaries, were treated for injuries and no less than eighty four protestors were arrested."

"The deployment of private security officers from Trident Security to assist the police and army in Scotland has been highly controversial, with several complaints being made about the high-handed behaviour of officers. But the Government is adamant that use of private security staff to support the police is here to stay. Sky News interviewed the Home Office Policing Minister, Luke Outram, this afternoon. This interview will follow the headlines."

"Meanwhile, in Wales, there were angry scenes in Tywyn when officers from another private security company, Black Prince, were called in to evict squatters who had occupied holiday homes owned by absentee landlords. Thirty arrests were made and twenty two protestors and twelve auxiliary police officers were taken to hospital with injuries."

<h3 style="text-align:center">27 September 2020
Caledonian Stadium
Inverness</h3>

Doug Paterson, Trevor Rees and Gordon Ross were in a good mood as they left the Caledonian Stadium after the shinty match between Inverness Highlanders and Fort William Sharks had finished. That weekend, the SNLA General Council had received the master copy of a new pornography film, *Francine's Night In*, which they had funded from the proceeds of drug trafficking. Ross and fellow General Council member, Iain Murray, had sorted out the distribution in Scotland while Rees had agreed to do the same for Wales. Organised crime groups with whom the SNLA and WRA had done business would look after distribution elsewhere.

"Would you laddies care to join me for a wee drink?" asked the Chairman of the SNLA General Council.

"I would, Doug" replied Rees.

"So would I" added Ross.

As they reached the stadium car park, Paterson opened the tailgate of his Vauxhall Insignia and opened a coolbox. Inside were several bottles of Tennant's lager. Paterson withdrew two of them, removed the tops with a bottle opener and passed them to Rees and Ross. He then took out a third bottle which he opened.

"To an independent Scotland and Wales" they toasted.

Neither Paterson, Rees nor Ross noticed another Vauxhall Insignia parked 100 metres away on the other side of the car park. Inside were Tony Buck and Howard Rolfe.

Buck scanned the car park with his binoculars. Most of the spectators at the Caledonian Stadium had already gone home and there were only a few still left. Some, like Paterson, were enjoying post-match refreshments as the sun began to dip towards the western horizon.

"Howie, a hundred metres straight in front of us" said Buck. "Paterson, Rees and Ross, just as the coppers said."

"Start the car up, Tony" said Rolfe as he cradled an AK-47 assault rifle. A former soldier in the Green Howards, he was a crack shot.

Rolfe took aim with the AK-47. The three men were in his sights. It was like being back in Afghanistan fighting the Taliban eight years earlier. Ready, steady, fire.

Paterson took the first shot straight through the heart and fell to the ground, dead. Before either Rees or Ross could react, further shots from Rolfe's AK-47 felled them both. One shot went through Rees's left temple. He too was instantly dead. The last shot went clean through Ross's abdomen. He fell to the ground, blood gushing from where the bullet had gone in.

Buck then hit the accelerator and screamed away at top speed.

28 September 2020
Rydal Water
Robert Street
Camden
London

Miles Chaucer had enjoyed a good weekend. The production work he had done on *Francine's Night In* had been recognised in the sex film industry and he now had the offer of regular work and a good salary. That Saturday, he had been to a party up at Camden Town, which had been attended by two up-and-coming rock bands, the Ginger Toms and The Wrong Kind Of. He had gone back to the flat of a pretty publicist for the bands' record company and had enjoyed a night of great sex. As he didn't have to report in for work, he slept in late.

On getting up, he switched on the radio in his bedroom. Chaucer listened to Radio Clash, a pirate station named after the legendary 1970s punk rock band, and one with similarly spiky views.

It was already coming up to 9am, which was the time of their hourly news bulletins.

"This is Jez Ford on Radio Clash with today's news headlines."

"Two leading members of the SNLA and a leading member of the WRA were shot dead in Inverness last night. Doug Paterson, the Chairman of the SNLA's General Council, Trevor Rees, the Chairman of the WRA's General Council and SNLA General Council member Gordon Ross were gunned down in the car park of the Caledonian Stadium shortly after 6pm. Responsibility for the murders has been claimed by the EVF in a statement which said it was in revenge for the murder of their leader, Phil Barden, earlier this year."

"The car used by the killers, a silver Vauxhall Insignia, was found burnt out near Kinloss some twenty five miles away. Northern Constabulary . . . ."

Chaucer suddenly had a horrible thought. He had told the police that the SNLA would be meeting in Inverness that weekend and that Trevor Rees would be there. Surely they couldn't have tipped off the EVF? But as the horrible enormity of what had happened sank in, Chaucer remembered the words of a local left-wing activist. There was good reason to suspect that the army and the police were tipping off the EVF. And the nobbling of a high profile terrorist trial was an excellent motive for by-passing judicial niceties and resorting to direct action.

The more Chaucer thought about the murders of Paterson, Rees and Ross and the consequences of what had happened, the worse it became. One thing was certain; both the SNLA and the WRA would be on the warpath to avenge the murder of their leaders. And it would not only include those who carried out the act. Both the SNLA and the WRA were ruthless towards anyone who they suspected of betrayal. Victims faced torture and possible mutilation before being shot.

One thing was certain. The SNLA had reason to suspect he had informed on them. Adam Gilchrist had told him about the General Council meeting in Inverness and that Rees would be in Inverness over the weekend.

There was only one thing to do. To get out of the country as quickly as possible. Before the SNLA or WRA caught up with him.

CHAPTER 26

30 September 2020
Ministry of Defence
Whitehall
London

Chris Beal, the Minister of State for the Armed Forces and Baroness Hornby, the Minister of State for Homeland Security were jointly chairing a meeting to discuss the security situation in Scotland and Wales.

Beal invited Lieutenant-General James Lawson, the Commander-in-Chief of "Operation Saltire", the counter-insurgency campaign in Scotland and Lieutenant-General Andrew Wade, the Commander-in-Chief of "Operation Dragon", the equivalent campaign in Wales, to address the meeting on progress.

Lawson was first to speak. Tall with slicked-back dark hair, he looked like the stereotype of an Army officer.

"Thank you, Minister. Firstly, the good news. There is evidence to suggest that the joint efforts between us and the police, which has for the first time involved the use of a private security company, have started to make inroads against the organised theft of corporate property. No less than a thousand arrests have been made and the use of the Proceeds of Crime Act 2014 to confiscate property has sent out a message that breaking the law and aiding and abetting terrorists will be severely punished."

"Now for the bad news. This whole operation has been very costly in terms of damage to life and limb. There is no doubt that the SNLA were behind the riots that took place and they had snipers out. We've lost no less than ten soldiers in the past three weeks, while the police, including auxiliary officers from Trident Security, have also taken severe casualties."

Sir Roy Plummer, the Chairman of ACPO, agreed. Lawson continued.

"Next weekend is going to be a severe challenge because of the funerals of Doug Paterson and Gordon Ross. But I think we can handle it. A potential flashpoint may be the auctions of confiscated goods planned. The SNLA have threatened to disrupt them."

"Thank you, James" said Beal. "Andrew" he said, turning to Colonel Wade.

Wade was a contrast to Lawson, shorter, stockier, with a meaty face. He still had traces of his Birmingham accent.

"The biggest challenge for us has been illegal occupations of English-owned properties. This is clearly being orchestrated by the WRA and the troublemakers have been playing cat and mouse with us, occupying new properties after we've moved in to evict them. There's no problem with manpower from our perspective, but I think that the police are coming under pressure. It's not for the Army to maintain law and order. Roy, can you get any reinforcements?"

"Sorry, Andrew, we're stretched as it is" replied Plummer.

"Any chance of using your reserve?" asked Wade.

"They're all committed" said Plummer.

"Roy, have you considered using further auxiliary officers from Black Prince?" asked Hornby. "From what I've heard, they're doing a good job in Wales."

"Minister, you know ACPO's views on the use of private policing" said Plummer.

"Roy, it's the only option you've got" said Beal. "Leave it and you risk losing control of law and order in Wales."

"Very well, Minister. I will ask Black Prince for reinforcements. I take it there are sufficient funds in the police budget for this."

1 October 2020
near Tullybeg
County Donegal
Republic of Ireland

The SNLA and the WRA were taking no chances with their bilateral meeting. Holding it in the United Kingdom was too risky—the assassination of Doug Paterson, Trevor Rees and Gordon Ross in Inverness the previous Sunday had been proof that the EVF could hit them even on their own turf. So they had arranged to use the rural estate which Sinn Fein owned in County Donegal as the venue for the meeting.

Both organisations had wasted little time in finding replacements for their fallen colleagues. Iain Murray had been elected as the new Chairman of the General Council and Adam Lamont, the interim Chairman while the leadership had been held in custody and Allan Stewart, who had commanded the Glasgow Brigade of the SNLA were elected to the General Council. As for the WRA, they had elected Gareth Evans as Chairman of the General Council and Rob Mathias who, like Lamont, had headed the Council while the regulars had been in custody, earned a seat.

Several new recruits to the SNLA and WRA were staying at Tullybeg and were undergoing training. The General Councils looked on approvingly.

It was Iain Murray who opened the meeting.

"Gentlemen, I am most grateful for you attending at such short notice. Clearly, the loss of Doug, Trevor and Gordon is a major setback for both our organisations. But I feel that the tide of history is flowing in our favour."

Murray continued

"Recruitment is running at record levels and the quality of the recruits is high. We've got former soldiers and policemen, IT experts and bankers joining. International support for our cause is high and if Richard Williams wins the US Presidential Election next month, we will effectively have tacit support for independence from the world's most powerful country. The United Kingdom's economy is suffering from the cost of trying to contain us and there are signs that they are tiring of trying to keep Scotland and Wales in the Union."

"However, there is no time for complacency. The Brits are not good losers. If they look like they are in trouble, they will play dirty. Like colluding with the EVF. I would like to bet you all that the security forces had a hand in the murders of Doug, Trevor and Gordon."

Gareth Evans now took over.

"You will all be aware that the authorities have taken to using private security companies to provide auxiliary police officers for Wales and Scotland. There are two companies involved, Trident Security and Black Prince Security. They have been involved in the recent surge against us, which has involved arresting anyone considered to be helping us. They are using the Proceeds of Crime Act to confiscate property from people."

"This is an opportunity for us to hit back against the authorities. Both the WRA and the SNLA have made it perfectly clear before that any individual or company who gives assistance to the occupying forces in Wales and Scotland is complicit in the oppression of its people and is therefore a legitimate military target. My previous experience of the private security industry is that they will bottle out if they find themselves up against an enemy that means business. We should therefore target immediate operations against Trident and Black Prince. Three years ago, an American security company pulled out of a contract to police the Cardigan oil terminal after we bombed one of their coaches. If we force Trident and Black Prince to pull out, it will leave the authorities short-handed."

"Next, we need to target the confiscation of property. Next week, auctions of confiscated property begin across Wales and Scotland. Demonstrations or disruptions of auctions will not work. The authorities will ensure the police and armed forces protect them. But if we were to place a bomb in the auction rooms, the impact would be devastating. Not only in terms of people killed and injured, but it would frighten people from attending similar auctions, and the cost of running them would outweigh the benefit. Once they become loss-makers, that will close them down."

After the meeting finished, Adam Lamont buttonholed Murray.

"Iain, have you got a minute?" asked Lamont.

"Aye, Adam. Anything troubling you?"

"Yeah. Had a call from Adam Gilchrist. He thinks there's an informer in the ranks."

"Why?"

"Look what happened on Sunday. Under no normal circumstances should the EVF be able to pick off our leaders in our own backyard. The Brits must have tipped them off. And someone must have told them that we would be in town."

"Adam, give Gilchrist a ring and tell him we'll send someone down from Internal Security to help him."

2 October 2020
Stewart Terrace
Gorgie
Edinburgh

Adam Lamont rang Adam Gilchrist on his personal data assistant.

"Hi Adam. Adam Lamont here."

"Thanks for ringing. How did Tullybeg go?"

"Great. Now the reason I'm ringing is to follow up on your call earlier in the week. About a possible mole in the organisation."

"Adam, I think we've found who was responsible" said Gilchrist. "Guy called Miles Chaucer. Photographer and film producer."

"Didn't he produce *Francine's Night In*?"

"Aye. We thought he was on our side. But I had a call to say he'd been seen in a pub nearby the NATS headquarters two weeks ago talking to a guy who looks like a copper. Chaucer knew Doug's home address, that there was going to be a General Council meeting there last weekend and that Trevor would be coming up from Wales. I asked him to send the master of the film there."

"So you reckon it was Chaucer who grassed to the authorities?"

"Can't be anyone else, Adam" replied Gilchrist.

"Whatever you do, Adam, find Chaucer and take him out. You know what our constitution says about dealing with traitors and grasses."

"If I can find him, I will. Chaucer's done a runner and nobody knows where he is."

5 October 2020
A44, Blaenrheidol
west of Pantmawr
Ceredigion
Wales

Two coaches hired from International Coachways were making steady progress along the A44 towards Aberystwyth. On board were 80 security guards from Black Prince Security who were being deployed to West Wales as auxiliary police officers.

To the right, it was just about possible to make out the shape of Plynlimon, the mountain close to the source of the River Severn and the River Wye. However, it was shrouded in low cloud. The mood of the Black Prince employees on board was not helped as it started to rain.

As the coaches crossed the boundary between Powys and Ceredigion, there was a tight bend in the road. Unfortunately, progress was arrested by a broken down lorry which forced the drivers of the coaches to stop.

Steve Platt and Jamie Riddell, the drivers of the two coaches, got out. They walked up to the cab of the lorry and found no one there.

"Where do you think the driver's gone, Steve?" asked Riddell.

"He might be trying to phone for assistance, Jamie" replied Platt. "I know from previous trips that mobile phone reception's crap in the mountains."

"Steve, I reckon we could get the coaches round this rig on the wrong side of the road" said Riddell. "Otherwise, we'll be late in and face having our pay docked."

"I wouldn't try it, Jamie" said Platt. "The guy's broken down on a tight bend. We'll have difficulty in getting round him, and there's traffic coming in the other direction to contend with. I'll radio Aber and tell them what's happened."

Two hundred metres away, further up the mountainside, Gareth David and Emlyn Williams were watching intently. They had stolen the lorry from a lorry park at Telford two days previously. They had also planted by the side of the road, close to a rock face, a bomb which was disguised under PVC sacking.

"We've got them trapped, Gar" said Williams. "Ready to detonate?"

"Ready when you are, butt" replied Davies.

Davies keyed in a preset code into his personal data assistant. A split second later, the roadside bomb exploded, blowing the first coach across the road and blowing in all the windows in the second coach.

6 October 2020
Royal Highland Centre
Ingliston
Edinburgh

The first public auction of goods that had been confiscated under the Proceeds of Crime Act 2014 from people who had either provided material help to the SNLA or had stolen corporate property was due to take place at the Royal Highland Centre, standing in the shadow of Edinburgh Airport. Behind the auctioneer's podium were stored cars, motorcycles, television sets, personal computers, jewellery and other goods that had been seized.

David Wilson, the Chief Auctioneer, had arrived early and had checked that the PA system and overhead projectors were working. Forty years old, Wilson had taken the job in the face of considerable opposition from his family who felt it was unpatriotic for a Scot to participate in an exercise which was nothing more than punishment being inflicted by the English. But the pay was good and Wilson needed the money for a mortgage on his house facing the Pentland Firth.

By 11:30am, the auction was in full swing. Already, he had sold two BMWs, a Porsche, an Audi coupe and a Mercedes. Hi-tech televisions and video equipment had also been big sellers. For many of the people present, it had been an opportunity to buy goods at below the market rate.

Of course, not everyone was happy. The police and armed forces had been briefed to expect violent demonstrations from nationalist sympathisers and people who had goods confiscated. They were under orders to keep the demonstrators away from the entrance to the centre so they could not harass people attending the auction.

"Lot 51, a Mercedes-Benz C300 coupe" called out Margaret Carmichael, Wilson's assistant. A gleaming white nearly-new Mercedes coupe was driven into the arena.

Wilson picked up his microphone. "Can I have any offers for this 2020 Mercedes-Benz C300. Only done 10,000 miles. Leather seats, full air conditioning, Blu-Ray plus media. Capable of 150 miles per hour."

The Mercedes was worth £50,000 on the open market. After the opening bid of £25,000 had been received, steadily higher bids were received. Eventually, a price of £40,000 was accepted from Andrew Smith, a businessman from Penicuik.

"£40,000, going, going, gone" shouted Wilson. "Lot 51, sold for £40,000 to Mr Andrew Smith. Mr Smith, can you come up to collect your car?"

Andrew and Jessica Smith came up to the podium to accept receipt of the Mercedes.

"Mr Smith, would you like to test-drive your purchase?" asked Wilson.

"I would very much" replied Smith. Turning to his wife, he said "Jessica, what do you think?"

"It's lovely, Andrew" replied Mrs Smith.

"Here are the keys" said Wilson, handing the keys on a smart Mercedes-Benz fob over to the Smiths.

Andrew and Jessica Smith got into the Mercedes and Andrew Smith turned the ignition key for the car to fire up. What Wilson, the Smiths or anyone else present knew was that the car had been booby-trapped by the SNLA. In the boot was a suitcase filled with PECT. It was primed to explode when the ignition key was turned.

A split-second later, the Mercedes exploded in a massive ball of flame.

7 October 2020
Café Zwart
Dam 15
Amsterdam

Miles Chaucer was relieved to find a place where he was safe. The café and bar off Dam Square where he ordered an Amstel appeared to be such a place. Everyone spoke English but he was out of the clutches of the National Anti-Terror Squad. And, more importantly, the SNLA who were now after him following the assassination of their leader.

All he now needed was cheap accommodation. His experience with photography and film production should find him work. Only that he couldn't use his real name.

A pretty, blonde Dutch girl asked if she could sit at his table. Chaucer said she could.

"You are English, yes?"

"I am" replied Chaucer. "What is your name?"

"Anna. How about you?"

"Justin. Justin Lake."

8 October 2020
MI6 Headquarters
Vauxhall Cross
London

The phone in Claire Glanville's office rang. On the other end of the line was Simon Leech, an MI6 field officer.

"Claire, I'm sending through some highly sensitive photographs. Can you make sure they're received safely."

"Sounds like you've found something important, Simon" replied Glanville. "Can you tell me what it is?"

"I've just received photographs from a US spy satellite of the Sinn Fein rest and recreation centre at Tullybeg in County Donegal. Rest and recreation my arse. They're training terrorists there and the SNLA and WRA General Councils were passing through last week. And why does a rest and recreation centre require triple-A and SAM missiles?"

Once the photographs had been received, Glanville sat down to examine them and carry out checks against MI6 records.

It was clear from the photos that Tullybeg was more than just a rest and recreation centre for Sinn Fein. The site had defence radars and further inspection revealed that the missiles were Russian-built SA-17s. The most modern available and reckoned to be immune to electronic countermeasures.

As Glanville pored through the photographs that Leech had sent through, she found definite matches to SNLA and WRA terrorists. Not only rank and file but the leadership. There were clear images of Mark Podborski and Richard Thomas.

Glanville knew that the Foreign Secretary's notice needed to be drawn to the photos. She knew that the Republic of Ireland was ruled by a fragile coalition between Fianna Fail and the Green Party and that Sinn Fein held the balance of power. So the Irish government would be reluctant to upset them. But there was clear evidence that Sinn Fein were training SNLA and WRA terrorists on Irish soil.

Glanville began to draft a note to the Director-General, Sir James Beveridge to escalate the matter.

12 October 2020
Foreign & Commonwealth Office
Whitehall
London

Noel Dempsey, the Irish Ambassador, was somewhat puzzled by a request to attend a meeting with the British Foreign Secretary, Henry Arbuthnot. It took less than five seconds for him to find out.

Arbuthnot was known for his candour and directness and was not pleased.

"Ambassador, is your government aware that terrorists plotting to carry out atrocities on British soil are using your country as a training base? Because if they are not, here is the evidence."

Arbuthnot slammed down on the desk eight photographs of Sinn Fein's rest and recreation centre at Tullybeg in County Donegal which had been taken by a spy satellite. He continued.

"That, Ambassador, is a so-called 'rest and recreation centre' owned by Sinn Fein in County Donegal. The only rest and recreation appears to be paramilitary training of SNLA and WRA terrorists. Have a look."

Dempsey thumbed through the photographs.

"Foreign Secretary, how certain are you that those photographs are of the Sinn Fein property in whatever it's called? And how certain are you that those men and women are Scottish or Welsh rather than Irish? And that they're not doing nothing more harmful than a spot of clay pigeon shooting or paintballing?"

Anger was steadily rising in the Foreign Secretary.

"Ambassador, for the record, we obtained those photographs through the CIA. That is Tullybeg and our secret intelligence services have identified it as owned by Sinn Fein. And what's more, we've managed to obtain positive identification of wanted SNLA and WRA terrorists. Look at this one."

Dempsey looked at a photograph in which two men and a woman had been circled.

"Mark Adams and Graeme Muir, both SNLA, wanted for murder and causing explosions. Cerys James, WRA. Also wanted for murder."

"Foreign Secretary, I will send a report on this to my Foreign Ministry with a recommendation that the matter is put in the hands of the Garda. If anyone has been found to be committing an offence on Irish soil, our judicial authorities will see they are prosecuted. But until evidence of wrongdoing is found, there is nothing more I can do."

"That, Ambassador, is not good enough" shouted Arbuthnot. "I want immediate action from your Government to shut down Tullybeg and to arrest any non-nationals found there. If nothing has been done within the next week, then my Government will consider further action."

Dempsey was irked by Arbuthnot's arrogant attitude.

"Foreign Secretary, remember this. The Republic of Ireland is no vassal of Britain. You appear to have forgotten that we went to war with you a century ago to win our self-determination. My Government will do what it considers right, not what you want. Good day."

13 October 2020
Cabinet Room
10 Downing Street
London

"How did the meeting with the Irish Ambassador go, Henry?" asked Robert Delgado.

"Not well, Prime Minister" replied Henry Arbuthnot. "He's refusing to do anything about the Sinn Fein base at Tullybeg which is being used to train the SNLA and WRA. We've got no option but to escalate this further."

"Do you mean trade sanctions?" asked the Secretary of State for Trade and Enterprise, Darren Bramble.

"Or suspending the Common Travel Area and requiring all Irish nationals to take out visas to travel here" said Deborah Pearson.

"I think the time for Queensbury Rules are over" said Arbuthnot. "What will drive home the message to the Paddies that we're not going to tolerate the use of their territory as a base for terrorists is if we destroy Tullybeg altogether."

"How on earth are you going to do that, Henry?" asked Secretary of State for National Heritage Cheryl Parkinson.

"Quite simple, Cheryl" said the Secretary of State for Defence Jason Steer. "The RAF has the capability of wiping Tullybeg off the face of the earth."

"Are you being serious, Jason?" asked Parkinson. "This is the 21st century, not the 19th. Your approach went out with Lord Palmerston."

"For God's sake, don't be wet, Cheryl" replied Steer. "The Paddies probably think all we can do is create a bit of minor inconvenience for them. This'll not only remove the problem at source. It will also send a message to other countries of what they face if they harbour our enemies."

"And it will avenge the victims of the Blaenrheidol and Ingliston bombings a week ago" added Pearson.

Delgado rapped his gavel to summon the Cabinet to order.

"Henry, Jason, I recognise you're frustrated by the inaction of the Irish government. But there's a couple of factors you need to consider. The first is that the Irish government has got a very tenuous hold on power with Sinn Fein holding the balance of power in the Dail. If the Government falls and there's new elections, there's a high risk of Sinn Fein increasing the numbers of seats and even winning a place in a future Government. That's the last thing any of us wants. The other is that the US Presidential Election takes place in three weeks time. I don't have to tell you about the big Irish-American vote. At present, it appears that Philip Odell's got a small lead and that should be sufficient to put him into the White House. But if we do anything to piss off the Irish-Americans, they'll all vote for Williams and we'll lose our main high profile ally."

"Henry, have another go at getting a diplomatic agreement with the Irish for the closure of Tullybeg. If it's a no-go, then I fear we may have to use the RAF. But not before the US votes."

Later that day
Satellite Sports Bar
Leidseplein
Amsterdam

Graeme Macpherson found the Satellite Sports Bar with little difficulty. He had flown in from London on an Easyjet flight earlier that day.

Macpherson guessed correctly that Sandy Douglas, an old mate of his from Airdrie, would be watching football. Glasgow Rangers' European Cup match against Sparta Prague was on.

"Sandy, how youse doing?"

"OK Gray" replied Douglas. "Great to see you out here."

"Can I get you a beer?"

"Another Amstel would be fine."

Macpherson joined Douglas at the table to watch Rangers grind out a 2-0 win. Once the match was over, Macpherson explained the purpose of his visit.

"Sandy, I wonder if you could help me? I'm looking for an English guy who's just moved out here. Name of Miles Chaucer. About five foot seven, average build, long hair, scruffy appearance. Works as a photographer mainly but also does some film production work."

"Doesn't ring a bell with me, Gray" replied Douglas. "There's a lot of people from the UK out here, you know. Not just Scots and Welsh, English too. A lot of them like Delgado as much as we do."

"I've got a photo of the guy, if that helps" said Macpherson. He pulled out a photo from the pocket of his jacket.

"Nope" replied Douglas. "Could be anyone."

"Did you say he worked as a photographer?" said Shona Mackay, another Scot in Douglas's party.

"Aye, I did" replied Macpherson.

"Might be able to help you" said Mackay. "By the way, what's your name?"

"Graeme. I'm an old mate of Sandy's from back home."

"I'll see what I can do for you, Graeme" said Mackay.

18 October 2020
Satellite Sports Bar
Leidseplein
Amsterdam

Graeme Macpherson had already spent nearly a week in Amsterdam without any success in tracking down Miles Chaucer. He did not want to return to London and tell Adam Gilchrist that his trip had been a waste of time. So when Shona Mackay phoned him earlier that day with news of a lead, he was excited.

Sunday was relatively quiet at the Satellite Sports Bar and he had no difficulty in locating Mackay.

"Hi Shona. Hear you've got some news for me."

"Aye, Graeme" replied Mackay. "I think I've found a lead to your Mr Chaucer. There's this guy called Justin Lake who arrived out here three weeks ago. Claims to be a photographer. He's found work with a film company which produces sex films and I've heard he's supplementing his income by working as a freelance photographer."

"Any idea where I can find this Mr Lake?" asked Macpherson.

"He quite often drinks at the Café Zwart near Dam Square" replied Mackay. "He's got a Dutch girlfriend now. A blonde, called Anna Sleuuwenhoek."

"Thanks, Shona."

21 October 2020
Café Zwart
Dam 15
Amsterdam

Miles Chaucer bought an Amstel for himself and a cherry brandy for Anna Sleuuwenhoek. The couple settled down at a table overlooking the street. It was clear that romance was in the air.

Five tables away, Graeme Macpherson and Scott McEwan were seated.

Macpherson leaned over and whispered "That's Chaucer, Scott. That's the bastard who grassed up Dougie Paterson and Gordon Ross. We owe him."

"Now's not the best time, Gray" whispered McEwan. "There'll be witnesses. Not only that, we would be forced to kill the bird to stop her identifying us. That will bring the Dutch polis down on us like a ton of bricks. Kill a foreigner of dubious repute and all they'll do is a short report for the coroner. But hit one of their own and they'll be all over the place."

"Okay, Scott. We'll bide our time until Chaucer's alone. But we can't wait forever. Gilchrist will think I'm playing around with the whores if I don't report something positive."

22 October 2020
Cureton Street
Pimlico
London

"Jason, is that you? Henry here."

Jason Steer had a good idea why Henry Arbuthnot was on the phone. He had been meeting the Irish Ambassador again.

"How did the meeting with Dempsey go, Henry?"

"Not well. He's refusing to budge about Tullybeg. Or at least his government is. Confirms what the PM said at Cabinet a week ago. That Sinn Fein's got them by the short and curlies."

"Shit. What do we do now, Henry? I'd be all for bombing the crap out of that Sinn Fein base but for the fact my Cabinet career will probably be over. You heard what Delgado said."

"Jason, I think Bob's under a bit of pressure. He's worried about the US Presidential Election and the possibility that Williams might win. The USA's been a valuable friend to us under Kate Whitney and supported us when the rest of the world hasn't. We'll lose that if Williams becomes President. That's why he's twitchy about bombing Tullybeg."

"Tell you what, though, Jason. If we do go ahead and whack that Sinn Fein base, it'll boost the Government's popularity at home and scare the shit out of the EU. Imagine the headlines in the *Sun* and the *Mail*?"

"What do the rest of the Cabinet feel, Henry?"

"Deborah will definitely in favour, as will Darren and Dominic. Bob Manson and Mark Taylor will back us as well. Only doubters are Villiers and Parkinson."

"Henry, I think it's a gamble worth taking" replied Steer. "I don't think Delgado will dare sack either of us without risking a major Cabinet split."

26 October 2020, 8am
off the coast of Northern Ireland

The RAF Boeing RC-135W Rivet Joint electronic warfare plane piloted by Group Captains William Lawrence and Patricia Robinson was patrolling at 30,000 feet above the Irish coast. Back in the electronic warfare suite, Flight Sergeant Ashley McGibbon was scanning for radar emissions.

"Jesus Christ, I'm getting some strong signals coming from twelve miles inland" shouted McGibbon.

"That's got to be Tullybeg" said fellow Flight Sergeant Deepak Kumar.

"Skipper, we're getting strong radar reports from the Sinn Fein base" said McGibbon. "Orders please."

"Put the jammers on, Ash" said Lawrence. The Flight Sergeant immediately turned on the big plane's electronic jamming equipment which blinded the radar at Tullybeg.

Approaching the coast of Northern Ireland in an arc were two Lockheed Martin F-35A Lightning fighter-bombers and four Panavia Tornado GR4 strike bombers.

"Big Bird to White Lightning and Big Wind" said Robinson into her radio. "Big Bird's jammers are on. Prepare for attack."

First to go in were the two Lightnings, piloted by Squadron Leader Mike Ruston and Flight Lieutenant Sharon Gault.

The Lightnings were armed with two of the latest Aries anti-radar missiles and a single 2,000 pound JDAM guided bomb. Their targets were the air defence radars which defended the Tullybeg site and the SAM and AAA installations. Five miles out, they vectored their attack radars onto the Tullybeg defence radar which had been blinded by the Rivet Joint and launches the Aries missiles. Travelling low and at twice the speed of sound, the missiles smashed into the large Russian-copy defence radars purchased from Iran and put them out of action. Ruston and Gault then released their JDAM bombs which took out the SAM and AAA installations.

Inside Tullybeg, there was panic as soon as they realised they were under attack. There were no less than 200 SNLA and WRA members present undergoing training. Most of them were eating breakfast in the main hall. The alarms came on, followed by a tannoy announcement for everyone to head for the air raid shelters underneath Tullybeg.

Before anything more than a handful of the people present could get into the shelters, the four RAF Tornados were fast approaching a now defenceless Tullybeg. Each of the four bombers was carrying four JDAM guided bombs which they released a mile out. Guided by the Tornados' radars, the bombs fell in a line, destroying Tullybeg and the outlying accommodation blocks.

"Mission accomplished" radioed Squadron Leader Gary Oldfield in the lead Tornado. The four bombers then turned and headed for home.

Later that day
10 Downing Street
London

The first Robert Delgado heard about the Tullybeg raid came that afternoon when he had an irate US President, Katherine Whitney, on the phone.

"Robert, what the hell did you guys think you were doing?" raged the US President. "Ireland's hardly an unfriendly country."

"Katherine, I'm sorry we didn't let you in on this. But we've had problems over the use of a Sinn Fein so-called rest and recreation centre for training SNLA and WRA terrorists. The CIA gave us photographs from a satellite which confirms this. The Irish government did nothing about it when we approached them."

"Yes, but do you realise the current political circumstances?" continued Whitney. "The Presidential election's just a week away and it's too close to call. Williams has managed to convince a lot of Middle America that the Republicans have stolen the American Dream and the Democrats will give it back. We need to votes of Irish Americans if Phil Odell is to win. You bombing Ireland will hand the White House to Williams lock stock and barrel."

"Katherine, there's something you should know" said Delgado. "I did not approve this act. I was aware that it had been proposed. Arbuthnot and Steer were the proponents of it. But I told them to hold off until after the election for the reasons you gave. I regard breaches of Cabinet discipline very seriously and will be taking appropriate action."

"Robert, you're missing the point" said Whitney. "The fact is, your guys have just bombed Ireland. I've just had Senators Arnott, Keegan and Murphy demanding sanctions against you. Do you realise that every Irish-American voter will be reminded that it was Britain who bombed the land of their fathers? And reminded that it was the Republicans who have regarded Britain as their special friend. You have probably cost Phil Odell the chance of becoming President."

27 October 2020
10 Downing Street
London

Henry Arbuthnot and Jason Steer had been summoned to a meeting with the Prime Minister before the full Cabinet meeting began. Arbuthnot and Steer were in the same position as Stuart Grieve and Jonathan Morgan had been six months previously and for the same reason, namely breach of Cabinet discipline. But, unlike Grieve and Morgan, Arbuthnot and Steer were expecting the summons and were prepared for it.

"Henry, Jason, good morning" said the Prime Minister. "I have asked you to come in before Cabinet meets to explain why you both have acted in breach of Cabinet protocol by authorising military action against a foreign country."

"Prime Minister, we had no choice but to go for military action" said Arbuthnot. "I met Dempsey again last Thursday and got no joy from him. The choice was either do nothing and risk having trained and hardened SNLA and WRA terrorists killing people or wipe Tullybeg off the face of the earth. We chose the latter."

Steer slammed down on Delgado's desk copies of that day's *Sun* and *Daily Mail*. The *Sun* headline read **PADDYWHACKED** while the *Mail* headline read **RAF SMASH TERROR CAMP**.

"Prime Minister, there's the evidence of how the papers have taken it. We're seen as national heroes. Try sacking us now."

"Gentlemen, do you realise I had Katherine Whitney on the phone yesterday?" said Delgado. "Worried that we've just handed the White House over to Richard Williams. If Williams gets in, the United Kingdom will have no high-profile allies left. On top of that, the EU's voting on whether to launch military action against the United Kingdom in response to an attack on a member country. Explain that."

"Prime Minister, the American people haven't forgotten how useless their last black President was" said Arbuthnot. "When push comes to shove, they'll stay with the Republicans."

"And if the EU dare to think about attacking us" said Steer, "they will face massive retaliation."

"It seems I'm wasting my time in trying to reason with either of you" said the Prime Minister. "I want your immediate resignation from the Cabinet."

"Out of the question" replied Arbuthnot.

"Then I've got no choice but to dismiss you."

Later that morning
Cabinet Room
10 Downing Street
London

The mood at the Cabinet meeting was terse. The second agenda item was 'Matters Arising' and Deborah Pearson chose her moment to go on the attack.

"Prime Minister, I understand you intend to dismiss Henry and Jason from the Cabinet. Don't you realise that they've been responsible for neutralising a major terrorist training base and for wiping out a large number of the SNLA and WRA?"

Robert Delgado was irritated by this display of insubordination from the Home Secretary.

"Deborah, Henry and Jason acted without Cabinet authority. That is a breach of Cabinet discipline, which is why I dismissed Stuart Grieve and Jonathan Morgan from the Cabinet earlier this year. Furthermore, you may have forgotten the reason why I asked for nothing to be done at this stage. Next week, the USA votes to elect a new President. There was a reasonable chance that Philip Odell would win until yesterday. Now it looks like all the Irish-Americans are going to turn out and vote for Williams."

"Haven't you seen today's papers, Prime Minister?" said Attorney-General Dominic Collins. "The *Sun, Mail, Express* and *Telegraph* all approve of what we did. People are ringing in to Sky's talk hosts to register their support for us."

"Dominic, the fact remains that Henry and Jason breached Cabinet discipline. If I do nothing, my authority as Prime Minister will be undermined, as will the principle of collective Cabinet responsibility."

Delgado continued.

"Haven't any of you realised that I've got to take account of issues a long way from this room? I'm as committed as anyone in this room to defeating the SNLA and WRA and making the United Kingdom peaceful again. But yesterday was not the time for military action against the Tullybeg base. The USA is the only high profile ally we've got in the world at the moment. If Richard Williams becomes President, we will lose that. He's committed to forcing us to negotiate with terrorists. He's blatantly cashed in on the Scottish-American and Welsh-American vote. If the Irish-Americans decide to vote for Williams as an act of revenge against the Republicans for supporting us, we can kiss goodbye to having the USA as a friend."

"Prime Minister, I need to make myself clear on this" said Pearson. "If you dismiss Henry and Jason from the Cabinet, I intend to resign too. There are several colleagues who are prepared to do the same."

"I certainly will" said Collins.

"Will all those intending to resign please stand up and identify yourselves" said Delgado.

To his horror, more than half the Cabinet stood up. Pearson and Collins were joined by Secretary of State for Trade and Enterprise, Darren Bramble, Chief Secretary to the Treasury, Mark Taylor, the Leader of the House of Lords, Lord Manson and five other Cabinet members in Roger Best, Secretary of State for Northern Ireland, Ben Clarke, Secretary of State for Employment, Iain Donaldson, Secretary of State for Scotland, Lawrence Fisher, Secretary of State for Transport and Caroline Johnson, Secretary of State for Environment and Local Government.

Before Delgado was able to come to terms with the fact he would lose more than half of his cabinet, he was interrupted by the appearance of his Private Secretary, Jenny Mitchell.

"Sorry to disturb you, Prime Minister. Sir Gerald Hamilton has asked for an urgent meeting."

"What about, Jenny?" replied Delgado. "Is it important?"

"It's about the dismissal of the Foreign and Defence Secretaries from the Cabinet. He says the back benches are in revolt over it."

"Jenny, tell Hamilton I'll see him tomorrow at 4pm."

"Prime Minister, he's insisting on a meeting today."

4 November 2020
Governor's Mansion
Miami, Florida

The US Presidential Election had gone down to the wire. With one state left to declare, the two main candidates, Philip Odell and Richard Williams were neck and neck. Williams had managed to gather more votes than his Republican rival—he had got 62 million votes against Odell's 59 million. But it was the number of electoral college votes that counted, and Odell was leading by 259 votes to 252.

The pattern of voting had been predictable. Williams had carried the North East, the Midwest and the West Coast but, in the South and the West, Odell had largely cleaned up through taking the white, 'Bible-Belt' vote although Scottish-American and Welsh-American voters switching to the Democrats nearly caused upsets in the Carolinas, Georgia and Tennessee.

As the case twenty years earlier, it was to be Florida which would decide the outcome of the election. The state was already on its third recount and it was now 9pm. Nerves in both parties' political camps were jangling.

The appearance of Florida's Attorney-General, Jose Cardenas, suggested that a result might be ready to be announced.

Cardenas, a Republican of Cuban origin, asked for microphones to be set up. He was ready to announce the result.

Thirty seconds later, the Florida Attorney-General was standing on the podium. Everyone fell silent.

"Ladies and gentlemen, the result of the election for President of the United States of America from the polls in the State of Florida is as follows."

Cardenas announced the results for the three independent and minor party candidates before coming to the two main rivals. He was now ready to announce how Odell and Williams had fared in Florida.

"Philip D'Arcy Odell, candidate for the Republican Party. Four million, one hundred and thirty five thousand, four hundred and sixty six votes."

A muted cheer went up from Republican supporters. It would only be enough to win if Democrat voters had not turned out in sufficient numbers. Evidence from the polling stations suggested otherwise.

"Richard Franklin Williams, candidate for the Democratic Party. Four million, one hundred and ninety thousand, two hundred and thirty two votes."

A massive roar of approval from the Democrat supporters swept through the Governor's mansion. Williams had collected the twenty seven electoral college votes and was now the USA's second black president ever.

5 November 2020
Café Zwart
Dam 15
Amsterdam

A massive party was in progress to celebrate the election of Richard Williams as the 46th President of the USA. The mainly youthful and multi-national clientele were delighted to see the end of Republican rule in the world's most powerful country.

Inside Café Zwart, Miles Chaucer had joined several of his colleagues in the film and photography industry to celebrate Williams' victory. He was without his girlfriend, Anna. Two nights earlier, they had rowed. Chaucer planned to call round and see her the following night and make things up.

Willem van Breukelen, one of his film production colleagues, returned from the bar with a round of Amstels. It was to be the first of many that night.

Two tables away, a group of Welsh lads were also celebrating Williams' victory. Three of them, Alun Bevan, Gareth Howells and Tom Michael, had evaded National Service in the United Kingdom and were working illegally in the Netherlands. But the fourth, Mel Davies, was there as a member of the WRA.

Two nights previously, Davies had been in the Satellite Sports Bar in Leidseplein and had met two Scottish lads from the SNLA who were looking for a suspected grass who was living in the Netherlands under a false identity. When Davies had mentioned to them that he would be drinking in the Café Zwart on Thursday night, they had asked him to keep an eye out for the guy. Name of Miles Chaucer, used the name Justin Lake. About five foot seven. Long hair, scruffily dressed.

Davies looked over at the party two tables down. They were Dutch, but he heard this small, scruffy guy speak with an English accent. Then he heard one of the Dutch guys refer to him as 'Justin'. Jesus Christ, thought Davies, that's the guy Graeme and Scott were talking about.

He withdrew his personal data assistant from his pocket and walked out into Dam Square. He dialled up Graeme Macpherson's number.

"Hello."

"Graeme, is that you? Mel here. Remember I was in the Satellite two nights ago. Got some news."

"Go ahead Mel."

"Chaucer. He's drinking in the Café Zwart. Doesn't appear to be with any bird so I assume he's alone."

"Nice work, Mel" said Macpherson. "We'll be up there in a few minutes."

"Need a hand, Graeme?" asked Davies.

"Could be useful."

6 November 2020
Elandsgracht, Amsterdam

A happy and somewhat drunk Miles Chaucer was making his way back to the tram stop to catch the late night tram back to his apartment. The good mood he was in following the election of Richard Williams as US President and the copious amounts of Amstel made him forget the fact he was a marked man. He therefore ignored the three men trailing him.

As Elandsgracht crossed the junction with Marnixstraat, there was a bridge over a canal. There was virtually no one else about. Macpherson gave the thumbs up to McEwan and Davies.

"Hey, what do you guys want?" slurred Chaucer. "Isn't it great news about Williams?"

Macpherson slammed a fist into Chaucer's solar plexus. The photographer doubled up and fell to the ground. As he fell, McEwan kicked him in the face while Davies added a boot into his kidneys.

McEwan seized the photographer and hauled him up onto his feet by his lapels.

"Well, Mr Chaucer" sneered McEwan. You thought you could avoid the SNLA by running away. No such luck. We'd find you if you went to live on fucking Mars."

"Look Guys, I'm sorry I set your leader up for a hit. The fuzz were onto me for blackmailing Sellers. They said if I didn't co-operate, they would send my down for twenty years. I thought all they'd do was lift Dougie Paterson, not take him out. Please, let me go."

"Too late for apologies, Mr Chaucer" said Macpherson. "The penalty for grassing on the SNLA is death."

Chaucer realised the seriousness of the situation. While a student, he had learned self-defence. He suddenly jabbed his fingers in McEwan's eyes and made a run for it.

McEwan staggered backwards, stunned by the sudden attack by Chaucer. "You little cunt, you're in for it now" he shouted.

Macpherson and Davies gave chase to Chaucer. He was fast on his feet and was already halfway to the bridge over one of Amsterdam's main canals, where Elandsgracht gave way to Kinkerstraat. But Davies was even faster and had played rugby at a good standard. He lunged at the fleeing Chaucer and brought him down from behind with a textbook tackle.

As Macpherson and Davies hauled Chaucer to his feet, McEwan arrived on the scene. Boiling with anger at having been poked in the eyes, he brought his knee up sharply into Chaucer's stomach. Chaucer screamed in agony.

"Alright, Scott, let's finish him off" said Macpherson.

McEwan pulled out a double edged knife used for cutting fabric and slammed it into Chaucer just under his ribcage. As blood poured out from the wound, he slumped forward in the grip of Macpherson and Davies.

"What shall we do with him now, guys?" asked Davies.

"Chuck him in the canal" replied McEwan.

Macpherson and Davies hauled Chaucer's limp body to the railings by the canal and threw him in.

CHAPTER 27

26 December 2020
"Windermere"
Gerrards Cross
Buckinghamshire

Deborah Pearson had invited Henry and Catherine Arbuthnot, Jason and Miranda Steer and Dominic and Laura Collins over for Boxing Day lunch. With them were Arbuthnot's son, Simon, an Army officer and his wife, Gemma, Steer's daughter, Charlotte, who worked in the music industry and Pearson's son, Ben and daughter, Lucy, both of who had followed their parents into the banking world.

In what had been a challenging year for the British government, there had been a personal triumph for Pearson two months previously. She had organised a Cabinet revolt when Robert Delgado had threatened to dismiss Arbuthnot and Steer from the Cabinet after the unauthorised Tullybeg bombing raid. She had also tipped off the backbenches through contacting Gravesend MP Spencer Parmenter, and Delgado had faced in addition a revolt from the 1922 Committee. Faced with opposition on two fronts, Delgado had reinstated the Foreign and Defence Secretaries in the Cabinet.

After lunch, the party retired to the lounge of Pearson's palatial house. For once, everyone could relax and avoid talk about politics. Invariably, the conversation focused on children and what they were doing now.

Arbuthnot knew that the music industry had a reputation for being left-wing in views and he asked Charlotte Steer how she was coping in such an environment.

"I'm getting on okay, Uncle Henry" replied Charlotte Steer. "Truth is, most people keep their politics to themselves. No one's had a go at me because of what Dad does."

"What are the artists like to deal with, Charlotte?" asked Collins. "A lot of them strike me as egotistical and neurotic."

"Some can be, Dominic. Particularly the women. Sara Greenfield was a complete nightmare to deal with. And don't get me started on Roxanne Singletary." Charlotte Steer was referring to the notoriously temperamental lead singer of Sincronicity.

"Another thing that pisses me off is the hypocrisy of so many people in the industry. Not just the performers. They always support these trendy, left-wing causes and keep on going on about how we should pay more tax, use our cars less and provide more aid to the Third World. Yet they demand five-star treatment wherever they go and, if they don't get it, throw tantrums that would make any two-year old seem reasonable."

"Typical of lefties all over the world" said her father.

"Charlotte, do you know of anything big coming up in 2021?" asked Deborah Pearson's son, Ben.

"On Saturday, 13 February, Ben" replied Charlotte Steer. "Only you'll have to go to New York for it."

"What is it, Charlie?"

"A benefit concert for Scotland and Wales. It's going to take place at Madison Square Garden. They've already lined up Full Metal Jacket, the Green Mile, Ringer and the Everlasting and they're trying to get Sincronicity to join the bill. Have a look at the publicity."

This was the most heavyweight rock music lineup that had ever been assembled in one venue. Full Metal Jacket, a heavy metal band from San Francisco, had four double platinum albums behind them and were acknowledged as the most successful rock band in the world. Sincronicity were a Nu-Soul band from New York and were the world's biggest-selling pop group. The Green Mile hailed from Portland in Oregon and their West Coast-flavoured alt-rock head earned them two double platinum albums.

There were two British bands on the bill. Or rather, one Scottish band and one Welsh. Ringer, who came from Glasgow, played jangly country rock and were Britain's most successful rock band and were one of the few who had been successful in the USA. The Everlasting hailed from Swansea and their rabble-rousing, anthemic rock was also starting to break the US market.

Henry Arbuthnot was somewhat disturbed to hear what had been planned. He asked Charlotte Steer for a copy of the publicity.

"Charlotte, do you know who's organised this?" asked Arbuthnot.

"Harvey Walker's the promoter, Uncle Henry. But I don't know who's put the money up. Is there a problem?"

"Could well be, Charlotte" replied Arbuthnot. "I'm concerned that the money raised will end up in the hands of the SNLA and the WRA. Apart from being a propaganda opportunity for them. I'll be having words with my officials when I get back."

4 January 2021
US Department of State
2201 C Street NW
Washington DC

Larry Horvath, the US Secretary of State, was in the final three weeks of his term of office before he gave way to Clint Romney, the nominee of incoming President, Richard Williams. Like many of Katherine Whitney's cabinet, he was winding down before starting a new career as a director of a leading US corporate law firm.

Horvath was an early riser, a habit instilled since boyhood, and this had served him well in a stellar career that had seen him through Harvard and Wall Street. He was however surprised to receive a call at 8:30am. When his secretary said the call was from the United Kingdom, the penny dropped. They were over five hours ahead and it would be early afternoon there.

"Foreign Secretary Arbuthnot on the telephone for you, sir" said his Personal Assistant, Donna Reames.

"Hi Henry, how are you?" asked Horvath. "Have a good Christmas?"

"Personally, yes Larry" replied the British Foreign Secretary. "Very enjoyable. Simon was over with Gemma on Christmas Day and we spent Boxing Day over at Deborah's."

"How's Simon doing?"

"Very well, Larry" replied Arbuthnot. "He's a Major in the Household Cavalry. Expect him to be going for Colonel in the next couple of years."

"What can I do for you, Henry?"

"Larry, on 13 February, there's going to be a massive benefit concert for Scotland and Wales at Madison Square Garden. Celtic Aid, they call it. Claims to be to raise money for people facing hardship because of the troubles in Scotland and Wales. The truth is that it will be a massive propaganda exercise for the SNLA and the WRA. I reckon all the money raised on the night will go to the SNLA and the WRA to fund further acts of terrorism. As well as acting as another propaganda tool to undermine our case for maintaining the territorial integrity of our country."

"Is there anything you can do to stop the concert going ahead? For example, under the Patriot Act?"

"Very difficult, Henry. Unless we have incontrovertible evidence that the purpose of the concert is to raise revenues for terrorist purposes, we are unable to use the Patriot Act. And, bearing in mind the difficulties we've had in tackling Caledonian Aid and Cambrian Aid in the past, I don't hold out too much hope. On top of that, by the time the concert takes place, we'll have Williams in place in the White House. He and Romney will be able to overturn anything I do before Katherine hands over the Presidency."

Horvath was referring to Clint Romney, his successor as Secretary of State.

"Damn!" swore Arbuthnot. "Any chance of New York State or City banning the concert, Larry?"

"You can ask, Henry" replied Horvath. "But I don't hold out too much hope. "New York State's got a Democratic governor. Janet Lombardo. And the Mayor's another Democrat. Edwin Barkley. Doubt if either will be too sympathetic to Britain."

Later that afternoon
Foreign and Commonwealth Office
Whitehall
London

Sir James Beveridge, the Director-General of MI6, had taken part in several meetings at the Foreign and Commonwealth Office since he had taken up the post seven years earlier, but he could tell from the tone of Henry Arbuthnot's voice that he was wanted urgently.

"Foreign Secretary, what do you need the SIS to do? From your call half an hour ago, it seemed urgent."

"It is, James" replied Arbuthnot. "Next month, there's a big benefit concert in New York to raise money for Scotland and Wales. They've got five of the world's leading rock bands to take part. The organisers claim that the money will be used for welfare for people suffering headship as a result of the Troubles. But Caledonian Aid and Cambrian Aid are involved, which means almost 100% that the money is intended for the SNLA and WRA. As well as being a massive propaganda coup for them in the USA."

"I spoke to Secretary of State Horvath earlier today to see if they could ban it under the Patriot Act. Didn't get a helpful reply—he basically said no chance."

"I'm not surprised, Foreign Secretary" said Beveridge. "Horvath's only got three weeks left in post. He's effectively doing nothing more but to clear his desk. Little point in him doing something that will be turned over by the incoming administration."

"James, is there any chance that SIS could arrange to put a spanner in the works and disrupt the arrangements for the concert?" asked Arbuthnot.

"It would be difficult, Foreign Secretary" replied Beveridge. "Firstly, the promoter, Harvey Walker, is a known supporter of the Democrats and will be organising the Inauguration Concert for Williams when he takes up the Presidency. He will have full co-operation from the authorities. Secondly, we'll have the New York Police Department to contend with. Historically, they've had a lot of Irish-American cops whose sympathies will be with their Celtic cousins. If they sense someone is trying to sabotage the concert, they'll come down like a ton of bricks. And finally, we've had good relations with the CIA and the FBI over the past ten years and would be reluctant to upset that."

"James, defending the United Kingdom's interests is difficult" said Arbuthnot testily. "But we do best when faced with adversity. The Battle of Britain showed that. As did the Falklands. Don't tell me that SIS don't have the wherewithal to bring Celtic Aid shuddering to a halt. Just do it."

"And James, I want fortnightly reports on how things are progressing" added Arbuthnot.

5 January 2021
MI6 Headquarters
Vauxhall Cross
London

"Ben, can you come in?" asked Sir James Beveridge. "It's urgent."

Ben Osgood, the Head of Section B, the North America desk at MI6, walked down the corridor and entered the office of the Director-General.

"Thank you for coming in, Ben" said Beveridge. "Now listen carefully. We've got a new assignment and there's just over five weeks to complete it."

"What's the rush for, Sir James?" asked Osgood. He had just turned forty and was highly ambitious.

"On 13 February, a charity rock concert is being held in Madison Square Garden to raise money for people in Scotland and Wales suffering hardship as a result on the civil unrest there. Here is a publicity flyer for the concert."

Beveridge handed Osgood an A4-sized leaflet with details of the concert.

"Wow, they're certainly pushing the boat out" said Osgood. "Managing to get Full Metal Jacket, Sincronicity and the Green Mile all in the same venue. Each of them could headline by themselves."

"Ben, this concert's almost certainly got the hand of Caledonian Aid and Cambrian Aid pulling the strings. Apart from being a massive propaganda coup for the SNLA and WRA, it's almost certain that the money raised will be destined for them rather than ordinary people. The Foreign Secretary made it clear to me yesterday that we've got to stop this concert going ahead."

"Madison Square Garden, eh. From my recollection, right above Penn Station."

"Ben, I don't have to spell out the consequences of what might happen if we upset the USA. They've been our main ally in the world in recent years. If we piss off the CIA and FBI, bang goes most of our vital source of intelligence information."

"Don't worry, Sir James. I'm well aware of this."

7 January 2021
British Embassy
Massachusetts Avenue
Washington DC

Ben Osgood had flown in to Washington DC the previous night and had arranged a meeting with Angela Thompson, a Third Secretary at the British Embassy and a fellow MI6 agent. A taxi ride from his hotel on the Beltway took Osgood to the Embassy, which had been rebuilt and fully restored after having been burned down by protestors five years previously following Bloody Sunday.

"Hi, Ben, how are you doing?" Angela Thompson was a strikingly attractive blonde four years younger than Osgood.

Osgood and Thompson made their way to a meeting room on the first floor. Coffee and biscuits were already provided.

"What brings you here at such short notice, Ben?" asked Thompson.

"Angela, the DG's given me an urgent job. Or rather, the commission's from the Foreign Secretary. He wants me to stop the Celtic Aid concert going ahead."

"Oh my God, the one at MSG" said Thompson. "You know Harvey Walker's the promoter, Ben? Which means he'll have the protection of all the king's horses."

"You mean the FBI and NYPD, Angela?" said Osgood.

Walker, the leading rock music promoter in the USA, was a high profile supporter of the Democrats.

"Angela, I believe you advised me a couple of months back that there's an active EVF over here."

"I did, Ben" replied Thompson. "They've now got over five thousand members. Leader's an ex-Marine, Harvey Treadwell."

"Have they done anything yet, Angela?" asked Osgood.

"Nothing major" replied Thompson. "But they've had several rallies and demonstrations and there was an ugly clash in Chicago three months ago when they clashed with SNLA and WRA sympathisers after mounting a counter-demonstration to one of theirs. However, I've heard that EVF volunteers have undergone military training. You ought to know that Bill Fraser and Ben Meredith are both under police protection after receiving EVF death threats."

Fraser and Meredith were the Chairmen of Caledonian Aid and Cambrian Aid, which the British government suspected of funding the SNLA and the WRA.

"Angela, I am going to ask a favour which is going to be highly controversial. Can you keep it a secret between you and me?"

"I think I know what you are going to say, Ben."

"Our one hope of stopping Celtic Aid going ahead will be if the EVF disrupt the preparations. Forget going through legal channels. By next month, Williams will be in the White House. We'll get no change out of him. It'll be the same with Congress, the Governor of New York State and the Mayor of New York. All Democrats and sympathetic to the cause of Scottish and Welsh independence."

Osgood continued.

"What I'm thinking of, Angela, is to use the EVF to disrupt the planning for Celtic Aid. There's many ways they could do this. Damaging MSG's infrastructure is one. Because of health and safety regulations, if MSG is made unfit to hold the concert, it will have to be called off. Then there's sabotaging the PA or the bands' equipment. Finally, the location of MSG above Penn Station could make it vulnerable to a bomb hoax. I'm not thinking about loss of life, just inconveniences which will prevent the concert going ahead."

"Ben, have you cleared this with Sir James?" asked Thompson. "I'm worried about involving the EVF. Remember what happened in Spain last year."

"No need to worry, Angela" said Osgood. "There'll be no body count on this operation. We'll be pulling all the strings. If the EVF don't do as they're told, we'll shop them to the US authorities."

9 January 2021
Banyan Drive
Springfield
Illinois

Gary Aldridge, MI6's lead field agent in the USA, had little difficulty in finding the commander of the EVF's US brigade, Harvey Treadwell. On his front lawn, a St George's flag flew alongside the Stars and Stripes. The one-time US Marine, now in his mid-40s, lived in a suburban street in the Forest Park district close to the eastern shore of Lake Springfield. He rang the doorbell of the Treadwell family residence. A plumpish blonde woman in her early 40s opened the door.

"Is Harvey Treadwell there?" asked Aldridge.

"I'll call him. By the way, who are you?"

"Gary Aldridge. British Embassy, Washington. I've arranged to meet him."

Thirty seconds later, Treadwell was at the front door.

"Mr Aldridge?"

"That's right. Good to meet you, Mr Treadwell" replied the MI6 agent.

The two men headed for Treadwell's "den". Mrs Treadwell brought in a couple of beers, a dip and a bag of tortilla chips.

"Thanks, honey" replied Treadwell.

The British agent set out the reason for his visit and how Treadwell and the US branch of the EVF might be of help.

"Mr Treadwell, you may be aware that, next month, a charity rock concert has been organised at Madison Square Garden to raise money supposedly for people in Scotland and Wales who are suffering from hardship arising from the civil unrest there."

"Celtic Aid. Heard all about it, Mr Aldridge. Nothing more than a blatant fundraising exercise for the SNLA and WRA."

"Exactly what HMG thinks. Strictly speaking, it should be banned under the anti-terrorist provisions of the Patriot Act as its giving aid and comfort to terrorists undermining the territorial integrity of a friendly country. But there's no chance of that with a Democrat President about to take office, a Democrat-controlled Congress . . . ."

"With those SOBs McAllister and Hopkins in charge" said Treadwell, referring to the Leaders of the Senate and the House of Representatives.

"And with the Governor of New York State and the Mayor also being Democrats with misguided sympathy towards what they consider to be the underdog" continued Aldridge.

"The reason I've come to see you, Mr Treadwell, is to enlist the co-operation of the EVF in ensuring that Celtic Aid does not take place. We've tried the legal channels and no one's playing ball."

"What do you want us to do, Mr Aldridge?" asked Treadwell.

"A bit of industrial sabotage, Mr Treadwell. MSG needs a Safety Certificate before the concert can go ahead. A bit of strategic damage may prevent that happening. Or sabotaging the electrics or the bands PA so they can't perform. Finally, you know that a major station is underneath MSG."

"I didn't" replied Treadwell.

"Pennsylvania Station. A major commuter thoroughfare. An emergency to coincide with the concert might cause it to be abandoned."

"What's in it for us, Mr Aldridge?" asked Treadwell. "Remember, me and many of my members have got wives and kids. If we get caught, we stand to go down for twenty years or more."

"Don't worry, Mr Treadwell" said Aldridge. "We'll ensure that our agents will remove any incriminating evidence."

11 January 2021
Manor Road
Lynbrook
New York City

The leadership of the US brigade of the EVF gathered in the lounge of Wayne Brooks's house. Brooks, a Londoner who had emigrated to the USA with his family in the 1990s, had married an American woman and stayed.

Harvey Treadwell, the Brigade Commander, called the meeting to order.

"Gentlemen, you will have heard that the British government has asked for our help in sabotaging Celtic Aid. They want, in their words, the concert to be sabotaged so it cannot go ahead. I think we are planning on going a bit further."

"Absolutely, Harvey" said Bob Lear, an Arkansan. "Some of the guys are thinking about planting a bomb. Just think of the impact that would have."

"Many people are laughing at the English because they think we won't fight back" said Brooks. "If we blow that fucker up, that will drive home the message over here that the English aren't to be fucked with. I reckon a lot of Americans will be scared off supporting the SNLA and WRA."

"Hold on, fellas" said Ed Sansom, another British émigré who was living in California. "Didn't the MI6 guy say that we were to restrict ourselves to stopping Celtic Aid going ahead, not to bomb the place. If the EVF bomb MSG and cause loss of life, we won't be seen as heroes. We'll be public enemy #1 and all we'll succeed in doing is taking Anglo-American relations back to the War of Independence. Better stick to what the intelligence guy asked us to do. Watching the abandonment of Celtic Aid will be a big embarrassment for the organisers and give everyone in the USA a laugh."

The other Brigade leaders were not impressed by Sansom's lack of enthusiasm.

"Ed, it would be nice to let everyone go home unharmed. What you forget is that the organisers of Celtic Aid, the musicians taking part and many of the audience attending couldn't care less about the plight of the English. When our countrymen and women are shot or blown up by the SNLA and WRA, they just shrug their shoulders and take the attitude "get over it". By supporting the cause, they are just as guilty as the terrorists. Remember, we were formed to defend England because the British government won't do it, nor will the US government help us. We've got one choice Ed, and that's to defend ourselves by any means possible."

There was a round of applause for Treadwell from the other Brigade leaders.

"Can we now turn to the logistics of smashing Celtic Aid" said Treadwell.

"First issue is how do we obtain explosives? We'll need a large amount to cause damage in a venue the size of MSG."

"I'm able to obtain explosives" said Ray Duffield, a West Virginian who was an engineer in the coalmining industry. "PECT. Let me know how much you need, Harvey."

"Second on the list is have we got any expertise in priming devices?" asked Treadwell.

"Try Sam Holmes" said Brooks. "He programmes mobile phones for a living."

380

"Finally, how do we manage to get the explosives into MSG? I bet security will be tight."

Mark Freeman indicated he wished to speak. Originally from Stoke-on-Trent and in his late-20s, he had been working in the USA for three years. Originally a computer mechanic, he had overstayed his Green Card and was working as a doorman at a bar near Times Square.

"Harvey, I reckon that'll be easier than many think. MSG don't have regular staff anymore to run events. Everything's sub-contracted now—catering, security, front of house. We should be able to infiltrate brigade members into MSG without any difficulty. The management is more concerned about profits and turnover that they'll turn a blind eye to security. I've worked gigs there before and loads of other Brits have also worked at MSG."

"One last word, guys" said Treadwell. "Keep this to yourselves and tell no one. Even to MI6. Otherwise, we all risk spending the rest of our lives in the slammer."

13 February 2021, 12pm
Madison Square Garden
New York City

The doors at Madison Square Garden were due to open at 1pm to admit the first customers for Celtic Aid. This promised to be the largest indoor rock concert ever held, surpassing the George Harrison-organised benefit concert for Bangladesh nearly fifty years previously. All the main US television channels, CBS, MBC and CNN, were to cover the concert although a notable absentee was Fox Television as the organisers specifically prohibited what they considered to be a hostile channel from being in attendance. Also covering the concert were the newly-formed European Broadcasting Corporation, which ensured that British fans could see the concert after the Government had banned domestic channels from screening the event.

Behind the scenes, team of staff had been hard at work since the morning preparing Madison Square Garden for Celtic Aid. Food and drink had been supplied, not only for the customers but also for the performers and VIP guests. The staff responsible had been told by their managers to follow the terms of the performers' riders to the letter. Full Metal Jacket and Sincronicity were, in particular, known to be difficult and demanding customers, especially their lead singers, Joey Bonavia and Roxanne Singletary. Meanwhile, the stage crew were ensuring that the venue's electrics were in sound mechanical order. An hour later, the road crew of the Everlasting would be arriving to set their equipment up.

Harvey Walker, the promoter, was pacing the floor nervously. There would be five bands at the top of their profession playing in the venue. And having to manage the clashing egos. The first one, the Everlasting, would be on in three hours time. They would be on for an hour, to be replaced by Ringer, who would also play for an hour. At 6pm the Green Mile would be on and would play for an hour and a half. Then Sincronicity would be on to play for an hour and three quarters. Finally, the headliners, Full Metal Jacket, would be on and would play up to the midnight closing time. Walker knew there would be no room for delays or overruns.

Downstairs in the cellars where the drinks were stored, Mark Freeman, Sam Holmes and Ross Wainwright had helped fill the beer kegs and to stack the bottles of beer, wine and spirits to supply the bars in the auditorium. Another hour to go and their shift would finish.

"Hey guys, what on earth possessed you to come and work at a gig like this? You must have known that it was going to be anti-British?" Brad Frinkel, like many of the Americans working for the day at Madison Square Garden, was a college student who was paying his way with casual work at the weekends and evenings.

"Brad, like you, we need the money" said Holmes.

"Mind, I agree that this gig sucks" said Wainwright. "How about the likes of Full Metal Jacket playing a charity gig for all the Brits killed or injured by the SNLA and WRA?"

Freeman remembered that Ray Duffield would be on the way in from West Virginia. He needed to check where he was.

As Freeman left the cellar, he was confronted by the Duty Manager, Lisa Murkowski.

"Mark, where do you think you're going? There's still an hour to go on your shift."

"Lisa, I need to check on two late deliveries and find out where they are and how long they'll be. The guys said they'd be in by 12:30 but you know what the traffic can be like."

"Okay, Mark. Don't be long. We need to be ready when everyone arrives."

Outside Madison Square Garden, Freeman dialled Ray Duffield's number.

"Ray, Mark here. How long before you arrive?"

"Another hour and a half, buddy" replied Duffield. "It's absolute shit on the Interstate."

"You know where to park, don't you, Ray? Round the back, in the service bays."

"Loud and clear, Mark. See you at half past one."

Later that afternoon

Ray Duffield's Mack truck was parked in the service bay, and Freeman, Holmes and Wainwright were all helping him and his mate, Barney, to unload it. The modern service lifts installed at Madison Square Garden enabled the three Britons to unload the cargo of PECT and transfer it into the cellar. By 2;45pm, the entire cargo had been unloaded, and Duffield could return to West Virginia.

"Good luck, guys" shouted Duffield as he backed the truck out.

"Cheers, Ray" shouted Freeman.

"Alright guys" said Freeman, turning to Holmes and Wainwright. "Time to get rocking. Lets get going."

The cellar area contained fifteen pressurised tanks for holding beer. There were three main suppliers—Budweiser, Coors and Miller. However, on the day, only twelve were in use; the other three were sealed of for a routine cleaning to ensure that beer supplies did not get contaminated. Freeman intended to use these for storing the PECT. Once inside, he planned to pump in pure oxygen. When the explosive was detonated, this would make the impact of the detonation even more damaging. Finally, it was to be the job of Holmes to prime each of the explosive devices to go off at 11:55pm. The three EVF members anticipated that Full Metal Jacket would be about to start their final encore. All five bands would be present, while the VIP seats close to the stage would contain celebrities like Hollywood actors, members of other rock bands and several leading politicians including Senator McAllister and Representative Hopkins.

Above them, Freemen, Holmes and Wainwright heard guitar chords followed by the compere's voice.

"Ladies and gentlemen, will you welcome the first band on the bill. From Swansea, Wales, the Everlasting."

The same evening
8:15pm

Harvey Walker's worst nightmare appeared to have happened.

The Green Mile had just finished their set. Lead singer Janet Evans and lead guitarist Doug McCulloch were heading for their dressing room. It was fifteen minutes before Sincronicity were due to take the stage, and Roxanne Singletary was in the first stage of a massive hissy fit. The band's lead singer was temperamental at the best of times but she was now in a filthy mood and threatening not to go on stage.

Part of the rider in the contract for Sincronicity's appearance stipulated that no one was to use the corridor outside their dressing rooms while they were preparing for the concert. Unfortunately, a sub-contracted member of staff who was new to the job took a wrong turning. And found himself outside Singletary's dressing room just as she emerged.

"Hey, calm it down, Roxy" said Walker. "The guy made a genuine mistake and got lost. He's really sorry. It was his first day in the job."

"I don't fucking care, Harvey" spat Singletary. "The contract for our appearance categorically said that no one—I mean, no one—was to go near our dressing rooms before the concert. And what did this asshole do but that."

"I want a full search of the entire MSG, Harvey. Otherwise, the gig's off."

Walker realised the seriousness of his predicament. It was fifteen minutes before Sincronicity were on stage. Any delays to the timings and there would be hell to pay. Not only from Sincronicity if their act was cut short but also from headliners, Full Metal Jacket, who would be arriving in twenty minutes time. Walker was also aware that standing next to Singletary was a gigantic minder. He did not fancy having the meathead start on him.

"Okay, Roxy. I'll get NYPD to carry out a thorough search of MSG. Is that alright?"

Michelle Alston, one of the band's other two singers interjected.

"Hey, come on Rox. That seems a fair deal. This is our home city and we've wanted to do this gig for ages. We can't walk out now."

"Alright, Harvey, I'll go on this time" said Singletary. "But if you fail to carry out the search I've requested, I'll never appear for you again."

Sincronicity were about to go on stage when Sergeant Jay Murphy of New York Police Department arrived. He was accompanied by Officer Kelly Maguire and Officer Dino Valentini.

"Hi there, Mr Walker. How can I help?" Murphy was in his late 40s, a veteran officer with nearly 30 years service.

"Thank you for coming so quickly, Sergeant" said Walker. "One of the artists appearing thinks there may be intruders on the premises. Is it possible to carry out a search?"

"Guess so. Kelly, Dino, we'll search the backstage area first. Is there a store room here, Mr Walker?"

"If you mean the cellar area downstairs, yes."

"We'll search that next. Does that sound okay?"

"Should be, Sergeant."

At that point, four men in their 30s, accompanied by a phalanx of hulking security men, walked by. Full Metal Jacket, the headliners had arrived. Lead singer, Joey Bonavia, guitarist, Rick Camilleri, bassist Glen Moreno and drummer Ed Symanski were wearing their customary leather jackets and dark glasses.

Ten minutes later
underneath Madison Square Garden

Freeman, Holmes and Wainwright had found the task of setting up and priming the explosives a longer task than expected. They were thankful that no one had disturbed them.

"Mark, can you pass me another length of copper wire?" asked Holmes. He was struggling to prime the second device.

"Christ, Sam, how much longer are you going to take?" said Freeman. "It's already quarter to nine and we've only got one bomb primed." Freeman was concerned that, if they left the premises shortly before the bombs were due to go off, they would attract suspicion.

"Nearly there, Mark" said Holmes. "Done it! Now for the final bomb."

Suddenly, the door to the underground cellar room opened and three shadows could be seen.

"Shit, we've got company" said Wainwright.

"Get down, fellas" said Freeman. "If we're not seen, whoever it is will leave."

The three Britons heard voices that were clearly American. And when they heard the sound of a two-way radio, their worst fears were confirmed.

"It's the cops, guys" whispered Freeman. "Have your guns ready."

Wainwright noticed there was better cover at the far end of the cellar and motioned for the three EVF members to head that way.

"There's definitely someone in here, Sir" said Valentini. He was the youngest of the trio, at 20 years old, and had only been two months out of the police academy.

"I think you're right, Dino" said Murphy. "Kelly, can you take the right hand side, Dino, take the left. I'll hold the centre and keep you covered."

Officer Maguire moved towards the right hand side of the cellar when she suddenly saw some movement. She shouted "Armed police—freeze!"

Holmes withdrew his Heckler and Koch pistol and returned fire.

"Shit, they mean business!" exclaimed Valentini.

"Hold your position there, Kelly" shouted Murphy. "Dino, edge forward. I've got you covered."

"Aye aye, sir."

Murphy and Valentini crept forward, guns cocked. As soon as Murphy saw movement, he opened fire. Valentini followed suit.

"This is New York Police Department. Whoever you are, surrender now. If you don't, I'm calling for reinforcements. There's going to be only one winner in this."

"Come on then, copper" snarled Freeman. "There's three of us here and we're all armed. See how brave you are."

Valentini now had a good sight of Freeman and moved forward to get a shot in. The big Midlander fell to the ground, dead. Unfortunately, he did not notice Wainwright who opened fire. The rookie cop fell to the floor, mortally wounded.

"Kelly, radio for an ambulance. Dino's been hit."

Murphy and Maguire were now intent on avenging their young colleague and had scant regard for their personal safety.

"Alright, you son of a bitch" shouted Murphy. "If that's the way you want it, that's the way you'll get it."

Maguire saw Wainwright move for just a split second. It was sufficient time for her to get a shot in.

Holmes was now the only member of the EVF cell left standing. Recovering Freeman's gun as well as his, he opened fire in the direction of Murphy and Maguire. Murphy successfully took cover but Maguire took a ricochet which hit her left arm.

"I've been hit, sir."

"Hold on in there, Kelly" shouted Murphy. "Reinforcements should be here anytime now."

"Come on, coppers" snarled Holmes. "See if New York's finest can get the better of the EVF."

"This is your last warning" shouted Murphy. "Throw down your gun and surrender now or we shoot to kill."

"Let's see you try it, pig" retorted Holmes.

Murphy edged forward slowly. Again, he was forced to fling himself to the ground as Holmes fired.

"Sir, I've got you covered" shouted Maguire.

Suddenly, Murphy saw his opportunity. Holmes moved once too often and could now be seen. The veteran Irish-American cop opened fire and saw Holmes fall to the ground.

"Got him" shouted Murphy.

At that moment, police reinforcements arrived in the shape of four officers under the command of Sergeant Pat Sheahan. He was an old buddy of Murphy.

"Too late for action, Pat" said Murphy. "We've managed to bag all three bad guys. Call the ambulances and CSI and we'll be out of here."

"Any casualties, Spud?" asked Sheahan.

"Afraid so, Pat" replied Murphy. "Maguire took a shot in the arm. She's on her way to hospital but it's not too serious. Sadly, Valentini's dead."

Murphy's boss, Lieutenant Bruce Kosar, turned up next. While Sheahan and his squad of officers searched the cellar area, Murphy gave Kosar a debrief on events.

"So Jay, you're saying those guys were English. Are you certain?"

"Yes sir" replied Murphy. "Could tell by their accents. One of the guys said he was from the EVF. Officer Maguire will back me up on this."

Sheahan, along with Officers Lee Carlin and Delroy Funches, made their way gingerly through the cellar. They were aware that one of the bad guys could still be alive and pose a threat to them. Their guns were therefore withdrawn from their holsters and uncocked.

Funches saw the first body. A large, muscular, shaven-headed man. It was Freeman. He waked over and checked his pulse.

"Dead, sir."

A second body lay five feet away. It was Wainwright.

Holmes, although bleeding heavily from a bullet wound, however, was still alive, if only just. He still had the personal data assistant which was programmed to detonate the bombs, and started to dial in the number to prime the detonation.

Officer Carlin was walking slowly through the cellar when she saw Holmes' arm moving. She was about to shout 'Freeze' but was too late. Holmes had hit the Enter button as his last act on the planet.

On the stage at Madison Square Garden, Sincronicity were in the middle of one of their biggest hits, "Mad at You" when half a ton of PECT exploded in three massive blasts. The resultant fireball consumed the entire stage and backstage area and the VIP seats at the front, before fanning out into the confines of Madison Square Garden. Sincronicity were blown to pieces, as were members of the Green Mile, Ringer and the Everlasting, who were relaxing backstage after playing their sets, and Full Metal Jacket who were getting ready for their headlining performance later that night. The roof of the auditorium, weakened by the blast, collapsed, dropping tons of shattered concrete and steel onto the panicking audience who were trying to escape.

Within minutes, all of New York City's Emergency Services were on the way to Madison Square Garden. It was an eerie repeat of events twenty years earlier.

CHAPTER 28

14 February 2021, 4:30am
10 Downing Street
London

"Prime Minister, it's President Williams on the phone. He's demanding to speak to you urgently."

The duty staff at the Prime Minister's residence seldom received calls in the early hours of the morning and any requesting the Prime Minister to be present were normally handled by taking a message for the Prime Minister or an official to ring back. But President Williams was insistent that the Prime Minister was raised from his sleep.

Robert Delgado was clearly irritated that the US President had disturbed his sleep. Didn't he know that the United Kingdom was in a different time zone?

"Prime Minister Delgado here, Mr President. You do know that its half past four in the morning here?"

"You've done it now, Delgado" said Williams in a slow and menacing tone.

"What the hell do you mean?" asked the British Prime Minister.

"Two and a half hours ago, a bomb went off in Madison Square Garden. Planted by the English Volunteer Force."

"Good God!" exclaimed Delgado. "How bad is the casualty rate? And can the United Kingdom offer any assistance?"

"The death toll could be as much as eight thousand, Prime Minister. That's more than twice as many as 9/11. Not only that, the dead include three of the country's leading rock bands, no less than twenty Hollywood actors and actresses and eight Senators and fourteen Congressmen and women, including the leaders of the Senate and the House of Representatives. And no, I do not need the help of the United Kingdom. The Emergency Services in New York City are coping admirably and are receiving help from the National Guard from Connecticut, New Jersey and New York State."

"Look, Mr President, I'm really, really, sorry that this terrible act has happened. I can assure you that if any of our nationals are involved in this, that we'll assist you in bringing them to justice."

"It's too late for apologies, Prime Minister" said Williams. "Your intelligence services seem to have been working with the English Volunteer Force. If I were you, I'd check what's going on in your own backyard."

Delgado went into his study and switched the television on. He turned to CNN as he knew they would offer a different slant on the events to Fox News.

What Delgado saw horrified him. A pall of smoke was rising from the huge edifice of Madison Square Garden. Outside there were legions of vehicles from the police, fire and ambulance services, all with blue lights flashing.

"This is Kirsten Lesniak of CNN News, live from outside Madison Square Garden."

"The rescue operation to locate and remove survivors of tonight's terrorist bomb blast at Madison Square Garden is now in progress, and the authorities are optimistic that they will be able to retrieve survivors from the outer edges of the venue. Behind me you will see rescue teams from New York Fire Department and the fire departments of Albany, Buffalo and Rochester who are starting to enter Madison Square Garden. However, it is believed to be a hundred percent certain that Full Metal Jacket, Sincronicity, the Green Mile, Ringer and the Everlasting all died in the massive blast which consumed the entire stage and backstage area. Likewise it is believed that the Senate Leader, Senator Brad McAllister and the Leader of the House of Representatives, Representative Graydon Hopkins, along with actors Ethan Blake, Alastair Carlyle, Otis Franklin, Mickey Redmond and Rob Young and actresses Sarah Dorff, Catherine Lewis-Jones and Grace Nelson, also perished as the VIP seats took the full force of the blast."

"The FBI's search for the perpetrators of the explosion is being hampered by the fact that little is known about the English Volunteer Force in the United States. However, the English Volunteer Force has gained notoriety in Britain and Europe over the past year after planting a bomb at the Benicassim Rock Festival in Spain which killed over eighty people and through the murders of the SNLA and WRA commanding officers and of rock star Sara Greenfield."

Jesus Christ, thought Delgado. Three leading US rock bands and two leading British rock bands, dead. No less than eight leading actors and actresses. Several Senators and Congressmen. The EVF will have succeeded in taking Anglo-American relationships back to 1776. I hope that Arbuthnot's got a good explanation and the claims of MI6 collusion with the EVF are nothing more than tittle tattle.

16 February 2021
Cabinet Room
10 Downing Street
London

It was clear from the agenda that the Cabinet meeting was to be dominated by a single issue. The EVF terrorist attack on Madison Square Garden three days previously and the implications for the United Kingdom.

Robert Delgado's fears that 2/13, as the Madison Square Garden atrocity was now being referred to, would have negative implications for the United Kingdom economically and politically, were being realised. There was a run on the pound as US investors started selling British shareholdings. The previous day, Ford announced that they would be closing their British factories and there were widespread rumours that General Motors and IBM were going to follow suit. The US Congress were due to vote on a motion to impose trade sanctions on the United Kingdom and the US government had tightened visa rules for British nationals. The previous day, the Director-General of MI6, Sir James Beveridge, had resigned from his post in the wake of internet rumours about collusion between them and the EVF.

Delgado formally opened the meeting and, following the minutes of the previous meeting and matters arising, moved straight to the main issue.

"It will be no surprise to you that the first item on the agenda is last Saturday's dreadful bombing in New York City and the impact it will have on the United Kingdom. We are facing trade sanctions from the USA and the prospect of US-owned companies following Ford and withdrawing their investment here. Darren, what's the latest news on GM and IBM?"

"It looks like bad news, Prime Minister" replied Darren Bramble, the Secretary of State for Trade and Enterprise. "They both plan to close their factories and offices here, and other US companies seem to be minded to follow suit."

Delgado then turned to the Chancellor of the Exchequer, Ed Villiers.

"Ed, have you been able to estimate the impact of the US business disinvestment and trade sanctions on the economy?"

"Not yet, Prime Minister" replied Villiers.

"Can you prepare one for the next Cabinet meeting."

Delgado then turned to the Foreign Secretary, Henry Arbuthnot.

"Henry, there have been some extremely disturbing reports about collusion between the secret intelligence services and the EVF. What are you doing to investigate this?"

"I have asked the Acting Director-General, Felicity Turner, to carry out a thorough investigation into this and have given her authority to hold individuals to account for their action. Which includes dismissals of anyone found guilty of gross misconduct."

The next Cabinet member to be questioned by the Prime Minister was the Home Secretary, Deborah Pearson.

"Deborah, I take it you've ordered a similar investigation at MI5."

"No, I haven't, Prime Minister" replied Pearson. "MI5 weren't involved in 2/13."

"That's beside the point, Deborah" said Delgado, testily. "The allegations of collusion with the EVF go beyond MI6. If any part of the security apparatus are found to have worked with a terrorist organisation, the credibility of this Government stands to be damaged permanently. Tell Nicola Martin to open an inquiry and report back to me."

Delgado then moved onto the next part of the agenda, labelled 'A Fresh Start'.

"Ladies and gentlemen, this Government is now entering the sixth year of the conflict in Scotland and Wales, and it appears to be no closer to defeating the SNLA and the WRA. When the conflict began in 2015, we were in a fortuitous position. There were friendly governments in place in the USA, Australia, Canada and New Zealand and most governments in Europe were centre-right. We had just discovered oil reserves worth £100 billion per year to the economy. The tectonic plates have now shifted. It now seems that most of the world has been seduced by the dangerous creed of socialism and even the United States has now elected the most left-wing President in its history. The United Kingdom is in danger of becoming politically isolated."

"Prime Minister, you appear to have forgotten that there is a legal challenge to President Williams' victory" said Deborah Pearson. She was referring to an attempt led by Senator Troy Burton, the Republican minority leader in the Senate and supported by several leading businessmen, to declare the result void on account of claimed votes cast by illegal immigrants and convicted felons debarred from voting.

"Deborah, I am aware of Senator Burton's challenge" said Delgado. "But it's not likely to get very far in the wake of 2/13. You do realise that many Americans were impressed with the way Williams has handled 2/13 and his approval ratings are sky-high. Not only that, a lot of Americans are outraged at what the EVF did because they killed several of their leading politicians and celebrities. Williams is moving to hold the by-elections for the Senators and Representatives who died next month and every prediction is that the Democrats will win. And as for Senator Burton, I take it you've heard that he's now got FBI protection because of threats to his life."

Delgado continued.

"Over the next year, we are going to have to face up to some unpalatable truths. One is that a purely military response to the SNLA and WRA is not going to succeed. We are going to have to consider how we can engage with the nationalist community in Scotland and Wales and negotiate a way back to peace."

"I don't believe I hear what you are saying, Prime Minister" shouted the Secretary of State for Defence, Jason Steer. "You appear to be suggesting appeasement of the SNLA and the WRA."

"Prime Minister's there's no way that the Party will tolerate giving in to terrorists" shouted Arbuthnot.

"Jason, Henry, be quiet" shouted a reddening Delgado. "You might want to take the United Kingdom downhill on a spiral of economic decline just to say we've beaten the SNLA and the WRA. But I won't. We've got to be realistic and the reality is that much of the world has little sympathy with us now."

17 February 2021
10 Downing Street
London

"Prime Minister, do I hear you right?" Tim Budgen, the Prime Minister's chief political adviser was astounded to hear the suggestion that the Government should open talks with the SNLA and the WRA.

"Absolutely right, Tim" replied Robert Delgado. "If we can bring the SNLA and WRA in from the cold, we might stand a chance of getting a ceasefire. And of ending the United Kingdom's international isolation. What's more, there's a chance of opening up splits in both organisations."

"It won't go down well with the party or the British public, Prime Minister" said Joel Durelle, another of the Prime Minister's advisers. "Too much of what the SNLA and WRA have done is still fresh in people's memories."

"It was the same over twenty five years ago when John Major opened up talks with the IRA" said Delgado. "And, on that occasion, Major's judgement was proved right in the face of many sceptics. He got a ceasefire with the IRA and that ultimately set the road to the Good Friday Agreement."

Delgado continued.

"What I want you chaps to do is, firstly, to find out whether the SNLA and WRA leadership are ready to meet to discuss the possibility of a ceasefire. And, secondly, if they are, to set up a secret meeting. We can use Chequers. By the way, not a word to anyone outside this room."

28 February 2021
"Chequers"
near Wendover
Buckinghamshire

"Prime Minister, your guests are here." The door staff ushered in Iain Murray and Gareth Evans, the Chairmen of the SNLA and WRA General Councils.

Robert Delgado noticed how ordinary Murray and Evans looked out of combat fatigues and balaclavas, which they were normally photographed in. Both men were wearing smart, casual clothes and, as Delgado thought, would not look out of place at a golf club.

"Mr Murray, Mr Evans, thank you for accepting my invitation to attend talks."

"Thank you, Mr Delgado" replied Murray and Evans.

"Gentlemen, the reason I've asked you here is to find out what terms the SNLA and WRA might be able to accept for a ceasefire."

"A ceasefire, Mr Delgado?" said Murray. "It appears it would be of more benefit to you than to us."

"We are only prepared to consider laying down arms if the British government pulls its troops out and agrees to full independence for Wales and Scotland" said Evans.

"Come on, gentlemen" said Delgado, "you've got to be realistic. The Government's not going to pull our troops out without a guarantee that the SNLA and WRA will disarm. And as for independence, I think the least you should offer is being willing to have a referendum on the subject."

"Very well, Mr Delgado" said Murray. "If the British government is prepared to be serious in the long term about demilitarising Scotland and Wales and letting their people decide their destiny, I think this could offer a basis for a possible SNLA ceasefire. Geraint, how would the WRA feel?"

"The same" replied Evans.

"Good" said Delgado. "We can now start talking more about specifics."

2 March 2021
MI5 Headquarters
Millbank
London

James Furnival, the Deputy Director-General of MI5 was a frustrated man. He coveted the top job in the agency, the post of Director-General, having spent eight years in the Deputy post. At the beginning of the year, it was expected that the current incumbent, Dame Nicola Martin, would retire. She was now 61. The previous week, Furnival had found out that Martin had obtained a two year extension to her contract. By the time she retired, Furnival would be 59. The Government would surely by-pass him and appoint a younger man or woman to the post.

Furnival was acknowledged to have a razor-sharp analytical mind and he had a reputation a man of action rather than words. But his impatience with office politics and in the importance of stakeholder management gave the impression that he was abrasive and impulsive. Nicola Martin had privately voiced doubts about whether he was the right material for the top post.

The phone rang in his office. Richard Donovan was on the other end. Furnival had little regard for Donovan. He was not an MI5 man by origin, having been seconded in from the Home Office and he was too obsessed with procedure and protocol. A 'do it by the book' man.

"James, have you got a minute?" asked Donovan.

"Is it important, Richard? I'm a busy man."

"It is. One of the field agents has just passed me photographs of the Prime Minister meeting with the Chairmen of the SNLA and WRA General Councils."

This certainly woke Furnival up. "Bring them through, Richard."

A minute later, Donovan was in Furnival's office.

"Jesus Christ, Richard, that's Chequers, isn't it? And yes, that's Iain Murray and Gareth Evans."

"James, we've got to make sure these don't get into the Press" said Donovan. "It could bring down the PM, if not the entire Government. Is Nicola around today?"

"She's at a conference in Paris, Richard, and won't be back until Thursday. I'll take charge of them."

After Donovan left the office, Furnival pulled out his directory of contacts. He had no intention of passing the photos to Dame Nicola when she got back. He rang the number of Spencer Parmenter, the Conservative MP for Gravesend. Parmenter was a well-known extreme right-winger who had been a strong advocate of ramping up the campaign against the SNLA and WRA to include more moderate nationalists and sympathisers in other parties. He was well-placed amongst the hierarchy of backbench Conservative MPs to escalate the issue.

"Is Spencer Parmenter there?"

"He is, sir" replied his secretary. "Who shall I say is phoning?"

"James Furnival."

5 March 2021
10 Downing Street
London

"Prime Minister, Sir Gerald is here to see you."

Robert Delgado's visitor was Sir Gerald Hamilton MP, the Chairman of the 1922 Committee, the official forum for backbench Conservative MPs. He had been surprised at the request late the previous day for an urgent meeting. Delgado routinely had monthly bilateral meetings with Sir Gerald to discuss issues that were concerning the backbenches and, in the 10 years he had been Prime Minister, most of the meetings had been friendly. The arrival of a red-faced Sir Gerald in his office suggested the meeting would be everything but.

"Good morning, Sir Gerald."

"Good morning, Prime Minister" replied Hamilton.

"You've asked for a meeting at short notice, Sir Gerald" said Delgado. "What is troubling you."

"Prime Minister, yesterday, the 1922 Committee found out that you had engaged in meetings with the leaders of the SNLA and the WRA last weekend. Is that right?"

Delgado was stunned. Someone in his team must have leaked details of the meeting. After a pause, he replied.

"Sir Gerald, I know what you're thinking. May I explain the reason why I had this meeting?"

"You must surely have noticed that a purely military solution to the insurgency in Scotland and Wales is not working. The SNLA and WRA are as resilient as ever and overseas support for the independence cause is growing. With Richard Williams winning the US Presidential election last year, we now have virtually no allies in the world. And this is before you take account of what the EVF have done."

"The USA and the EU have now imposed trade sanctions and an embargo on weapons sales on us. Following 2/13, Ford, General Motors, IBM and several other American companies with UK investments have pulled out. The Chancellor's latest economic report does not make good reading, Sir Gerald. We are facing the prospect of a full-blown recession. Many of our brightest young people are leaving the country to work abroad. Next year, we were planning to hold the next General Election. We may have to postpone that now. Even if we go to the country in two years time, it's unlikely that things will have improved. Do you really want Labour to get back in, Sir Gerald?"

"I'm afraid we've got no choice but to cut our losses and consider building in a political solution to Scotland and Wales. And this means being ready to talk to the SNLA and WRA, no matter how distasteful it might seem. But we have a precedent. In 1994, John Major opened talks with the IRA and managed to get a ceasefire that year. Although it didn't last, it helped pave the way for the Good Friday Agreement four years later."

Hamilton was not impressed.

"Prime Minister, the thought of anyone from the Party talking to those bastards makes me want to puke. Do you realise how many people the SNLA and WRA have killed and maimed over the past five years? I hope you've got a satisfactory answer to tell their relatives. And don't forget David Pickavance."

Hamilton was referring to the outspoken Conservative MP for Basildon South who had been murdered by the SNLA in a car bombing in the summer of 2017.

"The mood in the party is very angry at what you've done, Prime Minister. And even more so that you've concealed it from your Cabinet colleagues, officials and party members. You have not heard the last of this."

7 March 2021
Dolphin Square
Pimlico
London

No less than four Cabinet Ministers had gathered at Deborah Pearson's flat to discuss what to do after the news that the Prime Minister had engaged in secret talks with the SNLA and the WRA. They were Henry Arbuthnot, the Foreign Secretary, Darren Bramble, the Secretary of State for Trade and Enterprise, Dominic Collins, the Attorney-General and Jason Steer, the Secretary of State for Defence. Also present was Conservative Party Chairman, Sir Anthony Simmons and the Chairman of the 1922 Committee, Sir Gerald Hamilton.

Deborah Pearson opened the discussion.

"You will all know why I've asked you to come round today. I think you were all horrified to find out last week that Robert had been in talks with the SNLA and the WRA without letting any of us know. The only way we got to know was when Spencer Parmenter was tipped off. Isn't that right, Gerald?"

"Indeed so, Deborah" said Hamilton.

"I understand you met the PM on Friday about this" said Collins. "How did the meeting go?"

"Not well" replied Hamilton. "The PM's refusing to budge on this. He thinks it's the only way he'll win back overseas support for the United Kingdom."

"That's absolute poppycock!" thundered Arbuthnot. "Eighty years ago, Winston Churchill decided to stand alone against Nazi Germany when no one else would back him. And five years later, was on the winning side. Everyone knows this country shows its true colours when backed against the wall."

"I think Bob's lost his nerve" said Steer. "All because of 2/13. If he bides his time, he will find that Williams's popularity will drop like a stone when he presents Middle America with the tax bill for his crazy schemes. And the Yanks will forget 2/13 when they start reading about the decadent, debauched lifestyles of the celebs who died. The Republicans will have Congress in their hands in two years time and the Presidency in four."

"What I'm going to propose may sound controversial" said Pearson. "But I think it is time to remove Robert from office. He's lost the steel and resolve that led us so well through the last decade."

"The other Cabinet Ministers nodded their approval.

Sir Anthony Simmons was the only dissenter.

"Deborah, do you realise that replacing a party leader is not as simple as reshuffling the Cabinet? There has to be a formal leadership contest and if there's more than two candidates standing, the contest will have to run until there's two candidates left, when it's thrown open to all Party members to vote. This could leave us without a recognised leader for months at what is going to be a critical time for the Government. If we lose direction, Labour will pounce like a shark and we could lose the next General Election as a result. I'm sure no one here wants that."

"What's more, Robert has been an outstanding Prime Minister over the last ten years. It was he who led the party out of the doldrums and back to power. He won us three elections on the trot. A lot of people in the country recognise that, no matter what he's done now. The last time the Party removed a sitting Prime Minister was thirty years ago. You will surely remember that was the start of our long march to the wilderness."

Simmons was referring to the events surrounding the resignation of Margaret Thatcher as Prime Minister back in 1990.

"Tony, none of us are denying what Bob's done for the Conservative cause, the cause of free enterprise and for national pride" said Steer. "But we all think he's badly mistaken in opening dialogue with murderers and gangsters."

"The leadership election rules were drawn up over twenty years ago" said Collins. "Tony, what's the possibility of them being changed to speed things up?"

"That would have to be put to members" replied Simmons.

"Why can't we call an immediate leadership contest to take place in the next month?" asked Collins. "That way, we won't have to vote on changes to constitutional rules and we can have a new PM in place by April."

"I suppose we could do that" conceded Simmons.

"Are we all agreed then?" asked Pearson. "If a majority of MPs have lost confidence in Robert, we'll ask for his resignation."

11 March 2021
10 Downing Street
London

Robert Delgado was a worried man. The front page headline in the *Daily Telegraph* summed it up: **TORY REVOLT GROWS OVER DELGADO TALKS WITH SNLA AND WRA.** His mood was not helped by the news that a senior delegation from the Party hierarchy wanted to see him urgently.

At 2pm, the delegation arrived. They comprised Lord Strathendrick, the President of the Conservative Party, Sir Anthony Simmons, the Chairman and Sir Gerald Hamilton, the Chairman of the 1922 Committee. The so-called 'men in grey suits'.

Delgado suggested they should meet in his study. The three men agreed.

"Prime Minister, you will know why we are here" said Lord Strathendrick. "Bad news, I'm afraid. A majority of Conservative MPs have lost confidence in your ability to lead the Party. Not just because you've been speaking to terrorists but because the way you've done it behind everyone's back."

Delgado feared that the result of the confidence vote would be negative, but he was determined not to go without a fight.

"John, I know what I did has upset a lot of people. But, as with every decision I've taken since becoming Party leader fifteen years ago and Prime Minister ten years ago, it was taken for the right reason. We are having to operate in a hostile world environment where many governments are openly sympathetic to the cause of Scottish and Welsh independence. Our biggest trading partners, the EU and the USA, have imposed sanctions on us. The damage to the national interest of treating Scotland and Wales as a purely military problem means we have no alternative but to consider talking to the nationalist community. A ceasefire may go some way to addressing our economic and diplomatic problems."

"I'm sorry, Prime Minister" said Simmons. "That argument will not disguise the fact that you have spoken to men responsible for the murder and maiming of many innocent civilians here, as well as one of our MPs and several councillors. And, on top of that, responsible for trafficking hard drugs into the country and undermining the economy through counterfeiting, identity theft and contraband."

"I am afraid you have lost the Party's mandate to continue as its Leader. If you wish to spare yourself, and the Party, further pain, I would suggest that you offer your immediate resignation as Prime Minister."

12 March 2021
Sky News

"This is Daniel Merryfield with the lunchtime headlines on Sky News."

"The world of politics was stunned today by the resignation of the Prime Minister, Robert Delgado. It follows a week of turmoil in the Conservative Party about secret talks he held with the leaders of the SNLA and WRA which have upset many in the party."

"Mr Delgado has been Prime Minister for just under eleven years and, after Margaret Thatcher, has been the longest-serving incumbent over the past hundred years. His Premiership has not been without difficulties: in the early years, he had to cope with industrial unrest, a recession and Al-Q'aida terror attacks on London. But his aggressive commitment to a free-enterprise economy helped deliver growth of 6% a year up and made the United Kingdom the envy of the developed world. His robust approach to crime and national security has also proved popular with voters and, in 2013, he committed United Kingdom forces in the Third Gulf War which neutralised the threat from an increasingly dangerous Iran."

"The battle Mr Delgado has not been able to win has been the domestic insurgency in Scotland and Wales which began six years ago following the discovery of large oil deposits there. The SNLA and the WRA have managed to obtain support across a broad coalition ranging from conservative nationalists to extreme Marxists. The fight has not been helped

by the recent proliferation of left-wing governments across the world who have offered aid and comfort to the insurgents. It is believed that Mr Delgado was seeking to change his formerly hard-line approach towards the insurgency in the hope of achieving a ceasefire and in regaining overseas support."

CHAPTER 29

3 April 2021
Yellowcliffe Bay
American Virgin Islands

Deborah Pearson and her husband chose to take an Easter break at the villa they owned on the eastern side of the Virgin Islands. The villa was halfway up the side of a steep hill and had the advantage of being relatively secluded.

She was even more thrilled when her husband called in to say that Senator Trent Burton was on the phone.

"Thanks, Henry. Can you transfer the call to my line?"

"Will do, darling."

"Hi Trent" said Pearson. "How are you doing?"

"Debbie, you won't believe this, honey. I'm already out here."

Pearson was astounded. She thought that Burton was phoning from the USA.

"Troy, are you free this afternoon? If so, come over."

"You bet!"

An hour later, the bulky figure of the leader of the Republican minority group in the USA Senate was sipping a cold daiquiri on the verandah of the Pearson family villa.

"So Debbie, I hear you're acting Prime Minister" said Burton.

"I am, pending the outcome of the leadership contest. By the way, how's things with you? Last I heard, the FBI were giving you a guard because of death threats."

"That's still the case, Debbie" said Burton. "All because I told Americans the truth. That the SNLA and WRA are not national liberation heroes or romantic revolutionaries but vicious criminals and terrorists in cahoots with enemies of the USA. But I managed to give the FBI the slip for the Easter break."

"Let's drink to that."

After lunch, Pearson and Burton retired to Pearson's study in the basement. It was the coolest part of the house during the hottest part of the day.

The discussion switched to Senator Burton's efforts to force a recall election on the grounds of electoral irregularities. Pearson knew too well that a change back to a Republican administration would make the United Kingdom a preferred US ally and trading partner again. But Senator Burton's news on this front was disappointing.

"I think it's going to be a long haul to get Williams out of office, Debbie" said Burton. "The Democrats won all the by-elections last month and the new Leaders of the Senate are Mike Loughran and Dan Carroll. Both Irish-Americans, one from Chicago, the other from Frisco. And both anti-British."

"Is there any sense that the antipathy to the United Kingdom following 2/13 is fading, Troy?"

"It's starting to, Debbie" replied Burton. "2/13 wasn't like 9/11. 9/11 was targeted at US business and it was done by a bunch of ragheads. Different race, hostile religion, they purposefully went for what they considered to be the symbol of US capitalism and their aim was to subjugate the USA to Islam. 2/13 was carried out by white, Christian Brits, not by ragheads. And it was not targeted at the USA or anything which symbolised it, just at a particular group of people. A lot of people are now finding out what assholes those celebs who died were. Joey Bonavia and Rich Camilleri, both with Mafia links. Roxanne Singletary, an ex-prostitute. Janet Evans and Doug McCulloch, both hard drug users. In about 6 months time, 2/13 will be forgotten by most Americans."

Burton had referred to the lead singer and lead guitarist of Full Metal Jacket, the lead singer of Sincronicity and the lead singer and lead guitarist of the Green Mile, all of whom had died in the 2/13 atrocity.

"Another thing you should know, Debbie" continued Burton. "Already, the US business community is unhappy with the trade sanctions imposed on Britain. For them, it's damaging their business. Quite a few are ready to break those sanctions."

"Any names, Troy?" asked Pearson.

"Chevron, Exxon, Texaco from the energy industry. Boeing and Lockheed Martin in defence and electronics. AgriCorp in food production. Others are likely to follow suit. By the way, Debbie, how's the leadership battle going?"

"I should get the PM's job, Troy. My only opponent's Christian Vale. Remember? The former Foreign Secretary who walked out of the Government after Bloody Sunday six years ago."

"Yes, I do" said Burton. "Bit of a panty-waist."

"A good Minister for us, Troy. He got us out of the EU without tears. But misguided."

"There's something I want to ask you, Troy" said Pearson. "You were once on the Armed Forces Sub-Committee. Where does the obligation of NATO members stand in respect of fellow members?"

"Any reason for asking that, Debbie?"

"Yes. Henry Arbuthnot's been looking into this. You know he used to be in the British Army. He believes that the US Government, in common with all NATO members, is bound by obligations in the NATO Treaty to offer military assistance to any member state if there is a serious threat to their internal or external security. And that would include the United Kingdom. Henry also considers that the embargo on the supply of military equipment imposed by President Williams is in breach of that treaty."

"Problem is Debbie that the Democrats have got control of Congress as well as the Presidency. Chances of using Congress to twist Williams's arm is zero. Particularly now they've got Loughran and Carroll running Congress."

"Troy, you've said that business leaders are unhappy with Williams for putting sanctions on us" said Pearson. "Surely Wall Street can force Williams on this?"

"Debbie, there might be one last hope" said Burton. "If US interests are put at risk by Williams's refusal to provide the United Kingdom with military assistance, it might be possible to impeach him. Better still, the threat of impeachment might be a lever to force his resignation."

"Surely Williams won't resign?" said Pearson. "The Democrats are sitting on a solid majority."

"Wall Street are unhappy with him" said Burton. "So are the Joint Chiefs of Staff of the military. They carry a lot of weight as you know, Debbie. I think we could get rid of Williams in a palace coup without having to involve Congress."

21 April 2021
Conservative Party Headquarters
Millbank
London

The Press Suite at the Conservative Party's headquarters was packed solid with journalists from the United Kingdom and other countries. Television crews from the BBC, ITN, Sky News, EBC, CNN and Al-Jazeera were all present to cover the announcement of the result of the leadership contest.

Just two candidates had put their names forward. One, and the favourite to win, was Deborah Pearson, the current Home Secretary. The other was the former Foreign Secretary, Christian Vale.

On the top table, Party Chairman, Sir Anthony Simmons, was ready to read out the results.

"Ladies and gentlemen, I am now ready to announce the result of the contest for the leadership of the Conservative Party."

"There were two candidates who were nominated to stand—Deborah Helen Pearson, MP for North Worcestershire and Christian Michael Vale, MP for West Wiltshire. The first ballot was conducted under Party rules on votes cast by Members of Parliament."

"The results were as follows:—Deborah Helen Pearson—233 votes. Christian Michael Vale—86 votes. I therefore declare that Deborah Helen Pearson is the winner and is the new leader of the Conservative Party."

27 April 2021
Cabinet Room
10 Downing Street
London

Deborah Pearson had wasted little time in carrying an axe to the Cabinet. No less than five Ministers had been sacked. Perhaps the biggest surprise was the Chancellor of the Exchequer, Ed Villiers. Although a sound monetarist, Villiers was more liberal on social issues and Pearson considered him to be too close to former Prime Minister

Delgado. The others to go were Secretary of State for Health, Adrian Penfold, Secretary of State for Education, Jennifer Chadwick, Secretary of State for National Heritage, Cheryl Parkinson and Secretary of State for Wales, Catriona Evans.

Jason Steer was the new Chancellor of the Exchequer. Pearson's old Home Office protégé, Darren Bramble became the new Home Secretary, although now divested of its responsibility for national security. That had passed to Henry Arbuthnot who became Secretary of State for Defence and Homeland Security, and had prime responsibility for tackling the insurgency in Scotland and Wales. Dominic Collins was now Foreign Secretary while, to address concerns about the loss of female Cabinet members, Caroline Johnson became Attorney-General.

The first Cabinet meeting of Deborah Pearson's premiership started with a round the table roundup. First up was Jason Steer.

"The economic news is not good, Prime Minister. Although the FTSE and the pound both revived last week after the announcement of the leadership contest, growth is virtually static at 0.07% and the deficit has grown to £105 billion. The markets are starting to get restive. We are going to have to consider austerity measures, like a public sector pay and recruitment freeze, an increase in National Insurance and VAT and public spending cuts. We may also have to consider further contraction of the public sector and privatisation of services."

"Not really what we want to hear in the year before a planned Election, Jason" said the new Prime Minister. "Can you report back on options?"

Next on the agenda were foreign affairs.

"Prime Minister, there might be some rays of light from the USA. It appears that several large corporations are most unhappy with the trade sanctions the Government has placed on us. They've been lobbying Congress and Senator Burton's agreed to raise the issue with the President."

"That's encouraging, Dominic" said Pearson. "Do you think the public's starting to get over 2/13?"

"Not in New York or on the West Coast" replied Collins. "But in the South and the West, there's signs that white Middle America's falling out of love with President Williams. The old Tea Party's active again and they're making an issue of supporting the country's natural allies. Like the United Kingdom."

Then came the turn of Henry Arbuthnot, now back in the area of business he loved most.

"Prime Minister, in two days time, I, along with Chris Beal, Ed Starling, Duncan Moore, Mike Woodcock, James Lawson and Andrew Wade will be meeting General Gideon Bar-Levy, the former Commander-in-Chief of the Israeli armed forces. General Bar-Levy, as you know, was responsible for Israel's offensive defence strategy against Hamas and Hizbollah which helped put down the *intifada* seven years ago and probably secured the country's security for many years to come. He will be advising us on the successful counter-insurgency strategy he deployed in Israel against Palestinian terrorists and their sympathisers and supporters which brought the *intifada* to an end."

"Excellent news, Henry" said Pearson. "Can you let me know what comes out of the meeting with General Bar-Levy."

29 April 2021
Ministry of Defence
Whitehall
London

"General Bar-Levy has arrived, Secretary of State." The voice of Damien Kelly, Henry Arbuthnot's Principal Private Secretary, was on the other end of the line.

"Excellent, Damien. Show him to the main conference room."

Arbuthnot headed down to the large conference facility in the basement of the Ministry of Defence headquarters, where he was joined by Chris Beal, Minister of State for the Armed Forces, Ed Starling, Minister of State for Homeland Security, General Sir Robin Peacock, the Commander-in-Chief of the Army and the Commanders-in-Chief of the counter-insurgency campaigns in Scotland and Wales, Lieutenant-General James Lawson and Lieutenant-General Andrew Wade.

Bar-Levy was shown into the room by Kelly and introduced to Arbuthnot, his Ministers and the two senior Army officers. He was a short, stocky man of 61 years whose short, close-cropped hair was now white. Despite his age, he still looked the buccaneering officer from the Israeli armed forces which had struck terror in the hearts of their Arab adversaries.

"General Bar-Levy, I am most grateful to you for making the time to visit me and my colleagues" said Arbuthnot. "I look forward to learning from your experience in fighting the PLO, Hamas and Hizbollah and the lessons we can learn in fighting the SNLA and the WRA."

"Thank you, Secretary of State" said Bar-Levy.

"I do not have to elaborate on the fact that Israel has been fighting for its survival ever since it came into existence seventy three years ago. Our enemies, whether they have been the Palestine Liberation Organisation, the Popular Front for the Liberation of Palestine, Hamas or Hizbollah, have all had a single aim. The destruction of the state of Israel. Our enemies have been well-armed, receiving their weapons from the former Soviet Union and then from Russia, China and Iran. They have received diplomatic support from communist and so-called 'progressive' states as well as the Islamic world. They have received funding from legal means, through donations from friendly countries, and illegal means like trafficking of narcotic drugs. In contrast, Israel is not allied to anyone. It has had to fight hard to receive the most modern weaponry from Western countries, as well as the technology transfer so it can develop its domestic armaments industry. And unlike its adversaries, Israel, as a democratic country, has been subject to scrutiny of all its actions to defend itself."

"Ten years ago, Israel was facing an uncertain future. It had suffered military defeat at the hands of Hizbollah in the Lebanon in 2006. The strategy of engagement with the PLO and agreeing to an independent Palestinian homeland was doing nothing more than providing Hamas with a base to carry out attacks against us. Every time we launched a crackdown against Hamas or Hizbollah, it was filmed and screened on prime time television across the world, which weakened international support for us. We had conditional support at best from the then US President. Meanwhile, Iran was building up its nuclear weapons programme and purchasing long-range bombers from Russia, as well as providing material support for Hamas and Hizbollah. The prospect of Israel being attacked from several fronts simultaneously was real."

"The threat of facing possible annihilation put a stop to the squabbling amongst the political parties forming the ruling coalition and the Government agreed on a programme to tackle the threats facing Israel from both domestic insurgency and hostile foreign intervention. They agreed to give the armed forces, backed up by the police and the security services, a free hand to tackle Arab militants, unencumbered by the need to comply with laws, to regard suspects as innocent before proved guilty and to grant human rights to anyone arrested. We modified the courts system to introduce military tribunals for terrorist cases. We tightened the laws on national security and sedition to make it illegal to publish anything which denigrated our armed forces, police and intelligence agencies or which was helpful to hostile countries. We censored the Internet as well as press and broadcast media."

"We installed listening devices in Palestinian areas and supported these with surveillance drones. If there were riots or disturbances, we did not just bother to break them up. We sent snatch squads in to arrest the perpetrators and put them on trial. If any of our soldiers, policemen or intelligence agents were kidnapped, we replied in kind and seized members of Hamas or Hizbollah. If there were any properties being used for terrorist purposes, we destroyed them. We used armed aerial support. We allowed our nationals living in hostile areas to build defensive barriers to protect them against terrorist attacks. We required all Palestinians or Arabs living in Israel to carry identity passes and we reserved the right to refuse entry on security grounds. Finally, we were ruthless towards any of our own citizens or foreigners who carried out activities which undermined our security operation and ensured they were either imprisoned, deported or, in some cases, had their Israeli nationality removed. And we ensured that all our domestic opponents were subject to control orders and intense surveillance if it was felt they were giving aid and comfort to our enemies."

"We faced a lot of international opposition to our security strategy when we put it in place. Israel was suspended from the United Nations, you may remember. People were calling us Nazis and comparing us to Apartheid-era South Africa. And why? For defending our right to exist. Regrettably, there were lives lost, both on our side and on the Arab side. But, eventually, the tide turned in our favour. Hamas and Hizbollah both lost many of its best men and women. Either killed in action or taken prisoner by us. Their foreign sympathisers soon got the message that Israel wasn't messing about. By 2014, both Hamas and Hizbollah were pleading for a ceasefire."

Arbuthnot felt it politic not to mention the fact that the defeat of Iran in the Third Gulf War in 2013 had removed a significant overseas threat from Israel.

"General, once again, many thanks for your most helpful presentation. Once again, Israel has shown the Western world what can be done through resolve and determination."

All six British attendees had received a copy of General Bar-Levy's presentation. They retired to Arbuthnot's office to discuss the lessons that could be learned.

"I was rather impressed with what General Bar-Levy had to say" said Lawson. "I still feel we've been fighting this campaign with one arm tied behind our back. There's still scope for us to be more ruthless in tackling the SNLA and the WRA."

"I liked what he said about the armed forces, the police and the intelligence services fighting an integrated campaign" said Wade. "And on fighting the enemy on their own terms."

"Secretary of State, you realise that anything like destroying people's homes or introducing pass laws will be contentious" said Beal. "It depends whether the Government has the appetite to implement what General Bar-Levy has described."

"I think it has, Chris" replied Arbuthnot.

11 May 2021
Cabinet Room
10 Downing Street
London

Jason Steer, the Chancellor of the Exchequer, had prepared his report on the economy and the options for dealing with the deteriorating economic position.

"Jason, can you please summarise the main points of your report?" asked the Prime Minister, Deborah Pearson.

"Thank you Prime Minister" replied Steer.

"Ladies and gentlemen, you will have before you a report summarising the current economic position and the options that the Treasury has identified for both reducing the deficit and kick-starting economic growth. What is in this report is top secret and no one must discuss anything outside this room."

"The proposals contained all work on the premise that the budgets for defence, policing, prisons and national security are all ring-fenced. I take it everyone is in agreement."

The Cabinet indicated their approvals. Steer continued.

"Firstly, I consider that a freeze in public sector pay for the next three years, coupled with a recruitment freeze in the civil service, will yield savings of around £20 billion each year. I know that we went through a similar exercise between 2010 and 2015 and there are people who consider there's no more fat to cut. But this presents an opportunity for the Government to consider what scope there is to outsource some of the civil service's policy making functions in the same way that we have done for front-line service delivery and back office support. Many think tanks contain high calibre staff who are perfectly capable of providing policy advice to Ministers. I consider there is scope to reduce the civil service headcount even further without a detrimental effect upon policy advice to Ministers."

"Next, we should consider increasing National Insurance contributions by another penny in the pound and increasing VAT to 22.5%. VAT increases are never popular as they impact upon consumption. But such an increase would yield additional revenue of more than £20 billion a year."

"Finally, I think we seriously need to consider what services are being provided free of charge and whether we can afford to do so in the future. I'm specifically thinking of health and education. How I can speak as someone who was born in an NHS hospital and who was educated free of charge to my parents from the age of five to sixteen. But I think that the time of universal free provision must come to an end, as we can no longer afford it. We must therefore start considering charging people at the point of use."

"There will be many people who will say that such a move would discriminate against those who are least able to afford the cost and that it will increase inequalities in educational achievement and health. But we must seriously consider how many of the people who use those free services genuinely appreciate them. Look at our schools. Despite free provision, we still manage to produce armies of illiterate and innumerate school leavers who are of no value to employers or this country. And we still have people who cost the taxpayer money for medical treatment due to their feckless and irresponsible lifestyles. If people had to pay for those services, I believe they would appreciate them more."

"Thank you, Jason" said the Prime Minister. "Any views, please?"

The Cabinet agreed to Jason Steer's proposals to tackle the fiscal deficit. The next item was the Bar-Levy report and Henry Arbuthnot's proposals to escalate the fight against the SNLA and the WRA.

"Henry, can you please summarise the key points arising from General Bar-Levy's presentation and the conclusions you have drawn" said Pearson.

"Thank you, Prime Minister. On 29 April, I, along with Chris Beal and Ed Starling, General Peacock and Lieutenant-Generals Lawson and Wade, attended a presentation by General Gideon Bar-Levy, the former Commander-in-Chief of the Israeli armed forces. General Bar-Levy described how the Israelis successfully put down the terrorist insurgency by Hamas and Hizbollah between 2011 and 2014. Apart from our role through the Third Gulf War in 2013, all of this was achieved by the Israeli Defence Forces themselves."

"There are four main lessons that came out of General Bar-Levy's presentation" continued Arbuthnot. "Firstly, the total integration of the armed forces, the police and the security and intelligence services in the fight. Secondly, the Government granted the armed forces, the police and the security and intelligence services a free hand in the fight against terrorism, unencumbered by the need to be accountable to the law. This sent Hamas and Hizbollah the message that the gloves were off. Thirdly, a ruthless response to anyone helping the terrorists. In practice, this meant imposing summary justice and confiscation and destruction of property if there was strategic value in doing so. And finally, an iron control of communications. The Israelis successfully censored the Internet and arrested news teams from Western countries whose reporting was considered to be helpful to Hamas and Hizbollah."

"I would like to propose similar measures for tackling the SNLA and the WRA."

The Cabinet voted to agree to Arbuthnot's proposal.

17 May 2021
Craigmillar
Edinburgh

The Craigmillar Estate was not on the visit itinerary of the thousands of tourists who visited Edinburgh each year. The vast post-war housing estate was one of the Scottish capital's more deprived areas with high rates of crime and drug abuse. Following disturbances in the 1980s, efforts had been made to regenerate the estate but the good work done in the 1990s and 2000s ended up being dissipated after recession struck again early in the 2010s.

The Green Howards were patrolling the estate along with officers from Lothian and Borders Police and from English forces as part of Operation Clean Sweep. For the past week, the armed forces and the police had gone into known SNLA and WRA strongholds in force to arrest known terrorist suspects and sympathisers helping them, and had rounded up no less than 300 suspects. Furthermore, they had confiscated the homes of terror suspects and sealed them up so they could not be used for illegal purposes again.

The exercise had been costly, both in terms of human casualties and in further damage to the United Kingdom's reputation as a democratic country. There had already been riots in another part of Edinburgh, Wester Hailes, over the weekend, and further disturbances had taken place in Aberdeen, Cardiff, Dundee, Glasgow, Swansea and Wrexham. Seven soldiers and four policemen had been shot dead, along with seventeen members of the public. And there were rumours that the European Union, with support from Russia, China and Iran, was going to advance a motion at the United Nations calling for the United Kingdom's suspension.

A convoy of police cars and vans and British Army Saracen armoured cars rolled eastwards along Niddrie Mains Road. Inside the lead Saracen was Captain Tim Brennan of the Green Howards, who was in charge of the patrol.

Brennan radioed Chief Inspector Doug Gillies who was in a BMW 530 of Lothian and Borders Police to let him know they were closing in on a key suspect.

"Doug, we're going into Hay Drive. Next on the left. Suspect lives at number 45. Richard James Irvine, born 6 September 1992. Please confirm his details."

"Irvine is a known SNLA member, Tim" replied Gillies. "He's wanted on charges of attempted murder and causing explosions. We're ready to go in."

As the convoy turned into Hay Drive, they were met by a mob. Stones and petrol bombs started to be thrown.

"Oh shit!" said Lieutenant Ben Girling, second in command to Brennan.

Brennan was however prepared for trouble. He barked into his microphone "Saracen Two and Three, prepare to disembark and deploy crowd dispersal tactics." Then back on the radio to Chief Inspector Gillies, "Doug, prepare the TSG to go in."

Several soldiers jumped out of the second and third Saracen and, using the armoured vehicles as protection, opened fire with a volley of plastic bullets and CS gas at the crowd. Several rioters fell to the ground. Within seconds, the Territorial Support Group waded in, batons swinging, to make arrests.

Without warning, several gunshots rang out from the upper storey of a house in Hay Drive. Two soldiers and a policeman took direct hits.

"Sir, we're under fire" shouted Sergeant Chris Oldfield of the Green Howards.

"Return fire, Sergeant" shouted Brennan.

After the first return of fire from the Green Howards, they were scattered again as a couple of mortars landed close to the Saracens.

"Phew, that was close!" said Corporal Ryan Hawley.

Worse was to follow. In the top storey of 72 Hay Drive, Archie Munro aimed an RPG-9 rocket launcher. On the end was a Russian-built RPG-9 grenade capable of penetrating armour of 18 inches in thickness. Munro was a former corporal in the Royal Regiment of Scotland and had served in Afghanistan and had joined the SNLA four years previously. Munro pressed the launch button and the rocket-powered grenade smashed into the second Saracen standing 400 metres away and set it on fire.

Brennan realised the danger that his men and the police were in, and radioed his base for help.

"Tango Alpha 45 to base. We're under attack from the SNLA. Gunfire reported and we've lost a Saracen to a rocket-powered grenade."

"Read you loud and clear, Tango Alpha 45. Help is on the way."

Less than a minute later, the clatter of two Army Air Corps Boeing Apache helicopter gunships was heard over Craigmillar.

"Tango Alpha 45, please give location of the bad guys" said the lead pilot, Captain James Grabham.

"Positive identification on numbers 45 and 72—shit, there's your evidence" said Brennan as he ducked to avoid another round of gunfire.

"Big Bird Two, this is Big Bird One" said Grabham to Lieutenant Mark Kendall in the second Apache. "Prepare to engage targets."

Both Apaches were loaded with Hellfire missiles and each helicopter launched two missiles at their target. Numbers 45 and 72 Hay Drive were destroyed as the Hellfire missiles struck home and exploded.

Standing at the southern end of Hay Drive and filming the events of the day was a film crew from EBC News along with EBC Reporter, Asif Ahmed. Ahmed had formerly worked for BBC in the days before they were downsized and turned into a Government broadcasting agency, and had left following a disagreement with his bosses over editorial content. He had found a home at the EU and European government-funded corporation which had been modelled on the old BBC.

"This is Asif Ahmed of EBC News, live from Edinburgh."

"I am standing on the Craigmillar Estate where I have just seen the British Army destroy two houses following a confrontation with the SNLA. This will hardly endear an increasingly isolated British government with the international community . . . ."

Ahmed and his film crew found themselves starting at three large and clearly annoyed police officers.

"Can we see your identity and permission to film here" said Sergeant Wayne Goodbody of Staffordshire Police, who was on secondment to Lothian and Borders.

Ahmed produced his Press pass. "European Broadcasting Corporation. We're legal and permitted to work over here."

"You are not permitted to film the police and armed forces carrying out counter-terror activities, sunshine" replied Goodbody. "Government Emergency Powers. You're all under arrest. Constable Rogers, handcuff them."

19 May 2021
United Nations General Assembly
New York City

"The next motion to be discussed is Resolution 1042, which has been submitted by France and is supported by Germany, Greece, Italy, Spain and Sweden." The voice of the Secretary-General, Pretash Joshi, was the signal to the French Ambassador to the United Nations, Paul Haget, that he would be speaking next.

Haget's motion was a highly controversial one. It formally condemned the conduct of the United Kingdom government for its actions in expelling people from their homes on the pretext of being terrorist suspects and in arresting journalists in the course of doing their job, and called for the suspension of the United Kingdom from the United Nations for being in breach of the terms of its charter. Events had been brought to a head two days earlier when the British Army had responded to coming under fire by destroying two houses in Edinburgh and killing all the occupants, and following this up by arresting a news crew from EBC under emergency powers. To France and its fellow EU members, it smacked of the worst excesses by Israel and, in previous years, South Africa.

Haget stood up to speak.

"You have before you Resolution 1042 which the Government of France has tabled with the support of fellow governments from the European Union."

"My Government has not taken the decision to table this motion lightly. The United Kingdom may be our longest-standing rival, but they are also a close neighbour. The French people have not forgotten that the United Kingdom came to our assistance twice in the last century when both our countries were threatened and, despite our differences, there has been mutual respect between us. Like the United Kingdom, France has its own national minorities—the Basques, Bretons, Catalans and Corsicans—all of whom wish to preserve their national identity and who at times have challenged the rule of our Government."

"However, our Government cannot stand idly by and see one of our neighbours display a cavalier contempt for the rights of its own national minorities. During the past six years, the United Kingdom has sent its armed forces into Scotland and Wales, it has arrested and held in custody people without charge, it has presided over blatant miscarriages of justice, it has harassed campaigners and journalists who are trying to tell the truth and it has colluded with a terrorist organisation which has caused loss of life in both EU member countries and in the USA."

"The United Kingdom has shown contempt for international relations. Three years ago, it tried to arrest on French sovereign soil five men and women it suspected of murder rather than leave the matter to the Surête. As many of you know, that mission ended in tragedy when the plane taking them out of Paris crashed into an incoming airliner which came down in Saint Denis. In the same year, it used its air force to destroy a so-called pirate radio station which was causing it some embarrassment rather than seek the co-operation of our fellow European Union member, the Netherlands. And, most seriously, last year the United Kingdom was responsible for another hostile military act against another fellow European Union member, Ireland."

"The final straw was the events in the past week where the armed forces and the police have been forcibly evicting people from their homes on the pretext of being a terrorist suspect. That alone is contrary to the United Nations Charter which states that member countries should grant its citizens access to a free and fair trial if they are suspected of wrongdoing. This was compounded by the tragic events in Edinburgh two days ago where nine people were killed after helicopter gunships opened fire on two houses."

"The United Kingdom has also shown contempt for the freedom of the press. A news team from EBC News which filmed the attack in Edinburgh was arrested under the United Kingdom's security laws."

"The United Kingdom claims to be a democracy, but it has shown scant regard for the rights of people in Scotland and Wales, or for those people who do not agree with its policies. It operates a security apparatus that would be more at home under a military dictatorship. For these reasons, I do not consider that the United Kingdom's continued membership of this august body is compatible with its principles, and I call upon you to support this motion."

Sir Dennis Falconer, the United Kingdom's Ambassador to the United Nations, indicated that he wished to respond to the motion. He stood up.

"You will have heard M. Haget's reasons for putting this motion forward. I should be grateful if you could now listen to the reasons why you should reject this ridiculous motion."

"Anyone listening to M. Haget's emotive and hysterical speech would think that the United Kingdom has been under the heel of a brutal dictatorship for the past eleven years. He appears to have forgotten that the current Government has been elected on no less than three separate occasions under a franchise which has been open to all adults over the age of eighteen. Hardly the mark of a despotic regime."

"M. Haget has also forgotten that the people of the United Kingdom have faced the depredations of two vicious terrorist organisations. The SNLA and the WRA. It is those organisations who show utter contempt for democracy. It is those organisations which have killed innocent civilians by the gun and the bomb. It is those organisations which have run a reign of terror in their own countries and have killed and maimed anyone who does not pay tribute to them. It is those organisations which have robbed banks, peddled drugs and laundered money, thereby undermining the stability of society. And the United Kingdom has received scant support from its fellow governments in bringing the men and women of terror to justice."

"Do any of you seriously expect the United Kingdom to have abrogated its responsibility to its citizens and allowed the SNLA and WRA to continue their reign of terror without challenge? I do not believe that any of you sitting here today would have allowed such events to have happened in their own country."

"Fighting terror is not pretty. Sometimes, governments have to get down in the mud and play as dirty as their adversaries. I will admit that the United Kingdom has not always played by Queensbury Rules in its fight to keep the country safe. But to have played strictly by the rules would have risked capitulation to the men and women of violence. The people of the United Kingdom, who voted for a government that would not shirk from tough decisions, would not forgive us if we gave in. I therefore ask you to reject this Motion."

As the session wore on, Sir Dennis began to get the feeling that the tide was turning against the United Kingdom. No heavyweight countries were offering their support. The United States, Australia, Canada and New Zealand were all remaining neutral. The European Union had rallied behind France and had gained support from Russia, China and Iran. Argentina, Brazil and South Africa had all thrown their lot in with the motion.

At 5:30pm, the vote was called. UN Secretary-General Joshi took his seat to announce the result.

"I hereby announce the result of the vote on Resolution 1042. Those in favour—one hundred and seventy nine. Those against the motion—nine. Those in abstention—twenty five. I hereby declare that Resolution 1042has been passed."

The United Kingdom had been suspended from the United Nations.

CHAPTER 30

22 May 2021
Lindisfarne Grove
Clondalkin
Dublin

Iain Murray and Gareth Evans had switched their planned bilateral from Martin Hallinan's house in Drumcondra to fellow Sinn Fein member Michael O'Shea's house in one of Dublin's western suburbs. They reckoned it would be safer and that there was less of a chance of being watched by MI6 agents. O'Shea was lower down in Sinn Fein's hierarchy than Hallinan and the satellite town on Dublin's western fringes was less likely to be a magnet for MI6's attention.

The Chairmen of the General Councils of the SNLA and the WRA were sitting down in the lounge of O'Shea's house, drinking cups of tea brought in by Bridget O'Shea. On the agenda for discussion was the two organisations' response to Operation Clean Sweep.

"How's Clean Sweep impacted on the WRA, Gareth?" asked Murray.

"Much the same as for the SNLA, Iain" replied the Chairman of the WRA's General Council. "We've had a lot of our best men and women picked up. And by the way, there's another trial on at the Special Criminal Court."

"Who's on trial?" asked Murray.

"Anna Michael from us and Nicola Reid from the SNLA. Facing murder charges. They could face the rope."

"Who's the third girl?" asked Murray. "You said there were three."

"Sarah Bebbington. English, but a sympathiser with our cause. She's facing lesser charges of assisting terrorist organisations. You know what the media have dubbed them? The Angels of Death."

"Gareth, we've got to consider a big move to counter Clean Sweep" said Murray. "Something that will rock the British government to their foundations."

Evans was not wholly convinced.

"Not sure we really need to press that hard, Iain. The British government's got no friends left in the world. The Yanks have imposed trade sanctions on them, as have the EU and half the world, it seems. And Britain's just been suspended by the UN. I reckon Britain will collapse before the year's out and that bitch Pearson will have no choice but to go. And any new government will have to negotiate with us."

"I'm less convinced, Gareth" replied Murray. "The Brits are bloody resilient. If Operation Clean Sweep proves to be a success, Pearson will be a national heroine, just like Thatcher was. Also, there's signs that the Yanks are getting over 2/13, at least outside the North East and the states where there are a lot of Scottish and Welsh-Americans. All it will need is a change of political control in the USA and the EU and they'll lift trade sanctions. Just like what happened with Israel in the last decade."

Murray continued.

"What I'm thinking of is pulling off a mass escape from Foulness."

"Foulness? Jeez, Iain, I hope you know what you're letting yourself in for" said Evans. "They don't call it Alcatraz for nothing. It's in the middle of a fucking army gunnery range, you know. Only one way in and out and patrolled by a mean bunch of fuckers. No less than twenty of our guys have died trying to escape from there."

"I know it's a tough call, Gareth" said Murray. "But no security system's impenetrable. Some of our London Brigade have found major security weaknesses in the main contractor for prisoner escorts there. Securitas. I reckon it's possible to get some of our guys onto their payroll without challenge. They will find out the operating procedures for Foulness. Once we've done that, I reckon all we need to do is to kidnap one of the senior managers and hold his family hostage, and he will have no choice but to release our guys from custody."

"A tiger kidnap?" said Evans. "That sounds a great idea. Count me in."

2 June 2021
Department for Justice
Petty France
London

Staff at the Department for Justice were coming to terms with the news announced in the Emergency Budget that 33% of civil service jobs were going to be axed over the following year. In addition, salaries were to be frozen for three years and recruitment was to be suspended for the same period. The Chancellor of the Exchequer, Jason Steer, had also announced that a further wave of privatisation was to take place, with policymaking functions no longer exempt from the brisk winds of the marketplace.

Matthew Rhodes felt particularly vulnerable. An Executive Officer working for Courts Service Finance, he was in his sixth year of service and had twice been turned down for promotion. Six months earlier, he had a messy break-up with his girlfriend. She got the flat they shared and the episode left him with further debts on top of those he had incurred at university. Several of the colleagues who had joined at the same time as him had either obtained promotion or were in the field for promotion. And a year earlier, he had been forced to leave a job he enjoyed as a result of a restructure and take up a post he did not like. Nor did he like his line manager, Justine Wilkes, who he found officious and petty-minded. His last report was the first one he had received in his career that was less than glowing, and he knew that the next one would be similar.

The Public Services and Commercial Union, which represented the majority of civil servants, had held an open meeting that day, and Rhodes had been one of the attendees. On leaving the meeting, Rhodes approached Neil Duggan, a PCS representative.

Duggan was a known left-wing activist and Rhodes felt he might be sympathetic to his plight.

"Neil, have you got a minute?"

"Sure have, Matt" replied Duggan. "Have you got problems?"

"That's an understatement, Neil" said Rhodes. "I've got £20k of debts, some from university but most arising from when I split with Debbie earlier this year. I'm having difficulty in paying them off now and I'm starting to get letters with red ink threatening to take me to court. You don't need to be a rocket scientist to know that if I lose my job, I'm as good as bankrupt."

"You went for promotion twice" said Duggan. "You ought to be safe."

"A year ago, I would have agreed" said Rhodes. "But I was forced to move and I've got a fucking bitch as a line manager. What's worse, everyone knows she got her position by sleeping with the boss so he's on her side. And, as you know, Neil, there's a lot of high calibre staff working up here. Get one slightly less than brilliant report and you're in the relegation zone."

"Where are you living at present, Matt?" asked Duggan.

"Renting a flat on the Stockwell Park Estate. It's a complete fucking toilet. One of my neighbours is a crack dealer, the other's done time for armed robbery."

"Have you thought of moving back with your parents?"

"Neil, that's a complete non-runner" said Rhodes. "My mum doesn't even live in the UK anymore. She divorced my dad while I was at university and she's remarried. She and my stepdad now live in Marbella. In any case, I can't stand him. He's a typical smug, self-righteous expat arsehole who doesn't think I'm doing a proper job because I'm in the public sector."

"Matt, I'll ask around and find if there's anything that PCS can do to help you" said Duggan. "We may be starting up a hardship fund. We'll also be helping anyone made redundant find work. I'll be in touch."

"Thanks, Neil."

Later that day

Neil Duggan was home at last after a long day. Queries from worried PCS members at the Department for Justice had kept him busy.

He pulled out an old iPad which he used for emergency calls. He had it reprogrammed with the SIM card of another mobile, which made it difficult to track him. Duggan was more than just a trade union activist. His father and two of his uncles had been members of Sinn Fein and a third uncle had been a member of the IRA. Duggan himself was aligned to the Hard Left Caucus in the PCS but, unknown to his colleagues, had built close links with the SNLA and the WRA, and their political wings.

The phone rang. A man with a Welsh accent answered it.

"07799 515887."

"Is that you. Ed?" asked Duggan.

"Neil, it is. Got any news for me?" On the other end of the line was Ed Thomas, a Deputy Commander in the WRA's London Brigade.

"Ed, listen to this. There's a bloke at Department of Justice who might be open to persuasion. Basically, he's in shit street. His girlfriend dumped him, he's left with loads of debts and his career's going nowhere. He's also got access to Crown Courts and might be able to fix you up with passes to get in."

"Fucking brilliant, Neil" said Thomas. "Have you got his details?"

7 June 2021
Securitas plc
Southfields Business Park
Fenton Way
Basildon
Essex

The ten new recruits for Securitas reported to the Human Resources office to collect their passes and to attend an induction session.

Securitas were a large, multi-national security company and were proud that they had obtained the contract for the escort of prisoners to and from HMP Foulness, the country's first 'supermax' prison. For this reason, they were punctilious about who they recruited to make sure that no one working for them either had links or could be compromised by criminal or political extremist elements.

All ten had been recruited locally from South Essex and had passed security screening. Four of the ten, Lee Henderson, Mickey Jones, Liam Strachan and Guy Williams were joining as security guards. Two more, Richard Adamek and Trevor Byrne, were joining as drivers. Another two, Tom McGinlay and Donato Marinello, were joining as service engineers. And the two women in the party, Bethan Carver and Sheena Matthews, were joining as customer service assistants.

Each of the new recruits was shown the way into a lecture theatre. The room darkened as a video screen lit up to show a film about the work of Securitas. After the film ended, the company's security officer, a retired Chief Inspector from the local police force, gave a talk about security and reminded the new recruits that they would all be required to sign the Official Secrets Act. Before leaving to take up their posts, each of the new recruits was given an information pack and duly signed the Official Secrets Act.

After the recruits left, the Security Officer, Gordon Disley and the HR Manager, Helen Firmin, had a short chat about the new recruits.

"Gordon, I'm rather impressed with the calibre of the latest batch of recruits, don't you think? All look well-qualified and hard-working. They'll do well for us."

"I've got to admit that I agree with you, Helen" replied Disley. As a former policeman for thirty years, he was naturally suspicious of human nature but he admitted that the ten new joiners all looked good assets for Securitas.

Little did Disley or Firmin know that all ten recruits were members of the SNLA and the WRA and had slipped through security screening through being English-born and raised and not arousing suspicion.

8 June 2021
Wynter House
Aytoun Road
Stockwell Park Estate
London

Matthew Rhodes had gone through what is referred to as a "groundhog day". Delays on the Victoria Line meant that he was late into work. He'd had a blazing row with his line manager, Justine Wilkes, over a minor issue of presentation. The accumulated pressures of the break-up with his girlfriend, the forced job transfer he didn't want, debt and the news about forthcoming redundancies led him to blow his top and tell Justine exactly what he thought of her. He thought nothing more of the issue until later that afternoon when he was told that the Head of Unit, Simon Hutchinson, wanted to see him at 9:30 sharp the following morning. Hutchinson was someone who seldom engaged with staff in junior grades unless they were joining or leaving or to give a bollocking. Or worse. Rhodes knew that Justine Wilkes was a favourite of Hutchinson. He feared the worst—that disciplinary proceedings were to be taken against him.

At 8pm, Rhodes was surprised to hear the front door bell go. He went to answer it. There were two white men standing outside, one dark-haired, the other sandy-haired.

"Mr Rhodes?" asked the fair-haired man. He had a Scottish accent.

"Yes. Is there anything you want?"

"We might be able to help you, Mr Rhodes" said the darker-haired man. "Is it OK if we come in for a chat?"

"Can you explain why you're here first?" asked Rhodes.

"Sure" said the darker-haired man. Rhodes noticed he had a Welsh accent.

"Mr Rhodes, I've heard you're facing difficult circumstances" said the Scot. "In debt, facing possible redundancy. Me and my mate might be able to help."

"Okay, come in" said Rhodes. "By the way, what's your names?"

"Ed Lewis" said the Welshman.

"Craig Walker" said the Scot.

The three men were sat on the sofa in Rhodes' lounge. It had seen better days. Lewis was the first to speak.

"Mr Rhodes, er, what's your first name?"

"Matt."

"Okay, Matt, Craig and I want to visit a Crown Court for the day. We're researchers working for a consultancy. I understand you can fix us with access."

"You don't need to come here to ask that, Ed" said Rhodes. "DfJ can fix you up with tickets on application."

"It's no ordinary Crown Court, Matt" said Walker. "Ed and I want to attend the Special Criminal Court."

"You mean Woolwich Crown Court, Craig?" said an incredulous Rhodes. "There's no way I'm able to fix you up with admission for Woolwich. Security's now

415

tight as a drum there. The only guests they let in are a few embedded journalists who face very strict reporting restrictions."

"Matt, Craig and I are ready to offer you money if you get us passes" said Lewis. "How does £20k grab you?"

"Guys, you know what you're asking me to do?" said Rhodes. "I'm already facing a possible disciplinary at work. If I give you passes to get into the Special Criminal Court and get found out, it'll be more than a sacking. The Government's paranoid about security there, particularly after the nobbling of three of the Court's judges last year. I'm facing ten, maybe fifteen years in jail if I get caught."

**Later that night
A WRA safe house
Steventon Road
Shepherd's Bush
London**

Ed Thomas dialled Neil Duggan's number into his Personal Data Assistant.

"Neil, that you, Ed here."

"How did it go, Ed?" asked Duggan.

"Hard work. You can tell that Rhodes is pissed off with everything, but neither I nor Craig managed to persuade him to take the money and get us passes. He's frightened of getting caught and sent down."

"Keep plugging away, Ed" said Duggan. "Rhodes is facing possible serious disciplinary charges at work. He had a row with his boss and he basically told her to fuck off. She's gone and reported him to the Head of Unit."

**9 June 2021
Department for Justice
Petty France
London**

"Come in, Matt." The voice of Simon Hutchinson summoned Rhodes into the meeting room.

Hutchinson, a tall, broad-shouldered, balding man in his late 40s and the Head of Rhodes' Unit, looked like a former rugby player. He had been recruited to the Department from private industry six years earlier and, although the signs of middle-aged spread were starting to set in, he was still physically attractive to women. It was common knowledge that he had been involved in affairs with several of his female staff. One of whom was Justine Wilkes, Rhodes' line manager.

Hutchinson opened a sheath of papers on the desk.

"Matt, there have been allegations of gross misconduct made against you. Your line manager, Justine Wilkes, claims that, yesterday, you were verbally abusive towards her. Verbal abuse of a colleague is a breach of the Departmental code of conduct. Verbal abuse of a superior officer counts as insubordinate conduct."

"Had this been an isolated incident, I would have been content to go no further than to issue a verbal warning about your conduct. But Ms Wilkes had advised me that you have been unco-operative towards her since you joined the Unit a year ago and that you have been making unpleasant and totally false allegations about her to other colleagues behind her back. The Department has to take a serious view about the conduct of its staff whom it expects to behave in a professional manner. For these reasons, Matt, I'm going to have to issue you with a formal written warning about your conduct. This warning will remain live for a year. If there are no further complaints against you during the twelve months the warning is live, it will expire and will not be held against you in your career. But if there are any further complaints about your conduct during the next twelve months, the Department will have no option but to consider formal dismissal procedures. Do you understand?"

"Simon, this is a complete travesty of justice" shouted Rhodes. "If you bothered to get out and actually meet your staff, you would find that Justine's had it in for me ever since I joined Courts Service Unit. Other members of staff feel the same about her. You've completely overlooked the fact that managers in my previous Unit had no problem with either my work or conduct, and supported my applications for promotion. If you go ahead with this written warning, I'm going to take the matter up with PCS and, furthermore, I'll take out a grievance against you and Justine."

"Don't push your luck, Matt" said an increasingly red-faced Hutchinson. "You're already in the last chance saloon. Taking out malicious grievances is now a disciplinary matter. If you go ahead, all you'll be doing is signing your P45. Understand?"

The same evening
Wynter House
Aytoun Road
Stockwell Park Estate
London

Matt Rhodes got home to find a voicemail message on his telephone. It was from Ed Lewis.

Rhodes was still seething from the high-handed treatment he had got from Simon Hutchinson earlier that day. What was worse, he knew what the effect of a live disciplinary warning would be. Later that year, the Department for Justice would be requiring all staff to re-apply for their jobs as part of the exercise to reduce the headcount. The last two reports and the mid-year appraisal would carry a lot of weight. As would any live disciplinary action. Even if he got through the year without falling foul of Justine again, it was now highly likely that he would be a candidate for compulsory redundancy.

Sod it, he thought. Standing up to a bullying line manager and what does the Department do? Put him on notice that he faces dismissal next time he speaks out of turn. It was just as Hutchinson said. Defend yourself and the management closes ranks.

The two guys who called the night before were offering to clear his debts. He had strong doubts that they were researchers as claimed. How after all do they have

£20k on them? He guessed they either might be linked to criminals. Or the SNLA and the WRA. After all, Ed was Welsh and Craig a Scot.

Rhodes reached for the phone and dialled the number Ed had left.

"Is that Ed? Matt Rhodes here."

"Thanks for ringing back, Matt. Got something that might interest you."

"Go ahead."

"Matt, we're ready to offer you £40k if you can get us passes for Woolwich Crown Court. Interested?"

"Yes, I am."

12 June 2021
Kilworth Avenue
Brentwood
Essex

"Nearly there, David. Tom and I won't be more than another half an hour." The voice of Donato Marinello called out from outside the front of David Bovington's detached house.

David Bovington was the Area Manager for Securitas covering Essex and East Anglia and worked at the Securitas offices in Basildon. Earlier that week, his Mercedes-Benz E320 had developed a fault. The dealers told him they would be unable to take the car in for at least a week, which meant that he would have to either borrow a pool car or use his wife's Volkswagen Prinz.

Many of the managers at Securitas asked their staff to carry out jobs for them out of office hours and for payment. It was against company rules as there was a risk of compromising security, but the practice was so widespread that no one risked bringing disciplinary proceedings for fear that their own indiscretions might be brought up.

Bovington realised that, if he asked Securitas's service engineers to come out and see to his car, it would be back on the road. He therefore asked Donato Marinello and his colleague, Tom McGinlay, to come out and service his car that Saturday morning. The two engineers were only too keen to help.

Securitas had sophisticated portable service equipment in their vans. Although most of the service work was done at Basildon, there were occasional callouts if vans broke down whilst out on the road. As Securitas's business was security and the transport of highly risky cargos, whether money or people, they could not risk having vans immobile and at risk of attack.

Marinello and McGinlay had replaced the faulty part and all they had to do was a systems test on the computer. Then to run the engine on the Merc to check it was okay.

McGinlay ran the computer. As each system was checked, either a green tick which indicated it was working or a red cross which indicated a fault showed up. He looked pleased as a succession of green ticks showed up.

"All systems okay, Don" shouted McGinlay. "Try the engine."

Marinello turned the key in the ignition switch. The V6 engine started first time and ran smoothly.

"Looks like David's car's fixed" said Marinello.

Bovington was delighted when he saw that his car was working.

"I'm really grateful to you chaps for giving up your Saturday morning and coming out to do this. How much do I owe?"

"Five hundred quid okay?" asked McGinlay.

"Easily, Tom" replied Bovington. "That's half what the garage would have asked."

Bovington had online banking access in his study and he processed a pair of e-cheques to the accounts of Marinello and McGinlay.

Later that day
Whitmore Way
Basildon
Essex

Tom McGinlay pulled up outside the house of Donato Marinello's parents.

"Don, that went sweet as a nut" said McGinlay. "We've found out where Bovington lives, the layout of his house, the names of his wife and kids. All we've got to do now is to brief our commanders. I'll be getting in touch with Dougie Callender."

"And I'll let Gareth Higham know" said Marinello. "Have we got a date planned yet for Foul Play?"

Marinello was referring to the SNLA and WRA codename for the planned escape from HMP Foulness.

"I've heard 17 June is likely, Don" replied McGinlay. "Apparently, the Governor and Deputy Governors will both be out that day. Attending a conference about possible job cuts. Dougie's arranged for a fake prisoner transfer notice to be prepared—he's got an insider in the Prison Service looking after this. All we'll have to do is take Bovington and his wife and kids prisoner for the day. We've got Ricky and Trev on hand to drive the vans."

17 June 2021
Kilworth Avenue
Brentwood
Essex

David and Shirley Bovington were both early risers, a habit ingrained during their army service almost two decades earlier. Shirley had prepared breakfast for their two children, Henry, who was nine years old and Alison, who was six. In a month's time, the school year would be finishing and the family would be off to Marbella.

The chimes on the doorbell sounded. Both David and Shirley Bovington were surprised that someone would be calling at such an early hour.

"I'll go, darling" said David Bovington, as he made his way to the front door.

He opened it to find eight men, all wielding Glock machine pistols and dressed in black, with balaclavas hiding their faces. They burst into the Bovingtons' suburban home.

"What the hell's going on, Dave?" cried a frightened Shirley Bovington.

"Quiet!" shouted the leader of the gunmen, a stocky man with a Welsh accent. "Over there, in the corner. Now!"

The Bovingtons complied.

"Mr Bovington, if you want to see your wife and kids again, you will do what we tell you." The second man, who was taller, had a distinctive Scottish accent.

The leader of the gunmen gave further instructions to his colleagues.

"Elwyn, Gareth, can you stay with the Bovingtons. Euan, Hamish, the same. Mr Bovington, come with us. And no tricks. You stitch us up or call the fuzz, that will be the last you see of your wife and kids."

Bovington followed the four men to a silver Ford Mondeo parked in Kilworth Avenue. A black Vauxhall Insignia with four more masked men was parked behind. He got in the back.

"Mr Bovington" said the Welshman as the car pulled away, "we want you to dispatch two of your high security prisoner transports to HMP Foulness. On arrival, you will meet the Assistant Governor there, Ms Katie Lear, and present her with the prisoner transfer order I've got here."

He pointed to an official HM Prison Service order for the transfer of forty SNLA and WRA prisoners from HMP Foulness to HMP Woodhill and HMP Whitemoor. It was an excellent forgery prepared by a corrupt official in the Prison Service for the payment of twenty thousand pounds.

"If Assistant Governor Lear asks why you've applied for this transfer, you will say that the security services have found out that an attempt is to be made to spring the prisoners from custody. For the record, I know for a fact that a top secret communication is awaiting the Governor's notice on his return."

"Jesus Christ!" exclaimed Bovington. "Are you crazy or something? You do realise that Foulness is probably the world's most secure prison. All those guys you're trying to get out are some of the hardest core terrorists in the UK. As soon as the authorities realise an escape's happened, they'll shut the borders and there'll be NATS and the SAS running about armed to the teeth. If they catch your guys, they won't bother to say hello. They'll probably shoot them on the spot."

"Which is why we've asked you to co-operate with us, Mr Bovington" said the Scotsman. "The Prison Service will trust you. Ex-Army, senior manager with a leading security company. And, I'm afraid we'll have to hold your wife and kids until our guys are clear. Sorry."

The Welshman then addressed the Securitas Area Manager.

"Once the prisoners are in the Securitas transports, the drivers will take them to Rainham Marshes Nature Reserve where our colleagues will be waiting. The transfer of prisoners will take place there. We will collect you at Rainham Marshes and escort you back to Brentwood. Unfortunately, as my colleague said, we will be unable to release you or your family until our men have managed to make good their escape."

"Finally, a word of warning, Mr Bovington. If you let us down or tip off the authorities, it won't just be your wife and kids who will get it. It will be your last move too."

<h3 style="text-align:center">The same day
HMP Foulness
near Southend-on-Sea
Essex</h3>

David Bovington drove his Mercedes-Benz through the inner security gates at HMP Foulness and into the guest car park. He was followed by a pair of Volvo trucks that had been fitted out as high security prison transport. At the wheel were Richard Adamek and Trevor Byrne.

Katie Lear, an Assistant Governor at HMP Foulness, was effectively in charge for the day as the Governor, James Pocock and the Deputy Governor, Tony Caplin, were attending a conference in London. It was on the programme of staff cuts being imposed on the Civil Service to help manage the growing budget deficit. Foulness would not be exempt, despite its status as a supermax prison.

Lear knew Bovington well but she was completely taken aback when he presented her with a prisoner transfer order for forty of the country's most dangerous terrorists. They included Peter "Killer" Kane and Owen "Mad Dog" Williams, who had earned particularly unsavoury reputations for grisly murders.

"David, what on earth is Prison Service thinking of in transferring these guys to a less secure prison? It doesn't make sense—Foulness was set up to be the most escape-proof prison in the world."

"I know it sounds crazy, Katie" replied Bovington. "But I'm only doing what I've been asked to do. There's something else you need to know."

Bovington made sure that all the doors and windows in Lear's office were shut and no one was passing by.

"Katie, MI5 have just got hold of intelligence about a planned escape. The SNLA and WRA were going to obtain Prison Service accreditation from a bent official and spring a load of their prisoners being held here. The Governor will find a top secret memo waiting for him on his return about this. But we've had to act quickly and move these guys to secure accommodation before anyone has a chance to spring them. Once the insiders have been identified and arrested, it will be safe to return these guys to Foulness."

"David, I'll need to check with James Pocock first" said Lear. "This is a request which would normally not be cleared below full Governor level."

"We've got no time to lose on this, Katie" said Bovington. "Wait for Pocock's return and there's a risk that those guys will be out. This authority has gone to the top of Prison Service."

"Very well, David. I'll arrange for the named prisoners to be released to your custody."

Later that afternoon
Rainham Marshes Nature Reserve
Essex

No one had paid much attention to the four Ford Transit minibuses parked by the Nature Reserve. The only people using the Reserve that day were school parties and they assumed that the buses had been hired to take other school parties to visit the Reserve.

At 2:55pm, a silver Mercedes-Benz E320 drove into the Reserve's car park, closely followed by two security transports bearing the markings of Securitas plc. The SNLA mission commander, Dougie Callender, gave the thumbs up sign to his WRA counterpart, Gareth Higham.

David Bovington got out of his car and walked over to Callender and Higham.

"There you are" said Bovington. "All forty prisoners delivered to you as requested and at the set time."

The Securitas drivers opened up the back of the vans and forty of the most dangerous terrorists in the country walked into the Essex sunlight. They boarded the minibuses which started to leave one by one.

"Well done, Mr Bovington" said Callender.

"What about my wife and kids?" asked Bovington. "Are you going to release them?"

"We can't do that yet, Mr Bovington" said Higham. "We'll be holding them for another six hours. That will give our guys time to disperse before the authorities come looking for them."

"During that time, you should act as nothing has happened, Mr Bovington" said Callender. "And don't think about going to the polis. Remember what we said earlier in the day."

18 June 2021
Sky News

"This is Sara Ratcliffe with this morning's headlines on Sky News."

"Earlier today, forty highly dangerous terrorists from the SNLA and the WRA escaped from the country's most secure prison at Foulness after the wife and children of a senior manager at Securitas, the company responsible for escorting prisoners, were held hostage in a 'tiger kidnap'. The police and armed forces are continuing to search for the escapees and high-level alerts are in place at all air and seaports and at the four international railway stations serving Eurostar. It is however feared that the fugitives may have now fled the country."

"A spokesman for Essex Police said that officers are investigating the possibility that Securitas has been infiltrated by members of the SNLA and the WRA. Two Securitas employees and a member of Prison Service were arrested late yesterday for suspected complicity in the escape, and they are being interviewed at the National Anti-Terror Squad's headquarters at Nine Elms."

"The escape is an embarrassment for the Government as Foulness was claimed to be the most secure prison in the world. The Home Office is reviewing procedures for authorising prisoner transfers and is expected to impose tighter staff recruitment procedures for contractors."

Later that morning
Home Office
Marsham Street
London

David Rimington, the Director-General of the Prison Service, had erroneously thought that he might have an easier time with Darren Bramble than he did with Deborah Pearson. He was sorely mistaken. The new Home Secretary was boiling with fury over the Foulness escape.

"David, what happened yesterday was a national embarrassment" shouted Bramble. "Foulness was supposed to be a 'supermax' prison, completely escape-proof. And what happens? Forty SNLA and WRA prisoners walk out in broad daylight."

"Home Secretary, the circumstances were exceptional" replied a flustered Rimington. "Securitas's Area Manager and his family were kidnapped at gunpoint and he was forced to co-operate with the SNLA and WRA. If he hadn't done so, his wife and kids would have been killed."

"Where the hell were the Governor and Deputy Governor?" raged Bramble. "They're paid good money to keep that prison secure."

"Governor Pocock and Deputy Governor Caplin were attending the conference on managing the cuts. The one which all Prison Service governors and deputy governors were ordered to attend."

"David, it looks like Prison Service's procedures are not fit for purpose" continued Bramble. "It seems like one of your staff produced a fake prisoner transfer request after being tapped up. In future, I want such orders to be signed in person by yourself and by the Director of Custody before they become valid and for the transfer to be put on record so that staff at prisons can check first. Then I want management cover arrangements at all prisons changed. In future, if a Governor is not on duty for any reason, there must at all times be a Deputy Governor on duty. And finally, I want contractors to be forced to tighten up their staff recruitment procedures and submit them for positive vetting by the Security Services and the National Crime Agency. Understand?"

"Home Secretary, do you realise the impact such changes will have on our day-to-day business? Several prisons are going to be cutting senior management posts in the forthcoming restructure. Some may not have Deputy Governors to provide cover. Requiring the Director of Custody and myself to sign all prisoner transfer requests will slow down the processing of such requests and may endanger security if it involves transferring a high risk prisoner to more secure accommodation. And requiring our contractors to submit all new staff to MI5 and NCA vetting will slow down the process of filling vacancies and result in them not being able to fulfil their key duties."

"David, do I make myself understood?" growled Bramble. "This is not a request. It is an order. You and several of your colleagues in Prison Service are drinking in the last chance saloon."

**The same morning
Woolwich Crown Court
Belmarsh Road
Thamesmead
London**

The three judges sitting in the trial of *R v Bebbington, Michael and Reid* returned to the courtroom to deliver their verdict and sentence. Seated in the dock were the three defendants, Sarah Bebbington, Anna Michael and Nicola Reid.

Nine months earlier, Michael and Reid had been part of a joint SNLA and WRA team which had planted a bomb on board a bus being used to transport members of the Metropolitan Police's Territorial Support Group, which had been tasked with breaking up a banned demonstration in support of Scottish and Welsh independence. Twelve officers had been killed and another 28 had been injured. Bebbington, who was an activist with the Socialist Alliance, had obtained information about the movements of Metropolitan Police vehicles for the day after sleeping with a civilian employee at New Scotland Yard and had passed it to Michael and Reid.

The Chairman of the panel of judges, Mr Justice Leakey, prepared to read out the verdict and sentence.

"Ladies and gentlemen, I along with my learned colleagues, have considered the evidence presented by both the prosecution and the defence and through the cross-examination of witnesses from both sides."

"The prosecution's evidence is most compelling. There is forensic and DNA evidence that links both Michael and Reid to the planting of the bomb on board the bus LJ71EXY, as well as CCTV evidence which shows their presence in the locality. The alibis offered by the brother and sister of the accused, namely Gary Michael and Alison Reid, are found to be unreliable and without foundation."

"There is also DNA evidence that links Bebbington to the act of obtaining without proper authority the duty roster for the Territorial Support Group on 17 October 2020 and the transport schedule. Bebbington has admitted to sleeping with Mr William Farrell, a civilian employee of the Metropolitan Police Service. Her attempt to implicate Mr Farrell in passing on this information to Michael and Reid is not considered to stand up on further investigation. Mr Farrell has admitted to a sexual liaison with Bebbington, which he now regrets. He also admitted to taking the duty roster and transport schedule home with him, in breach of Metropolitan Police Service rules, but his motive was to clear a backlog of work and was not dishonourable. There is only one conclusion that I and my learned colleagues can draw, and that is that Bebbington removed the papers from Mr Farrell's abode."

"Anna Elizabeth Michael and Nicola Karen Reid, this court finds you guilty of the capital charges of the murder of the following persons on 17 October 2020: Sergeant Daniel Jefferies, Sergeant Jason Millington, Police Constable Marcus

424

Adams, Police Constable Suzanne Charles, Police Constable Robert Jackson, Police Constable Alexander Milward, Police Constable Ian Perkins and Police Constable James Tapolczay, all of the Metropolitan Police Service. The mandatory penalty for the murder of members of the police service in the execution of their duty is death. You will be taken from this courtroom to a place appointed, where you will be hung by the neck until you are dead."

"Sarah Jane Bebbington, this court finds you guilty under Section 4 of the Terrorism Act 2012 of having procured and made available to members of a terrorist organisation information which was material to the cause of the loss or endangerment of life, involved serious violence against a person, serious damage to property and interference or disruption to electronic systems for the purpose of advancing a political cause. You are hereby sentenced to a term of imprisonment of ten years."

"Take the prisoners down."

The three prisoners were led out of the courtroom under armed police escort. They would be taken back to the female prisoners wing at HMP Belmarsh, which was connected to the court by a tunnel.

Before the escorted journey back to the confines of HMP Belmarsh began, PC Tim Hollington, PC Carol Mansfield and PC Luke Walton had to book out the prisoners through the court staff. The three constables led the prisoners into the Court Office.

Awaiting them in the Court Office was not the court administration staff, who had been held at gunpoint and locked in a storeroom, but Ed Thomas and Craig Forrest, both brandishing Walther machine pistols. Thomas and Forrest had obtained access to the court through passes issued for the payment of £40,000 by a Department for Justice civil servant.

"Put your hands up now!" shouted Thomas. "And no funny stuff. Try anything on and you get both barrels."

"You don't seriously think you're going to get away with springing two convicted terrorists from this court, do you?" asked Mansfield. "As soon as you get out the door, every copper in London will be after you."

"Shut up!" snarled Forrest.

Hollington saw there was one chance. There was a panic button within reach. If he could press it, reinforcements would be summoned and there would be enough of them to cope with both Thomas and Forrest.

While Thomas and Forrest were looking at the corridor outside to see if anyone might be walking past, their attention was temporarily diverted. Hollington saw his chance and dived for the panic button.

"Look out, Ed" shouted Forrest, "the cunt's trying to raise the alarm."

Thomas reacted by opening fire on Hollington. Forrest then opened fire on the two remaining officers. All three were dead.

"Craig, keep me covered while I get the cuffs off Anna and Nikki" shouted Thomas.

Within seconds, Thomas undid the handcuffs on Michael and Reid. The two girls seized the Heckler and Koch machine pistols from the holsters of the dead police officers and followed Forrest and Thomas towards the exit. They fired warning shots to keep at bay anyone tempted to have a go and stop them.

Parked in Belmarsh Road was a silver BMW 530i. At the wheel was Noel McKilvey, who had acted as getaway driver for the Yardies. Thomas leapt into the front passenger seat while Forrest, Michael and Reid leapt into the rear seats. The BMW then sped away.

Thirty minutes later
Home Office
Marsham Street
London

Darren Bramble was clearing his last papers before departing for his constituency for the weekend, when the phone rang. It was Sir Philip Roebuck, the Commissioner of the Metropolitan Police.

"Sorry to disturb you, Home Secretary. Bad news, I'm afraid. There's been a courtroom escape at Woolwich Crown Court."

"What!" exclaimed Bramble. This was following on top of the escape from HMP Foulness.

"It seems that terrorists from the SNLA and WRA somehow got court passes. They've sprung two prisoners facing the death penalty. Three of our officers were shot dead trying to stop them. All Met units are in pursuit and National Police Air Service have sent two helicopters up."

"Thanks, Phil. Do what you can do. I'm sorry to hear about the three officers who died. Can you provide me with their details so I can write letters of condolences to their next-of-kin."

"I'll do that, Home Secretary" replied Roebuck.

Bramble then dialled the telephone number of Kevin Lazenby, Head of the National Anti-Terror Squad.

"Kevin Lazenby. Oh, hello, Home Secretary."

"Kevin, we've got another fucking emergency" said Bramble. "SNLA and WRA prisoners are on the run from Woolwich Crown Court. Both are facing the death penalty and armed. I don't have to tell you how dangerous they'll be."

"We've just heard, Home Secretary" replied Lazenby. "With your permission, can I put a full national lockdown into place?"

Lazenby was referring to co-ordinated action by the National Anti-Terror Squad with all territorial police forces in the United Kingdom and the Border Police Force to shut all airports, seaports and the four international railway stations. In addition, the harbourmasters at small ports and managers of private airfields were ordered to close down all movements.

"Absolutely, Kevin" said Bramble. "Can you keep me informed of progress every hour?"

"I'll do that, Home Secretary" replied Lazenby.

"One thing more, Kevin. I want those prisoners back in custody, whatever it takes. If they resist arrest, don't hesitate to shoot them."

The same day, 12:45pm
Redhill Aerodrome
Redhill
Surrey

Mark Birkenshaw, the General Manager at Redhill Aerodrome, took a telephone call. It was from Surrey Police.

"Is that the General Manager of Redhill Aerodrome?"

"It is. Mark Birkenshaw here. How can I help?"

"This is Inspector Jo Penrose, Surrey Police. Bad news, I'm afraid, Mr Birkenshaw. Two SNLA and WRA terrorists are on the run. We've got reason to believe they might try to escape by using an aeroplane. Can you suspend all flights until further notice."

"I'll do that immediately, Inspector."

Before Birkenshaw had a chance to put into action a general suspension of flights, he received another call. It was Ed Newman, the chief air traffic controller.

"Mark, thank God I've got through."

"What's up, Ed? Sounds like the bomb's dropped."

"I think one of the planes has been stolen."

The same day, 1pm
Apeldoorn Way
Wallington
Surrey

Melanie Kilminster was preparing lunch for herself and her three year old son, Alfie. The wife of a policeman serving at Croydon Police Station, she was on maternity leave from her job at the London Borough of Croydon, having given birth to a daughter, Kelly, six months earlier.

Alfie Kilminster was transfixed at the sight of a light aircraft coming into land behind the house. The site where the Kilminsters' house was built had formerly been part of London's main airport in the days before Heathrow was opened. It had been closed over sixty years previously and, in the intervening years, housing, a school and an industrial estate had been built on part of the site while another part had been levelled and converted to use as football pitches.

"Look Mummy, a plane!" cried an excited Alfie.

"Don't be silly, darling" said Melanie Kilminster. There's no . . . ."

Melanie Kilminster then realised that her son was telling the truth.

Most people would have thought nothing more than it was a one-off, probably a forced landing because of engine trouble. But Melanie Kilminster had heard from her husband about the tricks that criminals used. Her immediate reaction was that it might be drug traffickers. She had read in the *Daily Mail* that traffickers often used light planes and unofficial landing strips like waste ground.

She reached for the telephone.

The same day and time
Hadfield Machine Tools Ltd
Minden Road
Sutton
Surrey

Bradley Seaman, the Head of Security at Hadfield Machine Tools, was having his lunch. The CCTV monitor in the security gatehouse was switched on.

Seaman paid little notice to the silver BMW pulling up until he noticed two men and two women get out and then get into a blue Ford Mondeo. Both the men and the women were smartly dressed, and his first reaction was that they might be sales representatives from another company returning. But it seemed odd that they were going off in a beat-up old Mondeo.

The radio in the office was playing Magic FM, a radio station that largely played middle of the road pop and soft rock music. Suddenly, the music was interrupted for a newsflash.

"We are interrupting the programme for an important newsflash."

"Two convicted terrorists, Anna Michael and Nicola Reid, are on the run after accomplices held up Woolwich Crown Court at gunpoint. Three police officers, PCs Tim Hollington, Carol Mansfield and Luke Walton, were shot dead in trying to prevent the escape."

"The escapers got away in a silver BMW 530i, registration number LC20 AMU which was last seen heading for the South Circular Road. If anyone sees this car, can they please telephone the following number. 0845 3000 6210. Whatever you do, do not approach any of the suspects. They are known to be armed."

Seaman was jolted into action. CCTV should be able to identify the registration of the Beemer. He pressed the playback button.

The television monitor showed the silver BMW pulling up. He could see the two women and two men getting out. The numberplate came into focus. He pressed the Expand Image button.

Jesus Christ, thought Seaman. That's it. LC20 AMU.

He then focused on the blue Mondeo and again pressed Expand Image. LD58 OXY. He reached for the telephone and dialled the number given on the radio bulletin.

"Metropolitan Police. How can I help?" trilled a female voice.

"Hadfield Machine Tools, Sutton here. It's regarding the radio message about escaped terrorists."

"Go ahead sir."

"The BMW pulled up here five minutes ago and two women and two men got out. It's the registration you gave out—I've got CCTV footage to prove it."

"Thank you, sir. I'll pass your message on."

"There's more you need to know" said Seaman. "They got into a blue Ford Mondeo, registration number LD58 OXY."

**Five minutes later
National Anti-Terror Squad Headquarters
Nine Elms Lane
Battersea
London**

Chief Inspector Rob Beckett, leader of the National Anti-Terror Squad's Special Weapons and Tactics Team—commonly referred to as SWAT—had just arrived back from lunch when the telephone rang.

There were six SWAT teams in the National Anti-Terror Squad. All were trained in both weapons handling and unarmed combat to SAS-standard and were deployed in dangerous situations, such as tackling armed terrorists.

"Rob, Russ Colbourne here. Important news—listen up."

Superintendent Colbourne was Beckett's boss in the National Anti-Terror Squad.

"The two terrorists who were sprung from Woolwich Crown Court have been spotted in Sutton. We reckon they're going to attempt an airborne escape from the old Croydon Airport. A light plane stolen from Redhill Aerodrome was seen landing there five minutes ago. Z Division are out in force to try and kettle all routes into the old airport, but they'll need specialist backup. The terrs are armed and fucking dangerous, Rob. Two of them have just been sentenced to death, so they've got no incentive to surrender."

"No way we can get the squad cars or vans down there in time, sir" replied Beckett.

"Rob, take the choppers" said Colbourne. "And be quick. We reckon the bad guys will be there in fifteen minutes."

After ringing off, Beckett hit the emergency response button.

"SWAT One and Two, get ready to embark for takeoff. We've got a job to do."

With that, the two SWAT teams raced out of the building towards a pair of Sikorsky S-60 helicopters and leapt on board. Beckett joined them. Within seconds, the two choppers were airborne and heading for Croydon.

**The same day, 1:30pm
Hannibal Way
Wallington
Surrey**

"Next right, Kenny" said Ed Thomas.

Kenny Groves, the driver of the Ford Mondeo carrying Craig Forrest, Anna Michael, Nicola Reid and Thomas, had been for many years a getaway driver for London's criminal underworld. He had served three prison terms during his life. Although now semi-retired, he had been tempted by the job the SNLA and the WRA dangled before him. That was to provide the second leg of the getaway run that was to finish with the four terrorists flying to freedom in a stolen Cessna Criterion.

429

The first driver, Noel McKilvey, had done a good job. By heading further west than anyone expected, he had shaken off his pursuers. The police had concentrated their efforts on locking down Gatwick Airport and Ebbsfleet International Station. Even if they thought an attempt might be made to use the old Croydon Airport for a getaway flight, they would surely be expecting an approach from the east. Not the west. As Groves' dad would have said, "Sorted!"

Groves swung the Mondeo out of Stafford Road into Hannibal Way when Forrest suddenly noticed an unwelcome sight several hundred metres up the road.

"Jesus Christ, Kenny. Pull up."

"What's the problem, Craig?" asked Michael.

"Polis. Loads of them up ahead" replied Forrest.

"Why don't we turn round and try another entrance?" asked Reid. "There's two more possibilities—Roundshaw Park and the southern end of Plough Lane."

"Nikki, all we'll do is draw attention to ourselves" said Thomas. "And there's no guarantee that the plods haven't staked out those entrances."

"Fellas, I reckon I can get through that blockade" said Groves. "Did it several times in the past on bank jobs. You up for it?"

"Aye, Kenny" said Forrest. The others all signalled their agreement.

"Hold on tight" said Groves as he revved up the Mondeo.

Groves accelerated the Mondeo up Hannibal Way so, as it approached the line of police cars and vans forming the blockade, he was doing over 80 miles per hour. The police saw him coming.

"Everyone out the fucking way" shouted a sergeant.

Police officers scattered as Groves tried to force the speeding Mondeo through a gap between a Ford Focus and a Mercedes Sprinter van. There was a sickening sound of metal on metal as the Mondeo hit the Focus and Sprinter broadside. It lost its nearside front passenger door and offside rear passenger door in the impact. The Focus was flipped onto its side but the Sprinter stayed upright although having the driver's door ripped off.

Groves started to accelerate the battered Mondeo again as he approached the southern end of Hannibal Way. The road curved round towards a private health club, but Groves' aim was the playing fields where, further on, the Cessna was waiting to whisk the four terrorists on the run over the Channel to France. The only problem was that there was a steep bank to get up to reach the playing fields. At low speed, it was possible, but Groves was hitting 60 miles per hour as he reached the end of Hannibal Way.

The Mondeo took the bank at full speed and catapulted into the air before landing on its roof and rolling over twice. Forrest, Michael and Thomas were hurled out of the Mondeo, while Groves was crushed against the steering column and dashboard.

First on the scene were the two SWAT teams from the National Anti-Terror Squad. They were armed to the teeth with Heckler and Koch sub-machine guns. Immediately, they surrounded the wrecked car and the bodies of Groves, Forrest, Michael, Reid and Thomas.

"Looks like we're too late, guv" said PC Dave Bickley of SWAT Team One to his sergeant, Neil Rogers.

"A pity, Dave" said Rogers. "I was looking forward to wasting those scumbags."

The SWAT officers wanted revenge. They had not forgotten that Michael and Reid had murdered twelve Territorial Support Group officers the previous October when their bus was blown up. In addition, Forrest and Thomas had accounted for three more police officers earlier that day.

Chief Inspector Beckett arrived on the scene.

"I guess there's not much left to do now, sir" said Rogers.

"No, we can leave it to the coroners now, Neil" replied Beckett.

"Sir, one of the suspects is still alive" shouted Bickley. He had seen Reid move.

"Take her out, lads" said Beckett.

PC Justin Morris and PC Mickey Burns pinned Reid's arms down by her side so she couldn't move. Bickley then placed the barrel of his gun against her temple and fired.

"Done, sir" replied Bickley.

Three minutes later, the contingent of Press reporters, film crews and photographers who had been informed that the terrorists were going to fly out from the old airport were on the scene, and were interviewing Chief Inspector Beckett. Beckett was explaining to the world's viewers that the terrorists had died after crashing their car after trying to breach police lines.

There was one journalist who did not make his presence known to the police. Hidden behind the bushes adjacent to the health club was Greg Chaucer, a freelance photographer who had tacked along with the main body of reporters and then detached himself when the police were more preoccupied in stopping the terrorists get away. He had just taken a whole string of photos of the day's events. But the jewel in the crown was the photo of the National Anti-Terror Squad shooting dead Nicola Reid.

Chaucer had little reason to love the police. The previous year, his older brother had been forced to become an informer against the SNLA by the National Anti-Terror Squad after they fingered him in connection with a plot to blackmail High Court judges and pervert the course of justice. It had ended in tragedy when the SNLA tracked him down to Amsterdam and murdered him.

Chaucer's photos were not intended for the mainstream Press. He knew that no mainstream paper would dare publish a photograph showing the British police carrying out an extrajudicial execution. None would risk falling foul of the iron hand of the censor. Instead, they were destined for the website Whistleblower. Based outside the United Kingdom and away from the grasp of its law enforcement officials, it had made a career of publishing embarrassing information about Western governments and politicians, their business leaders and corporations and their police and security services.

CHAPTER 31

21 June 2021
Sky News

"*This is Daniel Merryfield with this morning's headlines on Sky News.*"

"*The fall-out from the shooting by the police of SNLA terrorist Nicola Reid in Croydon last Friday continues to dominate the headlines. Photographs taken by a freelance photographer of members of the National Anti-Terror Squad shooting an apparently unarmed and defenceless Ms Reid appeared on the Whistleblower website over the weekend. The Home Secretary, Darren Bramble, has condemned the publication by Whistleblower of the photographs as malicious mischief-making which has put the lives of officers from the National Anti-Terror Squad at risk. The Commissioner of the Metropolitan Police, Sir Philip Roebuck, said in an interview that the person responsible for taking the photographs and circulating them on Whistleblower faced arrest under the Terrorism Act. However, Opposition MPs have called for a debate on the shooting, and Independent Labour MP Jeremy Sanderson called the shooting 'extra-judicial murder by a fascist state'.*"

"*The worldwide response to the shooting of Nicola Reid has been hostile. The governments of France, Germany, Iran, Italy, Russia, Spain and Sweden have all condemned the United Kingdom government for allowing extra-judicial executions by the police to take place, as have the US Senate. The controversial French judge, Marcel Auriol, has indicated that he will seek to bring criminal charges against members of the National Anti-Terror Squad. A spokesman for the Prime Minister said she would robustly resist any meddling by foreign institutions in the United Kingdom's domestic affairs.*"

"*The police have made further arrests in connection with both Thursday's escape by SNLA and WRA prisoners from Foulness Maximum Security Prison and Friday's escape from Woolwich Crown Court by Reid and WRA terrorist Anna Michael. Following arrests made by Essex Police over the weekend of six Securitas employees, the Metropolitan Police arrested two civil servants from the Department for Justice in dawn raids, including one official of the Public Services and Commerce Union.*"

The same day
Portcullis House
Westminster
London

Anthony Rawlinson was reading his way through the morning papers that he had borrowed from the House of Commons Library. It did not make happy reading.

The economy remained in negative growth. Another round of public sector cuts was going through. The United Kingdom had become an international pariah. Many of its young people had fled abroad because they saw no future.

Rawlinson was the Conservative MP for South Northamptonshire and had first been elected in 2005. Firmly on the left of the party, he had been hopeful during his early years in the house that the party would become a modern, tolerant, diverse party which could attract votes from young people, ethnic minorities and public sector workers. There were signs in his first years in the house that the party was changing. But, after the 2008-09 recession, the party reverted to its old mantras. Low taxes, minimum regulation, aggressively pro-business, anti-EU, pro-American, tough on immigration and law and order. It had delivered three General Election victories. But, in his view, at a cost.

The United Kingdom should have been one of the world's wealthiest countries, able to provide jobs and housing for all its citizens. It was sitting on massive oil deposits. Rawlinson was in a minority of Conservative MPs who thought the Government were wrong to have denied the devolved governments in Scotland and Wales the chance to benefit from that oil wealth. And wrong to have closed them down and jailed their leaders after they defied Westminster. He had said six years previously that such action would lead to terrorism. And he had been proved right.

His secretary, Suzanne Beer, was typing out a reply to a constituent's letter when the phone rang.

"Anthony Rawlinson's office" said Beer. "Can I help you?"

"Simon August. Can I have a word with Tony?"

Simon August was a fellow Conservative MP and represented South Kesteven. Like Rawlinson, he was on the left of the party.

"Hello, Tony" said August. "Are you free this afternoon?"

"Should be, Simon" replied Rawlinson. "What's on?"

"The Fresh Start group's having a meeting."

Fresh Start was a grouping of moderate Conservative MPs who were opposed to the Government's harsh interpretation of Conservative philosophy and wanted the party to go back to one-nation Conservatism.

"Count me in, Simon" replied Rawlinson.

Later that afternoon
The Albert
Victoria Street
London

The Albert was well-known as a pub frequented by MPs and even had a Division Bell located in its bar and restaurant to notify MPs of an impending vote at the House of Commons.

The Fresh Start group had hired out one of its function rooms for a meeting. Some 20 MPs were present. Although the majority were backbenchers, there were four who had served in Government, including the former Foreign Secretary, Christian Vale.

Simon August called the meeting to order.

"Ladies and gentlemen", he began, "I am most grateful for you deciding to attend the first meeting of the Fresh Start group."

"Like myself, I believe all of you decided to enter politics for the same reason. To serve your country. To fight for the cause of freedom. To promote opportunity. That is why we joined the Conservative Party and that is the underlying core reason that distinguishes us from the Labour Party and the Liberal Democrat Party."

"However, what concerns me is that the Conservative Party is no longer seen as the party of freedom by many of our citizens. It is seen as the 'nasty' party. The party of military and police oppression. The party that denies life opportunities to its less fortunate citizens. The party that forces young people into unpaid servitude. The party that defends the unacceptable face of capitalism."

"For the past six years, we have watched helplessly from the sidelines as the Government run by our Party has wasted the golden inheritance from the North Atlantic and Celtic Sea oil on preventing the Scots and the Welsh from deciding their own future. And, in the process, we have eroded the United Kingdom's reputation for being a free and democratic country to the point that we are now an international pariah. No one abroad wants to do business with us. We've therefore lost out on incoming investment. We are subject to an arms embargo, which means we're having to sustain our armed forces with outdated equipment. Other countries are refusing to co-operate with us on judicial matters, which means that we are unable to bring criminals and terrorists to face justice. And, finally, the United Kingdom is facing a tourist and cultural boycott. All of this means that a country which should be one of the world's richest is in recession and having to impose swingeing cuts to public expenditure."

"I and fellow Conservative members have made repeated pleas to our leadership for a change of direction in their policies. And, what have we received in return? At the best, total indifference. At the worst, abuse and hostility of the lowest order. Bullying by the Whips' Office. Denunciation by fellow Conservative MPs. And scurrilous media campaigns against us."

"I think the time has come to say 'no more'. I am not going to recommend that we form a breakaway party. Bitter experience from the past has told us that Conservative splinter parties never succeed. You will know that Conservative voters are clannishly loyal to the Party and would never support anyone who might let Labour in through the back door."

"Instead, I am going to recommend that we table a Vote of No Confidence in the Government."

There was silence in the room, broken by only a few muffled gasps.

"Are you being serious, Simon?" asked Anne Tremain, the MP for Barnet North. "You do realise that it will need almost a third of the Party's MPs to support the motion."

Christian Vale stood up.

"It won't be as difficult as you think, Anne" said Vale. "All we need is 301 votes to win a no confidence vote. Assuming all the Labour and Liberal Democrat MPs vote with us, all it will take is for 62 Conservative MPs supporting the motion. And less if the Democratic Unionists support us."

23 June 2021
Prime Minister's Office
10 Downing Street
London

Mike Ward, the Conservative Party's Chief Whip, had prepared thoroughly for his meeting with the Prime Minister. He had a full dossier on the rebel Conservative MPs who were supporting the Vote of No Confidence, which was scheduled for Prime Minister's Questions the following Tuesday.

Ward was 59 years old, of average height but stockily built and, like the Prime Minister, came from Yorkshire. A successful businessman and farmer before becoming MP for Skipton and Ripon eleven years previously, he had served as a Minister of State at the Department of Trade and Enterprise and the Ministry of Defence before becoming Chief Whip three years earlier. As befitting the stereotype of his county, Ward was a tough, no-nonsense character who had earned a reputation as a brutal enforcer of Party discipline.

"The Prime Minister will see you now, Mr Ward" said Assistant Private Secretary, Liam Rippingale.

"Good morning, Prime Minister" said Ward.

"Good morning, Mike" replied Deborah Pearson. "I see you've come prepared."

"I was a Boy Scout, Prime Minister."

"Mike, I don't have to explain how serious the threat of a confidence vote against the Government is. All it will take is sixty two of our MPs to support the motion and we'll be out."

"I quite agree, Prime Minister" said Ward. "If Labour get in, we can kiss goodbye to the United Kingdom for evermore."

"So what's the position with the MPs supporting a confidence vote, Mike?" asked Pearson.

"There's a group called Fresh Start, Prime Minister. Formed by Tory wets. They want the party to go back to the failed model of One-Nation Conservatism. You know. Supporting higher taxes and public spending, a less punitive approach to law and order, being ready to talk to terrorists and kow-towing to international bodies like the UN and the EU. Our supporters will never stand for it."

Ward continued.

"Most of the supporters of Fresh Start are backbenchers whose careers have got nowhere. The leaders are Simon August and Anthony Rawlinson. But they've managed to get Christian Vale onboard."

"How many MPs might support the motion, Mike?" asked Pearson.

"Could be as many as eighty or ninety Prime Minister. But I reckon that no more than forty are hard core. We should be able to fight again."

"What do you plan to do, Mike?"

"Prime Minister, being an MP carries loads of privileges with it that are not available to Joe Public" said Ward. "And being an MP in the governing party carries even more privileges. Not only for the MPs but for their families as well. Like seats on Government bodies. Tickets for events like Wimbledon or Buckingham Palace garden parties. And finally, it's well known that Conservative MPs are almost guaranteed directorships in the City at the end of their political career. If we threaten to take those perks away, I reckon the rebellion will collapse."

"What about the likes of Vale?" asked Pearson. "He's unlikely to be put off by the threat of being unable to attend Royal garden parties."

"I told you I was prepared, Prime Minister" said Ward. "I've already been in touch with the constituency parties of the known ringleaders. They're very unhappy that their MPs have been engaged in an act of gross disloyalty. If the confidence vote goes ahead, Prime Minister, at least ten constituency secretaries have told me that they'll deselect their MP if they vote against the Government."

"Thank you, Mike" said Pearson. "Keep me advised of what's going on."

The same day
Labour Party Headquarters
Victoria Street
London

Jane Duffy, the Labour Party's Chief Whip in the House of Commons, was expecting the visit from the Party leader, Iain Turner.

"Jane, very important news" said Turner. "Next Tuesday, there's a Motion of No Confidence in the Government being tabled. Make sure there's a three-line-whip on."

"A Motion of No Confidence?" said a stunned Duffy. "From whom, Iain?"

"A group of rebel Tory MPs, Jane" replied Turner. "The Fresh Start group. All on the Party's left and dissatisfied with the Government's handling of the Scotland and Wales crisis. They're blaming the Government for the economic mess that's resulted."

"Surely they're not going to vote against their own Government?" asked a surprised Duffy. She had been an MP for twenty years and was familiar with past Tory rebellions that had fizzled out.

"This time it's serious, Jane" said Turner. "I've just had a meeting with Christian Vale. Remember him, the former Foreign Secretary? He's told me that as many as eighty four Tory MPs are ready to support the no confidence motion. All we need is a full turnout from our side and from the Lib Dems and Pearson's toast."

"Iain, what about other MPs?" asked Duffy.

"If you mean the SNP, Plaid Cymru and Sinn Fein, don't bother with them, Jane. They can't vote in any case because they've refused to swear an oath to the Queen. And even if they did, their presence would result in most of the Tory MPs bottling out of their commitment to topple the Government."

25 June 2021
Portcullis House
Westminster
London

Chris Lawler was in the process of packing up his papers and preparing to leave for the weekend when the Conservative party Chief Whip, Mike Ward, walked into his office.

"Afternoon Chris" said Ward.

"Hello Mike. How can I help?"

Ward sensed that Lawler might be vulnerable to pressure.

"Chris, I understand you've got involved with Fresh Start."

"That's right, Mike. I think the Government and, I'm sorry to say, the Conservative Party, is on the wrong track. All we're trying to do is to turn the Party back in what it should be. A party that everyone in the United Kingdom feels is looking after their interests."

Ward kept the pressure up.

"And, Chris, I understand you're planning to support a Vote of No Confidence in the Government."

"I'm sorry, Mike" said Lawler. "I feel bad about doing this. But I think a no confidence vote may be a blessing in disguise for the Conservative Party. For over ten years, I've felt that the Party's been taking the wrong direction. Championing the rich and powerful against the powerless. Dismissing half of the electorate as a bunch of feckless losers not deserving of support. Pandering to the greedy and bigoted. And where has it landed us? A civil war at home. No support on the international front. A country which should be one of the world's richest in recession with a massive budget deficit. Don't you realise that we could be out of power for generations as a result?"

"Chris, you've appeared to have forgotten something" said Ward. "You've done well out of being a Conservative MP. Trips abroad, all paid for by the taxpayer. A guaranteed directorship in the City on your retirement. That pretty wife of yours got onto the board of English Heritage thanks to your position. And tickets to the Wimbledon tennis and Royal garden parties. If you go ahead and bring down the Government, all that will end. You've seen Labour's manifesto. And don't forget this. I don't think your constituency party will be too pleased at what you're doing. The men and women there are the bedrock of Middle England. Hardworking, decent people who treasure loyalty and steadfastness in the face of an enemy. They won't want a traitor to represent them in Parliament, will they?"

The same day and time
Portcullis House
Westminster
London

"Thanks for the advice, Mel" said Jeremy Sanderson. "Geri and I will be supporting the no confidence vote next Tuesday. By the way, how about contacting the SNP and Plaid Cymru?"

"Jeremy, they can't vote. Remember they refused to swear an oath of loyalty to the Queen."

"If the prize is the fall of Pearson, they'll swear an oath to Beelzebub if necessary" replied Sanderson. "Be bold, go for it Mel."

Mel Stoddart had taken a calculated risk. As one of the Labour Party's whips, he had disobeyed the instructions of Chief Whip Jane Duffy by getting in touch with the two Independent Labour MPs, Geraldine Partington and Jeremy Sanderson, of the forthcoming no confidence vote against the Government. The Party leadership were terrified of the prospect of the two spikily left-wing MPs, both of whom had been stripped of the Labour whip, turning up to vote. If anything was guaranteed to result in undecided Conservative MPs to bottle the revolt, that was. But Stoddart felt that the leadership was being too timid. The more MPs that could be persuaded to support the no confidence vote, the better.

Stoddart, a Mancunian in his late 30s, had been an MP for only three years and had been appointed a whip three months earlier. The son of a bus inspector with Stagecoach Manchester, he was a rising star in the Labour Party and was considered to be a potential Cabinet Minister of the future. But many of the Labour Party hierarchy had concerns about Stoddart. He had a reputation for being headstrong and impulsive and, in tight or sensitive situations, a liability.

Stoddart had a train to catch later that afternoon. He was due in his constituency, Wigan, where he would spend the weekend dealing with the complaints of constituents about potholes in the road and anti-social behaviour by youths.

He thought about what Sanderson had said. There were fourteen SNP MPs. Eleven Plaid Cymru. The claim that eighty Tories were ready to topple their own Government seemed laughable. Half that number would be an over-estimate. But if the SNP and Plaid could be persuaded to add their weight. And the eight Sinn Fein MPs too. That would be 272 MPs. All it would need was for 29 Tory MPs to put their money where their mouth was, and Pearson would be gone.

He opened his phone book and found the number of the SNP parliamentary leader, Gordon Bremner. He then dialled a number into his telephone.

"Gordon Bremner."

"Gordon, Mel Stoddart here. Got something that might be of interest."

"Go ahead, Mel" said Bremner.

"Gordon, there's a no confidence vote in the Government on Tuesday."

"Are you serious, Mel?" asked Bremner.

"Gospel" replied Stoddart. "You know the SNP will have to swear an oath to the Queen to take part?"

"We do" said Bremner. "But it'll be worth it."

Stoddart then looked again in his phone book. His next target was Eifion Jones of Plaid Cymru.

He rang Jones's number.

26 June 2021
Greengates Farm
near Skipton
North Yorkshire

Mike and Angela Ward were preparing to go out for the evening when the phone rang. Mike Ward, who had got ready first and was waiting for his wife to finish applying her make-up, answered the phone.

"Mike, is that you? James Furnival here."

Ward was slightly puzzled why the MI5 Deputy Director should phone him at a weekend.

"James, you realise that if you had rung fifteen minutes earlier, I'd have still been in the bloody shower. What can I do you for?"

"Got something of potential great interest for you, Mike" said Furnival.

"Go ahead, James" replied Ward.

"Anthony Rawlinson. You're not going to believe what we've found on him."

"Don't tell me, James" said Ward. "An affair? He's gay? Knocking off rent boys? Money troubles?"

"Right first time, Mike" said Furnival. "What's more, it's not just with his secretary or an intern. He's been shagging Stephanie Washington for the past three years. You know, the singer."

"Who's Stephanie Washington?" asked Ward. His musical knowledge was restricted to heavy metal bands like Def Leppard and Iron Maiden, whom he was a fan of during his youth.

"American R&B star. Very colourful past to put it mildly. Was a crack addict once. Her stage shows have been banned in some parts of the USA for offending public decency."

"So it sounds like Rawlinson's local constituency party won't be too thrilled by his latest squeeze? What do you plan to do, James?"

"If you're agreeable, Mike, we're going to plant stories in the *News of the World*, the *Mail on Sunday* and the *Sunday Express*" said Furnival. "Should make a few people choke on their Sunday lunch."

"Too bloody right, James" said Ward. "That'll finish Rawlinson's political career as well as his marriage. And it'll send a message to the other MPs in the Party considering voting to bring us down what lies ahead if they step out of line. Come to think of it, I'll buy the *News of the World* and the *Mail* tomorrow."

Ward was normally a reader of the *Daily Telegraph* and the *Sunday Telegraph*.

As Ward put the phone down, his wife came down the stairs.

"Who was that, darling?" asked Angela Ward.

"Only the local constituency party, Angie" replied Ward.

439

29 June 2021
House of Commons
London

The House of Commons had been packed solid for the debate on the Vote of No Confidence. The Conservative, Labour and Liberal Democrat parties had all issued three-line whips on their MPs to attend, and the House was so crowded that not all the MPs could gain access for the debate.

The Speaker of the House of Commons, George Franklin, signalled it was time for the MPs to file through the voting lobbies.

The leaders of the Tory rebellion, Simon August and Christian Vale, noticed that the number of fellow rebels appeared to have fallen significantly. Several of them had received visits from the Chief Whip, Mike Ward, in person the previous week and the weekend had seen the stunning revelation that Anthony Rawlinson had engaged in an affair with a well-known American soul singer. Even so, twenty nine Conservative MPs were still ready to support the motion and followed August and Vale through the Ayes lobby.

The 220 Labour MPs then followed party leader Iain Turner through the Ayes lobby, followed by the Liberal Democrat leader Nick Moss and the other 16 MPs from his party. Finally, six of the nine Democratic Unionists from Northern Ireland trooped through the Ayes lobby, the party having had a free vote.

On the other side, the 290 Conservative MPs who remained loyal to the Government followed Prime Minister Deborah Pearson through the Noes lobby, followed by the three remaining Democratic Unionists who chose to support the Government. Most Conservative MPs smugly felt that the rebellion had been seen off.

Few people saw the twenty seven additions to the queue of MPs passing through the Ayes lobby but Spencer Parmenter, MP for Gravesend and a fierce Government loyalist on the backbenches did. He noticed the two Independent Labour MPs, Geraldine Partington and Jeremy Sanderson in the queue. But he also noticed the SNP and Plaid Cymru MPs in the House for the first time during the current term of Parliament and following their leaders, Gordon Bremner and Eifion Jones, through the Ayes lobby.

Having voted, Parmenter approached the House of Commons clerks.

"Madam, have you noticed that MPs from SNP and Plaid Cymru are in the lobby? They're not eligible to vote surely because they've refused to swear an oath of allegiance to the Queen."

Rachel Mannion, one of the Commons clerks found herself faced with the red-faced MP for Gravesend towering over her.

"I'll check the position for you, sir, and let you know" replied Mannion. "Can I have your phone number?"

"No, not later, young lady" boomed Parmenter. "Now!"

Mannion went off to confer with colleagues to find out why SNP and Plaid Cymru MPs had been allowed to vote. She knew from bitter experience that MPs had the power to get officials sacked if they felt they had been treated with less than due

440

deference, and Parmenter was one of the worst. He could ask the Prime Minister and Cabinet Ministers to pull rank.

A couple of minutes later, Mannion was back at her desk.

"Well" said Parmenter. "Why were the SNP and Plaid Cymru in the voting lobby?"

"Sir", replied Mannion, "I've had confirmed that earlier today, all the MPs from the Scottish National Party and Plaid Cymru swore oaths of allegiance to Her Majesty. They were therefore perfectly eligible to vote."

As the MPs returned to their benches, the Speaker read out the vote.

"The vote on the Motion, 'This House declares it has no confidence in the ability of Her Majesty's Government to govern the United Kingdom', is as follows. The Ayes, two hundred and ninety nine votes. The Noes, two hundred and ninety three votes. The Motion is therefore carried."

Later that day
Prime Minister's Office
10 Downing Street
London

Deborah Pearson still had a shocked look more than three hours after the vote of no confidence in the Government. She could not believe that members of the Conservative Party had helped vote her out of office.

Pearson's trusted inner circle of Cabinet Ministers were trying to help her come to terms with the cataclysmic consequences of the day's events.

"Do you realise what will happen if Labour get in?" slurred Pearson. She had already knocked back three large whiskies. "They will nationalise the banks and many of our key industries, take us back into the EU and allow rogue states to be set up on our borders. It will be the end for this once great country."

Pearson was aware that Labour held a ten point lead in the opinion polls.

"Where's Mike Ward?" shouted Pearson. "I thought he had put an end to the rebellion by Fresh Start."

"He had, Prime Minister" replied Chancellor of the Exchequer, Jason Steer. "Only twenty nine of our MPs backed the motion. The rest all voted with the Noes."

"Then how did we lose the vote?" wailed the Prime Minister.

"I've heard rumours that the SNP and Plaid Cymru mob turned up to vote" said Secretary of State for Defence and Homeland Security, Henry Arbuthnot.

"That's where Ward has gone, Prime Minister" added Foreign Secretary Dominic Collins. "He's trying to find out whether there have been any irregularities."

At that point, Mike Ward entered the Prime Minister's office.

"Got some news, Prime Minister" said Ward. "The reason we lost the no confidence vote was because all the SNP and Plaid Cymru MPs turned up. Spencer Parmenter told me he saw them join the back of the queue."

"I thought they couldn't vote" said Home Secretary Darren Bramble. "After all, they all refused to swear an oath of loyalty to the Queen."

"According to Parmenter, they all swore oaths in the House yesterday" replied Ward. "Very convenient. However, I'm proposing to challenge the validity of the oaths."

"Can you do that, Mike?" asked Collins.

"I think we may have good grounds, Dominic" said Ward. "It may be possible to argue that the oaths sworn by SNP and Plaid Cymru members carry no legal weight. Firstly, both parties are committed to separating Scotland and Wales from the United Kingdom, so it's technically impossible for them to be loyal to the Crown. Secondly, the timing of the swearing in. For anyone who has previously refused to swear an oath of loyalty and does so the day before an important vote which could bring down the Government suggests that their motive for swearing oaths was suspect."

"Prime Minister", Ward continued, "I have referred the matter to Roland Beaufoy for further opinion." Beaufoy was the Senior Treasury Solicitor and the Government's Chief Legal Adviser.

"I expect Beaufoy to deliver his advice some time tomorrow."

"Thank you, Mike" said a rather emotional Pearson. "You've probably saved this Government. Can you ask Beaufoy to let me know his verdict."

"I'll certainly do that, Prime Minister" replied Ward.

30 June 2021
Prime Minister's Office
10 Downing Street
London

"Roland Beaufoy to see you, Prime Minister" said Liam Rippingale.

"Thank you, Liam" replied Deborah Pearson. "Can you show him in."

Beaufoy was sixty years old, slim and grey-haired. He had been recruited as the Government's Chief Legal Adviser six years earlier from a leading firm of solicitors.

"Roland, many thanks for doing this so quickly" said the Prime Minister.

"Prime Minister, here is my considered legal opinion, which has been backed up by Helen Russell, with whom I conferred today."

Helen Russell was a Queen's Counsel and one of the country's foremost legal brains. Beaufoy continued.

"The fourteen MPs from the Scottish National Party and the eleven MPs from Plaid Cymru were all technically within their rights to cast votes in yesterday's no confidence vote against the Government. However, there are two material pieces of evidence which I consider constitute sound grounds to challenge the validity of the act of swearing an oath of allegiance to Her Majesty."

"Both the Scottish National Party and Plaid Cymru are political parties whose constitution and policies are centred around one primary aim. That is to seek independence from the United Kingdom. The fact that their methods are peaceful are irrelevant. I do not consider it is possible for someone who represents a political party with the aims of political separation of territory from the United Kingdom to pledge their loyalty to the United Kingdom or either its Head of State or Government."

"The other relevant consideration is the timing of the swearing of the oaths of loyalty. You will be aware that all twenty five MPs from the Scottish National Party and Plaid Cymru swore their oaths on 28 June 2021. I have the records from the House of Commons clerks. The fact that the following day there was going to be a vote of no confidence in the Government and that they were potential supporters of the motion is highly material in this context. I consider it is possible to argue in a Court of Law that the MPs from the Scottish National Party and Plaid Cymru chose to swear an oath of loyalty to Her Majesty on that day, not out of loyalty or devotion to the Crown but for the sole reason to enable them to participate in the vote of no confidence against the Government."

"Roland, it sounds like the Government has a very strong case for treating the votes cast by the SNP and Plaid Cymru as invalid" said Pearson.

"That is exactly what I'm saying, Prime Minister" replied Beaufoy.

"Do you realise that you've just saved the Government?" said a highly relieved Pearson.

The same day
Sky News

"This is Sameera Ahmed with this evening's headlines on Sky News."

"The main news item is the decision by the Prime Minister, Deborah Pearson, to defy yesterday's vote of no confidence against the Government and remain in office."

"A spokesman for the Prime Minister told Sky News earlier that the Government has refused to accept that the vote of no confidence was valid because of participation of MPs from the Scottish National Party and Plaid Cymru in the vote. The fourteen MPs from the Scottish National Party and eleven from its Welsh equivalent, Plaid Cymru have not been permitted to vote since they were elected to the current Parliament because of their refusal to swear an oath of allegiance to the Queen. Without the votes of Scottish National Party and Plaid Cymru MPs counting, the Government majority would be nineteen."

"The day before the vote of no confidence, all twenty five Scottish National Party and Plaid Cymru MPs hurriedly swore oaths of allegiance, which enabled them to participate in the vote. However, the Government does not accept that the oath of allegiance sworn by the MPs from the Scottish National Party and Plaid Cymru are legally valid because their party's constitutions prevent them from showing allegiance to the United Kingdom. The Government also argues that their sole reason for swearing oaths of allegiance was to enable them to take part in the vote of no confidence."

"The Government's decision to defy the vote of no confidence is likely to be contentious. Already, the Government has been condemned by Iain Turner, the Labour leader and Nick Moss, the Liberal Democrat leader for contempt of Parliament and democracy."

"Now for further news. The Labour Party has also had problems. Today, the Party dismissed one of its Whips, Mel Stoddart, for an act of gross indiscipline. Further details are not yet available."

"Before his dismissal, Mr Stoddart, the MP for Wigan, was regarded as one of the Labour Party's most promising young MPs and had been tipped for high office."

CHAPTER 32

**Handbill issued by the Joint Council for
Democracy in the UK**

SHOW PEARSON THE RED CARD

DEMONSTRATE ON 5 JULY

Over the past 11 years, the Tory Government has shown a cavalier contempt for the rights of the British people. It has repeatedly passed repressive laws reducing the rights of workers and trade unionists, students, young people, ethnic minorities and the Scots and the Welsh. It has used the armed forces, the police, the security services and the courts as the iron heel to put down opposition to its partisan and unfair policies. It has acted in breach of international conventions and defied its own laws when they fail to produce a convenient result. But last week's decision by the Government to remain in office in defiance of a Vote of No Confidence by Parliament is the final straw.

On Monday, 5 July, the Joint Council for Democracy in the UK has organised a march to show the discredited Tory Government that the British people no longer want them to rule over them. You are urged to join this march if you feel that the Tory Government has exceeded its mandate to rule.

The march starts at Hyde Park Corner at 12pm and will finish at Parliament Square.

Signed:

The Trades Union Council	Liberty	The Tribune Group
Fair Trials UK	Muslim League of Britain	Scottish National Party
Plaid Cymru	Jeremy Sanderson MP	Geraldine Partington MP
Celtic Solidarity Campaign	Socialist Alliance	

2 July 2021
Home Office
Marsham Street
London

"What do you mean that I've got no power to ban the demonstration?" asked an incredulous Darren Bramble.

On hearing that a demonstration calling for the Government's resignation had been called for the following Monday, the Home Secretary had convened a meeting with the Government's Chief Legal Adviser, Roland Beaufoy, the Chairman of the Association of Chief Police Officers, Sir Roy Plummer, the Commissioner of the Metropolitan Police, Sir Philip Roebuck and the Director-General of MI5, Dame Nicola Martin. Also present was the Permanent Secretary, Sir Richard Benson.

Bramble was irritated that Karen Bishop, the Mayor of London, was allowing the demonstration to go ahead.

"I'm afraid that's right, Home Secretary" replied Beaufoy. "Nine years ago, a whole raft of powers were devolved to the Mayor of London, including powers over policing in the capital. This included the right to permit or ban demonstrations."

"Philip, Roy, I guess it's over to you" said Bramble. "How do you intend to handle it?"

"The Met's got plenty of experience in managing hostile and potentially violent demonstrations" said Roebuck. "We'll escort the demonstration for its length but we're taking no chances. We've got mobile CCTV cameras in place to pick out troublemakers. NPAS have been asked to send a chopper up. Special Branch are working with Five to identify any plans for violent disorder. TSG are being deployed in case things turn nasty. And we're sealing off Parliament Square. If the demonstrators don't disperse, we're ready to kettle them. Roy, how's ACPO likely to view things?"

"Can't see any reason for objection, Phil" said Plummer. "Looks like you've got things worked out."

"Nicola, any reports on subversive involvement?" asked Bramble.

"Not yet, Home Secretary" replied Martin. "But our field agents are tailing the usual suspects like Trotskyist and anarchist organisations. And they're also looking out for possible SNLA and WRA involvement and are trailing suspected Al-Q'aida sleeper agents. Intelligence reports suggest that all three might use the demonstration as cover for terrorist activity."

3 July 2021
Fitzroy Avenue
Drumcondra
Dublin

The Sinn Fein driver dropped Iain Murray and Gareth Evans outside Martin Hallinan's house in Dublin's Northside. They looked round and were encouraged to se that no other vehicles were present.

"Looks like your idea of sending body doubles of us to Michael O'Shea's place has worked, Iain" said Evans. He was referring to a decoy ploy worked out by the SNLA which involved fitting two of its members with prosthetic disguises so they looked like doubles of Murray and Evans and sending them over to the home of another Sinn Fein member Michael O'Shea in West Dublin. It appeared that the British Secret Intelligence Service had fallen for the ploy.

"Good afternoon, gentlemen" said Hallinan. "We've got some guests to see you."

Murray and Evans followed Hallinan into the lounge of his home to find seated three men and a woman.

Zahir Mahmood was a senior Al-Q'aida commander in the United Kingdom. Susie Mendes of the Socialist Alliance, Dave Copeland of the Revolutionary Communist League and Zak Moody of Class War were also present.

Mendes opened the discussion. In her early 30s, Mendes was short and dark-haired. Even through she was wearing jeans, a black T-shirt and Doc Marten boots and her hair was cropped, she was quite an attractive woman.

"Iain, Gareth, you will probably be aware of the big demonstration in London on Monday."

"We are, Susie" said Murray.

"We're planning to use that as cover to start an insurgency that will overthrow the Government" said Copeland.

"Have you got anything planned, Dave?" asked Evans. "Knowing the authorities as Iain and I do, they'll surely have planned for that possibility."

"It's more than starting a few riots or smashing up buildings" said Moody. "We've got guns, bombs and missiles at our disposal. Also, we've got assistance from several of London's street gangs. The fuzz won't know what's hit them."

"The demonstration will provide cover for our fighters" said Mahmood. "The plan is to attack and occupy Government buildings and immobilise police stations and army barracks. We're also planning to blow open several of Her Majesty's prisons. The authorities won't know which way to turn as they'll be under attack from all sides."

"Any plans to attack the City of London?" asked Murray. "That's where the real power in the country is."

"We have, Iain" replied Mahmood. "The police and armed forces will be so preoccupied in defending Whitehall that they won't be able to defend the City as well as they would otherwise. On top of that, it's next door to our power base."

Mahmood was well aware that there were active Al-Q'aida cells in Whitechapel.

"On top of that, guys, we've turned a load of National Servicemen and women" said Mendes. "They're going to be used to augment the police and military in protecting the Houses of Parliament. You know that many of them don't want to be doing National Service. A load of them are going to help us on Monday."

"I take it you're looking for the SNLA and WRA to help" said Murray.

"Indeed we are, Iain" said Copeland. "How quickly can you guys mobilise your forces in London?"

"Very quickly, Dave" replied Evans. "All it'll take is a quick phone call to our commanders."

There was a ring at the doorbell. Hallinan went to the front door.

A few seconds later, a short, dapper man in his 40s entered the room. Mansour Kardooni was a Third Secretary at the Iranian Embassy in Dublin. His real role was as an agent of VEVAK, the Iranian intelligence agency.

"I hear you're planning an insurgency in the United Kingdom" said Kardooni. "I'm here to help you in any way I can. My masters in Tehran will be delighted if the Little Satan falls."

Kardooni continued. "Tomorrow, two Hizbollah agents will be arriving in the United Kingdom on false passports. Zahir, they will be arriving at Khalid Butt's home. It is your task to brief them on the plans for Monday and to touch base with Susie, Dave and Zak."

"Iain, Gareth, tomorrow a pair of merchant ships, *MV Orion* and *MV Ariadne*, will be putting into, respectively, Mallaig and Aberaeron. They will be carrying in their cargoes AK-47 assault rifles, Uzi machine pistols, RPG-11 rocket launchers and SA-15 missiles. It will be the task of the SNLA and the WRA to ensure their distribution to combat units in London."

5 July 2021
Whitehall
London

About 500,000 people had joined the demonstration calling on the Government to resign. By 3pm, there was a solid bank of demonstrators from the police barriers blocking the way into Parliament Square back to Trafalgar Square.

At the front of the demonstration were several of the luminaries who were in the forefront of the campaign for the Government to resign. Brendan Heenan, the Secretary of the TUC was there. So was Jenny Topliss of Liberty. Jeremy Sanderson and Geraldine Partington, the two Independent Labour MPs were there. From the world of celebrities, Matt Brazier and Johnny Bassett of the rock band, the Ginger Toms, and model Kate Regan were present.

Behind them, there were a forest of placards. Many read **PEARSON GO NOW, GET PEARSON OUT** and **GIVE THE TORIES THE RED CARD**.

Behind the barriers, Commander Ben Richman had the Gold Command for the day, and his task was to ensure that the demonstrators did not get into Parliament Square and, more importantly, the Houses of Parliament. The Metropolitan Police were supported by detachments of National Service personnel from the armed forces. This had been a controversial decision, not least because there were several senior members of the armed forces and the police who did not trust the loyalty of conscripted soldiers. They knew that many of the National Servicemen and women did not want to be there and were potentially sympathetic to the demonstrators.

Richman took a call on his radio. It was Deputy Commissioner Darren Charnock.

"Ben, what's it like out there?"

"Been peaceful up to now, sir, but it's starting to get a bit hairy. Some hard-core agitators have been identified in the crowd and I think it could kick off."

"Just had the Commissioner on the line, Ben. He wants everyone cleared out."

"Roger that, sir. We'll seal off all exits from Whitehall and send snatch squads in to nick any troublemakers."

Richman then sent out orders to the Silver and Bronze Commanders. Within seconds, police cordons had sealed off all roads leading from Whitehall. Some 500,000 demonstrators were corralled in.

The Territorial Support Group were ready. They had been issued with CCTV footage and had identified target demonstrators to arrest.

At the front of the demonstration by Parliament Square, the mood of the demonstrators started to get ugly. Egged on by activists from the Socialist Alliance and Class War, they started pushing at the police lines. The police responded with baton charges, following which the Territorial Support Group raced into arrest the demonstrators concerned.

Standing next to their Iveco personnel carrier was Private Jack Pike, one of seven detachments of National Service personnel who had been charged with protecting Parliament Square and the Houses of Parliament in the event of the police lines being breached.

Pike was 19 years old and resented the fact that he had been forced to do National Service. Failure to obtain the necessary A-levels to get into university and the inability to find a job in the shrinking job market had condemned him to a forced spell in the Army.

Pike knew that some of his friends were on the demonstration and he shared their views in wanting the fall of the Tory Government. The sight of the police violently batoning demonstrators was more than he could stand. He raised his L-115 Sniper rifle and opened fire on the police lines.

"What the hell do you think you're doing, Pike?"

Corporal Darren Rostron, who was in charge of Pike's unit, was furious that one of his men was firing on the police. He felled Pike with the butt of his rifle, then turned to Privates Lee Schofield and Rosie Williams.

"Schofield, Williams, don't just stand there" yelled Rostron. "Give me a hand with this fucker."

"No fucking way, corporal" shouted Private Lee Schofield. He pulled out his Sniper and opened fire on Rostron. The short, stocky corporal from Manchester fell to the ground, dead.

"Sir, we're being fired on. One of our men's dead and three more are wounded." The fear in the voice of one of Ben Richman's Silver Commanders, Superintendent Ed Cundall, was real.

"Who was it, Ed?"

"Came from Parliament Square, sir" replied Cundall. "We think it's the National Servicemen."

"Ed, you have authority to return fire" replied Richman.

No sooner than Cundall had finished his call when another Silver Commander radioed Richman. It was Superintendent Gary Knowles.

"Sir, we can't hold them anymore. The demonstrators are breaking through."

The same day
Committee Room 7
House of Commons
London

"It is essential that the Train Operating Companies are given contracts of this duration. Without this certainty, they will not feel it is worth their while in investing in new stock, and the passenger will suffer as a result. I therefore strongly recommend that this Committee approves Clause 69 of the Transport Bill."

Spencer Parmenter, the MP for Gravesend, had just spoken on proposals in the Transport Bill to give Train Operating Companies twenty year franchises. A fierce right winger, both on economic issues and on law and order and national security, he was one of the most trusted backbenchers in the Conservative Party and had a key role on the House of Commons Transport Committee which was considering the clauses in the Transport Bill currently going through the House.

Doug McLauchlan, the Labour MP for Glasgow East, motioned that he would speak next. A former train driver and official in the Rail, Maritime and Transport Workers Union, he felt that the proposals for long contracts were a 'wrecking ball' proposal by the Government to ensure that an incoming Labour government would be unable to renationalise the railways without having to pay crippling compensation to the Train Operating Companies.

Before McLauchlan could speak, the alarm siren sounded, followed by an announcement.

"The Houses of Parliament have come under attack by intruders. Will all Members and Strangers make their way to the basement and go to the safe rooms marked."

"Good God, Spencer, looks like that bloody rabble have got into Parliament Square" said Elizabeth Maynard, the Conservative MP for South Staffordshire and a fellow member of the Transport Committee.

Near panic ensued as MPs, civil servants and researchers all rushed out of the various rooms, looking for a way to the basement. Clear directions were missing, a casualty of spending cuts.

Maynard and Parmenter realised they were lost. Suddenly, their worst nightmare appeared. They were confronted by five of the demonstrators who had got into the Houses of Parliament.

"That's Parmenter" snarled a man in his early 20s, his long hair styled into dreadlocks.

"Who's the bitch?" shouted a colleague. "She looks like a Tory too."

"Let's get 'em."

"Get back, Liz" shouted Parmenter to Maynard. "I'll take on this lot."

449

Parmenter was a big man at six foot three and nearly seventeen stones in weight, and he could pack a punch. He felled the first attacker, the man with the dreadlocks, with a right hander and sent the next attacker reeling with a left hook. But all this did was to enrage the other three demonstrators.

Danny Brooks had a knife on him. With Parmenter engaged in fighting off his colleagues, he advanced from the side and rammed the knife into Parmenter's ribcage. The MP for Gravesend fell to the ground as Maynard screamed.

"Got the bastard!" shouted an elated Brooks.

"Let's get the bitch" shouted Charlie Rushton, one of Brooks' accomplices. Elizabeth Maynard stood no chance as the five men grabbed hold of her. A knife thrust under the heart from from Brooks brought her life to an end.

The same day
CNN News
Atlanta

"This is Kirsten Lezniak with the lunchtime news headlines for the Eastern seaboard."

"Severe rioting has broken out in London after an anti-Government demonstration was prevented from approaching the British Parliament. Demonstrators have occupied or ransacked several Government buildings and other buildings and cars have been set on fire. There are unconfirmed reports that demonstrators have broken into the Houses of Parliament and that two Members of Parliament have been murdered."

"The demonstrators were calling for the resignation of the Prime Minister, Deborah Pearson, following a vote of no confidence in her Government last Tuesday. Although the organisers of the demonstration claimed that their motives were peaceful, Government sources claimed that hard-core troublemakers intent on the violent overthrow of the Government were involved."

"The latest reports are that Ms Pearson has flown to her country residence outside London where she will convene the Government and organise operations to restore order."

Later that day
Chequers near Wendover
Buckinghamshire

Deborah Pearson had wasted no time in setting up an emergency Cabinet at Chequers. Henry Arbuthnot, the Secretary of State for Defence and Homeland Security was present, as was Darren Bramble, the Home Secretary. Also in attendance were General Sir Robin Peacock, the Chief of Staff of the British Army, Sir Roy Plummer, the Chairman of the Association of Chief Police Officers and Dame Nicola Martin, the Director-General of MI5.

"Darren, can I have a latest update of the position in London?" asked the Prime Minister.

450

"Grim reading at the moment, Prime Minister" replied Bramble. "Mobs have been rampaging through Whitehall and the West End. Shops have been looted and businesses set on fire. Several hole in the wall cash machines have been raided. Demonstrators have occupied the Home Office, the Department for Justice, the Department for Trade and Enterprise and the Department for Transport. There are reports that some civil servants have colluded with the mobs and helped them get in."

"I wouldn't be surprised if some of those facing the sack were involved" said Plummer.

"Roy, I understand we're getting reinforcements from provincial forces" continued Bramble. "When do you expect them to arrive?"

"This evening, Home Secretary" replied the ACPO Chairman.

"Commissioner Roebuck has imposed a dusk to dawn curfew in London and armed patrols will enforce that. Also, we've made available some five thousand places in our prisons" added Bramble. "And we've found holding accommodation at Dunsfold and Manston if we're faced with an overflow."

"Thank you, Darren" said Pearson. "Henry."

"Prime Minister, I am sorry to say that several members of our National Service battalions disgraced the Army today by helping the rioters. I have therefore decided to stand down all National Service personnel from security duties and confine them to barracks."

Arbuthnot continued.

"To cope with the collapse in law and order in London, I've managed to get hold of regular battalions from the Rifles, the Royal Anglian, the Royal Mercian and the Duke of Lancaster's Regiments. We can't release the Green Howards or the Wessex Regiment as they're needed in Scotland and Wales."

"I'm also proposing we commission Local Defence Volunteers to guard vital installations, Prime Minister. Although many of those likely to join might not be in the first flush of youth, it has been proven that volunteers have the commitment and energy to be a real asset. Apart from the fact that many of them are likely to be retired soldiers or policemen."

"I think that's an excellent idea, Henry. How soon can you put it into force?"

"I think the first battalions can be made ready in two days time, Prime Minister" said Arbuthnot.

"Nicola, any developments on the intelligence front?" asked Pearson.

"We're watching the main subversive groups, the Socialist Alliance, the Revolutionary Communist League and Class War, Prime Minister. And we've also followed up on leads about the involvement of the SNLA and the WRA and Al-Q'aida. We're in close contact with NATS and the Met's Special Branch and we reckon there'll be arrests in a day or two."

"Thank you, Nicola" said Pearson. "Keep Henry, Darren and myself posted on developments."

6 July 2021
HM Prison Wandsworth
Heathfield Road
Wandsworth
London

The prison authorities had been caught on the hop. Shortly before light out, five prisoners had overpowered a guard and grabbed hold of his keys. Other prisoners joined in and, before long, three wings at the prison were under the control of the prisoners.

At 6am, a white Nissan Cargo van pulled up opposite the main gates. In the back were Shafi Ahmed, Habibur Rahman and Mohammed Sadiq, three members of Al-Q'aida. In the back of the van, they were carrying Russian-built RPG-11 rocket launchers.

All three men had undergone military training in a camp on the Pakistan-Afghanistan border and were familiar with the RPG-11.

Attached to the RPG-11s were high explosive devices capable of blowing a hole in doors two feet thick. Ahmed sat in the driver's seat ready to make a quick getaway while Rahman and Sadiq primed, then aimed the RPG-11s.

Two streaks of flame shot from the back of the Cargo and simultaneously hit the outer doors of HMP Wandsworth. A massive blast shattered the doors. Wandsworth was now open to the world.

Ahmed hit the accelerator of the Nissan Cargo and was gone from the scene. A few minutes later, prisoners started streaming out of HMP Wandsworth for unscheduled freedom.

The same day
Birmingham City Council
Council House
Victoria Square
Birmingham

Jane Entwistle, the Chief Executive of Birmingham City Council, emerged from the city's Management Board meeting. They had discussed and agreed plans to make no less than 40% of their remaining employees compulsorily redundant. She knew that the main public sector, Unison, would make a fuss and threaten industrial action. But they had few levers. There were restrictions on the ability of public sector employees to go on strike and the threat of summary dismissal without compensation was sufficient to make employees think twice about withdrawing their labour.

Earlier that day, the Borough Commander at the city's main police station had been on the phone to warn her that there had been an escape from Winson Green Prison after suspected insurgents had blasted open the doors. But there seemed no cause for alarm until Entwistle heard the sound of breaking glass.

Within a minute, masked and hooded men and women were overrunning the Council House. Before Entwistle and fellow Management Board members had a chance to escape, they had been surrounded. A hooded youth called 'Zeb' appeared to be in charge of the intruders.

"Ms Entwistle, you are now in the custody of the Birmingham Provisional Revolutionary Committee" said Zeb. "You will now carry out the following instructions. Firstly, you will cancel all planned redundancies that the City Council was planning to issue. Secondly, you will remove all CCTV cameras from Birmingham's inner suburbs. And thirdly, you will reopen all libraries and leisure centres that you have closed over the past five years."

"Young man, I don't know who you are" said Entwistle. "But I should remind you and your colleagues that you are falsely imprisoning myself and my fellow Management Board members. If you want to avoid a lengthy prison sentence, I suggest that you release us now. And, for the record, there is no alternative to the redundancy measures proposed. The money isn't available."

Zeb pointed his gun menacingly at Jane Entwistle.

"Don't push your luck, lady. Me and my mates are armed. Piss us off and we'll use them."

Entwistle saw there was no point in trying to be a heroine and paying with her life.

The same day
Parliament Square
London

Parliament Square was packed solid with anti-Government demonstrators, who had returned for the second day. A forest of placards and banners identified them, ranging from the trade unions Unite, Unison, RMT and PCS, through to Liberty, the Socialist Alliance, the Muslim League of Britain, the Celtic Solidarity Campaign, Clann na h-Albann and Meibion Cymru. The chants continued:-

"WE WANT PEARSON OUT, WE WANT PEARSON OUT"

The police had given up on trying to protect most buildings around Whitehall, but a heavily armed presence surrounded the Houses of Parliament. Along with Buckingham Palace and 10 Downing Street, this was the building that the Government desperately wanted to hold control of. Elsewhere in the district, banners flew from the windows of the Government departments which had been occupied by anti-Government demonstrators.

At 2pm, a column of armoured personnel carriers from the Rifles and the Duke of Lancaster's Regiment rumbled down Victoria Street. Meanwhile, on the other side of the Thames, another column of armoured personnel carriers from the Royal Anglian and Royal Mercian Regiments rolled along York Road towards Westminster Bridge. Some fifty unmarked police vans containing members of the National Anti-Terror Squad's SWAT Team and the Metropolitan Police's Territorial Support Group moved along Millbank from the South and Victoria Embankment from the north. Above Parliament Square hovered Sikorsky S-92 helicopters of the National Police Air Service along with Westland Super Lynx helicopters of the Army Air Corps.

Major Ashley Bridge of the Rifles switched on the public address system in the lead APC standing at the western entrance to Parliament Square.

"This is an illegal demonstration which is in breach of martial law Regulations announced by the Government yesterday. You are all ordered to disperse and leave Parliament Square immediately. If you fail to comply with this order, we have no alternative but to use force to ensure its compliance."

"Go fuck yourself, soldier boy" shouted a voice from the throng of demonstrators.

Major Bridge radioed Major Pete Roberts from the Duke of Lancaster's Regiment, Major Julian Blair of the Royal Anglian Regiment and Major Richard Cork of the Royal Mercian Regiment, as well as Superintendent Alexandra Wall of the Territorial Support Group and Chief Inspector Rob Beckett of NATS.

"It looks like they're not going to budge. We've got no choice but to go in. Let's do it."

The Army fired tear gas canisters into Parliament Square as troops leapt out of APCs and police leapt out of vans and started to hit demonstrators with their batons. A hail of bricks, cans and bottles flew back in the direction of the Army and the police in reply. As the main body of demonstrators broke up and started to run, the police turned on their water cannons, each carrying water dyed red so that fleeing demonstrators could be identified. Snatch squads from the Army and the Territorial Support Group started seizing demonstrators and threw them into the arrest vans.

In the mayhem that followed, no one noticed Jamie Strachan unloading a Russian-built RPG-11 rocket launcher and taking aim at the lead APC parked at the end of Victoria Street. The RPG-11 was small and easily portable, yet the warhead on the end could destroy a Challenger or Abrams battle tank. Strachan, a member of the SNLA's London Brigade, was under orders to infiltrate the demonstration and launch attacks on the Army and the police.

A whoosh of flame streaked from the RPG-11 and hit the APC clean through its front window. The APC exploded in a ball of flame, instantly killing Major Bridge and his crew.

Major Cork radioed HQ immediately.

"Indigo Alpha here. There are bandits loose in the Square with weapons. An APC has copped it already. Permission to use lethal force."

Colonel David Preston came on the line.

"Permission granted Indigo Alpha."

The same day
Sky News

"This is Sameera Ahmed with this evening's headlines on Sky News."

"The second day of anti-Government demonstrations in London turned violent as police and troops were forced to fire on demonstrators in self-defence after coming under attack. Reports suggest that as many as twenty demonstrators have been shot dead in the

clashes, which started after an armoured personnel carrier of the Rifles was destroyed by an attack using a rocket-powered grenade. Seven members of the Rifles died as the vehicle exploded, while six policemen and women were also shot dead after coming under attack by small arms fire."

"It has been reported that over two thousand demonstrators have been taken into custody. However, attempts by the police and army to apprehend rioters have been hampered by cat-and-mouse tactics used by the rioters and assistance given by sympathisers who have occupied Government buildings."

"The security services are investigating rumours that terrorists from the SNLA, WRA and Al-Q'aida infiltrated the protests and carried out attacks upon the armed forces and the police under cover."

"Now for the remaining headlines. The disturbances which have racked central London for the past two days have now spread out into the provinces. Protestors against plans for public spending cuts have occupied council offices in Birmingham, Leeds, Liverpool and Manchester and are holding chief officers hostage. They have demanded as conditions for their release the immediate cancellation of the cuts and planned redundancies of staff. There are reports that some of the protestors are armed, and the police have held off attempting to retake the buildings."

"Brent Cross and the Valley Park shopping centres have spent today clearing up after looters attacked shops last night and made off with property worth over six million pounds. The owners believe that the diversion of local police to deal with the anti-Government protests in London was exploited by criminal elements. CCTV footage has been passed to the police."

"The police are appealing for public assistance in tracking down escaped prisoners after last night's assaults on eleven prisons by suspected anti-Government protestors. Although the majority of prisons targeted were Category B and C prisons, it is known that a large number of prolific and violent offenders are on the run. Details can be found on www.police.uk/mostwanted.

"Volunteers have been flocking to sign up to the Local Defence Volunteers after the Government's announcement of the scheme today. The last time that the so-called "Dad's Army" was activated was eighty years ago during the Second World War. The current State of Emergency, which has seen the police and armed forces put under pressure by the insurgency in Scotland and Wales and the violent anti-Government protests in London, have made it necessary for an additional layer of security to be put in place to protect homes and businesses."

That evening
MI5 Headquarters
Millbank
London

"F6 haven't exactly covered themselves in glory over the past few days, Richard" shouted MI5 Deputy Director, James Furnival.

Richard Donovan, the Section Head, was however defiant.

"James, you more than anyone should realise the difficulties in getting good quality human intelligence in the field" replied Donovan. He was referring to Furnival's past history at GCHQ.

"We are dealing with ruthless terrorist organisations who not only have no compunction about killing innocent civilians, they will do the same to anyone they think is a spy. Over the past six years, we've lost eleven agents in the field who've been murdered by the SNLA and WRA after their cover was blown. And that's not counting another six murdered by Al-Q'aida. On top of that, you've got to remember that extreme left organisations have infiltrated the Civil Service and have no hesitation in passing sensitive information to terrorists. And you can't blame me for the Dublin cock-up. That was MI6."

Donovan was referring to the embarrassing failure by MI6 agents to track SNLA and WRA commanders Iain Murray and Gareth Evans on a visit to Dublin through getting fooled by two low level agents who donned prosthetic disguises and went to a different address.

"Richard, I'm getting sick and tired of excuses" said Furnival. "Over the past two days, we've had attacks on eleven prisons and no less than three hundred lags on the run. Which appears to be the work of the SNLA, WRA or Al-Q'aida or possibly all three. And now the attacks on the police and Army in London."

"I'm holding a briefing meeting at half past eight tomorrow morning. Darren Charnock and Kevin Lazenby will be there. I want an up-to-date report on the progress of field agents in tracking the moves of subversives and terrorists and what the next suspected targets will be. If I don't feel your reports cuts the mustard, I'll be considering your future here."

Later that night
10:50 London Victoria to Sutton train

Richard Donovan had obtained an update from Peter Firth of the field team's progress in tracking the movements of the hard-core of subversives involved in the anti-Government protests.

Half an hour earlier, Firth had e-mailed him a report giving details of the organisations and persons involved and their planned activities. Firth's report confirmed that the SNLA, the WRA and Al-Q'aida were not only helping the hard-core troublemakers, but were also using cover of the protests to carry out terrorist acts. He found out that the SNLA and WRA had taken delivery of a frightening arsenal of weaponry that Hizbollah had smuggled in. It meant they could destroy helicopters and armoured vehicles. And the next intended target of the anti-Government protestors was the City of London. He had wasted no time and informed Russell Colbourne at the National Anti-Terror Squad and Paula Wakeham at New Scotland Yard.

Donovan was still fuming. Furnival was the know-all brought in from outside and he had effectively threatened Donovan with the sack if his report was not up to scratch. It would mean typing out a report when he got home. He would have barely four hours sleep before having to get up so he was in for Furnival's 'breakfast' briefing. Only there would be no breakfast available. Economy rules.

Donovan knew he was not supposed to bring the official laptop and papers out of the office. Especially those marked 'Top Secret'. But he had no choice.

The train pulled out of Balham Station. Another twenty five minutes and he would be home.

There was hardly anyone on board the train. Because of the curfew, only people whose work made it necessary for them to travel after dark and had passes, were out and about.

Suddenly, Donovan felt a chill go through his blood. He sensed trouble. A group of five youths entered his carriage. Four males and one female. All about 17 to 19 years old, he guessed. And not looking very friendly.

Three of the four boys were black and the fourth was mixed race. All were wearing track suit tops with hoods, baggy jeans and trainers. The girl was white, blonde-haired and wore a denim miniskirt and black knee-length boots and would have been attractive apart from the spiteful scowl on her face.

The five youths prowled up and down the carriage of the train, eyeing up Donovan more than once. They appeared to be heading for the next carriage, so Donovan picked up his case and started to move towards the carriage in front.

Donovan's worst fears were suddenly realised as he felt a hand roughly grab his shoulder.

"Where do you think you're going, you cunt?" snarled the mixed race youth. He was six foot tall and appeared to be the leader of the gang.

Donovan knew he had two options—fight or flight. He was in his late 50s, two inches shorter than the youth, carrying surplus weight around the midriff and had last been involved in a fight over forty years earlier when he was at school. But the knowledge and instinct that had served him well in several schoolboy scraps a lifetime away hadn't deserted him. With his left hand, he seized the collar of the youth's sweatshirt, pulled him off balance and delivered a powerful head-butt to the bridge of his nose. He heard the crack of the nose breaking.

Within a split second, the rest of the gang set upon Donovan, punching and kicking. Donovan used his beefy forearms to deflect many of the punches and rolled with them to make him a harder target, but he still took a couple of powerful shots to the cheek. If he could get his own punch in, that might remove another of the assailants from the fight.

Donovan dropped his shoulder and unleashed a thunderous straight right which connected against the jaw of the tallest youth in the gang. The youth was some six inches taller than Donovan, but the power of Donovan's punch sent him crashing to the floor.

Donovan had taken two kicks to the shin from the girl. She was obviously trying to prove herself to her boyfriend. But Donovan remembered another trick he had learned all those years ago. He brought his right knee up and connected with her upper thigh at great velocity. It was called a 'dead leg' and was highly effective in disabling assailants. The girl fell to the ground, screaming in agony.

The gang leader was enraged. He was still streaming blood from a broken nose. Their quarry, a fat, balding, middle-aged man, was putting members of the Streatham Hill Posse to flight. If word got out on the street that they had come off second best against this old bloke, their credibility would be permanently ruined. He resorted to his trusty back up. A double-edged hunting knife bought over the Internet.

The other two youths in the gang had already been on the receiving end of Donovan's punches and were starting to think about splitting when their leader went into a crouch and brought his knife sharply up into Donovan's ribcage. The MI5 man staggered under the blow. Two more knife thrusts left him on the ground, as his life started to ebb away. His Personal Data Assistant fell out of his top pocket.

"Jermaine, we've got his bag. Grab the PDA and fucking leg it" shouted the shortest of the four youths.

As the train approached the embankment near the Streatham Park Estate, the gang forced open the train doors, jumped down onto the embankment and ran away with their ill-gotten gains.

7 July 2021
Victoria Park Gardens
Bethnal Green
London

Asif Mahmood had managed to give members of the local Al-Q'aida cell the slip. He needed to contact MI5 headquarters immediately as there appeared to have been a leak. Somehow, Al-Q'aida had managed to get hold of classified MI5 information about the plans by anti-Government protestors to storm the City of London. He had been in the flat of Al-Q'aida's Whitechapel commander, Habibur Rahman, when they had phoned the group of activists from Class War and the Revolutionary Communist League to warn them that a police raid was planned at 5:30am on the warehouse in Olympic Way which they were using as a base. Mahmood knew that the activists would be dispersing and that the police would be going on a wild goose chase.

It was already 4:30am and starting to get light in the eastern sky. Victoria Park Gardens, opposite Bethnal Green Underground Station, looked a suitably quiet spot to call in.

The quiet was broken by the sound of a two-stroke engine of a scooter heading down Cambridge Heath Road. Probably someone going to work. Mahmood withdrew his encrypted Personal Data Assistant and started to type a message. He knew that the duty staff at Thames House would pick it up.

On the 200cc Kawasaki scooter was Habibur Rahman's son, Mohibur, and Lutfur Choudhury. Choudhury was armed with an AK-47 assault rifle.

"Mohib, there's Mahmood. Stop now, man" said Choudhury.

Rahman pulled the scooter to a halt. Meanwhile, Choudhury lined up the MI5 agent in the sights of his AK-47 and opened fire. Mahmood took two bullets to the abdomen and one to the head and fell to the ground, bleeding heavily. As his life ebbed away, Rahman and Choudhury made their getaway.

An hour later
Olympic Way
Stratford
London

The sun had already risen when Commander Paula Wakeham, the chief officer in the Metropolitan Police for territorial policing and the Gold Commander for Operation Hoover, received the news that both ends of Olympic Way had been sealed off. A vacant warehouse had been identified as the base for the protestors intending to storm the City of London later that day.

Wakeham was in her early-40s and was the highest ranked female officer in the Metropolitan Police. She was ambitious and was hoping to become the first female Commissioner of the Metropolitan Police.

He picked up her police radio and called Chief Superintendents Barry Caswell and Ryan Rossiter, her Silver Commanders.

"Barry, Ryan, are you ready to go in?"

"Ready, Ma'am" replied the two Silver Commanders. "Okay, guys, let's go."

Five lead officers, selected because of their size and physical strength, sledgehammered the shutters to the warehouse open. Then no less than a hundred officers, all dressed in riot gear and wielding batons, burst into the warehouse, only to find it empty.

Wakeham's radio started bleeping. On the other end was Rossiter.

"Ma'am, are you sure we've got the right building? No one's here."

"Ryan, I was advised by the Deputy Commissioner that we were to raid 362 Olympic Way. It's got to be the right one."

Meanwhile, inside the building, the frustrated officers were preparing to leave. None was in a good mood, having had to get up at an unearthly hour and for nothing. One of the officers, PC Phil Atherton, saw some graffiti painted on the wall. It read **HA HA COPPERS. WE'VE GIVEN YOU THE SLIP.**

"Sir, have a look at this" said Atherton, motioning to his Sergeant. "Looks like those bastards knew we were coming first."

Later that morning
MI5 Headquarters
Millbank
London

"Marcel, where the hell's Richard? I told him to be in for an 8:30 meeting."

James Furnival, the Deputy Director of MI5, was furious that Richard Donovan was not in. He had a report to deliver on the field section's monitoring of terrorist involvement with the anti-Government protests.

"Don't know, Mr Furnival" replied Marcel Francois, Donovan's deputy. "Richard's normally in by now."

"When he comes in, tell him to report to HR" said Furnival.

"Marcel, I've got two urgent messages" said Emma Richardson, one of Francois's team of monitoring officers. "Russ Colbourne and Peter Firth. They can't wait."

Jesus Christ, thought Francois. The one day Richard's not in early and I've got two high level calls to deal at once.

"Put Russ Colbourne through, Emma. Tell Peter I'll deal with him next."

"Hi, Marcel, is Richard around?" asked Colbourne.

"Not yet. Any problem?"

"That's an understatement, Marcel. I fear there's been a leak somewhere along the line. Earlier today, the Met were going to bust a load of the Commie and Trot activists who were holed up in the Olympic Business Park before they trashed the City. When they got there, all the soap avoiders had buggered off. Someone must have tipped them off."

"I'll raise it as a high level alert here" said Francois. "What's the Met and NATS doing?"

"The same" replied Colbourne.

Next up was Peter Firth. With more bad news.

"Marcel, thank God I've found someone" said Firth. "I fear that the cover of our field team's been blown."

"Why, Peter? What's happened?"

"Asif Mahmood was shot dead earlier today. He was investigating Al-Q'aida involvement with the protests. Someone must have tipped off his killers."

Francois realised the seriousness of what had happened. There was a potential mole in MI5. He would have to let Furnival and Dame Nicola know.

Francois went into Furnival's outer office where his PA, Debbie King, sat.

"Debbie, is Mr Furnival free? I need to speak with him urgently. We've got a potential mole."

"I'm sorry, Mark" replied King. "Mr Furnival has got someone with him. I'll let you know when he's free."

Fifteen minutes later

Detective Chief Superintendent Trevor Ramsden, from the Metropolitan Police's Special Branch, was standing in Debbie King's office, flashing his warrant card.

"Can I see the Director-General or the Deputy Director please?"

"I'm sorry, sir" replied Debbie King. "The Director-General's on leave and the Deputy Director is busy."

"I'm afraid it's extremely urgent, miss" replied Ramsden. "There's security implications."

"Very well, sir, I'll ask the Deputy Director to see you."

A minute later, Ramsden was seated in Furnival's office.

"Good morning, Chief Superintendent Ramsden" said Furnival. "I understand you want to see me about a security issue."

"Mr Furnival, I've got some bad news. Last night, one of your officials, Richard Donovan, was murdered. A gang of youths tried to rob him and he put up a fight. Unfortunately, one of them had a knife and used it."

"Oh, my God!" exclaimed Furnival. He was feeling guilty about forcing Donovan to work late.

"Do you know if Mr Donovan was carrying any official papers, Mr Furnival?"

"I don't know, Chief Superintendent. Why are you asking?"

"Because CCTV footage clearly shows the robbers running off with Mr Donovan's briefcase. If he was, there's a risk those papers will be in the hands of insurgents and terrorists by now."

Furnival's heart sank. He knew there was a high probability that Donovan had taken papers home with him. After all, it was only yesterday that he had asked Donovan for a report on the monitoring of terrorist activity in the anti-Government protests.

The phone rang again. It was Debbie.

"Mr Furnival, Marcel Francois wants to see you. Urgently."

"Can't he wait, Debbie?"

"Apparently not, sir. He's had calls from the field teams and from NATS which suggest there's been a breach of security."

"Very well, Debbie. Send him in."

**The same day
Chequers
near Wendover
Buckinghamshire**

"Anti-Government protests in the United Kingdom have continued for the third day. Protestors have returned to Parliament Square and have been engaged in running battles with the police and the Army. Occupations of central and local Government buildings across the country have continued, with offices in Bristol, Leeds and Nottingham now being occupied."

"The protests took an alarming turn earlier this morning as demonstrators breached the 'Ring of Steel' around the City of London and have occupied offices belonging to Barclays, BNP Paribas, Deutsche Bank, Goldman Sachs, HSBC, Morgan Stanley and RBS, along with the offices of several leading corporate law firms. The Stock Exchange was forced to stop trading at 10am. Officials at the Bank of England are taking precautionary measures to remove the country's gold reserves to a more secure location."

The Sky News broadcast was the last thing Henry Arbuthnot and Darren Bramble wanted to hear. It suggested that the anti-Government protestors were running rings round the police and armed forces. The Prime Minister had arranged a briefing session at 12:30pm. She was not going to be happy at hearing the latest developments.

A flushed and tense Jason Steer entered the room. He had been fielding calls from anxious investors and businessmen about the security of their assets.

"Looks like you've had a bad morning, Jason" said Bramble.

"If the police had done what they were supposed to and pulled in that leftie mob in Stratford, we wouldn't be in this fucking mess" snapped the Chancellor of the Exchequer.

"How bad is it, Jason?" asked Arbuthnot.

"When you've had to explain to investors, bankers and hedge fund managers why their accounts have been cleaned out, perhaps you'll understand, Henry" replied Steer.

The 12:30 security update meeting which the Prime Minister chaired was tense. As well as the Prime Minister, Arbuthnot and Bramble, Jason Steer was invited, as was Foreign Secretary Dominic Collins and Sir Robin Peacock, the Army's Chief of Staff, Sir Roy Plummer, the Chairman of the Association of Chief Police Officers and Dame Nicola Martin, the Director-General of MI5.

Henry Arbuthnot was first to speak in his capacity of having responsibility for homeland security.

"Prime Minister, I'm afraid the news is not good. Protestors are still at large in Whitehall, occupations of official buildings are now spreading across the country and, this morning, they have broken into the City of London and taken control of buildings there. Jason has advised me that confidential details of private bank accounts have been placed on the Internet and have been plundered."

"Henry, you realise the damage this has done to the United Kingdom's reputation" said Deborah Pearson. "Possibly forever. What were you doing to prevent it happening?"

"A lot, Prime Minister" replied Arbuthnot. "Darren will fill you in with the details."

"MI5 field agents managed to track down the location of a team of insurgents from Class War and the Revolutionary Communist League who were going to storm the City of London. They were camped out in a warehouse in the Olympic Business Park and the police were planning to bust the lot of them earlier today. But someone tipped them off and they scarpered before the police were due to arrive. Which suggests that MI5 have got a mole in their ranks."

"There's no mole in MI5" replied Martin. "One of our officials took work home with him last night to produce a report for my deputy, James Furnival, on the involvement of the SNLA, WRA and Al-Q'aida with the protests. Unfortunately, he was murdered on the journey home in a botched robbery. We believe the robbers got hold of a laptop, papers and a PDA and passed them to either terrorists or anti-Government protestors. I will be taking disciplinary action against Furnival for recklessly forcing a subordinate to put himself and the country at risk."

"Has there been any other implications of this compromise of security, Nicola?" asked Pearson.

"I'm afraid so, Prime Minister" replied Martin. "Three of our field agents have been murdered."

"I'm sorry to hear that, Nicola" said the Prime Minister. "Henry, what do you propose we should do? We appear to be rather stretched."

"Prime Minister, our first priority should be to regain control of the City of London" replied Arbuthnot. "I propose that we send the SAS in. Secondly, to regain control of Whitehall. This could be a job for the Paras and the Marines, along with NATS' SWAT Teams. Finally, regaining control of the rest of the country. We're going to be a bit stretched but the Local Defence Volunteers should be able to take a lot of the pressure off the Army and the police."

Turning to Peacock, Arbuthnot asked him "Robin, how's recruitment going with the LDVs?"

"Rather patchily, Secretary of State" replied the Army Chief of Staff. "In rural areas and the South and South West, very well. But in the main cities and much of the North, it's poor. What's more, too many of the volunteers are middle-aged or elderly. Several are ex-forces or police but they'll be up against much younger people. A lot of the protestors are nothing more than a rabble but I fear there's SNLA and WRA embedded with them."

"If we manage to take control of the City and Whitehall, the rest of the country should be relatively easy" said Plummer. "Regular police and soldiers, supported by the reserve, should be able to achieve that."

Pearson's impatience showed on her face. She summoned the meeting to order.

"Henry, I fully agree about using the SAS. But we need to mobilise them now. Can I leave that to you?"

"Roy, I fully appreciate what the police are doing in these difficult times, but the challenge is the worst this country has faced for eighty years. We need the support the Local Defence Volunteers can offer. Robin, can you push this a bit harder."

Later that afternoon
Grange Road
Ealing
London

Gareth Appleyard took a call on his Personal Data Assistant. It was from Alun John, the West of England WRA commander.

"That you Gareth?"

"Yeah"

"Can you get ready. Two Chinooks will be on the way over Ealing Common in fifteen minutes. All carrying SAS on their way to the City. We reckon they'll be flying directly over you."

Appleyard called out to his flatmate, Mike Havard.

"Mike, get the SA-15s ready. Target overhead in fifteen mins."

Havard unzipped the neoprene containers which contained the SA-15s and lifted them out carefully. He then unzipped a similar container holding the missiles and, before loading them, ensured the batteries were still in working order. Appleyard then made a quick recce of the back garden to make sure there were no prying eyes who might give them away.

The SA-15 was one of the world's most feared missile systems because it was lightweight and could be mounted on a person's shoulder, yet its missiles were immune to most electronic countermeasures in the West. It was popular with guerrilla movements across the world, and the SNLA and WRA had both used them.

"All clear, Mike" shouted Appleyard.

Havard brought out the two SA-15s. He then heard the distant clatter of rotors.

"I think our target's about to come over, Gar" said Havard.

Appleyard looked up to the north west and saw two Chinooks in close formation.

"That's them. Ready, Mike."

Appleyard and Havard lifted the SA-15s onto their shoulders, turned the barrels towards the direction of the Chinooks and launched the missiles.

The missiles streaked upwards and accelerated to twice the speed of sound before smashing into the hot exhausts of the two General Electric turbine engines. The two Chinooks went into a dive as they lost power and crashed onto Ealing Common before bursting into flames.

That evening
London Road
Thornton Heath
London

Earlier that afternoon, detachments from the Parachute Regiment, the Royal Marines and the National Anti-Terror Squad's Special Weapons and Tactics Teams had taken control of the Government buildings in central London occupied by anti-Government protestors. And not without a struggle. Some of the protestors were armed, having obtained weapons through London crime gangs or disaffected National Servicemen. No less than fifteen protestors had been shot dead as the authorities stormed the occupied Departmental offices, along with another thirty three as battles with protestors took place in the streets outside. And another two thousand had been arrested.

With military and police numbers stretched, the Local Defence Volunteers were deployed to escort the prisoners to holding facilities set up at Biggin Hill, Kenley and Redhill airfields.

Local Defence Volunteers from Purley and Coulsdon were taking a detachment of 500 prisoners to Redhill. The ten Iveco military lorries were proceeding in formation down London Road towards Thornton Heath Pond, where they were to take the Croydon by-pass.

As they approached the one-way system round the former Pond, which had been filled in for years, they encountered a roadblock. Behind it were groups of menacing-looking youths. Most were black or Asian, but some were white.

The Commander of the Purley and Coulsdon Local Defence Volunteers was Alan Merrick, a big, meaty-faced man who had been a former Chief Inspector in the Metropolitan Police. To him, the youths behind the roadblock were what he termed 'police property' from his days in the force. What he and fellow officers termed 'scumbags' who lived a criminal and parasitic lifestyle and were justified targets for harassment and arrest.

Merrick radioed Captains Roger Jeffreys and Matt Durkin for support. Jeffreys was short and stocky, in his 60s and ran a construction firm. Durkin was an investment banker in his 30s, tall and built like a rugby back row forward.

Merrick, Jeffreys and Durkin uncocked their Sniper rifles and walked towards the makeshift barrier blocking London Road.

"What the fuck do you think you're doing?" snarled Merrick to three youths at the front of the barrier. "We're Local Defence Volunteers on Government business, escorting prisoners. If you don't remove that crap from the road in the next minute, I'll give my men orders to drive straight through it."

"We're the North Croydon Provisional Defence Committee, man" replied Connor Sealy, a dreadlocked black man in his early 20s. "We decide who passes through."

"And you're part of the fascist polis" added Abid Khan, a Pakistani youth with a sneering demeanour.

"Listen, son, what part of 'get this crap off the road' don't you understand?" shouted Jeffreys. "We're part of the security services of this country and we're ordering you to clear the road. Now!"

"Matt, call up reinforcements" said Merrick. "Looks like we're going to have to use force to get through."

Durkin followed Merrick's order and, within thirty seconds, another ten Local Defence Volunteers were standing at the barricade.

"Right, your time's up" shouted Merrick. "Local Defence Volunteers, prepare to drive through."

The engines on the Ivecos began to rev up as the lorries started to move. Suddenly, a hail of bricks and stones started to fly in their direction from behind the barricade.

Merrick had his orders. If there was any violent resistance and a threat to the safety of the Local Defence Volunteers, he could open fire. That situation had arisen. Merrick gave the order "Open Fire."

The first volley of gunfire from the Local Defence Volunteers cut down Khan, Sealey and nine other youths manning the barricade. This however enraged the other protestors. Suddenly, petrol bombs started to accompany the bricks and stones. Then gunfire from a flat on the corner of London Road and Brigstock Road. Three of the Local Defence Volunteers, including their Commander, Alan Merrick, fell to the bullets of an AK-47. Matt Durkin was seen desperately radioing for reinforcements when he, too, was cut down.

In the first lorry were fifty prisoners, now under the guard of only one Local Defence Volunteer. Rob Springall saw he and his fellow prisoners had a chance for freedom.

"Dave" he whispered to Dave Lawson sitting next to him, "I think the LDVs are under attack. Here's our chance to make a break for it."

Lucy Hynes, a sales representative with IBM and a member of her local Conservative Association, overheard the whispering.

"Silence!" snapped Hynes. "Anymore talking out of place and you'll get some of this." Hynes was brandishing a long side-handled baton that the police had issued to the Local Defence Volunteers.

Springall seized his opportunity. As Hynes returned to her position at the front of the lorry, Springall stuck his leg out and tripped her. Hynes fell to the ground.

Under normal circumstances, Hynes would have had two heavily armed colleagues with her and they would have had little difficulty in dealing with Springall. But she was on her own. Before she had an opportunity to use her panic alarm, she was writhing in agony from a boot in the kidneys and was powerless to stop the prisoners escaping.

Thirty minutes later, the skirmish was over. Twenty five of the prisoners had been shot while escaping but all the rest made it to freedom.

CHAPTER 33

8 July 2021
Chequers near Wendover
Buckinghamshire

Henry Arbuthnot and Darren Bramble had agreed to meet Business First, a pressure group formed by several of the United Kingdom's leading businessmen who were concerned about the collapse of law and order over the previous four days. Several members had reported serious damage to property, loss of business caused by illegal occupations of business premises and theft from private bank accounts. In addition, that morning's news had reported that squatters had taken over several vacant houses.

Business First's Chairman, Sir Martin Weighill, the Chairman of a leading investment bank, was a forceful man at the best of times. Many of his members had suffered occupation of their offices and the embezzlement of their assets as confidential commercial information was put into the public domain, and he was demanding robust action to restore order.

"Secretary of State, Home Secretary, my members are extremely concerned about the Government's apparent inability to defend life and property" said Weighill. "Both Whitehall and the City of London are in the hands of, to put it lightly, brigands. So it seems as well are Government and commercial premises in the provinces. And from the news, it appears that the insurgents are getting the upper hand over the Government."

Weighill was referring to the shooting down of two Chinook helicopters carrying the SAS on a mission to regain control of the City of London and the ambush of Local Defence Volunteers in Croydon the previous night.

Sir Bruce Capon, a publishing magnate, was next to speak.

"Gentlemen, what Business First is proposing is that we raise our own privately-funded army who will provide support to regular forces in putting down this revolt."

"Sir Bruce, I appreciate your concern" said Arbuthnot. "This idea has been previously suggested before. Thing you chaps need to remember is that the regular armed forces and police are all highly trained and are far better placed to tackle unrest of this kind than civilian volunteers, no matter how well-motivated they may be. And you need to be aware that you won't just be facing spotty-faced adolescents. Hardened terrorists have embedded themselves with this revolt."

"Secretary of State, you don't understand" said Weighill. "The men we will be recruiting will all be professional soldiers with military experience. And we will be making available the maximum resources necessary so they will be as well trained and equipped as regular soldiers. If not better."

There was a knock on the door of the meeting room. It was Katherine Skinner, Arbuthnot's Senior Private Secretary.

"Sorry to interrupt you, Secretary of State. General Peacock needs to see you. It's urgent."

"Sorry, Sir Martin" said Arbuthnot. "I better see what Peacock wants."

Peacock's office was fifty yards down the corridor.

"Secretary of State, you better see this" said Peacock. He pointed to charts on the video screen which were backed up by photographs.

"Military forces from EU countries have been observed carrying out manoeuvres in the Pas de Calais region in France. Satellite photos clearly show tanks, helos and infantry practising. Secondly, French Air Force Rafales and Luftwaffe Typhoons and Tornados have been practising mock combats and bombing runs over Luneberg Heath. Universal transports have been practising cargo drops. Neptune maritime patrol planes from the French and German navies have been carrying out reconnaissance flights along the British coastline. And finally, the *Charles de Gaulle* carrier group have been observed passing through the Irish Sea and appear to be en route to Dublin."

"Good God!" exclaimed Arbuthnot. "It looks like there's a possibility of EU military intervention. That's all we need. We'll have to let the PM know."

Deborah Pearson meanwhile was pursuing her own line of enquiry. She had remembered that Henry Arbuthnot had established that all countries signatory to the North Atlantic Treaty Organisation were duty bound to provide military assistance to another member country facing either hostile military action or domestic unrest.

Earlier that day, she had phoned President Williams to point this out and demand NATO assistance to suppress the insurgency taking place. Williams had rebuffed her, pointing out that the United Kingdom was under suspension from United Nations for breaches of its human rights covenant.

Pearson then remembered her meeting with Senator Troy Burton in Yellowcliffe Bay three months earlier. She reached for the telephone.

Burton's secretary answered the phone.

"Can I speak to Senator Burton?"

"Who is speaking?"

"Deborah Pearson, Prime Minister of the United Kingdom."

A few seconds later, Burton was on the line.

"Hi, Debbie, how's things in the UK?"

"Not good, Troy" replied the Prime Minister. "We're having trouble in containing the unrest that's occurred over the past week. Protestors have taken over the City and council offices in several provincial cities and towns. We've got control of Whitehall back but I understand there've been fresh clashes there. The protestors are using the Internet and mobile communications to plan their moves. We've tried shutting them down, but we're unable to prevent them using dial-up lines and mobile phone networks have been illegally brought back on line. But what's tipped it has been a mutiny by National Servicemen and help from the SNLA, WRA and Al-Q'aida. This has given the insurgents access to weapons. And things weren't helped when they got hold of details of our intelligence communications earlier this week."

"How did that happen, Debbie?"

"An MI5 official was murdered on the train journey home earlier this week. Unfortunately, he was carrying highly sensitive information and that's found its way to the insurgents. They now know our every move."

"What reinforcements have you got, Debbie?"

"Not as much as I want, Troy. We're going to have to call on the Green Howards and the Wessex Regiment, who are up in Scotland and Wales. If we pull troops out of there, we risk losing control to the SNLA and WRA. The Government's tried commissioning Local Defence Volunteers, but recruitment's been patchy. There are a lot of people who would like to see us fail. Arbuthnot and Bramble are currently meeting a group of leading businessmen who want to recruit a private army to assist."

"Have you spoken to the President yet?" asked Burton.

"I have, Troy. A complete waste of time. He would be content to see our Government fall. If that happens, US business will lose out massively. A Labour Government here would strangle business with red tape and regulation, they would be back in the EU in a flash and there's a risk that they'll consider trade deals with Russia and China. And that is before you consider the implications of an independent Scotland and Wales."

"I don't think our business leaders are happy with Williams's inaction, Debbie. They see him as damaging US interests."

"Is there any chance you can force Williams's arm, Troy?" asked Pearson.

"If you mean by threatening to use the Twenty Fifth Amendment, Debbie, yes."

As soon as Pearson put down the phone, Arbuthnot was waiting to see her.

"Prime Minister, can I have a word? It's urgent."

"Go ahead, Henry" replied Pearson.

"You better see this, Prime Minister" said Arbuthnot, laying down photographs and printouts from the charts General Peacock had shown him.

The same day
Oval Office
White House
Washington DC

"Senator Burton to see you, Mr President" said Chief of Staff Larry Hendricks.

"Send him through, Larry" replied Richard Williams, President of the United States of America.

The Senator for Mississippi was accompanied by fellow Senator Byron Mitchell, Representatives Phil Krebs and Kay Navarro, retired General Donald England and

Admiral Stephen Graf, the former National Security Advisor to President Whitney, Harley Drake and six business leaders, Louise Anderson, the Chairman of General Electric, Greg Connor, the Chairman of AgriCorp, Bruce Hellstrom, the Chairman of Exxon, Bob Murdoch, the Chairman of Texaco, Milton Spector, the Chairman of Chevron and Jane Tarantini, the Chairman of Morgan Stanley.

Burton addressed the President.

"Mr President, I and my colleagues are here today in our capacity as patriotic Americans to register our displeasure at your failure to act over the unrest in a NATO ally country, the United Kingdom. I understand you advised Prime Minister Pearson that the United States Government would be offering no military assistance, despite the fact that the United Kingdom is facing a domestic insurgency."

"That is correct, Senator" replied Williams. "If you recall, the Government of the United Kingdom has been suspended by the United Nations for breaching the terms of its charter. It has breached the norms of every human rights convention through the use of torture, by imprisonment without trial, the use of military force against civilians and the denial of fair trials to suspects. The United States Government has felt it necessary to suspend arms sales to the United Kingdom and it is supported by both Houses of Congress. If you are seriously suggesting that I order the deployment of US military personnel to save Deborah Pearson's hide, then you've got another think coming."

"No, Mr President, it's you who've got another think coming" shouted Spector. "You are putting at risk US business investments worth trillions of dollars by doing nothing. If any of us lose money over this, we'll see that you get impeached for gross dereliction of duty."

"Furthermore, Mr President, you are putting US national security at risk by allowing Britain to fall to insurgents" added Drake. "Don't you appreciate the help that Britain has given us in the past, when the rest of the world didn't want to know. They helped us win three Gulf wars. What's more, they've allowed us to use their bases for over seventy years and that's helped keep the West free from tyranny. If Britain breaks up, we could lose that. And Russia, China and Iran will be laughing their way to the bank."

"Mr President, may I remind you that the NATO Treaty obliges the US Government as a signatory to offer military assistance to any fellow signatory facing hostile military action, whatever the source" said Burton. "You have no choice but to give the United Kingdom military assistance."

"And if I don't?" said Williams.

"Then we will ask for your resignation, Mr President" replied Burton. "Under the Twenty Fifth Amendment, the powers and duties of your Office will automatically devolve to Vice-President Gould, who has agreed to serve as the new President."

"You're wasting your breath, Senator" said Williams. I have no intention of resigning."

"Then you will face impeachment for dereliction of Office, Mr President."

Later that day
Oval Office
White House
Washington DC

General Edward Connolly was surprised to be summoned at short notice to see President Williams.

Connolly, an Irish-American from Boston, was Commander-in-Chief of the US armed forces' Atlantic Command. The son of a policeman, he had chosen a military career instead of following his three brothers into Boston Police Department and had risen to high command above the sons of generals and colonels by his sheer ability and energy.

"Ed, how quickly can you mobilise a task force to assist the British Government?"

"You did say Britain, sir?" asked an incredulous Connolly. He knew that the current administration was not well-disposed towards its transatlantic partner.

"I did, Ed" replied the President. "As much as I dislike the current Government in London and what they stand for, they are a fellow signatory to NATO. Furthermore, US commercial and military interests are served by having a stable Government there. So I've got no choice but to go in."

"It's going to be tough, sir" said Connolly. "The *Kennedy* and *Stennis* carrier groups are ready to sail from Norfolk and we've got infantry ready at Fort Bragg and Fort Sumner. But the *Reagan* and *George H W Bush* carrier croups are in the South Atlantic and it will take two weeks to get them in the combat zone. Air support's more of a problem. We need fighters and attack planes to secure UK airspace and the nearest land base we can use is Keflavik. Otherwise, we risk having our transports shot down. Fortunately, Canada should allow us to use Goose Bay for B-1 and B-52 flights."

"Ed, I know it's tough, but if we lose the United Kingdom to civil war, the consequences for us will be worse. Just do it."

"Aye aye, sir" said Connolly.

"Sir, there's one thing more you should know" said Connolly. "A lot of our men and women, both enlisted and officers, are of Scottish or Welsh ancestry. Seeing us go in to help out the Government that's oppressed the lands of their forefathers will stick in their craw. I'm worried that some will desert."

"Ed, I know how you and many of the armed forces feel about this" said Williams. He knew many Irish-Americans and they all held the same long-standing grievance against the British and, particularly, the English for what they saw as historical oppression of their homeland.

"But there's times where duty has to override personal convictions. Believe me, I cannot stand Deborah Pearson or the British government. But they're fellow NATO members and facing insurrection. We've got no choice but to help her."

The same evening
Yellowcliffe Bay
American Virgin Islands

Juanita Nelson, the housekeeper at Virgin Islands villa of Henry Bergesen and Deborah Pearson, had called in the repairmen from CNT Electronics when one of the servants reported a malfunction on the CCTV security system which protected the property. Elmore Reynolds, a tall local man in his 30s, was carrying out repairs.

It had taken Reynolds five hours to put the malfunctioning system right, but he was now close to confirming that everything was working.

"How long do you think you'll be, Mr Reynolds?" asked the housekeeper.

"I'm nearly there, Ma'am" replied Reynolds. "I'm going to carry out one more full system run and should be completed in half an hour's time."

"Let me know when you're ready" said Nelson.

Reynolds decided to carry out a windback to test the CCTV system again. He chose the camera in the basement for the test as it would show how effectively the system worked in less than optimum light. He pressed the 'rewind' button, then randomly stopped it. He then pressed 'play'.

Reynolds saw a man and a woman seated in the basement talking to each other. They looked familiar. He stopped the test and walked into the lounge. The sun had just set and darkness was quickly falling outside.

"Mrs Nelson, have you got a newspaper I could borrow for a minute?" asked Reynolds. "By the way, I'm in the middle of the final test. I should be out of here in about twenty minutes time."

"There's a Wall Street Journal, Mr Reynolds" said Nelson.

"Thank you. Just what I need."

Reynolds looked at the front page. On it, the leading article read

Business leaders slam Williams for inaction over Britain

Leading US businessmen and women, including Bruce Hellstrom of Exxon, Milton Spector of Chevron and Jane Tarantini of Morgan Stanley, are up in arms over the refusal by President Williams to commit military support to Britain, where the fourth day of unrest by anti-Government protestors has seen occupations of business and Government buildings continuing. Their views have been echoed by the leader of the minority Republican group in Congress, Senator Troy Burton (pictured) who says that US commercial and security interests are at risk.

Britain's Prime Minister, Deborah Pearson (pictured below) has vowed to stand firm in the face of the unrest which, in a statement given to Fox News, she said was being organised by Marxist and anarchist troublemakers and that the SNLA, the WRA and Islamic extremists were using the protests as cover to further their aim of overthrowing the British government.

Jesus Christ, thought Reynolds. That's Pearson and Burton on the video.

Reynolds started up the CCTV playback and heard the contents of the conversation. But it was as the conversation came to an end that his interest rose.

"Debbie, there might be one last hope. "If US interests are put at risk by Williams's refusal to provide the United Kingdom with military assistance, it might be possible to impeach him. Better still, the threat of impeachment might be a lever to force his resignation."

"Surely Williams won't resign? The Democrats are sitting on a solid majority."

"Wall Street are unhappy with him. So are the Joint Chiefs of Staff of the military. They carry a lot of weight as you know, Debbie. I think we could get rid of Williams in a palace coup without having to involve Congress."

Many of the Virgin Islanders were content to remain a US colony. Reynolds was one of the minority who wasn't. He was in favour of independence. He was aware who Senator Burton was. A Southern Republican senator. Probably one who disliked blacks and wanted Williams out of the White House because of his colour. The likes of him had finished off one black President already. He sure didn't want a second to go the same way.

He searched in his case for a USB stick and plugged it into the mainframe. He identified the date of the footage. 3 April 2021. He now had evidence that Senator Burton had engaged in espionage and, possibly, treason. The USB stick was not destined for the local FBI. A lot of them were unreconstructed Republican supporters and he would probably be arrested under the misuse of telecommunications laws. Instead, it would be destined for the subversive website, Whistleblower.

9 July 2021
Federal Bureau of Investigations Headquarters
935 Pennsylvania Avenue NW
Washington DC

"Brad, it's Jan. Have you got a moment? Something really interesting has come up on Whistleblower."

Janet Ricardo, an intelligence analyst, was following up on a lead on the latest story to emerge from the controversial website which specialised in leaking sensitive Government and commercial information in the Western world. To some people, Whistleblower was a crusader for freedom and people's rights in a world increasingly dominated by governmental and corporate high-handedness. But to others, Whistleblower were nothing more than traitors who put people's lives at risk. It was perhaps significant that they were based in Islamist-run Algeria and were believed to receive a substantial income from Al-Q'aida through their drug-trafficking operations.

"Sorry, Jan, I'm rather tied up with work" replied her Section Leader, Brad Hoffmann. "We might be onto a breakthrough in finding EVF cells based here."

"Brad, it's about Senator Burton. The former Senate leader."

"Not more tittle tattle about which nubile young secretary he's screwed."

"Much worse than that, Brad" said Ricardo. "There's video footage of him discussing with the British Prime Minister about overthrowing President Williams. It's on YouTube and is set to be headline news in tomorrow's newspapers. We need to alert the White House before this happens."

"Jan, everyone knows that Senator Burton cannot stand the President and would be delighted if he could force a re-run of last year's election. But overthrow him? Even Burton can't be that crazy."

"Brad, that's what Burton and Pearson were saying. Forcing the President's hand over providing military assistance to Britain, with the threat of impeachment if he refuses. Burton actually refers to removing the President in a palace coup. That's surely evidence of his complicity."

"Are you sure it's genuine, Jan?" asked Hoffmann. "There's been hoaxes in the past."

"It is, Brad. Come and see for yourself. By the way, it answers a query that Special Agent Doyle wanted to find out."

"What was that, Jan?" asked Hoffmann.

"You know that the FBI were detailed to provide Senator Burton with protection following 2/13? Early in April, he went missing for four days. Now we know why."

Later that morning
Oval Office
White House
Washington DC

"Mr President, Mike Farkas to see you." Larry Hendricks, the President's Chief of Staff, showed the FBI Director into the Oval Office.

"Good morning, Mike" said Williams. "Understand you've got some interesting news about Troy Burton."

"Indeed I have, Mr President" replied Farkas. "Here are the details."

Farkas, a tall, now balding former police officer from Cleveland in his mid-50s, plugged a USB stick into the computer in the Oval Office and pressed 'play'.

"Jesus Christ!" exclaimed the President. "So that's why Pearson was so keen to have US troops sent over to Britain."

"Has she formally asked for that, Mr President?" asked Farkas.

"She most certainly has, Mike" replied Williams. "And to reinforce the message, I have a deputation of retired Whitney administration officials and business leaders led by Senator Burton yesterday to twist my arm and threaten me with impeachment or forced resignation if I did not comply with their demands."

"What do you intend to do now, Mr President?" asked the FBI Director.

"I haven't made up my mind, Mike" replied the President. "But one thing's for certain. I won't be bailing out Prime Minister Pearson. How about you?"

"I think the FBI may have some questions to ask Senator Burton" replied Farkas.

After Farkas left, Williams summoned Larry Hendricks on his internal phone.

"Larry, can you get hold of the following people. Immediately."

"Fire away, Mr President."

"Firstly, George Savlakis, the EU Ambassador. Secondly, General Connolly. And finally, Christian Vale."

"Who's Christian Vale, Mr President?" asked Hendricks.

"The former British Foreign Secretary, Larry. Served under Delgado from 2010 to 2015 when he resigned over the Government's policy in Scotland and Wales. He's in New York on a lecture tour of the States."

<h2 style="text-align:center">The same day, 10:30am
Chequers
near Wendover
Buckinghamshire</h2>

Deborah Pearson reached for the telephone in her study and called the White House on the special line. Surely President Williams would be ready to send military assistance after Burton had done his work?

"President Williams here. Good morning, Madam Prime Minister."

"Mr President, I am phoning regarding my request yesterday for military assistance under the terms of the NATO Treaty. Have you reconsidered your position?"

"Madam Prime Minister, I am prepared to send US military assistance to Britain under the terms of the NATO Treaty. But under the following conditions."

"What do you mean 'the following conditions', Mr President?" rasped a tetchy Prime Minister.

"Firstly, any assistance that my country will offer will be in a peacekeeping capacity only. And, furthermore, the United States will not be acting alone. The US peacekeeping force will be accompanied by a similar force from EU countries but will be under the overall command of General Edward Connolly, the Commander-in-Chief of the US Atlantic Command. I secured an agreement with EU Ambassador Savlakis this morning."

"The EU. Don't you realise, Mr President that they were planning to invade the United Kingdom?"

Williams was in no mood to respond to Pearson's points and continued.

"And, secondly, Madam Prime Minister, I want the immediate resignation of your Government, including you as Prime Minister. I will make arrangements for a caretaker administration to take control after you've gone."

"What did you say, Mr President?" Pearson was now white with fury.

"I, Madam Prime Minister, will repeat myself for the last time. The offer of assistance from my country is on condition that you and your Government resign. Understand?"

"And if I don't?" said a defiant Pearson.

"Then you will be left to your own devices" replied Williams.

Pearson slammed the phone down. She then immediately dialled the number of Senator Troy Burton. His secretary answered the phone.

"Can I speak to Senator Burton immediately? It's Deborah Pearson here."

"I'm most sorry, madam" replied the secretary. "Senator Burton is not available to speak to anyone."

There was a knock on the door. It was Liam Rippingale, the Prime Minister's Assistant Private Secretary.

"Prime Minister, have you got a minute?"

"What is it, Liam? I'm busy."

"It's about Senator Burton. Just seen the latest bulletin on Sky News. He's just been arrested by the FBI on treason charges."

Later that day
Chequers
near Wendover
Buckinghamshire

Deborah Pearson had convened an emergency meeting of the full Cabinet to consider the offer that President Williams had made. In reality, it was an attempt by Pearson to get a vote of confidence in her plan to stay put and see off the uprising.

The logistical problems of getting Cabinet members to Chequers because of the disorder meant that it was not possible to start the meeting until 5pm. The day had been humid and sultry and dark clouds were building up over the Buckinghamshire countryside. The first peals of distant thunder could be heard.

At 5pm, Pearson signalled that the Cabinet meeting was open. As soon as it started, there was a blinding flash of lightning followed by a cacophonous roll of thunder.

"There will be just one agenda item for this afternoon" said Pearson. "Earlier today, President Williams gave me the terms of his offer to provide military assistance to the United Kingdom. He has agreed to send US troops to restore order, but on two conditions. One is that they from part of a multi-lateral force shared with the EU. The other is that this Government resigns and hands over power to a caretaker administration whom I believe President Williams is selecting. This will also mean my resignation as Prime Minister."

"My view is that President Williams is in breach of the NATO Treaty signed seventy two years ago, which commits all member states to provide military assistance to fellow members facing a threat to its security. The fact that the United Nations has suspended us—for what I consider to be an unwarranted intrusion in our domestic affairs—should have no bearing on the Treaty's application."

"You will be aware that many of the business leaders in the United States and worldwide think that the international trade and arms embargos on the United Kingdom are a waste of time and money. Yesterday, Senator Burton led a delegation consisting of business leaders, retired senior military officers and three Congressional colleagues to meet President Williams to explain the error of his ways. His reward has been to be arrested by the FBI in what was a blatantly political act designed to remove a key critic of the Williams administration."

"Today is the most critical day this country has faced since either the Spanish Armada in 1588 and the Battle of Britain in 1940. On both occasions, the country was alone, facing a well-armed enemy. No one thought we would survive. But can I say this. The British are fighters, not quitters. It is my intention to continue as Prime Minister in this Government. Through guts and courage, we will prevail, whether or not the USA or anyone decides to help us. What I'm asking you to give me is your unconditional support."

Even with the lights turned on, the room was lit up by another flash of lightning. Three seconds later, a deafening peal of thunder followed.

The body language of the Cabinet suggested that Deborah Pearson would have a struggle to obtain support.

First to speak was Henry Arbuthnot.

"Prime Minister, I have been a loyal member of this Government since they were first elected to office eleven years ago. But I see the odds against which we are faced. I'm afraid to say that the insurgency's getting support from ordinary people. And not just through active participation in acts of disorder. Many people are either refusing to support us or are giving help to the insurgents. Just look at the pathetic enrolment for the Local Defence Volunteers. If we accept Williams's offer, at least we'll get some degree of normality restored."

Jason Steer was next to speak.

"Prime Minister, like Henry, I've given long and loyal service to this Government. But I too think we need to face up to reality. I know you can't stand Williams. Nor can I. But unless we get the country back to work, we'll go bust."

"You also need to look at the bigger and longer-term picture, Prime Minister" said Dominic Collins. "Any caretaker Government will almost certainly contain a lot of Labour MPs. If they are responsible for the break-up of the United Kingdom, the English electorate will never forgive Labour. We'll be back in power and, without all the Labour and nationalist votes from Scotland and Wales, we'll have a permanent majority."

Next to speak was Darren Bramble.

"It's also worth remembering that, even if Scotland and Wales get independence, they will still be dependent on England for finance and communications. If they get the wrong side of us, we'll be able to squeeze the life out of them."

"Hold on a minute" said Lord Manson. "It's starting to look like rats deserting a sinking ship. Only three months ago, we voted for the Prime Minister because of her resolution in the face of fire. We've faced worse challenges over the past eleven years. The mass strikes and riots in 2011. The Al-Q'aida bombings in 2012. The Third Gulf War in 2013 where the United Kingdom and Australia were the only countries to support the USA. Just because the rest of the world refuses to support us is no excuse to throw in the towel."

"Come on, Robert, face reality" said Ben Clarke. "Insurgents have got control of Parliament Square, Whitehall, the City and most provincial towns and cities. There have been reports that soldiers and the police are now refusing to move against insurgents. And we're facing possible invasion by the EU. Look what we've got to fight them. Apart from the regular police and army, a bunch of dogs of war recruited by business and Dad's Army. What Jason and Dominic said is right. Let the caretaker Government break up the United Kingdom and Labour will cop the blame from the electorate. Play the long game and we'll be back in a few years. And probably for good."

At 6:25pm, the Cabinet moved to vote on the motion of accepting President Williams's offer of military assistance. By sixteen votes to two, the Cabinet voted to accept the offer. The moment the result of the vote was announced, a loud blast rocked Chequers. A bolt of lightning had struck the roof.

10 July 2021
Sky News

"This is Daniel Merryfield with this morning's headlines on Sky News."

"The main news item has been the announcement of the resignation of the Government. Less than an hour ago, Prime Minister Deborah Pearson flew by helicopter to Buckingham Palace to hand in her resignation and to advise the Queen that the Government would be standing down."

"The news of the Government's resignation was greeted by jubilation by protestors in Parliament Square."

"It has been announced that former Foreign Secretary, Christian Vale, is going to act as Prime Minister under an all-party caretaker administration. Mr Vale, who has been on a lecture tour of the USA, is expected to return to London tomorrow to take up his post."

"The final act of the outgoing Government was to agree to a joint US-EU peacekeeping force, which will be arriving in the United Kingdom from tomorrow to help restore order in the United Kingdom."

"London and the South East is clearing up after violent thunderstorms crossed the region yesterday evening and night. Over two inches of rain was recorded in places and buildings in Croydon, Slough and Tilbury were damaged after being struck by lightning. Striking firefighters abandoned their picket lines to help fight a blaze on an industrial estate in Purfleet after lightning struck oil storage tanks."

12 July 2021
The Kremlin
Moscow

Hamidreza Yazdani, the Iranian Foreign Minister, looked like the cat that had got the cream. He had just signed a contract with Russia for the supply of an aircraft carrier, ten *Sovremenyy*-class destroyers, ten *Sochi*-class submarines, fifty Su-37 fighters, eighty MiG-39 fighters, of which fifteen were to be equipped for carrier operation, fifty Su-34 strike bombers, ten Tu-22M long-range bombers, ten Tu-142 maritime reconnaissance planes, twenty five Il-176 transports, fifty Yak-130 advanced trainers and forty Mil-28 gunship helicopters. In addition, Iran would be supplied with the jigs to build an indigenous attack bomber based on the Su-25, a tactical transport plane and a basic trainer.

Yazdani knew that the President, Mohammed Khoramzadeh, was terminally ill with cancer and would almost certainly be dead later that year. With the weapons deal in the bag that would once again make Iran the major Islamic power, his chances of getting the top job were much enhanced.

Yazdani and his Russian counterpart, Igor Stepashin, walked out of the Kremlin into the Moscow summer sunlight.

"Tell me, Hamidreza, what made you think that you could sign such a deal without attracting the notice of the USA or Britain?" asked Stepashin. "After all, you were at war with them only eight years ago."

"Igor, have a look at this" said the dimunitive Iranian who was dwarfed by the tall Russian who stood a good foot taller. Yazdani handed him a copy of the *International Herald Tribune*.

Stepashin read the leading article.

US and European troops move into Britain as Vale takes charge

LONDON 11 July The prospect of peace in Great Britain grew as US and European Union peacekeeping troops under the command of US General Edward Connolly started to arrive in the country last night. Already, the offer of an amnesty from prosecution and a review of grievances by the caretaker Government has led to the departure of the protestors who have occupied Parliament Square for almost a week.

The new Prime Minister, Christian Vale, has started appointing his Cabinet. Former Chancellor of the Exchequer, Ed Villiers, has been re-appointed to the post he held until April this year while Labor Party leader, Iain Turner, has been appointed Home Secretary and Liberal Democrat leader Nick Moss has been appointed Foreign Secretary.

Mr Vale's main priority will be to find a political solution to Scotland and Wales, where pro-independence insurgents have been fighting a war for the past six years. As a first step, Mr Vale has announced an amnesty for all insurgents from the SNLA, the WRA and the EVF who surrender their weapons to the peacekeepers.

"You can see, Igor, that the Great Satan and the Little Satan have matters on their mind other than us" said Yazdani. "With their attention focused on what has happened in Britain over the past six years, we've been able to start the process of re-arming without them noticing. Remember what the Chinese philosopher Sun Tzu said on the art of war. 'Break the will of the enemy to fight and you accomplish the true objective of war. Cover with ridicule the enemy's tradition. Exploit and aggravate the inherent frictions within the enemy country. Agitate the young against the old. Prevail if possible without armed conflict. The supreme excellence is not to win a hundred victories in a hundred battles. The supreme excellence is to defeat the armies of your enemies without ever having to fight them'. And that is what we have done."

"Hamidreza, good luck for the future" said Stepashin as he shook the hand of the Iranian Foreign Minister.

CHAPTER 34

13 July 2021
HM Prison Woodhill
Milton Keynes
Buckinghamshire

"Prisoner Ferguson, the Governor would like to see you now."

Alastair Ferguson was slightly baffled by the news from Officer David Kynaston. He had not done anything that might attract disciplinary sanction.

The former Scottish First Minister was in the sixth year of a thirty year prison sentence following conviction for treason in October 2015. Years of incarceration, a lack of sunshine and a poor diet had left the one-time Dundee United triallist looking older than his 56 years. He had put on weight and his hair had not only turned grey but he was starting to go bald.

"Do you know the reason, Mr Kynaston?"

"Sorry, Ferguson, no idea. Might be good news in any case."

Ferguson followed Kynaston along the corridors to the Governor's office. He was surprised to find former Transport Minister Jim Donnachie and the former Welsh Agriculture Minister Hywel John, also inmates at Woodhill, seated there.

Governor Graham Colgan walked into the room and sat down at his desk. His body language suggested he was in a good mood.

"Prisoners Donnachie, Ferguson and John, I've got some good news for you. The new Government has decided to release from prison all former members of the Scottish and Welsh governments currently serving sentences. You are therefore being released with effect from today. If you follow Officer Kynaston to the Custody Office, he will return your civilian clothes and issue you with money and train tickets so you can return home. All your families have been notified."

"Ferguson, can you remain here for a further minute?" asked Colgan. "I've got a further request. The Prime Minister has invited you to meet him at Chequers to discuss a review of the constitutional position in Scotland. Are you willing to take part? If so, I'll let his office know and you'll be picked up."

"Governor, do you mind me asking a question? Are you telling me there's been a change of Government?"

"Indeed there is, Ferguson" replied Colgan. "An all-Party administration took office at the weekend following the resignation of the previous Government. The former Foreign Secretary, Christian Vale, is now Prime Minister."

"Tell Mr Vale I'd be delighted to meet him" said the former First Minister of Scotland.

That afternoon
Prime Minister's Office
10 Downing Street
London

Emyr Roderick had also aged during his incarceration. He, too, had put on weight through inactivity and his formerly dark hair had gone grey. But Alastair Ferguson had little difficulty in recognising the former Welsh First Minister who had been voted into power at the same time, declared independence on the same day and had been sentenced to an identical term of imprisonment almost six years earlier.

"Long time since we last saw each other, shipmate" said Ferguson, shaking the Welshman's hand.

"Remember the last time we were here, Ally" said Roderick. "Almost exactly six years ago. Delgado reading us the Riot Act over us taxing the oil industry."

"Should be different with Vale, Emyr" replied Ferguson. "He was always one of the few reasonable Tories."

"Will you gentlemen like to come through?" asked the Prime Minister's Assistant Private Secretary, Liam Rippingale.

Ferguson and Roderick followed Rippingale into the Prime Minister's office where, seated before them was the tall, blond-haired figure of Christian Vale.

"Good afternoon, gentlemen" said Vale. "I'm really glad you accepted my invitation for a meeting."

"Thank you, Prime Minister" replied the two former First Ministers.

"Alastair, Emyr, you may or may not be aware what has happened in the past few days" continued the Prime Minister. "You may have heard that the previous Government lost a no-confidence vote in the House two weeks ago. Initially, they refused to stand down but, following a week of protests, they agreed to stand down last weekend. My Government is an all-Party coalition which will act in a caretaker capacity until a constitutional agreement is found for the future of Scotland and Wales. That is why I've invited you along today."

"What have you got in mind, Prime Minister?" asked Ferguson.

"I'm planning to hold a peace conference" replied Vale. "Aidan Daly, the Irish Prime Minister, has offered to host them at Slane Castle and Senator Bruce Farah, President Williams's envoy, will help facilitate them. I hope you will participate."

"You can guarantee on that, Prime Minister" said Ferguson.

"Me as well" added Roderick.

"By the way, Prime Minister, what about the WRA and SNLA?" asked Roderick. "Can't see them putting their weapons away unless something juicy's on the table."

"Actually, they have, Emyr" replied Vale. "Both the SNLA and WRA declared a ceasefire last night and the EVF followed suit this morning. All warring parties have been asked to surrender to the US and EU peacekeepers who've been brought in to help restore order. First signs look most encouraging."

"I will be inviting the SNLA and WRA to join the talks on the constitutional future of Scotland and Wales" added Vale.

Thirty minutes later
Prime Minister's Office
10 Downing Street
London

"This is not good enough, Prime Minister" raged Philip Waldron, the Chairman of the hedge fund iBIS. "My Company's account has suffered embezzlement by suspected UK residents on this list." He slammed down a sheath of papers on the Prime Minister's desk. In it were the account numbers of persons who were recorded as having drawn money from iBIS's Zurich-based private bank account after the details were stolen the previous week during the occupation of the City of London.

"Mr Waldron, as I've previously told you, the new United Kingdom Government is doing all I can to reunite its nationals with assets that have been stolen or misappropriated. It will take time. But I cannot give special treatment companies like yours who clearly moved their investments abroad in order to avoid paying United Kingdom taxes. I am sorry that you have suffered financial loss. But if we were to reclaim the monies embezzled, I should remind you that we would be justified in deducting what you owe in tax."

"Christian, do you realise you are damaging the reputation of the United Kingdom and the City of London as a place to do business?" shouted former Foreign Secretary Dominic Collins, who was accompanying Waldron.

"If you don't co-operate with us in arresting and charging the individuals responsible, we'll have no hesitation in hiring asset recovery officers to arrest the individuals under Swiss law and to take them back to Switzerland to face trial" said Waldron.

Vale's goodwill had now vanished.

"Listen, Mr Waldron" growled Vale, "you have benefited very nicely from being both a UK citizen and resident without making any financial contribution towards the country's upkeep. For you, it's the 'little people' who pay taxes and suffer from being thrown out of work whenever you asset-strip some company you've taken over. Very few people in this country will have any sympathy for you. Learn to get over it. And one last warning. If you send any of your dogs of war into the United Kingdom, *they* will face trial under our law for false imprisonment if they seize any of our citizens. And remember that US and EU peacekeepers are in charge of public order. General Connolly's men have orders to shoot anyone who threatens that."

"Christian, have you gone totally crazy?" shouted Collins. "Do you realise that Philip Waldron is Chairman of the UK's biggest private investment company? You can't talk to him like that."

"Dominic, remember this" said Vale very slowly. "You are no longer a Government Minister. I am now in charge of the country. And remember to call me 'Prime Minister' in the future."

24 July 2021
Slane Castle
County Meath
Republic of Ireland

Alastair Ferguson and Emyr Roderick had agreed to be the main spokespersons and negotiators for the SNP and Plaid Cymru at the peace talks aimed to end the conflict in Scotland and Wales, and had taken their places at the table. Sitting further over to the right were Iain Murray and Gareth Evans, representing respectively the SNLA and the WRA. To the left sat Christian Vale, the British Prime Minister and Nick Moss, the British Foreign Secretary, who would be leading the official British delegation.

At 10:30am, the two facilitators for the peace conference walked in. The Taoiseach, Aidan Daly, was accompanied by a short, swarthy man. Bruce Farah, a Lebanese-American from Detroit and a Democrat Senator from Michigan, had been appointed by President Williams to oversee the peace conference.

"Good morning, gentlemen" said Daly. "My apologies for the late start, but we have one further delegate to arrive."

At that moment, Daly's Private Secretary, Bernadette Callaghan, came in with an important message.

"Taoiseach, your remaining delegate has arrived."

"Thanks, Bernie" said Daly. "Send him up."

Two minutes later, Callaghan accompanied a tall, muscular man into the room.

"Gentlemen, out last delegate is here" said Daly. "May I introduce you to Mr Glenn Nicholls, who will be representing the English Volunteer Force."

There was an immediate expression of discontent, not only from Evans and Murray, but also from Ferguson and Roderick.

"Taoiseach, what the hell are you doing inviting the EVF to attend?" shouted Ferguson. "They've got the blood of hundreds of my countrymen on their hands."

"Not forgetting over six thousand Americans who died in 2/13" added Roderick, pointedly looking at Senator Farah.

"We're not taking part if that bastard's allowed to stay" growled Murray, rising from his seat. "Gareth?"

"I'm with you on this, Iain" said the Chairman of the WRA's General Council, also getting up.

Daly and Farah walked over to the door of the Conference Room and stood in front of it. They were joined by Vale. There was no way out.

"Gareth, Iain, may I remind you this is a peace conference" said Daly. "Prime Minister Vale, Senator Farah and I are trying to find a political solution to Scotland and Wales that is acceptable to all parties. And that includes the English. It is therefore proper that all warring parties are invited to this conference. And that is why the EVF are here."

"No one is going to leave this Conference until a political agreement to which all parties are content has been signed. Prime Minister Vale and Senator Farah are in agreement with me. Furthermore, I have the full support of the Presidents of the

United States of America and the European Union. I would therefore suggest that you return to your seats."

Both Daly and Vale were big men. Evans and Murray saw little point in continuing with their rebellion.

26 October 2021
Slane Castle
County Meath
Republic of Ireland

"Do I therefore take it that everyone's agreed?" asked Senator Farah.

There were universal expressions of agreement round the table.

"All that needs to be done is for the final draft Agreement before you to be signed. A signature copy will be brought in during the next few minutes. Once this has been done, you will all be free to go home."

An ironic cheer went up.

Actually, Senator Farah was not a hundred percent correct in saying that everyone could go home immediately. There was to be a press conference to announce the Treaty.

The look of relief on Christian Vale's face was clear for all to see. He had obtained an historic peace agreement and could now focus his attention on getting the United Kingdom back to prosperity before his period as caretaker leader came to an end.

The previous three months had been the tensest time of his life. Although he delegated much of the day-to-day responsibility of the negotiations to the Foreign Secretary, Nick Moss, he had got personally involved when it looked like deadlock was going to stall the talks.

At the start of the Conference, the British Government had offered Scotland and Wales full devolution in domestic affairs with only foreign policy, trade, defence and national security remaining the preserve of Whitehall. This would have been an effective restoration of pre-2015 devolution but with even more powers. Vale did not expect the SNLA and WRA to agree to this, but neither did the SNP and Plaid Cymru. From the start, their aim was full independence from the United Kingdom.

Another difficult moment had been when the SNLA and WRA demanded reparations from the United Kingdom, including territorial concessions. Had they got their way, most of Northumberland north of the River Wansbeck and the northernmost part of Cumbria north of the River Eden, along with Carlisle, would have been transferred to Scotland, while the western parts of Cheshire, Herefordshire and Shropshire, along with Chester, Hereford and Shrewsbury, would have been transferred to Wales. But neither Taoiseach Daly nor Senator Farah considered this to be either workable nor sensible, and the SNP and Plaid Cymru did not support it either.

The discussion of travel and settlement rights also threatened to become acrimonious. The SNLA and the WRA wanted to restrict the rights of their nationals to hold dual nationality, to make it compulsory for all Scottish and Welsh residents to take out Scottish and Welsh citizenship and to impose restrictions on the rights of

British nationals to work or own property in Scotland and Wales. Both Ferguson and Roderick showed some sympathy to this view as absentee landlords was a contentious topic. This provoked Glenn Nicholls of the EVF to demand a guarantee from an incoming Scottish and Welsh government to protect the rights of English residents and that, if not, that Scottish and Welsh residents in England should be made subject to immigration control. It took skilful prompting from Farah and Vale to guide the squabbling parties towards agreeing on a Common Travel Area, dual-nationality and the right to continue to hold British citizenship and the rights of the English to reside, work and own property in Scotland and Wales and, vice-versa, the rights of Scottish and Welsh nationals to travel freely and work in the rump United Kingdom.

At 3pm, the news conference began. Journalists from across the world were gathered in the Main Hall at Slane Castle. At the top table, Daly, Farah and Vale were all seated in the middle. To the left sat Evans, Ferguson, Murray and Roderick, while Nicholls sat on the right.

Vale indicated he was ready to speak.

"Ladies and gentlemen of the media, I am most grateful for your attendance on what is an historic day for the United Kingdom."

"Earlier today, the Government of the United Kingdom, along with representatives from the Scottish National Party, Plaid Cymru, the Scottish National Liberation Army, the Welsh Republican Army and the English Volunteer Force, signed an Agreement setting out the future constitutional arrangements for Scotland and Wales. Furthermore, the Scottish National Liberation Army, the Welsh Republican Army and the English Volunteer Force have agreed to cease all hostilities."

"From 1 April 2022, Scotland and Wales will both become fully independent countries and will, as a consequence, leave the United Kingdom. On 17 February 2022, elections will be held to determine who will govern Scotland and Wales. No decisions have been taken yet on whether Scotland and Wales will retain Her Majesty Queen Elizabeth II as their Head of State or whether they will become members of the Commonwealth. Those will be issues for the incoming Governments to decide. Likewise, it will be for the incoming Governments to decide other trans-national commitments such as membership of the European Union or the North Atlantic Treaty Organisation. Her Majesty's Government will offer them the opportunity to share their national defence with the United Kingdom, but this will be for the respective Governments to decide."

"It has been agreed that Scotland and Wales should benefit from a Common Travel Area in the same way that the Republic of Ireland has benefited since its independence almost a century ago. It will be open to residents of Scotland and Wales to either take out nationality of their respective countries, to remain citizens of the United Kingdom or to be dual-nationals. Likewise, it will be open to nationals of Scotland and Wales to live, work and own property anywhere in the remaining parts of the United Kingdom following independence and for nationals of the United Kingdom to do the same in Scotland and Wales."

"Finally, I would like to offer my special thanks to the Marquess of Conyngham for allowing the use of this marvellous venue for this conference and to the Taoiseach,

Mr Aidan Daly, and Senator Bruce Farah of the United States Congress, for their invaluable assistance in facilitating the talks that led to the signing of this historic Agreement."

27 October 2021
Daily Telegraph

Peace, but at what cost?
Deborah Pearson

Today, the Prime Minister will give a statement in the House of Commons on the peace agreement he signed at Slane Castle yesterday, under which the SNLA, the WRA and the EVF have agreed to hand in their arms. In inviting Parliament to endorse the Agreement, the Prime Minister will be emphasising the economic benefit to the United Kingdom and the British Isles that will arise from a peaceful settlement to the problems that have beset the United Kingdom over the past six years.

Many commentators, both in this country and internationally, are hailing Christian Vale as a visionary for having the courage to accept the division of the United Kingdom as a price of restoring peace and economic prosperity. There are already rumours that he is to be nominated for the Nobel Peace Prize next year. Since he succeeded me as Prime Minister three months ago, there can be no doubt that Mr Vale has obtained a "peace dividend". Today's quarterly report on the economy will state whether it has delivered economic benefits for the United Kingdom. But I will not be alone in questioning whether the Treaty of Slane will be, in the long term, a benefit or a millstone for the United Kingdom.

Mr Vale has argued that a return to peace will benefit the United Kingdom economy. I concede that the confidence of investors has returned. However, I consider that the following factors which Mr Vale appears to have overlooked may in fact weaken the United Kingdom's economic position in years to come. Firstly, he appears to have forgotten that the United Kingdom's economic and political strength are closely linked. The withdrawal of Scotland and Wales from the United Kingdom may only reduce its population by 8 million. But it will adversely affect its international political clout. Already, there are calls for the United Kingdom to surrender its permanent seat on the United Nations Security Council. Once the United Kingdom is removed from the top table of international diplomacy, its capacity to fight its economic interests are reduced too.

Mr Vale also appears to have given too much away on the obligations of Scotland and Wales to defend the West in the face of attack from hostile forces. The military strength of the United Kingdom and its commitment to the Atlantic Alliance have been the bedrock, not only of our freedom but also of the United Kingdom's position as a trading nation. Mr Vale has conceded demands from the Scottish and Welsh Nationalists for the right to choose their alliances and favoured trading partners. It is no secret that Russia and China would like to have a newly independent Scotland and Wales as trading partners. As previous experience with both countries has shown, military influence follows trade influence. Does Mr Vale recognise the possibility that there may be hostile military and intelligence forces stationed on the British landmass?

Finally, Mr Vale appears to have given little regard to the consequences of his agreement to the release of convicted terrorists from prison. Many of the men and women being released are convicted murderers guilty of the most heinous crimes against innocent civilians. Apart from the impact on the victims of the atrocities committed by the SNLA and the WRA, has he not thought that conceding to the men and women of violence will only encourage others to follow in their footsteps? I am thinking particularly of Northern Ireland. Sinn Fein and the IRA have not gone away and still aim to take Northern Ireland out of the United Kingdom. They can only be encouraged by the Government's lack of resolve demonstrated at Slane Castle.

The same day
Prime Minister's Office
10 Downing Street
London

Christian Vale slammed down the copy of the Daily Telegraph onto his desk. He had just read the article by his predecessor, Deborah Pearson, which effectively accused him of selling out the United Kingdom's national interests when he signed the Peace Agreement at Slane Castle the previous day. He was due to address the House of Commons later that day before the House debated and decided whether to ratify the Peace Agreement.

Seated to his left was Sarah Berne, his Principal Private Secretary, a former high ranking PR executive in the City of London. In her late 30s, tall, blonde and aristocratic, she had a reputation for coolness under pressure.

To his right was Andy Smallwood, his Press Officer. Smallwood, a Midlander from a council estate in Dudley and in his mid-40s, was heavily-built and abrasive, and had formerly worked on the *Sun*.

Vale was a worried man. Apart from the *Guardian*, the *Independent* and the *Daily Mirror*, the press were not exactly complimentary. The general tone appeared to be a grudging acceptance of the Peace Agreement, tempered by concern that too much had been given away. There were reports in the *Daily Mail* and the *Daily Express* that over 150 Conservative MPs were going to vote against ratifying the Peace Agreement and that the rebellion was growing. And it still had to clear the House of Lords before full ratification took place. If the rebellion grew, there was a risk of the Government losing the vote and of Vale's credibility as Prime Minister being terminally damaged.

"Sarah, Andy, I don't have to tell you that today is make or break. If I lose the Commons vote, I'll have to resign. And the country will be back to where it was three months ago."

"I don't think things will be as bad as you fear, Prime Minister" said Berne. "While you were on the way back, I spoke to Simon August. Simon is confident that at least 100 Tory MPs will back the Peace Agreement. Add in the whole of Labour, the Liberal Democrats, SNP and Plaid Cymru, you'll have a clear majority."

August, who had been part of the Fresh Start group which had instigated the No Confidence vote against Deborah Pearson earlier that year, was now Chief Whip in the all-party caretaker government.

"Thanks, Sarah. Can you ask Simon to ring me this morning and let me know how he's got on in persuading uncommitted MPs to vote Yes."

Smallwood was next to speak.

"Prime Minister, have a look at the *Financial Times*. The leading article should silence any doubters."

Vale read through the leading article on the front page. It was most encouraging. The next quarterly report on the economy was not due until the following week but the *Financial Times* reported with some authority that the economy had grown by 4% in the previous quarter, that orders were flooding into British companies and that foreign investment was returning. There was speculation there would be a fall in unemployment of over 250,000. The *Financial Times* was unequivocal in attributing the improved economic performance to the peace dividend that Vale had delivered since accepting President Williams' offer to head up a caretaker administration back in July.

"Andy, that's excellent news" said Vale. "But it still doesn't get away from the problem that many people think I've sold out the country."

"Prime Minister, the blunt truth is that people vote with their wallets" said Smallwood. "If people have got a job and money to spend, they couldn't give a shit about a break up of the UK. No Government that delivers economic growth and success ever does badly at the polls. And it's you who has achieved that. Tell that to Pearson, Collins and all the other flat-earthers who would take us back to civil war."

"And there's one more thing to tell anyone whingeing about the loss of national identity. Ten years ago, half of Middle England were in favour of Scottish and Welsh independence. In fact, several of them wanted English independence from the UK. They saw Scotland and Wales as a drain on their taxes. Remind them of that."

EPILOGUE

11 February 2022
Presidential Palace
Tehran
Iran

The President of Iran, Hamidreza Yazdani, had gone to bed the previous night a contented man. During the past year he had secured a multi-million dollar arms deal with Russia that would once again make Iran the most powerful country in the Islamic world, then won the Presidential election following the death of Mohammed Khoramzadeh the previous September. 11 February was the official anniversary of the Islamic Revolution which had brought Imam Khomeini to power forty three years previously, and Yazdani had made sure that the expensive military hardware bought from Russia would be on display.

There was however dissent from some quarters. Dissident students had demonstrated following the Presidential election, alleging that it had been fixed. Yazdani had ordered the Revolutionary Guard to break up the demonstrations and imprison the ringleaders. He regarded the students as tiresome, unpatriotic and supporters of the Islamic government's worst enemy, the Great Satan, the United States of America.

The students were not the only people unhappy with the Islamic government. Trade unions had been protesting about living standards. And there was the usual cohort of businessmen who wanted greater 'freedom'. Which to Yazdani meant freedom to trade with Iran's mortal enemies.

As far as Yazdani was concerned, he was safe. He had the unconditional support of the Supreme Council, and that was all that mattered. His enemies were the enemies of Islam. Infidels, who deserved to be treated like dogs. The Great Satan, the United States of America, had been emasculated. Discontent about falling living standards and corporate greed had delivered another black Democratic President for whom military might was not a major priority. The Little Satan, the United Kingdom, had been convulsed in civil war for the previous six years and was about to lose Scotland and Wales, who were about to gain independence. Yazdani had made a mental note to pay a visit to the new leaders of Scotland and Wales.

Yazdani wanted to leave a legacy. Of world Islamic dominance and with Iran at the vanguard. All Iran needed to do was to seize control of the Gulf first. Once Bahrain, Qatar and the Emirates had gone, Saudi Arabia would cravenly sign a peace deal. Then support Islamic agitators in North Africa. The Mediterranean Sea would then be an Islamic lake and all of Europe would be within range of its fighters and bombers. And the Great Satan itself, the USA would also be within reach.

The official celebrations for the 43rd anniversary of the Revolution would start after morning prayers had finished.

At 6am, there was a loud knock at the front door of the Presidential Palace. Yazdani's housekeeper, Mohammed, went to answer it. He was greeted by the sight of a large battalion of soldiers. A colonel in his late 30s was standing in the doorway.

"Is the President there?" asked the colonel.

"He is" replied Mohammed. "I'll get him for you."

Two minutes later, Yazdani was at the front door, dressed in a silk dressing gown.

"Good morning, colonel" said the President. "I hope you've got a good excuse for waking me up at 6am. Do you realise what today is?"

"I do, Mr President" replied the colonel. "On the orders of the Provisional Government of the Republic of Iran, I am placing you under arrest."

Later that day
The White House
Washington DC

Richard Williams was working on a box of papers before packing up to head off to Camp David for the weekend. At 9:30am, the Secretary of State, Clint Romney, walked in.

"Mr President, have you heard the latest news? There's been a coup in Iran. The armed forces have overthrown the Islamic government."

"What!" exclaimed Williams. "Clint, are you serious?"

"Absolutely" replied Romney. "Come to the Press Office to see for yourself."

A minute later, Williams entered the Press Office. All the staff stood up as he walked in.

The telescreens were showing CNN whose chief reporter, Dan Colbert, was in Tehran covering the events.

"This is Dan Colbert of CNN News reporting from Tehran."

"The Iranian capital is now calm following the military coup earlier today. There have been no reports of bloodshed across the country, apart from a detachment of Revolutionary Guards in Bandar Khomeini who opened fire on regular Army units as they moved in. Crowds have taken to the streets to cheer the soldiers, and it appears that there has been broad public support for the action of the armed forces."

"President Yazdani has been placed under arrest, as have members of his Cabinet, the Director-General of the intelligence service, VEVAK, and the members of the Supreme Council. No decision has been taken on whether they will face trial."

"The leader of the military council now ruling Iran, General Massoud Rostamian, has pledged to rebuild relations between Iran and the rest of the world and, as a first measure, has ended all support for overseas terrorist and subversive activity. There are reports that members of Al-Q'aida, Hamas, Hizbollah and the Taliban who have been

attending terrorist training camps in Iran have been rounded up and will face summary deportation."

President Williams had still not fully taken in the full implications of events in Iran earlier that day but to say he was ecstatic was an understatement. Iran had been a major foreign policy nightmare for US Presidents for the previous four decades. They had trained and funded terrorists all over the world, carried out acts of military piracy in the Gulf and it was widely believed they had helped traffick heroin to the West. For years, the Islamic government had seemed unshiftable because no one would move against the ayatollahs who effectively ran the country. And now, with one swift move, they were gone.

As Williams and Romney walked back to the Oval Office, they talked about the now imprisoned former Iranian President.

"Guess I'm kinda sorry to see what's happened to Yazdani, Mr President" said Romney. "He was very Westernised and was an intelligent and well-read man."

"Clint, the guy was no different to the rest of that crew" replied Williams. "He was good at turning on the charm but, at the end of the day, he was the same as the ayatollahs. They all had the same aim—global conquest in the name of Islam."

"I remember Yazdani liked quoting the Chinese philosopher, Sun Tzu" said Romney. "He always argued that the best way to prevail in conflicts was to do as little as possible and to exploit tensions and conflicts in the enemy. He persuaded Khoramzadeh and the ayatollahs to follow that line after the last Gulf War, and it seems he had a point. Without an enemy to concentrate minds, the American public started to agitate for a bigger share of the national wealth and that helped put us in. Even more so in Britain's case. I doubt if there would have been as much support for Scottish and Welsh independence if the Iranians had nuke missiles in Algeria and Morocco."

"Well it didn't do Yazdani much good, Clint" said Williams. "Like every country, if they are facing threat from an enemy whose way of life and culture is completely different, the people always rally behind its leaders. Look at us and the Brits nine years ago. All he managed to do by scaling down hostile action against us was to take the Iranian people's minds off the threat to Islam from the infidels. And when that happened, the students started to agitate for more freedom. The trade unions started agitating for better living standards. Businesses wanted greater freedom to trade with the West. Six years ago, a coup would have got nowhere and would have landed the perpetrators a one-way ticket to the gallows. But this time, there's popular support for it. You saw the people on that CNN report Clint?"

Williams and Romney were greeted by the President's Chief of Staff, Larry Hendricks.

"Mr President, have you got a minute? General Rostamian's on the phone."

"Tell him I'd be delighted to speak to him, Larry" replied Williams.

2015. The United Kingdom's just discovered enough oil to guarantee prosperity for the next 100 years. The Government sees this as the final cog in its project to make the United Kingdom the enterprise capital of the world and to restore the country's greatness.

The only problem is that most of the oil lies off Scotland and Wales. And the Scots and Welsh want their share of the bonanza.

Over the next six years, the United Kingdom descends into a spiral of conflict in which oil nationalisms re-emerge and threaten to drag in European neighbours and the United States as the violence spills over beyond the country's boundaries.

authorHOUSE®

ISBN 978-1-4567-821

52

9 781456 782115